# RESURRECTION OF THE EXPS

## BOOK 2

# THE HERO OF SEL

## Alexander J. McCarty

### Art by: William McCarty

RESURRECTION OF THE EXPS BOOK 2 The Hero of Sel. Copyright © 2016 by Alexander J. McCarty

ISBN 978-1-943733-033

Published by Sphere of Compassion, Inc.
authoralexandermccarty@gmail.com
alexanderjmccarty@facebook.com (updates often with excerpts and art).
alexander_j_mccarty@instagram.com
of_the_Exps@twitter.com
oftheexps@tumbler.com

Cover design by William McCarty

# Books from *Of the Exps*© Series

# Table of Contents

## Part 6: The Realm of Sellum

## Part 7: Trapped in Absence

## Part 8: The Goddess Shaped by Misfortune

# Part 9: The Lord of Hate

# **Acknowledgments**

First and foremost, I give a continuous and reverent thanks to my brother for bringing my characters to life with his art, helping me plan and flesh out scenes, providing feedback whenever I need it, and brainstorming with me to create new characters and hone old ones. I give thanks to my loving and supportive parents. I thank Luis Garced who read this book back when I first began writing it. Thanks also to my FB friend (and fellow writer) Aleah, who is supportive of me and my work. I thank my family and friends who read any part of this book either digitally or in manuscript form, particularly Gabriel, Ivan, Ken, Gabriel, John, Jesus, Tatiana, and Val who have all supported my book series for years. I give thanks to Andres, Adrian, Kevin, and my brother for looking over this book before its release.

Shout out to Dr. Steve Vose and Iqbal Aktar for answering questions I had about religious traditions. Special thanks to my wonderful editor, Rosemi, who, with her vast knowledge and research, has helped make this book more accessible and more real to my readers. I am grateful to the creators of clever, innovative, and thought-provoking anime, manga, videogames, scripture, and other visual literature.

As always, I thank my id for keeping me vital and driven, my ego for keeping me positive and critical about my work, and my super ego for directing my creative energies toward a better world for all living beings. Lastly, I thank you, the reader, for purchasing this book. I hope you enjoy it and continue to support me and my future books.

Thank you! =(:3)*   (That's a bunny, by the way.)

*This book is dedicated to heroes and prophets—from all creeds, cultures and species—who have fought against a system of exploitation and have stood up for those being oppressed. May we all follow their example and work toward a world without systemic violence and oppression.*

# **<u>Introduction</u>**

It's been over a year since the first book's publication. After getting the first book in print, the process of going from digital to physical took me far less time. Book 3 is coming along and will be ready by this fall. After that there is just one more book in the *Resurrection* arc. I've been marketing in new ways and have started my own YouTube Channel with my brother for discussions on our company's works and for reviews. This year also marks my first time boothing at a convention. On the side I've been working on a fan-fiction story, and it has been challenging but rewarding in its own way.

   I hope you will follow me on FB, Instagram, YouTube, and Tumblr, and feel free to message me. My Facebook group, Alexander J McCarty, updates often with quotes, excerpts, and character art from my book series. Please spread the word about my series, take a moment to give it (and the first book if you haven't already) a review (on Amazon or Goodreads) and enjoy. =(:3)*

# In the Last Volume:

# Book 1, *Exp 8*: Rebellion of the Exps

Devlin, a youthful and passionate inventor, created Exp 8, the ultimate weapon, and sought to awaken his creation's latent power through physical, mental, and emotional struggles. Exp 8 escaped, as planned, and formed his own team by turning Devlin's living weapons and modified assassins against him. Devlin sacrificed much for his cause and nearly lost sight of his goal when he became smitten with Kaity, an assassin prodigy who worked for Devlin's detestable brother. Despite interruptions by Senator Jo John and his elite spies, the dedicated inventor achieved vengeance on his family, lost his virginity while manipulating a beautiful assassin, and even persuaded the Goddess of Death to join him in his quest to become a god. Devlin married the love of his life, but this ended up being a ploy constructed by Etah that left Kaity as a mindless doll. In the end, despite all his planning and efforts, Exp 8's pre-programmed charisma and endless power led him to victory over the genius inventor. While the noble scientist was breaking down from within, he used the last of his strength to send Kaity, his dearly beloved, out of the range of Exp 8's explosion. The greatest inventor of all time was then consumed in his greatest creation's final blast.

# Agent Alpha's Recon Notes

Government Report: Contains SPOILERS (read at your own risk) :)

## DEVLIN'S EXPS

**NoOne**: Serial # Exp. 1; The Shadow Master
*Appearance*: A mobile goopy shadow humanoid; Bright eyes; Malleable body
*Personality*: Lacks confidence; Obsessed with heroes; Likes chilling with sheep
*Relations*: Devlin (creator); Wants relations with other Exps but feels undeserving
*Abilities*: Shape-shifting; Shadow bending & control; Harms shadow to harm body
*Recent Activity*: Went into Deceivant's lab alongside Exp 8—outcome unknown
*Artifacts*: **Shadow**–Sphalerite (black)
*Threat Level*: Very high (not sure I can take this one down)


**Karson**: Serial # Exp. 2
*Occupation*: Devlin's friend and bodyguard; Currently a soldier for Freedom Forcers
*Appearance*: Construct of weapons with humanoid shape; Head is a British missile
*Personality*: Brave; Honorable; Militaristic; Refuses to attack opponent's weak point
*Relations*: Devlin (ex-commander/creator); Pharma (rival)
*Abilities*: Varied artillery; Ejects and redeploys head missile; Particle beam cannon
*Recent Activity*: KIA by Bob under Devlin's orders
*Threat Level*: Low (due to self-destruct button, otherwise high—it's a weapon depot)


**Nina**: Serial # Exp. 3
*Appearance*: Long purple hair; Satin scarf; Lightly tanned skin; Curvaceous figure
*Personality*: Narcissistic; Attention seeker; Tactical tease; Sees sexuality as a weapon
*Relations*: Devlin (ex-partner/creator); Ada (teacher); Matteria (rival); Kaity (fan-girl)
*Abilities*: Incapacitates through erotic poses; Explodes and regenerates clothing
*Recent Activity*: Sent away by Devlin after fighting him—whereabouts unknown.
*Artifacts*: **Gravity**–Barite (white); **Ice**–Frozen water; **Slow-mo**–Amphiboles (white)
*Threat Level*: Very Low (I can shoot her while she's posing)


**Matteria**: Serial # Exp. 4
*Occupation*: Celebrity; Model; Idol; Actor; Porn star; Made to be Devlin's sex partner
*Appearance*: Teenage girl; Rainbow-colored hair; Makeup that alternates colors
*Personality*: Playful; Strong libido; Free-loving but loyal; Likes getting into scandals
*Relations*: Devlin (master/creator); Reflector (current boyfriend); Nina (current crush)
*Abilities*: Matter manipulation—bends matter and changes states of matter
*Recent Activity*: KIA by Demonica
*Artifacts*: **Matter Change**–Moonstone (white)
*Threat Level*: High (hard to kill and hard to capture; thankfully lacks combat skill)

**Reflector**: Serial # Exp. 5

*Occupation*: Living museum sculpture

*Appearance*: Shiny; Rectangular; Reflective; Angular head; Tiny arms and legs

*Personality*: Needy; Cowardly; Voyeur; Lacks self-confidence; Wants a harem

*Relations*: Devlin (creator); Matteria (girlfriend); Nina (crush)

*Abilities*: Creates glass constructs; Reflects damage; Shoots lasers

*Recent Activity*: Trapped in Kanasta's Death Die after paying the assassin to kill him

*Artifacts*: **Mirror**–mineral unknown; **Create**–Galena (silver), **Darkness**–Tiger's Eye

*Threat Level*: High (how do you hurt it without injuring yourself?)


**Anthrax**: Serial # Exp. 6

*Occupation*: Doctor (works for free; no insurance needed)

*Appearance*: Human boy; White hair and eyes; Oversized lab coat;
Can change into a diseased monstrosity; I'd rather not go into further details

*Personality*: Helpful; Prideful; Emotionally detached but tries to connect with patients

*Relations*: Devlin (creator); Matteria (girlfriend)

*Abilities*: Psychological and physical treatments (said to be able to cure anything)
Combines, spreads and injects disease when in sick form

*Recent Activity*: KIA by Demonica

*Artifacts*: **Sickness**–Sulfur (yellow)

*Threat Level*: Very Low/High (physically weak/sick form is invincible)


**Violet Gold**: Serial # Exp. 7

*Occupation*: Spiritual Mentor; Devotee

*Appearance*: Light blue skin; Golden hair; Amethyst eyes; Wears rags

*Personality*: Compassionate; Dutiful; Blindly devout to Devlin; Loves rituals

*Relations*: Devlin (creator/god); Sees Exps (and all life-forms) as her soul siblings

*Abilities*: Belief manipulation (brainwashing); Skilled with blades

*Recent Activity*: Committed suicide while fighting Kaity; RIP

*Artifacts*: **Belief**–Lazurite (color unknown)

*Threat Level*: High (but you can catch her by surprise if you act friendly)


**Exp 8**: serial # Exp. 8; The Ultimate Exp

*Occupation*: Leader of the Freedom Forcers

*Appearance*: Cat-like humanoid with concave chest; Has a tail; Platinum coated armor

*Personality*: Strong will; Freedom obsessed; Firm morals; Cherishes sunsets

*Relations*: Kawai (sister); Atatasuki (brother); Devlin (creator); Sees Exps as family

*Abilities*: Ejects energy as orbs; Jetpack; Turrets; Minor gravity manipulation

*Recent Activity*: Battled Devlin near lab he was imprisoned—outcome unknown

*Threat Level*: Priority One; The Ultimate Exp (but not the most deadly in my opinion)

**Pharma**: Serial # Exp. 9 (created while working on Exp 8)
*Occupation*: Devlin's personal stash/drug buddy
*Appearance*: Humanoid composed of addictive pharmaceuticals; Bong for head
*Personality*: Addictive; Competitive; Carefree; Suicidal (by toxic overdose only)
*Relations*: Devlin (creator); Karson (rival)
*Abilities*: Bleeds alcohol; Increases speed & durability; Intoxication; Injects drugs
*Special Weapon*: Nicky—a bastard sword colored like a cigarette with smoking tip
*Recent Activity*: Accidentally exploded himself with Nicky while fighting Karson
*Threat Level*: Very Low (he's a bumbling idiot who killed himself)

**Riufen**: Serial # Exp. 10; Dragon fencer (but misspelled, should be Ryufen)
*Occupation*: Samurai; Devlin's trainer/bodyguard
*Appearance*: Rock-like skin; Headband of teeth; Armored with own skeleton
*Personality*: Stupidly obedient; Polite; Strong sense of honor despite misunderstanding
*Relations*: Devlin (creator)—calls him Devlin-sama; Bob (rival/teacher)
*Abilities*: Manipulates and weaponizes body; Wields spinal cord as sword; Immortal
*Recent Activity*: Battled Exp 8 and NoOne alongside Bob—Outcome unknown
*Artifacts*: **Life**–Coal (black)
*Threat Level*: Very High (if I can get rid of his artifact, then he can be killed, right?)

**Exp 11**: Serial # Exp. 11; Opti/Pesi
*Appearance*: Changes based on which personality is in control
Opti: Humanoid with long white hair; White comedy drama mask; White feathers
Pesi: Humanoid with spiky black hair; Black tragedy drama mask; Black feathers
*Personality*: Changes based on who is in control
Opti: Cheerful; Fun-loving; Simple-minded; Easily deceived; Loves fluffy animals
Pesi: Grim; Sadistic; Redundant ignoramus; Refuses to be subservient; Hates life
*Relations*: Devlin (creator); Opti/Pesi (sees other personality as nemesis)
*Abilities*: Influences reality through force of will; Can resurrect dead if recently killed
*Recent Activity*: KIA by Demonica
*Artifacts*: **Influence**–Garnet (burgundy)
*Threat Level*: High/Low (not too skilled in combat despite absurd power of artifact)

**Demonica**: Exp. 12?
*Appearance*: Long black-and-red mane; Dark horns; Scarlet fingernails
*Personality*: Sadistic; Manipulative; Erotic; Sexy; Forceful; Psychotic crush on Devlin
*Relations*: Devlin (creator/obsession) Etah (employer)—supposedly a god (yeah right)
*Abilities*: Flight; Shapeshifts; Manipulates blood; Whatever she touches turns to blood
*Recent Activity*: Vanished while fighting Ada—whereabouts unknown
*Artifacts*: Unconfirmed–Blood?
*Threat Level*: Very High (killed multiple Exps in seconds). Can we recruit this vixen?

# DECEIVANT'S EXPS

**Ada**: Serial # Exp. 03; A.D.A.
*Occupation*: Loving Mom; Dutiful Wife; Computer database
*Appearance*: Blue sphere; Materialized Exp form: humanoid woman made of digits
*Personality*: Always cheerful; Air-headed; Unconditionally loving; Inferiority complex
*Relations*: Deceivant (husband); Devlin (son); Kanasta (son); Deceivant's Exps (kids)
*Abilities*: Inserts into Exp 8's chest; Levitation; Flight; Wi-Fi; GPS; Holograms
*Recent Activity*: Murdered by Devlin (her own son)
*Artifacts*: **Illusion**–Jasper (red brown)
*Threat Level*: Very Low (too kind to be a threat); Support type; Lacks combat skills

**D.S.**: Serial # Exp. 04; Supply Master (at least that's what he calls himself)
*Occupation*: Reformed gangster; School security guard
*Appearance*: Bald muscular man; School uniform; Correction tape around face
*Personality*: Grade-school mentality; Gullible; Friendly; Loves learning
*Relations*: Ada (mother); Deceivant (father/creator); Kanasta (brother/rival)
*Abilities*: Heals; Erases; Weaponized school supplies (mainly giant scissors)
*Recent Activity*: KIA by Demonica
*Artifacts*: **Erase**–Plume Agate (pink); **Storage**–Gold (color is self-explanatory)
*Threat Level*: Medium (surprisingly skilled in battle and tactics but easily deceived)

**Devlin Kagaku**: Serial # unknown (created after Ada and before Atatasuki)
*Occupation*: Scientist (self-employed)
*Appearance*: Black-plated feline; Composed of wires; Acts as male human inventor
*Personality*: Vengeful; Romantically obsessive; Paradoxically loves & kills creations
*Relations*: Ada (mother); Kanasta (brother); Deceivant (father); Kaity (wife?!)
*Abilities*: Command over wires; Melts host to absorb energy, will, and possibly powers
*Recent Activity*: Battled against Exp 8 near his father's lab—outcome unknown
*Artifacts*: **Teleport**–Traveler's Stone (color unknown)
*Threat Level*: Priority (likely has many hidden artifacts; Exp and creator in one bundle)

**Atatasuki**: Serial # Exp. 05; First (semi) functional prototype of Exp 8
*Occupation*: Microwave oven (seriously, I'm not making this up)
*Appearance*: Feline humanoid; Copper armor; V-shaped head; Oven in chest cavity
*Personality*: Comical; Passionate; Fixated with muffins & sister; Sees flaws as identity
*Relations*: Exp 8 (brother); Kawai (sister/crush); Devlin (creator); Violet (best friend)
*Abilities*: Superheat body; Jetpack (dysfunctional); Tactically modifies his memories
*Recent Activity*: KIA by Violet Gold on orders from Devlin
*Threat Level*: Low (prolonged fighting leads to overheating and potential death)

**Kawai**: Serial # Exp. 07; Prototype of Exp 8

*Occupation*: None (she's a kid)

*Appearance*: Feline humanoid; Pink pedomorphic body; Gold armor; Little slippers

*Personality*: Insecure; Sadistic; Loyal; Cute; Obsessively infatuated with Exp 8

*Relations*: Exp 8 (brother); Atatasuki (bro); Deceivant (creator); Devlin (benefactor)

*Abilities*: Floatation; Laser net; Gives or takes energy; Strong tail (1.5 x body length)

*Recent Activity*: KIA by Bob on Devlin's orders; RIP

*Artifacts*: **Sound**–Crystalline Quartz (clear); **Shield**–Calcite (blue)

*Threat Level*: High (re-energizes allies so should be taken down first if in a group)


**Demo**: Serial # Exp. 08

*Appearance*: Baseball-sized silver ball

*Personality*: Speaks in geometric turns; Not much else is known

*Relations*: Deceivant (creator)

*Abilities*: Levitation; Multiplies to create various shapes

*Recent Activity*: KIA by Kaity Rin Rainbow Viper—nice job :)

*Artifacts*: **Multiply**–Gypsum (grey)

*Threat Level*: High (fast and can multiply in an instant)


**Fusion**: Serial # Exp. 09

*Appearance*: A sticky ball of various colors.

*Personality*: Unknown

*Relations*: Deceivant (creator)

*Abilities*: Can merge and control (I saw it take over Deceivant's lab, turrets and all)

*Recent Activity*: KIA by Demonica

*Artifacts*: **Fusion**–Copper (color is self-explanatory)

*Threat Level*: Medium (might be tricky to kill, but nothing I can't handle)


**Bob**: Serial # Exp. 10; Befriender of Betrayal

*Occupation*: Deceivant's spy; Self-proclaimed actor

*Appearance*: Beach-ball-sized floating eyeball; Lucid green iris; Intense blue pupil

*Personality*: Playful; Cruel; Sarcastic; Manipulative; Bored easily; Values trust;
Enjoys betraying but dutifully acts as an ally until signaled otherwise

*Relations*: Deceivant (creator); Sees others as playmates, but will kill them if ordered

*Abilities*: Flight; Pass through objects; Lasers; Clear appendages; Summons minions?

*Special Weapon*: Atma Blade: Sword of swirling energy made from Bob's essence?

*Recent Activity*: Vanished after confronting Devlin—whereabouts unknown

*Threat Level*: Very High (unsure if he's a strong as he says, but still has many abilities)

# ASSASSINS

**Kanasta Kagaku**: Real name unknown; Called the Boss by his co-workers
*Occupation*: Official: Combat trainer; Unofficial: Leader of the Viper Squad Assassins
*Appearance*: Skintight suit; Spiky hair; Blood-red eyes; Carries steel-plated suitcase
*Personality*: Stoic; Competitive; Fatherly; Capitalistic morals; Strong love of family
*Relations*: Deceivant (father); Ada (mother); Kaity (protégé); Viper Squad (family)
*Abilities*: Super strength; Varied arsenal; Mixed martial arts; Creates custom weapons
*Recent Activity*: Vanished after joining Freedom Forcers—whereabouts unknown
*Artifacts*: Unknown (I seriously have no idea)
*Threat Level*: High (I think I can beat him, but honestly it could go either way)

**Tempo:** Real name unknown
*Occupation*: Viper Squad's 2nd in command; Cleaner
*Appearance*: Mid-forties; Biker jacket; Spiky red and blue hair; Shark teeth
*Personality*: Values money; Enjoys killing more than other assassins (even Kaity)
*Relations*: Kanasta (boss); Ego (best friend): Kaity (competition)
*Abilities*: Temperature manipulation (can melt a building and freeze a lake)
*Special Weapon*: The Termometer: dual-ended staff-like thermometer
*Recent Activity*: KIA by Exp 11 (Opti at the time—I know shocker)
*Artifacts*: **Temperature**–Mercury (crimson)
*Threat Level*: High (should be a fun fight)

**Ego**: Real name unknown
*Occupation*: Viper Squad Assassin; Mechanic; Lookout; Driver
*Appearance*: Young man; Punk green Mohawk; VR visor; Neon nose piercings
*Personality*: Narcissistic; Brotherly; Surfer bro; Obsessed with training and experience
*Relations*: Kanasta (boss); Tempo (bro); Sees the Viper Squad as his family
*Abilities*: Drives vehicles; Master of all sports; Can grow or shrink body and objects
*Recent Activity*: KIA by Nina after an insult battle
*Artifacts*: **Size**–Feldspar (beige)
*Threat Level*: Medium (overconfidence is his greatest downfall)

**Kaity Rin Rainbow Viper** (real name)

*Occupation*: Viper Squad Assassin; Sniper

*Appearance*: Preteen; Purple skintight bodysuit; Folding robotic cat ears; Metal tail

*Personality*: Playful; Clingy; Free-spirited; The thankless conscience of Viper Squad

*Relations*: Kanasta (dad); Sefiwah (lover); Devlin (husband?!)–calls him Devi-kun >:(

*Abilities*: Super hearing; Super agility; Expert marksmanship; Magnetism <3

*Recent Activity*: Missing after Exp 8's battle against Devlin–whereabouts unknown

*Artifacts*: **Love**–not sure what mineral or color

*Threat Level*: High (there's a reason she's been chosen as the next Viper Squad boss!)


**Sefiwah**: Real name unknown

*Occupation*: Viper Squad Assassin; Spy

*Appearance*: Clad in bandages; Pale skin; Eye patch; White pupils; Spiked belt

*Personality*: Remorseless killer; Sadomasochistic; Obsessed with white; Fears blood?

*Relations*: Kanasta (employer); Kaity (soul mate)

*Abilities*: Nimble; Snake-style; Fingers pierce flesh; Resurrects targets if near death

*Recent Activity*: Died in battle against Ada (whether suicide or homicide is uncertain)

*Artifacts*: **Revive**–unknown mineral

*Threat Level*: Medium (I'd shoot her down as soon as she enters my range)


**BoneSaw**: Real name unknown (just kidding it's a robot)

*Occupation*: Viper Squad Assassin; Covert ops

*Appearance*: Compact and portable boxy robot; Circular saws and chainsaws roll out

*Personality*: Kills the target

*Relations*: Kanasta (creator)

*Abilities*: Saws; Chainsaws; Self-replication; Skilled at covert ops (it's a freaking box)

*Recent Activity*: Destroyed by Atatasuki

*Threat Level*: Low (electromagnetic discharge has proven to disable it)

# HUMANS

## Deceivant Kagaku
*Occupation:* Scientist; Inventor; Pedophilic Philanthropist; Daycare franchise owner
*Appearance*: Short black hair; Rectangular glasses; Golden eyes; DNA Necklace
*Personality*: Relaxed; Intellectual; Elitist; Lolicon; Follows science religiously
*Relations*: Ada (wife); Devlin (son); Kanasta (son); D.S. (son); Kawai (daughter)
*Recent Activity*: KIA by Demonica
*Threat Level*: Priority (can make new Exps, but physically weak)

## Senator Jo John
*Occupation*: Democrat; Senator; Veteran; World Bank corporate lobbyist
*Appearance*: Black suit; Red, white, and blue necktie; Jagged eyebrows
*Personality*: Easily angered; Polished political charisma; Desires Exps as weapons
*Recent Activity*: Left Deceivant's lab after Exp 8 broke out from his incubator
*Threat Level*: Low (sorry boss but it's true, a bullet to the head would end your career)

## Black Suit Commander: Agent Alpha; Real name is a secret, sorry ladies :)
*Occupation*: Leads Senator Jo John's special forces; Governmental spy
*Personality*: Handsome: Charming; Playful; Manipulative; Strict humanitarian diet
*Recent Activity*: Goaded Exp 8 into battle against Devlin; Made a quick report
*Threat Level*: High (I'd honestly like to place myself higher, but I'm not immortal like some of these freaks)

# Part 6
# The Realm of Sellum

# Chapter 51: The Realm of Sel

The light of life was vanquished as the vast void exploded, forcing all it touched into immediate demise. The souls were instantly spirited away to the world beyond.

"Freedom is a shackle."

In the silence of his demise, this familiar phrase cycled though Exp 8's mind.

Two portals appeared, one on either side of Exp 8. To his left was a corrosive black vortex. He could feel it gently tugging his soul into the darkness. On his right was a blindingly white portal. He did not feel his spirit being drawn to this one. He reached his arm out to the white portal, trying to touch its light. The world beyond it felt unattainable. The portal of light faded away like a wall of mist, leaving him in total darkness. In the distance, he saw a red glint of light. The crimson flame then vanished before he could confirm its existence.

A sudden sense of plummeting took over him.

Exp 8's slender, muscular body smashed against an unseen barrier. A powerful heat seeped through his inch-thick quicksilver platinum-colored armor, melting the flesh beneath it. The cybernetic living weapon shifted his helmet around, trying to release the heat residue trapped within. He could feel his breath hindered as pieces of ash entered through his mouthpiece filter. His eyes shot open, seeing the scorching world of torment for the first time. With a struggle, the leader of the Freedom Forcers stood up, still feeling an inner flame permeating his armor.

The air was a mix of ash and steam, creating a blinding mist from the soles of his feet to the top of his head. A monstrous flame abruptly pierced through the steam and enveloped him. He thought his body would be rendered to ashes in the blaze. He collapsed on all fours. The pain of the flame had released him as swiftly as it had seized him.

The metal tendrils branching out from his helmet felt a sudden shift in the air around him.

A short figure with a black hood appeared once the flames vanished. It bowed down to Exp 8. Tears flooded down its silver cheeks.

Exp 8 scanned the area with his night vision. "Where is Kaity?" he asked, turning to the hooded figure.

"Welcome to Sel, the realm of the sinners," said the figure in a soft childish tone with forced malice.

"This place...am I dead?"

"Welcome, Destroyer! It is a pleasure to meet you." The figure bowed.

"Who the hell are you?" asked Exp 8 in his strong-willed, gruff, and demanding voice.

"I am one of Etah's many followers. He has sent me to get you acquainted with our home."

Exp 8 crouched down to the figure. "Why am I here?"

"Etah was most pleased when you sacrificed yourself to eliminate the one who dared to stand against him. I can't believe that stupid human, trying to defy a god. How dare he even ask for Lord Etah's help," said the resident of Sel with resentment.

A symphony of screams leaked out from the ground.

"So this…this is the afterlife?" Exp 8's body trembled.

"There's no need to be afraid. You are here as our ally. You alone shall be excluded from torture."

"This can't be it. Are we all to be enslaved even in death?"

"You don't know anything, do you?"

Exp 8's eyes peered beyond the molten hills. "At least I killed myself before my soul was bound to Devlin. So, if I'm dead, where is Kaity?"

"She and Devlin have been detained for their transgressions," said the dark follower with a sharp grin.

"Why are they being tormented? Kaity has done nothing against Etah; if anything she has sent him souls."

"Despite killing so many, she had a clean slate relatively free of sin."

"How is that possible?"

"Who knows?" said the hooded figure with a shrug.

Exp 8 gripped the figure's shoulders. "If she has a clean slate, why must she be tortured?"

"Devlin's deepest desire is to protect Kaity. So, Lord Etah, God of Hate, will torment her to torture him," said the hooded figure with a hop of excitement.

"That isn't fair," said Exp 8, clenching his fist.

"All are punished in Sel. Is that not fair?" asked the figure with a dagger-like grin.

"Where are the rest of the Freedom Forcers?"

"Who knows?"

"Is this place abandoned?"

"Not at all. Recently, the realm of Sel has been running out of room," said the figure before vanishing in the steam.

The smoke cleared from the ground, allowing Exp 8 to see the vastness of the world he was in. Volcanoes erupted on the horizon.

Exp 8 looked into the sky to see a blanket of black mist.

He ventured onward, careful of the geyser blasts.

Blue and green flames shot out at random from the cracks in the molten ground several meters ahead. They were the only light source he had. Without them, he would be traveling through this barren world blind.

"Why is the ground so soft? It's nothing like the metal floor at Devlin's lab." Exp 8 looked at his feet. His piercing black eyes widened.

The ground was composed of bodies, their flesh searing from the heat of the atmosphere.

Exp 8 activated his jetpack and soared up into the sky. He stopped once he reached the ominous coat of black fog and gazed upon the landscape below.

Bodies stretched along the plane as far as he could see.

He flew back down and landed. "Is this really where living beings go after death? Is this the afterlife?"

There was a strained grunting noise coming from beneath his foot.

"Are you alive?" he asked, crouching to the floor.

A head with melted cheeks peered up at the newcomer. "If I were alive, would I be here?"

"How long have you been in this place?"

"Time is irrelevant here. There is no sun nor moon, neither day nor night; you're in Sel," said the head.

"Do you feel pain?" asked Exp 8, noticing his foot was on top of a scorched torso.

"Once you get used to burning, once you've accepted the agony...that's when they sprinkle you."

"They sprinkle you?"

"The fluids increase our capacity for pain so that we never become numb to the agony. Each time the pain increases. I've gotten used to even that though," said the head with a crispy smile.

"What kind of life is that? You're left with no choice but to adapt to suffering."

"Yep, the oldest of us are on the top and have joined with the flames. That's why we look like molten ground. Don't worry about walking around. We can barely feel pain anymore. Don't tell the demons, but I'm a pyrophile. I love the pain of burning. Oh yes. The more they burn me, the happier I am."

"So what's your name?"

"Do bricks have names? What about tiles? I am part of a landscape. I don't have a name. I wasn't always a pyrophile, but I've adapted to it. It's the only way to keep your sanity."

"I'll call you Brick then. If you've been here awhile, why aren't you on the bottom?"

"Well, that's the way I would have done it, a sturdy foundation makes a sturdy building. However, since the flames burn hottest at the top, they plant the newcomers beneath them. When I died, I arrived at the bottom, but as we suffer, we slowly rise up," said Brick.

"What happens to the people who reach the top?"

"If you stay for a bit, we'll both find out. So, what's your name?"

"I'm Exp 8 and I'm here to free—" said the Ultimate Exp before being cut off by dozens of voices.

"It's him! He stopped Devlin! He's a hero! Save us! Free us! Savior! Warrior of the light! He stepped on my face! Well, he fell on my back!" exclaimed various voices.

"All these people are trapped here? What the hell kind of world is this?"

A line of disfigured humans paraded down the hillside.

"Are they the oppressors? I thought this nightmare would end after I defeated Devlin," said Exp 8, his body sinking down.

The warrior of freedom went into a fighting stance and engaged his elbow talons once the tormented humans came within range.

The demons lowered their heads with respect.

"Humans? You were all once human?" asked Exp 8.

"Welcome, Destroyer! On behalf of all of Sel, we thank you for eliminating our enemy."

"I did not do it alone."

"Free us too! I love you! Have my babies! You can eat my arm! Save us from this torment! Sign my back!" exclaimed various voices beneath him.

"Silence!" yelled the charred human leader, who was crispier and quite a bit larger than the others. "The Destroyer lays waste to those who dare defy Lord Etah! He isn't concerned with you sinners."

The charred human with a bladed arm stabbed it into the fleshy ground.

"What are you doing?" asked Exp 8, gripping the charred human by its shoulders.

"This does not concern you. Stand aside." He poked the visitor with his bladed arm.

Exp 8 grabbed the blade, spun it around, and tripped the charred human.

The leader stood in the way as the charred human rose to retaliate. "We are demons. It is our duty to tend to the sinners. We are not your enemy," he said, calming his ally with harsh hand gestures.

"That is for me to decide," said Exp 8, standing tall.

"We are both followers of Etah. There is no need for opposition," said the demon leader.

"I did not kill Devlin because he opposed Etah. I killed Devlin, my creator, because I oppose slavery," said Exp 8, clenching his fist.

"This isn't slavery. All residents of Sel are united for a common goal."

"And what goal is that?"

"Existence."

The demons with the sharpest blades sliced into the ground. They carved between the fused bodies, separating them from one another.

The sinners screamed and cried.

Exp 8's long metal tail tapped against the ground, but he did not intervene.

Three demons pulled Brick's body out of the fleshy mesh of agony.

"This is our daily regimen. There is no need for concern," said the demon leader.

Exp 8 watched as Brick was yanked out of the ground.

The victimized pyrophile crawled on his scorched limbs. "I forgot what freedom felt like," he said with tears overflowing.

"You're freeing them? Then you aren't oppressors. But who put these living beings in the ground?" asked Exp 8.

"They did it to themselves, through their own actions and choices in the pre-life."

"I don't understand. Why are these life-forms melted into the ground?"

"That is the way of this world. Follow and watch. Soon you will understand," said the demon leader. He signaled three demons to go up the hillside.

The demons lifted up two charred humans each and ventured over the hill.

Exp 8 followed behind the demons, traversing beyond hills of flesh and through gusts of ash. They arrived at the peak of a volcano.

"What are we doing here?" asked Exp 8.

The demons tossed the sinners off their shoulders and into the lava pit.

Exp 8 leaped into action but was blocked by the demons.

The bodies combusted before they even touched the lava. Their screams erupted as synchronized agony.

"What have you done!" yelled Exp 8, gripping onto the arm of the closest demon.

"This is the conversion process. There is no need to fret," said the demon with a dismissive wave of the hand.

"You just killed them! How about I throw you in?" asked Exp 8, grinding his teeth.

"Death does not exist here, only rebirth," said the shortest demon.

23

The tallest of the group dropped his hook-like arm in the lava pit.

The large hook pierced through the sinners, but what it pulled out were demons. The new demons plopped onto the scorched ground.

"Are they alive?"

"Nothing in Sel is truly alive, but it would be strange to say they are dead. They merely exist and they will do so throughout time," said the shortest demon.

"They've been reincarnated as demons," said Exp 8 with wide eyes.

"You are beginning to understand. The residents who reach the top are ripe and ready to become demons. Once they are reborn as demons, they sprinkle pain on the residents to help culture their agony. Every demon was once a resident and every resident will become a demon. The more pain you receive, the higher rank you are. That's why Lord Etah harbors so much anger," said the demon.

The leader signaled the group and then turned to the visitor. "Get behind me."

"What are you afraid of?" asked Exp 8.

A battalion of demons charged up to the peak of the mountain.

"What do they want?"

"You." The leader turned to his squad. "Do not let them take the hero. We have the high ground. We will not lose!"

"I know a way around this problem." Exp 8 jet-boosted into the crowd of incoming demons.

"The fool! After him!" yelled the leader, signaling his squad to charge.

Exp 8 landed in front of who he assumed was the leader—a demon nearly his height and hidden under a shroud. Swords pierced her front and back, a battle's worth of arrows decorated the sides of her legs, and daggers were sheathed in each of her major joints. A dagger with a crimson grip was lodged in her head, holding the cowl of the shroud in place.

"So who are you guys?" asked Exp 8.

"Sinner's Fury. We are the only rebel group in Sel. We fight against the twisted system of this psychotic world," said the demon leader.

"Sounds good to me. This place…it shouldn't exist," said Exp 8 with a clenched hand.

"Pain Forest is at the base of the mountain. A second group is waiting for you there," said the demon in a raspy but proud womanly voice. "I'll hold them off." She unsheathed two swords and rushed up the mountain, slicing a volley of arrows directed at her.

Three demons escorted the stranger down the mountain side while the rest provided their leader protection.

"How many of you are there?" asked Exp 8, slowing down a bit to keep pace with them.

"Not many. But we will fight till the end."

Once they arrived in the mist, Exp 8 could make out over thirty clouded figures.

The demons split up into ten different groups, each heading a different way.

"Are you guys going to take me to your boss?" asked Exp 8.

"You're looking at him," said one the demons. The obese demon leader was reclined in a velvet bed, made mobile by four pointed metal legs. A crown was fused into his head and each finger had a ring he acquired from one of his many patrons. Heated gold leaked from his belly button, having coated his belly in its rich splendor. Resourceful metal hands came out from his stubby legs and motioned the newcomer to approach.

"You're the leader?"

"In a manner of speaking. So, are you really strong enough to take down Etah?"

"It's not a matter of strength. He's got to go down. Simple as that."

"Good attitude," said a sly feminine voice that sounded a bit forced.

Exp 8 turned his head to see a misshapen mess of a living creature that could be viewed as neither male nor female. Half a woman's face was sewn onto the demon's fleshy head and bare breasts were seared onto its charred chest. It had arms instead of legs and four extra arms in its back.

"Who are you?" asked Exp 8.

"I'm the leader too. Eheheh," said the mishmash demon with a smile.

"How many leaders are there?" asked Exp 8.

"Seven. One for each region of sin. Keep up the pace, you're almost there," said the mishmash demon.

"Having only one leader makes us predictable, so we alternate. Plus, with more leaders, the resistance is harder to break," said the golden demon with a regal and boisterous flamboyant voice.

"Don't you bicker with each other?" asked Exp 8, jogging alongside them.

"We have certain ways of solving disputes. And here we are. Welcome to our base: Traitor's Trench," said the mishmash demon.

Exp 8 stepped into what looked like more mist and fell through. He landed on his rump in a dark pit. "I was far too trusting. Ada, can you...oh yeah. You're not here." He groped around in the dark.

It wasn't long before Exp 8 noticed a light in the distance.

"You've finally arrived. You had better not let us down, hero!" yelled the light source in a loud voice.

Balls of fire shot to the sides and lit up the torches.

The area slowly came into view.

The ground was fleshy but not alive and had a golden layer on top of it. The walls were the same, with a torch placed every eight meters along it. The place was nearly empty, but Exp 8 could see some connecting tunnel entrances past what was likely yet another leader.

This demon was coated in flames, orange at his legs, red at his torso and blue on his bald head. He was shorter than the others, but his intense red eyes gave him plenty of presence.

"I'm Exp 8."

"I damn well know who you are. Everyone does. Etah made sure of that," said the demon.

"Didn't expect to be so well-known down here," said Exp 8, scratching the side of his helmet.

"We don't need you. You're too much of a liability. I voted against rescuing you," said the flaming demon.

"Why?"

"You're going to repurpose the rebellion. That's what Etah wants. Repurpose it and then fail. We can achieve victory without you."

"Do all the leaders feel that way?"

"They've told you too much already. If only I was chosen today, things would have been different. You wouldn't be here!"

"Chosen, who chose you?"

"Fate," said a demon, coming out from the shadows.

"You're the one who welcomed me here. You're with the rebellion?" asked Exp 8, crouching down to get a look at the figure's face.

"If Etah knew how far our reach is, he would wipe us out in one fell swoop," said the short hooded figure, turning away from his gaze.

"Are you a leader too?"

"Nope. I'm their mediator. I was promoted due to my ability to avoid conflict."

"Hells yeah. Congratulations."

"You're making me bwush," said the figure, turning away.

"So what do we do now? Or did you not plan ahead?"

"You're going to follow our orders, unless you want to be stranded in this hellhole," said the fiery demon lord.

"I appreciate the sentiment, but I am in command of my own actions. I'm open to suggestions though," said Exp 8 with an implied smile.

"I want you to take on Etah, right now. Hurry up and die," said the fire demon.

"What?" asked Exp 8, wide-eyed.

"That's enough of that," said the gold demon, approaching from behind.

"You were right with me. Why did it take you so long to find this spot?" asked Exp 8.

"Had to take a detour. We were being followed," said the mishmash demon.

"Wait, so which one of you decided to rescue me?" asked Exp 8.

"That would be the Baroness of Blades, who is most likely fighting right now. All of us leaders are demon lords, merely one level below gods. She felt that getting you on our side was of pivotal importance. I am the Duke of Deception," said the mishmash demon lord.

"Führer of Fortune is what I am known as. And our hot-headed equal is the General of Genocide," said the golden demon.

"He wants me dead. What about you two?" asked Exp 8.

The Duke of Deception grabbed the metal man's arm. "If it were up to me, you'd be a diversion. And if you died, I'd turn you into a helpful martyr."

"I'd use you as a bargaining tool to exchange for something more useful," said the Führer of Fortune.

"I'm wasting time here, for all of us. Tell me where Etah is and I'll take him down," said Exp 8, cracking his knuckles.

"The momentary leader tasked us with keeping you here. You aren't going anywhere!" yelled the General of Genocide in a loud, cracking voice that broke out into a high-pitched squeal.

"You want me dead, right? Well, either I die fighting Etah and you spin it to your liking or I take him down," said Exp 8, stretching his arms behind his head.

"I am going to take him down!" exclaimed all the leaders, their voices merging into an explosive growl.

"Stay calm, my demonic brethren," said the hooded demon.

"Wait, you all want to kill him. Don't you see how that is problematic?" asked Exp 8.

"I want his kingdom!" yelled the Führer.

"I want his still-beating heart!" yelled the General.

"I desire his status," said the Duke.

"Then why do you need to be the ones to kill him?" asked Exp 8.

"They each have their own motives and goals. It was hard bringing them together," said the hooded demon.

"I like you. What's your name?" asked Exp 8.

"Oh, uh, call me the Mediator. I wike you too," said the hooded demon, shuffling its feet.

"Everyone calm down. I'm going to assume that the other four leaders are on their way. I'll wait here until then. Promise I won't go after Etah until I hear you all out," said Exp 8.

"Ah, such a reasonable fellow," said the Führer.

"Indeed," said the Duke.

"If you think we are equals, you are wrong," said the General.

Exp 8 teared up.

"You made him cry!" hissed the Mediator.

"What? How?" asked the General.

"Sorry. For a moment there you reminded me of someone I miss dearly. He was a brother to me," said Exp 8, wiping away his tears.

"Too emotionally unstable. We may have to reconsider," said the General.

"That just makes him easier to mold to our whims," said the Führer.

"Here I am, trapped in Hell. But at least I'm not alone," said Exp 8, hugging the short demon.

The Mediator was unable to reach all the way around his back with a reciprocal embrace.

"Do you know me?" asked Exp 8.

"I've been waiting for a hero to come. And here you are—strong, cunning, and kind. I know that spirit. It won't be crushed," said the Mediator with a razor-sharp grin.

"That's right. In fact, it is my free spirit that will crush Etah's world!"

# Chapter 52: Where is Everybody?

Atatasuki awoke in a crystal clear pond. He thrashed around, splashing the water around him. Water moccasins, frogs, and lily pads were all pushed away. He frantically made his way out of the lake. After drying off, he stood up, looked left to right, up and down.

"Where is everybody?"

Atatasuki peered into the disrupted pond. "Brother?"

As the water calmed, he gradually recognized the figure.

Rusty copper armor, muffin brown skin, and a V outcropping on the helmet clearly distinguished Atatasuki from his less faulty brother.

"Hey, it's me! Where is this place? It feels different than the frungle. I don't remember the wind being so comforting," said Atatasuki, breathing in deeply. He opened the large hatch on his chest.

There were no muffins inside his beloved microwave.

Sweat dripped down his forehead. His tail shook back and forth as he relentlessly searched the white landscape.

Exhausted, he collapsed on the ground. His eyes widened.

He dug up the soft dirt and endeavored to shape it into a muffin. It collapsed in his grip, seeping out between his thin fingers.

"Alright. I can figure this out. Ingredients for muffins: batter and love. Batter consists of water, flour, and egg…uh…no, wait…what was it? Okay, love and batter plus oven equals muffin! Oh hallelujah, I remembered!"

Atatasuki raced around the area. "Okay. I have an oven and love. Need something to keep the mix together and I need to find the flour too. Oh my dear Muffin God, save me!" The muffin addict rushed through the swampy mangrove. He stopped in his tracks.

A chicken sat before him.

The passionate prototype took a deep breath, calmed his shaking hands and crouched down.

"Excuse me miss, I uh…need your uh…egg. Can I have it?"

The chicken scurried off.

Atatasuki jumped and captured the chicken.

It struggled in his grip, clawing and pecking to escape.

"Come on! Give it to me!" He shook the chicken up and down.

The chicken screamed and squirmed.

Atatasuki opened the hen's cloacae with his fingers and shoved them inside. There was rustling in the bushes.

A figure emerged, stopped in place and carefully examined the scene.

"Do you realize you're raping a chicken?" asked the figure with a raspy, congested voice.

Atatasuki looked up at the figure, his amber eyes over-laid with velvet veins. "This woman is refusing to give me what's mine!"

The figure was entirely composed of pharmaceuticals. His head was a bong, his fingers and toes were cigars, cigarettes and injectors and the rest of his body was concealed under a white coat of cocaine powder.

The man made of drugs crouched down. "You need to chill. Right now you are going through withdrawal."

"I'm not crazy! You're crazy!" yelled Atatasuki.

The drug man pulled the addict's fingers out of the hen's cloacae and pried her out of his shaking hands.

"You don't need this."

"I don't?" asked Atatasuki as he wrestled the figure to get hold of the feathered woman.

"Nah man. That shit won't bring you happiness. Have you looked around?"

"Yeah and…I couldn't find what I need!"

"First rule of addiction man: don't harm others. You terrified this chicken and you put your fingers in her piss, baby, shit hole just so you could taste her period. You got some serious problems man."

"Wow, I didn't realize it." Atatasuki sat down on the grass. "You're right. I'm a bad person."

"You were withdrawing. It's not easy man. I'm going through it too."

"So there are precepts for addicts to follow?"

"Of course, we're spiritual, ethical creatures who embrace our habits! You and I are cut from the same hemp plant."

"What's the second rule?"

"Share with fellow users." He passed his brother-in-drugs a Bufo toad.

"Okay. Is this some sign of friendship?"

"Lick the toad. It will send you to Heaven."

Atatasuki pet the toad. "Thanks, but I'll pass."

"Alright. Your loss."

The addict's bendy straw nose-sticks went up and down the toad.

"Hmm. Not as potent as I expected. Must not be the only user around."

"So, how many precepts of addicts are there?" asked Atatasuki, drawing in the sand.

"Three."

"What's the third?"

"Enjoy freely and continuously." He snorted the amphibian's secretions.

"Hey you know, I was thinking," said Atatasuki.

"Yeah, about what?"

"Well, you. You seem familiar. Do I know you from somewhere?"

"I'm Pharma!"

"Oh yeah! You died! I remember now. Yo, do you know where we are?"

"No idea, but as long as I got a fix. It doesn't matter."

"I didn't know addicts were so responsible."

"We have to be. There's so much slander against us users, so we had to step up and create a moral code. Now we…well, we're still not all that popular, but progress is progress."

A young man landed in front of them. He had a punk green Mohawk, sideburns, and a goatee. He was holding headphones in his hands but still had his visor over his eyes.

"Yo dudes, have you seen Kanasta? The squad has been looking around and no luck yet," he said in a young, hip, and stylish voice.

"I can't even walk in a straight line right now," said Pharma, holding his head.

"Forget them, Ego. We must keep searching," said a pale woman, peering beyond the grass.

The woman had a meaty but slender build and was covered head to toe in bandages. Deathly white skin could only be seen around her eyes, one of which was white with a black iris and the other covered by a white eye patch. Short white hair covered half her face, allowing her to see everything with strands of white.

"And your name is Sefiwah, right? I kept it in mind because you're really pretty. Why are you here? I thought you died," said Atatasuki

"And?" The pale killer stared into his eyes.

"Am I dead? Are we all dead?" he asked.

"Last thing I remember is a woman's clothing covering my face. She was naked, aw yeah," said Ego with a grin.

"We can't ask BoneSaw, so there's no way to confirm it," said Sefiwah.

"Oh, it died. I killed it, so I remember," said Atatasuki.

BoneSaw turned to the one who had beaten it. Its treads pushed off the ground, raising its box-like metal body.

"Don't worry, BoneSaw isn't vengeful. He only kills for the mission," said Sefiwah in a cold, gentle tone.

"He probably doesn't even remember. As for me, I don't remember dying, but I forget things all the time," said Atatasuki, scratching the side of his head.

"I wish I could forget some things," said Sefiwah softly.

"Never thought I would die. I thought, I dunno, I was invincible," said Ego with a half-hearted smile.

"As an assassin you see death daily. Can you really be that foolish?" asked Sefiwah.

"Hey, I'm young in spirit. Give me a break," said Ego.

"So, how long have you guys been wandering around?" asked Atatasuki, waving to the birds in the white trees.

"Couple hours. The Boss is not in this area. We must move out of the swamp," said Sefiwah.

Ego took cover behind a mangrove tree and the other assassins quickly followed. "Hey, I found someone!"

Sefiwah pulled in Atatasuki and kept her hand over his mouthpiece.

"I think she's a foreigner or something. Hey babe, what are you doing here?" asked Ego, combing his Mohawk.

The blue-skinned woman turned around. She was cloaked in white rags. Tears poured down her light blue cheeks. Golden hair dropped down to her thighs. Her third eye resonated with a faint light that shone through her tilak, making her amber eyes sparkle. The devotee's see-through cloth covered her mouth from doing harm all the while displaying her radiant smile.

She rushed up to Atatasuki and looked up at him in tears.

"Looks like you know her," said Ego, elbowing his fellow man.

"Of course I do. She's my friend. Why are you crying, Violet?" asked Atatasuki, his voice a bit goofy but with an inner strength and a hint of sadness.

"I sinned grievously against you. I cannot ask for your forgiveness, but please know it was done out of absolute necessity. I will make amends in any way I can," said Violet, pressing her head to his feet.

"I have no idea what you're talking about. Forget and forgive, I suppose. But if it will make you feel better, I would like a hug to re-instill our friendship," said Atatasuki with open arms.

Violet stood up and embraced him with a face full of tears. "Forgiveness truly is divine." She spoke in a wispy voice filled with love.

"No need to cry. It couldn't have been that bad if I don't even remember it."

Violet lowered her head. "It was bad. Very, very bad."

Atatasuki put his arm around her. "My dear friend, I may not remember what great transgression you committed against me, but I do remember something else."

"And what is that?" asked Violet, her tears falling to the damp grass.

"You made it so I would never be alone. You showed me that the Muffin God is a real and forgiving being. You showed that even someone like me, who can only hurt the ones he loves, is eternally and unconditionally loved. I can't ever repay you, my friend, but I can say thanks a lot!" Atatasuki gave her a thumbs-up.

Violet put her hands around Atatasuki's. "You are forever welcome," she said, her watery eyes now shimmering.

Ego elbowed his fellow man. "Very smooth. Go for it, dude. She likes you," he said, raising his eyebrows.

Atatasuki embraced Violet tightly who returned the embrace. He was then knocked off his feet by a blurry projectile. The glitch-ridden prototype landed in a moss-laden puddle.

A floating girl pounded his chest with her gentle hands. "Don't you ever leave me again!"

Violet jumped back, bumping into Ego.

"Whoa, lady. Are you afraid of that little girl? Kawai is harmless, right?" asked Ego.

Atatasuki looked down at his pink-skinned sister. Her massive glittering eyes were welling up with tears. The young girl's mouthpiece opened up, revealing her tiny mouth. At the top of her helmet her golden cat ears drooped. Kawai's tail, which was 1.5 times her body length, wagged back and forth as she wailed illegibly.

Atatasuki patted her head, caressed her green hair and smiled. "Whoops, did I go into a coma again? I'm sorry, Sis, I must have gotten overwhelmed. I'll try to take it easy."

"Promise me you won't die ever again," said Kawai in a cutesy mumbling voice, grabbing his cheeks.

Atatasuki grabbed her pink shoulder guards. "I promise. Hey, wait. When did I die?"

A mesh of metal shaped like a human popped out of the ground and brushed off the dirt.

The proud gunman had the colors of Britain adorning his missile head. He tilted his head and shook it, trying to clear out his shotgun barrel eyes. The soldier coughed up a ball of dirt from his grenade launcher mouth. He shook the soil off his feet, revealing they were Uzis. Though covered by a dirty British cadet uniform, the shapes of guns could be seen beneath his clothes.

"Yo, Karson," said Atatasuki, looking up for a moment before redirecting his attention back to his cuddly sister.

"Is it still there?" asked Karson, turning around.

Violet stepped up to the honorable soldier.

In the hole on the back of the gunman's uniform there was a bright red protruding button.

"I'm sorry, my brother, but it has not vanished."

"No surprise," said Karson, his shoulders drooping.

"Why would it disappear?" asked Atatasuki.

33

"You haven't figured it out? We're dead. None of us know for certain when we died, but all of us are here because we are casualties of war! Welcome to the afterlife, my fellow soldiers." Karson spoke with a British soldier accent that exuded pride.

"Please, do not say such things so passively," said Violet with a calming hand.

"I'm dead! Kawai is dead! That's totally absurd!" yelled Atatasuki.

"We already discussed this," said Sefiwah.

"Don't think of it as death. Think of it as a rebirth. We are all in a new and glorious world. My dear brothers and sisters, we have arrived in Heaven!" Violet embraced Atatasuki and Kawai together.

Kawai squealed and pushed Violet off.

A man dropped down from above. He was in his mid-forties and held a thermometer with his stiffened jaw. His hiking boots with crampons crumbled the grass below. A biker jacket was worn over his black skin suit. The assassin's hair was blue and red, jetting upward like a flame.

"Then why am I here? There is no way I'd make it to Heaven," he said, grabbing Violet's arm with his thick fingers.

"You underestimate the forgiveness of an all-loving God."

"I deserve to suffer! I won't accept this!" He displayed his filed teeth as he screamed to the sky. Even when ignited by fury, he spoke with a dark gruff voice.

"Tempo, is that you!?" An eight-foot man rushed through the woods and arrived before the group. Metallic board games were worn around his chest and back as armor, above a black, skintight bodysuit. His slicked back, checkerboard designed spiky hair had twigs and leaves in it. The assassin boss' blood-red eyes gleamed with hope and compassion.

"Kanasta, have you seen Kaity?" asked Sefiwah, stepping up to him.

"I…I saw you die. Ego, Sefiwah, you're all alive," said Kanasta, his stoic, deep, fear-invoking voice tinged with subtle joy. He walked up and embraced them one by one, never releasing his iron grip on his steel-plated suitcase.

"They are here because they are dead. Did Bob kill you too?" asked Karson.

"Ah, yes. I remember now. My brother, Devlin…he killed me." Kanasta's face remained stoic as his eyes watered up.

A small smile grew on Sefiwah's face.

"Sis, I need your help. We need to make muffins pronto! Do you see me shaking? I'm totally shaking. You have to help me!" yelled Atatasuki, trapping her in a tight embrace.

"Let go of me! Stop freaking out! You don't need ingredients to make muffins. You're a walking bakery remember?"

"Oh yeah, my body makes them! Whoops, guess I forgot."

"You are such an idiot sometimes. Heeheehmph."

"You laughed. I made you laugh," said Atatasuki.

"Yep, I guess you did," said Kawai, burying her blush under her tail.

"We're almost out of the swamp. There's a forest not too far from here. Stay low and out of sight," said Sefiwah.

"What are we hiding from?" asked Violet, trailing behind.

"From the unknown," said Ego, covering himself in mud and grass.

"Follow my lead," said Kanasta.


The group ventured out of the swamp and into a thick forest.

"How are we going to locate our friends in this place?" asked Atatasuki, carefully traversing around anthills.

"This way," said Tempo, pointing down a grassy path.

"Everyone, follow the man," said Ego, rushing to catch up to his fellow assassin.

"How many are there?" asked Kanasta.

"Four. They arrived recently," said Sefiwah.

"You all are so amazing. Can you sense their energies?" asked Violet, walking side by side with the repentant pale mystic.

Sefiwah stopped as soon as her eyes met Violet's.

"Is everything okay?" asked Violet, touching the woman's fragile hand.

"Fine. I'm fine. Let's keep moving."

"How many more of our allies were killed? Please, at least let Kaity be safe," said Kanasta softly.

"Where's mom! Have you seen my mom? Where's my mommy?" asked an approaching figure in tears, its rows of sharp and pointy teeth fully exposed.

It was a big, muscular man. He was wearing a school uniform that barely fit. Blue-striped shorts and awesome light-up sneakers made him look really cool. He was bald and had correction tape wrapped around a lot of his face. The man's innocent light blue eyes were flooding with tears.

"Good to see you, little brother," said Kanasta with a smile.

"Welcome, brother D.S.," said Violet with a nod.

"Brother, have you seen Mommy?" asked D.S. in a deep but childlike voice.

"My friends! We have found you!" exclaimed a happy-go-lucky voice.

The owner of the voice's long white hair swayed in the wind along with his snow white feathery robe. A white drama mask with a blue line around the eyehole covered half his face, but the other half was bursting with joy.

"Hey Opti," said D.S., waving with both hands.

Tempo snapped a tree branch and lunged at Opti.

Sefiwah tripped him and pinned him to the floor. "What if they can sense violence? What if the angels can smell your aggression?"

"That hippie bastard killed me with a big smile. I'm going to rip his face off." The seasoned killer jumped back to his feet.

"Tempo, restrain yourself," said Kanasta.

"Yes, Boss. I'll try," said Tempo with heavy breaths.

"I didn't want to kill you, but you guys refused to come home. It's all okay though, because we're all friends now!" Opti hugged everyone one by one.

"Touch me and I'll tear off your arm," said Tempo with flaring nostrils.

A young boy rushed into the scene, dragging his oversized lab-coat pant legs along the ground. "Tempo, calm down. Anger has been clinically proven to be detrimental to your health," he said, holding his long white hair. The small doctor pulled up his sleeves and rummaged through his medical bag.

"How can you guys trust this two-faced murderer?" asked Tempo.

"That's actually a fairly accurate psychological evaluation," said the doctor before tossing the sadistic assassin a stress doll.

"Anthrax, right?" asked Tempo.

"Correct," said the child doctor.

Tempo popped the doll in his grip. He crouched down to the white-haired child. "Are you mocking me?"

"Of course not! I'm just working on group cohesion," said Anthrax in a distinguished yet childlike voice.

"Hey, Matteria, how's it going, friend?" asked Opti.

"Don't get too close, Thraxy. He killed you too," said Matteria, standing between his boyfriend and Opti.

Bedazzled hearts and stars along with scarlet blush decorated Matteria's cheeks. His pink hair had bows and was in pigtails. Around his neck was a pink, rainbow-sprinkled cupcake emblem choker. His slim figure was held up by a multi-colored, self-designed corset. Below the diva's rainbow-striped mini-skirt was a pink-and-white garter belt with matching leggings. Just below the leggings were high-top Goth boots. The gender bender's glittery nail polish and lipstick alternated colors at will.

Tears poured down Anthrax's cheeks as he hugged his beloved.

"Aww, I love you too. What do you say we get naked?" asked Matteria in a chipper girly voice imbued with arousal as he opened up his adorable boyfriend's lab coat.

"Hey, what are you doing?" asked Anthrax, pulling away. He lost his balance and fell flat on his butt.

"Are you okay?" asked Opti, approaching his little friend.

"Stay away!" yelled Matteria, lashing his claws at the killer.

"Friends, please do not be upset. It hurts me to see you frown," said Opti.

"It hurts me to see you breathe," said Tempo with clenched teeth.

Opti took in a deep breath and held it in.

"Can I kill him later?" asked Tempo.

"Only if you are paid," said Kanasta sternly.

"We need to keep moving, there are four more nearby," said Sefiwah.


Sefiwah led them around the tree and into the next group.

Riufen was in a firm stance, practicing forward jabs with his spine. The warrior's silver hair showed both age and vitality. His empty white eyes hid every emotion while brimming with determination. The samurai's topknot was wrapped in bones. A bony helmet and a headband made of teeth further distinguished him as a follower of Bushido. The swordsman's skin was firm and had the appearance of stone.

NoOne was sulking. The Shadow Master was a pitch black shadow man with long fingers and no legs.

Fusion was rolling around, its myriad of colors gleaming in a ray of sunlight.

Deceivant was on the ground in a patch of grass. His short black hair moved with the wind. Beneath his rectangular glasses were two peaceful golden eyes. Deceivant's hands were firmly clenched around his double helix necklace.

"Hey NoOne," said Matteria with a wave.

"Oh, you are talking to me," said NoOne in a wispy voice, his void-like eyes widening.

"Hi friends!" exclaimed Opti, waving at them.

"Greetings," said Riufen with a strong, devout, and stoic tone while bowing.

At that moment Bob appeared. The beach-ball-sized pearl-white eyeball looked beyond the clouds with his lucid green iris and serene blue pupil.

Kawai screamed. Karson jumped for cover.

Digit by digit Ada materialized on the white grass next to Bob. Her nude motherly figure came into being. Once fully materialized, she leaned to her side and stared at Deceivant.

Bob rose up, floating about a foot above the ground. "Friends, why do you show such fear?" he asked with an innocent blue eye.

"What did you do to my sister?" Atatasuki rushed at Bob and pummeled him. Each punch phased through the treacherous sphere.

Ada stood in front of Karson. "Everyone please, Bob is our friend. He helped us save Devlin," she said in a cheerful, motherly voice.

"Our friend? He ruthlessly slaughtered us!" yelled Karson, raising his Gatling gun arms.

"I was not ruthless. I rather enjoyed myself," said Bob with a sly voice and slightly nasal but dignified tone.

"You…killed my sister, didn't you!" yelled Atatasuki.

"Actually, I made Exp 8 do it. But I was merely following orders. Deceivant told me to obey Devlin until he gave the signal. You expect me to go against my programming. Let's put this behind us," said Bob, embracing the defective weakling with spectral tentacles.

"Wait, so this was his fault. I should have known! He's the reason for the Button, he's the reason Matteria is a guy, he's the reason Devlin became obsessive, so of course he's the reason we were all killed!" Karson turned his guns on Deceivant.

Ada threw herself on top of her husband as Karson revved up his Gatling guns.

Kanasta slammed the guns down before they could fire. "Do not attack my family."

"Sir, yes, sir," said Karson with a sudden salute.

Kawai grabbed her other brother's arms with trembling fingers. "Don't fight him! Stop being so impulsive! I don't want you to die again," she said in tears.

Atatasuki's head turned around to face her. His eyes were watering and his mouth had curved into a wide smile.

Kawai smiled back at him nervously. She then turned to Bob. "Where is my brother? Did you kill him?" Her tail stood on end.

"Aww, what do you think?" asked Bob, patting her head.

"Was…was it painful?" asked Kawai, wiping her nose.

"Come now, Bob. You shouldn't joke like that. You didn't kill him. He was with us when you came back to your family. So…is my little boy alive?" asked Ada.

Bob shrugged. "Who knows?"

"We are wasting time with him! Sefiwah, where are the others?" asked Tempo.

"The last one rushed off to the East. No point in following. Wait, there is one more. This way," said Sefiwah.

"My wonderful husband, it's time to get up," said Ada, running her hand's through his gorgeous black hair.

"Mika, Mika, Mika," said Deceivant under his breath over and over.

"I'll carry him," said Bob, lifting up the dazed inventor.

"Hey Bro, can you carry me?" asked Kawai with a nervous smile.

Atatasuki turned around, saw no one behind him, and then turned back. "Me? You want me to carry you?"

Kawai held her cheeks and nodded.

Atatasuki plucked his adorable sister out of the air and into an embrace. "Of course I will."

"Do you see it too?" asked Kawai, gazing up at the clouds with a dazed look of bliss.

"Yeah, but this one's my favorite," said Atatasuki, patting his sister's head.

Kawai buried her blush under her tail.

"Hey Boss, how long are we going to stay with them?" asked Tempo.

Kanasta turned to face the group. "We must find Devlin. Our next course of action can be determined then. If this is Heaven, then that woman who had Devlin sacrifice me is likely a demon. I won't let her corrupt my brother further. We will save Devlin. I will not fail him again."

# Chapter 53: The Realm of Lum

Moments after Devlin's death, Nina, who was on the roof of the lab, was engulfed in Exp 8's explosion.

Silence became all pervasive.

A black portal appeared to her left. She felt shivers as she stared into the pure darkness of the void. She looked away and squinted, trying to see her reflection in the clear portal. All the while she was slowly dragged into the vortex of light. The light completely surrounded her, blinding her momentarily.

Nina felt a cushioning on her smooth back. Once her dazzling eyes adjusted, a world brimming with life appeared before her. She leaped to her pretty feet, standing in a flower bed of dandelions, buttercups, lilacs, and daisies, all of which were bleached white. The sensual survivalist sat down in the flower bed and looked up.

An ever-flowing stream of multi-colored clouds passed above her. The clouds broke out of their routine and came together. Soon the clouds morphed into the shape of her bodacious body.

The clouds mimicked her long, dark-purple hair but failed to imitate its silky texture. The white clouds and caramel clouds joined to present her lightly tanned skin. The collection of clouds adjusted its shape, trying to capture all the nuances of her curvaceous figure. Amethyst clouds rose out and formed eyes for the cloudy figure. Lastly, two small purple clouds joined from opposite sides to form the sexy warrior's light purple lips. Despite their relatively decent accuracy, the cloud figure was missing something. The goddess of gorgeousness' clothing— her lilac overshirt that split in the middle to expose her zip-up tank top; black latex gloves that rode up to her youthful shoulders; violet skirt that rode down over the top of her knees and her lavender thigh-highs—it was all missing. Her entire sexy, curvaceous, luscious, natural body, even parts that had only been witnessed by her and Devlin, were displayed in the sky for all to see.

Nina panicked. She rushed around the flower bed scaring off squirrels, bunnies, and chipmunks who were staring into the sky. She rushed to the tallest tree in the area. Leaping and climbing from branch to branch, she swiftly made it to the top.

There was a sea of white trees in every direction. Birds of all kinds, monkeys, lizards, snakes, frogs, various insects, and many other animals covered the trees, gazing up into the clouds.

Nina fainted, falling all the way down the tree.

"There she is!" yelled a familiar voice.

Atatasuki crouched over the beautiful woman and grabbed her shoulders, shaking her to her senses.

Once her eyes opened, Nina rolled into a ball. She felt exposed no matter how hard she tried to cover herself.

"Don't look at me," said Nina, her bodacious body shivering.

"Wow, you're even more paranoid than usual."

Nina sat up, her hands still shaking. "Wait, you're looking at me…not the clouds?"

"Well, I was looking at the clouds on the way here."

"Then you've seen it?"

"Yeah…wait, you mean you saw it too."

Nina nodded with a light blush.

"It was so beautiful."

"But the real thing is better, right?" asked Nina, slightly pushing up her breasts.

"Yeah, it's waaay more tasty! A thousand times more!"

"Oh…uh, thanks," said Nina with flushed cheeks.

"Um, you're welcome? I didn't know you liked muffins so much. Or were you talking about Kawai?" asked Atatasuki, tapping his chin.

"What? Wait; look in the sky right now. What do you see?"

"A blueberry, no carrot, now it's an apple muffin!" cheered Atatasuki.

Nina leaped to her feet. "So you don't see my bare naked flawless body, perky purple nipples, full gorgeous breasts?" she asked in a pompous, seductive voice.

Atatasuki looked at her up and down. "No, but I would like to," he said with an open mouth.

"Only I see it! Wonderful!" exclaimed Nina with joyful tears welling up in her amethyst eyes.

"Oh, I get it! You see yourself and I see muffins and Kawais. We must see what we love! That's why Kawai was staring off into the clouds; she must have been gazing up at Exp 8!"

"Kawai? Are the others are here as well?" Nina closed her overshirt.

"Not everyone. Exp 8 must still be fighting Devlin. If Exp 8 wins, then that means I'll be trapped here with Kawai, just the two of us. Is it bad to hope he wins? Oh, I really hope he pulls through."

"What are you talking about? Go signal the group so we can figure things out."

"Hey guys! Over here!" shouted Atatasuki, jumping up and waving.

The group came down from the hillside and met up with them.

"Good to have you back, soldier," said Karson with a salute.

"Have you seen Devlin?" asked Matteria.

"Don't talk to me about him," said Nina with a quivering lip.

Kawai pulled her other brother up to her with her tail. "Don't you go running off again."

"You've all come together! Welcome to Lum, children of light," said a soothing voice, overflowing with adoration.

Violet leaped to her feet, brimming with joy. She bowed her head as soon as her eyes met the ball of pure light hovering before them.

"An angel! Are you an angel?" asked Violet, jumping up and down.

Deceivant broke out of his trance, hopped to his feet and turned to the artificial zealot. "Come now, angels are mythic beings. They aren't real," he said with a relaxed tone outlined with philosophical skepticism and a dismissive wave of the hand.

"I am a deity," said the pink ball of light.

"Evol, correct?" Violet's eyes were shimmering.

"Yes, Violet, it is me," said the orb.

"I am honored to meet you in person," said Violet bowing repeatedly.

"How do you know Violet?" asked Deceivant.

"As a mother cares for her baby with instinctual love, I cherish and connect to all living beings."

"We have conversed before. You can put your faith in Evol," said Violet.

"Where is Exp 8? Where is my brother?" asked Kawai to the sphere.

"He has been sent to Sel by special orders."

"And you didn't rescue him!" yelled Kawai.

"We want our relations with Sel to remain positive. Our prayers are with him."

"Wait, Sel? That must be like Hell, isn't it?" asked Violet with wide eyes.

"I suppose so."

"You didn't even try to save him, did you? Now he's in Sel, all alone. What about your rules, huh? What about good people go to Heaven and all that? Why would he even go to Sel! He's a hero!" yelled Kawai.

"That's why. The gods of Sel see him as a hero because he surpassed Devlin," said the ball of light.

"That's not fair! Why didn't I get to go? I've committed lots of sins." said Kawai with a frown.

"No you haven't; unless being adorable is a sin," said Atatasuki, rubbing her head.

"I can be really violent, just ask Violet," said Kawai, her tongue between her teeth.

"You stood up to Devlin. That alone has set you on the path to salvation," said Evol with a spin.

"So how do I get there? To Sel, I mean. Come on, you have to help me!"

"I wish I knew how to help."

"Then what, I'm supposed to be stuck here for the rest of my life with a half-baked copy!"

"Sis, how can you say something so mean?" asked Atatasuki in tears.

"I…miss him so much. I feel so alone," said Kawai, crying into her tail.

"I'm here for you. And he's our brother, so there's a bit of him in both of us," said Atatasuki.

"You are so right! I guess even though you're a failed copy, you're a failed copy of him, auuh," said Kawai, holding her chest.

"Don't worry, dear sister. I promise you, right here, right now: I am not going to give up until I have freed Exp 8 from the prison of Sel," said Atatasuki, throwing his fist into the air.

"Damn right we aren't, we're never ever ever ever going to give up," said Kawai grabbing his fist.

Atatasuki turned red and overheated, collapsing to the ground.

Ada approached the radiant sphere of light. "If I may be so rude as to ask: do you know where Devlin is?"

"His presence is outside Lum's borders and not on Earth; that's all I know."

"What about Kaity; is she here? Did she die as well?" asked Kanasta.

"Son, please don't tell me you believe in this nonsense," said Deceivant, combing his hair with his hand.

"I was told Kaity had arrived recently, but Etah came here and carried her to his home. We allowed him to do so. After all, she had already bound her soul to the realm of Sel," said Evol.

"No. That can't be true. I cleansed her of all sin. She should be here with us," said Violet.

"She was on Devlin's side in the end. I wish she had stayed on the side of the light."

"Can you take me to Devlin? Please. I want to see my son, if only for a few minutes," said Ada.

"Your love shines into me. I will ask the other goddesses if they know where he is. I'm sure it will be a pleasant visit."

"It isn't safe. I'll come with you," said Deceivant.

"I'll stay here. Devlin won't want to see me," said Kanasta.

"I will make the arrangements for your trip," said Evol before zooming off into the sky.

"Wait a moment! I, NoOne, made it to Heaven!" The shadow man's arms flailed around joyously.

"We all did," said Bob with a smile.

"You killed my sister!" yelled Atatasuki, jumping at Bob with blind fury.

"That was only me playing a role. Deceivant created this body and thus I did as he asked," said Bob, holding the prototype's arm back with spectral hands.

"I won't trust anyone who would hurt my sister," said Atatasuki, struggling to break free.

Bob released his grip and put a spectral hand on the temperamental defect's shoulders. "I am deeply sorry for what I did. Please keep in mind that I did it all to aid your brother's efforts in stopping Devlin." He turned away as his eye flashed red.

"Bro, you can't hurt Bob. You'll only put yourself in danger, so stop," said Kawai.

"You're right. I'm okay," said Atatasuki, clenching his fists.

"Thanks, my love." Kawai leaned over and kissed Atatasuki's lips.

His whole body became enflamed and he collapsed to the ground, unconscious.

"Heeheehmph! I feel so warm," said Kawai with flushed cheeks.

"Stay calm! Dr. Anthrax is on the scene!" The young doctor rushed to the heat-stricken patient's side as he rummaged through his medical bag.

"I'm so happy you're alive," said Matteria, hugging his adorable little doctor from behind.

"Well, actually I'm dead. We're in Heaven, remember?" asked Anthrax, putting ice packs all over Atatasuki's body.

"Anywhere with you is Heaven," said Matteria, kissing him on the cheek.

"Wait, come to think of it, what happens when you die in Lum?" asked Anthrax, pausing for a moment before continuing the procedure.

"You're a doctor, how can you believe this nonsense?" asked Deceivant.

"You mean you aren't the least bit curious about the afterlife? Come on! It's the great unknown, the realm beyond, the final destination!" Despite his excitement, Anthrax stayed wholly focused on the task at hand. "Ow." He pulled his finger away from Atatasuki's forehead.

"I'll take care of it," said Matteria, licking the burnt finger.

"You assume that's where we are. I've chosen to remain skeptical. Brash assumptions impede proper scientific investigation," said Deceivant.

Evol dropped down from the trees and turned to Anthrax. "What is this 'death' you speak of?"

"You don't know? Then is this place an eternal paradise?" asked Matteria with shimmering eyes.

"It's a transit point for your next existence."

"Airport?" asked D.S.

"Your concept is foreign yet your intent rings true," said Evol.

"Yay! Past lives are now proven! You heard her, right?" asked Violet, turning to Sefiwah.

"Testimonies are not proof; they are hardly evidence," said Deceivant with a smirk.

"Gather around. I shall tell you all about the world of Lum," said Evol.

"Before you do that, mind telling me why my headsets aren't working?" asked Ego.

"That's because they are figments of your imagination."

"A dream. That's a rather simple explanation, but I suppose it will suffice," said Deceivant, leaning against a tree.

"What about the clothes I am wearing?" asked Nina, covering her voluptuous chest.

"Projections of your thoughts and unnecessary," said Evol.

"Then these ice packs won't save him?"

"Save him from what?"

"This suitcase and its precious contents…are figments?" asked Kanasta.

"I'm made of guns, does that mean I'm not real?" asked Karson.

"Relax, my dearly beloveds! All will be explained promptly," said Evol.

"I am ready to learn, great teacher," said Violet with a bow.

"When you ascend from the world of the living and if you were a very kind person, or in your cases had last-minute atonement that annulled all your past deviations, then you go to the wonderful world of Lum."

"What nonsense!" Deceivant walked out of the group and up to the anomaly. "Are we really supposed to buy this? The whole idea of sinning and atonement only exists as a tool to control the ignorant masses. 'Religion is the opium of the people', after all."

"Who said opium?" asked Pharma, his head darting left to right.

"Religion is much more than a drug," retorted Violet.

"It's for those who are too afraid to live with doubt," said Deceivant, gripping his pendant.

"I'll have you know that doubt is an integral part of many of my belief systems," said Violet.

"Religion—root word ligare—means to bind. It's a form of mental bondage that creates dogmatic ideological frameworks that don't make sense in a globalized society."

"Religion is all the more needed in a global community. And just so you know, ligare is the same root word for ligaments. It means to hold together, while still allowing for movement."

"Even so, if the skeleton of the idea is nonsense, then no progressive thought can come from it."

"We'll talk later. Evol, please continue," said Violet with a bow.

"It is wonderful to see you two speak so passionately. Everyone, look around you. The world you see here is Lum, the land of desires. Whatever you desire will be formed in the clouds."

"Mere hallucinations," said Deceivant, staring off into the sky with a smile.

"Then we can materialize things at will?" asked Pharma.

"My dear, only items that you hold great attachment to are recreated and only upon your initial arrival. Your current thoughts are intangible."

"So if I lose these clothes, that's it? I'm naked?" asked Nina, clenching her chest.

"Most certainly. Whatever item you desired or had attachment to at the moment of passing—for example, clothing—will form with you. This ensures new souls will be more at ease upon arrival. It perturbs some of the visitors to be frugal in the afterlife, and we are happy to harmlessly adhere to their desires," said Evol, sending rays of her love to those with concern.

"And are these figments eternal?" asked Matteria.

"Until they are shed, yes."

"That's a relief, I would die without my makeup," said Matteria, patting his cheeks.

"Ugh, how absurd! This is your chance to stop covering your natural face with that filth," said Nina, dragging her finger down his cheek.

"You have no idea how expensive this stuff is, do you?" asked Matteria with a blank stare.

"Shall I continue?" asked Evol.

"Please do," said Ada.

"As long as you are all here you are under our protection."

"I'm being protected by angels! This is really happening?" asked NoOne with wide eyes.

"Then we're trapped here?" asked Kawai.

"Trapped?" asked Evol with a twist.

"How much longer are we going to listen to this ball of hot air?" asked Tempo, clawing at his leg.

"Of course!" Kawai floated up to Tempo. "Please, save my brother!"

"Family is important. I'll do what I can. Hey doc, move aside." Tempo flung Anthrax off his patient.

"Hey, I wasn't done!" yelled Anthrax.

Matteria grabbed his lover's hand. "Just let him handle it. It's best not to argue with a killer."

Tempo released a cold wave from his hand. "Heh, looks like we've switched roles, eh Doc."

"Must we stay here?" asked Violet.

"Only for the time being. Etah's forces want you just like we do. That means you'll be getting extra protection, my dear ones. Oh, I am being called upon. Ada, Deceivant, please follow me."

Deceivant grabbed his wife's hand and walked forward.

"Wait a minute. You do know where he is. Where's my brother!" exclaimed Kanasta.

"I was recently informed of his whereabouts. He is in Absence. Enjoy your stay in Lum. Your special heavenly protector will arrive shortly," said Evol before leaving with the married couple.

# Chapter 54: The Realm of Absence

At the moment of Exp 8's demise, Devlin was enveloped in darkness. A pure black portal appeared to his left.

The vengeful scientist wanted to enter and see what was beyond it but could not move. A bright light appeared on his right, which he turned his head away from dismissively. Devlin could feel no gravitation from either side but instead felt it from his front. As he was absorbed into an invisible portal, he gazed upon the dark vortex, yearning to reach where it led.

Devlin suddenly felt a sharp pain in his head. Gravity was pulling him down. He fell backward onto the ground of this new realm. He stood up in a daze.

Not only had his body healed, he was fully clothed.

Each time he walked forward he felt a sinking sensation as if he had missed a step. While standing still, Devlin felt a continuous sense of falling. The curious creator walked onward into what seemed to be nothingness, but his feet did not slip. Suddenly he felt a constriction on his wrists. The youthful inventor fell to the ground, pulled down by an unseen force. His legs felt cold steel wrap around them. Soon his whole body was bound by unseen chains.

"Where is Kaity?" yelled Devlin into the indiscernible void above.

Not the slightest reverberation of sound was heard. His words disappeared almost as he spoke them.

Unable to hear even his own words, Devlin checked his ears for damage.

"Where's my wife!" called out Devlin. He looked to his feet. Unable to move, he sobbed. Time seemed meaningless as his cries were silenced by the atmosphere.

Devlin clenched his teeth.

Peering down on him was a man with short black hair, rectangular glasses, a well-groomed goatee and golden eyes. The man was dressed in a lab coat, black disco pants with glitter stars, and white light-up sneakers. The DNA strand necklace was the only thing the two of them wore in common.

"I'm in Hell," said Devlin, his vitality sapped.

Deceivant shrugged his shoulders.

"Screw you!" yelled Devlin.

Deceivant pointed to his ear, signaling that he could not hear him.

Devlin's hand trembled, but he managed to bring his middle finger up.

Deceivant nodded his head and smiled in acknowledgement. He placed a hand-crafted bell-shaped receiver on the angry boy's face and held the other side to his ear.

"I knew you would go to Hell. I knew that justice would win in the end," said Devlin in a dramatic, youthful voice.

"I'm here too," said Ada, snatching the receiver from her hubby.

The woman before him was covered in a white robe. Even with the robe on, her loving, motherly figure shined through. Ada's exposed hands, feet, and face were composed of blue numbers. Her long green digitized hair floated freely in the airless void. She smiled warmly at her little boy, her light blue lips lighting up from within.

"Good. Now you see that abandoning your child is a sin," said Devlin through his teeth.

Deceivant pressed his cheeks against his wife's. "I take it you lost to Exp 8."

"Shut up! I don't need you to rub it in," said Devlin.

"We're not here to fight with you. We found out where Kaity is, and we thought you should know. But if you want us to—" said Deceivant.

"Where is she!" yelled Devlin, standing up before being pulled back down by the chains.

Deceivant turned his gaze away. "Kaity is in Sel," he said with a heavy breath.

"Impossible, I sent her halfway across the globe where she would be safe," said Devlin with clenched teeth.

"Well, one way or another, she arrived in Sel," said Deceivant.

"Oh, don't worry, son. I'm sure you'll find her," said Ada, patting her little boy's head.

"Kaity," said Devlin with teary eyes.

Ada went down to her knees. "We will find a way to free both of you," she said before embracing him.

"I have to save her," said Devlin with trembling hands, struggling to break the chains.

"You're stuck here. According to Efil, there has never been an escape from this place. It is hopeless to try. We're working on a way to save Kaity, but you're doomed. You can't rescue her if you can't go to Sel," said Deceivant bluntly.

"Wait, where? I thought this was Sel," said Devlin.

"No, this place is for special cases. You are in the realm of eternal boredom, not suffering. Unlike Sel, this place was made to be a prison. You can never escape here," said Deceivant with a sudden dark tone.

"Don't pull that crap with me! If you had to escape to save Ada, you would try until you were dead. No matter how hopeless it was."

"Yeah, that's probably true, heheh." Deceivant wrapped his arm around his beloved.

"I won't give up either," said Devlin with a determined fist.

"I knew you wouldn't. We're both hopelessly stubborn. Good luck son," said Deceivant, holding his lover's gentle hand.

"What are you so happy about? You were condemned to this place as well. Both of you were. You're stuck here just like me," said Devlin with a smirk.

"Oh, is that what you thought? No, no, we're only visiting. We both arrived in Lum. You thought we were sent here…with you? Preposterous, haha," said Deceivant, patting the lost child's head.

"What! That's not fair! How come you were sent to Lum!" asked Devlin, writhing around on the ground.

"Funny story. Turns out that by fighting against you, I atoned for my sins. At least that's what the so-called goddess said. They believe in such nonsense," said Deceivant, twirling his DNA pendant.

"You're a pedophile! You don't belong in Lum!"

"I've given children across the globe another chance at life. My nonprofit group has found many homes for so many orphans. I've empowered children to see themselves as independent entities, capable of complex thought. There's no reason I shouldn't go to Heaven."

"You abandoned me!"

"You don't understand. Things aren't so simple."

"What about the others? Are all of the Exps in Lum?" asked Devlin.

"I've seen most of them," said Deceivant.

"They should be safe there. I suppose it worked out. By defying Etah I saved their souls," said Devlin with a warm smile.

"Aww, that's my boy. Worry not, my precious little boy, I will not rest until I've found a way to free you," said Ada, holding him lovingly to her chest.

Devlin teared up. "Stop pretending you care about me! I don't love you, so just stop it! I killed you! I smashed your head with my foot!"

"You did what?" yelled Deceivant.

"It doesn't matter what you did; you're my son and I love you," said Ada, grabbing her husband's fist.

"Of course it matters! We're going back to Lum now," said Deceivant, pulling his beloved close to him.

Ada peered over her shoulder. "I'll save you," she said, walking through the white portal.

"Don't think this means I forgive you!" hollered Devlin.

They then disappeared from sight, leaving Devlin all alone.

Devlin stared into the sky, but there was only a void. It seemed to continue for infinity. He was suddenly seized by an all-pervasive feeling of insignificance. "So meaningless! How pathetic was my rebellion against this fractured world? I was a mere speck battling the laws of the universe. Ahehehehehahahaha-hughu-hugh!" He began to sob.

The charismatic creator shook away his tears. "No! I won't let them hurt Kaity. I don't care if I'm condemned to this place till the end of time. Kaity will not suffer!" he yelled, fighting against the invisible force pinning him down.

The chains tightened their grip, bringing him right back down.

"A mere nuisance." Wires shot out of the pores in his skin and tore the chains apart.

Now free, Devlin searched the area. In the distance was an infinite void, just like the sky of the realm. There was no horizon. If not for gravity, he wouldn't even be able to distinguish the ceiling from the floor. He squinted and noticed a dot in the distance.

"I'm not the only one here." Devlin ran on all fours up to the figure, his hope increasing with every leap.

"Hey! Who's there! Hello!" yelled Devlin running all the way up to the shadowy figure.

The figure had a long clear cloak around it. In its cupped hands was a human skull.

"It's just a statue." Devlin looked on the ground to see a cord attached to a funnel. He put it to his ear but heard nothing. "Great. I'm alone! In the middle of nowhere! With no escape!" He slammed his fist into the skull.

The statue sprung to life and placed the other end of the cord to the skull's mouth.

"Who dares strike a guardian of Absence?" asked the skull, having the figure turn it to look around.

"Isn't it obvious?" asked Devlin with a smirk.

"So it was you. You admit to your aggressive outburst! You must be a complete idiot! Tehtehtehtehteh!" exclaimed the skull in a shrill mocking voice.

Devlin stood up proudly. "You have no idea who I am, do you?"

"Let's see: youthful, neither teenager nor adult, full of rage, brooding, black hair covering one intense golden eye, black lab coat, red undershirt, obsessed with revenge, oh, and a one-track pedophilic mind…you must be Devlin. Tehtehtehtehteh!"

"Shut it." Devlin punched the skull, spinning it around in place. "I want some answers," he said, aggressively pointing at the skull.

The hooded figure pressed his pointer finger against the skull's crown to cease the rotation.

"Which is it? Silence or answers? Tehtehteh."

"I want answers!"

"Of course you do. One as forwardly brutal as you must have need for my intellectual prowess. Ask away, prisoner."

"Why am I here?"

"Oh, that's a bit too philosophical, don't you think?"

"Fine. Where am I?"

"In Absence, the sanctuary of Sellum. Well, it could be seen as a prison too, depending on whether you see the universe as mostly dark matter or full of planets. This is a special place where those who aren't permitted to incarnate—the really mischievous ones—and those dedicated paragons of existence who want to reach enlightenment are both welcomed and—to put it in kind words—trapped for all eternity! Tehtehteh!"

"Where's the exit to this prison?"

The figure slowly spun the skull around. It shifted it up and down. It then removed it, examined itself, and then inspected the mortal.

"There is no escape! You will be trapped in here forever! Tehtehtehthehteh!"

"Okay, no exit. Well then, how do I get out of here?" asked Devlin, with a sly grin.

The skull was shifted to face the figure and the two nodded in synch. "Ah, now he's asking the right questions." The skull was abruptly turned to the ill-tempered boy. "The only way to get out is to defeat all the guardians!"

"How soon can I fight them? Where are they?"

"Don't waste your time. You died at the hands of your own child. Someone so pathhhhhetic will never be able to defeat the guardians. Even the greatest warriors have never accomplished such a feat."

"Aren't you a guardian?" asked Devlin.

"Very, very, very, very, very, veeeery observant! Yes, indeed! I am Eil, Guardian of Annoyance."

"Aptly named." Devlin backhanded the skull.

The hooded figure grabbed the skull and set it on the ground. It planted its feet into the ground and held out its cloaked arms.

"Ooooh, you're in trouble now," said Eil, chattering his teeth in delight.

"In trouble—I don't think so. Your protector is just going to keep me interested. Without getting my blood pumping I'll turn into a mindless drone. Time to get pumped," said Devlin, hopping in place.

The guard's fist launched at the resident, who slid out of the way.

Devlin kicked off the ground and slammed his feet into the hooded figure's shoulders. His legs then sandwiched his opponent's head.

Two thick spines came out from the sleeves of the guard.

The nimble scientist kicked off and landed on the ground with a wobble. "That's going to take some getting used to," he said, peering at the solid nothingness below his feet.

The figure rushed at the resident.

Devlin knocked one arm aside with his elbow and ducked under the other.

He watched the spike pass just above his head and smirked. After wrapping his arm around the protector's arm, he swung himself into a multi-kick directed at the figure's face. Once the quills were about to pierce him, the nimble scientist jumped off the guard's head.

The hooded figure leaped off the ground and thrust a spike at the resident's chest.

Devlin stopped the thick needle between his palms and tumbled to the ground along with the guard. He was gripping the spike in his palm and held the other arm back from gouging out his eye. "I was raised alongside an assassin. Don't feel too bad when I beat you."

The single spike split into three within the mortal's hand.

Rather than pressing forward, the figure pulled the needles out of the resident's grip.

Devlin kicked off.

The quills elongated and pierced the resident's shoulders.

Devlin hit the ground hard. After reorienting himself, he looked up to see that his opponent was gone. "What the…? He ran away? Things were just getting good." He hopped back to his feet.


"You find amusement in your own agony. How perplexing," said Eil.

Devlin crouched down to the skull. "Your bodyguard, where is he?"

"He was summoned. We are more than mere defenders of this realm; we keep it in balance."

"Is that so?" Devlin smacked the skull.

"Would you stop hitting me!" yelled Eil.

"What if I don't?" asked Devlin.

"I will…well, you're already in Absence. How would I punish you?"

"Exactly," said Devlin before hitting the talking skull once more.

"But, just because there is no greater torment awaiting you, does not mean you should continue this senseless mild violence."

"Why not, it's keeping me entertained," said Devlin, timing his punches to see how fast he could spin the skull.

Eil eventually stopped spinning and landed, staring right into Devlin's eyes with its bony sockets.

"Oh, I haven't heard that word in forever. Enter-tain-mentah! Simply saying it brings me joy. But you're a fool if you think you can keep this up. Soon you will grow tired of violence and must turn to something else."

"Is there anyone else here?" asked Devlin.

"Nope. Only you."

"Then no one has ever escaped because nobody has ever been banished from here, right?"

"Don't get your hopes up. There are billions of residents here."

"Where?"

"They are invisible. The only way for you to meet one would be to bump into them. Considering I don't even know how vast this plane is, the chances of a confrontation hardly exist."

"Then why am I visible?"

"You're an extra special case, though everyone here is special in some way or another. We have been ordered to make you visible so that you could later be found. You should feel quite good about it considering you are the first ever to have this privilege. Many, many, many, many, many congratulations!"

"Can you see them? Can they see you?"

"Most souls cannot see me, making my job here deathly boring. But every so often there is a problem child in need of correction."

"I'm not just another problem child. You were ordered to make me visible? Who made the order?"

"Lord…I mean Neutral. Yes, simply Neutral. It has a name as boring as this realm. Honestly, Devlin, I rather enjoyed it when you struck me. I may not have been able to feel the pain of the blow, but I felt the fear it brought."

"What are you going on about now?"

"Well, no amount of time can age emotions to death. I felt fear as freshly as a human child being spanked by their parents for the very first time," said Eil, bliss etched into his shrill voice.

"Don't talk to me about parents!"

"Ooooh, touchy, touchy."

"So, you just let the souls wander this void for eternity. What do you do exactly? Don't you have some sort of role to fulfill?"

"Most of my time is spent staring out into this void. I'm supposed to monitor and uphold the neutrality of the realm. But honestly, I don't think it needs much help. I used to have a grand old time tormenting the residents with songs, riddles, insults, paradoxical questions and obnoxious noises. Nowadays I don't do much of anything. Oh woe is me! I am forever cursed to be trapped here for all of time, looking out into an infinite span of nothingness."

"I refuse to stay here. Hope you enjoy your quest to find refuge in your pitiful existence," said Devlin before turning around.

"This little kitty has quite the bark! You really think you will escape here? Etah has tasked us with keeping you extra confined to this place."

"So this is his doing. Regardless, this isn't his realm. There's no point in convincing him. I need to talk to Neutral," said Devlin, looking around.

"Oh, it's useless to try, but keep up your wiggling. A good, hearty struggle provides me with some entertainment. Never give up! Tehteh, it keeps things fun."

"Where is he?"

"Oh, he's talking with Etah, they should be done soon. But soon is relative, after all. And as such, it is relatively insignificant. Tehtehteh."

"Ugh, so I have to wait. In the meantime, I'm going to let off some steam." Devlin began punching Eil again.

# Chapter 55: The Three Regions

"They want to hold us here. Perhaps they are still debating on what to do with us. I don't think it's safe. Let's get moving," said Kanasta.

"Agreed. Exp 8 is counting on us," said Kawai, floating above her unconscious brother.

"Are you saying we should betray Evol's trust? Its love is unconditional. The Deity of Love would never bring harm upon us. Do what your spirit tells you, but I will stay here," said Violet.

"They aren't upset at the moment. We shouldn't provoke them. It's useless to try to fight a deity," said Sefiwah.

"Any other cowards among us?" asked Bob.

NoOne raised his hand.

"I for one outright refuse to sit here and allow myself to be imprisoned," said Bob.

"I'm scared of prison. There are bad people there. They're gonna get me," said D.S., hiding behind his blue-skinned buddy.

"Only meritorious souls are here. Nobody in Heaven would harm you," said Violet, placing her hand on her brother's scalp.

"Do you think they allow smoking in Heaven?" asked Pharma, about to light his finger.

"More importantly are you allowed to inspire lust in the hearts of mortals? Because if not, then I'm a criminal," said Nina, squeezing her breasts.

"It doesn't matter what's allowed! What matters is that we are going to be imprisoned and then I can't save my brother," said Kawai, whining into her tail.

"As long as I'm locked up with you, I don't care," said Atatasuki, sitting up caressing his dear sister.

"Don't even joke about that! We have to free Brother. He fought for our freedom and now it's our turn! I refuse to fall in love with you again. You are merely a temporary substitute, got it?" asked Kawai, grabbing his head with her tail.

Atatasuki nodded.

"Good. So what's the plan?" asked Kawai.

"I don't get it. You couldn't stop Devlin. What makes you think you can stop a deity?" asked Sefiwah.

"I promised Sis, so therefore I will! It's as simple as that," said Atatasuki.

"I thought that was how it worked, but it's not quite so simple," said NoOne, seeping into the ground.

"Hey, nice job saving Atatasuki," said Ego, slugging Tempo.

"Never thought I'd use my powers to save a life. Hugh-hugh-heheheheh, maybe this place is getting to me," said Tempo, holding his sides.

"Thanks. I won't forget this," said Kawai, bowing to Tempo.

"Well I didn't forget that fight you gave me! Eheheheh, that was quite the thrill," said Tempo, his fist heating up.

"Hey!" Kawai spun around to face her faulty brother. "Do you think Brother beat Devlin?" asked Kawai.

"Of course. He promised he would, right?" asked Atatasuki.

"You're right, he must have," said Kawai, floating through the air in bliss.

"Not really. Evol said he's in Sel, right? Doesn't that mean he lost?" asked Bob.

"Don't you care?" asked Riufen.

"I'm sorry, what?"

"About Devlin…at all?" asked Riufen.

"How many times must I explain myself? I was following Deceivant's will. I would have killed Devlin myself if I was ordered to," said Bob with a grin.

"You pretended to be Devlin's ally. You betrayed his trust," said Riufen, stepping up to the ball of dishonor.

"But of course, I am obedient only to my true master," said Bob.

"It is a shame to lose to one without a shred of honor," said Riufen, looking down.

"Don't you talk, you disobeyed my direct order!" exclaimed Bob.

"That's enough, we cannot fight amongst ourselves," said Kanasta.

"Who died and made you leader? I am not afraid of the power of some deity," said Bob, circling around the assassin boss.

"Wait a minute. Bob, how did you die?" asked Atatasuki.

"I didn't. Devlin used the Teleport Artifact to send me away. Such a cheap trick," said Bob, his veins intensifying.

Atatasuki stood on top of a rock. "Everyone, may I have your attention? We need to elect a leader since Exp 8 is currently trapped in Sel. I nominate Kawai. After all, she's a prototype of him and she's incredibly adorable."

"That she is. Alright, I agree," said Deceivant, raising his hand.

"Why would she lead us?" Bob circled around the scrawny little girl. "I killed you, so I outrank you."

"I never told you to kill my wittle Kawai!" exclaimed Deceivant.

"When did you get back? Is Devlin okay? Does he miss me?" asked Matteria.

"We arrived recently. Devlin is unharmed," said Deceivant.

Matteria turned to Ada. "Where did you get that robe?"

"Evol gave it to me. The deity didn't want my body to inspire passion in the visitors of Lum. I said there was no need to worry before happily accepting her gift," said Ada with a twirl.

"Hey where's Demonica? Is she hiding somewhere, waiting to strike?" asked NoOne, keeping away from the bushes.

"She vanished in a beam of light back on Earth," said Ada.

"May she never return," said NoOne.

"Stop talking. Look," said Sefiwah, pointing to a white portal.

Efil emerged before the gathering of Exps.

The Goddess of Life had a meek body that was covered in moss, emanated a soothing white aura, and naturally bent like a flower. In her seaweed hair was her cherished white Madonna lily. Two gentle green and brown eyes complemented her beaming smile. The pink lotus lilies protecting her chest had yet to bloom. A light-pink Canterbury Bell flower grew from her hips and stretched over her fragile knees. Dandelion wings, radiating light from within, naturally bent in reverence to Lum.

Violet fell to her knees as she spontaneously worshiped.

"Do not praise me, please. Pride is a sin," said Efil, speaking in a humble whispery tone that lacked self-assurance.

"Hey, I know you," said Deceivant.

"Yes and I know you. You're the one who broke our covenant," said Efil with a somber look.

"How did I do that?" asked Deceivant.

"You handed my powers down to Ada. They were supposed to return to me after you died," said Efil, making a flower bloom on her finger.

"Well then punish me how you see fit, because there was no way I was going to leave Ada unprotected," said Deceivant, pulling his beloved in close.

"Punishing you will solve nothing. I will take your infidelity as grounds to be more wary of the legitimacy of the promises you make from here on out," said Efil with an unsettled smile.

"So, why are you here?" asked Kawai suspiciously.

"There's no reason for any unrest. I am here to integrate you into Lum. Exps are living creatures and will be treated like everyone else."

"This is the place our brother was fighting for. This is a land of freedom and equality," said Atatasuki in a blissful daze.

"Let's not jump to any conclusions," said Kawai with a discerning glare.

"What sort of integration?" asked Kanasta.

"We will have you properly monitored; there is no reason for concern. No harm will come to you under the light of Lum's oversight."

"And what if we don't want to integrate?" asked Ego, lifting his visor and revealing his blue eyes.

"I don't see why you wouldn't. Integrating means being assigned to specific regions, and each region is watched by a group of guardian angels. I'll try to keep all of you as undivided as I can."

"Why split us up at all?" asked Deceivant.

"It is part of the integration process. But also, Sel feels threatened by your presence," said Efil, looking to the ground.

"So then, you work for Etah now?" asked Deceivant.

"Never! The only reason we listen to his demands is to keep the peace."

"And you want to keep the peace because your flower attacks are completely useless," said Bob, watching Riufen's forward thrusts.

"We are worried. The slightest disturbance could set off Etah. I will need you all to comply with any orders I give. Know that Lum wants you safe and will do nothing to endanger you."

"What if we don't want to stay?" asked Kawai.

"I don't understand why you—"

"And if we don't?"

"Let's hope it doesn't come to that."

"Atatasuki and I are going to Sel to rescue our brother. You can't bribe us with this false paradise. Our only paradise is together, as a family," said Kawai, her tail on end.

"You can't leave. It isn't safe. I am tasked with protecting all of you," said Efil with shaky hands.

"My brother died so that we could all be free to go wherever we wanted. I won't let you put his efforts in vain."

"At least hear me out before you turn down my offer. I'll talk to Lum about a possible escort to Sel."

"And Absence," said Matteria.

"Not a problem. The only means to gain access to Sel is from Absence anyway. Just realize that once you arrive in Sel you will be on your own. The angels will not assist you in rescuing your allies," said Efil.

"So, why don't you explain what you mean by integration," said Tempo, his back against a tree and a twig clenched between his sharpened teeth.

"Yes, of course. I'll give you the routine rundown." The goddess took in a deep breath and worked up the energy to form a gentle genuine smile. "Greetings, wayward souls. Congratulations on your benevolent life and welcome to Lum. Here, all live in God's grace; there is no violence or competition. This is a realm of peace and of freedom. But this peace can only be maintained as long as the visitors follow simple but extremely important rules. Due to certain rules being broken in the past, changes were made in order to prevent the inclinations that led to this rule-breaking. Rule number one: No unwelcomed physical contact. Any contact must be made with consent of both parties. Rule number two: No acts of procreation or intentional displays of erotic nature."

"Go ahead, lock me up. My body is a beacon of arousal," said Nina, covering her breasts all the while caressing them.

"You haven't broken any rules. Please let me continue," said Efil with a smile.

Nina stepped back, ashamed that she would not be promptly incarcerated.

"Wait, so sex is forbidden here, in this pseudo paradise?" asked Deceivant.

"Completely. The only time sex is necessary is when there is a shortage of a population. Sex is punishable by banishment. Virgins in Lum stay virgins, understood?" asked Efil, surveying the crowd.

"I suppose that is understandable," said Ada, biting her thumb.

"Hmm, makes sense to me," said Deceivant with a shrug.

"So in the land of desire you can't have sex? That's not fair at all," said Matteria.

"Desire and fulfillment are two very different things, after all," said Anthrax with a big smile.

"Rule number three: No acts of violence or provocation of violence are allowed. This rule can be broken if the need for self-defense arises. Rule number four: Visitors must be actively conscious of where they step, doing their best to avoid stepping on other living beings, such as insects, grass, and flowers."

"But there's grass everywhere," said D.S., sucking on his thumb.

"Tread lightly and compassionately. Rule number five: No alteration to the environment is permitted, each soul must be respected as a self-determining individual; this is not limited to breaking twigs, carving on trees or displacing snow in a frivolous manner."

"This is really it. A paradise for all souls," said Violet, her cheeks rosy with joy.

"Rule number six: No profanity or violence-inspiring words in any language. Rule number seven: All angels must be obeyed. If there is a question about a specific order given by an angel, a second angel may be called in to mediate the disagreement. Rule number eight: Visitors will not speak or act in a way that undermines the glory of Lum. Rule number nine: When the call to prayer comes, made apparent by the radiant pillar of light in the sky, all visitors will pray for as long as the sky remains alight. Rule number ten: If any of the rules are broken once, the perpetrator may or may not be pardoned. If the act is deemed intentional, they will be punished."

"Punished how?" asked Deceivant, tilting his head to get a peek at Kawai's pink panties.

"That depends on the act committed and the circumstances surrounding the incident. There are no trials, and only the gods of Lum are authorized to punish rule-breakers."

"I don't like all these rules," said D.S., crossing his arms.

Efil flapped her wings, releasing dandelion seeds coated in her white aura. "There is no need for concern. Preventative measures have already been taken on behalf of the safety of the visitors. Due to the excessive breaking of rules one and two, Lum has been divided into three regions. There is Femina, Masculino, and Complex. We keep the women in Femina and the men in Masculino. Complex is for beings like snails or other hermaphroditic creatures; it is also for non-gendered species, including those that asexually reproduce. You are all currently in Femina."

"Could you elaborate a bit more on the reason for this division?" asked Deceivant, sitting down before shifting his gaze back to Kawai.

"Certainly. Lum was originally undivided, but once humans started gaining access to Lum, a lot of them desired…well…sexual experiences. We didn't want Lum to get crowded, so we separated the two sexes. The other animals, with notably few exceptions, obeyed the law. We separated them as well to maintain equality. We keep a close eye on everything happening in Lum. And I must say I am ashamed of some of your behavior," said Efil with a slightly raised voice, glaring at Atatasuki. She stood up straight and stiffened her spine. "Let me be clear. Fighting Devlin has not atoned for your sins. We are keeping you in Lum to protect you from Sel's grasp. Though I won't reprimand you for your actions in the past, future transgressions will not be ignored. This is your chance to start anew. Don't squander it."

"Is there money here?" asked Kanasta.

"Of course not! Money is the source of such horrid sin! It creates greed and is formed from the dead skin of trees and the pillaging of the Earth. The only good money does is keep humans away from the sin of sloth. Farewell for now. Some angels will be here to escort you to your new homes. May Lum's blessing be with all of you," said Efil before vanishing.

The team was suddenly surrounded by wolves, tigers, bears, deer, and alligators, all with radiant white wings of light erupting from their backs.

Violet bowed down reverently.

"Are these the angels?" asked Riufen.

"It would appear so," said Sefiwah, getting into a fighting stance.

"So many fluffy creatures!" cheered Opti, rushing up to hug the bear.

D.S. grabbed Opti before he could reach the bear. "No hugs. Remember?"

"What is wrong with this place?" asked Opti in tears.

The tigers and wolves began to separate the males from the females by nudging them to different sides of the grassy field while the other angels stayed on the lookout.

Atatasuki held his sister's hand tightly. "I'm never leaving her alone again," he said to himself.

"Ow, don't clench your hand so hard," said Kawai, whacking him with her tail.

The tiger growled at Atatasuki.

"We are family. You can't tear us apart," said Atatasuki.

"All the more reason to separate you," said the tiger.

"Whoa! I understood that! Did anyone else hear him talk?" asked Atatasuki.

"I am Ada. It is a pleasure to meet you," she said to the wolf in front of her.

"A pleasure to meet you as well. Leave the man and come with me. We will lead you to the other females," said the wolf.

"I don't want to leave my husband, is there any way you could reconsider?" asked Ada.

"We cannot."

"What should I do?" asked Ada, pulling her lover close to her.

"Go with them. As long as Violet follows along, I don't think it will be an issue," said Deceivant, blowing his beloved a kiss.

"I will keep her safe," said Violet with a smile.

"As will I," said Sefiwah.

"Hey kitty, how are you talking?" asked D.S.

"I am an angel. Do not speak to me in such a demeaning way. All angels are able to communicate with those going through transition. We can all speak in a mutually intelligible and instantly translated language. Without communication, the system of Lum would be ineffective. Misinformation can lead to great calamities."

"Cool. So are you like, psychic?" asked D.S.

"I speak telepathically utilizing my soul energy."

"That's incredible!" cheered D.S.

"It's a rudimentary soul power. I do it all the time," said Bob.

"Whoa. What am I thinking about right now?" asked D.S.

"How cool I am," said Bob with a smirk.

"Yeah, that's right. You are psychic!"

"Hey, Boss, what do we do?" asked Tempo, refusing to budge.

"Play along for now," said Kanasta, joining the male side.

The female wolf and the male tiger stopped when they reached Matteria.

"This is a tricky one. It is male, but…" said the wolf, looking up at the bulge in Matteria's striped rainbow panties.

"It appears female," said the tiger.

"What? I am obviously a guy!" exclaimed Matteria.

"Let's put it in Femina. It will cause the least disruption there," said the wolf.

"Yes, no doubt it would create unrest in Masculino," said the tiger.

"The fact that you are even having this argument shows how outdated and inapplicable gender boundaries are," said Matteria, sticking out his tongue.

"Come on, Matteria, join us!" cheered Ada.

"Alright, I'll go," said Matteria, dragging his feet to the female side.

"Matty, don't worry, I'm sure we'll meet again," said Anthrax as he was escorted to the male side.

"Just be careful, ok?" asked Matteria.

"I will. I love you!" exclaimed Anthrax, giving his boyfriend a big air hug.

"I love you too!" exclaimed Matteria, blowing multiple kisses to his lover.

The angels stopped once more at Bob.

"Male or female?"

"I transcend such concepts," replied Bob, forming a male and female sign with his soul energy before evaporating them.

"To Complex then. You'll be grouped with the other asexual creatures," said the wolf.

"Whatever, come along, BoneSaw," said Bob, lifting up the little robot.

"What is the problem with you?" asked Karson, being pulled away from the male side.

"Not male, artificial, join your eyeball friend," said the wolf.

"I am a man! Metal or flesh, I know what I am!" exclaimed Karson with a proud pose.

"You tell them!" cheered Matteria.

"Why must you of all people agree with me?" asked Karson, his hand to his forehead.

"Get over here. We don't have time to waste," said Bob, pulling Karson to his side.

"These creatures are so complicated. What do we do with this one?" asked a tiger, looking up at NoOne.

"Just put it with the males," said the wolf.

"What? How come the shadow is a man, but the gun is put with the asexual people? A gun is a phallic symbol! This is bloody ridiculous!" yelled Karson.

"I bet if they saw your cannon they wouldn't argue!" hollered Matteria.

"You bet your sweet arse they wouldn't!" hollered Karson.

"Are we going or not?" asked Bob with irritated look.

Once Atatasuki was pried away from Kawai by a bear angel, the entire team had been segregated.

"Let go of me!" yelled Atatasuki, struggling in the bear's grip.

"Don't bother fighting them. Efil is forwarding our request. For now we stay put and follow their orders. Stay put, got it?" asked Kawai with wide eyes.

"Understood. I'll never forget you!" yelled Atatasuki as he was pulled away.

"You had better not!" hollered Kawai.

"Females, stay here. The men and asexual visitors will be moved elsewhere," said the lead wolf.

"Will we ever see them again?" asked Ada, looking longingly at her husband.

"Separation is necessary for the transition into your new lives," said the wolf.

The other groups were escorted out of the forest clearing.

"Okay, so now what do we do?" asked Nina.

"Stay within the forest. If you leave Femina, we will be alerted. That is all."

Violet rushed up and tapped the angels' back. "Wait, I just need to know. Is this it?"

"What?"

"Are there other destinations? Um…is there only one Heaven?"

"There are three realms of the afterlife: Sel, Absence, and Lum. There is no Heaven."

The female angels left the area.

"We aren't going to play along with this, are we?" asked Nina.

"We died. Might as well make the best of this new life," said Sefiwah.

"Transitioning into a new life means they want us to reincarnate. If I'm not keeping this bodacious body, then I don't want to go back," said Nina.

"They won't force us to do anything we don't want to. Let's just try and enjoy ourselves," said Ada.

"You don't mind reincarnating, do you?" asked Kawai.

"That isn't what I said. I just think we shouldn't upset our new friends," said Ada.

"Well I'm not even going to worry about a new existence till I've rescued my brother. In the meantime, I'm sticking with mom," said Kawai, sitting on Ada's shoulder.

"That's wonderful news," said Ada, patting her daughter's head.

"You can stay here. I'm going to practice my poses…alone," said Nina, walking off.

"I'm going to examine the forest. We may need a quick escape later," said Sefiwah before rushing out of sight.

Matteria stepped up to Violet. "You want to rescue Devlin too, don't you?"

Violet did not respond. She was muttering below her breath.

"Of course she does, we all do, right?" asked Ada, poking Kawai's belly.

"Yeah, but Brother's rescue comes first," said Kawai.

"But if we rescue him first, he won't help us save Master Devlin," said Matteria.

"My brother isn't like that. He helps those who are imprisoned. Once he sees I'm alive and well, I'm sure he'll forget all about his silly grudge with Devlin," said Kawai.

"I hope so," said Matteria with a worried look.


The males and NoOne were escorted all the way out of the forest and into a jungle.

"Do not leave this jungle," said the lead tiger.

"Understood," said Kanasta.

The tigers left the area.

"Okay, so while we wait, let's figure out a plan for when we get to Sel," said Atatasuki.

"Nobody knows anything about Sel, and we aren't going on your pointless journey. I already died once," said Tempo, eyeing his cheerful killer.

"Then what's the plan? We just stay here and wait to be judged? We're assassins. Who knows what they'll make us reincarnate as? I mean if karma carries over, we'll probably be born without arms or legs," said Ego, staring into a puddle.

"What's wrong with that? Rather have a crippled body than a mind bound by society's ideals. Look, if we are going to reincarnate, we're doing it together. And I doubt the Boss has any plans for that," said Tempo, putting his arm around Ego.

"We are not reincarnating. We have a job to do," said Kanasta.

"Agreed. Devlin-sama needs us," said Riufen.

"As does Kaity. Worrying about reincarnation is just what these angels want. The more we think about it the easier it will be for them to manipulate us," said Deceivant.

"That's right. Don't let them get in your head," said Pharma, hunched over and shivering.

"But angels are the good guys, right? Hey, if we're good guys now, will we come back as good guys?" asked D.S.

"Of course we will! Soul memory is a powerful thing! I hope I come back as something super fluffy and herbivorous. Speaking of which, who wants to come with me to find fluffy creatures?" asked Opti, peering at his friends with hope brewing in his eyes.

"I'll go. Don't forget we can't touch them," said D.S.

"I'll come along as well. Perhaps we will run into some sheep," said NoOne.

"Sheep in a jungle? You're stupid," said D.S.

"Now, now, behave," said Deceivant with a stern finger.

"Okay. I'm sorry, NoOne," said D.S, lowering his head.

"Not a problem. You'll be the one feeling stupid once we find some sheep," said NoOne.

"Betcha we won't find any."

"Bet we will."

"Loser has to…hug a bear."

"You're on."

"Sheep in a jungle…why does that seem familiar?" asked Atatasuki.

"Kanasta, would you go along and accompany your brother?" asked Deceivant.

"I must work on enhancements. If we are to break Devlin out, I will need to grow stronger."

"What am I supposed to do? This place is boring," said Tempo.

"I agree, dude. What's the point of being in Heaven if you're stuck with a bunch of guys?" asked Ego, needlessly mucking about with his headset.

"I think I finally understand how they feel. The patients on their deathbeds, I mean. They want a second chance. They don't want to leave their loved ones behind. I want to go back to Earth and continue my life. I don't ever want to move on or be stuck in this paradise. Here I can't help anyone. I feel useless," said Anthrax.

"Heeeey, don't say that. You got drugs in that bag?" asked Pharma with a toothy grin.

"Prescription drugs, though they aren't real. Even my nametag isn't real," said Anthrax, pushing out his bottom lip.

"If they aren't real, then hand them over!" yelled Pharma, lunging at the supplier.

Kanasta pinned the addict to the ground. "Calm yourself."

"I don't even give patients placebos without diagnosing them first. Sorry, it's against my code as a doctor," said Anthrax, pulling his medical bag in close.

"You're not a doctor anymore! Here you are just another soul, getting prepped for a new existence," said Pharma, clawing at the ground.

"I've been a doctor since the day of my creation. It's more than a career for me. I won't let being dead end my way of life. There has to be someone injured here," said Anthrax, searching the grass.

"Just hand them over!" yelled Pharma.

"If there were any injured here, then I believe the angels would take care of them," said Riufen.

"That's it! I could become an angel. Then I could be of some use to this place. How do I become an angel?" asked Anthrax.

"Listen to yourself. You're a doctor; you shouldn't be talking about angels," said Deceivant, looking up at the sky.

"Exps can't dream, so whether it makes sense or not, this place is real. I'm going to go look for some angels. Anyone want to come with me?" asked Anthrax.

"Can't let a kid wander off alone. I'll come along. Besides, there are some tests I'd like to try out on these so-called angels as soon as I'm done with this," said Deceivant, examining a white petal that fell into his hand.

"I'm going with the nature group then. Hey, big guy, that means you can get off," said Pharma, trying to steady his breaths.

Kanasta released him.

"Hey guys, while we look for sheep let's keep our eyes peeled for some Bufo toads!" hollered Pharma, rushing to Opti's group.

"You know, Atatasuki, if you would like to help your brother…" Riufen pulled out his spine and pointed it at his ally, "spar with me."

"Sorry, but I'll decline. I need to go through my memory and delete some sound bites, pictures, and video clips," said Atatasuki, sitting down and leaning against a tree. "Um, does this count as nonconsensual contact?"

"You're not cutting up the tree. I doubt it is offended," said Riufen.

"Hey Tempo, mind giving me some fighting tips?" asked Ego.

"Why the hell not? There's not much else I can do."

A monkey angel dropped from the trees and approached Tempo.

"What the hell do you want?" asked Tempo, chewing on the twig in his mouth.

"No violence." It pulled the twig out from his teeth. "And do not speak of the dark realm."

"I'm not gonna last here. Not without busting some skulls open," said Tempo with a clenched fist.

"Hey, uh, you're an angel, right?" asked Anthrax.

"I am," replied the monkey.

"Is there a training course for angels or were you born an angel?"

"Birth is not allowed in Lum. No exceptions. I chose to become an angel."

"Can I become an angel too? I only want to help people. I think becoming an angel is the best way."

"There has never been an Exp angel before. Are you prepared to uphold Lum's values and abandon all connections?"

"I want some information, that's all. Don't want to make the change until I'm sure it's what's best."

"Come with me. I shall see if I can schedule you an appointment with a goddess."

"Sure, thanks a lot."

"My pleasure."

"I'll join you," said Deceivant.


The final group was escorted to a swamp.

The angel escorts left in the mist.

"Okay, so any ideas where Demo might be?" asked Bob, turning to face Karson.

"Not a bloody clue. Why do I have to be stuck with you of all people?" asked Karson, pointing his gun at the floating safety hazard.

"I'm not going to kill you again. We should split up into two groups and look for Demo. Fusion, lead the way," said Bob.

"BoneSaw, you come with me. Let's get away from that one-eyed lunatic. I can't wait till we reunite with our fearless leader," said Karson.

# Chapter 56: Sinner's Fury

Previously: Exp 8 met with Sinner's Fury, the only rebel group in Sel. He decided to wait for the other demon lords to arrive before leaving to fight Etah.

"She's late again. I suppose such a pretty little morsel has to have some undesirable qualities. Still waiting on her to agree to our wedding. She must feel so honored to have the Prince of Pleasure doting on her. Well, words can't do her fortune justice," he said, adjusting the heart lapel on his suit.

The demon lord sitting next to Exp 8 was slender, dressed in a tuxedo made of the finest skin and had a contorted grin, making him unnaturally alluring.

"Doting eh, that's a bit of a misrepresentation don'cha think?"

Seated next to the Prince of Pleasure was a muscular demon lord. Bulging eyes, nostril holes, and an open mouth made up its face. Its pot belly made a boiling sound, and its fingers had been replaced with cooking utensils.

"Don't pretend you can understand the longing I feel," said the Prince, gripping his lapel.

"That heart you have looks, mmm, rather appetizing. What do you want for it?" asked the gluttonous demon.

"I apologize, but I already have my eyes on the Princess of Insight," said the Prince in a suave, sultry voice that almost masked his dark tone.

"So, Duchess of Desire, what are your plans for me? The Prince seems a bit preoccupied to have an agenda," said Exp 8.

"I'd rather like to have you as my servant. I've heard all about those energy orbs you create, they sound positively scrumptious," said the Duchess in a slobbery, deranged tone oozing with desire.

"Are any of you in this for the residents? You all went through the same process, didn't you?" asked Exp 8.

"Sentimentality is what ruins a rebellion," said the Führer, polishing his golden belly while hoisted by his portable throne.

"I disagree," said the Baroness of Blades, sharpening the tip of a sword protruding from her chest.

"Then why did you join this rebellion?" asked Exp 8.

"I only feel alive when I fight for a cause. Battle without purpose feels empty. That said, I have been known to start a battle and add meaning in the midst of the bout." She flicked her wrist, causing blades to shoot out of her fingers.

"And what are your plans for me?" asked Exp 8.

"To not let you steal my kill. Etah must die by my blades. I've been fighting as Sel's hero long before you came along. Besides, I can slice you to ribbons anytime I please," she said, flashing her bladed fangs.

"I'll be the one to remove the king from his throne. He's a battle-hardened warrior. Only a subtle approach can do him in," said the Prince, pressing his finger against his glowing purple lips.

The Duchess of Desire stood up. "Give it to me! Give me that heart!" She lunged at the prince, stabbing his back with the hooks embedded into the top of her hands.

"Mind your manners, filth!" The Prince smacked the Duchess across the face. He bit his finger and then jabbed it into her eye. "Maybe you wouldn't be so picky if you couldn't see." His lusty pink eyes caught something in the distance. He removed the hooks, pushed off the Duchess, and straightened his lapel. "The Princess has arrived," he said with a wide grin and a gentlemanly bow.

The Princess of Insight was a sluggish young woman. She dragged her broken leg behind her and was pulled along by two helper demons. Her hair reached the ground and covered her face. Beneath the hair were two rows of sharpened teeth. One final hand came out from behind her like a tail and limply swayed back and forth.

"Absolutely stunning! No fire in Sel burns hotter than my passion for you," said the Prince, gripping his lapel in euphoric agony.

"I beg to differ," said the General of Genocide, throwing a fireball at the Prince.

The Prince need not even move.

The Princess skated into the fireball's trajectory and was knocked off her feet.

The Prince caught the star-crossed damsel in his arms and twisted her around into a passionate kiss. "Nothing more beautiful than someone willing to die for you," he said, her extra long tongue clenched between his teeth.

"Just don't expect me to fall for you. I died unmarried," said the Baroness of Blades.

"So then you remember, don't you? Was it an enjoyable death?" asked the Prince, now sucking on his princess' supple neck.

"No. I don't remember. But I just know it. I'm independent. Always have been. Most likely I was an orphan," she said, juggling a knife with one hand.

"So none of you remember why you were sent here? Doesn't that upset you?" asked Exp 8.

"Come now, do you question why you were born where you were born, with those particular parents, in a specific time? My mistake, you weren't born at all, were you? Such a wretched creature," said the Duke of Deception, adjusting the skin on its face.

"I asked all those questions and you should too. Why should you be punished for doing something you can't even remember?" asked Exp 8.

"It would be nice to remember, wouldn't it? Sure would make rediscovering your specialty a bit easier. Though mine was exceptionally easy to decipher," said the Prince, caressing his princess' smooth back.

"All of you rule a different region, right? You're all demon lords, one step below gods. If that's true, does that mean together you own all the land?" asked Exp 8.

"Not yet," said the Führer, admiring his rings. "There are roughly five demon lords per region. I'm the only one here who rules an entire region."

"So then, you killed your competition?" asked Exp 8.

"Not at all. I merely shifted their wealth up the ladder," said the Führer with a solid gold grin.

"If it wasn't for this delectable little treat, I wouldn't have joined. But she has captured my heart," said the Prince as he lifted up the Princess by her squishy bottom into a near kiss.

"Hey Princess, what about you? What do you want with me?" asked Exp 8.

The Princess stared at him blankly.

"She doesn't even know who you are. Can't imagine how she became a demon lord," said the Duchess, tapping her spoon fingers together.

"The previous demon lord of her city was poisoned, the other potential candidates died by various accidents. Providence protects her from those who wish to do her harm and from those who stand in her path. She was called the Princess of Misfortune beforehand, but after we met up and fell for one another, I gave her a name worthy of her talent."

"I'm done asking questions. We should start the meeting," said Exp 8, leaning back in his fleshy chair.

"Getting you acquainted is part of the meeting. But we should decide our next course of action. Mediator, you may proceed," said the Duke of Deception.

The Mediator got up from the floor and dropped an object from its sleeves.

It was a searing hot thorn.

Each demon lord pierced their palm and filled the Mediator's bony bowl with three drops of blood.

"What are we doing?" asked Exp 8, picking up the thorn.

The Mediator gazed up at the hero with a wide smile.

"Giving the Mediator a paycheck," said the Führer.

"This place has strange customs." Exp 8 pierced his hand and gave the bowl his blood.

Once the last bit of blood was collected, the Mediator brought the bowl up to its lips and drank the contents while swaying its hips. Once finished, the Mediator dropped a seven-sided die from its sleeve.

"So this is how you settle disputes?" asked Exp 8.

"Even in Sel, there must be a modicum of fairness. We all agreed to the terms, let's see who it lands on this time," said the Prince.

The die stopped on a seven.

"Congratulations on your first time being chosen. What is our next move, leader?" asked the Prince, turning to his damsel.

The Princess stared at the dice as if not comprehending the outcome.

"Does she talk at all?" asked Exp 8.

"Do you not see the holes in her throat? She had her vocal cords removed by one of the other candidates. It's a miracle she's still alive," said the Prince, petting his doll with the tips of his fingers.

"What shall we do now?" asked the Duke, fiddling with its eyelashes.

"Well, as her fiancé, I'll decide in her place, naturally," said the Prince.

"Fiancé? She hasn't agreed to marry you yet. We aren't fooled so easily," said the Duchess before biting into his tantalizing lapel.

The Prince grabbed the cretins head and flung her aside. "I think we should host a public execution of Etah's hero," he said, half-grinning at Exp 8.

"He has far too much potential value to be eliminated," said the Duke.

"I've decided. As the leader, my word is final," said the Prince.

"You're not the leader. Roll the dice again," said the Baroness, practicing her quick draw.

"Don't even bother!" yelled Exp 8, standing out of his chair. "I only wanted to know what this rebellion stood for, I never agreed to help. You're all out for your own special interests or for some kind of sick thrill. Is this honestly your answer to the people's suffering?"

"If you're going to try and leave, you may want to reconsider," said the Baroness, holding a sword to the deserter's throat.

"Apprehend him. We'll need him subdued for the execution," said the Prince.

"You weren't chosen!" yelled the Duchess.

"Put down your sword!" The Prince slammed his arm into the Baroness, getting sliced by her heated blade in the process.

"Forget your squabbling; he's trying to escape! **FLAME CANNON!**" yelled the General, ejecting fireballs from his hand.

Exp 8 swerved out of the way and stopped all movement. "What the hell is this?"

"It's something special I created. Practically invisible and infinitely powerful. Plus…" the Duke pulled in the string from its pretty fingertips, tying the hero up without a scratch, "I am in complete control of them."

Exp 8 fired orbs out from his hand.

The Prince grabbed the Princess and leaped to the ground.

The Duchess grabbed the orbs with her hooks and plopped them in her mouth. "Aaah. Delicious!"

"I'll make sure he doesn't struggle," said the Führer, gold dripping off his back onto the hero.

Exp 8's talons sliced through the string.

The Baroness slammed a sword against his arm as soon as he got to his feet. "Let us fight to the death," she said, her eyes gleaming like a blade.

Exp 8 took two steps back, despite blocking with his elbow talons. He slid his foot back, allowing the weapon to push through and slam against the ground.

A fireball barrage sent him smashing into the wall.

"Let's hold the execution right here!" yelled the General of Genocide.

"We can't see where he is. You made too much smoke," said the Duchess.

A laser net shot out from the smoke and wrapped around the Duke.

"To think I was captured so easily. How shameful," it said with hollow eyes.

Exp 8 fired orbs into the roof, causing a collapse.

"My beloved, we must move," said the Prince, hoisting the Princess up like an umbrella.

Exp 8 zoomed out of the opening and into the foggy forest. "Damn this place. Even the rebels are corrupt," he said, scanning the area for movement.

The freedom fighter slammed into a thorny tree, broke it, and collapsed to the ashy floor. "Damn it. I'm sorry. I didn't see you there. Are you okay? Are you even alive?" He pulled out a metal thorn from a gap in his armor.

The ground shook and came up. Ten demons encircled him.

"There's no need to fight. Just tell me where Etah is, okay?" asked Exp 8, engaging his elbow talons and turrets.

A great flame emitted from the ground and spiraled upward, followed by screams of agony. The flame dispersed the surrounding fog and revealed Lord Etah.

The ruler of Sel was twelve feet tall and had pulsating muscles that bulged out of him, ready to burst out with his temper. Lord Etah was encompassed by molten armor that had been seared against his black-as-coal skin. The God of Hate had neither hair nor eyebrows. His eyes were swirling suns of dark red energy.

The Deva's body was branded with jagged glowing red tattoos shaped like various weapons. The warrior god's teeth were sharp as axes.

The screams of agony instantly died out. Even the wind was silenced.

Etah gave Exp 8 a toothy grin. "I hope you weren't troubled by their incessant blathering." He glared into the eyes of a protruding head in the ground. "You needn't worry yourself with the sinners nor these lowly demons. This realm now has had many new residents, and the sinners get a little claustrophobic and try to distract themselves with gossip. All of you, leave us!" The god's deep, rough voice echoed throughout the realm.

The demons scurried away, vanishing in the fog.

"A ruler must lead with strength!" Etah slammed his foot down.

A flame geyser erupted between Etah and Exp 8, ascending from the orchestra of agony below.

Etah breathed in deep with his large nostrils. "Ah…each scream fills me with power."

"You feed off their suffering?" asked Exp 8.

"No, I feed off their hate."

"Then why make them suffer?"

"It is my duty to make sure they suffer. All are bound to their duty in Sel. Without sufficient agony, this world would die."

"What kind of world is this? Did Devlin know? Did he seek to change this place?" asked Exp 8, staring off into space.

"Don't be so idealistic. Devlin seeks what we all seek: power!" Etah tensed his fingers.

"Is he here? Is he a part of this world?"

"No. He is a special case. He is a traitor."

"What about Kaity, is she here?"

"No."

"And the other Exps?"

"You're alone here. All your friends have been sent to the realm of light, regardless of what side they were on. Well, except Kaity, that is," said Etah.

Exp 8 felt the gap of his concaved chest where Ada once resided.

"Are you getting sentimental?" asked Etah.

"Why are they all bunched together? Doesn't it matter what they did beforehand?" asked Exp 8 with a trembling fist.

"Of course it matters, but since Devlin created them, they had no choice but to assist him. The blame falls upon him," said Etah.

"They have individuality. They willfully chose to support or defy Devlin. Exps aren't slaves; we are independent living beings."

"It sounds like you want some of them here? Are you feeling lonesome?"

"You isolated me, didn't you?"

"Perhaps, but what does it matter? You aren't a resident here. You're a visitor."

"Does that mean I'm free?" asked Exp 8.

"Of course! You are a hero!" exclaimed Etah, putting the full weight of his arm over Exp 8's shoulders.

A few bodies rose up, forming a chair. "Sit," said Etah with a slight nod.

Exp 8 sat down reluctantly, looking into the eyes of one of the bodies.

"Welcome to Sel!"

"I don't feel welcome. This place is miserable."

"In this place we are all interconnected. Our dependency on one another sustains this realm. The bodies of the sinners have melted together to create a massive island floating above a sea of lava. Is it not beautiful? We are standing on an ever-growing construct of sinners. Their screams of agony keep it afloat. This world truly relies on suffering. It is a glorious cycle that has been in existence far before my time and will continue for all eternity," said Etah, raising his arms in honor of the magnificent splendor of it all.

"Why did you bring me here?" asked Exp 8 with slanted eyes.

"You needn't be so skeptical." Etah smacked the hero on the back, knocking him out of the chair.

Exp 8 stood up firmly on his tippy toes. "You have an agenda. What is it?"

Etah gripped the hero by the shoulders and pressed him down to the soles of his feet. "You are here to inspire hope into this world."

"Then you do recognize the injustice of this place."

Etah grabbed the hero's head. "Hmmhmmhmmm! Don't think me merciful. I want you lifting their spirits so that I can squeeze more suffering out of them once despair sets in. When someone is overtaken by despair, they let out a burst of misery like no other. Not only that, but they begin to curse their very existence. This potent self-loathing enters through my whole body, not only filling me with power but increasing my threshold. I want you to make these sinners believe that you will save them." The god made the mortal's head pan over the landscape of tortured bodies.

"Then…you're just using me. You're using me to hurt others," said Exp 8 with watery eyes.

Etah released his grip. "I want the sinners to believe they have a messiah. I want them to radiate with hope and look toward salvation. Then I want them to realize how unimportant they truly are. I want this entire realm to exhale profound misery. You are a warrior of freedom, the fabled leader of the Freedom Forcers. You are their only hope. You are my greatest ally."

"I won't let you do this to them."

Etah pushed the mortal to the side. "I am the God of Hate! You can't oppose me! And there's no reason you should." The Deva brought up more bodies, enlarging the chair. He sat down and glared at the hero. "We can help each other. You can play the hero, as you so dearly enjoy, and I can become even more powerful. Bow down to me as your god and I shall give you a role to play; a role that will nurture this land with faith. Bow down to me, and I will make you a god here and now."

"Despite being an omniscient, you haven't been paying attention. I was born into slavery. I broke those chains so I would never have to serve anyone, so I could find my own purpose and forge my own path. I escaped Devlin's control by surrendering my life. What makes you think that in death I will bow down and go right back into servitude? I won't give you the satisfaction of my respect. I would rather burn for eternity than assist you in crushing the souls of the imprisoned," said Exp 8, standing firmly.

"Hmmhmmhmmhmmmhuhuh! A rebel to the bitter end and after! I must admit I am moved by your fortitude. I thought power was what all slaves desired, to feel the might of controlling destinies," said Etah, wiping a molten tear off his chin.

"I only want freedom."

"You do not know what you want. Why do you covet freedom so vehemently? Freedom is an unattainable goal. The concept of freedom is always subjective and has been imposed upon those who were already content with their existence. You come here as an outsider; you have no right to judge the way this realm operates."

"Any system that enslaves its people is inherently corrupt. The desire for freedom I have is not something I impose upon others. This feeling, which pushes me forward, is the instinctual pull that every living being shares!"

"Enough of your preaching."

Etah's aura slammed into Exp 8. The incredible force of the blow momentarily clouded the hero's vision.

Exp 8 activated his jets, zoomed behind Etah and slammed a soccer-ball-sized orb into the god's exposed back.

The orb didn't make contact; it was held back and then devoured by the god's dark red aura.

Etah slammed his fist into the rebel, imprinting him in the ground.

The Exp's turrets opened fire, but none of the bullets could make it through.

"If you want to oppose me, you'll need more power. The pain this place offers becomes strength for those who conquer it," said Etah.

"Is that so? I've seen those who've mastered the inherent violence of this realm; they weren't strong at all. They were selfish and misguided," said Exp 8, firing a laser net at the tyrant.

The God of Hate grabbed the web and rolled it up. "So you've already met them. Hmmm, this isn't the proper place. This is a battle that needs an audience. There are some rebels in a city to the west called Respite. It's occupied with residents of all kinds. My forces are already on their way. They are going to melt Respite and all its occupants to cinders. You best hurry and save them, hero." Etah slammed his foot down, triggering a burst of flame followed by tortured screams.

By the time Exp 8 made it back on his feet, the God of Hate had vanished.

"I'll show the people what a real hero is like," said Exp 8, activating his jets and heading west.

Exp 8 arrived at Respite without any disruptions.

The rooftops were burning and spikes outlined the perimeter, fencing in the people. Lamps were situated in patterns, creating various paths and intersections within the complex.

Exp 8 zoomed through the city, looking for a sign of struggle. "Damn it! How the hell am I supposed to know where they're attacking from? What if this whole ordeal was a lie?"

There was a scream in the distance.

Exp 8 flew over the pool of blood, getting noticed by a few demon children taking a bath, and navigated through the stampede of residents.

A flaming demon commander, along with ten other ignited demons took notice of the hero.

Exp 8 landed and walked up to them. "I don't want any trouble. Leave this place now."

A symphony of screams came from a nearby building.

Four demons came out from a stampeding group and opened fire on Etah's army.

Exp 8 took off, heading toward the building. He slammed into an attacker and knocked him to the ground. "Stop this now!"

"What are you doing? I'm with the rebellion," said the demon, firing an arrow from the crossbow on his arm.

The arrow pierced a fire demon's throat.

Exp 8 pushed off the ground and fired an orb at the fire demon, blasting him out the window. "Sorry about that. Is he the only one?"

"He was with six others. They were headed to the top floor, where all the children are," said the rebel, rushing up the stairs.

"I'll take care of them. Look for anyone who is wounded. Honestly, it's hard for me to tell who is and who isn't in this place." Exp 8 soared up the stairway, firing orbs at any demons that fired at him first. He swerved out of the way of a fireball and was pierced in his side once he reached the top.

Four demons encircled the children.

"Your hero has arrived," said the demon commander, plunging the blade in deeper.

Exp 8 gripped the hot steel and struggled to pull it out.

One of the children screamed as he was being roasted alive.

Exp 8 let go of the blade and slammed his fist into the commander's face.

The blade twisted as it slipped out, leaving a nasty scarlet wound.

The hero rushed at the demons as his turrets opened fire.

They dispersed and fled once he started shooting orbs their way.

Exp 8 grabbed the burning child and rolled him on the ground.

It was no use; the flames stuck like napalm.

The warrior of freedom grabbed the kid, cringing as the fire scraped against his wound. Without a second to spare, he jetted out of the building and slammed into the pool of blood.

Now coated red, Exp 8 lifted the kid out of the pool. "Are you alright?" he asked, not sure if the kid's skin was any more burnt than it used to be.

The kid nodded and smiled at him.

"Hero! Congratulations on saving one child. Now, what are you going to do about all these?" asked a deep voice.

Exp 8 turned to see a massive bulky demon, nearly sixteen feet tall and eight feet wide. The creature was in a long black cloak, concealing potential weapons within. Its head poked out from the cloak. The demon lord's one eye focused on the hero. Beyond the demon lord were eight other demon soldiers, each holding two children hostage.

"Let's make this entertaining. You have eight minutes to take me down. Each minute that passes by means a beheaded hostage. If you attack anyone but me, they all die. Come on, hero, fight with all the hope you can muster."

Exp 8 flew circles around the demon, firing energy orbs out like machine-gun fire.

A grappling hook slammed into the hero's face, causing him to lose trajectory and crash to the ground.

Exp 8 quickly reoriented himself and then swerved out of the way of a volley of arrows.

The demon lord removed what remained of his cloak. "I am the Baron of Brutality!" Four arms, each pulsing with muscles and wielding a different weapon, aimed at the hero.

Exp 8 changed course and shot toward the Baron. He slammed one fist against the five-foot bastard sword and the other into the demon's chest.

"Kill one," said the Baron, turning his head to his soldiers.

Exp 8 heard a slice followed by a roll. All sound was blotted out by the screams of children.

The demon lord backhanded Exp 8, sending him tumbling into the pool of blood.

"Kill another one when he resurfaces. There are plenty more," said the demon lord, firing a volley of arrows into the crimson pool.

The pool lit up from below.

"Lord Etah places too much faith in this hero," said the demon lord.

Exp 8 emerged, wielding an orb the size of a car.

The demon lord impaled a sword through his own foot, prepping for the impact.

Exp 8 flew up, swerving out of the way of an anchor and then smashed the orb into the demon lord's face. He slammed the orb against the demon lord repeatedly, all the while being assaulted by arrows. "𝐵𝐼𝐺 𝑂𝑅𝐵!" He ejected from the orb and zoomed out of range as the orb exploded.

Once the smoke cleared, it was clear there was nothing left of the Baron of Brutality.

Exp 8 zoomed up to the demon soldiers.

One of the soldiers tossed the hostages and ran as fast as he could. Two froze up in fear. The last one killed the other hostage under his watch with his guillotine arm.

"Let them go now," said Exp 8, wielding an orb in each hand.

The other two demons fled and the last one charged at the hero.

"I have no remorse for murderers," said Exp 8 with a vicious glare.

The orbs shot out and burst the demon to pieces.

Exp 8 held the two limp bodies to his chest. "I'm sorry. I wasn't strong enough. I should have saved you." Tears gushed out of his helmet.

It took some time before Exp 8 heard the synchronized call of the people. "Hero! Hero! Hero!"

He looked out to see demons of all ages, shapes, and sizes beaming at him with hope twinkling in their eyes.

An outstretched hand lifted up the Hero of Sel.

"You saved my beloved's city. I can't express my gratitude," said the Prince of Pleasure, bowing to Exp 8.

"This is where the Princess of Insight came from. She must have joined the rebellion to protect these people," said Exp 8 to himself, wiping away his tears.

"I suppose it's possible. You know, you should wave at them," said the Prince, still bowing.

Exp 8 stood up and raised his fist in the air. "I will take down Etah and free everyone from this corrupt world!"

The audience fell silent. One by one they raised their fist in the air.

"I think you just recruited a whole city. Perhaps we could stage some attacks elsewhere," said the Prince, straightening his shirt.

"You're playing with people's lives. Don't forget that," said Exp 8 with a glare.

"I'm well aware. I've been playing the game for as long as I can remember. Come with me back to the trench. This development calls for a change of plan," said the Prince, grabbing the hero's hand.

"Lead the way."

Exp 8 left the city alongside the Prince.

"So, tell me the truth. Did my act of heroism move you at all?" asked Exp 8, trying to wipe the blood off his armor.

"He only attacked the city because you showed up in Sel. As far as I'm concerned, you started the problem. If you had just stayed with us and gone along with the execution, you could have avoided casualties," said the Prince.

"Who in their right mind would agree to their own execution?" asked Exp 8.

"You don't get it at all. It's the perfect move. Etah would be caught in a stalemate. He would have to come to your rescue, but in doing so he would have to give up his plan to make you a hero. Simple tactics won't work against him. You shouldn't have willingly followed his advice. You should have let us handle the protection of the city."

"I didn't see you fighting that massive demon lord."

"I was waiting for an opportunity," said the Prince with a shrug.

"I thought you said you were indebted because I saved your beloved's city. You were moved. I saw it in your eyes."

"I merely changed strategies. If we can use your heroism to round up more allies, then we can shift the tides. I was pandering to you. The people love me and by giving you my support, by submitting publicly, I made you look incredibly desirable. I sent my own messengers out to spread the word to all the corners to Sel. You'll be an overnight success."

"Etah wants me to give the people hope. Can't this plan backfire?"

"Only if you engage him in open combat. If you see him, leave as swiftly as possible."

"I promised those people I would take him down," said Exp 8, raising his fist in the air.

"So the thumb is right on the pointer finger's joint. That's a nice little gesture you created. You're not as simple-minded as I had thought. I won't deny there is a chance you can beat Etah, but if you fail then that will cause irreparable damage," said the Prince.

"Then I'll try again."

"Hah. And what if he kills you?"

"He won't. Like Devlin, he has plans for me."

"If you're going to be that stubborn, I suppose I'll have to concede."

Exp 8 turned to his unlikely ally. "Do you know where he is?"

The Prince sliced his finger on his spiked bracelet and placed his hand over the hero's mouth.

Exp 8 knocked him aside, but not before getting a mouthful of poison. "What the hell did you put in me?"

"Something to sedate you, that's all. I'm surprised you can still stand."

Exp 8 uppercutted the Prince's chin, knocking him out cold. "Bastard. Got to find cover," he said, wobbling back and forth.

The hero tripped on something and tumbled to the ground. Within a second, he was wrapped up in string.

Exp 8 writhed around and activated his jets, slamming into a tree before falling unconscious.

# Chapter 57: A New Life

Nina was naked under a waterfall in Femina, balancing on one foot while arching her back forward. "Being loud and boisterous will only cause problems. I need to follow Ada's wisdom. I need to practice silent sexiness." The graceful warrior leaped up and landed in a cat crawl, making a splash in the process. "Not good enough. The slightest noise could give me away. I need to soften my movements, making the allure of my body all the more potent." The flexible bombshell back flipped into the rocky wall behind her. She pushed off of it with her pretty feet and landed gracefully on her tip toes as she shook her long hair sensuously. "I've learned all I can from Ada. It's best to distance myself. I won't stay trapped in this place. And to get out I'll likely have to use force. If I am to survive, I must be independent. I must live solely for myself." The sexy survivalist gazed up at the waterfall and smiled. "Hmm, I could use that," she said with a sly smile.


Meanwhile: a few dozen trees away, Violet was shivering and muttering to herself.

Kawai leaned up to her mom's ear. "Is she having a religious experience?"

"I'm not sure. Normally she dances around when the spirit of religious ecstasy takes over. This is something new. Perhaps a spiritual revelation!" cheered Ada, clapping her hands.

"Violet, are you okay? If something is bothering you, tell us. And if you're worried about Devlin, don't be. We'll definitely rescue him," said Matteria, lifting up her beautiful blue chin.

Violet's eyes were hollow and her lips were dry.

Kawai straddled her mom's arm. "Was she attacked?"

"I don't know, but she looks dreadful. We should get her some water," said Ada.

"No. We don't want to upset the angels. Drinking water is viewed as a form of un-needed violence. We should look for an angel and see if they can help," said Kawai, releasing her grip.

"Wait, she's speaking. Violet, can you hear me?" asked Matteria.

"Matteria, go fetch her some water. Just a little bit," said Ada.

Matteria nodded and sped off.

Kawai held the distraught woman's head up. "Hello. It's me, Kawai. Anybody home?"

"It's real. This place…it's the afterlife," said Violet in tears.

"Yeah, seems so. Are you feeling better now?" asked Kawai.

Violet held her shivering chest. "Proof. Undeniable proof."

"I'm sure my husband would disagree," said Ada, running her fingers through her granddaughter's golden hair.

"This is it. This is it," muttered Violet.

"She was happy a moment ago. What happened?" asked Kawai.

"Didn't you hear the angel? There is no Heaven. Only Sel, Lum, and Absence. There is no Heaven, no Hell, no Hades, no Sheol, no spirit world, and no nirvana! None of it's true!" Violet yanked out clumps of her hair.

Kawai wrapped her tail around Violet's arms and held her down. "Don't freak out. What does it matter, anyway? What matters is that we stay calm and wait for Efil to come back with our answer."

"The saints aren't real either, are they? Nor is Gilgamesh, Set, Odin, Isis, Satan, Dionysus, Allah, Xenu…they are all figments, storybook characters. They are all a lie," said Violet, her pupils quivering.

"What is wrong with you? Heaven exists. You were right. You should be happy. There's a world that rewards the good, and you made it here with your family despite killing my brother. Isn't that worth celebrating?" asked Kawai, glaring through a fake smile.

"The Muffin God. I told your brother it was real. I spoke a falsehood to him. I swear, I didn't know. I'm so sorry," cried Violet.

"Atatasuki won't lose faith and you shouldn't either," said Kawai.

"How can't I? Feel the ground. Look at the clouds. I touched an angel. This is no mere hallucination. This is reality. This is without a doubt the afterlife. The one true afterlife. All the prophets were wrong. Faith can't exist alongside certainty. How can I doubt the world I live in? How can I rationalize beyond this reality?" asked Violet, breaking down into tears.

"Mom, I tried really really hard. It didn't work. Can you help her?" asked Kawai.

"You can offer me a shoulder to cry on, but you can't solve this. No amount of love can cure an existential crisis," said Violet softly.

"Only doubt can. I know who can help you. We have to get to Masculino," said Ada.

"Uh-uh. Efil said to wait here for my answer. The angels said 'do not leave the forest.' I'm sure Violet will get over this. She's strong," said Kawai with a smile.

"I understand. You stay here with Matteria. I must help her," said Ada.

"Do you even know how to get to the boy zone?" asked Kawai.

"No. I don't," said Ada.

"Then you'll just get lost."

"I suppose so."

Matteria came out from the trees, holding a banana leaf with some water in it. He rushed up to Violet and tilted the water into her mouth.

"Dreams and stories, that's all they are," said Violet softly.

"Did you find out what's wrong with her?" asked Matteria.

"I think the certainty of this place is threatening her other beliefs. It's complicated," said Kawai with a shrug.

"Matteria, do you know where Masculino is?" asked Ada.

"No, but I'm sure Violet could find it. She is exceptionally receptive to energy," said Matteria.

"She doesn't seem receptive to anything right now," said Kawai, wagging her tail in the spiritualist's dreary face.

"Then how are we going to get there?" asked Ada.

"No idea. Let's just stay put until Efil arrives with our escort," said Kawai, lying on a nearby tree branch.

"You two wait here. I can't stay put. Not with her like this. I may get lost, but I'll find it eventually," said Ada, pulling her beloved friend off the ground.

"Alright, I'll come along. Brother wouldn't be happy if I met with him at the expense of our ally," said Kawai, sliding off the branch.

"We should find Sefiwah first. She's an assassin. Maybe she could follow their tracks," said Matteria.

"No time for that. Hit me."

"What?"

"Hit me. We'll need an angel to guide us. One is sure to come if there's violence. So, hit me."

"I can't just hit you out of nowhere."

"Fine then. I'll go first." Kawai's tail slammed into Matteria's chest.

He fell to the ground, cringing in pain.

A hawk clad in white armor swooped down and landed before them. "No violence is to be permitted. If this continues, you will be punished," said the hawk, staring at the small one.

"That was fast. Hey, um, Mrs. Angel, did Efil send you to escort us to Absence?" asked Kawai.

"I have not spoken with Efil. I came here to tell you to cease your violent activities," said the angel.

"Our friend Violet is unwell. The only man who can help her is in Masculino. Can you lead us there?" asked Ada.

"You are to stay in this place. No exceptions," said the angel.

"But do you know how to get there?" asked Kawai.

"Of course I do, but you must not leave thi—"

Kawai wrapped her tail around the angel and pulled her in. "Lead the way."

"Are you threatening me?" asked the angel with wide eyes.

"Nope, but I'll hold you here until you show us the way," said Kawai.

"Trying to hold an angel hostage is foolish. We are wholly devout to Lum. You should have stayed put. The gods are keeping a close eye on all of you," said the angel.

A portal of light appeared before them.

The angel hawk slid out of Kawai's grasp and flew out.

Efil emerged from the portal. "Such acts shall not be permitted in Lum. Come with me, Kawai."

Violet grabbed onto the goddess' legs. "Is Dionysus here? Is he a god of Lum? What about Cronos? Archangel Michael? Vishnu?"

"Never heard of any of them. Are you alright?" asked Efil, pulling her leg out of the visitor's grip.

"Yeah, uh, I kind of hit Matteria so an angel would help her. She's having a mental breakdown, or maybe a spiritual apocalypse is a better term," said Kawai with a mumble.

"You broke the laws to help your ally. Such loyalty. I shall forgive your outward violence, but sadly I can do nothing to help her at this time," said Efil.

"She needs to see my husband. Please, Efil," said Ada.

"I am busy negotiating for an escort to Absence, but I shall send an angel to lead you," said Efil.

A shadow came from above. A pterodactyl landed before them.

"Using another living being as a form of transport is explicitly forbidden in Lum, but this is in an emergency. Take them to the World Tree," said Efil before reentering the portal.

Violet let out a soft sigh. "At least dinosaurs are real. Not all my faith is misplaced," she said with tearful eyes.

"Never thought I would ride a real dinosaur," said Matteria, climbing up the angel's wings.

"Do not think yourself an exception because you are an Exp. Efil helps all those in need, but is loyal to Lum above all else," said the angel.

"Get some rest. We'll get there soon," said Ada, laying her dear friend down on her lap.

Kawai held on to her mom's back.

The angel flapped its wings gently and took to the skies.

Meanwhile: in Masculino, Tempo's fist stops right at Ego's chin.

"How are we supposed to spar without hitting each other? I hate this place!" yelled Tempo.

"Even without contact, it's good to practice. I'm sure the Boss will figure out what the best course of action is. Till then, might as well buff up," said Ego, sliding into a handstand and padding his partner with rapid kicks.

"I don't know how long I can wait. The urges are killing me," said Tempo.

"Tell me about it. If only Matteria came with us. I always perform better when there's a pretty lady watching," said Ego, pushing off the ground with one hand into a dropkick.

Tempo smacked the leg aside and pressed his fellow assassin to the wet grass. "I was talking about other urges," he said, his rough hands quivering.

Ego hopped off the ground. "Whoa man, keep it together. If you kill someone here, who knows what the angels will do to us. Bide your time for now. Wait a while and maybe the angels will hire us to take care of some obstacles for them." He flashed his bro a sly smile.

"It isn't easy to hold back. My head is throbbing. My hands are itching. My blood is boiling!" yelled Tempo.

Kanasta peeked up, an assortment of metal in his lap. "Is something the matter?"

"We're merely enjoying the sparring match," said Tempo with a smirk, gripping his buddy's throat.

"Good." Kanasta buried his head back in his work.

"Yo Boss, weren't you supposed to be sparring with Riufen?" asked Ego, struggling to escape Tempo's grip.

"If we can't make contact, I won't grow stronger. I need physical strength if I am to crush the target back on Earth." Kanasta flipped a switch on and off.

"That's our boss, already preparing for our journey home. Are you going to enhance the Power Glove?" asked Ego, fake slamming his knee into Tempo's chest.

"First things first, I need to keep up my drive. Without purpose, my strength will deteriorate. Damn, still no signal." Kanasta fiddled with the antenna.

"What are you building then?" asked Ego, finally released from Tempo's neck hold.

"A portable gaming system. But there are no outlets in Lum. I'll have to improvise." Kanasta stabbed the plug into his chest. "Success! The first console to be powered by the gamer's energy. That's odd, the screen is blank."

"All the stuff we brought with us isn't real, remember? If it was, I'd be listening to some Hendrix right now," said Ego, tapping his headphones.

Kanasta's eyes became hollow. "We have to get out of this place."

86

"Glad we agree." Tempo grabbed Ego's arm and rushed out of the area.

After going down a hill a few miles away, Tempo released Ego's arm and sat on a rock. His legs were trembling.

"Whoa, you really aren't doing well. You should lie down."

"You've kept my urges a secret from the Boss, right?" asked Tempo, clawing at his own arm.

"Of course. You're my best friend; always have been. Without you, I wouldn't have found my life's purpose. Has it been that long since you've, uh, satiated your...desires?" asked Ego, leaning in closer.

"It isn't about how long it has been. It comes out suddenly and without warning. When I saw that goddess, the glorified pink beach ball, I heard it."

"You heard it. You never told me you were hearing voices. That sounds serious, bro."

"I'm not hearing voices. It's my conscience." Tempo's finger bore into his arm, breaching all the way to the bone. "It begs me to kill."

Ego took a step back. "You need to get control over yourself. You don't have to listen to that voice. You're in command."

"This place is driving me insane. You know me; I like to confide in my targets. The killing is best when I really get to know them. That means they know my secret. They know money don't mean shit to me. Who's to say we won't run into one of my victims here? What if they tell Kanasta the truth about me?"

"Calm down. We haven't even seen any humans yet and we may never bump into any. Stay with me and pay no attention to that voice."

"I won't ignore it! I love to kill. It doesn't coerce me. The voice serenades me. It's a part of me. It fuels me. We savor the violence together. You should hear its voice. It's like a melody," said Tempo with a grin.

"Well right now, it's a problem. Can't you blot it out?"

"Can you blot out your own conscience? Temporarily maybe, but it doesn't last. The voice that punishes and rewards your actions always returns. Only true psychos don't have a conscience," said Tempo, struggling to his feet.

"I should get Kanasta. Maybe he'll know what to do," said Ego, turning away.

Tempo gripped Ego's arm. "You're going to satisfy my urges. Your broken body will quench my thirst for violence." He slammed his head into his frustration outlet.

Meanwhile: about half a mile from the assassins' current location, Riufen was practicing kata. Each slash of his spinal cord was swift and precise.

"I did it!" exclaimed Kanasta, holding up his latest invention.

"You did what?" asked Riufen, his training unhindered.

"Look. Haha! It works!" Kanasta held up a metallic device.

The device had six ledges and two pressure sensitive bumpers.

"I made Pachinko! Real or not, these metal spheres have weight to them. I won't let this paradise break me," said Kanasta, shooting the ball into the center ledge. "Perfection."

"When do we leave to save Devlin?" asked Riufen.

"We are awaiting Efil's response. Without a means to get into Sel, we can't reach him. For now we should prepare for the coming battle," said Kanasta, placing his new device back in his suitcase.

"I am used to a far more…immersive training regimen. Repeated strikes may aid with muscle memory, but they are monotonous."

"What about poetry?"

"I don't understand."

"Many daimyos were both swordsmen and wordsmiths. They wrote poetry when they weren't fighting, fortifying their spirit with a tranquility gained through artistic expression," said Kanasta, using his finger to write symbols in the air.

"I never knew. Where did you acquire this information?"

"My father was born in Japan and proud of it. And it's not as if I don't find samurai warriors interesting, though misguided."

"And they were poets as well as warriors? Hmm. I thought Bushido was life for the samurai."

"That's anachronistic thinking. Bushido is a term created later on in order to parallel the well-known concept of chivalry held by medieval knights. That's not to say that samurais didn't live by a code, but it was one that was unspoken. It wasn't cemented in an ideological framework till much later."

"Such wisdom. Their way of life united them. Truly honor flows through their actions. For me to encounter Bushido on my own, I must follow in their footsteps. If poetry is a gateway to reach this ideology, then a poet I shall become."

"My brother loves poetry. I'm sure the same creative spirit flows through you," said Kanasta with a smile.

Riufen bit his finger and let the blood drip onto his spine. "To discover Bushido firsthand, I must master this art. Hmm…what should I write about?"

"Nearly all feudal Japanese poetry was centered on nature and the seasons. You may want to start there," said Kanasta as he reconfigured his mechanized glove.

"Hmm…I shall give it my all," said Riufen, placing his spinal brush against a large leaf. "I don't know any kanji. How can I cast the spell without knowing the runes?" His shoulders drooped.

Kanasta stood up. "Drawing kanji is art in itself." He sat down next to the great warrior. "I can teach you."

"You know kanji? All I know is giri and ninjo," said Riufen, tapping his headband.

"I know enough. The lessons passed down to me from my father shall now be forwarded to you," said Kanasta.

"I shouldn't disrupt you from your activity. I can learn on my own."

Kanasta put his hand on Riufen's head. "You underestimate my ability to multitask. It would be my honor to help my nephew," he said with a warm smile.

"And it would be an honor to learn from you, my exalted uncle," said Riufen with a growing smile.


Meanwhile: deeper in the jungle of Masculino, D.S., NoOne, Opti, and Pharma come across their first furry creature.

"It's a bunny!" screamed Opti.

The bun covered its ears as it rushed off.

"You moronic buffoon. Don't scare away my victims!" yelled Pesi before Opti came back into control.

"I caught it!" cheered D.S., cupping his hands.

"Caught what?" asked Pharma, peeking over his shoulder.

The moment D.S. opened his hand, Pharma snatched the animal.

"It's a Bufo toad!"

"Yep. It's not slimy like I expected, but it's still way cool," said D.S. with a smirk.

"Hmph, I thought you wouldn't even know the difference between a frog and a toad," said Pharma, petting his addiction.

"My mom is a biology teacher. Course I know what a Bufo toad is," said D.S., pushing out his chest with pride.

Opti leaned down to get a better look at the toad. "It isn't fluffy at all…but it's soooo cuuuute!"

Pharma brought the toad to his chest. "I didn't want this big guy because I think he's cute. I want him for his bufotoxin. Take too much and he'll lose his protective coating, but taken in moderation and the toxins will replenish themselves."

"Toxins. You eat poison. You're stupid," said D.S.

"Staying in a static state of mind is boring. There are so many substances that can create a gateway into new worlds within this one," said Pharma, placing his bendy straws against the toad's back.

"That sounds super cool," said D.S. with wide eyes.

"It is. Wait, you've never had drugs before?" asked Pharma, looking up at the poor wretch.

"Well, my mom does give me chocolate every so often. Does that count?"

"What about sodas?"

"Nah, that stuff is unhealthy."

"Your parents never gave you drugs? Not a cigarette, bottle of wine, coffee, or even morphine?"

"Ew, no. That stuff is gross."

"Don't you want to see the world in new ways?"

"That's what pretend is for."

"Yes, but if you play pretend when you're high, it makes it even more fun," said Pharma with a shaky grin.

"Really!? Wait, how do I know you aren't making stuff up? You just want my money, don't you?"

"I can't let my little cousin live a life free of psychedelics. Here, you get the first dosage. This is nature's bounty; it belongs to no man and it's free of charge," said Pharma, pushing the toad in D.S.'s face.

"Um guys, I think Mr. Toad wants you to let go of him. He's squirming around a lot," said Opti with worrisome eyes.

"I'm not letting him go…ever. This big guy is my lifeline. He is the only way I can survive in this drug-free hell!" yelled Pharma, taking another snort.

"That's your problem, not his," said Opti, reaching for the toad.

Pharma tripped his enemy and slammed his foot down on him. "This is self-preservation! I'm not doing this just for kicks. Hey, little cousin, are you going to try it or not?"

"I'm older than you, by a lot," said D.S.

"Who cares about that?"

"I…think Opti's right. He seems scared. Mom says good boys are nice to the animals."

"I'm proud of you," said Opti, giving his childish pal a warm smile.

"Fine then, more for me," said Pharma, snorting the toad's back. His eyes shrank. "Nothing."

The Bufo toad hopped out of his grip and vanished in the jungle.

Pharma fell to his knees. "Last time, there was a toxin. Now it's gone! What gives? There's no escaping reality in this place. I'm going to die."

"Not on my watch," said D.S., pulling the crazy guy back to his feet.

"Leave me here. Without drugs I can't connect to my soul. And without that connection, I'm hardly alive," said Pharma before retching.

NoOne sunk into the ground and sped off.

"Friends, NoOne just up and left. I'm going to go find him. Be right back," said Opti before rushing off.

"Violet says meditation is the best way to reach your soul. She said that intoxication is a shortcut. And everybody knows: only cheaters take shortcuts," said D.S.

"Some of us don't have the patience for self-intoxication. Normally I can overdose on my own body, but in this place my blood is tasteless, my cigarette fingers have no nicotine, and my needles have no potency. This place is eternal rehab," said Pharma, his shakes returning.

"Then we'll just have to find another way to make you happy."

"Shut up! Just leave me alone!"

D.S. spun and spun in circles until he collapsed to the ground. "Haha. Now it's your turn," he said, wobbling into a stand.

"This is idiotic."

"Whoa, the world is spinning," said D.S., still wobbly.

"Alright, I'll do it!" Pharma spun around for a minute straight. He careened into D.S., knocking him down with him to the grass.

"So...."

"I suppose it will have to do for the time being," said Pharma with a shaky smile.


Meanwhile: Opti was searching for NoOne.

"Hello, NoOne? Where are you?" he asked, careful not to step on any insect visitors.

"Shh! Get over here!" whispered NoOne.

Opti went to his shadow buddy and crouched down. "Why are we whispering?"

NoOne peeked through the foliage. "We don't want to startle them."

"Startle who?" Opti parted the leaves. "They are so fluffy!" he exclaimed with shimmering eyes.

"They are wooly, actually, and keep it down. To think I could find a whole herd this quickly. When you meet up with D.S., tell him I won the bet," said NoOne with a jagged smile.

"Why don't you tell him?"

"I'm not going back to the team."

"I don't understand."

NoOne put his arm over the optimist's shoulder. "These are my people."

Opti examined his friend's shadowy body. "Sorry. I don't see the resemblance."

"It's not like that! Sheep don't judge you for being worthless; they give you unconditional love. Once I've changed my shape, they will welcome me with open arms," he said, rounding his body.

"But we're your family too," said Opti, hugging his sibling.

"I'd only get in the way if I stuck with you guys. Besides, I want a simple, peaceful life…one where I'm not constantly confronted by my own inadequacies. One where I can graze and commune with others in peace," said NoOne, shrinking his arms down.

"I won't let you leave us just like that."

"It isn't your choice. What do you care anyway? You hardly know me," said NoOne, sinking out of the hug.

"Well you don't know them at all! You're my friend, all the Exps are. We're all family. If you think about it, I'm basically your little brother," said Opti with a nod.

"You're right, I don't know them. But they are kin to me. We may not be the same species, but I relate to sheep more than I do Exps. You don't need to take it personally."

"We are going to rescue Devlin, our father, together. At least stick with us until then, brother."

NoOne started carving hooves into his hands. "I'm not going to go on a perilous quest to save Devlin. I love him and I wish him well, but I'm simply not cut out for being a rebel. We are in Lum now. We died. This is our new home. I want to make a new life here, with my people. I don't want to get dragged into another series of unwinnable battles. I know it won't be forever. This body will fade and I'll be reborn. But hopefully when I get my next life, it will be a peaceful one, free of struggle." NoOne smiled at the one who called him brother.

"Okay, I can't stop you. But I won't accept you going like this."

"Then don't."

"If they are your true family, then you shouldn't have to morph your body to look like them. I'll only accept you leaving if they accept you as you truly are. Go to them as an Exp, not a sheep."

Black tears oozed from NoOne's eyes. "You think this isn't hard enough as it is? I'm already riddled with doubt. I don't think they'll accept me, even looking like a sheep. I'm not like you, I don't have confidence…I fear rejection like death itself."

"If they reject you, then we'll just have to keep searching for a herd of sheep that doesn't," said Opti, hugging his brother tightly.

"Let me do this my way."

"Why lie to them? If you want people to trust you and welcome you, then you shouldn't deceive them. You can leave us behind, but don't run away from who you are, from what you are."

NoOne reconfigured his body to its original shape. "You are right. There's only one proper way to do this. But what if it's not just them? What if none of the herds we find accept me?"

"Then you'll have to stay with the people who do," said Opti, helping his dear friend mold his hands back to normal.

In a secluded spot near some palm fronds, Atatasuki sat alone.

*Then what, I'm supposed to be stuck here for the rest of my life with a half-baked copy*! Kawai's voice emitted from the holes in the prototype's mouthpiece.

Atatasuki tapped his forehead, ending the memory. "Hmm, that's no good. She sounds angry. Delete. Okay, what comes next?" *Sis, how can you say something so mean*?

*I...miss him so much? I feel so alone*, said the Kawai recording.

He flicked his forehead. "Yeah, both of these can go. I'm getting sad just thinking about it. Okay, what's next?"

*I'm here for you. And he's our brother, so there's a bit of him in both of us.*

"Oh yeah, very smooth, that's a keeper. Proceeding onward."

*You are so right! I guess even though you're a failed copy, you're a failed copy of him, auuh.*

*Don't worry, dear sister. I promise you, right here, right now: I am not going to give up until I have freed Exp 8 from the prison of Sel.*

*Damn right we aren't, we're never ever ever ever going to give up.*

Atatasuki tapped his forehead. "Saved and stored for revisiting. Okay, now I just need to erase our recent separation. Or should I keep it? It may complicate things if I don't know where she is or why she isn't here. I'll keep the rest for now. Let's see...ah, there it is."

*Thanks, my love*, said the Kawai recording.

"So cute."

*Thanks, my love. Thanks, my love. Thanks, my love.*

"I could listen to this for the rest of time." Atatasuki pulled his hand off his chest. "Or not, I'm already starting to overheat. Better go cool off." The glitch-ridden individual stood up and walked off.

Meanwhile: Anthrax and Deceivant arrived at a massive tree.

At nearly four hundred feet tall and fifty feet wide, the tree had a powerful presence. Fruits of all types sprouted from the ancient branches of the tree. The top of the tree was clouded in bright particles of light, making it impossible to see its true shape. Around the perimeter of the tree were fields of veggies, freely growing wherever their seeds had fallen.

"Whoa, Violet should see this. It's like Yggdrasil," said Anthrax, looking at protruding roots larger than buildings. A current of light spiraled down the roots and into the ground. "Truly miraculous!"

"It's simply an ancient mangrove tree, nothing mythical or miraculous about it," said Deceivant, rubbing luminescent moss off the roots and examining it.

"I shall return shortly," said the angel monkey before rushing inside a crevice in the tree.

"You shouldn't throw away your mortality. Being an angel may be more trouble than it's worth," said Deceivant, twisting a feather of light between his fingers.

"I haven't made up my mind yet; I'm only getting information. But if I do become an angel, I'll use my status to help us rescue Devlin in any way I can," said Anthrax.

"Devlin is in Absence; he is beyond Lum's jurisdiction. I doubt becoming an angel will help his predicament."

"As an angel I could help keep the team safe so they can rescue Devlin. But like I said, I'm not going to jump into this."

The angel came out from the tree. "I have duties elsewhere. Some insurgents are causing trouble nearby."

"Wait, insurgents, but I thought Lum was without conflict," said Anthrax.

"Even in this land of peace, there are those who rebel. Their self-centered way of living makes them nearly incompatible with this realm. The goddess inside will tell you what you need to know. Perhaps we will meet again once you're an angel."

Deceivant and Anthrax carefully lifted a line of branches covering the entrance.

They met face-to-face with Efil who was at the very center with her hands above her head. Energy came out from her fingers and shot into the walls of the tree.

"That was your energy?" asked Anthrax.

"All light and energy come from Lum. Welcome to the World Tree, the center of Lum and the only place where the different sexes can mingle."

Anthrax now noticed there were various reptiles, insects, and even a few mammals inside the room within the tree, interacting in various ways. Vines covered the walls and balls of light floated around the area like dandelion seeds.

Deceivant tried to grab one of the orbs, but his fingers passed through them.

"So Anthrax, I hear you want to become an angel," said Efil with shimmering eyes.

"I want to know more about angels, but I may consider it," said Anthrax.

"First things first. Do we have an escort?" asked Deceivant.

"I filled out the request and have sent it to Lum. I was waiting for a response when I heard about the first ever Exp angel!"

"Calm down. I only want to know what becoming an angel entails. I haven't decided on anything," said Anthrax, raising his sleeves.

Deceivant walked up to Efil and plucked one of her feathers. "Hmm. This one is more radiant than the one from the angel," he said to himself.

"Okay, first off, you can't become an angel. True angels are born by the union of two angels, authorized by Lum."

"Then how were the first angels created?" asked Deceivant, lowering his glasses to examine the aura from the feather.

"Um…I'm not sure. Angels have been around for a very long time."

"The angel we met up with said they aren't born. This contradicts his statement," said Anthrax.

"Well, they aren't born anymore. All new angels come out from the pool of Lum visitors. Lum found it unfair to permit the bonding of angels but not the bonding of others and did away with the old system," said Efil.

"So if I can't become an angel, what can I become?" asked Anthrax.

"A mawali."

"Is that African?"

"Arabic, actually. A mawali is a new angel; they aren't the chosen ones like true angels, but they are all in service to Lum and are treated with equal respect and dignity. After awhile, mawali become indistinguishable from angels and lose their mawali status."

"Were you ever an angel, or were you born a goddess?"

"I became a goddess after living as an angel, but I was a visitor before that."

"Fascinating," said Deceivant, looking at the feather glow beneath his shirt.

"Glad to see you're taking interest. Though I am a bit surprised," said Efil.

"When a scientist encounters something new, he or she is called to explore it." Deceivant put his hand through Efil's aura.

"Are you coming to grips with being dead? This is a huge step for you. Many congratulations," said Efil with a bow.

"Don't get ahead of yourself now. I'm just gaining data since I'm here. I can worry about the ramifications of this place's potential existence at a later time."

"Let's get back on topic. What does becoming a mawali entail?" asked Anthrax.

"Hold that thought." Deceivant butted in front of the youthful doctor. "The angel's feather is losing light. Why is that?"

"Well it's because—"

"Silence. Let me forge my own hypothesis before you sway me with your all-knowing bias," said Deceivant with a wave of his hand.

"If I become a mawali, will I lose my memories?" asked Anthrax.

"Yes, but you'll need to leave them behind if you are to reincarnate anyway," said Efil, making a flower in her palm.

"Will I forget about Devlin, about Matteria?" asked Anthrax, his voice dropping into worry.

"The bonds you have with them will stay, but the memories won't. That is the way of reincarnation. This is something all who die go through," said Efil, regressing the flower into a seed.

"Hmm, science doesn't support or deny reincarnation. Do you have any evidence to back up your claim?" asked Deceivant.

"It isn't a claim. It's the way of life. Do you doubt me?" asked Efil.

"Yes, I do. Though there's no reason to let that bother you. I doubt everything," said Deceivant, twirling his DNA pendant.

Anthrax stepped up to the goddess. "If I'm going to lose my memories regardless, then I'll do it. I'll become an angel."

"That's wonderful news!" exclaimed Efil with a leap of excitement.

"But I'm not ready yet. I want to spend as much time as I can with Matteria. Once I've forgotten him…then I'll undergo the transformation. I'll help those in need all across Lum!" exclaimed Anthrax with great conviction.

"Don't you think you're deciding on this too soon? Who knows if what she says is even true?" asked Deceivant.

"I would never lie. Well, unless Lum commanded it, but she never would," said Efil, shaking her hands in a dismissive way.

"And you expect us to take your word on this?" asked Deceivant, lowering his glasses.

"I'm not a liar," said Efil with a pout.

"Efil, can you bring Matteria here? He doesn't belong in Femina anyway," said Anthrax.

"Actually, Matteria is already on his way here. Along with Ada and Violet," said Efil.

"Ada is coming?" asked Deceivant.

"Yes, and apparently she thinks you're the only one who can help Violet," said Efil.

"What happened to her?"

"Well she—"

"It doesn't matter. I can handle any sickness. Is she nearby? Should I get ready?" asked Anthrax, slipping on his gloves after rolling up his sleeves.

"I sent a message to meet here. They should arrive any minute now," said Efil.

"Fantastic! I finally get to help someone!" cheered Anthrax.

Meanwhile: in Complex, Bob and Fusion locate Demo.

"Wait." Bob's spectral tendril grabbed onto Fusion. "It seems our little friend isn't alone."

Demo was encircled by angels. The softball-sized black dot searched for an opening.

"Do not move. We have orders to take you in." The tiger angel commander concentrated light in his mouth, forming a luminous blade. The other angels formed arrows of light and aimed at Demo.

"Well, this is rather peculiar. Seems the angels have ulterior motives," said Bob.

Fusion tried to escape Bob's grip to rescue Demo.

"Hold still. Let's find out what they want before we intervene," said Bob.

The tiger angel lunged at the metal ball which slammed into his exposed belly before he could make contact.

Demo became a ray and zoomed through the light arrows.

The arrows swerved past the spherical Exp and collided above it. They then formed a cage of solid light, trapping the threat within.

The tiger condensed the cage and placed it on his back.

Demo slammed against the sides but was unable to break through.

"Keep it fortified. We don't want it breaking out before we can deliver it," said the commander.

Snail angels landed on the light cage and filtered their energy into it as the tiger left the area.

"As soon as they go around the bend, we'll follow suit," said Bob, picking up his adhesive comrade.

"Freeze, visitor!" exclaimed an angel from behind.

Bob's pupil slid to the back to face the human angel. "What seems to be the problem?"

"I have orders to bring you in. Stand down and follow me."

Bob fired a laser that pierced through the angel's chest. "I'm fine where I am, thank you very much."

Light arrows rained down from above.

Bob tossed his spherical sibling and seeped into the ground before the light cage could form.

"**FUSE**." Fusion crashed into one owl angel, combined him with another, and then slammed them both into a third angel.

Bob peeked out from the ground, firing lasers before digging back in.

"Reinforcements! We need reinforcements!" yelled the human commander, his chest already healed.

Bob came out from below the commander and ensnared him in spectral tentacles. "Stand down or he dies."

The angels fired their arrows into the commander. The arrows were absorbed into his aura.

The commander created two spears of light and stabbed them into the threat.

"Accursed angel!" Bob lifted the ascended human up with his telekinesis and bludgeoned the approaching angels with their commander's body.

"Retreat!" yelled the commander.

The angels released their light auras into the air, blinding Bob momentarily.

By the time Bob regained sight, they were gone. "Fusion? Hello? Are you there? Curses, it was captured. I better go find the others before the same happens to them."

Karson and BoneSaw rushed up to Bob.

"What in the bloody hell happened here?"

"Ah, you're here. That's good," said Bob, patting the patriot's missile head.

"Where's your little partner?" asked Karson.

"Captured I'm afraid."

"Says you. For all I know you killed it."

"Didn't you see all the angels flying around?"

"No. I saw lasers in the air. Who's to say you didn't stage the whole thing? Why would angels kill Fusion anyway?"

"They captured Fusion and Demo. Who knows why? Maybe they want some leverage against us. They should have captured someone a bit more important."

"We didn't break any rules, so there's no reason for them to attack us. You're a liar and a spy," said Karson, pressing his guns up to the round traitor.

"Why would I kill off my own teammates? You sound like an imbecile," said Bob, glaring at the trigger happy buffoon.

"I can't figure out what's going on inside that twisted mind."

"Whether you trust me or not, I suggest you follow me."

"Where are you going?"

"To Masculino, where the majority of our team is. It's best we stick together."

"But weren't we ordered to stay here?"

"Suit yourself," said Bob with a shrug.

"No. Uh, I'm coming along. The team needs their gunman, after all."

"Splendid. Don't fall behind," said Bob, rushing ahead.

# Chapter 58: A Pointless Happiness

Near the waterfall in Femina, Nina lands in the crystal clear lake without a sound. "Hmm, am I getting better or am I just channeling her skill? I ought to be careful." On the tips of her toes, she walked out of the lake and turned around. "Let's see if I can do it." After a slow inhalation, the seductive warrior sprinted on top of the water all the way up to the waterfall. She kept her footing, running six feet up the stream of water before kicking off. Upon impact, she transitioned into a sprint and silently rushed out of the lake. "Alright, time to get dressed." The sensual survivalist walked around the tree. "Where are my clothes?" She rushed around other nearby trees. "They aren't here. Okay, not a problem. I can grow them back…except I'm in Lum. Damn it! And I can't make new clothes without breaking some rules. They were stolen. I'll just have to track down the culprit and withhold my urge to slit their throat."

Something was moving in the corner of her eye. It was a human woman with Nina's clothes in her arms.

The naked ninja rushed up to her and knocked her down, using her enticing legs to pin down the culprit's arms.

"Don't move." The voice was behind her.

Nina spun around, catching a wooden arrow in her hand.

There were twelve women. They were armed with crossbows and in white cloaks that covered everything but their eyes.

"I want my clothes back, that's all," said Nina, putting her hands over her erogenous zones.

"We don't want to hurt you. We want you to come with us. We want you to join us," said the extra tall woman.

"Maybe I'll consider it after I've got my clothes back. I really don't like being exposed," said Nina, scooting over to her clothes ever so slowly.

"We need every human we can get. Only we possess the reason to see the flaws of this world," said the tall woman.

"Or so you claim. I have plenty of problems with this place. Inspiring lust in others is a sin here. And that means the slightest exposure could result in my incarceration, so I need to get dressed," said Nina, trying to flatten her breasts.

"You should join us. Only united can we gain freedom. We are all human and we are all women."

"I am one hundred percent woman. But I'm not a human." Nina kicked her clothes into the air and leaped up. Once her feet touched the ground, she was fully clothed.

"What are you?" asked the tall woman.

"I'm an Exp, obviously. No mortal could ever attain a body as enticing as mine," said Nina, squeezing her breasts.

"I've never seen an Exp in person before."

"Well then I've spoiled you. They don't get any prettier than this," said Nina, running her finger across her bottom lip.

"You may not be a human, but you must join us. We will take you by force if need be," said the tall woman.

Nina snatched an empty bottle from the closest woman. She slid across the ground, collecting water from a nearby puddle. She leaped over the arrows and dripped the water on her shirt. The femme fatale then landed, pushing out her chest. She then ducked under the second volley of arrows and tripped all the women.

By the time the women hit the ground they had all been disarmed.

A polar bear angel leaped into action. "Who caused the disturbance?"

"Sorry, I was fooling around with my friends. That's all," said Nina with a smile.

"This is sacred land. It's not a place for games. Your kind will submit to Lum's will. I'll let you off with a warning this time." The bear cautiously left the area.

"Thanks, but for what reason did you protect us?" asked the tall woman as she helped her allies back to their feet.

"You've got me curious. I'll come along, but don't expect me to stay," said Nina, adjusting her bra.

"If you choose to, you are welcome to leave."

"Good. Now lead the way," said Nina, filling up four more bottles with water.

Previously: fueled by his murderous conscience, Tempo lunged at Ego with killing intent.

Ego felt his skull crack upon impact. His mentor's fingers were pierced into his chest and ignited him from the inside.

Ego enlarged his hand and punched his bro's face.

Tempo tumbled backward, sending a fireball with a thrust of his hand.

The extremely rad assassin fell into a handstand to dodge the first fireball and leaped up to dodge the next one. "I won't hesitate to defend myself. GROWING SELF-RESPECT!" He enlarged his foot and slammed it into his bro once he was within range. "Calm down, bro! What if Kanasta sees you like this?"

Tempo sent a heat trail up the grass into his victim while tumbling backward.

"He can't hear me anymore." Ego put out the flame with a freestyle break-dance and ran up a nearby tree as his attacker charged once more.

Tempo tossed heat waves at the tree, igniting its snow white leaves.

Ego shrank the tree till it resembled a bonsai plant and leaped over his crazed bro. He tumbled to the ground, picking up some grass that he quickly enlarged to deflect the next flame volley. Once he ran out of green, he tumbled to the ground, doing a summersault halfway through and gripped the mini tree. "I didn't want to hurt you, bro." The stylish assassin raised the tiny tree.

By the time the tree hit the psychopath, it was back to its regular size.

Tempo placed his arms over his head and melted through the tree.

Ego enlarged his hand and blocked his face from his bro's heated barrage.

Angels swooped down from above to intervene as Tempo's arm caught aflame.

The angels fired arrows of light into the rampaging visitor's eyes, momentarily blinding him.

A massive arrow shot into Ego's chest, healing both his heated insides and the holes in his flesh.

A polar bear angel jumped on Tempo's back as soon as he started to stand up.

"Don't kill him!" yelled Ego.

The polar bear looked up at him curiously. "If I'm not mistaken, he started the fight. He made an attempt on your life."

"He has issues, but look…I'm fine. I'm begging you guys, please don't kill him. We went to grade school together. We may not be related, but he's my big brother. If you kill him…I'll kill you," said Ego, enlarging his fist.

Tempo thrashed around from under the polar bear. His body heated up, causing the bear angel to withdraw.

"He's my responsibility. We've been through a lot together. This isn't the first time he's tried to kill me and hopefully it won't be the last." Ego slammed his fist into his heated bro's head just as he was rising up.

Tempo collapsed to the ground, knocked out cold.

"Augh! That burns," said Ego, trying to shake off the pain.

"Thank you for preserving the peace. We will not kill him, but we must relocate him," said the polar bear angel.

"If he is getting relocated, then so am I," said Ego, hoisting his bro up.

"We shall bring him to Efil, and she will decide where to place this hazard."

"Then I'm coming along."

"So be it."

Previously: NoOne prepared to face the rejection of a herd of sheep.

"Alright! I'm fired up! Let's do this!" exclaimed NoOne, standing tall.

"That's the spirit," said Opti, patting his pal's back.

"I don't even know where this feeling came from. Did you force your optimism into me?" asked NoOne with slanted eyes.

"No. I believed in you. I guess my familial love rubbed off on you."

"You're my little brother after all. Even so, this feeling, this determination…ahh, it feels excellent," said NoOne.

"Best feeling in the world, isn't it?" asked Opti, hugging his brother tightly.

"Second best actually." NoOne broke out of the warm embrace.

"Oh, do tell! You've got me so curious!"

"Well, you know how it is…that special someone," said NoOne with an embarrassed slanted smile.

"Special someone," said Opti with shining eyes.

"Yeah, someone who makes you feel, well, special."

"I'm not sure I have one of those. I mean. I already feel super special. And I love all my friends so much," said Opti, giving himself a hug.

"But isn't there one you love the most? One that makes you feel worthwhile, maybe even loveable?" asked NoOne, tapping his brother's chest.

"Hmm. Well there's only one person I have a really special bond with and that's Pesi. Though I can't say I love him or he loves me, it's more of a mutual desire for the other's elimination. Oh, but I don't want to hurt him. I simply want to be in control of my body."

"You really don't know the feeling? Not to worry; there are plenty of loving people, whether Exps or assassins, in the group. Maybe you'll find that special someone one day, maybe soon," said NoOne with a smirk and a shrug.

"Not sure I want to. Love just means thinking about or spending more time with one person over another. I'd rather give my love to everybody and have fun with them all," said Opti, gazing up at the clouds.

"You may change your mind one day, but I suppose it's possible you may not."

"So tell me about this special someone," said Opti, his hands on his cheeks.

"Well, it's a girl. She has the most innocent eyes, like a brand new soul. They are always looking to the future. And when they met mine, they transformed. Love overflowed them, oozing out as a fountain of tears. She looked at me as her salvation. I've never felt so good in my entire life," said NoOne, grasping his chest.

"Wow! That's sounds incredible. What did she look like? All you've talked about so far is her eyes."

"I was so captivated by them. I didn't really get a chance to behold anything else, though I'm sure that she was beautiful through and through. She only saw me for a moment, but that moment has stayed with me through it all."

"Do you want to kiss her?" asked Opti, pursing his lips.

"Whoa there, calm down. I only want to look at her looking at me again. I want to gaze into her eyes as she is peering into mine. We can make love through sight alone," said NoOne, wispily shifting side to side.

"Wait, but if you stay here, in Lum, with a herd of sheep, how will you ever meet her again?" asked Opti with a sad look.

"I won't and I don't expect to. It's merely an impossible wish I hold dear, that's all."

"Where did you meet her?" asked Opti.

"Perhaps in a dream. Yes, she's a dream, that's all," said NoOne, his body dripping to the grass.

"No! She's real! The connection you have is totally real. You have to find her."

"Even if I did, she probably wouldn't even remember me. For all I know, she could be dead."

"I hope so."

"What!"

"If she died, then she is definitely in Lum. I hope I'm there to see the reunion," said Opti, bouncing in place.

"There won't be a reunion. By joining the herd, I am moving on. I am transitioning to a new life."

"Well then I hope your bonds lead you two together once more," said Opti with a great big grin.

"One last encounter. A final look. Maybe I'll catch her smile this time. Yes, that sounds pleasant. Thank you, friend. I may not have known you for long, but the moments we've shared have resonance. I wish you luck in all your future ventures, though coming from me it might be taken as a curse, keheh."

"I take it as a blessing. You have my blessing too." Opti leaned over and kissed his brother's cheek.

"Um, thanks?"

"Are you ready?" asked Opti, gripping his pal's shoulders.

NoOne looked at the herd of sheep. "I am." He went to the herd, his confidence rising as the distance shortened.

The sheep were uneasy.

Taking notice of this, NoOne slowed his pace. He crouched down and opened his arms.

One sheep approached and nudged him.

NoOne patted the sheep's head.

The other sheep came and examined the strange new creature.

NoOne hugged one of the sheep and the others gathered around.

Opti watched from behind the bushes. "Maybe we're the foolish ones, refusing to accept this paradise before us. It would be nice, living here with all the fluffy creatures. But first we have to save Devlin. I should go find D.S. and Pharma."

Meanwhile: elsewhere in Masculino, D.S. and Pharma were sitting cross-legged with their eyes closed.

"Imagine a big crystal. That crystal is the real you. It shines with your true light. Uh, look into it and see yourself. Now…time to go back to your body. You don't need to look. Your true self is connected. Find the bond and follow it back. Enter your body slowly. Now um…open your eyes." D.S. leaned over to his scary-looking nephew. "Welcome back."

"I think you missed a few steps," said Pharma with a smirk.

"Well, yeah. Violet is much better at it than me. So, how was it?"

"It was relaxing, but I never left my body."

"Yeah, me neither, but do you feel the energy?"

"Yes, from the tip of my cigarette toes to the top of my bong."

"Want to go another round?"

"Not really. To me, the mind is both sacred and inseparable from the body. I wouldn't want to leave my body. To abandon it would mean to leave behind all self-indulgence. That is something I would never do willingly."

"Ok. I understand. But I wouldn't mind. Because of this body, I can't play with the other kids. They think I'm scary. And their parents think I'm a criminal. Also because of this body, I got caught up in organized crime. I was a bouncer for a gang called the Empty Hand."

"A drug lord and a gangster, no wonder we get along. Honestly, I'm surprised Ada allowed you to join a gang."

"Mom didn't know until after I quit. Big Bro Kanasta helped me get in the gang. It didn't last long though. Once things got too violent, I left. I mean I like shooting guns, but I don't like shooting people. Rival gangs are one thing, they are the bad guys. But if I shoot people using the sidewalk, well, then I'm the bad guy," said D.S. softly.

"You seem down."

"Well yeah. I never shot nice people, but I saw my friends do it. It was really scary," said D.S., looking down at his folded hands.

"How do you cope with that? Are you still haunted?" asked Pharma, leaning in closer.

"I try to forget about it. My new job is a security guard. I protect kids from bad people…like the people who were my friends," said D.S. with a solemn tone.

"No. No. That will never do. Deflections and rationalizations can only minimize our misery. Satisfaction can only diminish the pain. Only intoxicants get rid of it. They make our bodies and minds immune. They fill the wounds with bliss. Intoxicants block off all current and future pain."

"You sound kinda religious."

"Drugs are my god. No matter the situation, no matter the severity of the pain, narcotics offer me refuge. They can counter fatigue, pain, insomnia, anything. Drugs allow us to keep on sinning against our bodies; they allow us immediate respite. We don't have to stop what causes us pain or damage; we can always create new drugs to remedy it. Who needs prevention, when you have the all-in-one cure? If I had a religion, it would be pharmaceutics."

"Well, I think you're crazy."

"Oh, do you? Why's that?"

"If that's true, then rather than quit the gang I would just take a pill. I'd be killing good guys and then taking medicine to make the guilt go bye-bye. That's scary."

"Whoa, whoa. I said sinning against our bodies, not others. A lot of druggies have taken it upon themselves to use responsibly. We believe in sharing, helping our fellow users out when they need a fix. And we don't harm others."

"But, you know, the plants are alive. If you aren't eating them to live, then it's wasteful and mean," said D.S. with a frown.

"Depends on what you mean by living. Without drugs, I don't feel alive. What I meant by don't harm others is…well, for one, smoking near kids is bad, so is using a product that didn't come straight from the earth—like grinding up rhino horns for an aphrodisiac. No animal testing either. Why even test drugs on rats when humans are going to be the ones using them? It makes no sense. Consent is important to us users. We draw the line when our addictions harm others."

"You don't support those mean rat-stickers. So, you're the good guys?"

"Well, I wouldn't say that, but we've got standards, morals, and shit like that."

"That's a bad word. You shouldn't say that."

"Whatever. You get the point."

"Violet says that your body is a gift from God. It's a temple and you shouldn't harm it."

"She takes narcotics during rituals too, you know."

"I didn't know that."

"Many religions implement drugs in their rituals. Various indigenous groups, Vedic, Rastafarians, Catholics—"

"Catholics don't, do they?"

"Though taken in small quantities, wine is a mind-altering drug. Why do you think some people call them spirits?"

"I didn't know that either," said D.S. with wide eyes.

"Oh, but it's more complex than that. There is favoritism, for a long time, Rastafarians weren't allowed ritual use of marijuana. Freedom of religion doesn't matter when your religion is viewed as an obstacle."

"I mean if it's someone's belief system, then they should get permission."

"We shouldn't need permission to eat what comes from the earth!"

"But what if it's bad for us?"

"The banning of marijuana has more to do with race than the actual substance being harmful."

"What do you mean?"

"Rastafarians tend to be of a darker color and as such they aren't given the same considerations. They are suppressed both knowingly and unknowingly. But race shouldn't matter at all. When I'm riding a real high, I don't even notice what color you are or anything is, really. The war on drugs and the war on race are one in the same."

"Then by fighting for drug rights, you're a hero! You're making a stand against injustice!"

"Calm down. Racism is a human problem and I'm an Exp. Still, a user is a user and we deserve the right to indulge. Getting locked up because you use a color-coated drug makes the drug war all the more sickening to me."

"You're super smart. You know like a lot of history and stuff."

"Yep and as the war on drugs became a global issue, it became an excuse for white colonial intervention."

"Whoa, I have no idea what that means, but it sounds good."

"It's not. It's horrible. It's like the popular kid who breaks all the toys, taking them away from you because he says you're gonna break them."

"What!? That's not good at all. When you said white, I was thinking like good. You know, white good, black bad."

"Yes, funny how convenient that distinction is. The Arians symbolize purity and culture and the Dravidians are viewed as dark and barbarous. I don't think it's a coincidence that the gods of the Dravidians are the Asuras of the

Arians. If I've learned anything from the war on drugs, it's that the ones claiming purity aren't the good guys."

"So then, what about this place?" D.S. gestured to the pure white jungle around them.

"Exactly my point. Despite all its claims of being a sanctuary, Lum won't even allow a desperate user to indulge. I'd rather have lungs black with tar than live a virtuous white life. Though, I do love me some white powder." Pharma snorted up some cocaine off his arm. "With enough imagination, I can still taste it. Still, we've got to get out of here," he said, standing up.

"Hey look, Opti's back!" exclaimed D.S., waving at him.

"Any luck finding NoOne?" asked Pharma, approaching his ally.

"Yeah, I found him." Opti started tearing up. "And he found a new family." He smiled despite the tears pouring down his cheeks.

"Wait, you mean he found a sheep?" asked D.S.

"A whole herd."

"And he's living with them?"

"That's right."

"Aw man, now I gotta hug a bear," said D.S. with a pouty face.

"So, what's the plan?" asked Pharma.

"You're asking me?" asked Opti.

"Yeah, why not?"

"Okay, then let's go meet up with the others."

"Sounds good. Do you know where they are?"

"Not a clue. Sorry."

"If you fly up high, maybe you can spot them," said D.S.

"Good thinking!" Opti flew over the tree tops, seeing a group of angel birds to the north. He landed in front of his friends. "Follow me. Something is going on. I hope nobody is hurt."

"Hey, little cousin," said Pharma with a smirk.

"I'm your uncle, not your cousin. And like I said, I'm way older than you," said D.S.

"Yeah, yeah. Thanks for helping me. Withdrawal isn't fun, but you made it bearable."

"Bear-able, funny. Cuz I gotta hug a bear."

"What? Ugh, no. That isn't what I meant."

"I had fun too," said D.S. with a toothy grin.

Previously: Kanasta decided to teach Riufen calligraphy.

"Not, bad. You've got the order down and everything. Good balance of light strokes," said Kanasta, peering over the samurai's shoulder.

"It's rather like carving up an enemy, I think I understand," said Riufen, finishing a kanji in an instant.

"Yes, shall we go for the next one?"

"I'd rather not." Riufen turned away.

"Why not? You're a natural."

"I don't enjoy this. It feels dishonorable."

"How so?"

"I'm slicing up a defenseless victim. The canvas has no way to fight back, no way to decorate me with wounds. I feel as if I am violating someone, not practicing for an honorable duel."

"Isn't it the same as slicing up a tree, or punching a target?"

"Yes, but I don't enjoy that either. The holograms I battled in Devlin's lab, they reacted, they attacked, they learned. If the battle is not alive, then I can learn nothing from it. That is how I feel," said Riufen softly.

"Then let's try poetry, look at your surroundings and make a haiku."

"The seasons unchanging, my sword in its sheath, paradise is false."

"It's easier to see on paper and you may not have had the proper number of syllables, but that sounded pretty good."

"I can make words connect, but it doesn't bring me and my sword any closer. I need combat. Everything else is a distraction. I'm sorry for wasting your time, my most honored uncle," said Riufen with a bow.

"Any time spent with my nephew is time well spent in my eyes," said Kanasta, putting his arm around his brother's creation.

Karson rushed up to them, breaking some branches in the process. "Hello comrades!"

"Where is Fusion? Did you find Demo?" asked Kanasta, grabbing Karson's shoulder.

"Well, that's the thing; I think the treacherous beach ball ki—"

Bob popped out from below. "They were captured by angels. We need to inform the others."

"Angels, you mean they can fight?" asked Riufen.

"In a manner of speaking," said Bob.

"Why should I believe anything you say?" asked Riufen with a glare.

"Sounds suspicious, right? I think Bob was the one who killed them," said Karson.

Kanasta's fingers pierced into the deceptive Exp's sides. "If you killed them, I will end you."

"Ugh, believe what you want. Either way we need to join up with the others. Most of them have gathered at the big tree; let's join them and figure out our next move," said Bob, passing through the assassin boss' grip.

"And you just happen to know where they are? How convenient," said Karson.

"Unlike you mortals, I can see souls. That's how I knew where these two were. Now, are we going or not?" asked Bob.

"Yes. We shall present the others with both stories and see which they find the most believable," said Kanasta.

"If it turns out Bob is lying, please allow me to cut him down," said Riufen.

"Oh yes, because you've beaten me soooo many times," said Bob, rolling his pupil.

Kanasta picked BoneSaw up. "I think it's time for an upgrade."

Opti, D.S., and Pharma rushed up to the group.

"Are you alright? There were a bunch of angels and some smoke. I think there may be a troublemaker nearby," said Opti.

"Don't worry, I can handle it," said D.S., cracking his fingers.

"Those were the angels that captured Demo. Maybe if you were paying attention like these three, you would have noticed," said Bob.

"Demo was captured? Who is Demo?" asked Opti.

"Our little ally who I did not kill," said Bob, seeping into the ground.

"I think he's telling the truth...this time," said D.S. with slanted eyes.

"Where are you guys headed?" asked Pharma.

Bob popped out of the grass. "Most of our team is at the big tree. It isn't too far. We're going to meet up with them—"

"And decide whether Bob is lying about Demo or not," said Kanasta, detaching BoneSaw's treads.

Riufen approached Opti. "Where is NoOne? Wasn't he with you?"

"He's decided to live with the local sheep...permanently," said Opti.

"Not surprising at all. Come on, let's get moving," said Bob.

Meanwhile: Ada, Violet, Kawai, and Matteria were dropped off by the World Tree.

"Thank you so much for your help," said Ada, hugging the pterodactyl angel.

"Release me. My every action is merely the reflection of Lum's will. I have done nothing," said the angel.

"Oh, sorry," said Ada, pulling away.

"Then thanks for nothing!" exclaimed Kawai, waving with a smile.

"Enter the tree and you will meet with the Goddess of Life. She will assist you from there." The angel took flight and disappeared in the clouds.

"Violet, can you stand?" asked Kawai, pulling her up with her tail.

"Why bother? It's all so meaningless. My opinions and beliefs have no stake in reality," said Violet.

"You killed my brother and now you want me to carry you!" yelled Kawai, livid with rage.

"Ohm. Ohm. Ohm. Ohm," said Violet softly.

"Rgh! What now?" asked Kawai, clenching her hands.

"She's chanting to keep herself together," said Ada.

"It's called japa, a recitation of sound. Mother Mary. Mother Mary. Hare Ram. Hare Ram. Hare Krishna…."

"Hey, let's take it easy," said Matteria, having Violet lean on him.

The group pushed through the foliage and entered the tree.

"Ada!" Deceivant rushed into a tight embrace.

"I missed you too," said Ada with a smile before kissing his lips.

"Where's my kiss?" asked Matteria, sticking out his tongue.

"Matty, I'm so happy to see you!" exclaimed Anthrax, hopping into his lover's arms and kissing him on the cheek.

Matteria rubbed noses with him all the while smiling.

Anthrax blushed bright red and rubbed back with a smile.

"Ah, Kawai, I am overjoyed to be reunited with you!" exclaimed Deceivant, hugging her from behind.

"Hey, watch where you put your hands," said Kawai, covering her chest.

Deceivant pinched her cheeks. "You are so adorable."

"I am, but we came here for a reason…not to cuddle," said Kawai, pushing the pervert off with her tail.

"That's right. I heard Violet isn't feeling well. Lie her down and I'll fix her up," said Anthrax, struggling to reach his medical bag.

Matteria set down his boyfriend. "I'll be outside. That way our allies will know where we are," he said as he walked off.

"What is wrong with her?" asked Anthrax, helping Kawai place Violet down.

"She's having a spiritual apocalypse. All her worldviews are falling to pieces," said Kawai.

"That sounds serious. I've never had to cure something like that before, but I'm willing to put my all into helping her through this," said Anthrax, checking if the patient's pupils were dilated.

111

"Here I thought she of all people would find solace in this place," said Deceivant.

"Hey, hey, Efil. Did you forward my question? You know, about the escort to Absence?" asked Kawai.

"Of course I did. You'll be happy to know that the request was sent and a response should come soon," said Efil, folding her hands.

"Thank you so much!" exclaimed Kawai, stopping in place before her hug connected. She retreated, covering her embarrassed face with her tail.

"You are most welcome," said Efil with a bow.

"You can help her, can't you?" asked Ada, grabbing her husband's arm.

"Me? How do you expect me to help her? When we talk we tend to aggravate each other, not mend wounds," said Deceivant.

"I believe in you," said Ada, giving her beloved a gentle kiss on the cheek.

"Belief makes more problems than it solves…as you can see," said Deceivant, eyeing the broken zealot.

"Does that mean you won't even try?" asked Ada.

"No. No. No. Of course I'll try. But I'm going to need the conversation to be uninterrupted. Politics, religion, and ethics are always a touchy subject," said Deceivant, cleaning his glasses.

"Ada, the escort has arrived," said Efil.

A figure in a clear cloak walked up to Ada.

"Hey, what about me? I'm the one who wanted to go to Absence. It's the only way to get to Sel. It's the only way I can see my brother again," said Kawai, floating right up to the goddess' face without making contact.

"I'm sorry, but if you go to Sel you would be either captured or killed. If you want to leave, I won't stop you, but I suggest you convince some of your friends to come along with you."

"Efil is taking me to visit Devlin again. I'll be back shortly," said Ada.

"Okay, but you'll help me save Brother, right? He's basically your grandson. You won't leave me to do it by myself, right?" asked Kawai.

"I will help in any way I can. He's my friend too," said Ada with a smile.

The figure in the clear cloak opened up a portal.

The portal blocked all behind it from view, but had nothing within. It was a floating void.

"Come back safely," said Deceivant, hugging his beloved.

"I'll be fine," she said, returning the hug.

Ada entered the portal with a wave.

# Chapter 59: Torment

Ada emerged on the other side of the portal, arriving four feet in front of her son, who was whacking a human skull like a top.

Upon noticing her, Devlin rushed into the portal to Lum. The sound of a collision against a brick wall preceded him toppling over. He looked up to see the skull guardian.

"I told you it was impossible to leave. But you just had to see it for yourself. Oh scientists are such fun!" exclaimed Eil.

Devlin stood up, adjusted his neckline and turned to the treacherous woman with a glare.

"So, you came back from your wonderful vacation in Lum. How come you and Deceivant can enter and leave Absence all you want?" asked Devlin, his gaze intensifying.

"They each have a visitor's pass embedded into their souls. Your parents can only stay here for a limited time due to the fact they are eternally linked to Lum. Just as you are forever bound to this realm," said Eil.

"Well isn't that just terrible?" said Devlin, circling around the detestable woman.

"Your father and I are going to convince the others to rescue you. I have faith that with Matteria doing his part, we can all unite under a common goal," said Ada sweetly.

"I don't need their help. All I need to do is kill all the guardians of Absence. Isn't that right, Eil?" asked Devlin, digging his finger into the skull's forehead.

"Kill us…that is impossible. You must merely provide us enough entertainment," said Eil.

"So there you have it, I will escape on my own accord," said Devlin.

"About that, fighting all of the Absence guardians will merely allow you to leave this realm for a limited time. You have already been bound here. How like a scientist, being told what he already knows thousands of times before he realizes it's a law," said Eil.

"So I'm stuck here forever!" yelled Devlin.

"Watch out!" yelled Ada.

A hand gripped Devlin by his head and lifted him off the ground. With a snap, Devlin's head twisted 180 degrees. He was met with the heated gaze of the Lord of Hate.

"You thought that you could announce treason without repercussions. You wanted to escape Absence, how about a vacation in Sel!" Etah slammed the defiant child against the ground and then tossed him forward.

Devlin soared directly into a black portal.

Ada rushed in after him, before being knocked down by the back of Etah's hand.

"Forget about your son! His body is now my meat puppet," said Etah with a growing smile as his body permeated the portal.


Devlin shot out of the portal and tumbled down scorched earth. Everything around him was clouded in darkness. He grabbed a glowing tree for support, gouging his hand in the process. Feet pressed into the ground, he waited for Etah's arrival.

A drop of blood tapped his forehead. Before he could think, his head jerked upward.

Two spiked, almost metallic, trees towered above him. In the center, wrapped in metal vines was a naked figure. Slim body, bloodied arms, wide eyes, metal tail—Kaity!

Before Devlin could register his horror, Kaity's lifeless lips opened.

"Master! Master! You're here!" she exclaimed, tail on end and eyes gleaming with excitement.

The tension left his face, tears dripped down his cheeks. "Thank goodness."

"Master, you look so small from down there. Grr, mmh! I'm kind of stuck."

"Don't move!" Devlin gripped the thorny trees and scaled all the way up to his lifeline.

"Master, you're bleeding," said Kaity, slicing her arm as she reached out to her precious owner.

"I'm sorry." Devlin's arms slid under the thorns and pulled the injured girl into a loving embrace. "I'm here now. I'm here." He cradled her closer to his chest.

"Aww, I love you too, Master," said Kaity with a lick.

"How did they find you? I sent you halfway across the world. What happened?"

"I dunno. My memory's kinda hazy," she said, sticking out her tongue.

Something made the ground quake. The metal trees reverberated, making the love-stricken scientist lose his footing.

Devlin twisted to face Etah the moment his toes touched the ground. He crawled to the one who dared to hurt Kaity and grabbed his molten feet. "Please. Let her go. I'll take ten times the torture. Just, please, let her live," he said, his tears evaporating before they could fully form.

"Making her suffer is the greatest way to cause you harm. She won't die though. This is a special torture chamber! I made it specifically for traitors! Hmmhmmhmmmhuhuh."

A black iron whip coiled around Devlin's chest.

"And guess who has the pleasure of torturing you," said a breathy voice that trailed off the end of each utterance in a bewitching whisper.

"You!"

Demonica's purple skin shimmered in the ashy air, exposing her busty build. Six dark horns erected out from her black-and-red mane. The dark goddess' misty purple lips kissed his neck while her scarlet fingernails clawed at his chest. True to her nature, she was in an iron dominatrix outfit complete with a jagged mistress mask and nipple spikes. Her mountainous bosom was held up with thin strings and was now pressed against Devlin's face.

"That's right." Demonica pierced her spiked stiletto heel into his foot.

Etah spit out a charred rock, singeing the vengeful boy's face. "Only torture the girl; Devlin will be of great use to us. I'll leave you to it," he said before disappearing into the darkness.

"Demonica, please, have mercy! Whip me, boil my insides, rip off my skin. Don't hurt Kaity!" Devlin sobbed at her feet.

"Now you get on your knees and beg! Now that I'm not permitted to play with you, you desire it. Not fair at all!" Demonica took flight and grabbed the face of Devlin's obsession.

"Don't do this," said Devlin, rising to his feet.

"Sorry, orders are orders." Demonica yanked on the metal vines.

Kaity screamed out in such a high pitch that her voice gave out.

"Oh, what a pleasant sound. Shall I have her sing for you?" asked Demonica with a flick of her serpentine tongue.

"Stop! If you love me, how can you do this to me? If you loved me as truly as I love Kaity, you wouldn't hurt me like this. Please, Demonica, I'm at your mercy," said Devlin in tears.

"I've had enough of your sniveling." She sliced the vines around the little tease, grabbed onto her and landed in front of Devlin. "You are not the Devlin I fell in love with. You're a pathetic broken coward. I haven't even sliced off her fingers, and yet here you are, kneeling down on the floor and begging for mercy. You disappoint me." Her bladelike fingers jutted out.

"Why are you being so cruel?" asked Devlin.

"Master, it hurts," said Kaity in tears, reaching out to her salvation.

Demonica tossed the girl to the floor. "Why aren't you!? You're supposed to be cruel, egotistic, powerful, and sexy. It seems the brave Devlin died in that abominable explosion. If the love of my life is dead, then so shall be the love of yours. Say goodbye to your little squeeze; you have broken my heart, so I'll rip hers out," seethed Demonica as her fingertips became blood red.

Wires wrapped around her leg and pulled her in.

"I told you not to hurt her," said Devlin, his wires piercing past skin and through organs.

"What's this? The freak has a backbone. Wow, this is scary, are you going to cry on me? Your love for that child has made you so weak," said Demonica, curling her bottom lip in disgust.

Devlin slammed her repeatedly against the scorched ground.

"The outcast has a temper! Sehuhuhuhu!"

"Shut up!" Devlin completely wrapped her in wires.

"Oh yes, rip me to shreds! Unleash your anger! Bathe in my blood! This is the brutal Devlin I love!"

"You aren't going to love it when you're only blood on my wires."

"Oh yes, I can feel my body being ripped apart!"

Demonica's body was torn into five bloody sections.

"Yaaay! Master is my hero!" cheered Kaity.

Devlin crouched down and started untangling the metal vines. "Don't move, okay?"

Kaity nodded with a big grin.

Demonica's fleshy bits collapsed into blood. After pooling into one large puddle, the blood hardened and reformed her body. "Auuuh! That felt amazing! But you should be more careful. I'm the one who put that incantation on Kaity. If you had killed me, that kitten would remain your slave forever after! And for some reason you don't want that," she said with a grin.

"I'd find a way to save her. No matter what."

The wires seeped back into Devlin.

"Wow, when you ripped me to pieces, I got such an erotic thrill. Just the thought of being torn to shreds by your powerful body…ahh!" exclaimed Demonica, running her hands across her body.

"Free Kaity's mind!" ordered Devlin with fierce eyes.

"Oh, I love it when you're assertive." said Demonica, stroking her beloved's chest.

Devlin slapped her across the face. "I said free her!"

Demonica gave him a joyous hug, a single tear falling from her eye. "I knew the Devlin I loved was still alive. I knew you hadn't abandoned me."

"Free her," said Devlin, softly pulling away.

"Why should I? She's quite the cuddly little torture doll the way she is."

"How can you even say that?"

"You know, you shouldn't assume that the love I have for you is like the love you pester her with. It's totally different. I don't mind hurting you. In fact, seeing you cry gets me going," said Demonica, dragging her nails down the living doll's back.

"Master, make the pain go away!" cried Kaity.

A single wire sliced off Demonica's hand.

"You sicken me."

"That said, I also get off on your happiness." Her fingernails moved in a flash.

The vines fell to pieces.

Devlin grabbed hold of his dear Kaity.

"I could break the incantation, hmm, but what should I ask in return?" Demonica paced around him.

"I don't need your help." Devlin wiped the blood off the little girl's mutilated arms. "Kaity, it's me. You need to wake up."

"Aww, Master is so funny. I already wakey-wakey! Hee-hee!" Kaity pinched her own cheeks.

"Please. Seeing you like this. It's all my fault. You have to be in there somewhere."

Kaity put her hands over her eyes and then pulled them away. "Ta-da! I'm right here, silly Master."

Devlin's head turned to the dark goddess as his fingers tensed up. "What do you want?" he asked in a growl.

"Aw, that's no good. You look so grumpy," said Demonica, reconnecting her hand.

"Why did you do this to her? You knew this would happen."

"Perfect isn't it. Killing her wouldn't end your obsession, but losing her, being unable to reach her when she's right in front of you—oh it must feel so bad. Won't be too long before you can't remember who she was. You may have noticed she's acting a bit different now. I lightened the incantation a bit so I could get more satisfaction out of torturing her, but I can turn her back into a doll if you upset me."

"What's she talking about, Master?"

"Was it your idea to do this to her?"

"Maybe. Keep in mind I was ordered to make you succeed. Can't let you get distracted by a one-sided romance when you have such an important task ahead of you." Demonica snapped her fingers.

Kaity's eyes became hollow.

"See? Now she's a doll," said Demonica, pulling at the girl's limp face.

Devlin bowed his head. "What do I have to do so you'll free her?"

"Well, for a start, what do you say we have that date you owe me?" asked Demonica, turning away slightly with a light blush.

"I don't owe you anything. My plan never succeeded," said Devlin with a grimace.

"I spared Kaity's life, doesn't that count for anything?" asked Demonica.

"You're also the one who controlled her," said Devlin, malice entering his eyes.

"You were the one who was in such a rush to get married. Trying to fulfill all your boyish fantasies without any consideration for the consequences," said Demonica, caressing Devlin's crotch.

"You don't understand love," said Devlin, turning away.

"Then teach me," whispered Demonica, with an enticing breath that pressed into the boy's ear.

Devlin moved away. "First of all, you don't rape someone you love. If I did anything with Kaity right now…even a hug, it would be rape," he said, grabbing Demonica by her wrist.

"Sehuhuhuhu! Oh my. You're serious?"

Devlin stared her down.

"Ooh. Still a child I see. Think about it. If you truly love someone then you cannot contain your feelings for them. They erupt out of your body into pure passion." She pressed up against Devlin. "To deny the fulfillment of that passion is to deny love itself," she said, caressing his innocent lips.

"True love is not possession. I would never think of doing anything against her will."

"That isn't love. It's self-righteous nonsense. True love is beyond control. It is untamable." Demonica's serpentine tongue bit into his tender cheek and then gave it a kiss.

Devlin grabbed her tongue. "I'm the teacher here! The second rule of love is your own desires come second to that of your loved one. This rule supports my first point. This means you don't kill or break the person that they love!"

Demonica pulled her tongue in. "I had no intention of killing Kaity. I only wanted to play with you for a bit. You are so incredibly adorable when you're angry. Mmmm, like a cornered kitten," she said, patting Devlin's head.

"If you truly love someone, all you will care for is their happiness. You should do what is best for them, despite your own interests."

"What you speak of is selflessness. Love is not as noble as you claim it to be. Love is an act of pure ego. You desire to be with a person to make yourself happy. Their joy is your joy and thus you wish them to be joyous."

"Do not be ridiculous! Demonica, you know that love is something deeper than that. You can't deny that your desire for me is true. I can tell that you may not understand love, but you have it."

"You're such an idealist. Normally I detest stupidity, but the more innocent you are, the more I can enjoy corrupting you."

"Do you truly believe your feelings for me are purely selfish?"

"Oh if only I could be naïve like you. Teach me your ways of denial. Release them into me so that I too may live in your world of obliviousness," said Demonica, leaning back into his arms.

Devlin dropped her and she collapsed into blood. "You're a lost cause. I hope one day you will understand the depth of your obsession. Deep down you must feel it, you must!"

Demonica reformed, her body grinding against Devlin's. "Oh my! I feel it! I feel the need to have my every orifice penetrated."

"One day you will realize how just love is. I cannot teach you anymore," said Devlin, turning away from her.

"I doubt I can transcend my Sel heritage. Regardless, for your sake, I hope there is goodness in me."

"Your desire for righteousness proves just how righteous your love is."

"You think you know so much about me. You've barely breached the surface," said Demonica, pressing her lover's fingers against her moist gateway.

"I recognize that love-stricken look, that's all."

"How does it make you feel?" Demonica pressed his fingers in all at once.

Devlin pulled out his fingers and flicked off the filth. "Lesson's over. Free her."

"Are you sure you don't want to have some fun first?" asked Demonica, raising her eyebrows.

"I'm married!" yelled Devlin.

"Don't act like a conformist, it doesn't fit you," said Demonica, playing with her hair.

"I may be rebellious, but I'm respectful. I would never dream of breaking the vows I made to Kaity," said Devlin, smiling down at his beloved.

"Don't say such altruistic things, my heart cannot bear it!" gasped Demonica, falling over dramatically. She exploded into blood when she hit the floor.

"Break the hex!" yelled Devlin.

Demonica reformed in front of the temperamental teenager. "Funny thing about that. The only way to break her out of my hex is to give her a deep passionate and messy kiss," said Demonica, flicking her tongue up and down.

"Enough of your games. This isn't a damn fairytale," said Devlin.

"I'm serious. Having you waste your time trying to bring her back is too heartbreaking, even for me. If you want to save her, you'll have to break your own rule. You'll have to force your tongue into her unwilling mouth. But, you know, you could keep her like this. She would make an adorable pet," said Demonica, patting the girl's head.

Kaity rose from the ground and got all fours. "Nya, nya," she mewed playfully.

"I suppose I have no choice but to believe you," said Devlin, turning to face the lost child.

"Take my advice. Have fun with her now while she's…relatively willing. You won't get another chance like this," said Demonica, giving his ear a lick.

"You don't understand at all. I love Kaity. This isn't her. It's a doll," said Devlin, turning his gaze away.

"Well unless you force your tongue into her mouth and press your body against hers, I can't break the hex," said Demonica with a shrug.

"No. I refuse to take advantage of Kaity, no matter what."

"Then I'll get the leash."

"You do it. Go on," said Devlin.

"Are you serious?" asked Demonica with wide eyes.

"It doesn't have to be me."

Demonica's fingers bore into Devlin's shoulders. "You have the perfect opportunity to fulfill your deepest desires right here and now! She won't remember anything you do to her! This is your greatest chance for sexual fulfillment!"

"I love Kaity. A one-sided kiss is empty. When I kiss her, I want her to kiss me back," said Devlin, his cheeks a bit flushed.

"Hrrgh! I don't even know why I love you. You're more goodhearted then those blessed angels. This is a golden opportunity and you refuse it!" yelled Demonica, cringing with frustration.

"Please hurry. I want to see Kaity again," said Devlin with an airy smile.

"Oh! Your purity is turning me on. You want what you can't get I guess." Demonica coated her hand in black fog and passed it between the star-crossed lovebirds. "The bond is broken. Congrats on your divorce. I'll let you two settle things together in Absence."

"You're leaving me to explain things to her on my own?" asked Devlin.

"He's coming back. You need to go," she said in an intense whisper.

Devlin grabbed Kaity's hand and vanished in an instant.

The married couple landed on the invisible ground and Kaity awoke, stretching like a kitty.

"Is it really you?" asked Devlin.

Kaity's eyes burned with rage as their focused deepened on Devlin. She leaped on him and put her fist to his throat. "You brainwashed me!"

"Welcome back." Devlin wrapped his arms around her and engaged her in a tight embrace, letting his tears flow freely.

Kaity's plasma claws shot out and burned the tip of Devlin's neck before she pulled out of the embrace. "Why did you do it?" she asked in tears.

"I didn't…I would never…I love you for who you are," said Devlin.

Kaity shot him a hostile glance.

"It was Demonica who controlled you. Etah told her to. I don't think she had a choice. The God of Hate thought that you would get in the way of my plan, his plan." Devlin's shoulders drooped. "I know why you married me and so did he. You did it to stop me. You pretended to love me, pretended that you cared. I understand your perspective. Please Kaity, believe me when I say I didn't know what would happen to you. My plan was made in part by Etah. I played him and he played me." He bent down and hugged her tightly. "I'm so sorry! I never meant for you to lose your free will. I'll never hurt you again," he said, crying over her shoulder.

"What happened? Where are we? Is this your lab? Did you win?" asked Kaity, looking around.

"I lost, but I teleported you away safely. I sent you to Akihabara. It's the only place I thought you could blend in, heh," said Devlin.

"Well I don't remember that at all. What about you? Why are you…wherever we are?"

"I was killed in Exp 8's explosion. I have no idea how much damage it caused." Devlin looked up at Kaity with a gentle smile. "You're safe. That's all that matters."

"You're done pursuing vengeance?" asked Kaity.

"Yes I am. My new purpose is to fulfill your happiness. What greater purpose can there be?" asked Devlin, touching her cheek.

"I haven't forgotten how you murdered Kanasta," said Kaity with a glare.

A black portal appeared a couple feet in front of them.

"No, it can't be him…not now," said Devlin, trembling with fear.

# Chapter 60: The Crimson Coliseum

Previously: Exp 8 was knocked out by the Prince of Pleasure's poison. He awoke on the ashy floor of a dark room. "Where the hell am I?" He rattled the searing hot iron bars.

"Calm down. Wait your turn," said a demon.

Exp 8 recognized him.

It was the same crispy demon captain that had led him up the mountain.

"Where is this place?" asked Exp 8, pulling his hands off the bars.

"The center of entertainment, the Crimson Coliseum!" The crispy demon pulled a lever that rose the iron bars up.

"Don't die, alright? You did a good thing in Respite, saving those kids. Beg if you have to. Strike a deal. Don't piss him off," said the charred demon commander.

Exp 8 stepped out of the prison cell and entered the Crimson Coliseum. The structure itself was made from bones, making it more durable than the fleshy buildings he had previously encountered. Tens of thousands of demons were stationed at the pews. Nearly all of them cheered when Exp 8 rose up his fist. There were only a few thousand that raised their fist in solemn silence.

Exp 8 got into a fighting stance as the bars of a nearby cell opened up.

The Baroness of Blades emerged, leaping onto the blood-soaked fleshy arena stage.

"What are you doing…?"

"As Etah's proudest warrior, I will strike you down, hero." She gripped the hilt of one of her rear swords and rushed up to her competitor.

"We can take him on together," said Exp 8, skipping back while using his jets.

"My pride will not allow it. *IGNITION!*" The Baroness unsheathed a sword, super heating it in the process. The blade missed Exp 8's head but sliced off one of his tendrils. She swerved out of the way of an orb directed at her face and slammed her bladed foot into her rival.

Exp 8 slid back, directing the momentum to get behind her.

The Baroness grabbed the hilt of a blade at her front and gouged it in.

Exp 8 ducked under her reverse jab and used the opening to stab his talons into her legs.

She ripped the dagger out of her head and jabbed it at his throat, blocked by his arm at each thrust.

Exp 8 gripped the arm holding the dagger and slammed his head into her face. "If this is some kind of ploy, best to end it soon. I don't want to kill you by accident." His turrets rose out from his shoulders.

The Baroness stopped all movement. "I may be incognito, but this fight is real. The winner gets to face Etah. This may be my one chance at taking him down. *IGNITION!*" She pulled out a dagger from her knee, set aflame by her boiling blood.

The blade slid up Exp 8's torso and sliced open his shoulder.

Exp 8 gripped onto the blade and twisted the talons he had imbedded in her leg.

The Baroness collapsed to the ground alongside her rival.

Most of the protruding blades slid off Exp 8's armor, but two or three found the gaps and pierced his flesh.

"I don't believe you. You've had plenty of chances to fight Etah." Exp 8 twisted her arm, making her drop the dagger.

"Calling me a coward!" she yelled, biting into his neck.

Exp 8 slammed her against the bloody floor. "You want an audience! You need someone to see your victory. It's not tactics; it's your inflated ego!" He created an orb, gripped it with his gravity field and slammed it into her head repeatedly.

"That's right! Everyone is watching! I won't fail now!" She twisted one of her blades as she tore it out, blinding her rival with a gush of steamy blood.

Only able to see red, Exp 8 felt something slam into his chest. He was rolled onto his back. His vision adjusted through the blood to see a long slab of steel between his fingers. "Make it look good."

The blade slid through his fingers and into his chest.

The Baroness plunged the blade all the way through. "It's over." She stood up, yanked the sword out from his chest and raised it. "I won! I am the greatest warrior."

A few members of the audience cheered. Most were either silent or weeping.

Etah leaped off from his decorated podium.

The impact from his landing splintered the ground.

The God of Hate backhanded the defiant demon lord. "What have you done?"

The Baroness slid back and jabbed a sword into the ground, slowing herself to a halt. "They're all watching. All of them! My pride is at stake!" She rushed at the Deva, wielding two swords in each hand.

"He was supposed to win! To triumph against an unstoppable force! How dare you deny these people their hero!" Etah's aura was sucked into his bulky body. "Death would be mercy. You shall be disgraced!"

The Baroness ducked under his fist and sliced his belly.

Etah's legs slammed into her body like battering rams.

The Baroness jabbed two blades into the Deva's knee and kicked off the ground. She rode the momentum, slicing the god's shoulders and positioning herself behind him.

Etah spun around. "All of it ruined! You want to be a hero so badly! Hmmhmmhmmmhuhuh! The job is yours!" He parried each strike with an equally powerful punch. His foot slammed down on hers, flattening it along with her pride. "Everyone behold! This is the embodiment of your hopes! She alone can save you from your judgment!" The god gripped her swords between two fingers each.

Nearly the whole stadium cheered for their new hero.

"You've taken up their dreams. You've stolen Exp 8's mission by striking him down. Can you live up to their expectations?"

"You will fall with all of Sel watching!" The Baroness dropped the swords and stabbed a dagger into Etah's throat. She twisted it as she ripped out the scorching blade. Lava gushed out of the deity's wound. "Never underestimate me!" she yelled in a frenzy, stabbing his throat with various daggers.

Etah knocked her off.

The Baroness rushed up to the Deva, her hands ready to unsheathe two more swords.

Etah's aura burst out and gripped her hands. His tattoos lit up once she was within range. His hands went around hers. "And so the rebellion dies!"

"*IGNITION!*" The Baroness pulled her blades out halfway before they were pushed completely through her.

Etah twisted the blades and cleaved her body in two.

The Baroness joined the blood-soaked floor.

Moans, screams, and anguish from the pews blotted out all noise.

"This despair, it's superficial. Not nearly enough," said Etah with a clenched fist.

Exp 8 spat out blood.

Etah turned his attention to the fallen hero. His grimace shifted into a wide grin. "Still alive! Heal him!"

Four demons with white wolves and tigers on a leash came out from the sidelines. They went to Exp 8's side and placed their paws on him.

"I'm sorry, I couldn't free you," said Exp 8, tugging at their collar.

White energy poured out from the paws and entered Exp 8.

Within seconds his wounds had closed. Within half a minute, he was glowing with energy.

Etah pulled the leader of the Freedom Forcers off the ground. "Residents of Sel! Your hero has returned from the dead! The battle you came for will now commence!"

The stadium shook, each cheer contributing to the quake of support.

"Come, hero! Fight me here and now in the Crimson Coliseum! End my reign, if you can," said Etah with a beckoning hand.

"No."

Etah took a step forward. "What?"

"I won't move a muscle until you heal her. I know you can do it," said Exp 8, patting his helpers on the head.

"You think a warrior like her would die so easily?" asked Etah, lifting up the demon lord's upper half.

The Baroness ripped out an arrow and jabbed into the tyrant. "Die! Die! I'm not done yet! I won't lose to you!" she yelled, unable to pierce his hardened muscles.

Etah flung her aside.

"Heal her or I'm out."

The God of Hate glared at the defiant hero. "You don't get to command me."

"Have it your way." Exp 8 flew off the ground. He slammed into a thin red aura.

"As if I'd risk letting you leave. Come down here and face me!" yelled Etah.

"Look everyone! See your ruler! Look how he struggles when things don't go as he plans. Marvel at his frustration," said Exp 8, flying circles around Etah.

The deity bit his lip. "Heal her." He turned his head to the demons. "I said heal her!"

The demons dropped their leashes and picked up the Baroness' halves.

"Wait. Stop." Etah looked at the hero and smiled. "I have a better plan. Either fight me…." His red aura shot out like a bullet. It exploded into the crowd like a grenade, killing seven demons immediately and injuring eleven more. "Or I'll dispose of the audience. It's your choice." The merciless tyrant gathered energy in his hand, aiming it at a group of child demons near the front.

Exp 8 sent a volley of orbs at the detestable deity while making circles in the air.

Etah redirected the blast at the Exp, followed by a volley of smaller bursts.

The Ultimate Exp enlarged an orb as he swerved around the attacks, all the while firing at the god's face to disrupt his aiming.

"Your hero will do anything to protect you! Come down, hero, or face the consequences," said Etah, aiming his aura at the audience.

Exp 8 swooped down and slammed into the deity. "I will take you down! 𝔹𝕀𝔾 𝔹𝔸𝕃𝕃 𝕊ℍ𝕆𝕋!" He fired off the orb, sending his enemy back a few feet. After reengaging his thrusters, he pummeled Etah's chest, keeping steady fire on the god's face.

"Stop! I'm not done! He's mine!" yelled the Baroness, using her dagger to scale up the arena.

Etah's aura gripped the orb and rammed it into Exp 8. He then grabbed onto the hero's leg.

Exp 8 slammed his talons into the arm holding his leg. He twisted out of the iron grip after firing a pebble-sized orb point blank at the god's face.

"Better hurry," said Etah.

The massive orb from earlier was now heading to a crowd that wasn't dispersing fast enough.

Exp 8 supercharged his jets and slammed his body into the orb, redirecting it to the ground. His jets flipped and backed him out, but he was still caught in the periphery of the blast.

Etah leaped off the ground. His massive hands grabbed onto Exp 8's torso. "You should pay attention."

The hero's jets flipped around again and blasted the god's face.

Exp 8 zoomed by, slicing Etah's back with his elbow talons. "Stop dragging this out. The longer it goes on, the more casualties there will be."

"Hmmhmmhmmmhuhuh. I'm well aware." Etah fired out heated blasts at the hero.

Knowing that a misfire would result in a casualty, Exp 8 slammed into each blast. The freedom fighter then crashed to the ground.

"Even when his life is on the line, the hero defends you! He protects people he has never met! Such valor!" Etah pinned down the mortal with his foot.

"These people aren't strangers. They're enslaved...like I was. We are made kin by our oppression!" Exp 8 struggled beneath the Deva's foot.

"Such powerful words! Though you could have picked a better time for them," said Etah, stepping on the hero's legs with his other foot.

Exp 8 punched the god's foot with great strength but it wouldn't budge. His tail smacked against the God of Hate's leg.

"What was that? Are you mocking me?" asked Etah, glaring down at the nuisance.

"Haven't quite gotten the hang of fighting with my tail, that's all," said Exp 8, struggling to push the god's foot off him.

"Behold: the Hero of Sel is unable to move! I could crush him at any moment! And if he dies! All of you die!" yelled Etah.

Exp 8 supercharged his jets yet again, sliding out from beneath the powerful legs and then quickly turning around to punch the god's face.

A stray arrow pierced into the gap in Exp 8's arm.

"I told you. I will kill Etah!" yelled the Baroness, ripping out another arrow from her body.

"How are you still alive?" asked Exp 8, rapidly dodging the tyrant's punches with properly timed jet-boosting.

"You know so little." Etah opened his fist and grabbed the hero's head. "Demons don't die, only suffer. Those children you failed to rescue. The ones you saw beheaded before your eyes, they are alive. I don't kill rebels, merely repurpose them! That's what happened with the Baroness! I break wills, not destroy lives. You are fighting to save them from nothing. What will you do now, hero?" asked the Deva, smearing Exp 8 with the blood of the wounded.

The Hero of Sel wrapped his legs around Etah's left arm. "Everyone dies. That's not what I'm against. Everyone suffers. Trying to stop that is pointless. What I fight for…what I died for is freedom! Slavery takes the meaning out of life and the purpose out of suffering! As long as living beings, whether sinners or saints, are trapped in a system of exploitation…as long as willful beings are treated as property, not people, I will keep on fighting! Until the system falls, I will stand and fight!" His jets went into overdrive.

Etah's arm twisted up and then back. The sound of it snapping ringed across the Crimson Coliseum.

Exp 8 careened into the ground and slammed into the wall of the arena.

Etah's left arm shook but he could not raise it.

The people cheered. They climbed out of their seats and charged into the arena, raising their blades, fists, and tendrils as weapons.

"Enough!" Etah's aura burst out from his body, melting anyone who entered it. He stepped up to the defiant hero who was still getting back on his feet.

"The people have stood up to you. You lost. The rebellion won," said Exp 8, gripping one massive orb in between his palms.

"Not another word!" Etah's aura burst out and slammed into Exp 8 from below.

Before the hero could reorient himself, the god gripped his arm.

Exp 8's eyes went blank as his left arm was torn from its socket.

Etah slammed the hero back and forth against the ground by flailing him around by the dismembered arm.

Exp 8's working hand disengaged his grip on the orb. He fell flat on the ground, his palm facing up.

Etah's aura crept out from his feet and held the hero's legs in place.

Exp 8 stood up in a daze, his eyes fixated on the god. His still-attached arm was too weak to form a fist.

Etah's aura shot into the mob. It pulled them in and contorted them into a chair.

The God of Hate created a barrier between him and the mob with his aura. "Listen to your hero now. You'll find his words deficient in valor now that his life is in my hands," said Etah, his aura climbing up the broken mortal's body.

"I can't move," said Exp 8, tears dripping from his helmet.

"Hero. You may live yet." Etah sat down in his living chair and assumed a lax position. "I'm going to give you one chance. Abandon your ideals. Let go of your morals. Stand by my side as a new god of this world. All you have to do to rule alongside me, almost as equals, is lower your head. Bow down to me or perish," he said, staring at Exp 8 with his eyes aflame.

"In that simple gesture lies the injustice of surrender. I will not bow to anyone, neither mortal nor god."

Etah's fiery aura came out from his hand and pressed down on the hero's back.

The Ultimate Exp fought against the weight. He pressed off the ground and looked up at the tyrant, crouched on one knee.

"Ah, much better."

Exp 8 raised his head, his body still held in place by the god's aura. "I will not bow down to you. Even if you break my neck, my willful spirit will wholeheartedly oppose you," said the leader of the Freedom Forcers, his resolve firm and tall like a mountain.

"A fool in the realm of the living and beyond. Such a shame. Your false hope has brought you so much determination, yet in the end, you had to surrender your life to be free."

"I chose to die. I did not surrender. I died for freedom! I am liberated now!" exclaimed Exp 8, raising a defiant trembling fist at the tyrant god.

"Utter nonsense! If you were truly free, you could have chosen to enter the portal of light like you desired. You were brought here by my willpower. Your freedom is an illusion. I own you, body and soul! You do not choose what path you take; I do," said Etah, clenching his fist.

"You may have sent me here, but I choose my path. I also decide what actions I take," said Exp 8, creating an orb in his fist.

Etah snapped his fingers. A figure in a clear cloak came out of the audience and rushed to his side.

"Such a blessed shame! You would have been perfect. You believe in this freedom so fervently you have deceived yourself into thinking you have attained it. Logic and reality have no power over your delusion. It matters not. By opposing me you have become a hero. All sinners, behold: the Hero of Sel stands against me even now! He values your freedom above his own life!"

Sinners throughout the arena raised their fists in solemn silence.

"By refusing me you have created a burning hope. A hope that is inextinguishable no matter what truths ram against it. You are a threat, a true threat. A psychopath who can deny the facts of life can only be tamed with insanity. Soon, you shall become like all the rest here, a brick supporting my foundation. All sinners, behold: I banish this hero to the realm of Absence! When your hero returns, he will be my new footstool!" Etah punched the Hero of Sel, his massive fist a blur.

The legendary leader of the Freedom Forcers was sent flying back. He was gobbled up by an unseen portal and vanished from the Crimson Coliseum.


Previously: After Devlin rescued Kaity from the realm of Sel, a black portal appeared.

"No, it can't be him…not now," said Devlin, trembling with fear.

"Can't be who? It's him!" Kaity hopped to her feet.

Exp 8 emerged from the blackness of the portal, landing on his knees so he didn't fall flat on his face. He stood up, holding his head with his only arm. "I thought Etah would send me here. I'm glad my inference was correct. He sent me right, uh, where am I?" He turned to Kaity. "Hey, good to see you. Mission accomplished," he said with a bloody thumbs-up.

"You saw Etah?" asked Devlin.

"Yep. I fought him. I'm lucky to be alive," said Exp 8, his arm limply sliding down.

"Damned to Sel, were you? Heh. What sort of hero are you?" asked Devlin, holding his forehead.

"I was sent there for my heroic deeds. I'm a hero in Sel because I stopped you," said Exp 8, rolling his neck.

"And so that makes me the villain? Think of what you are saying," said Devlin.

"You were sent to…what did he call it? Oh yeah, Absence. That's a far greater sentence than mine," said Exp 8, as Kaity examined his wounds.

"Only because I defied Etah. That makes me the hero, doesn't it?"

"Yeah, a failed hero. Like me," said Exp 8, falling to the ground in exhaustion.

"Ugh, I suppose you're right," said Devlin with a grimace.

"Who cares? What matters right now is ending Etah's dominion of Sel," said Exp 8, peering up at the blank sky.

"What are you talking about?" asked Devlin.

"I'm talking about freedom, same as usual. As long as Etah draws breath, all of Sel's residents are trapped."

"Most of which are human. What do you care?"

"All I see are victims. And if Etah has his way, he'll no doubt attack this place too. All of Sellum is in danger as long as he lives," said Exp 8 with a clenched fist. "Good, at least I can use one arm," he said to himself.

"So now you're an expert on the afterlife?"

"I wasn't in Sel for long, but it was long enough to see that it operates on an oppressive system."

"And you expect to change it with blind courage alone? Baseless heroism and empty valor weren't enough to stop me, and from the way you look, it seems they weren't enough to stop Etah," said Devlin, putting his foot on the Ultimate Exp's chest.

"This time will be different," said Exp 8, turning to Kaity with an assumed smile.

"Kanasta, did you see Kanasta in Sel? What about Sefiwah? Nina? Anyone?" asked Kaity, leaning in closer with hope.

"Sorry, it's only me. But I heard the others are in Lum from Etah. If they aren't here or in Sel, then that means they are safe," said Exp 8, rising back to his feet.

Kaity embraced him with tears in her eyes. "They're all okay."

"Yeah. Not sure if I'm to thank though," said Exp 8, cringing as he pulled away.

"Only one way to find out. We've got to get to Lum," said Devlin.

"Any ideas so far?" asked Exp 8.

"Nothing solid yet, but now that Kaity is back, I'll figure something out," said Devlin.

"The three of us will figure it out." Exp 8 turned to face Kaity. "We'll get you back with your team, that's a promise," he said with a thumbs-up.

"Thanks. With you leading us, I'm sure it will work out." Kaity looked at the vast expanse of nothingness. "I can't believe the afterlife is real. I thought, once you died, that's it, game over. Makes me feel a little less bad about all the targets I took down."

Exp 8 stood up. "I've been given a second chance. This time I'll make sure nobody dies."

# Chapter 61: Those Who Rebel

Previously: after nearly overheating from hearing Kawai's sweet words of love, Atatasuki looked for a place to cool down.

"Oh, great Muffin God. Thank you for this bounty!" exclaimed Atatasuki, gazing upon a mossy lake. He carefully entered, trying not to disrupt a sleeping frog on a lily pad. "Ah, this is nice. Still, it's not the same without my little sis." The steamy prototype sunk in till only his head was above water. His head then perked up. "But as long as I'm here in this chilly lake, I can't overheat. Alright, time to test out my 'Love, Love, Little Sis,' slideshow or is it more of a soundtrack? Either way, let's have a listen.

*Don't you ever leave me again! Promise me you won't die ever again. You're a walking bakery... You are such an idiot sometimes. Heeheehmph. I don't want you to die again. Hey Bro, can you carry me? Don't you go running off again. You are so right! I guess even though you're a failed copy, you're a failed copy of him, auuh. Thanks, my love. Our only paradise is together, as a family.*

"So much adorable! So much love. And it's all directed at me. It also serves as a reminder; don't leave her again, don't die again, those are promises I must keep. I should stay here as ordered. Maybe a little time away from me will mend her wounds a bit."

"Hey, are you an angel?"

Atatasuki looked at the edge of the bath to see a bare-chested muscular man with an untrimmed beard, dark blue turban, and thick eyebrows.

"Are you flirting with me?" asked Atatasuki, backing up a bit.

"Are you an angel or not?"

"No."

"Then what are you?"

"I'm an Exp."

"Pah, as if I'd believe that. Exps are immortal, or was that only a marketing ploy?" asked the man with a wise and friendly old voice.

"Most of us don't age once we're at our prime, but we can die. I don't know how I went out, but I am sure it was way cool," said Atatasuki, putting his hands behind his head.

"I refuse to forget how I died," said the man, pulling his arms out of the water. Two large circular shackles were on his wrinkled arms.

"Was it cool?"

The man swam closer to the Exp. "It was kind of cool."

"How cool?"

"I died defending a total stranger. He was being attacked because of his religion. He was a Muslim, and there was a lot of fear about Islam going around at the time. I stepped in but got mistaken for a Muslim myself. They shot me first, right between the eyes, thinking I was some sort of terrorist. I don't regret it, but I didn't expect it either. I thought it was a regular scuffle. Should have drawn my kirpan faster."

"You mean sword? Are you like a samurai?" asked Atatasuki, pantomiming sword swings.

"My name is Rambir. I'm a Sikh and a defender of the weak."

"I'm Atatasuki and I'm good at baking. Oh and I love muffins."

"Didn't know Exps ate. Isn't that seen as wasteful?"

"Yeah, I know. It's more than food to me, though. It's like my identity."

"So, can you fight?"

"Yeah, I use my passion to fuel my fists."

"That's interesting. Hey, you should come meet my friends. I bet we could put your skills to use."

"I would, but I'm not allowed to leave this place. I don't want to make the angels or my sister upset."

"It's not far. You wouldn't be breaking any rules."

"Okay then, sure."

"I like you, you've got dedication."

"Thanks, you're cool yourself. Violet—she's an Exp too and she's like my spiritual advisor—anyways, she told me a bit about Sikhs. You guys were in World War I and II. How do you manage to always be on the right side, the winning side?"

"We fight for the freedom of minorities. It's not about what's right; it's about what's righteous. Let's get going. The angels should be scouting this area soon," said Rambir, getting out from the pond.

"Is that a problem?"

"Only if they find me. I'm the leader of a group of rebels, but I'm no terrorist. Love is my weapon of choice."

"That's so cool! My brother was a rebel leader too! I was a tag along, but a really badass tag along." Atatasuki climbed out of the mossy lake.

"Then you understand. Many people are depending on me to come back safely. Follow me," he said, putting on his deep blue robes.

Previously: after reclaiming her stolen clothes, Nina tagged along with the rebel group in Femina.

"We are being followed. That angel brought reinforcements. You, Exp, get behind me," said the commander, her tone brisk and her voice a bit hoarse.

"My name is Nina."

"Not if you join us. Hmm, I'm thinking Pink Lightning," said the commander.

"Purple, first of all, secondly, what are you going on about? What's your name?"

"I used to carry my birth name, but once I became a soldier and swore allegiance to Allah, I was given a new name. Heaven's Thunder is what I am called now," she said, her amber eyes glistening and resolute.

"That's some name," said Nina, leisurely putting her hands behind her head.

"Stay close. We haven't lost them yet," said Thunder.

"Who cares if the angels follow us? You haven't done anything wrong. They can't attack you without reason."

"You're new here. You haven't heard of the Preemptive Suppression Act. It allows for angels to capture anyone for any reason, as long as they deem it necessary."

"Angels are infidels who lay claim to this paradise," said another woman.

"This land belongs to Allah!" exclaimed another.

"I wasn't sure you two could speak. Do you have fancy names too?" asked Nina.

"Enough talking. And stick close to me." Thunder grabbed the warrior woman's arm.

"I can distract the angels if you want," said Nina, yanking her arm free.

"No need. We have arrived," said Thunder.

Arrows came out from the bushes and shot into the air.

"Leave angels. Come too close and you will be invading our sovereign land," said one of the rebels, hiding in the thicket.

"All land beneath this sky belongs to Lum!" yelled the polar bear angel.

Angels of all types came out from the surrounding trees and encircled the women.

"I thought angels were supposed to be peaceful. Efil would be ashamed," said Nina, shaking her head side to side.

"You only live because Lum allows it!" The polar bear angel snarled and then led her group out of the area.

The rebels came out from their hiding spots and approached Thunder's group.

"Who is she?" asked one of the women, eyeing the foreigner.

"She is an Exp and a great fighter. Is the Imam at base?" asked Thunder.

"Yes. There will be a meeting shortly. You must make haste."

"I'm not just an Exp. I'm the most gorgeous Exp in existence," said Nina, twirling a lock of hair between her fingers.

"All that Allah creates has beauty in his eyes."

"Then I must be the pinnacle of creation."

"Are you sure it is okay to let one like her in? She is of man, not of Allah."

"Nina is a woman, whether she is or isn't human does not matter. We women must stand together, despite our backgrounds, despite our faith," said Thunder, smiling at her new comrade.

"So, where is your base?" asked Nina, trying to peek through the bleached leaves.

"First things first. We need to cover you." Thunder grabbed some clothes from one of the rebels. "We are going to dress you in the niqab and chador."

Nina swiped the outfit. "Hmm, not much maneuverability. Great at covering the body, but perhaps it covers too much. Curves are only useful if they can be seen. I'll pass," she said, handing the clothes back to the grumpy commander.

"You will not be allowed in the base with the clothes you are wearing. Modesty and chastity are important to us. These clothes show our dedication to our path."

"Modesty's not my thing, but I'm all about chastity. Alright, I'll put it on. But once I leave, I will wear what I want," said Nina, starting to pull up her shirt.

"Thank you for understanding."

"Um, are you all going to keep staring at me?"

"There is no need for worry. We are all women here. Our thoughts are pure."

"I don't care. I won't strip bare naked in front of anyone. Don't know if you ladies have ever heard of the collective unconscious, but basically the more anyone sees my body, the less enticing it becomes. Turn around. Yeah, all of you. Good." Nina pulled off all her clothes in one quick motion. She slipped into her new clothes without letting even the trees witness her beautiful bare breasts. "On second thought." The sexiest Exp stripped out of the white clothes and back into her old ones. She then put on the rebel's uniform. "I feel trapped," she said, her voice muffled by the cloth.

"It may take some getting used to," said Thunder with a veiled smile.

"I'll say. I don't feel like a liberated woman. I feel like my existence is being censored." Nina pulled up the bottom so she could see the curvature of her legs. "Not sure how long I can last in this."

"Then we better get moving. Here, put this on," said Thunder, holding a white piece of cloth.

Nina grabbed the cloth and put it around her neck.

"It's not a scarf; it's for your eyes," said Thunder with a light chuckle.

"I can take this off after we've arrived, right?" asked Nina, fastening it around her head.

"Yes. We cannot trust you with the location. We must be cautious."

"Don't the angels know where it is?" asked Nina.

"Yes, they do, but the fewer who know, the better. Angels aren't the only enemy of the rebellion. And the Exps aren't on either side yet, so I don't want you telling your friends where we are stationed."

"I don't have friends. I'm a survivalist. I rely only on myself."

"All the more reason for you not to know where the base is. Grab my hand and I'll lead you the rest of the way."

"So I'm supposed to trust you, but you won't trust me?"

"We can offer you refuge. As a survivalist you should realize this is your best option."

"Fine. Fine. Lead the way," said Nina with a shrug.


Previously: Deceivant asked to be alone while he tried to fix Violet's trauma.

"I'm not a counselor, but I'll try my best. What's bothering you?" asked Deceivant, sitting down next to the troubled zealot.

"Everything," she said, her purple face now pale.

"Come on, I'm sure you've worked through many troubles before. What do you usually do when faced with a crisis?"

"I pray to Ganesh to remove the obstacles that block me. After that I usually meditate. Meditation is how I gain new perspective. No matter the subject, I can unlock fruitful wisdom."

"Then there you have it. Pray to the beheaded son of Siva, sit down a bit and get over this slump," said Deceivant, putting his arm around her.

"He's not real. Ganesh isn't real."

"No arguments here," said Deceivant with a smirk.

"And I can't meditate out of this."

"Well when I'm faced with a problem, I use the scientific method. Experiments are like meditation in a sense. You come with a question and you let it lead you to a possible answer. It's only when that answer is cemented as truth that the discovery is polluted."

"I can't even meditate. My breathing is irregular, my mind is jumbled. I'm shaking. Everything I believed…it's wrong. It's all wrong. This is it. This is all there is," said Violet in tears, sprawled on her back.

"Spontaneous generation. Scientists once believed that flies could naturally come into being by leaving food out for extended periods of time. When they discovered this theory was false, they abandoned the notion completely. There was no emotional attachment to the theory, thus they moved on to discover more truths. Your expectations of reality let you down; happens every day in the system of science," said Deceivant, patting her head.

"That is the fault of science. Knowledge can only become right knowledge when tempered with proper faith."

"Let's not digress."

"This is different than a disproven scientific assumption. For me there is an emotional attachment. These weren't simply theories; they were the foundation for my identity. The scriptures were my truth and the gods were my very dear friends. Are you saying they are only figments of my imagination; that I just made them up to get answers to my questions?"

"You're making quite the assumption there. But yes, that is extremely probable."

"If they aren't real, then I don't even know who I am." Violet cried into his lap.

"This is why doubt is so important. Doubt keeps us open to new ideas, new information. It keeps us unbounded by our beliefs."

"So this is my fault, because I believed too much. I had too much faith?"

"Exactly. It's great that you're accepting it so readily."

"Bhakti is what gives me energy. Devotion fuels me. It shapes my very being."

"And it blinds you from the truth, even when it is right before your eyes. Maya means that our perception of objects and living beings as static is false. We live in a transitory world; it is a passage, or a samsara, of sorts. That doesn't make it any less real. Painting the entire world as an illusion Devalues the whole system of life. Surely you must have foreseen the danger of this."

"The physical world isn't maya, I agree, but it's not all there is either. It is the transient part of existence. The soul is the only thing that lasts forever."

"Wow, you say that with such certainty. Ugh, typical."

"How can you be certain it doesn't exist? Answer me. What makes the mind think but cannot be thought of? What makes the eyes see but is invisible? What makes you draw breath but cannot be drawn through breathing?"

"Certainty reduces all possibilities irrelevant when met with a single dominant truth."

"Unable to answer the question?"

"I don't bother with what can't be seen. Science has its field of operation, the perceivable, and it should stay within that field. I'm sure you can have a great conversation with plenty of psychologists about past lives, emotional states of being, behavioralism, and other unquantifiable data. Not me though. I study the material world. If it can't be perceived, then I don't believe it."

"But you forget, science is a sensory religion. The earliest religions were all sense-oriented."

"Yes, but the sensory religious devotees made haphazard logical leaps, astrology may have some scientific foundation, but it assumes relations that end up as either self-fulfilling prophecies or vague approximations. And for the record, I never said souls don't exist; I simply refuse to stake my reality on something that has no sensory evidence supporting it. As a scientist I can neither prove they exist nor don't exist. Saying it exists makes me a zealot and denying its existence makes me a Buddhist."

"So you do not know it, but can't say you know it not? That's Patanjali, by the way. Do you know who he is?"

"Yes, a writer who makes universal claims without proper analysis or procedure. I've read his work."

"He made yoga into the spiritual discipline it is today."

"Really? Nowadays yoga seems more like a weight loss program than a means to enlightenment."

"Yoga is fitness for the soul. The asanas may be only one facet of yoga, but that doesn't mean their exclusive practice is inauthentic. However a moral foundation and purification is necessary before practicing the asanas. The eight limbs of yoga are supplemental to one another but they also have a specific order to them. Though who knows if any of the three paths of yoga—karma, bhakti, jnana—are a proper means to enlightenment. I don't. Not anymore."

"To answer your earlier question, I don't know anything. As a scientist I am perfectly comfortable knowing that my beliefs are founded on theories not laws. Each well-researched assumption I hold is coated in a thin layer of doubt that lets it enter and leave my mind with equal ease. Even scientific laws are loose approximations at best. I'll agree with spirituality on one thing, the ego is quite dubious."

"Then you must understand that the intellect can never comprehend the Source, it can only be perceived through experience."

"The source? You mean the big bang? Well I agree that you can't know it, but I currently believe in it. Though I'm ready to abandon that belief should sufficient evidence to the contrary arise. As for perceiving it through experience, impossible. It happened in the past. Plus, experiences differ based on individuals. You can't draw worthwhile conclusions from testimonies."

"You're right. Thinking in truths has destroyed me. What happened to my non-absolutist way of thought? I'm supposed to follow the principles of anekānta. Wait, so you don't know anything, correct?"

"Never can and never will."

"Child abuse. Right or wrong?"

"What? Obviously child abuse is wrong. Any kind of abuse is."

"That's not a very scientific response. What observational data led you to come up with that conclusion?"

"Ah, I'm not falling for this. My moral system is something I created, and I recognize it as such."

"Then you wouldn't stop someone who violates that moral system?"

"Of course I would."

"Then you are forcing your belief upon them, right? Your untested, not reviewed, and biased truth would be forced upon them?"

"Ah, you think you've got me now. But you see, I don't have a religious laissez faire, non-judgmental idealism. My moral code is not violated by me forcing my views on others. If I see child abuse, I intervene with whatever force is necessary to stop it."

"Good. Morality is the only thing that is not subject to opinions. Ahimsa is the way of the world. Non-violence is the truth I hold above all others," said Violet with a smile.

"Then you are a Jain first and foremost."

"Yes, but even my Jain views are wrong. This place, Lum, is the afterlife. It's not only my eyes—my mind, body, and soul are all telling me this is no illusion. Lum is real and all other heavens are false. I can't deny it," said Violet with a fresh stream of tears.

"Why not? Isn't that the whole thing about religion, denying the perceivable in favor of the numinous?"

"I told you. This truth…no matter how destructive…it resonated with me. It resonated with the core of my spirit. It is truth and I have to accept that."

"Fine, let's assume this place is real. So what?"

"You wouldn't understand. Leave me be."

Deceivant lifted her off the ground and helped her into a seating posture. "I don't claim to understand, but I'm here to help. I want you to tell me how Efil being alive disproves Dionysus existing."

"I just want to be left alone. Please."

"Answer the question."

"The heaven here, it isn't like any heaven I've read about nor any heaven I've experienced. Why should I assume that the gods here would be the ones I believe in? I'm afraid to ask. It's the only doubt holding together what's left of me." Violet's body was shivering.

"You don't need to ask. You need to use logic to get out of this slump."

"Logic and reason may work for you, but they aren't enough for me."

"Come on, think about it. You believe in all these religions. You don't see conflicts between them?"

"I see differences but no conflicts."

"You have too much faith. Now that your opiate has run dry, you've lost your hold on reality."

"The opposite of faith is certainty. Faith is only dangerous when misinterpreted and repurposed as dogmatic certainty."

"Then you're letting the certainty of this place impinge on your faith. If uncertainty is found, create certainty. That's the trap of theistic thinking and it stunts creative thought. The omni-god is a false projection of certainty, and it has caused religious disillusionment to entire polytheistic cultures. Hmm, not sure if you're faith is too strong or not strong enough, heheh."

Violet turned away. "I'm done speaking with you."

Deceivant flicked her chin with his thumb. "Well, I'm not. You worship many gods, so what if Efil isn't in any pantheon you know of? She is a goddess. But just because she exists doesn't mean others don't."

"Do you think they're real, Zeus, Odin, all the others?"

"Stay with me for a bit longer. This is a heaven and maybe the angels think this is the only one. But that doesn't mean it is. How long did mankind think the Earth was flat; how many tribes thought they were the first people, the only people; how long did we think we were separate and superior to other animals?"

"A long time and many still do despite Darwin's discoveries. What are you getting at?"

"Limited knowledge, skewed scopes of reasoning, bias, false perception. There's no reason to think that only creatures in the realm of the living have these limitations. There is no evidence that the angels here are omniscient, nor the gods all knowing. Just because they say this is it, doesn't mean it is. If I told you that there is no soul you wouldn't believe me. Don't let your devotion misguide you. There may be many heavens and there may be more than one supreme god."

"I...um...I...I think you're right."

"Quite possibly so. I mean there are at least three supreme gods in the traditions of Hinduism; you've got Vishnu, Shiva and the Mahadevi. You know better than anyone that there are many geneses, many scriptures, and many truths."

"I do." Violet stood up straight. She turned to the devout scientist, her eyes brimming with hope.

"Don't ever let certainty make you forgot how to doubt."

"I...I won't. Thank you. You've helped me find my path again," said Violet with a bow.

"I couldn't let my granddaughter give up on life. Look, I know you get on my nerves and I frustrate you too. Science will never explain what religion claims to have uncovered, science has its limitations—that is exactly why it has endured. Only the material and efficient concepts are taken up by science, leaving out unquantifiable data such as purpose and function. They are ignored because they cannot be measured through physical means. Religion is for those who need answers now; it's for people without patience and devoid of a thirst for learning."

"Learning through scripture is a multifaceted, reflective, creative experience. And religion isn't stagnant. Though scriptures may not change, what the scripture means to the people, especially in the wake of new technology and social justice movements, undergoes constant transformation and reinterpretation. Both science and religion are in a state of flux. You've made a baseless logical leap."

"Heheh, perhaps you are right. I suppose it's a difference in technique, primarily. I follow the bottom-up, experimental approach. You follow the top-down, experiential approach. But as long as we both follow our path with integrity and some lubricating doubt, we can endure and we can discover. I'm glad I could help," said Deceivant, patting his granddaughter's head.

"Bottom-up approach assumes that all of life's mysteries can be explained through science and top-down believes all uncertainties can be rationalized through the existence of an external force, but neither seems sufficient to explain reality as it is. Neither science nor religion, bottom or top as you say, are sufficient to fully understand reality. Not even when combined are they enough. But they help us see part of the bigger picture and from different scopes. They both have their place. I'm no longer scared now. I'm excited. I get to learn about a whole new world. This is a chance to re-examine all my belief systems, not throw them away. And this is an opportunity for me to be a part of a new religion: Lum worship. Thank you, Deceivant. I won't forget this kindness."

"Great. Now let's join with the others and make up a plan of action."

"In a bit. I need to revitalize my chakras first. My heart-chakra aches when I haven't meditated in awhile," said Violet, her hand to her chest.

"Energy flow. Seems scientific enough to me," said Deceivant with a smirk. He sat down, crossed his legs and closed his eyes. "Shall we start with an ohm?"


Previously: Ada left for Absence, leaving Kawai and Anthrax with Efil.

"Okay, Anthrax, what's your plan to save my brother, who you gave amnesia to, by the way?" asked Kawai, poking him with the tip of her tail.

"Actually, I came here to learn more about becoming an angel," said Anthrax.

"You're just going to let my brother boil alive in Sel?" asked Kawai with wide eyes.

"No. We are going to save Exp 8 and Devlin. And I'll do what I can to help."

"Would you bring Matteria here? I would like to talk with the three of you together," said Efil.

"Sure. I'll be right back," said Anthrax, speed walking out of the tree.

"Let's get to the point. What's your agenda?" asked Kawai.

"I follow Lum's will," said Efil with a bow.

"Okaaay, so what's Lum's will?" asked Kawai.

"It's best if I discuss this once the others join in."

"Fine. I'll wait." Kawai crossed her arms.

Matteria and Anthrax walked in.

"You wanted to talk with me?" asked Matteria.

"I want to speak with all three of you. With Violet out of commission, you three are the only ones I can trust," said Efil.

"What, you can't trust Ada?" asked Kawai.

"She isn't here. And she isn't very subtle. It's best not to tell her secrets."

"Why do you trust us?" asked Anthrax.

"You want to be an angel, or are at least considering it. More than anyone, Matteria wants to save Devlin, and Kawai wants to save Exp 8," said Efil with a smile.

"So you trust us because we want something from you? Doesn't sound like we were selected for our virtues," said Anthrax, rolling his eyes.

"You make it sound so crude. I only thought that because you wanted something from me, you would be most likely to listen to me with an open mind," said Efil with a solemn glance.

"We will happily listen. You can trust us," said Matteria, stopping before his hand touched the goddess' shoulder.

"Understand that I am not becoming a mawali until I know what such a transformation entails," said Anthrax.

"A what?" asked Matteria.

"It's like an angel in training," said Anthrax.

"Did you forget we have to free Devlin? He's trapped, probably being tortured, right now," said Matteria, scratching his knuckles.

"Becoming an angel would allow me to help with Devlin's rescue—"

"And Exp 8's," added Kawai with a glare.

"It's the only way I can help rescue both of them. Besides in the end, it's my choice. I just want to make sure it's the proper one," said Anthrax.

"So Efil, what is Lum's agenda?" asked Kawai.

"The preservation of this realm and its people," said Efil.

"How can we help?" asked Matteria with a warm smile.

"Wrong. First question is: why should we help? Until I am in my brother's arms, you're on your own," said Kawai, turning her head and raising her nose.

"If you don't help me, then you will never see him again. That isn't a threat; it's the truth. Sel's forces have waited for this moment. They want you in their army, fighting against Lum. They took your brother in only to crush him. Sel is a world that is fueled by despair. What could create more despair than a hero being broken before their eyes?"

"Don't worry then. My brother won't break. He'll fight. I just hope he doesn't die in the process," said Kawai softly.

"You split us all up. Told us to forge a new life here. Is that what you want? Or do you want to recruit us? If so, how are you any different from Sel?" asked Anthrax.

"We split you up to protect you. That way, if Sel's forces breached the barrier, they wouldn't be able to round you all up in one fell swoop."

"Didn't you allow Kaity to be captured to keep the peace?" asked Anthrax.

"There were reasons for that. I know it sounds horrible, but it was a sacrifice that had to be made."

"Oh really? And why is that?" asked Kawai.

"Kaity was corrupted by Sel's will. She was a liability. Keeping her in Lum would only incite more violence. We gave her up to protect everyone; not just the angels."

"She does have a point," said Kawai under her breath.

"What do you want us to do?" asked Matteria.

"I'll get to that, but I need to clear some things up first. My orders for all of you are on standby. I am to keep a close watch on all the Exps, but anything beyond that has yet to be determined. Lum and the other gods are deciding your fate as we speak."

"Don't we get to give our own input?" asked Anthrax.

"I have already spoken on your behalf. Once Exp 8 started that rebellion, we immediately started our deliberations."

"You knew we were going to die?" asked Kawai, through her teeth.

"We knew it was likely some of you would die. But we didn't think there would be so many lost lives, nor did we predict it would happen so quickly." Efil looked at the group and smiled. "I've been on your side since before we met. I've convinced many angels that you deserve the same treatment as any visitor does. It doesn't matter that you were made by humans, you are still alive. I've fought for you and I will keep fighting. But when Lum makes her decision, I will follow it. I won't hesitate. I have faith in Lum above all else."

"Thank you Efil for speaking out for us," said Matteria with a smile.

"I—of course I did. I'm the Goddess of Life. I can't play favorites. I don't know what Lum will decide, but I can give you the possibilities. We are currently voting on them," said Efil, shuffling her feet.

"What are the possibilities?" asked Kawai.

Ada jumped in between them. "Efil! You have to help my son! Etah dragged him off. He's in Sel now. My little boy is going to be tortured," she said in tears.

"I'm sorry, Ada. There is nothing I can do. Sending in any angels could incite war," said Efil.

"That's why you need us. You can't go in. But we're neutral, right?" asked Kawai.

"Why don't you go see your husband? He's in the back with Violet," said Efil, leading Ada along.

"She said she fought for us, but we have no proof. Can we trust her?" asked Anthrax.

"Why not? She's a good person. I can tell," said Matteria.

"It's good to be a bit cautious," said Kawai.

"That's right. As a surgeon, I know that the slightest error, the smallest assumption can lead to death. We need to see all the possibilities and foresee all the consequences of each one before we can make the proper choice," said Anthrax with an inquisitive gaze.

"Love the confidence," said Matteria, snuggling up to his beloved.

"And I love you," said Anthrax getting on his tip toes for a kiss.

Efil returned to the group. "As I was saying. I can tell you the possibilities. Though you may not like some of them…most of them. And you can't tell the others," she said, her gaze dropping to the ground.

"If you think it's best we don't, then we won't. Simple, right?" asked Anthrax, followed by nods from Matteria and Kawai.

"First option: you are split up, monitored by the angels and encouraged to make a new life in Lum. Second option: you move on and reincarnate as swiftly as possible. Third option: Anthrax convinces the other Exps to become mawalis and join Lum's forces. Fourth option: you all convince your allies to fight by Lum's side. Fifth option: you are banished to Absence, making it impossible for Sel's forces to reach you. Sixth option: you are placed in the most guarded facility in Lum until the tension between Sel and Lum dies down. Seventh option: certain members of your group are held captive and you follow Lum's orders to assure their safety."

"You forgot one. Option eight: you come along with your strongest warriors and help me get back my brother!" yelled Kawai.

"I wasn't done." Efil looked up at them with shaky eyes. "Last option: you are eliminated, making sure that Sel cannot use you against us."

Matteria grabbed Kawai before she could scratch the goddess. "Thank you for being honest with us. Now what do you want us to do?"

"I need you to convince the others that Lum is on your side."

"After what we just heard you say? You're kidding," said Anthrax with fierce eyes.

"It's the best option for both of us. If Lum sees that most of the Exps want to protect this realm and its people, then she will view Exps as potential allies rather than potential enemies. I believe that being in Lum's favor is your best option," said Efil, standing straight but trembling a bit.

"I agree. Thanks for all the help," said Anthrax, holding out his hand.

Matteria gently lowered his boyfriend's arm. "She doesn't do physical contact, remember?"

"Oh yes, of course," said Anthrax, pulling back his hand with a blush.

"I hope they haven't already been influenced to go against Lum," said Efil with a look of dismay.

# Chapter 62: Refuge & Lotus

Previously: Atatasuki met up with Rambir in a lake and decided to tag along to see his base.

"We've arrived, my friend," said Rambir, putting his hand on his newest friend's shoulder.

"What's a building doing in Lum?" asked Atatasuki, pointing way up.

The structure was pearly white and reached higher than the hills behind it. Grass covered the outside perimeter of the building and flowers sprouted on the lower walls of the structure. There was a long winding covered passageway that seemed to venture around the entire building, most likely so attendees could avoid stepping on the grass. At each corner of the pathway were mini-shrines, which likely paid homage to the prototype gods of the temple. Four pillars came out from the top of the shrines, each located at the corners of the building. One extra thick and particularly shiny pillar came out from the center. It had a rather rugged capstone, with a few marks and some wear on the sides. The roof of the building had several protrusions shaped like treasure chests. There were no windows and only one entrance to the main temple, keeping the secrets of the building away from curious angels.

"This is Refuge. It is our base of operations and a place for worship."

Atatasuki climbed the shimmering long stairs up to the porch of the building.

A studded canopy extended over the last few stairs and kept any invasive light from reaching inside. Standing at the corners of the wall were two white lion statues.

Atatasuki jumped back when the statues suddenly sprang to life.

Rambir raised his palm out. "He's with me," he said, rubbing the top of the head of one of the lions.

"Are these angels?" asked Atatasuki, noticing a white aura flowing out from the big cats.

"Yes, but they are on our side, and they aren't the only ones. We even have a goddess who supports our movement." Rambir walked in front of his metal friend and slid open what looked like a wall.

"You have a cool team name right? I'm part of the Freedom Forcers. My bro came up with the title. Pretty sweet, right?"

"Haha. It's a rather odd name. A bit contradictory, don't you think?"

"Nah. Freedom at any cost. That's the idea behind it, I think."

"Outside the temple you can call me Rambir. But inside, call me Singh."

"Do you like singing?"

"I do, but that is unrelated. My friend, there are some among us who have forgotten their names. This is very distressing. To accommodate them, all males are called Singh and all females are Kaur."

"Sing and car? I don't understand, but I'll keep it in mind," said Atatasuki.

"Singh means lion. It transcends caste."

"Then car must mean lioness? Wait, there are women here?"

"Princess, actually. And no, crossing over to Masculino is a crime after all. Don't worry, Singh, I'm sure you'll pick it up in no time." Rambir patted him on the back.

Atatasuki nearly slipped on the polished granite as he walked through the doors and entered a new community.

"Careful, we clean it daily."

"Yeah, I can tell."

Rambir opened the iron door. "We are Refuge of the People."

"Oh yeah! I knew you'd have a cool team name!"

There were males, young and old, sitting in a circle on the ground with their legs crossed. They were eating and conversing, all with handcrafted swords attached to their pants.

"Would you like some?" asked Rambir, taking a white and shiny pomegranate from the table and offering it to the friendly Exp.

"Sorry, but I was told eating is against the law," said Atatasuki.

"Relax, my friend. This food is provided by our angel friends. It is called light fruit and is made of entirely out of light. There is no harm in eating it."

"I'm more of a muffin kind of guy," said Atatasuki with a grin.

The group in the back of the table turned around, staring at the newcomer.

"You have muffins?" asked one of the youngest members, not even a third of Atatasuki's size.

"Baked them on the way here." Atatasuki opened his chest. "Made with my own power and with lots of love."

Before he realized it, Atatasuki was surrounded by kids. They weren't jumping at his muffins though. Instead they opened their palms and looked up at him with hope.

"One for you. And one for you. Umm, can you guys split them in half? I don't think I have enough," said Atatasuki with a nervous grin.

Before long his chest was vacant.

"I'll get to work on another batch," said Atatasuki, closing his chest.

"Shall I introduce you to everyone?" asked Rambir, guiding his new friend by the shoulder.

"I can't stay too long. Can you tell me more about this group? What you're fighting against or for? How you fight? Stuff like that," said Atatasuki.

"First I must show you the temple," said Rambir, navigating through the standing crowd up to the doorway. "This building is the first temple ever built in Lum." He took a deep breath before passing through the open doorway.

The temple was wide and glistening, but there were no devotional icons to be seen.

"Cool. I have a friend who is way deep into religion. She would love this place," said Atatasuki, peering up at the lotus leaf dome.

"Once there is no longer a border separating men from women, extend her my invitation," said Rambir with a bow. "Before this temple was built there were huts and igloos but nothing that was devoted to a higher cause. The founder of this temple was a friend to the angels and believed that through devotion he could speed up the reincarnation process. He rounded up humans all across Lum, and with permission from the Goddesses, this place was built." The Sikh leader led the visitor around the empty altar and around a circular path.

"This is a Jain temple, right?"

"Correct, my friend. The founder was a Jain himself, and he united people of many faiths in Lum. The temple was mainly built by deceased Hindi architects. Without them and that monk, religion might never have developed here. There were once icons here from all different traditions, but that didn't last. The Goddesses decided that any worship was idolatry and that all devotion belonged to Lum. Later on, the Goddesses decided that religion should exist and that through religion the humans could be controlled. And so they adopted the religion of Islam, perhaps due to its global appeal or because of the power of the Quran itself."

"Is the book powerful?"

"All scripture is. But the Quran is written from God's perspective, making it particularly useful. After the Goddesses modified the laws to suit their purposes, they praised Lum as Allah. All are forced to follow these modified Quranic laws. Whenever the sky lights up, everyone in Lum must bow east and pray to Lum. We have no choice." Rambir stopped walking and turned to face his friend. "That is what we fight against."

"Against praying?"

"We are against religious intolerance, of any kind. As a Sikh, I fight for minorities, for justice. Here, humans are the minority and justice is not given to us. We are all forced to follow laws we do not believe in, taken and modified from a book that means nothing to some of us. Prayer must come naturally. It cannot be imposed."

"Why would the goddesses allow it? Efil seemed nice enough."

"Yes. She has always fought for us. Despite this, there are many who doubt her virtues."

"Why is that?"

The smile faded from Rambir's face. "During one of our peace meetings, there was an incident. The other angels stormed the building and captured all those inside. This was a time where there was great fear coming from both sides. There was a rebellion led by a different group of humans. Still is. Some think Efil knew about the plan to trap the rebels. They believe she lured us out for this purpose. I choose to trust her," said Rambir, his smile returning.

"Why? I mean, you don't know for certain."

"Many problems begin when there is no trust. Fear leads to conflict and conflict can result in war. And…when I look into her eyes. There is such sadness. She has gone through great loss. I trust the look in her eyes," said Rambir, nodding to himself.

"But the Goddesses are the ones who made all these discriminatory laws and she is a goddess, right?"

"I fight against oppression, not oppressors. And I do not generalize."

"You are so wise! How did you get to be such a scholarly badass?"

"We are all students. We all learn from one another. I only know what I have been taught." Rambir put his hand on his dear friend's shoulder. "Singh, if you treat every being you meet as a teacher, you will be amazed at the lessons you learn."

"You keep dropping the wisdom bombs. Saved and stored for revisiting. Hey, but what do you do if the angels attack?"

"If they attack, we retaliate, but otherwise we simply hold our ground."

They had made their way around the altar and were now back at the front.

Atatsuki noticed something new. At the exact center of the altar was a three-inch tall clay figure, poised like a pillar. It had eyes painted on it and a third eye carved and painted on its forehead. "Is this the god of the temple?"

"It is whatever you worship. To me, God is Guru Nanak's teachings. To you, well that is for you to decide."

Atatsuki folded his hands and prostrated himself. "Thank you, God of Muffins, for creating this world and everyone in it." He then stood up, beaming with energy. "Thank you, uh, Singh. I've learned so much from you."

"You are most welcome, Singh. Now, earlier you asked me how we fight. Let me show you." Rambir led Atatsuki out of the place of worship and up the stairs.

They climbed to the second floor of the palace and entered a room guarded by more lions.

Swords lined the walls, along with daggers, all handcrafted and polished.

148

"We fight when we must; but most of our battles are peaceful. I, along with some of the other spiritual leaders, schedule meetings with the Goddesses to try and change these laws. If we are attacked, we retaliate. We do not attack without provocation. I can give you a kirpan, but you must use it wisely," said Rambir, placing a silver blade in the noble warrior's hands.

"You're giving it to me? Or lending it? I have a tendency to forget what I've borrowed."

"There is no need to worry, my friend. It is yours now."

"Thanks." Atatasuki gripped the blade. "This is super cool. You know, I'm kind of the same. I can't fight without passion. I need to be emotionally fired up to do battle. Devlin told me humans are intolerant and untrustworthy, but I think what you guys fight for…it's good."

"Thank you, my friend. But be wary. Not all humans in Lum fight for religious freedom. There are many groups. Some are peaceful; some are violent. One in particular is dangerous. They want to overthrow the Goddesses and claim this realm for humanity. You best be careful."

"Of course. I'll keep my eyes peeled. But there's no way a bunch of humans could ever beat a goddess. I doubt I could and I'm a fighting machine," said Atatasuki, punching the air.

"You're right. Alone, they stand no chance. But they don't fight alone. Hmm, do you know how to use a kirpan?"

"Never used a sword, but I'm strong enough so it doesn't matter. Swoosh! Swoosh! Jab!"

Rambir ducked under Atatasuki's unpolished swordsmanship. "I could teach you. Unless you have to go."

"I'd love to learn. And then I can show off my new skills to my little sister," said Atatasuki.

"Yes. It is important to protect those we love. But remember that those we love can become both victims and victimizers. That is why you should only draw your sword to defend the oppressed."

"I understand," said Atatasuki with a bow.

"Good." Rambir drew his jewel-encrusted, slanted kirpan. "Come at me."

Previously: after being covered up in a white garment, Nina continued her journey to the rebel base in Femina.

"We've arrived." Thunder removed the blindfold from the non-human woman. "Take off your shoes."

"Don't rush me. These things take time," said Nina, running her hands down her thighs all the way to her feet. "It's just not the same when I'm in this Puritan wedding sheet," said the disgruntled warrior, rolling her eyes.

"You have beautiful eyes," said one of the rebel girls, seemingly a teenager.

"Thanks for noticing," said Nina with a wink.

The girl covered her blush with her hands.

"Cute. But your face is already covered," said Nina with a smile.

"Yes. Uh, you're right."

"This mosque, our base, was created before the Goddesses decided to hijack our religion. It is called Lotus," said Thunder, gesturing to the structure.

Nina passed through the elongated gateway, which had a vine design and some fancy letters traveling up it. "Is that it?" She looked up at the building, but seemed unimpressed.

Lotus was a massive structure no doubt, but it lacked color—the whole thing was white, like everything in Lum. A recently trimmed garden, designed around the pathway in large rectangular clumps, made it look a bit too orderly. The one-way windows were made out of a special glass to keep prying eyes from peeking in. There were four pillars, one for each corner of the building. The pillars were a mishmash of different stones; it was clear that this temple was built under a time crunch. Holes had been carved out of the midsection of each pillar where pairs of women armed with bows were keeping watch. At the center of the building was a protrusion of the top portion of a pillar, sealed off with what looked like an upside-down acorn. Nina sighed as she looked at this part of the building; it reminded her of her now barely visible bust.

Nina was about to take a step but was stopped by the grumpy commander's hand.

"Follow my lead. Step exactly where I step, understood?"

"You women are so uptight." Nina dropped to the ground into a handstand and propelled herself over the stairway, landing at its top.

The young rebel girl was clapping excitedly, silenced when the leader glared in her direction.

Thunder went up the steep stairs in a roundabout way, sometimes going down one step to get around an unseen disaster. The other rebels followed suit.

"Ohohoho, you all look so funny," said Nina.

"My name is Fatima. What is your name?" asked the young rebel, beaming at Nina.

"Named after the founder's daughter?"

"You know of the Prophet?" she asked with wide amber eyes.

"Yeah. One of my uh…allies is his follower. But she follows many prophets, not just the mainstream ones. I'm Nina. Always a pleasure to meet a fan," she said, starting to comb back her hair before realizing it was covered.

"You are going to love it here. I know it," said Fatima in a gentle voice brimming with joy.

"I'm not lovin' it so far." said Nina, waving at a bird that flew by the outpost.

The women in the pillar fired their crossbows near the bird, causing it to rush off.

"Do I have to wear this thing the entire time I'm inside this outpost?"

"Not everywhere. Inside, past the altar, there is a communal bath. We could take a bath together," said the young girl, her beaming smile visible through the cloth.

"I don't do communal bathing. I wash this heavenly body all by myself," said Nina, making her strut extra seductive to compensate for her undesirable outfit.

"Heehee. She walks so funny," said Fatima to herself.

Nina was stopped by six guards, pointing their spears at her before she could open the door. "They don't seem friendly."

"Calm down, sisters. She is with me." Thunder rushed to the front and opened the door.

The young rebel rushed ahead with a twirl into the communal hall.

"I'll go find my friends. You must meet them," she said, grabbing Nina's hand.

"Fatima, she must speak with the Imam. She can meet your friends another time," said Thunder.

"Yeah I've got business, sweetie. But we can hang out later. Maybe you can rub my feet," said Nina, patting her little fan's head.

"I look forward to our next meeting," said Fatima with a curtsy.

"Come with me," said Thunder, grabbing the Exp by the arm.

Nina pulled her arm out of the inelegant grip. "Geez, don't bruise me. You're so brutish. Very unladylike," she said, her nose held high.

"I doubt you bruise so easily. You are a lady and a warrior, as I am," said Thunder, hitting the fighter's back.

"Let's get moving." Nina was led past the altar, which had an image of a complex geometric symbol above another bundle of fancy letters. She followed the grumpy commander up the staircase, looking up at the lily pad dome on the ceiling. She went down another corridor, past no less than fifty guards and finally arrived at the room all the way in the back. "Ugh. You shouldn't put my enchanting feet through such an ordeal," she said, stretching her toes.

"Great Mother, I know that we are having our meeting soon, but I found an Exp. She may be able to help us. She can fight," said Thunder, now speaking in a reserved tone.

"With grace, power, elegance, and finesse," added Nina.

"She may enter," said a firm commanding voice from behind the door.

"I will be in the meeting room; it is halfway down the hallway. Do not wander around. Go straight to the communal hall after she is done talking to you," said Thunder, gripping the womanly warrior's shoulders.

"Got it. See you then. You know, just because we can't see your mouth doesn't mean you can't smile," said Nina with a veiled smile.

"I hope you will consider joining us." Thunder turned to the door, bowed to the Imam inside and then left.

Nina opened the door.

There was a woman dressed like all the others, though a bit meatier, seated on her knees. Behind her were stacks of scrolls.

Nina sat down on her knees, careful not to step on the cloth over her legs.

"Welcome to Allah's Jannah," said the Imam, who had brown eyes.

"So that's what this sorority is called."

"You are not the first."

"But you are, right? The first female Imam, I mean. Violet said that women weren't allowed to be leaders of an Islamic religious community. Hmm, when did she say that again?" asked Nina to herself.

"Allah cares not whether the leader is female or male. If they can effectively lead the community, with strength and cohesion, nothing else matters. What I meant was: you are not the first Exp."

"You've seen others?"

"Yes. I have been a leader for a long time. The Exps are no longer here. Some say they moved on. Others say they became angels. Fewer still say they are the gods and goddesses that currently preside over the realms. One thing is for certain, when they came, change soon followed."

"We aren't fond of rules. Makes sense to me," said Nina.

"What about angels, Goddesses, are you fond of them?" she asked, her gaze unshaken.

"Don't trust them. I don't trust anyone. Trust has to be earned. And nobody has quite earned mine yet."

"That is good. You should be wary. Angels have authority in this realm. They follow the will of the Goddesses and some are less virtuous than others."

"Hmm…from my understanding they followed Lum, not the Goddesses."

"Ah yes, of course. But no one has ever seen this god. Lum is a leader without a face, but it has a voice. Do the Goddesses take turns becoming that voice? That would make this Lum appear less conflicted; it would serve a purpose. Or are they all fooled by one goddess playing the role of leader without their knowledge? It is possible that Lum exists, but I am skeptical of this."

"Oh, I get it. If you make it to the throne room you become Lum. Is that it? No one would be the wiser. And then everything under the clouds would be yours, right?"

"You are a clever woman. But no. My place is here, at this mosque. I cannot go outside. I will not."

"Why not? Shouldn't the leader be at the battlefield, cheering on the warriors and upping their morale?"

"I must remain pure. I do not trust the light of this realm. I don't trust anything the angels or goddesses give. Whenever they give something, they take away something precious."

"Like what?" asked Nina, scooting in closer.

"They give bliss, overflowing, profound joy, but in the act of giving they take away a memory or a simple thought. It is subtle, but soon the images become hazy and then eventually they vanish. That is how they force us to reincarnate. They make us forget who we are. It is also how they prepare us to become angels. None of the angels are to be trusted and the Goddesses even less so."

"You're totally paranoid. Isn't reincarnation the way of life? Why fight what's part of the natural system?" asked Nina, looking at the thin white sheet which was presumably the Imam's bed.

"Do you know who or what you will reincarnate as?"

"I'm not planning on reincarnating. I'm staying in this body till I cease to exist. You would understand if you could see the splendor of my physique. But you can't…because of this," said Nina, tugging at her clothes.

"No one wants to start over. And here's the thing that is most peculiar about it. The angels say that it is our soul that chooses our next incarnation. But it is a goddess who tells us what our soul decides. How can we know if our soul is making the choice when they are the only ones who can translate the language of our spirit?"

"You make an excellent point. But let's talk results. Do you have any reason to think the angels are against you? Are there grounds for all your paranoia?"

"Most certainly. The Goddesses adapted the holy religion of Islam. They modified our scripture, Allah's sacred text. They call it Allah's Nur, and then they claim Lum is Allah."

"That is tricky. Hmm, so any guesses which goddess is acting as Lum? Or do you think it's all of them."

"There is one above all that cannot be trusted. She cowers behind Lum's word and claims innocence. She has even bent some of my people to her will. Her humble nature makes me most suspicious of her. Not only that, but she stays close to the most dangerous of all the Goddesses, the ruthless slayer of my people, Etaf."

"If Efil is life, then Etaf is fate. The Goddess of Fate is your enemy? Heavy duty. I don't know about you, but I'd try not to get on her bad side."

"You'd be wise not to. She claims morality is an illusion conjured by humanity. Her angels are the most ruthless. I have seen them tear out babies from a mother's womb, oftentimes killing her in the process. It makes no difference to them whether the baby was forced upon the mother or from her consent. To them Lum is the only creator, the exclusive mussawir. They deem all products of creation as exclusive property of Lum. They have no mercy."

"Why do they kill these babies? Is it to make an example?"

"Sometimes yes. But other times they are taken away and perhaps become mawali, brainwashed by Lum's lies."

"The land of milk and honey indeed," said Nina, rolling her eyes.

"Your words ring true. Our children are the milk, taken from us to be used for their own devices. And the honey is the scripture, Allah's Nur, regurgitated over and over and forced upon all of us. Equality and freedom are mere words here. They have no substance. Do you know who they put at the front lines of the battlefield?"

"Nope."

"Human angels. Every time, without fail. They see us as expendable. No, not even. They want to get rid of us without dirtying their hands."

"Quite crafty."

"You have heard me talk and I could continue, but it is all meaningless if you do not stay with us and fight." Her wrinkly hand rose from her lap and was gently placed on the warrior's hand. "Please. We need your help."

"Sorry. No can do. It's suicidal. Nothing to gain and everything to lose," said Nina with a shrug.

"Ah. You don't know then? Of course you don't. I cannot say when it is, but during the next battle we will strike back. We will storm the portal to Earth. If you help us, and we win, I can give you what you want."

"But I don't want to reincarnate," said Nina, rolling her neck.

"If you make it to that portal, you will return to Earth in this body, as you are right now. I must stay here, but there are many here who miss their families, especially the children," she said with a soothing tone.

"If you're telling the truth, then you've got yourself a new warrior. But shouldn't you think this through? When your rebel pals come back from the dead, that's sure to get some unwanted attention."

"They will have the attention of all the people of the world. They will tell them how paradise has been hijacked by a self-proclaimed god and a band of false angels. When the next generation of women arrives in Lum, they will come prepared to battle the injustice. We make it through and we turn the tide of the revolution. We have tried before and failed, but each time we have come closer."

"Then hopefully you make it this time. I don't like it here. I'll be glad to leave it behind."

"You should join us for our meeting," said the Imam, standing up.

Nina leaped to her feet. "You trust me too quickly."

"You may be an Exp, but you are also a woman. We have always been victimized and here it is no different. You're a proud warrior. There would be no reason for you to sabotage our plan. We are your only means of leaving. Now come along." The Imam opened the door.

"Do I have to keep wearing this uniform until I get back to Earth?"

"I wouldn't recommend removing it if I were you. Those clothes protect more than your chastity."

"Well considering how everything in Lum is white and bland everything, I assume it makes for great camouflage."

"That is indeed true, but there's more to it. Light is most powerful here when it touches your head. It will change the way you think. The niqab and chador block off this light. It keeps our minds free of Lum's influence."

"Then I'll keep it on," said Nina, trying to rub away the wrinkles in the cloth.

"That would be best," said the Imam, opening the door to the meeting room.

"I'll pass on the meeting. Negotiating with others isn't one of my special skills. See ya around." Nina walked out the door and down the hall. After passing by the guards outside, she made her way to the stairs.

Fatima ran into the beautiful newcomer with a hug. "So, are you going to stay?" she asked, eyes alight with hope.

"Depends. I definitely want to make it to the portal to Earth. Do you?" asked Nina, crouching down.

"We could go together! You could be like my big sister!" exclaimed Fatima, grabbing her new friend's hand.

Nina slipped her hand out of her clingy fan's grip. "I'm a loner. Hey, can you do me a favor?"

"Of course!"

Nina picked up the teenage girl. "Those guards. The ones standing by the wall. Can you distract them for me?"

After Fatima was set down, she rushed by the guards.

The guards turned their head to face the girl before being jabbed in the neck.

Nina set the guards down gently as they collapsed. "I'll be back soon." The nimble warrior pressed against the wall, causing it to spin around. She arrived at a secret staircase. "Now what do we have here?"

Two guards at the bottom of the staircase caught a glimpse of the intruder and raised their crossbows. "What is the password?"

Nina rushed down the stairway, dodging three arrows and gripping the fourth. "Out of the way, I'm not your enemy." She slid under two more and jumped up.

The two guards slammed against the wall from the intruder's spinning kick, dropping their weapons.

The seductive survivalist pressed her fingers into a pressure point on their necks and knocked them out.

"What could they be hiding down here?" Nina looked to her left and right to see cages. They looked empty, but it was hard to tell with how dark it was.

She suddenly became aware of a low growling.

Gripping the bars of the fourth prison cell from the stairs was a tortured human. His flesh was scorched. Thorns held his mutilated body together. His eyes were vacant.

"What happened to you? Yeesh, these women are more brutal than I expected. Well, enough snooping about." Nina turned around and headed back toward the stairs. "This get up is perfect. It will be impossible for them to know who broke in," she said, skipping up the stairs.

Four armored women came out from the secret entrance and slammed into the intruder.

Two archers behind them put out the nearby torches.

"Put the light back on! I don't like the darkness," said Nina, wobbling as she stood up.

The armored women gripped the trespasser's arms and brought her to the secret entrance.

The wall flipped around and Nina saw light once more, along with the Imam, looking down at her.

"You saw something you shouldn't have," said the Imam, her eyes devoid of compassion.

"I was curious. There was obviously something behind that wall. I'm still game for storming the portal," said Nina, stretching out her hand.

"You have broken my trust. You must be held accountable," said the Imam, turning away from the traitor.

# Chapter 63: Angelic Intervention

Previously: Efil convinced Kawai, Matteria, and Anthrax to persuade their allies to see Lum in a positive light.

Kanasta came rushing into the World Tree, followed by Riufen, Karson, BoneSaw, D.S., Pharma, Opti, and Bob.

"Welcome. Have a seat. There is something I would like to discuss with all of you," said Efil with a smile.

"Likewise." Bob zoomed up to the flowery goddess. "Why did your angels capture our allies?"

"Wait, they did what? Where's my brother? You guys were with Atatasuki. Where is he?" asked Kawai, gripping onto the assassin boss' chest.

"He went off on his own."

"Great. Now we have another problem to deal with. Bob, do you think my brother got captured by angels?" asked Kawai with worrisome eyes.

"Not sure, but I know for certain that Demo and Fusion were both taken away," said Bob.

"Not true at all. We only know that Bob was with Fusion when we split up and the sticky ball was gone when he returned," said Karson.

"Why are we all just standing here? We need to find my brother," said Kawai.

"What about Nina? We need to find her too," said Matteria.

"I could locate them, but I doubt you would trust me to," said Bob with a sly grin.

"I could send you along with some escorts," said Efil.

"Great idea! But first, how about you explain to us why your angels kidnapped our people?" asked Bob, pulling the glorified angel up to the group with his spectral tentacles.

"We're wasting time bickering. Bob, lead me to my little brother...now," said Kawai with fierce eyes.

"By little, I assume you mean older. After all, Atatasuki's creation precedes your own," said Bob.

"Yeah him. Let's go," said Kawai.

"You can't go with him. He isn't trustworthy," said Karson.

"Where is NoOne?" asked Anthrax.

"He's kind of a sheep now," said D.S., shifting his feet.

"He decided he wants to move on," said Opti.

"Well so do I. But I'm not getting a new life until my comrades are free. Bloody coward," said Karson.

"We need to get everyone together if we are going to free Exp 8, Kaity, and Devlin. We need three groups to bring back the others. We will all meet back here as soon as possible," said Anthrax.

"Four groups. Sefiwah is missing as well," said Kanasta, reattaching BoneSaw's treads.

"I'll stay here," said Deceivant, holding his sobbing wife in his arms.

"I can sense spiritual bodies if I get close enough," said Violet.

"Hey, you're okay!" Matteria rushed in for a hug. "Good to have you back."

"It's good to be back," said Violet, returning her brother's gesture of kindness with a smile and a bow.

Efil looked at Violet, noticing some of her hair had been pulled out. She raised her hand and released light energy, regenerating the devotee's missing hair in seconds. "Welcome back."

Angels suddenly stormed into the tree, holding Tempo's arms behind his back.

Kanasta stood in their path. "Is there a problem?" He cracked each finger individually.

"So where are you going to put me?" asked Tempo, his head popping up.

The angels dropped him, took a step back and held out their natural weapons.

"Oh great, the bear is here." D.S. squeezed through the group, went past Kanasta and up to the polar bear angel. "Couldn't have been a sloth bear. This sucks." He opened his muscular arms as wide as he could.

"Stand aside," said the bear in a commanding voice.

D.S. wrapped his arms around the bear and embraced it tightly.

"Wh-what are you doing?" asked the bear, losing the intimidation in its voice.

D.S. was pulled off by another bear angel and pinned to the ground.

"Touching an angel is forbidden," she said with a snarl.

"Yes, but we can forgive children, can't we?" asked Efil with a calming tone.

"What? That's a child?" asked the bear with wide eyes.

"Exps are complicated. I give him full pardon, this time," said Efil with a smile.

"Will you give me pardon too?" asked Tempo, stepping up to the winged woman with a smirk.

The polar bear leaped onto his back and pinned him down.

"I knew this one would be a law breaker. What did he do?" asked Efil.

"He tried to kill one of the visitors. He was in a crazed frenzy and had to be subdued. It is not safe to keep him here. Where would you have us relocate him?" asked the bear angel.

"Wait up! Look, I'm the guy he attacked. No harm done. It happens sometimes. He was a bit restless, that's all. I'll make sure it doesn't happen again," said Ego.

"What happened?" asked Kanasta with a raised eyebrow.

"We were sparring and we both got into it a bit too much. No more sparring so no more problems; promise," said Ego with a nervous smile.

"Is this true?" asked Efil, looking down at the hired gun.

"Every bit of it, your highness," said Tempo with a nod and a grin.

"I'll make sure he doesn't repeat the same mistake," said Kanasta, pulling his subordinate away from the goddess.

"No. I can't let this slide. He will have to pay for his crime," said Efil.

"Pay, you mean like as in money?" asked Tempo, a drop of sweat sliding down his cheek.

"No. Hoist him up," said Efil.

The polar bears brought Tempo to his feet and held onto his arms.

"I'm his commander. I will pay whatever it is he owes you," said Kanasta.

"We are all individuals in Lum. And thus we must personally pay for our crimes," said Efil as light erupted from her hand.

Tempo slammed his elbows into the polar bears and leaped on top of them. "I'm not letting you touch me."

"You don't have a choice." Efil shot forward and plunged her hand into the lawbreaker's chest. She ripped out a bright swirling collection of light. She then tossed the criminal into his boss. "See to it that he causes no more problems." The swirling energy was then absorbed into her fingertips.

"What the hell did you do to me?" asked Tempo, flailing his arms as he tried to escape his boss' iron grip.

"I took your bliss. How do I explain this to a murderer, hmm? Well, in Lum, bliss is our currency. You paid the price for your actions. If you break another law, the consequences shall be greater. I must be off. Lum is calling for me." Efil created a white portal and entered.

Kanasta set his business brother on the ground and checked his pulse. "How do you feel?"

"I'm fine, Boss. A little drained is all," said Tempo, bobbing back and forth.

"You two weren't here earlier, so I'll fill you in. Four of our teammates are still out there, not counting the ones who were allegedly captured," said Kawai, shooting the treacherous eyeball a glare.

"Can't we get beyond this already?" asked Bob, rolling his pupil.

"No. I can't. Look, I can believe that you didn't kill them," said Kawai, circling around her killer.

"Great. Then what seems to be the problem?" asked Bob.

"Why did you let them get captured?" asked Kawai.

"Good question," said Kanasta, modifying BoneSaw's mainframe.

"I what? Ugh, more baseless accusations," said Bob.

"I agree. Bob is strong. He wouldn't lose to angels," said Riufen, glaring at the traitor.

"While it's true I am powerful, that doesn't mean I—"

"You weren't trying to protect them! Oh, it all makes sense now," said Karson.

"There are rules against violence in Lum, especially against angels. My hands were tied, so to speak. Not only that, but there were a lot of angels at the time, all of them militarized. They left with our allies after blinding me. Efil is the one you should be doubting. Why don't you ask her why her angels ambushed us?" Bob's spectral arms pulled in Kawai, Riufen, and Karson. "Oh, that's right, she isn't here. Convenient?"

Kawai shrugged off the wispy tendril. "I don't believe you. But…I need your help. You're the only one who can find my little brother."

"Ah yes. You need me. But, I can't very well go with you. Who knows, I may let you get captured by angels. I can't be trusted, right?" asked Bob with a watery gaze.

Deceivant gave his wifey a gentle kiss on the lips and then stood up. "Forget about him. I'll lead you to your brother."

"You don't know where he is. I'm Kawai's only hope," said Bob, grabbing her cheeks.

Kawai smacked aside the spectral hands. "We're wasting time!"

Deceivant whipped out a locator from his coat. The industrious inventor fiddled around with the controls. "Found him. Hop on and let's move out," he said, patting his shoulder.

Kawai hopped off the air, landing on his shoulder. She peered down at the device and the flashing dot way in the distance that symbolized her little brother. "When did you get this?" she asked, her eyes shimmering.

"I made it, a long time ago. Once we make it to Sel, we can track down Exp 8 with it too," said Deceivant, poking Kawai-chan's squishy wittle tummy.

"Aww, you're the best!" she exclaimed, kissing his cheek.

Deceivant blushed a bit as he smiled at her. "But wait, if you go with us, won't you be breaking the law? Perhaps you should leave the retrieval to me."

"I'll take the punishment. What I won't do is sit here while my brother is in danger. Let's move out," said Kawai, pointing at the exit.

"May I accompany you? If any problems come up along the way, I will cut them down," said Riufen.

"Sounds good. D.S., you should come too. You are my bodyguard, after all," said Deceivant, wiping his glasses.

"Of course I'm coming!" D.S. bent down to his mom and gave her a big hug. "We'll be back soon."

Led by Deceivant, Kawai's group left the tree and headed out to find Atatasuki.

"Bob, we could use your assistance," said Kanasta.

"Oh, you want my help? Really? Are you sure? I may lead you into forbidden territory and watch as you get abducted by angelic warriors," said Bob, circling around the malleable assassin.

"That is a risk we must take. Sefiwah is out there alone. It is not safe. We must find her. You will lead us."

"Us? So you're not the only one going?" asked Bob.

"BoneSaw, Ego, and Tempo are coming along as well. The plan is to find her and bring her back here. From there we will figure out how to rescue Kaity, my brother, and Exp 8," said Kanasta.

"Yeah, wouldn't be right making a rescue party for Kaity without her girlfriend," said Ego, stretching his arms back.

"Seems like a good enough plan. Follow me." Bob zoomed out of the tree, followed by the Viper Squad assassins.

"I'll lead the way to NoOne. Who wants to join the party?" asked Opti.

"I'll come along," said Anthrax.

"Got nothing better to do," said Pharma.

"In case we get attacked, we'll need someone who can fight," said Anthrax, looking over the group.

"I can fight," said Pharma with a shrug.

"Karson, would you come along?" asked Anthrax.

"You've chosen wisely. Sure I'll accompany you. I'll bring that coward back to us if I have to hold him at gunpoint." Karson cocked his shotgun arm.

"What? Why him? I already proved I'm better," said Pharma.

"Great. Let's move out," said Anthrax.

With Opti at the front, the group left the area to find NoOne.

"We have to bring Nina back. I can locate her energy trail if you can take me back to where you last saw her," said Violet.

"Sure. Follow me," said Matteria.

"I'll come along too. I'm sure we can convince her to help save my little boy. She's a loving person, after all," said Ada.

The last group left the tree.

Previously: Kanasta's group left in search of Sefiwah. Dashing through trees and rushing up hills, the Viper Squad assassins followed Bob's lead. After passing by some straw huts, their attuned leader stopped.

"She's down the hill in those bushes. Go in carefully, if there are enemies inside we could easily be ambushed. I'll cover you from here," said Bob, his pupil glowing with a light green aura.

"You can see souls, right man? Can't you see if she's alone?" asked Ego.

"Yes. I can clearly see she is not alone. There are three with her. But I don't know if they are friend or foe," said Bob, the aura around his pupil vanishing.

"Let's find out." Kanasta set BoneSaw down.

The little robot sped down the slope and into the bushes. It immediately zoomed out, waving its massive saw around frantically.

As Kanasta rushed in he noticed that the bushes had drops of blood on the tips of their leaves. He saw Sefiwah and three more, their hands pierced through her chest, above a damp puddle of blood.

Tempo slammed his body into one of the figures, causing the other two to pull away.

As the figures created weapons of light, the rest of Kanasta's group rushed in.

"Stop! They aren't your enemy!" yelled Sefiwah, her pale lips now a weak grey.

"Who isn't?" asked Tempo, setting his hand aflame.

Sefiwah turned to the angels. "These are my allies." She looked up into Kanasta's eyes. "These angels are trying to save me."

With a firm gesture, Kanasta signaled Tempo to stand down. Once the angels resumed the healing process, he crouched down to her level. "Who attacked you?"

"They tried to kidnap me. I defended against the first few, but they kept coming. They were women, wearing all white. Once they saw that I wasn't going to come peacefully, they attacked all at once." Sefiwah's bottom lip quivered.

"You let your guard down?"

"I was shot in the leg." Sefiwah gestured to the hole above her ankle. "These angels took the arrow out. If they hadn't found me, I would have died," she said, about to cry.

Kanasta put his hand on hers. "You are safe now. Once you've healed up, we'll join with the others."

"But wasn't the team split up?"

"Yes, and now we are coming together. All of us. We will free Kaity." Kanasta put his hand to his powerful chest. "I swear my life upon it."

"Hey, those women hurt my buddy. Do you angels know anything about them?" asked Ego.

"Yes. They are a group of extremist humans. They want to take over Lum," said the gazelle angel.

"Those who will not join them are viewed as obstacles. Your friend is lucky to be alive," said the badger angel.

"These humans have no place in Lum. They belong in Sel!" yelled the wolverine angel, her mouth quaking but her hands steady.

"Would you be willing to pay for them to go away?" asked Tempo, still wobbling a bit.

"Such things are against the laws of Lum. But…sometimes rules must be broken to uphold Lum's doctrine," said the wolverine.

The badger angel's eyes widened. "You mustn't say such things. Only a goddess can make such a decision."

The gazelle ended her Reiki treatment. She focused her light energy and materialized a document.

Kanasta peeked at the words but couldn't recognize any of them. "What does it say?"

"It is written in Luminous, only angels can read it and only angels are allowed to read it," said the gazelle, moving the document out of Kanasta's line of sight.

The angels read the document as they healed the pale woman.

"Well that changes things," said the badger with wide eyes.

"Does this mean we are getting paid?" asked Tempo with a grin.

"A year's worth of bliss for each of you…provided you dethrone the Imam of Allah's Jannah. You are also permitted to defend yourself as you see necessary."

"Allah's Paradise, such hubris," said Sefiwah.

"What do you say, Boss; a job in Heaven? Could be fun," said Tempo.

"You may decline if you wish. The choice is yours," said the wolverine.

"It isn't money, so no point in taking it up, right Boss?" asked Ego.

"Principle is what matters. We help those in need of our services. We will head out as soon as she is healed," said Kanasta.

"Then let's get moving," said Sefiwah with a weak smile. Her body no longer had gashes or holes. The assassin's thin fingers trembled as she wiped off the last bit of blood off her chest.

"Can I come too? It sounds like fun," said Bob with a cheerful smile.

"You are not an assassin. Do what you will, but don't get in our way," said Kanasta.

"On second thought, maybe I should go warn the others about these extremists. And make sure they know where to meet," said Bob.

"Do what you will." Kanasta shifted his attention to the angels. "Can you show us the location of the target?"

"Their base isn't far from here. Follow me and I'll lead you there," said the gazelle.

"The Viper Squad is back in business," said Kanasta with the slightest of smiles.


Previously: Deceivant left with his group to locate Atatasuki. It wasn't long before the rebel base was in sight.

"Whoa, that's mega big. Are you sure my brother's in there?" asked Kawai.

"Well you have to account for human error, but it sure looks like it," said Deceivant, holding up the locator.

"Was he captured?" asked Riufen, drawing out his spine and surveying the area.

"We mustn't jump to conclusions. We don't know what happened to him. He could be there willingly," said Deceivant.

"Uh-uh. No way. I told him to stay put. What, did he forget or something? Wait! Ugh! What a moron!" yelled Kawai.

"That's not very nice," said D.S., shrinking a little in response to her rage.

"I'll go check it out. If things get dangerous, I'm counting on you to come to my rescue." Deceivant's smile shifted from D.S. to Riufen. "You'll keep little Kawai safe while I'm away, right?"

"You have my word," said Riufen with a bow.

"You're going to have to keep Atatasuki safe from me! I told him one thing. One thing! Why can't he ever be dependable?" asked Kawai with a prolonged pout.

"At least he is alive," said Deceivant, giving his darling creation a pat on the head.

"Yeah. You're right," said Kawai with an itty bitty smile.

Deceivant came out from the trees and was immediately spotted by the guards.

The white lions followed him with their eyes as he made his way up the stairs to the front door.

Once his hand was about to touch the doorknob, he heard a growl.

Deceivant immediately pulled back. He realized the growl came from what he thought were statues a moment ago. "Oh…ah…um…greetings. I am here as a visitor. I mean you no harm."

The doors opened and a young man came out. He was dark-skinned, had dimples and a big smile. The top of his head was covered by a turban, and his hand was gripping the hilt of a sword. He saw fear in the visitor's eyes and relaxed his hand, though he did not remove it from the weapon.

"Do you speak English? Nihongo? Italiano? I speak all three," said Deceivant.

"I speak English. I am sorry, my friend, but we do not allow visitors here. You must be invited in," said the man, his words warm and welcoming.

"Well then, can you invite me in? I only want to see my friend. He's in here, according to this." Deceivant held up the locator.

"I can ask about your friend, but I cannot let you in. I will need your name and his name."

"I'm Deceivant. I'm rather well known in the scientific community. Well, not to brag, but I am a household name. My friend's name is Atatasuki. He's an Exp so he should stick out."

"Yes, my friend. One moment." The young man closed the door.

Deceivant backed away from the door and turned away so the lions couldn't see him. He gave a thumbs-up to D.S. who was watching from behind a nearby pine tree.

"So far so good." Deceivant brushed some dirt off his pants.

The door opened again. The same young man came out and was now smiling. "He says he doesn't trust you." The young man couldn't help but snicker a bit as he closed the door.

"What? Who said that? Your leader?"

"Your friend. He said, 'I don't remember why, but I don't trust that guy.' He is so funny."

"So then, I can't come in?"

"Sorry, but no. Wait, my friend. He was wondering if you have seen his sister?"

"Yes. She's with me."

"Sis!" yelled a voice behind the door.

Atatasuki burst open the door and rushed down the stairs. He turned to his creator. "Where is she?"

"Right…."

"I'm right here," said Kawai, coming out from the trees.

"Sis!" Atatasuki rushed into a hug.

Kawai slid out of the way, having her brother almost slam his face into a pine tree. "Do you know what stay put means?" she asked, pulling him in with her tail.

"I'm sorry, Sis. I can't remember why I came here, but I know it was for a good reason. I never left Masculino, so I didn't break any rules or anything. The leader here is ultra nice. You should meet him," said Atatasuki.

"Well because you ventured off, I had to cross over to the boy zone and now I'm a rule breaker. We are going home…now." Kawai wrapped her tail around the defect's throat.

Rambir came out from the temple and smiled at Deceivant. "Ah, I have heard great things about you from the young teachers. I am Rambir. Welcome to Lum, my friend," he said with a bow.

"Rambir! I want to introduce you to my sister!" hollered Atatasuki as he rushed up to the steps, bumping Deceivant aside.

Kawai did a mid-air curtsy. "Pleasure to meet you, sir. I'm Kawai. Thanks for keeping my idiot brother safe."

"You are most welcome. I never thought I would meet two Exps," said Rambir with a surprised smile.

"And their creator," said Deceivant, tapping Kawai-chan's itty bitty nose.

"What a wondrous day. I am sure you have much to teach me," said Rambir, looking out at the three of them.

"I'm sorry Rambir, but we told our allies we would meet up with them as soon as possible. At a later time, I'd be happy to chat," said Deceivant.

"If you must go, then go. All of you and your friends are welcome to come to the temple at any time. I hope we will meet again," said Rambir.

"Wait, you almost forgot your sword," said Atatasuki, pulling the blade out of his tail's grip.

"That is a gift. As is this." Rambir pulled up his sleeves, showing that his arm was covered in bracelets. "How many teammates do you have?" he asked, looking up at his newest friend.

"I'm the last person you should ask," said Atatasuki with a grin.

"Twenty-five. Though some of them are currently missing," said Deceivant.

"Take thirty." Rambir pulled off almost all his bracelets and pulled out some smaller ones from beneath his shirt. Only the two massive steel bracelets remained on his arms. "The karas will grant you entrance into this temple if I am away. Not only that, but most of the wrongs we commit are committed by our hands. Theft, murder, rape, our hands can be used for many wrong-doings. When we are in a dangerous situation, when we are about to do wrong, we look to our hands. Let these karas remind you that you walk a path of learning and teaching, not force. Remember to be aware of your options before you draw your weapon." The simple guru slipped the bracelet up Atatasuki and Deceivant's wrists. "I trust you will pass these down with my blessing." He handed the remaining bracelets to Atatasuki.

"Sis, is it alright if I—"

"It's fine. But hurry. We need to make a plan to rescue big brother," said Kawai.

Atatasuki placed the bracelet on his dear sister's soft hands.

"Oh yeah. I'm rockin' this," said Kawai, admiring the bracelet.

"Ooh! I want one!" exclaimed D.S., rushing out from cover.

"Yet another Exp. I am Rambir. It is an honor to meet you."

"Whoa! That's a long beard. Is that a sword?" asked D.S., reaching for Rambir's weapon.

"Such an innocent spirit this one has. Remember to choose your battles wisely, my friend," said Rambir.

"Friend! I'm your friend? Cool! You're like the oldest friend I have! I mean you're a new friend, but you're sooo old!" exclaimed D.S., shifting back and forth in excitement.

"It is a pleasure to meet you too. I won't keep you here. Hope we meet again," said Rambir, making his way back inside the temple.

"Come along, Mommy is waiting for us," said Deceivant, tugging at his creation's arm.

Bob popped out from the ground, causing Kawai to shriek and hide behind the living microwave. "Whoops, did I scare you?" he asked with an innocent gaze.

Deceivant stepped between Bob and Atatasuki. "I thought you were with the Viper Squad."

"I was. But I came here to tell you we have a new meeting spot. It's the rebel base in Femina. Follow Deceivant's locator to Nina. I've got to find Anthrax's group and inform them."

"Why should we trust you?" asked Riufen.

"Ugh, this again? Do what you want. I've got to tell the others." Bob vanished from sight.

"Our priority should be getting the team back together, even if we have to break a few rules. I say we go for it," said Deceivant.

"The quicker we get back together, the quicker we can rescue my brother!" cheered Kawai, throwing her arm in the air.

"Our brother," said Atatasuki, giving her a fist bump.

Previously: Opti volunteered to lead his group to NoOne. He was the team captain for their trip and led them through about three acres of trees until they arrived at the open grasslands.

"Are you guys sure about this? Who are we to tell him how to live his life?" asked Opti, turning to face the group.

"I agree. Live and let live," said Pharma, exhaling imaginary smoke rings.

"Devlin created him. He has obligations to his father," said Anthrax.

"Says you. Bird left the nest a long time ago, if you ask me," said Pharma.

"Anthrax is right. Exps are warriors, and no warrior should leave the battlefield when their commander is in enemy camp. I will gladly reincarnate once all this is said and done, but my duty to Devlin and Exp 8 comes first and foremost. He can't shirk his moral responsibilities simply because he's a bloomin' coward," said Karson, parting the bushes.

"Okay, but let me go talk to him. You'll probably scare off the sheep," said Opti, holding his hands to his chest.

"I'll come along too," said Anthrax.

The two of them entered the open landscape and immediately spotted NoOne.

The shadow master was on the ground between two sheep, taking in their warmth.

"We need to talk," said Anthrax.

NoOne's shadow moved across the ground up to the dutiful doctor. He rose out from it. "Talk about what? Can't you see I'm busy being eternally at peace?"

"Well, Devlin is busy being trapped in Absence. We need your help if we are going to rescue him."

"My help? What can I do? I'd only get in the way. I've never once succeeded in battle. I was deceived by Exp 8 into believing I won, but I won't fall for it again. Leave me here. It's best for all of us," said NoOne, sinking in the ground as he talked.

Opti grabbed his hand. "You can't live like this. You have to believe in yourself. You can be your own shining sun if you only believe."

"Ugh. Do you even listen to yourself? Leave me alone," said NoOne.

"These sheep…they are your new family?" asked Anthrax.

"That's correct," said NoOne with a blank stare.

"I talked with Efil. The forces of Sel are trying to break into Lum. If they succeed, then everyone in Lum is in danger. You care about these sheep, your new family, don't you? Fight with us to protect them," said Anthrax, making a punching motion.

"Wait? Fight for the defenseless…like a hero?" NoOne's pupils shrank. He brought his finger to his mouth. "You think I can do that?"

"Not alone you can't. This isn't like last time. Exp 8 is on our side now. All the Exps are united, along with the assassins. And Deceivant is with us too! We can do this," said Anthrax with a smile brimming with hope.

NoOne looked back at the sheep. "It is different. Bob and Riufen are with us this time. You're right. Okay. I'll help. To protect these people. To defend this land."

Opti jumped up into a hug with his shadow buddy. "Yay! I knew you would do the right thing!"

"You give me too much credit. I thought I'd be at peace with the sheep, but I can't get her eyes out of my head. Why did you have to make me remember her?" asked NoOne.

"Don't be such a downer. Cherish the memory. Use her loving eyes to push your forward as you stand up to protect Lum," said Opti, putting his arm around his shadow buddy.

"You're right. The fact that I still remember those eyes is a miracle and it should be treated as such," said NoOne with a blissful smile.

"Let's get moving. The rest of our allies are waiting for us," said Anthrax with a heartwarming smile.

"I'll be there in a bit. I need to tell them I'm going away for a while," said NoOne, sliding back toward his herd.

"Take your time," said Anthrax with a nod.

Anthrax and Opti met up with the rest of the group. Someone new had shown up.

"Bob, what are you doing here?" asked Anthrax.

"As I was telling the others, there has been a change in plans. We are all meeting up at the rebel base in Femina."

"Oh. Thanks for telling us," said Anthrax with a smile.

"You're welcome. Thanks for not making this difficult. You all probably need a guide to get there. I'll lead the way," said Bob.

"Wait up, NoOne is coming, but he needs a moment to say goodbye," said Opti.

"Stand ready. We've got company," said Bob.

Seven angels, all carnivorous and all heavily armored encircled the team.

"Flying bears…whoa man, and this is without drugs," said Pharma, holding his head.

"Keep your distance, angels. I won't hesitate to defend myself," said Karson, aiming each limb at a different body.

"Calm down. What seems to be the problem?" asked Anthrax, with the same relaxed tone he utilized with his patients.

"He is coming with us. He cannot be allowed in Femina," said the tiger angel, barring his fangs at Karson.

"Now you recognize I'm a male. Took you angels long enough," said Karson, keeping his guns poised.

"Your preferred gender is arbitrary. The reason you were kept in Complex was to keep you from being rounded up by the rebel groups in Femina and Masculino," said the tiger angel.

"Oh. Well, that makes me feel a bit better, actually," said Karson.

"Point is: you're coming with us," said the crocodile angel, poised to lunge at a moment's notice.

"I'm not going with anyone. I have to meet at the rendezvous point, and I don't care whether or not it's in enemy lines. Another step and I shoot," said Karson.

"No need," said NoOne, rising out from a black puddle.

"What do you mean? I'm not going to just give up!" yelled Karson.

"They can't move." NoOne pointed to the ground. "My shadow has their shadow in its grasp. They can't do anything. Let's get going," he said, parting the angels out of their way.

"Oh, well, yes…quite right," said Karson, hurrying along behind him.

Previously: Violet's group left to find their missing ally. They arrived at the lake where Nina had been bathing.

Violet closed her eyes. Her forehead resonated with an inner light. "I've found her trail. There are many souls around her but the area she is in…it's dead matter. She's in a building."

"Can you teach me that?" asked Ada, turning to her spiritually gifted friend.

"Most certainly, but can it wait?" asked Violet with a relaxed smile.

"Of course. No rush. Let's find Nina!" cheered Ada.

"Um, there's something I want to talk to you guys about. It's Efil. I think we can trust her," said Matteria.

"Absolutely! She is such a wonderful person!" cheered Ada.

"Efil is a goddess of Lum. I am now her devotee. Of course I trust her, though not blindly," said Violet with a bit of a blush as she navigated through the woods without stepping on her fellow Lumians.

"Thanks for understanding. The angels of Lum…they want us to feel safe. But I think they need our help. They have enemies who threaten this realm. I think we should defend Lum with them," said Matteria.

"I'm not all that good at battling, but I can convince the others to help out," said Ada.

"Violence is to be avoided whenever possible. But if I must draw out my spirit to defend the weak, then I shall do so," said Violet, touching the bracelet around her wrist.

Despite her careful steps, Violet swiftly guided the group to the female base.

"State your business," said a rebel, dropping down from the treetops, followed by three more.

"We are here to see Nina," said Matteria.

"And who are you?" asked a short woman, raising her crossbow.

One of the younger rebels rushed in front. "Matteria! Oh my! It's you, isn't it?" she asked, hyperventilating from excitement.

"A fan?" he asked with a smile.

"A huge fan!" she exclaimed with a hop.

"I'm sorry, who's Matteria?" asked the short woman, her weapon still poised.

"Only the greatest singer of all time!" exclaimed the girl in a speedy voice pulsing with excitement.

"Now, now. There is no best. We should cherish our differences, right?" asked Matteria.

"This is incredible!" she exclaimed, her blue eyes shimmering.

"Can Matteria be trusted?" asked the woman.

"Of course! Matteria is a rebel too! Your song about the hijab really opened up the eyes of my friends. One of them even adopted Islam as her faith! Thank you so much!"

"♫ Virtue, freedom, peace, that's what hijab means to me. ♫ That one?" asked Matteria, brimming with excitement.

"Fine. She may enter Lotus. But the rest of you remain here until she returns."

"Thank you so much for your consideration," said Ada with a bow.

Violet looked up longingly at the rebel base. "But (sniffle), I want to go too. It looks so beautiful."

"Do you know her?" asked the rebel leader to the younger woman.

"Can't say I do. But look at her. Her energy. She is so spiritual," said the young woman.

"As are you. All of you," said Violet with the slightest of bows and the warmest of smiles.

"What are the three pillars of Islam?" asked the woman.

"There is one God and Mohammed is his messenger. A pilgrimage to Mecca, which I have done numerous times. And giving alms to the needy. I'm Muslim!" exclaimed Violet.

"You may go in as well," said the woman.

"May I ask…um, why do you cover your bodies? Is it because your husband doesn't find you desirable?" asked Ada with a solemn tone.

"I have no husband. Men only complicate things. They distract us from seeing Allah's glory," said the woman.

"Ah, so you wear those clothes to keep your body free from their sexual intentions?" asked Ada with a curious look.

"There are many reasons. I will be happy to tell you. Miriam, they must be properly dressed before entering," said the woman, lowering her crossbow.

"I shall get them dressed," said Miriam, grabbing her idol's hand and rushing off. "Mama! Mama! Can you bring me two outfits? You won't believe who is here!"

The older woman came up to her daughter and looked up at Matteria. Tears flowed down her cheeks.

"What is wrong, Mama?" asked Miriam.

"Who killed you? Who would kill such a wonderful person?" she asked, looking up at the saintly young boy.

"No. I wasn't. Well, I was. Umm…this may sound strange. But it was a demon."

The mother's eyes enlarged with shock. "A demon on Earth?" she asked with a horrified look.

"Mama, I will get the clothes. You should sit down," said Miriam, leading her mother to the stairs.

"I've got what you're looking for right here!" exclaimed a lanky teenage rebel girl with hazel eyes. She looked from side to side. "It's best if you change in the bushes. I'm honored to meet you," she said with heavy breaths, peering up at the beautiful celebrity.

"Good thinking. Don't want to alarm anyone. It's great to meet you too," said Matteria, heading toward the bushes.

"I am Illiana. I'm not Muslim, but still they care for me here. The women here are so loving. Since I died before my mother, I would be all alone without them. I've thought about you…a lot. I've seen your videos. All of them! Even the ones I'm not old enough to see," she said with a sly smile and a whispery voice.

Matteria opened his arms and embraced her. "Thanks for all your support!"

"Thank you. Whenever I feel lost, I listen to you. You give me hope and now…here you are." Illiana started to tear up as she held up the outfits.

Violet took the sanctified cloth and placed it over her clothes. "Ah, I feel closer to Allah already," she said, holding herself in a loving embrace.

Matteria ended the hug and held up the garment. "I should get dressed too."

"Can I…" Illiana covered her cheeks with her hands, "watch?"

"Why not? I've got nothing to hide," said Matteria, stripping out of his skirt.

"I have a friend. She likes girls. She loves your music. You must meet her."

"Sure, I'm always up for meeting a fan."

"You helped her feel better about herself, about her preferences," said Illiana with a light blush.

"God's creation is truly glorious. We all have different likes and dislikes. We are as God makes us. God loves us all equally, from the largest whale to the smallest ant," said Violet.

"That is so beautiful. I am a Christian. You are Muslim, right? They are sister religions. That makes us sisters," said Illiana with a smile.

"Oh, I am Christian too. All prophets speak unique truths, so I follow them all," said Violet.

"You are so wise," said Illiana.

"She's my younger sister, by the way. We were both created by the same amazing man," said Matteria with longing eyes.

"I never knew you had a sister. So, how is the niqab? Do you like it? I didn't at first, but now I feel safe in it, not only safe but, more spiritual," said Illiana, smiling through her eyes.

"It's only my second time, but I kind of like it. I prefer something a bit flashy, but I also love traditional clothing. Let's go inside. We are looking for Nina. Do you know her?"

"Oh, she's rather sneaky, isn't she?" asked Illiana.

Matteria turned to his sibling with an estranged look. "Is she?"

Violet shrugged.

"Can you take us to her?" asked Matteria.

Illiana's expression turned grim. "She went to a place where no one is allowed. The mothers here were very upset. I don't know where she is now."

"Well then, we are going to find out," said Matteria.

The teenage girl cheerfully led them to the mosque's door.

"Wait." Violet was hyperventilating.

"Is everything okay? Are you still recovering from your breakdown?" asked Matteria, holding her up in case she fainted.

"I am going to a holy site, a mosque, in Heaven. I am so excited!" she exclaimed with a smile that kept expanding. She breathed in and out deeply. "Let me...center myself."

"Your friend is so passionate," said the Illiana, scooting in close to touch Matteria's hand. "You must meet Fatima. She is my best friend!" she exclaimed once her fingers were locked with her idol's.

"Then I'm sure we'll get along great," said Matteria.

"Ohm. Ohm. Peace. Peace. Okay. I'm ready," said Violet, putting her hand on the door knob.

The devotee of many faiths opened the door to see a room full of congregants. Some were praying on their own in a corner, other's playing with children and a few were standing upright and scoping out the new guests.

"Allahu Akbar! Allahu Akbar!" cheered Violet.

The women chanted back. "Allahu Akbar!"

"You know them?" asked Matteria.

"Yes, we are all sisters in faith," said Violet, rushing off to her new friends.

"Fatima! Look who is here!" exclaimed Illiana.

When Fatima saw the newcomer's mascara-coated pink eyes, she froze up. Her mouth opened, but no words came out.

Illiana rushed to her dazed friend and shook her. "I know, right!?"

"Thank you." Fatima kept bowing, stuck in a pattern.

"Happy to help."

"I don't hate myself. You...made it so I could love myself. Thank you," she burst into tears.

Miriam met up with the group. "So, I see you've already been introduced?"

"Yes, we have. Do any of you know where Nina is? She's my friend," said Matteria.

Fatima rushed up to her savior and grabbed his sleeve. "She was taken away. I don't know where. I'm worried about her."

"Hmm. I sense her presence underground. Let's go find her and then we can all visit the main temple," said Violet, bouncing in excitement.

"You aren't allowed down there. Only the Imam and the Caliphs can go to the bottom floor. But maybe you can reason with them. Nina didn't know. She didn't mean to break the rules," said Fatima.

"Shh, it is time for prayer," said Miriam, setting down her carpet and shifting it to face east.

"This time must be devoted to God. We will find Nina afterwards," said Violet, smiling at the young devotee.

Fatima nodded and adjusted her carpet.

"Is this facing the right way?" asked Matteria, pointing to his carpet.

"It makes no difference. We must face east toward Mecca. Toward the Holy Land," said Violet, graciously bowing after receiving a carpet from one of her sisters in faith.

Another woman entered the room, her pupils were white and her irises were black. "I need to speak with the Imam. The angels are coming here to exterminate us!"

"Evacuate the area!" exclaimed one of the guards.

The women jumped up and exited the room down the hallway.

BoneSaw slid in through the open door. Tempo and Kanasta entered. The mission had begun.

# Chapter 64: The Verdict

Heat and cold simultaneously poured out of Tempo, creating a spike in temperature. The shift in the air created a thick fog that permeated throughout the room.

"Let's make some noise," said Tempo, his grin visible through the clouded air.

"Wait, stop! This is a holy place!" exclaimed Violet.

"Are you going to stop me?" asked Tempo, lighting his hand aflame.

"No. I'm going to change your mind. *BELIEF CHANGER*. Wait, why isn't it working? I can't connect to my artifact."

"Don't get in the way!" Tempo slammed his knee into the nuisance, sending a cold wave that froze her on impact.

"Don't kill her! That's Violet!" yelled Matteria.

"She's not dead. But get in our way and she will be," said Tempo.

Kanasta picked up the table and flung it into the temple.

Once four guards passed by the entryway to check out the disturbance, Sefiwah slipped by. She raced up the stairs, keeping her head low where the fog was denser. She ran up the wall and onto the ceiling. A spear shot into the place where she had placed her foot a moment ago.

Four arrows then shot up her leg in a straight line.

The graceful assassin fell to the ground, kicking off on impact to the source of the arrows.

Her fingers slammed into her target like a burst of bullets.

Even when coated with armor, the guard was knocked down.

Sefiwah pulled the arrows out and flung them into four more approaching guards.

Direct hits were followed by a collapse to the ground.

The pale assassin was closing in. At the end of the hall, she spotted the Imam's room.

"Target acquired," said Sefiwah under her breath, if only to center her mind.

The tactful assassin opened the door with a bit of urgency. "Great mother! The angels are attacking!"

Five—no, ten guards, all armored and armed stood before her. The Imam was not in this room.

Thirty arrows in three seconds.

Sefiwah slammed the door, still getting pierced by six arrows, three in her right arm and three more in her chest. "So much red," she said, starting to wobble a bit.

The door swung open, slamming into her back.

Sefiwah toppled to the ground, rolled onto her back, and was looking up at five crossbows, all pointed at her head.

"Who are you?" they asked.

Sefiwah stayed silent. She needed to buy time.

Three chairs soared through the fog and slammed into her attackers. Five more archers busted out of the room and fired at the source of the attack.

A woman screamed.

A body was then hurled into the nest of archers, already pierced with arrows.

Kanasta rushed in as the body slammed into the guards. He hoisted Sefiwah onto his shoulder. "Not there? Any ideas where the target is?" he asked, wrapping his ally's wounds as he sped down the hallway.

"Don't know," said Sefiwah, her eyes a bit hazy.

"Should we retreat for now?" he asked, arriving at the stairway.

A figure approached them, just turning at the stairs. "Hey Boss, I found a secret room. Follow me," said Tempo.

The three of them made it to the staircase. They were faced with fifteen guards, all armed with crossbows.

"I'll lead the way." Tempo clenched his fist and held out his arm in front.

"**HEAT SHIELD!**"

Heat seeped out from his knuckles, forming a haze that passed over the killer's head and up to his knees.

Tempo came out from behind cover.

The first volley of arrows melted before they could reach their target.

One of the guards pulled out a spear and rushed the intruder.

Tempo's left hand peeked out from the side of his shield. "**ICE SHOT!**"

Six frozen bullets came out from his fingers and drove themselves into his attacker.

The spear wielder's hands were stuck to her weapon, and her feet were joined with the floor.

Tempo ripped out the spear with his left hand and her arms along with it. The masterful assassin readied the spear and searched for a target.

All the attackers suddenly collapsed, holding their wounded legs.

BoneSaw rode up the bumpy stairs and joined back with its team.

"Well done," said Kanasta.

Tempo dropped the heat shield and fired a full round of ice bullets into the downed guards. "Six went with the civilians, now dead. Four guarded the hallway.

And fifteen bodies here. That's twenty-five for me. How many did you take down?"

"Sefiwah took down five and I eliminated twenty."

"Sixty, either K.O. or dead. Yep, that should be all of them." Tempo's head jerked toward the Boss. "Don't you think we rushed this job a bit?"

"Couldn't be helped. We have prior arrangements. Once the leader is dead, we'll head back to the tree," said Kanasta.

"And here we are. The fog is seeping in through the wall, so there's obviously something on the other side. Ego could only count from the windows. Who knows how many are down here," said Tempo, knocking on the wall.

"Doesn't matter. That's where our target is." Kanasta flipped the wall around. "Get Sefiwah to safety. I'll handle things from here."

"Roger, Boss." Tempo picked up his wounded ally and made his way toward the exit.

Bob popped out from below. "Oooh, she looks pretty injured. Not going as planned?"

"Almost completed, though a bit sloppy for my taste. We should still be able to meet up with the others in time," said Tempo, stepping around the broken chairs.

"No need. I brought them here. Seemed as good a place to meet as any," said Bob.


Meanwhile: Kanasta descended along the stairs in total darkness.

"Perhaps Tempo should have been the one to finish the job," he said, squinting through the darkness.

A low growling was heard from below. It was gradually coming closer.

Kanasta disengaged a canister from his belt and tossed it into the darkness below.

The canister burst open, releasing a bundle of angel feathers.

At the center of the feathers were three tortured humans, crouched on all fours. Their eyes focused on the newcomer.

"Who sent you?" asked a voice even further down the tunnel.

The assassin boss stayed silent and calmly made his way down the steps.

"What are you doing here?" asked a voice which clearly belonged to Nina.

"You know him?" asked the Imam.

"He was hired by my creator at one point. Supposedly he's my uncle," said Nina.

"Tell him to stop this foolishness," said the Imam.

"You're here for her head, aren't you? Did the angels hire you?" asked Nina.

"I don't disclose the identity of my clients," said Kanasta.

"Well, the job is over. I'm not going to get into the specifics, but these human women, they know a way to get back to Earth. I won't miss this opportunity," said Nina, taking one step forward.

"Once a job has been taken up, it must be completed," said Kanasta, almost at the bottom of the stairs.

"Well, I tried," said Nina with an extravagant shrug.

The three tortured humans rushed at Kanasta, barring their sharpened teeth.

With a single motion, the assassin boss swiped the wretches off their feet and sent them tumbling down the stairs.

"Let me handle this," said Thunder, her voice coming from behind the Imam.

"Stand down. I can take him. Well, that is, if you'll still let me come along," said Nina.

"You'll be the first one out," said the Imam.

"I am more than capable," said Thunder.

"Let her go first," said the Imam.

Nina fired six shots from a crossbow.

Kanasta took the attack head on, not bothering to dodge as he rushed down the stairs.

Nina leaped off the ground, wrapped her legs around the muscle man's thick neck, pulled up his left arm and held it in place with her powerful legs. As soon as he reached for her, she swung behind him, still strangling his neck. She flung her nimble body backward, gripping onto his left leg with both hands. The brute grabbed onto her torso. As he pulled the kunoichi, she used his own force to pull his leg out from under him before finally bringing the giant to the ground. He spun around and as soon as his right arm reached for her, she jumped off. Pushing off the ceiling with both powerful legs, she slammed the sides of her arms into his chest.

Kanasta grabbed her waist and slammed her into the wall.

The wall crumbled on top of the beautiful warrior.

The Imam shrieked and ran as more tortured humans rushed out from the nearby cages.

One of them bit into the large man's arm.

Kanasta flung his arm back and forth, knocking aside the others with the body of their ally.

"I can get you out of here! You can return to Earth! Isn't that what you want?" asked the Imam.

"Sorry. Business is business. I'll make it quick," said Kanasta, cracking his knuckles.

Nina leaped up and slammed her leg into his stubborn head. "I won't let you ruin my only chance!" Her other leg then smashed into the back of the muscle man's neck.

Kanasta reached behind him and grabbed her leg. He spun the dedicated warrior around and then smashed her into the ground.

Thunder pierced him with a spear, followed by a line of arrows from his chest to his head.

Kanasta took a step forward.

"I lay my life down for the Imam!" Thunder rushed at the man, her dagger gleaming in the darkness.

Kanasta swiped his foot, but she leaped over it and stabbed the dagger into his chest.

The dagger became stuck in his hardened muscle.

Kanasta stepped toward the Imam, pulling the warrior along with him.

"That's enough!" yelled a voice from above the stairs.

"Efil! Did you send him here?" asked the Imam.

"Kanasta, for your continued acts of violence against the people of Lum, I hereby banish you!" yelled Efil, her voice still a bit shaky.

"I'll be with you in a moment," said Kanasta, stepping up to the Imam.

He vanished into thin air.

The Imam fell to the ground in relief.

"Are you alright?" asked Efil.

"Your timing was rather convenient. If you think saving my life from the man you sent to kill me will gain my trust, you are wrong. Leave now!" yelled the Imam.

"I...yes. As you wish," said Efil, turning away.

"Wait. Kanasta...he messed me up, pretty bad. I need you to heal me," said Nina, her bones cracking as she struggled to stand.

The goddess fired an arrow of light into the injured warrior's chest.

"Come outside once you've recovered. Your allies are waiting for you," said Efil.

"Damn well better be," said Nina, climbing up the stairs, while leaning against the wall.

Nina followed Efil outside and met up with her allies.

"Are you okay?" asked Anthrax, rushing to the victim's aid.

"Efil's arrow is healing me up," said Nina, holding her side in pain.

Ada rushed in and embraced her beautiful friend. "I am overjoyed to see you!"

"Nice to see you too," said Nina with a slight smile.

"That's an odd look for you," said Karson, approaching her.

"Thanks again for unthawing me," said Violet with a bow.

"Think nothing of it," said Efil with a smile.

"Is Kanasta on his way?" asked Ada, peeking over at the goddess.

"No, he was banished to Absence, along with the rest of his gang," said Efil.

"Oh," said Ada, taken aback.

"Anthrax, if you would like to become an angel, I will need to know soon," said Efil.

"You aren't still planning on going through with that, are you?" asked Matteria, looking down at his boyfriend.

"I was merely gathering information, as Nina was," said Anthrax.

"So, what is your answer?" asked Efil.

"It will have to wait. I'll decide after Devlin has been rescued," said Anthrax.

"Efil, how can we get to Sel? Devlin is all alone in that place," said Ada.

"You may be able to convince the escort in Absence to bring you there," said Efil.

"Well then we've got a plan. Devlin is counting on us." Matteria stripped out of his religious attire. "Who's with me?"

"Why should we help him? Exp 8, I understand. He only led you all to your demise and is the reason we are here in the first place. Actually, why bother saving either of them?" asked Bob.

"I'm sorry. I'm being called upon once more. Stay put. We can discuss this further once I've returned," said Efil before vanishing.

Deceivant stepped into the center of the group. "We need to free both Kaity and Devlin."

"But you told him it would be foolish to try," said Ada confused.

"I said that so he would try all the harder. Trust me. Nothing motivates Devlin like negative reinforcement from me. So who wants to help us?" asked Deceivant.

"Kaity was being controlled, so I guess she didn't technically betray us. And the more worshipers I have, the better," said Nina, combing her hair with her fingertips.

"Does that mean you're coming along?" asked Matteria.

"No, but I wish you all good luck. I'm staying here. Lum isn't so bad once you get used to it," said Nina, gazing up at the clouds.

"This place is magical! But I feel hesitant enjoying it while Devlin is imprisoned," said Violet.

"Devlin imprisoned us. I say it's his turn. Devlin is the reason we're all dead in the first place," said Atatasuki, his face steaming.

"But we are all children of God. It is our duty to help those in need," said Violet.

"He ordered Bob to kill my sister!" yelled Atatasuki.

"I'm surprised you remember that," said Kawai, her gaze drifting off.

"Agreed. He is such a cruel boy," said Bob, his spectral hands patting the steaming defect's shoulder.

"He's my little brother and he's super nice to me. We gotta help him," said D.S.

"He killed you!" exclaimed Kawai.

"Yeah, but I was being bad," said D.S., fiddling with his fingers.

"Devlin made all of us. We have an obligation to rescue him," said Matteria.

"Not all of us. Regardless, he's in need. Therefore we should help him," said Anthrax.

Kawai rushed into the center of the crowd. "Helloooo. I think we are forgetting our priorities. I mean, it's okay if we rescue Devlin. But what about Exp 8? He's the only one who truly matters! We need to help him first," whined Kawai.

"I wouldn't worry about him. Turns out he beat Devlin," said Deceivant.

"I knew it. Nothing can stop him," said Kawai, hopping in mid-air.

"Hey, if helping Devlin provides some entertainment, I'm up for it. This place is boring me to death," said Ego, drumming on a rock.

"How can you be bored? There are trees everywhere with a plethora of animals. Water, air, and earth-bodied beings exist all around us! This place is wondrous," said Violet, prancing through the grass.

"Yeah, it's beautiful," said Matteria.

"I see it as a signal of how prominent death is. Think about it: everything here was once alive," said Anthrax sadly.

"Wow, so instead of seeing life, we're seeing death, that's so depressing," said NoOne, pulling black tears out from his eyeholes.

Opti's eyes became filled with red hot hate. The white portion of his mask became black. There was now a flame design atop his club-shaped eyehole. His skin became black like ash as his wings molted and blackened. His white hair became spiky and black. His gentle hands grew sharp fingernails. The smile of his mask molded into a jagged white frown. "I will enjoy wiping out every dead thing from this sanctuary! Soon this disgusting forest will be annihilated!" he wailed in a furious raspy tone.

Kawai smacked the madman with her tail. "Try it and I'll break you."

Pesi crawled backward. "I can't stand to be in this field of pansies! It's too disgusting! Opti, you take control!"

"So, how are we going to escape? Evol is trying to keep us here," said Anthrax.

"Evol explained its reasoning. The Deity of Love cares deeply about us," said Violet.

"Well, Kanasta and his playmates were banished to Absence. I suppose we could do the same," said Ada.

"Let's ask Efil if we can visit. I'd rather not be stuck there," said Deceivant.

"I agree. If we are banished to Absence, then we will never again be allowed in Lum. I couldn't handle it," said Violet, still wearing her niqab.

"Mom, nobody is listening to me. We have to save my big brother, we just have to," said Kawai, tugging on Ada's arm.

"Not to worry, sweetie. We will rescue all of them. I'll make sure of it," said Ada.

"Whatever the team decides, I'll follow," said Riufen.

"Whoever comes our way first will be the first to be saved. Does anyone disagree with this plan?" asked Deceivant.

Only Nina raised her hand. "I'm staying here."

"Does anyone else object?"

"I totally forgot!" exclaimed Atatasuki.

"Whoopty-do. What else is new?" asked Kawai, rolling her eyes.

"I've got bracelets for everyone. We will look like a real team with these on," said Atatasuki, opening up his chest.

"It will have to wait. Looks like the goddess of flowers has returned," said Bob, gazing at Efil.

"That's Goddess of Life," she said, folding her hands.

"Am I the only one who sees spinning double rainbows?" asked Pharma, staring into the clouds.

"Efil, can you have the escort bring us to Absence?" asked Deceivant.

"I cannot," said Efil, looking at the ground.

"Why not?" asked Ada.

"Come with me," said Efil, turning around.

"I think I'll stay here, but thanks," said Nina.

The goddess tilted her head toward Nina. "All of you."

"Is something the matter?" asked Anthrax.

"Lum has made her verdict. Follow me," said Efil, her voice seeped in sadness.

"And what was Lum's verdict?" asked Matteria.

"I shall tell you once we've arrived," said Efil, keeping her gaze lowered.

"How about you tell us now or we don't follow you?" asked Bob.

"I hate to say it, but he's right. We want some answers!" exclaimed Karson, aiming his shotgun arms at the suspicious goddess.

Twenty angels came out from the trees and surrounded the Exps.

"You are all to be held prisoner until Lum chooses otherwise. Please, don't make this difficult." Efil turned to face them, her eyes on the verge of tears. "Just come peacefully."

"And what if we don't come?" asked Matteria.

"You will be subdued," said Efil.

"Why are we going to prison? We didn't do anything wrong," said Kawai.

"Would you like me to list all the laws broken by each of you?" asked Efil with a strained smile.

"It can't be that many, right?" asked Anthrax, looking out at his allies for reassurance.

"Here they are, in the order they were committed and not counting the ones I personally pardoned nor the ones broken before the rules were explained to all of you: Atatasuki grabs Kawai's hand without her permission; Kawai hits Atatasuki; Violet taps an angel; D.S. calls NoOne stupid; Tempo says hell; Tempo chews on a twig; Violet drinks water; Pharma and D.S. touch a toad; D.S. calls Pharma stupid; Deceivant plucks an angel's feather; Deceivant plucks my feather; Bob shoots an angel; Fusion makes contact with two angels; Fusion rams them into a third angel; Bob grabs an angel commander with spectral tentacles; Bob bludgeons five angels with their commander; Karson presses his guns up to Bob; Tempo head-butts and pierces Ego's chest with his fingers; Ego kicks Tempo; Tempo sets the grass and a tree on fire; Ego uses grass as a shield; Ego slams a tree into Tempo; Tempo sends multiple fireballs at Ego; Riufen desecrates a leaf with calligraphy; Karson breaks some branches while running; Kanasta's fingers pierce Bob; Ada hugs an angel; Bob pulls me in with his tentacles; Bob pulls in Kawai, Karson, and Riufen; Bob grabs Kawai's cheeks; Bob and BoneSaw cross the border and enter Femina; Karson crosses the border and goes to Masculino; Kawai crosses the border and enters Masculino; Bob crosses the border and enters Femina; all Masculino members and Karson cross the border and join up with the female members at Lotus; Tempo attacks and freezes Violet. The most recent crimes were all committed by the Viper Squad directly against the visitors. As they have already been banished, I see no reason to repeat them," said Efil, visibly shaken up.

Sweat dripped down Anthrax's cheek. "That's more than I expected…but Matteria didn't break any rules at all. And if you don't count us crossing borders, some of us are totally innocent. Like me, NoOne, Opti or…."

"Or me," said Nina with a smile.

"Demo never broke your silly rules and yet he was promptly captured. I wonder how many deals you've broken, how many of your own laws you've consciously bent," said Bob, glaring at the goddess.

"If Lum wants us imprisoned, then I think we should listen. Who are we to question a divinity?" asked Violet.

"Free spirits! My brother fought for our freedom. I died for his freedom. I won't let you make everything he strove for, all he's done, worthless!" Kawai zoomed up to the goddess and grabbed onto her.

"Do you want me to add this to the list?" asked Efil.

"*Energy Drain*" yelled Kawai, lighting up and squinting as she squeezed with added strength.

"Touching a goddess is forbidden," said Efil, lowering her head.

"Why isn't this working?" asked Kawai.

Lum's missionary pulled off the attacker and tossed her aside.

A hawk angel swooped down and pinned the defiant visitor to the ground.

"Get off her!" yelled Atatasuki.

Four human angels aimed their light arrows at the metal man.

"Enough! Come with me now! This is what I negotiated for. I had to compromise. It's either imprisonment or annihilation," said Efil with open arms.

"What!? We could fight for Lum. We could help you defend this land," said Matteria.

"Lum does not trust you. Those are your only options. Now come with me!" yelled Efil, tears pouring down her cheeks.

"Impossible. Lum should have nothing against us," said Sefiwah.

"Ada and I are no threat to you. Please, let us stay in Lum. We will follow your laws," said Deceivant.

"You create Exps. You're too valuable to be put in harm's way," said Efil.

"I know this may be a bad time, but hmm…looks like I wasn't lying. You heard how my attacking the angels was right before Fusion attacked them." Bob turned to Efil with a big smile. "Thanks for proving me innocent through my crimes. Demo and Fusion, they're already at the prison, aren't they?"

"Yes. By my orders. I needed to keep you all occupied while Lum decided your fate," said Efil.

Bob looked at the gunman with a grin. "I believe someone owes me an apology."

"No time for chitchat. We're surrounded," said Karson, his guns poised.

"In the prison, in Elysium, you'll be safe. Neither the rebels nor Sel's forces can capture you. Once the Forces of Hatred withdraw from the border, I will have you freed. It's only temporary," said Efil.

"Some of us are entirely innocent! Matteria, Ada, Opti, and I aren't a threat to anyone. What sort of system imprisons people based on species membership!" yelled Anthrax.

"You're wasting your time arguing with me. Justice is clear cut. Whatever Lum commands is just, whatever Lum prohibits is unjust. Come with me and you will not be harmed," said Efil, standing in a firm stance.

"This soldier doesn't surrender. You want me, you'll have to take me down first," said Karson.

Riufen drew his spine and held it out in front of him. "Let this battle decide what path we take."

"Are we the heroes or the villains in this situation?" asked NoOne.

"Doesn't matter. We've got friends to rescue," said D.S.

"Let's negotiate. I don't want to make the angels our enemies," said Nina.

"You've already chosen your side. I know all about your deal with the Imam," said Efil.

"What?" asked Nina.

"It's obvious why you don't want to leave Lum...yet," said Efil.

"Forget about what she says. We're all friends here. I thought Efil was our friend too. I was wrong," said Opti, readying his fists.

"You're all so selfish! Lum has given you a chance. She has shown you mercy and you've all squandered it. Fine then. **TIME LAPSE**." The Goddess of Life formed a wooden blade in each hand. She turned to face them. "Come at me!"

The team stood their ground.


Efil turned to face the angels. "Fire at them. We are wasting time here."

"They can't. I've got their shadows. They're kind of stuck. I've pinned your shadow too," said NoOne.

Riufen rushed at the warrior goddess.

Efil parried his jab with one sword and pierced the other sword into the ground. "**TIME LAPSE**."

A tree rose from beneath them, breaking the goddess free of the shadow-man's grip.

Riufen's spine pierced into the light warrior's chest as her weapons bore into his.

Vines came out from her weapon and wrapped around the swordsman.

Efil kicked him off the tree and swerved out of the way of Bob's laser. Green blood spurted out from her wound, sealing it up. Flowers emerged from the drops that had splattered to the ground.

"Everyone who raises a hand against me is a traitor to Lum. Banish any who dare attack!" exclaimed the Goddess of Life.

Kawai slammed her tail into Efil's side, knocking her off the tree.

D.S. jumped up, grabbed her, and slammed her to the ground like a football. "Touchdown!"

A figure in a clear cloak created a portal. It slammed into D.S., knocking him inside. The figure then shifted its gaze to Kawai.

Atatasuki leaped up to save her, but his sister vanished before he made contact.

Efil aged the tree and then toppled it on top of Atatasuki.

"She's gone! Give me back my sister! If she isn't here in three seconds, I'm going to bake your ass extra crispy!" yelled Atatasuki, his body melting through the tree.

"Profanity is such a pointless sin," said Efil, while countering the swordsman's onslaught.

Riufen slammed his knee into her chest and sliced off the warrior goddess' arm. He then leaped back to dodge the tree that sprouted from below.

"Stop!" yelled Ada, leaping in front of the hooded figure.

"Out of the way!" yelled Karson.

Bob knocked Ada aside just in time for Karson's missile to slam into the hooded figure. "Careful, you almost killed our ally. Or is that what you wanted?" he asked with a malicious glint.

A new head popped out from Karson's neck. "It was an obvious misfire! I was wrong about you, okay? I apologize."

The figure knocked the missile off without triggering it. After landing, it sent a portal out between Karson and Bob.

"Does he expect us to just walk through?"

A crystal wall rose out of the ground.

The figure rammed into the wall, knocking Bob into the portal and attaching the portal to it all at once.

Karson fired at the wall while running. "You're not taking me!" He slammed into an invisible wall before being sandwiched by the two walls and swallowed up by the portal between them.

Deceivant hoisted his beloved onto his back and made a run for it.

"None shall escape!" yelled Efil, her severed arm already sealed up.

"𝕿𝖎𝖒𝖊 𝕷𝖆𝖕𝖘𝖊."

Trees sprouted around what remained of the group.

Riufen leaped over the Absence portal wall and tossed his spine.

The spine pierced through the figure's cloak but not its skin.

With one arm, Efil stabbed the swordsman from behind. She then rolled out of the way of the oncoming portal.

Riufen vanished.

All who remained were Opti, Pharma, NoOne, Anthrax, Deceivant, Ada, Matteria, Violet, and Nina.

"Are they dead?" asked Pharma, taking a step back.

"They've been sent to Absence, where Devlin was," said Anthrax.

Efil reattached her arm, which was now held in place by vines. "Now, if everyone else would follow me, that would be greatly appreciated," she said, pointing her swords at them.

"Devlin is counting on us!" Matteria charged at the goddess but vanished before he could make contact.

"Absence has got to be better than this place," said Pharma.

"Leave the portal on the ground. Thank you for your services. You've done enough," said Efil to the figure.

After setting the portal wall face up on the ground a few feet in front of the Goddess of Life, the figure hopped in and vanished.

Efil peeked over her shoulder at an incoming battalion of angels. "Last chance. Will you cooperate?"

"All the strong ones are gone. I can't stick around here!" NoOne willingly entered the portal.

"And the rest of you?" asked Efil.

"Just so we're clear, I didn't attack you," said Nina before hopping in.

Efil looked back at the battalion coming down the hillside. "What are you waiting for? Get in," she said softly.

"It's our best bet," said Deceivant, worry seeping into his face.

"No time!" exclaimed Efil.

Vines sprouted from the ground and pulled what remained of the group into the portal to Absence.

# Part 7
# Trapped in Absence

# Chapter 65: Arrival

A white portal appeared and disappeared nearly the same moment. Kanasta looked up to see his fellow assassins, who were already scoping out the new location.

Sefiwah's head jerked toward the assassin boss. "Did you get her?"

"Not yet. But as long as the Imam draws breath, the mission is on," said Kanasta.

"Well, can we put it on the backburner for now? I don't even know where we are," said Ego.

"We're in Absence. According to Ada, Devlin was taken to Sel. Still, it's possible he's returned to this place. Fan out and search for my brother," said Kanasta.

"Why does it look like we're the only ones here?" asked Tempo, peering at the endless horizon.

Ego pulled out his binoculars. "Boss, see that dot way in the distance? I think that's him. He's with two other dots. Gotta be Kaity and Exp 8, right?"

Sefiwah swiped the binoculars. "That's Kaity alright. Let's get moving. If we keep up a steady pace, we may be able to get there in a few minutes."

"Agreed. Until we can find a way back to Lum, our job is on hold," said Kanasta.


South from the Viper Squad's location, a Lum portal dropped D.S. flat on his face. He looked around the strange looking place. "Hello?" The big guy crouched down and poked the invisible floor. "Whoa, cool!" He kept poking it until a light portal appeared not many feet in front of him.

Kawai came out of the portal but didn't land. She was upside-down and only realized this once her gaze met D.S. "Oh yeah! Score! Made it to Absence!" she cheered with a spin. She floated up to her ally and sat on his shoulder. "From now on you work for me."

Atatasuki dropped in front of them screaming in terror, able to see only nothingness below.

Kawai held him up with her tail. "What are you screaming about?" she asked, grabbing his face.

"Sis, it's you! You're okay!" he exclaimed, reaching out to hug her before being dropped on the ground.

"What the…it's solid," said Atatasuki.

"Yep, just like my plan. All we gotta do is find the Sel escort and then free our brother!" she cheered.

Another portal appeared and shot out Karson and Bob against the clear ground.

"What happened?" asked Karson, standing up in a daze.

Bob bounced off the ground. "Hmm. Seems we've arrived."

"Oh, great, he's here," said Kawai, peering at the murderous eyeball from behind D.S.'s broad shoulders.

Riufen was the next to arrive. He looked left, then right, then down. "I lost," he said, his eyes hollow.

"Am I glad to see you," said Kawai, floating up to the masterful warrior with a big smile.

"You are?" asked Riufen.

"Course I am. You're like my nephew. Yeah, my mega big nephew. Family's got to stick together, right?" asked Kawai, shaking his hand with her tail.

"Umm, yes. Indeed," said Riufen with a confused look.

"That's right. So, are you ready to fight to free our brother?" asked Kawai.

"Oh. Ah, well...yes, that's a good idea," said Riufen.

"With you guarding my back, I have nothing to worry about," said Kawai, leaning against her tail.

Matteria stumbled out of the portal. "Here, we are. Now, to find that escort," he said under his breath as his eyes scanned the area.

NoOne oozed out of the next Lum portal. "Hmm, not bad. Void of light, clear sky. I could get used to this place. Wait...no light. That means no shadows. Curses."

Nina dropped in from a portal above them. Just before hitting the ground, she landed in Kanasta's arms.

"Watch your step," he said, setting her down.

"And you watch where you put your hands," said Nina, wiping away his dirty energy imprint off her butt. "Don't all act chummy with me. I'm still aching because of you."

"I suggest you don't impede my mission in the future then," said Kanasta.

The last portal appeared on the ground. Deceivant, Ada, Opti, Anthrax, Pharma, and Violet came out almost at the same time.

"Well, we made it. Though not under the best circumstances," said Deceivant.

"This place looks kinda dull," said Opti.

"Matteria!" Anthrax rushed up to his boyfriend.

"Hope they don't mind if I smoke here," said Pharma, lighting up each of his cigarette fingers.

"Everyone, Devlin is here along with two others." Kanasta pointed in the distance. "We proceed with caution. We don't know what to expect here."

"If there are two others, then that means my brother might be one of them! Charge!" cheered Kawai, rushing off with Atatasuki, D.S. and Riufen.

"Follow her lead, but stay wary," said Kanasta.

The group's footsteps were silenced once they reached a certain distance. The sound then returned once they were close enough to Devlin, Kaity, and Exp 8.

Kaity went on all fours and rushed up to the team. "Nina!" she cheered, leaping into a hug.

"Been a while since I've seen you," said Nina with a smile as she shimmied out of the embrace. "Wait, how did you recognize me?"

"Nothing can hide these melons," said Kaity, grabbing her crush's squishy breasts.

"As nice as it is to have you fawn over me…" Nina knocked her kitty fan girl's arms off, "no touching, okay?"

"Are you still injured? Is that why you're hiding your body? Because of what Devlin did to you…to your face?" asked Kaity.

"No, that wound healed by the time I woke up here. Not sure how that worked actually," said Nina.

"The team is back together," said Kanasta, towering behind his pupil with a smile.

"Papa!" Kaity rushed into a hug. "You're back! I missed you!"

"Understandable. I did die," said Kanasta, petting her head.

"But you're here now. It's really you!" Kaity gripped her papa's hand with a wide smile.

Sefiwah gave a slight smile and waved at Kaity.

The nimble cat-girl hopped out from Kanasta's arms and pounced on Sefiwah. Her lips pressed against her beloved as her arms and legs pulled her into an embrace. Tears dripped down Kaity's face onto her partner's snow white cheeks.

Once the kiss ended, Sefiwah pet her lover and held her close.

"I'm never losing you again. I can't believe you were killed. How did you die?" asked Kaity.

"Not important. Tell me, how did you get placed here? I heard the angels did nothing as you were carried off to Sel by Etah. Is that really true?" asked Sefiwah, holding Kaity's cheeks.

"I…I don't remember what happened. I was under a hex. It's all so hazy."

"I suppose it's irrelevant now. You're here. With me. I'll keep you safe," said Sefiwah, her hand now caressing Kaity's ear.

"Buh-Buh-Brother!" exclaimed Kawai, slamming into her beloved and lifting him from the ground.

"Sister," said Exp 8 in tears.

"Mmhmm," said Kawai with a nod before smothering his chest with her face.

Devlin looked up at the team from his seated posture. "You're all alive," he said with a smile. "Wait, Bob, how are you here?"

"I escaped. Can't get rid of me that easily," said Bob.

Violet folded her hands and bowed to her creator.

Exp 8 took a deep breath and raised his head to face his fallen allies. "It's my fault all of you died. I don't expect forgiveness, but know that I will never put any of you in harm's way again."

"Brother, what happened to your arm?" asked Kawai.

"It doesn't matter. I can still hold you," said Exp 8, embracing Kawai with his battle-scarred arm.

"Anthrax, fix him," said Kawai.

"I can't without my powers," said Anthrax.

"It's okay. Devlin did all that could be done. I'll wait for it to heal. As for my left arm, I can still take Etah down without it. Now back to the matter at hand."

Exp 8 walked up to his victims and hugged them one by one.

"Kawai, I'm so sorry. I swore I would protect you and…I failed."

"You did your best." Kawai hopped out of his embrace and kissed his cheek.

Exp 8 crouched down to BoneSaw and put his hand on the robot's top. "I'm sorry you got mixed up in my feud." He stood up and hugged Ego. "That goes for you too."

"No sweat, dude. We were hired to kill you. Assassins kill, so we're prepared to be killed. And not that I like to brag, but my death was totally awesome," said Ego, eyeing Nina's legs.

"I stripped completely for strategic reasons. I didn't know the afterlife was real. I thought killing you would be enough to cover my tracks," said Nina before being gripped by Exp 8. "Let go."

"If you're here…then that means I killed you. My explosion was meant to take out Devlin. I never intended for you to get caught up in it."

Nina pushed him off. "If you want to apologize for murdering me, then you better find a way to get me back to Earth."

"It's a promise," said Exp 8, gripping her arm.

"We're all going back, right bro?" asked Atatasuki.

Exp 8 seized his brother in a sudden tearful embrace. "That's right! I'll take responsibility. I'll get you all back to Earth."

"Do I get a hug too?" asked Bob.

Exp 8 gradually released his grip on his brother and put his arm around Bob. "In the end, you fought with us against Devlin. That makes you my ally."

"I also killed a few of your comrades. Are you really going to overlook that so easily?"

"I'm the reason they died. Devlin and I are the only ones responsible."

Bob squeezed out of the embrace. "Hmph. No acknowledgment."

"Good to have you back commander," said Karson before being taken up in an embrace. "Hey, careful. Watch the Button!"

"I failed to protect you."

"As a soldier, I alone am responsible for my life. I chose my side. You're not to blame. Though you really shouldn't forgive Bob so easily."

"I'm glad you're back," said Anthrax, putting his arms around Exp 8's legs.

"Group hug!" cheered D.S., launching at the team captain from behind.

"Hey. One at a time," said Exp 8, almost tipping over.

"Whoa. You got beat really bad," said D.S., poking at Exp 8's severed tendril.

"Sorry, like I said, I'm a doctor, not a mechanic," said Anthrax, examining Exp 8's battle-worn arm.

"Allow me." Kanasta grabbed Exp 8's arm. "What happened to your other arm?"

"I left it behind where I fought Etah. Thanks, by the way. I don't know what happened to you, but you fought with us. No doubt you helped lead the team to this place."

"Actually he got us in trouble with the so-called goddesses. Anthrax and I took charge," said Deceivant.

"He really hurt you. Are you sure you're alright?" asked Ada, touching Exp 8's arm.

"I'm an Exp. I'll tough it out." He pulled his arm out from Kanasta's grip and put it around Ada's shoulders. "You did well out there. Can't believe I ever doubted you."

Ada embraced him tightly. "Stop being so serious. We're all alive!"

"Yeah. We are."

"For now," said NoOne, his gaze descending.

"Hey. Don't be like that. I beat Devlin, just like I promised I would," said Exp 8, pulling his shadowy comrade up.

"Don't. I…I wasn't killed by Riufen. After I was sliced to pieces…I took cover. I died from your explosion. Rather than being killed on the battlefield, I died a coward's death huddled in a corner."

"You fought bravely against Bob and Riufen. You were injured. There was no shame in retreating."

Riufen stepped up to the leader of the Freedom Forcers and bowed. "I apologize for my actions. My battle with you was dishonorable. You have taught me much." He walked up to Devlin.

"Hey, no need to apologize. Bob is powerful. Victory wasn't possible," said Devlin.

"Devlin-sama, I am no longer yours to command."

"What?" Devlin bit his lip.

"I must find my own path. Fight on my terms. I do not regret a single second under your command. I do this for my own reasons."

"Hey, maybe you're being a bit hasty," said Matteria, holding Devlin's hand.

"No. To follow the honorable path, I must choose my own battles. I have already tarnished Devlin's honor enough as it is," said Riufen, clenching his fists till they bled.

"Matteria. You always believed in Devlin and you still do. Take my word for it: you're more precious to him than you may think," said Exp 8.

Matteria looked away with a heavy blush.

"All my children are precious," said Devlin with flustered cheeks.

"Did something happen?" asked Sefiwah.

Exp 8 stepped up to her with his arm outstretched.

"Say what you have to say. Don't touch me," she said, eyeing his arm.

"Thank you for not killing Ada."

"It wasn't out of mercy. She…was trickier than I had imagined," said Sefiwah, feeling Kanasta's gaze behind her.

"Hey buddy. Why not have a smoke?" asked Pharma, shoving a cigarette in Exp 8's face.

"Buddy? You never joined my side. Not once. You were too caught up in a rivalry to even make a moral decision."

"What about me?" asked Opti.

"You were used by Devlin and you came to your senses. You fought with us and died for my cause. So did Pesi. I owe you both," said Exp 8, placing his hand on the shoulder two of his allies shared.

Nina grabbed Exp 8's side and spun him around to face her. "I…thank you. For killing me, I mean. The way I looked. The way Devlin made me look. I couldn't bear to live like that. Now I'm back and beau-ti-ful," said Nina with a hair flip.

"You fought bravely to the end. You're a true warrior," said Exp 8, knocking his fist against hers.

"You forgot sexy," she said with a smirk.

"There's something you should know! I killed your brother. I'm so sorry. You must hate me," said Violet with a wounded look.

"You fought for what you believed in. I can't blame you. I did the same. You're devoted to your beliefs and to Devlin. Just be sure to think things through this time around. Don't make the same mistake again," said Exp 8, grabbing her hand.

"I won't," said Violet, gripping her bracelet with a relieved smile.

"Tempo. I'm sorry you got caught up in this. And thanks for not killing my sister," said Exp 8 with a nod.

"You're not the one who's to blame," said Tempo, eyeing Opti.

"Well, that's everyone. Come to think of it. Why are you all here?" asked Exp 8, looking out at his allies.

"We came to rescue you," said Kawai, latching onto his arm.

"I appreciate the sentiment, but there's no need. No prison can hold me," said Exp 8, patting her head.

"Yo," said Atatasuki, smacking his brother on the back.

Exp 8 broke down into tears. "Guess I can't hold them in anymore. I thought I'd never see you again. Any of you. But you're all here, alive and well," he said, tightly embracing his dear brother.

"Their presence here proves that they're dead. You're not thinking straight at all," said Devlin with a smirk.

"Thraxy said the same thing," said Matteria, holding his master's hand against his cheek.

Kawai poked Atatasuki. "You were right. He won," she said, beaming up at Exp 8.

"Of course he did. But um, when did I say that?" asked Atatasuki.

"I was the one who went and saw Devlin to confirm whether Exp 8 was alive or not. I told you he had won, didn't I?" asked Deceivant.

"Yeah, yeah, I suppose you did. But seeing him now, alive and strong, it really cements the victory in my mind," said Kawai with a shrug and a grin.

"It's good to see you," said Kanasta, smiling at his little brother.

"Good to see—what? He killed you, remember?" asked Kaity.

"Yes. I suppose in the end, his path of vengeance was nobler than my life as an assassin," said Kanasta.

"Well, we're all together now, but how do we get out of here?" asked Anthrax.

"Hey, where's Demo, Fusion, and Reflector?" asked Exp 8, scanning the ground.

"Reflector is still on Earth, waiting for me to grow strong enough to fulfill my contract. That's two jobs on the backburner," said Kanasta, his shoulders drooping.

Devlin glared at Deceivant. "So, what's the reason you all came here? Is it to rub my failure in my face or just to laugh at me?"

"Can't it be both?" asked Bob, squeezing the boy's squishy cheeks.

Devlin pushed the spherical traitor off of him.

"We came here to rescue you," said Kanasta.

"What? Save him? Save Devlin?" asked Exp 8, looking back and forth between his greatest enemy and his allies.

"That's right," said Matteria. "And why should that be a surprise? He created most of us. And he created you too. We are all indebted to him."

"Atatasuki and I came for you, but Matteria has a point," said Kawai with a shrug.

"Don't you remember that he killed you? Almost all of us died because of him. You want to help him after all he's done?" asked Exp 8, quaking with rage.

"Didn't you just apologize for getting us killed?" asked NoOne.

"Yeah, I brought you into battle, but he's the one who called the order that led to your demise," said Exp 8, pointing at his captor with a rage-filled finger.

"I couldn't care less about the hormonal delinquent. I wanted to stay in Lum," said Nina.

"As did I. The sheep are defenseless without me," said NoOne, seeping into the ground.

"You sure seem fired up. Haven't been here that long, have you?" asked Bob, circling around the self-proclaimed hero like a guilty conscience.

"I haven't forgotten what you've done," said Exp 8, holding his sister close while glaring at her killer.

"As you know, I was following orders. Sheesh, touchy touchy," said Bob.

"You came around in the end but I still don't trust you, Bob. I don't want anything to do with you or Devlin. I have a mission to carry out, and I won't let anyone get in the way," said Exp 8.

"Ooh, ooh. Can I get in the way? Kidding. I do want to come along though," said Kawai.

"Out of the question. I'm going on my own," said Exp 8.

"What is this mission you assigned yourself?" asked Sefiwah.

"To take down Etah and free the residents of Sel."

Sefiwah's eyes widened.

"And you're going to go alone? Here I thought the Ultimate Exp would be more rational. You'll need all the help you can get if you are to kill a self-proclaimed god," said Deceivant.

"Etah is a god. Period," said Sefiwah.

"Believe whatever you want," said Deceivant.

"That isn't the problem here." Exp 8 looked at the group and then shifted his gaze to the ground. "I can't forgive Devlin after all he's done."

The youthful inventor stood up. "Why not? Once I become a god I'll have more than enough power to resurrect everyone here. You think I killed them all so carelessly just to help you unlock your latent potential. You sure are full of yourself."

"And what about me, huh? What's your excuse for trying to absorb me?"

"Simple. You were enslaved by your morals and your conscience. Becoming my energy was the only remedy for your affliction."

"Play it smug all you want. But you cried after your minions killed them. That wasn't fake," said Exp 8.

"Of course not! I care dearly for them and was ever aware that I may not succeed in becoming a god. That is why I planned out everything so meticulously. Once Atatasuki was dead, there was no turning back. I had to succeed," said Devlin, intensely wrapping his fingers together.

"You used your own concern and love for them to motivate you. You killed your creations, your children, to push you further in your ambition. Aaah. It was an honor to act as your ally." Bob bowed with watery eyes.

"He still trapped us! He still killed my family! I can't forgive him! It's impossible," said Exp 8.

"You make it sound like forgiving Devlin is an anomaly. And no one here wants you to forgive him. Put aside your blind rage and let's work together," said Deceivant.

"Are you offering to help?" asked Kawai with a curious look.

"No, not me. But it would be a real loss for the scientific community if this living marvel of science was destroyed by some mythic tyrant," said Deceivant.

"I think we should help him. In any way we can," said Ada.

"Wait, what's all this about becoming a god?" asked Anthrax.

"That was the reason for the whole ordeal. I was supposed to use Exp 8 to round up enough souls so that I could attain godhood. Then I would use my divine powers and god status to bring back all my fallen Exps," said Devlin.

"Even me?" asked NoOne with a blank stare.

"Yes, of course. All of you," said Devlin with a fatherly smile.

"And by rounding up, you mean killing, right? He was planning on murdering innocents!" exclaimed Exp 8.

"You had to ruin it," said Devlin with a glare.

"Always shooting for the heavens. That's our boy," said Ada, holding her hubby's hand tightly.

"Ugh, where did he get this obsession with mythos from? I'm surprised he didn't abandon science altogether to become a theologian," said Deceivant with a smirk.

"Gods are real. You're so drenched in scientific dogma that you fail to observe reality as it is," said Devlin, flicking Deceivant's DNA pendant.

Matteria grabbed his master's hand. "Whatever you want, I'm here to help you get it."

"As am I! This soldier needs a battlefield!" cheered Karson.

"Forget him. I've got you're back," said Pharma, walking out of a smoke cloud.

"You guys seriously want to help Devlin?" asked Exp 8 amazed.

"I only want to get out of here and back to Lum," said Nina.

"Me too," said NoOne.

"Don't be like that. Devlin can be nice. He's not always a bad guy," said D.S.

"I shall follow the majority, whatever their will may be," said Riufen with a reverent bow.

"Helping Devlin get in touch with his divinity was the reason I was created. Now more than ever he needs me. He needs all of us," said Violet.

"Speak for yourself. I'm not going to throw away my life for his mission. Didn't you all learn anything from Exp 8's mistakes?" asked Bob.

"He's right," said Exp 8.

"I suppose I am," said Bob, feigning embarrassment.

"If you follow Devlin, you'll end up dead…like when you followed me. Don't make this your last decision," said Exp 8 with a firm fist.

"Of course we're going to help him. He granted us the gift of life!" cheered Opti.

"I'm not going anywhere," said Kawai, snuggling up to her big, strong, sexy brother.

"Yeah, I've had enough fighting for a while," said Atatasuki, putting his arm around his bro's shoulder.

"I will be there when Devlin needs me. As for the rest of you, that's for you to decide," said Kanasta, nodding to the team.

"Geez Boss, you can't jump into things so quickly. We gotta weigh our options. We don't even know how Devlin can become a god. Who knows what this mission entails," said Tempo, igniting a twig he got from Lum.

"It matters not. My brother needs me," said Kanasta.

"I suppose I could pay for your services again," said Devlin with a grin.

"Pay us with what?" asked Tempo.

"Not now, obviously. But once I've become a god, I could easily procure your payment. How about we set up a retainer when we get out of this place?" asked Devlin.

"Nice try, but there's no way to keep track of time here," said Ego.

"BoneSaw has an internal clock. When are you going to hire us?" asked Kanasta.

"Well not yet. Gotta figure a way out of here, first," said Devlin.

"Easy peasy. We simply have to find the escort to Sel and convince him to help us," said Kawai.

"Why are you helping Devlin?" asked Exp 8, pulling his sister up to him.

"I know he ordered Bob to kill me, but that doesn't change that unlike some people…" Kawai shot a bladed glare at Deceivant, "he treats me like a person and he gave me a home."

"What is that supposed to mean?" asked Deceivant, holding his chest.

"Stubby arms and legs, I actually kinda like my little boobies, but then there's the tiny mouth, heavy head…I pee apple juice!" yelled Kawai.

"Wait, you what?" asked Exp 8 with wide eyes.

"And not without a struggle. You designed me to be Atatasuki's love doll. Well this little kitten wants to do more than just snuggle, and what I want to do should not be dictated by your pedo-morphic design choice. And another thing, I decide who I love!" yelled Kawai, seething with anger.

"Sis, you should love your body. It's what makes you who you are," said Atatasuki.

"No, it's what confines my personality based on the labels brought with it. If I was given a more mature body, I would have Exp 8 drooling at my feet. But no. I'm stuck with this. And Atatasuki, he can't even…he could die if he overheats. We are people not toys, you bastard," said Kawai on the verge of tears.

"My dear Kawai-chan, I never meant any harm. I just made you adorable," said Deceivant.

"You bound me to Atatasuki. Don't act innocent," said Kawai, seething with rage.

"Hey Sis, what's all this? Come on, we're together now. Forget about him," said Exp 8, cuddling her to his chest.

"Together," said Kawai, looking up at him with vibrant eyes.

"And I like you exactly the way you are. Couldn't be cuter," said Exp 8, his mouthpiece stretching as he smiled.

"Aww! You're the best!" squealed Kawai.

"And I know you were made to suit my preferences, but you far exceeded them!" cheered Atatasuki.

"Not right now. I'm bonding with Brother," said Kawai before resuming her smother session.

"So, this escort to Sel, where is it?" asked Devlin.

"Don't know," said Kawai with a shrug.

"And even if she did, she wouldn't tell you. Kawai is free; she doesn't work for you anymore," said Exp 8, hugging her tightly.

"Thanks for speaking up for me, but I'm also free to speak for myself. I don't see a problem with helping Devlin out," said Kawai.

"Does that mean you forgive me?" asked Devlin, his face lax with relief.

"Nobody forgives you! You don't deserve forgiveness!" yelled Exp 8.

"See, what did I tell you?" asked Matteria, looking at Kawai.

"I guess it will take some time before he can let go," said Kawai.

"There is nothing to forgive. Devlin acted on the behalf of everyone. He took so many possibilities into consideration." Violet turned to her god. "Can the Earth still be saved, without Exp 8's power I mean?"

"That is yet to be determined. Divine ascendance may yet make it possible," said Devlin with a sly grin.

"Listen to him. Still as psychotic as ever. We can't trust him and none of us should forgive him," said Exp 8.

"Forgiveness aside, we have a common enemy. I think we can all agree that stopping Etah is our top priority," said Deceivant.

"Does that mean you're going to help?" asked Ada, geared up to jump.

"I'll do what I can," said Deceivant with a sly, confident smile.

"Hooray!" cheered Ada, hopping into the air.

"Etah's the one who banished me here," said Exp 8, clenching his fist.

"So you were in Sel? How did you get out?" asked Anthrax.

"I refused to bow down to him and he banished me. It's almost uncanny that I get led right to Kaity. It's even more interesting considering all of you ended up here. It's too convenient to be a coincidence; I think Etah has something planned for us," said Exp 8.

"I came here willingly," said Violet.

"True, but only after Efil drove us into a corner," said Deceivant.

"She was following divine orders. Is servitude a crime?" asked Violet.

"Enforcing it sure is," said Exp 8, staring at his detestable creator with spite.

"Didn't you guys get banished on purpose?" asked Devlin.

"I was planning on following Efil and the other goddesses to get you divine assistance. I had no choice but to go here," said Violet.

"It was either get banished to Absence or be imprisoned in Lum. It's a miracle nobody got killed," said Kawai.

"Nobody got killed. Then Demo and Fusion, they were imprisoned, they aren't dead?" asked Exp 8.

"We don't really know. I only saw them abducted. Could be alive, could have escaped, could be dead," said Bob.

"Which reminds me…how quickly did the rest of you die? I was staring into Lum's beautiful sky for only a bit before the rest of you appeared. There were little muffins and Kawais floating in the air. Aaaah," said Atatasuki.

"Back to the matter at hand: Devlin is our enemy! I refuse to help him and you should too!" exclaimed Exp 8.

"Oh, stop being stubborn. We have a far greater enemy," said Deceivant.

"I'll be the one to take down Etah," said Exp 8.

"Can't allow that. I've only got one chance at gaining divinity," said Devlin.

"Then all the more reason I have to take him down first. Who's with me?" asked Exp 8.

"Um, do we have to pick a side?" asked Opti.

Riufen patted Opti's shoulder and then approached Exp 8. "I understand your intentions but at times like this you should follow the principle of nemawashi. We must put aside our differences and offer our support to a common cause."

"I'm not going to work for Devlin just so I can feel a bit of moral ease by posing as a peacekeeper," said Exp 8 with growing frustration.

"Brother, it's your decision, but I think you should carefully think this through," said Kawai.

"I've already made up my mind."

"Come on, how long are you going to resist? Listen to your teammates at least once in awhile. You were misguided; it's understandable. I forgive you for leading them to their deaths. It's in the past now. I personally have no problem with you joining me," said Devlin, outstretching his hand to his greatest creation.

"I never agreed to this. Besides, you'd be joining us," said Exp 8.

"Well if you want me that badly, then it's settled!" exclaimed Devlin, shaking Exp 8's only hand.

"Wait, what?" asked Exp 8, pulling his hand away.

"We are one force now. From now on we shall be called the Freedom Overseers. Hmm, no that sounds odd," said Devlin.

"We're keeping our name, and I never agreed to this alliance," said Exp 8 with a stern finger.

"I like the new name better," said D.S.

"Who the hell cares what you like! You guys can't seriously be considering joining up with him, right?" asked Exp 8, his words eroded by doubt.

"Destructus Supplious, do you have paper?" asked Devlin.

"Uh-huh, I have graph, construction, tracing, computer, line, and even sand paper," said D.S., rummaging through his book bag.

"Give me the lined paper," said Devlin.

"A formal alliance bound by a contract. Good thinking. We must sign this alliance in blood," said Kanasta.

"I have a pen," said D.S., whipping it out of his book bag.

"That works too, I suppose," said Kanasta, his shoulders drooping.

"When everyone signs, this will be the proof of our alliance," said Devlin as he passed the paper to his new ally.

Exp 8 gave the smug scientist an angry look, wrote something on the paper and then passed it to his motherly comrade.

"I'm so glad we reached a compromise," said Ada as she signed. She then joyously handed the paper to her darling little girl.

Kawai signed it and shoved it in her other brother's face. "Off on another dangerous quest. Don't you die again."

"I won't. And I agree that we should help Devlin. I don't remember all the good he's done for us, but I remember enough," said Atatasuki before passing it to the shadow guy.

"Why do I feel like we're filling out an attendance sheet for a cemetery?" asked NoOne.

"Come on, at least try to stay positive," said Anthrax.

"You're right. It's different this time around. I'm on the side of good. I shall surely have a fighting chance," said NoOne, turning his frown upside-down.

"I wonder how long it will be before one of us dies. Ooh, things are going to get interesting," said Bob, grabbing the pen and signing. "Here, Karson, sign it."

"Ex-Commander Devlin isn't the one who put this cursed button on my back, so I'd happily sign! Problem is, I have no fingers," said Karson, raising his pistols.

"Sign it already, I can't wait to write my sexy name," said Nina, hopping up and down.

Karson shot a hole in the paper. "All yours, soldier."

Nina was already gripping the paper. "This isn't about Devlin or some great battle for peace. The only reason I'm signing this is because I want everyone to see my curvaceous cursive handwriting."

"Let me sign before the tar in my lungs kills me again," said Pharma, singing the paper with a cigarette butt. He then passed it to the head of the assassins.

Kanasta's eyes remained stoic even as they watered up. "Before I sign, there is something I need to say. It doesn't matter what you've done in the past. I will help you because you are my little brother. I'm so proud of you. Killing is easy if you send someone to do it. However to murder your brother with your own hands, that's impressive, most impressive. You didn't do it for money, but I'm still so proud of you, Brother," he said with a bow.

"I'm not going to forgive you. Just sign it," said Devlin.

Kanasta bit his thumb and signed with his blood.

"Kaity, you're up next," said Kanasta.

"How can you forgive him? He killed you," said Kaity with tearful eyes.

"I bear no grudges. Are you going to sign?" asked Kanasta.

"Yeah. We're in this together, for better or worse."

BoneSaw bumped against Kaity's leg.

"Oh don't worry, I'll sign your name too," said Kaity, patting her robotic ally.

"Why ruin a perfectly white sheet of paper?" asked Sefiwah.

"So, is it true? What Ada said? Did you kill yourself?" asked Kaity.

"Does it matter?" asked Sefiwah turning away.

"Yes. I need to know what happened," said Kaity, coiling her fingers around her soul mate's.

"Yes…I killed myself."

"See, Kaity? Sefiwah isn't mean or bloodthirsty. She doesn't like hurting people at all. She's a loving, caring friendly person," said Ada.

"I realized that I was not skilled enough to kill the target. I failed in battle and had no other choice. You're wrong about me not enjoying pain. I relished my murder," said Sefiwah, using a bloody thumbprint.

Tempo looked at the sheet of paper. "Not so sure about this. Don't want to jump the gun. I like getting paid at least half in advance."

"Come now. We can return to Lum later. There has got to be a god of wealth, am I right?" asked Kanasta.

"We'll clip its wings and pawn them for cash. Alright Kanasta, you've got yourself a deal," said Tempo.

"Now, now. We only kill when paid. I wonder if Etah would hire us," said Kanasta.

Exp 8 leaned over to the cute assassin. "He's joking, right? I can't tell with him."

"Nope. He's serious," said Kaity.

"One step closer to killing the god of wealth," said Tempo as he signed in an instant.

"The battle awaits," said Riufen, spraying blood out of his fingertip. "It is done."

"Devlin, I thank you for bringing me into this world. Thanks to you I was able to meet the Gods. You gave me life, so I'm going to give my mind, body, and soul to you," said Violet as she elegantly signed.

"Such loyalty cannot be bought," said Devlin with a smile.

"Yeah, it was constructed," said Exp 8.

"It's time for the doctor to sign," said Anthrax, cracking his fingers.

"Who are you?" asked Atatasuki.

"I'm Dr. Anthrax," he said, fixing his collar with pride.

"Don't ask me, dude. I've never seen him," said Ego.

"I was at the big tree in the center of Lum," said Anthrax.

"You're kinda short for a doctor, aint'cha?" asked Ego.

"Well I know him very well," said Matteria, kissing his boyfriend and signing.

"Matty, not in front of everybody," said Anthrax, his hands over his flushed cheeks.

"Come to think of it, has anyone seen the living mirror around?" asked Nina, shifting poses to see which ones worked for her new outfit.

"We've been over this. He's alive, trapped for the time being in the Death Die," said Kanasta.

"Merely another victim of your business, no?" asked Devlin.

"He's a client and a target. I will return to Earth and finish the job," said Kanasta.

"I can't wait to get out of here and have a sleepover," said Deceivant as he signed.

"I'm the last one," said Opti.

"Don't forget me!" yelled Pesi.

"Don't forget him? How can you guys possibly forget Ego?" He snatched the paper out of Pesi's hand.

"As I thought, only the assassins and the samurai signed in blood," said Ego as he flipped the page around.

"Then that's everyone, right? You don't understand how much this means to me." Devlin went down on his knees. "I'm sorry for getting you, my beloved creations, involved with my revenge and my divine plan," said Devlin with a reverent bow.

"Yeah, yeah, keep playing them. They may forgive, but they won't forget," said Exp 8.

"Forget what?" asked Atatasuki.

"That he killed you!" yelled Exp 8.

"He did. Hmm, I didn't know that," said Atatasuki.

"Well, he sent Violet to do it, but that's beside the point," said Exp 8.

"Violet? She wouldn't hurt a root vegetable. You shouldn't try to trick your older brother," said Atatasuki.

"Oh yeah, I suppose you are my older brother. Wisdom and age aren't as correlated as I had expected," said Exp 8.

"There we go. Here," said Ego, holding his head and squinting.

Devlin took the paper before Exp 8 could. "I hope the power of peer pressure pulled through. Let's see. Devlin; Leader: Exp 8; Computer: Ada; Adorable Mascot: Kawai. Hmm, looks like he started a trend."

"A mascot? Why belittle yourself? Then again, other than a leech, I'm not sure what else to call you," said Bob.

"I am the mascot. I'm cute, small, and I look like a chibi of our leader," said Kawai.

"Are you okay with that? You're much more than that. You're my emotional support. You hold me together. You believe in me, more than anyone else," said Exp 8.

"Really? Is that true?" asked Kawai, hope brewing in her eyes.

"Of course," said Exp 8.

"The muffins agree and so do I," said Atatasuki, thrusting his arm in the air.

"Anyway, let me continue, the Microwave: Atatasuki."

"Oh yeah!" exclaimed Atatasuki.

"The Shadow Master: NoOne; the Backstabber: Bob...are you actually proud of that?" asked Devlin.

"Sorry, did I reopen a wound?" asked Bob with a mocking pout.

"Soldier: Karson; *Erotic Warrior*: *Nina*."

Nina gripped the paper. "Look at my handwriting! Stunning isn't it?" she asked, feigning embarrassment.

Devlin swapped it from her grip. "Stimulant: Pharma; Killer: Kanasta; Sniper: Kaity; Box: BoneSaw.... How come I don't get a cool title? I know, Master of Creation: Devlin. Yes, I like the sound of that. Moving along. Acupuncturist: Sefiwah; Assassin: Tempo; Swordsman: Riufen; Bouncer: Destructus Supplious; Devotee: Violet...what the hell is this?"

"I wrote in after Violet. It's my signature," said Anthrax.

"It is? It looks like chicken wire got caught in a tornado," said Devlin.

"Doctor and Virus: Anthrax. Can't let my other side feel left out or he might intrude," said Anthrax.

"Now I see why you're always practicing your sig. Anyway, Spectrum Superstar: Matteria; Pedophile: Deceivant. Did you just admit to—of course you did."

"Why be ashamed of love? Why not flaunt my love of children? Well not merely children, but everything associated with them. Innocence is truly a wonder," said Deceivant, patting his wifey's head.

"This body will never grow. I'm stuck being tiny…forever!" yelled Kawai.

"Eternal youth is a blessing. I only wish I got my capsule at a younger age," said Deceivant.

"Shut up. I need to make sure everyone signed. Let's see, Peace Spreader: Opti; War Bringer: Pesi; Amazing, Great, Super, Wonderful, Powerful, Undefeated, Ravishing…Ego you took up the whole back page!" exclaimed Devlin.

"Yeah, I'm feeling a bit woozy," said Ego.

"I'll fix you up," said Anthrax.

"Six assassins, sixteen Exps, and one useless father. So add it all up and we have a team of twenty-three members. That's quite a fighting force!" exclaimed Devlin.

"Yep! I'd say the Freedom Forcers are officially back together!" cheered Exp 8.

"There are only fifteen Exps, right?" Kaity started counting them beneath her breath.

"Well you see, this proud young scientist—" said Exp 8 before he was kicked.

"I forgot to count myself, and I counted Opti and Pesi as separate Exps," said Devlin.

"And you forgot me. How rude," said Demonica, suddenly appearing before them.

"Not another step!" yelled D.S., holding out his scissors.

"Demon!" yelled Opti, toppling to the ground.

Kanasta leaped at Demonica and slammed her to the ground. "You will not use my brother ever again."

"Stand down. She's with me," said Devlin.

"What? She murdered us!"

"I only did what Devlin wanted," said Demonica, sucking on her finger.

"You manipulated my brother to do your bidding. Killing you will be merely an act of self-defense," said Kanasta before slamming her against the ground.

"Riufen, make Kanasta stand down," said Devlin.

"I cannot intrude on their fight," said Riufen, standing with shaky legs.

Demonica burst into blood and then solidified behind Devlin's brother.

"Got your back, Boss," said Tempo, shooting heat bullets at the enemy.

"Ooh, that feels great," said Demonica before Kanasta's rock-hard fist busted open her face.

Sefiwah grabbed the beheaded body and tossed it to the ground. Her hands pierced through as the dark goddess' body liquefied.

Demonica became solid, holding her sharpened fingernails to Sefiwah's pale neck.

"Put her down," said Kaity, walking up to the enemy with her plasma claws engaged.

"Everyone stop!" yelled Exp 8, standing in front of Kanasta. "Demonica was following Devlin's orders. You don't have to trust her, I sure as hell don't, but fighting her is only going to put us at risk."

"Demonica is loyal to me above all else," said Devlin.

"If Master Devlin says so, then I believe him," said Matteria, holding Anthrax close.

"She is the reason Kaity is back to normal. Besides, she knows more about Etah than any of us. I welcome her to the team," said Devlin.

"Are you sure that's a good idea?" asked Ada.

"Yes. We'll most certainly need her help." Devlin grabbed the demon goddess' hand.

Demonica released her hostage.

"I was so worried," said Kaity, sobbing in Sefiwah's embrace.

Devlin twirled Demonica into and out of an embrace. "Happy to have you on our side. That makes twenty-four teammates then. Perhaps we do stand a chance against Etah."

"Don't be so confident. Etah has legions upon legions at his command. And what, you think a bunch of experienced humans and novice living weapons stand a chance against the gods of Sel? On his own Etah could probably wipe out everyone here," said Demonica, surveying the group.

"Doomed. Doomed. Doomed," said NoOne, sinking lower and lower.

"I'm watching you," said Matteria, holding Anthrax's hand while glaring at the demon.

"First things first, let's find a way out of here," said Devlin.

Demonica grabbed Devlin and pulled him aside. "Don't worry, I didn't tell Etah our dir-ty se-cret. He has no idea how powerful you are."

"And I'm supposed to take your word on this?"

"Come on. I'm tired of Etah's rule. It was fun at first, but it has become more and more monotonous. Sel needs a new leader and who better to lead it than you?" asked Demonica with an open hand.

"Shhh, he'll hear us," said Devlin.

"Don't worry; he can only see what is on Earth and in Sel. When you transformed, I entertained his body so he couldn't pay attention. I've made so many sacrifices for you," said Demonica, falling into her beloved's arms.

"Wait, isn't he your father?" asked Devlin, pushing her back on her feet.

"He's just the new ruler. I was the one who transformed into the God of Death. And Sel's previous ruler threw me into the Hellfire Pit. I remember when I was just a part of Sel, burning with the other residents. I was so pathetic back then," said Demonica with a grimace.

"We all start out weak."

"Not you, you were born to be a god."

"Shh! They can hear you," said Devlin, searching for nearby Absence gods.

"Can you promise me that date if I help you become Sel's ruler?" asked Demonica, stroking his hair.

"Fair enough but keep quiet. If Kaity found out what I am, my chances of her loving me would be even slimmer," said Devlin with a sigh.

"Deal?" asked Demonica.

Devlin outstretched his hand to her. "It's a deal."

"We are bonded by our goals!" cheered Demonica, gripping his hand.

"Indeed we are. So, do you know how to get out of here? Kawai mentioned an escort to Sel, do you know who she's talking about?" asked Devlin.

"Forget the escort. You have to convince the guardians for a pass to get out. That's only temporary though. Convincing Neutral, Lord of Nothing, is the only way to be free of Absence's pull," said Demonica.

"The Lord of Nothing, he sounds even weaker than Deceivant," said Exp 8, sliding in the conversation.

"Good one," said Devlin with a smirk.

"Neutral is the king of this realm. If he wanted to, he could erase our souls," said Demonica.

"Why are you two talking in secret?" asked Matteria, his gaze fixed on the dark succubus.

"Like I said, she knows more about this world than any of us. Thanks to her, we've got a game plan," said Devlin.

"My pleasure," said Demonica.

Devlin turned to address the team. Noticing some were off doing their own thing, he clapped his hands together. "Everyone, stay put. According to Demonica, there is no point in locating the escort to Sel. The plan for now is to gain favor with the guardians of this world. I'll try to convince Eil to offer us support." He split from the group and ventured where he intuitively felt was east.

A clear cloaked figure holding a human skull appeared out of thin air.

"Can you teleport?" asked Devlin, approaching the skull still held in the statue's hands.

"I merely hid my presence."

"And I see your protector is back from his errand."

"Correct. Hmm, your little minions are quite the colorful group," said Eil.

"Yeah, they light up the sky of my ambition. Wait, you heard us, right? Then you know what I want," said Devlin.

"I do, but I'm still going to make you ask."

"Ugh, of course. I want out. You know how. Tell me."

"So, you want to get out of Absence, do ya?" asked Eil, making his voice extra shrill.

"That's right," said Devlin calmly.

"Ha! I deceived you. That was a retractable question."

"Don't you mean rhetorical?"

"No...wait...yes, I mean no. I take it back! Ah, you see, it is retractable."

"Can we go?"

"No, you can't not."

"Wonderful, so how do we leave?"

"Well played. You can leave, for a bit, but only if you defeat me," said Eil, glaring at the delinquent with empty sockets of battle charisma.

"Why?"

"It's so boring doing nothing for eternity."

A figure of dashed lines appeared spontaneously, just barely visible.

"What is that?" asked Devlin.

"That is Neutral, ruler of Absence."

"There will be neutral-ity at all times," said Neutral in monotone.

"Come on, I'm bored. I want to fight," complained Eil.

"There will be neutral-ity at all times."

"Is that all he says?" asked Devlin.

Neutral approached the newcomer. "What is your reason for inspiring feelings?"

"We want to leave here. We won't inconvenience you any more if we're gone, right?"

"You think in such simple terms. As the God of Neutrality, I do not care if things are neutral."

"Great, neither do I."

"What do we have to do to get your pass?" asked Exp 8.

"A rainbow. It's been so long since I've seen one," said Neutral.

Matteria hopped up. "That's easy! Huh, there's no water in the atmosphere here."

"It is an impossible task," said Neutral, lowering his head.

"Not a problem!" Nina tossed Matteria a water bottle.

"Oh yeah, my powers…they don't work anymore. I didn't bring the artifact along with me when I died. I guess it makes sense," said Matteria.

"Mine still works," said Tempo, lighting his finger up.

"That's weird. What's wrong with me?"

"What's wrong is you aren't trying. Devlin needs you, are you really going to let him down now?" asked Nina, digging her finger in the powdered boy's chest.

Matteria took in a deep breath. "Okay. I can do this!" He sprayed the water in the air and then created a rainbow that arched over his head. After a timely wink, he blew a kiss at Neutral.

"Look at the vibrant colors. I've only dreamed of such beauty. Thank you," said Neutral, looking up in awe.

"I believe you're forgetting something," said Devlin.

"Oh yes, of course." Neutral handed him the pass, his eyes still fixated on the rainbow.

The pass was almost invisible with the words. *Get out of Absence: 2 Day Pass* in thin dashed lines.

"Not the control I'm used to, but it's fine for now. Thanks, Nina," said Matteria with a warm smile.

"Oh yeah, one step closer. Now let's find that escort," said Nina.

Demonica snatched the ticket out of Devlin's hand. "I'll lead the way," she said before creating a black portal.

"Wait, you're the escort?" asked Kawai.

"What, don't trust me?" asked Demonica.

"I don't know you. Do any of you?" asked Kawai.

Matteria held Anthrax close to him.

D.S. nodded with a look of fright.

Opti kept his gaze to the ground.

Deceivant glared at the hateful woman. "We know her, alright. She killed me."

"Just following orders, like this one," said Demonica, poking the round tactician with her long finger nails.

"Ow!" Bob brought out the Atma Blade. "Do that again and you'll lose your ability to move."

"Trust me or not, I'm your only means of getting into Sel. If we hurry, we can ambush Etah. Is anyone coming with me? The portal won't last forever." Demonica rushed into the portal.

# Chapter 66: Tickets

The Freedom Forcers looked at their heroic leader.

"Oh, uh. Yeah. Let's go in. Stay cautious," said Exp 8 before entering the dark portal.

The rest of the team rushed in the portal. The blackness of the portal vanquished their vision. They saw a burst of fire before they fell on the ashy floor of Sel.

"Sorry. Hey wait, it's just molten rock," said Exp 8, looking at the ground.

"Hey, this place isn't so bad," said Pharma, lighting up four cigarettes at once.

"Says you. I might overheat just walking around here," said Atatasuki.

"No need to worry about that. *TEMPERATURE FALL.*" Cool air seeped out from Tempo's fingers and coated Atatasuki. "I can regulate your temperature no problem."

"Thanks for helping him out," said Exp 8.

"No problem. It isn't his fault he was born inadequate," said Tempo, grinding his teeth.

"Then we'll have to make this a quick visit," said Exp 8, scanning the area.

"How do you come up with so many cool lines?" asked Kawai, bouncing up and down.

"You're so cute, Sis," said Exp 8, patting her head.

"Ugh, I'm all sweaty," said Nina, wiping her forehead.

"I think you look hot," said Kaity with wide eyes.

"You're right. Sweat simply makes my scrumptious body even more, mmm, enticing," said Nina, licking her pointer finger before pressing it against her bountiful booty.

"It's not the most comfortable place, but its home," said Demonica, a twinkling in her eye.

A whip suddenly fastened itself around Demonica's neck and pulled her away from the group.

"Stay alert! We've got company," said Devlin.

"It's her…again," said Deceivant.

"Who?" asked Exp 8.

"Tsul. How did she know where we would land?" asked Deceivant.

"Good question. Let's not forget who made the portal," said Matteria.

"You're right! Demonica must want us to meet her sister!" cheered Ada.

Tsul, the Sin of Lust and Demonica's older sister, was slender and curvaceous. Red tentacles protruded out of her dark pink skin, forming a fleshy suit. They spiraled around her six breasts and teased her nipples. A pulsating fleshy piston plunged in and out of her anus while her frontal cave was in a state of constant penetration by her tentacles. Red wax dripped down her sides, forming a descending trail of pleasure throughout her body. Her feathered legs moved back and forth, giving slight tingling sensations. Tsul's eyes bulged as she got more and more aroused by strangling her sister.

"You dare betray Etah!" yelled Tsul, her breath coming out as a pink puff of smoke as she tightened her grip.

"Devlin is so much sexier," said Demonica, winking at her beloved.

"No remorse for your transgressions. You're a traitor at heart," said Tsul, speaking in a commanding and composed voice despite the rage buried in it.

"And you're always such a prude," said Demonica, rolling her eyes.

Tsul's tentacles coiled around her arm, forming a pink spiked whip.

"You just want an excuse to play with me," said Demonica, kissing her sister's cheek.

"You're so arrogant. *CHAINS OF LUST.*"

Pink chains sprouted from the ground, rose up like pillars, and wrapped around the Freedom Forcers.

"Who do I kill first?" asked Tsul, scanning her victims. Tiny spikes formed around the lusty demon's whip-like fingers.

"Don't bother struggling, I've got this under control," said Demonica.

"With each thrust of my whip I can kill one of your precious toys. Now submit to me." Tsul caressed her thick black whip-like hair with her wavy suctioned fingers.

"Sorry, no deal. I have to be on top; it's genetic," said Demonica, before slipping out of the whip's grasp.

"Riufen, Bob, anyone, break out and attack her!" yelled Devlin, squirming around.

Riufen looked side to side. "If I broke out now, I would ruin the team's cohesion. I must be supportive of the consensus we as a team have reached."

"What the hell are you talking about!" yelled Devlin.

"Devi-kun, I'm scared," said Kaity, trying to turn her head to face him.

A few meters away, Tsul knocked Demonica down with a powerful crack of her whip. "With you dead, I will take my rightful place as leader of the Sinful Sorority," she said, thrashing her whip arm at the traitor.

"If it was your rightful place, then why am I Etah's queen?" asked Demonica as she was viciously assaulted.

"You won't be for long! I'm going to have your boyfriend here kill you," said Tsul.

"Sounds fun," said Demonica.

"Rrgh, you are so frustrating! I'm going to make you watch him suffer! All of your teammates shall die!" Tsul thrust her whip forward at the Freedom Forcers.

Wires shot out from Devlin's back, stopping the whip an inch before it hit Deceivant, who was standing right in front of Kaity.

"Phew. That was close," said Deceivant, holding his chest.

Devlin broke out of the chains as wires shot out from his body, wrapping around the enemy.

"You think I would love Devlin if he was a weakling?" asked Demonica.

"The next time we meet, you will regret this," said Tsul before vanishing into a portal.


The chains holding the Freedom Forcers shattered.

The team stood motionless.

Devlin's wires seeped back into his skin as he helped Demonica to her feet. His skin fell off, revealing his true form.

His body was sleek and his exposed flesh was black.

"I would have stopped her, you know. You didn't have to transform," said Demonica.

Devlin turned to face the Freedom Forcers, his pupils shrinking.

"M-M-Master Devlin?" asked Matteria with wide eyes.

"I'm confused," said NoOne.

"Are you one of us?" asked Riufen.

"Looks kind of familiar, actually," said Ego, tilting his head.

"It's best if you don't remember," said Tempo in a hushed tone.

"I thought you were a human!" exclaimed Atatasuki, eyes wide with shock.

"Doesn't look like a human to me," said Sefiwah, her gaze unwavering.

"He's clearly not. Wires aren't part of human anatomy. Seems Devlin is entirely inorganic," said Anthrax matter-of-factly.

Tempo bumped the Boss with his elbow. "I thought you said he was your brother."

"He is my brother. Always will be," said Kanasta.

"Dude, your brother looks badass!" exclaimed Ego.

"He does look pretty cool," said Kaity with a smile.

"Looks kind of like a cat without fur…it's kind of cute," said Opti.

"Yeah, it is," said Kaity, trying to hide her blush.

"Little brother is one of us! Yay!" cheered D.S.

"Sis, I thought you would be more surprised," said Exp 8.

"Well, I didn't know he looked like a kitty, but Atatasuki and I already knew Devlin was an Exp. Can't believe he forgot something so important," said Kawai, her gaze drifting.

"Must say, I'm impressed. Isn't easy to keep something like this a secret," said Nina.

"I thought it was obvious," said Bob with a shrug.

"Ex-commander Devlin is an Exp? Why have you been lolling about when you could have joined us in battle?" asked Karson.

"I know Master Devlin must have had a good reason to keep this from us," said Matteria.

"I too have faith in him," said Violet, her eyes filled with love and devotion.

"This form explains how he created us so quickly. He's got hundreds of appendages," said Pharma.

"That's a keen observation, Pharma." Anthrax folded his hands. "So Devlin, why didn't you tell us?"

"I don't have to answer anything," said Devlin, eyes focused on the ground.

"Oh sweetie, you've grown so much! Who's my big strong boy?" asked Ada, running to her son with open arms.

Wires jutted out and pinned the hateful woman to the ground.

"Stay away," said Devlin with a dark glare.

"Calm down. We're in this together now," said Anthrax.

"Why didn't any of you break free?" asked Devlin, his golden eyes tearing up.

Exp 8 smiled slyly. "While you were talking with Eil, I had a talk with my team. We agreed that in the next battle we would all act useless to test your loyalty, as well as Demonica's. She fought bravely; though I still don't trust her. " The leader of the Freedom Forcers walked up to Devlin. "You passed the test; I knew you would transform." He patted his fellow Exp on the back.

Devlin punched his creation with his metallic fist. "You idiot, you could've gotten Kaity killed!"

"How can you all be so mean to Devlin? And how could you try to hide that sexy transformation from me?" asked Demonica, stroking her beloved's sleek black chin.

"I couldn't risk letting Kaity get hurt," said Devlin.

"We're all here to support you. You can tell us anything," said Anthrax.

"I was oppressed because I was an Exp. It's as simple as that," said Devlin with quaking hands.

"Actually, this would be a great time to clear things up," said Deceivant.

"I have nothing to say to you!" yelled Devlin.

"Why did you try to enslave me if we're the same? I still don't understand it," said Exp 8 with a quaking fist.

"Our people are only seen as property. I thought I needed your power to become a god. You were the one sacrifice to put our people at the top of the world. We should be the sustainers of the Earth, not mere tools for mankind," said Devlin, charisma building throughout his being.

"What was all that about freedom being a shackle? Sounds to me like you value freedom," said Exp 8.

"Reverse psychology. I wanted you to grow stronger. That mantra was created to bring about internal conflict. It was all to shake up your psyche and awaken your true potential," said Devlin.

"That's absurdly convoluted," said Exp 8.

"Even so, I don't believe in absolute freedom. Discipline serves its purpose. I've seen firsthand how freedoms can take hold of one's life. Addiction is caused by lack of discipline. Take a look at capitalism, the free market. In that system the more freedom one has, the less responsibility they take upon themselves. Either way I'd rather be bound than abandoned. The Exps need a leader; they need guidance. Once I'm a god, I'll be ready to assume my role," said Devlin, standing tall with renewed determination.

"I'm only here to take down Etah. You can go through your apotheosis without me," said Exp 8.

"I suppose I'll have to reach divinity with only the Viper Squad and every other Exp at my side. It is quite a bit off from my original plan, but the end result is the same," said Devlin.

"Want to see a magic trick?" asked Demonica.

"Like what?" asked Devlin.

Demonica snapped her fingers.

Devlin was instantly blanketed in his human skin. Even his lab coat and other adornments had regenerated.

"You like?" she asked.

"How did you do that?" he asked with a blank stare.

"Secret," she said, kissing his cheek.

The fiery sky and molten ground morphed into a white void and clear floor as the team was teleported back to Absence.

"Time's up," said Eil.

"That wasn't even close to two days!" exclaimed Exp 8.

"Believe what you want," said Eil.

"No point in arguing about it. Absence tickets are meant to inspire hope simply so they can crush it after a few minutes," said Demonica.

"Why didn't you tell me?" asked Devlin, gripping the Demonica's arm.

"You were so happy; I didn't want to disappoint you. It's like telling a child the Easter Bunny isn't real," said Demonica with a fake pout.

"What do you mean he's not real!" exclaimed D.S. with wide eyes.

"She's merely giving an example. The Easter Bunny does exist! We had a deep conversation about the nature of creation a couple weeks ago," explained Violet.

"Oh my, there is nothing you won't believe, is there? Where does the bunny get the eggs from? Does he steal them from a birds nest? Once you start to think, even for a second, all this superstitious nonsense falls to pieces." Deceivant flicked Demonica's horn.

"That sounds evil! The Easter Bunny would never do that. He just hides candy from children in eggs. Wait, that's mean too," said D.S.

"The Easter Bunny is solely a metaphor about life. Easter symbolizes that you have to put forth effort if you want a reward," explained Bob.

"So he protects children from the sin of sloth!" exclaimed Violet joyously.

"Enough! I was just giving an example! I can't believe you people," said Demonica.

Exp 8 pulled Devlin aside. "Look, I don't want to alarm the others, but that guard, the one holding the obnoxious skull, I saw him in Sel. He was working with Etah. I don't know the details, but we can't be certain the guardians of Absence are a truly neutral group," said Exp 8.

"So that's where he went. I'll keep it in mind. I heard that it was Etah who placed me here, though it was from a less than reliable source," said Devlin.

"Just so we're clear, I don't fully trust you either," said Exp 8.

"Duly noted." Devlin walked up to the skull guardian. "So Eil, how do we get another pass?"

"Well, I'll give you another pass if you can answer three riddles," said Eil.

"Done," said Devlin.

"What?" asked Eil.

"I can answer the riddles in theory. That is what 'can' implies. As in, are able to. Now answering them is completely different," said Devlin.

"Oh, I think I'm rubbing off on you. But being able to answer won't be enough. You must answer all three of them! Riddle number one: what speaks but has no lungs, sees but has no eyes, hears but has no ears?"

D.S. jumped up, flailing his hand in the air. "Ooh! Ooh! I know this one! It's Ada! It's my mom!"

"It's you, the talking skull," said Devlin.

"Both are correct. The second one will be a bit harder. What moves all but does not move itself?" asked Eil, adding a mysterious tone to his voice.

"Is it gravity?" asked Devlin.

"It's the un-moving mover! It's God! The Tao. It's the unseen force behind everything!" exclaimed Violet.

"Very good. There's only a few here who have gotten that one," said Eil.

"Final riddle. How do you escape a box with no edges, no entrance and no exit?" asked Eil.

"How can it be a box if it has no edges?" asked Deceivant.

"Cocky bastard. If we knew the answer to this riddle, we wouldn't be here right now. You can't escape, that's the answer, isn't it?" Devlin massaged his temples.

"So ironic isn't it? Tehtehtehteh," said Eil.

"Is this a riddle or a joke?" asked Ada.

"I know the answer," said NoOne, stepping up to the wise skull.

"Wonderful!" exclaimed Eil.

"You can't escape. The box is your own body and you are forever bound to it," said NoOne before seeping back into the crowd.

"I see someone has come to grips with reality. Tehteh."

"You make your own exit!" cheered Karson.

"You pass through it," said Bob with a grin.

"Wrong and wrong. But points for trying."

"Transcendence," said Violet.

"What?" asked Eil, swiftly being turned to face the blue-skinned woman.

"You journey inward. You realize there are no boundaries. You become aware the true self cannot be confined. You move beyond the realm you are in and enter the space at the peak of the universe, the Siddha Loka," said Violet.

"Correct and properly explained. You must have quite a few lifetimes under your belt," said Eil.

"No, um. I was created with a spectrum of scriptural knowledge. I'm a new soul who is open to learning, that's all," said Violet, her cheeks turning purple.

"Then we're done here?" asked Devlin.

"No. You failed the second and third riddle. Shouldn't have let your allies answer for you, fool," said Eil.

"Okay, so give us the pass," said Devlin casually.

"What, but you were wrong. You shall get no ticket from me. You will be stuck here for eternity, tormented by my plethora of knock-knock jokes, riddles, and puns!" exclaimed Eil.

"You said you'd give me the ticket if I answered all three riddles. You said nothing about me answering correctly," said Devlin with a smirk.

"Oh...I did. You...you...you're right! Here, take it. But you have to wait till tomorrow to use it," said Eil before he coughed up the ticket.

"Good job getting that ticket. There aren't many who are crazy enough to actually ask for Eil's riddles. Your clever intellect really gets me going," said Demonica, rubbing up against her handsome leader.

"Leave me alone," said Devlin, turning away.

"Oh, no need to be shy. I think the real you looks majestic!" exclaimed Demonica.

"The real me? I've been using this shell for so long it's hard to tell which is the real me."

"Many gods take up a humanoid form. There's nothing to be ashamed of."

"When I've shed my disguise, I don't feel liberated. I feel like a slave, like I'm just property," said Devlin, his breath quivering.

"It's a horrible feeling," said Demonica, touching his chest.

"Hey, are we just going to sit around and wait? Ego spotted another hooded figure a couple miles down," said Exp 8.

"Let's get moving," said Devlin.

"Yes, let's." Demonica grabbed his hand.

The Freedom Forcers came together in front of the hooded figure.

"I'll take care of this," said Devlin before approaching the Second Guardian.

"One sec." Exp 8 stepped in front of Devlin. "Remember what I said earlier, about the guard holding the talking skull? Well...turns out all the guards wear cloaks. I can't be sure it was that one that was working with Etah."

"What about Etah?" asked Kawai, sitting on her brother's shoulder.

"Just planning ahead, that's all," said Exp 8.

"Basic planning. Nothing worth mentioning. Moving along," said Devlin, turning back to face the guard.

"The Second Guardian will give you a ticket for free. But you have to get his attention first! Tehtehtehtehteh!" yelled Eil.

The guardian was a smooth rounded rock. An assortment of symbols and mantras were painted across it.

"Hello," said Devlin.

There was no response.

"He's deaf. Obviously he has no ears," said Eil.

"Neither do you," said Devlin.

219

"True, true. But I once did, so therefore I can hear," said Eil.

"That doesn't make any sense," said Anthrax.

"Oh and even if he did hear you, he won't respond. He's also mute," said Eil.

"And how do you talk?" asked Deceivant intrigued.

"I use telepathy of course," said Eil.

"Ah yes, I use an internal microphone for Exps without mouths. The issue with telepathy is it is either picked up by everyone or only a select few. It's a rather ineffective form of communication," said Deceivant.

Bob rose out from beneath him. "Says you, hmph."

Devlin hit the Second Guardian, but there was no response.

"He can't feel either. Face it, you are doomed!" exclaimed Eil.

"I'll handle it from here." Atatasuki approached the Second Guardian. "I have fresh chocolate chip muffins! Are you hungry?" He opened up his chest and took out a steamy batch of pastries.

The Second Guardian made no indication of smelling the scrumptious muffins.

"He's no longer among the living," said Atatasuki.

"Moving along. Where is the next guardian?" asked Devlin.

"Is this him?" asked D.S., pointing to a hooded figure that had popped up behind them.

The Third Guardian, like the first, was a skull. He was much smaller than Eil and resembled the shape of a chameleon.

Before Devlin could approach the guardian, Neutral appeared a foot in front of him.

"Thanks for the ticket," said Devlin.

"I do not know what you are talk-ing about. I have never seen you before," said Neutral.

"There must have been an imposter!" exclaimed Eil.

"An imposter!" exclaimed the new skull.

"What guardian is he?" asked Devlin.

"He is Plagiarism, the Third Guardian. He is also the one who pretend-ed to be me," said Neutral.

"I wanted to see something with some damn color!" yelled the Third Guardian with an exuberant and shrill voice.

"I will not stand for a tone of voice. Guard, give him punishment," said Neutral.

The hooded figure holding the Third Guardian raised its hand and patted the top of the guardian's head vigorously.

"Stop! Stop! Please, I beg you!" yelled Plagiarism in agony.

"You continue to have pitch, this is un-forgiv-able," said Neutral.

The chameleon sucked up his pain as his head was patted ten more times.

"You may stop. Now behave, I must depart," said Neutral before vanishing.

"Where does he go?" asked Devlin confused.

"He is consulting with the other gods. You see my love, Lum and Sel are at the brink of war," said Demonica.

"How could Lum even think of fighting?" asked Exp 8.

"Why don't we ever get to fight?" asked Eil.

"It's because of that bore of a god, Neutral. Our last ruler was so much more fun," said the chameleon skull.

"So we didn't get Neutral's pass. That means we got the Third Guardian's pass instead," said Devlin.

"Correct. It gets so lonely here," said the reptilian skull.

"Poor little guy. How can you let him oppress you like that?" asked Opti.

"He's the god of this realm, hence known as a realm god. I'm only a demi-god, I wouldn't stand a chance against him," said the Third Guardian.

"Well, since we already got the Third Guardian's pass, let's see what the Fourth Guardian wants," said Devlin. "Wait!" yelled Eil.

"Why are you screaming?" asked Atatasuki.

"It's nightfall, we must rest," said Eil.

The Freedom Forcers looked up at the infinite nothingness above them.

"How the hell can you tell?" asked Exp 8.

"The moon is out. Obviously. Goodnight," said Eil.

"This place is absurd," said Devlin.

"No stupid response? Is he sleeping?" asked Exp 8.

"Evidently so. I better get some sleep too," said Deceivant, lying on the ground. "Hey Kawai, you want to snuggle with me?" he asked, giving her a charming smile.

"I'd rather cuddle with a porcupine! I'm going to sleep with my beloved brother!" exclaimed Kawai as she flew into Exp 8's powerful and loving embrace.

"Exps don't sleep, right?" asked Exp 8, looking down at the insightful inventor.

"Well it's not necessary for energy recuperation, but it does give them more concentrated energy and some extra vitality," said Deceivant.

"Reflector dreams all the time. He tells me about them," said Matteria.

"Fascinating! What does he dream about?" asked Anthrax.

"Umm, me," said Matteria, sinking into his shoulders a bit.

"Of course," said Anthrax.

Kaity stretched her back in an arch and yawned. "I'm tired too," she said, closing her eyes.

"Would you like to cuddle with me?" asked Deceivant.

"Nope, sorry," said Kaity with a nervous grin.

"Um Kaity, would it be alright if I gave you a hug goodnight?" asked Devlin shyly.

"Don't touch me, papa killer," said Kaity with sharp eyes.

Demonica pulled Devlin away. "You actually asked to give her a hug? I can't believe what a wuss you are. Pin her down and take her. You'd better hurry before I take your virginity," she said, flicking Devlin's crotch.

"You can't!" yelled Devlin.

"Why not?" asked Demonica with a curious look.

Sefiwah glanced at the dangerous boy.

Devlin turned away. "My body is my own. If you want it, then you'll have to beat me first."

"Are you trying to tempt me?" asked Demonica, gripping his manhood.

"Nina, can I get a kiss goodnight?" asked Matteria.

"You got yours when I slit your throat," said Nina with a dark glare.

"And it was incredible," said Matteria, gripping his sides.

"What! You kissed him! He's my boyfriend!" yelled Anthrax.

"It was purely tactical. There is nothing between us," said Nina with a glare.

"Ooh! Ooh! Nina! Can you give me a kiss goodnight?" asked Kaity, jumping on her back.

"Huhuhu-agheheheheh, no." Nina flipped her fan over her shoulders, toppling her to the floor.

Sefiwah picked her girl up and gave her a deep kiss. She set her down and then turned her sights on Nina. "If I wanted to I could pierce right through your cherished breasts and puncture your capsule. Don't hurt her."

"I'm fine. It's okay. Calm down."

"It hurts me to see you in pain," said Sefiwah with a tear.

"Come on, give me a smile." Kaity tickled her protector.

"St-stop. Not in front of the others," said Sefiwah, her snow white cheeks now tinted with a light shade of pink.

"But I missed you so much." Kaity nibbled on her soul mate's ear.

"I missed you too." Sefiwah lifted her lover up by her butt and gave her a deep kiss.

Kaity rubbed up against Sefiwah once the kiss parted. "I'm feeling really frisky right now."

"I can't continue. Devlin is watching," said Sefiwah.

"Do you want me to shoot out his eyes?" asked Kaity, whipping out her sidearm.

Sefiwah lowered the gun. "We can just ignore him, I suppose," she said, kissing her kitten's supple neck.

"Sefi-chan, that tickles," said Kaity, squirming in her lover's embrace. "Let's cuddle all night long."

"It's been too long," said Sefiwah, holding her girl in a snug embrace.

"She is so cute," said Deceivant.

"Yeah. Yeah, she is," said Devlin in a blissful trance.

"Ooh, ooh. Hey Brother, let's do what they're doing!" cheered Kawai, hopping up and down on his chest.

"Um Sis, could you give me the undeserved honor of your embrace?" asked Atatasuki.

"Shut up! I'm obviously busy!" yelled Kawai.

Exp 8 looked into his sister's aroused eyes. "You want me to be happy, right?"

"Uh-huh. More than anything in the whole wide world," said Kawai, holding her cheeks.

"Nothing makes me happier than seeing my family get along. So, give him a hug, for me," said Exp 8, tapping her nose.

"Yeah. Sure. Anything." Kawai flew up to her less important sibling in a daze. She wrapped her tail around him and hugged his chest with her stubby arms. "Is this good?" she asked, wagging her butt.

"It's great." Exp 8 joined in the embrace, sandwiching his sister between him and his brother.

"Huuuh, you're so close," said Kawai, her pink cheeks now red like strawberries.

Exp 8 let go and patted her head.

Once Kawai let go, her faulty brother collapsed to his knees, his eyes were drenched in tears.

"Thank you!" cried Atatasuki.

Matteria walked up to Anthrax, waving his hips side to side.

"Do you want a kiss?" he asked.

"Nope."

"What? Why?"

"Kissing is an easy way to spread disease."

"You think I'm sick?" asked Matteria, his head jerking back.

"Come on, I've told you before. I like to stay healthy."

"But I thought it would be different since we are dead now."

"Can't be certain, so for now it's air hugs and kisses," said Anthrax, giving Matteria a warm smile.

"But before, in Lum, we were kissing," said Matteria.

"I was planning on becoming a mawali. I wanted to be with you before I forgot you."

"Then you've decided against it?" asked Matteria with hopeful eyes.

"For the time being, yes." Anthrax held out his arms and embraced the air. "There we go. That's much less risky. If I got sick I could become Amthraahksh again, and that would be bad."

"That was so cute!" exclaimed Matteria, shaking his butt.


"Aw man, looks like everybody has a partner but me," said Ego, biting his thumb.

"Relationships only serve to stimulate. No need to envy them," said Tempo.

"Whoa, I'm not into love or anything. I want a hot babe to put my arm around, that's all bro," said Ego.

Tempo lifted Ego off the ground. "Then go for it." He pushed his friend, causing him to stumble.

Violet caught Ego before he fell over.

"Hey babe, nice catch," said Ego with a wink.

"I beg your pardon," said Violet with a curious look.

"Oh, I…well I, I was complementing you," said Ego as he backed up.

"Thanks for the compliment then." Violet smiled and then walked off.

Tempo put his arm around Ego. "See? Waste of time. She's totally clueless. Best you forget about girls and just hang with your old classmate."

"Yeah. I can try again some other time," said Ego, walking with his bro.

"Hey bro, sorry about attacking you. I lost control," said Tempo softly.

"You can't help who you are. Just try to keep it in check for me, okay dude?"

"Sure thing," said Tempo with a grin.


Violet approached Pharma.

"Something you want?" asked Pharma, chewing nicotine tar.

"You have such potential," said Violet, sitting down next to him.

"That's potency, not potential. Want one?" asked Pharma, offering her a cig.

"Not in a thousand lifetimes." She scooted closer to him. "What I meant was: your soul craves ecstasy. You're merely taking the wrong path to achieve it.

I'm sure that if you devoted yourself to a spiritual discipline, you would find greater fulfillment. I'm here to help you in any way I can."

"I'm not after a sense of purpose or some great fulfillment. I'm fine the way I am. Indulging is more than enough for me." Pharma popped a pill in his mouth.

"But that's all superficial. You can't even taste anything, can you?"

"Doesn't matter! The action itself is enough to satiate my habit! If you don't want a puff, then move along."

"Okay, I suppose you aren't ready yet. Perhaps in another life?"

"Go away. I'm not interested. Damn pusher," said Pharma with a grimace.

"Come here, my darling," said Deceivant as he patted the ground.

"Now you want me. Now that you couldn't get Kawai or Kaity to cuddle with you," said Ada, turning away with watery eyes.

"You misunderstand. I was going to sleep with all three of you," said Deceivant.

"You mean it?" asked Ada.

"Trust me," said Deceivant, curling his fingers enticingly.

"Oh, you are so sweet!" exclaimed Ada

"It's nice to relax," said NoOne, easing into a puddle.

"We should be training for the coming battle," said Exp 8.

"I agree," said Riufen, drawing his spine and taking a firm stance.

"Whoa, calm down. I've already got my training partner." Exp 8 looked down at his little sister.

"Me?" asked Kawai with shimmering eyes.

"Yeah. Actually, I was hoping you could teach me."

"T-teach you? You mean…about intimacy?" asked Kawai, her head going round in circles.

"Huh-heh. No. I mean combat. Specifically using your tail in combat. You control it with such power and precision. Mine kind of just wags around. It's an obvious weak point. When Etah had me pinned down, I could have escaped if I had proper control of it. I'm lucky it hasn't cost me my life already."

"Sure, I'd love to teach you. But not for free. You'll have to pay me in kisses!" cheered Kawai, opening her mouthpiece.

"Kissing makes me kind of uncomfortable. Can I pay you in hugs?"

Kawai nodded spasmodically. "Yeah! That works too. Okay, close your eyes, focus on your tail. Wag it. Oh yeah, you're working it," she said with a little drool.

"Yeah, I can wag it, but I can't bend it like yours."

"Change your attitude. This is merely another wall for you to smash through!" exclaimed Kawai, manually bending his tail.

"A change in perspective, heh, that's how I got NoOne to join me. Alright, let's do this. Hrrgh! Hey look, I'm hugging you with my tail. I'm really doing it."

Kawai's tail wrapped around his. "Let's do some physical training. We are going to tail wrestle until you beat me. Till then, my tail won't be letting go, got it?"

"Understood. I won't let you down," said Exp 8, raising his fist.

"Oh yeah, that's it. Grip me, hard," said Kawai, tightening her muscles.


"Time's up!" exclaimed Eil.

"What do you mean?" asked Devlin, rolling his eyes.

"It is time for you to leave."

"I thought you said it was nighttime," said Devlin.

"Did I?"

"You did. But BoneSaw's clock places us in the afternoon," said Kanasta.

"You lied! Liar, liar!" yelled D.S.

"Giving false information and lying aren't the same."

"He's got a point," said Bob.

"So, why not head out to your next journey? Those tickets expire rather quickly," said Eil.

"Let's go," said Devlin.

"We should be back in eight minutes, right?" asked Demonica, making the portal.

"More like a week," said Eil, before the Freedom Forcers entered the portal.

The boring whiteness of Absence transformed into the vibrant red of Sel around the Freedom Forcers.

# Chapter 67: The Sinful Sorority

Tsul was whipping a demon when the Freedom Forcers arrived. She cracked her whip at his neck, cutting his head clean off once she took notice of them. Taking her time, she licked the blood off the tip of her whip and then tossed the body aside.

The body groped around for its head, found it and reattached it by searing the flesh together.

The demon smiled and bowed.

"I knew you would show up soon enough. This time there will be no escape," said Tsul, savoring the blood all the way to the grip of her whip.

"You're the one who ran away last time!" yelled Devlin.

Kaity raised her pistol, but her papa lowered it.

"We cannot intervene without being paid," said Kanasta.

"But Boss, don't we work for Devlin now?" asked Tempo.

"We discussed the payment, but we have yet to be formally hired. I'll protect him if need be, but I won't kill without proper compensation," said Kanasta.

"Hey Tempo, can you do that thing again?" asked Kawai, tapping his shoulder.

"Sure thing," said Tempo, coating Atatasuki in cold air.

Demonica put her hand on Devlin's shoulder, gently pushing him aside.

"I've needed to settle this for a while. Don't interfere," said Demonica to the Freedom Forcers.

Tsul thrust her whip forward while Demonica had her back to her. The whip shot straight through the traitor's heart and then bore into her neck.

"Auuh!" Demonica grasped the whip and jerked it up and down. Spikes shot out and the dark goddess pulled the whip deeper into herself, moaning as her insides were being ravaged. "Auuuh! You always knew how to give me such incredible pain," she said with her tongue hanging out.

"*CHAINS OF LUST!*" yelled Tsul.

Pink chains shot out from her aura and wrapped around the traitor's torso.

Tsul's head spun around to face Devlin. "Now it's time for you to die." She snapped her arm-whip.

The chains around Demonica dripped down her body as blood.

"Don't think you're strong enough to kill Devlin if you can't kill me," said Demonica with a jagged grin. Her body liquidated into blood but kept its shape. She walked nonchalantly toward her plaything, passing through the whip.

Tsul tugged furiously, but the whip would not budge.

Demonica grabbed her prey's arm and licked it with her bloody serpent tongue.

"What are you doing?" asked Tsul, taking a step back.

The droplets of blood on her arm pierced into her skin. Blood then sprayed out from her arm and swiftly encased it.

"What's going on?" asked Tsul with shrunken pupils.

The lusty demon's arm fell to the crispy ground, evaporating into steam.

"You're still too weak to defeat me," said Demonica, gripping her sister's chin.

Tsul bit Demonica's hand and then jumped back.

"Earlier she said she was part of the Sinful Sorority. Does that mean there are more like her? How many? Seven? It's seven, right?" asked Violet.

"Yes! We are the Seven Deadly Sisters of the Sinful Sorority! Which reminds me, Deerg, stop them!" yelled Tsul, each whip of her hair pointing to a different Freedom Forcer.

"Yes! I knew it!" cheered Violet.

"Sinful Sorority. Is that a joke? Did you all go to the same university? Are there even schools in Sel?" asked Karson.

"Urgh. A sorority is a gathering of women who share a fellowship! We sisters fight for a common goal. Do not mock our bonds! Deerg, where are you?" asked Tsul.

A short figure leaped out from behind a living rock, climbed on top of it, and surveyed the opponents.

Deerg was three and a half feet tall. The slender imp's skin was made of tempered gold. Multiple lines of paper currency branched out from her scalp as hair. A golden crown grew out from her forehead, embedded with an assortment of rare minerals. Her emerald eyes gleamed and sparkled as they scanned the Freedom Forcers. A single diamond tooth poked out of her wide smile. Pennies were placed where her nipples presumably would be. Her tail coiled into a dollar sign and jiggled as she quaked in excitement.

"Beautiful," said Kanasta, staring deeply into the green gems imbedded into the solid gold figure.

"That she is, son," said Deceivant, looking through his vest for a gift.

Deerg caressed her hair. "Hmmm…1,000 U.S. dollars, 100,219 yen, 884 Euros, 67,107 Indian rupees, and uh, 100,000 grains of rice. Or you can just pay me in gold," she said in a squeaky voice, her tongue dangling.

Tsul's whip seized a stray bill that fell from Deerg's hair. "All I have is a twenty," she said, carelessly handing her little sister the money.

Deerg snatched the money out of the whip and added it to her hair, all the while breathing intensely.

"Are you alright?" asked Deceivant, stepping up to the cutie.

"Like a hundred bucks," said Deerg, a trail of golden drool coming from her mouth.

Tsul's whip wrapped around Deerg and pulled her in. "That's all I have. I'm sure Etah can pay you the rest. Right now we need to stay focused. Kill them," she said, patting the little one's head.

"I'm going to rip off all your heads and sell them to Lord Etah!" exclaimed Deerg, standing on her tippy toes.

"Aww, so cute," said Deceivant with shimmering eyes.

"Cute doesn't begin to describe her. She's a financial paradise," said Kanasta with watery eyes.

"Hey, I'm way cuter. And gold looks way better on me than her. She's just another poser. She isn't cute at all, right brother?" asked Kawai, tugging at Exp 8's arm.

"Can we please stay focused?" asked Exp 8.

"You're way cuter, Sis, but that diamond cat-tooth she has is pretty damn cute," said Atatasuki.

Kawai pushed her flawed brother away with her tail. "Hrrgh, who asked you?"

"Diamond tooth, hmm. Anthrax, my dear nephew, do you have pliers?" asked Kanasta.

"Hey, my tools are only to be used to help people," said Anthrax, hiding his bag behind his back.

Deerg's eyes shifted to face NoOne. "You, blacky, what are you made of? What's it worth?"

"I'm made of shadows," said NoOne, pushing out his chest.

"Everyone has a shadow. How pathetically common. You're worthless," she said, turning her head away.

"If I know it's true, why does it still hurt?" asked NoOne in tears.

"Other than the robot family, you all look pretty worthless," said Deerg with a shrug.

"Fu-fu-family! She said we're a family! Do we look like a married couple? Do we? Do we?" asked Kawai, interlocking her fingers with Exp 8's."

"Gold and quicksilver are melded together in my mineral mountain," said Deerg.

"Wow, that sounds like destiny. It is destiny!" cheered Kawai.

"As for the rest of you. Organ selling is quite profitable, but I've got a better plan. I will turn all your bodies into gems and add them to my collection," said Deerg with a wide smile.

"Wait a second," said Deceivant walking up to the little demon. He put his hand behind her pointed ear.

"What is it? Is it a blemish? Is it rust?"

"Viola!" exclaimed Deceivant, revealing a quarter in the palm of his hand.

"You can make money out of thin air! You're so amazing!" exclaimed Deerg as she applauded with the tips of her fingers.

"And you're so adowable," said Deceivant, wiping away a passionate tear.

"Do it again! Again!" she cheered.

"Very well," said Deceivant with a smile. He reached behind her other ear and pulled out another quarter.

She swiped the coin from between his fingers. "Wow, so where's the other one?" she asked, scanning his hand.

"Oh, I only have one. I borrowed it from my son," said Deceivant.

"And now I'm taking it back," said Kanasta, swiping the quarter out from her hands.

"Look what you've done. Now she's going to cry," said Deceivant.

"I know. She'll probably sob out diamonds," said Kanasta with the slightest of smiles.

"How can you be so cruel?" asked Deceivant, patting Deerg's head.

"I'm going to slit her throat and take all the money she has," said Kanasta, rubbing his hands together in anticipation.

"You are no longer my son!"

"I wonder if she bleeds rubies."

"Hey, who needs a god of wealth when you've got the Sin of Greed? I'm going to melt her down until she's just precious metals," said Tempo, his hand aflame.

Kanasta grabbed his greedy comrade's arm. "Stop. First we need to shave her. Her hair is cash! We can't let it go to waste."

"Duly noted," said Tempo, taking a step toward the living gold mine.

"Give me one moment." Exp 8 crouched down to the little goddess. "Want to see something cool?"

"Does it involve money? Do I get to keep it?" she asked with shifty eyes.

"Of course, but you can't tell anyone about it, okay?"

"I promise," she said, offering her pinky.

Exp 8 wrapped his pinky around hers, sealing the deal. "You're not above bribes, I take it." He put out his hand and a swarm of dollar bills poured out of it.

"Plenty more where that came from."

"Sorry, Tsul. Got to go. Forgot had a prior arrangement," said Deerg as she added the dollars to her hair.

"Threat neutralized," said Exp 8.

"How did you get her to surrender?" asked Deceivant, spinning around.

"It doesn't matter. She's safe now," said Exp 8.

"Where did she go?" asked Deceivant.

"Abandoning the battlefield is tantamount to treason! I demand that you destroy them now!" yelled Tsul, stretching out her whip to stop the imp's departure.

"I was sufficiently bribed and Etah never gave me an allowance," said Deerg, sticking out her tongue.

"I gave you an order. Kill them now!" yelled Tsul, pink smoke slipping out from her clenched teeth.

"If you want them dead, kill them yourself. I'm going back home." Deerg hopped up and rode a wave of coins out of sight.

"Kanasta, what happened to you not killing without a paycheck?" asked Exp 8.

"The job pays for itself. That puts it in a bit of a gray area. Still, perhaps I did get a bit carried away. Devlin, you said you would pay us once we were out of Absence," said Kanasta.

"I did indeed. Consider yourself on retainer. Six-thousand an hour. But only so long as we are outside of Absence. And don't kill unnecessarily. You fight for me now, so you play by my rules," said Devlin.

"Understood. BoneSaw, start the clock. Viper Squad, we're back in business!" cheered Kanasta.

"Are you all done now? Edirp, go and kill them," said Tsul.

The ground around the Freedom Forcers sank. A lone figure stood on a thin pillar of molten rock in the center.

Edirp was made tall like a pillar by her spiked stiletto boots. Her dark purple skin radiated from within. Short grey locks of hair were adorned with peacock feathers. Bracelets made of bone-marrow adorned her scrawny arms. Her left breast was nearly three times the size of her right. Her crooked spine was held in place by a corset of bone. Purple blood oozed out of her chapped lips. The demon's swollen eyes were emphasized by a thin layer of black smoke.

"Of course I'll kill them. After all, it's not like you could. You are just lust, while I am pride, the Queen of Sel. Avert your eyes, if you can. It is an insult for such lowly beings to even gaze upon my insurmountable presence. It would be taboo for you to even think about me. You are mere outcasts who have been sent here as punishment for your sins. You are a microscopic nuisance to me," said Edirp, her voice fast-paced, haughty, and narcissistic.

"She's going down!" yelled Ego and Nina simultaneously.

Nina compulsively took off her shirt and tossed it at the vanity queen.

231

"*GROWING SELF-RESPEKT. BOMB*," said Ego.

The bomb inside the shirt expanded, enhancing its power.

"*Dynamite Body, Explosive Clothes!*" Nina pulled the trigger and the explosion consumed the abomination in a fiery blast.

"Is that all?" Edirp stood on the podium unaffected by their attacks.

"Enemy in sight," said Karson's head missile before slamming into the enemy soldier.

"Meaningless. All of your attacks are utterly meaningless."

"I've had enough of her," said Bob, before firing a laser through her heart. The laser disintegrated on contact.

"So pathetic. You are all too worthless to be bothered with," said Edirp, turning around.

"Oh no you don't. You're going to destroy them!" yelled Tsul.

"I can't believe I was summoned to stop this…well, I don't even know what to call it. Does Etah attack the wind every time a gust comes along? Absurd. I've got better things to do," said Edirp before vanishing in a Sel portal.

"Pfft, unreliable as usual! Ynottulg!" yelled Tsul.

The ground shook violently and parted at various places. It rose up from beneath the Freedom Forcers, revealing it was alive.

The team fell off the creature and toppled to the scorching floor of Sel.

"Ynottulg, eat them alive!" yelled Tsul.

The brown skinned creature was an eighty-foot wrecking ball of lard, with two itty-bitty wings on her molten back. The massive demon moved the flab covering her eyes with her short arms. In the place of eyes were three smaller mouths. Ynnotulg opened her stomach mouth.

"Wow, Sis, way to go. You've lost a ton of weight," said Demonica.

"You poor thing!" exclaimed Anthrax, hugging the gelatinous blob of misfortune.

"How can you touch something that hideous?" exclaimed Nina, almost retching.

Matteria looked away with tear-filled eyes.

"You just need some liposuction. Then you'll be all better." Anthrax opened up his medical bag. He took out a large tube and shoved it into one of many flaps.

It started sucking up the fat like a vacuum cleaner. The folds of the beast then wrapped around the tube and consumed it.

Anthrax turned away with a clenched fist. He then walked to Demonica. "I did all I could. I'm sorry, but your sister isn't going to make it," he said, his head lowered.

"Watch out!" yelled Matteria.

Anthrax was suddenly bitten from behind by a mouth hidden within the folds of fat.

"Let him go!" Matteria solidified the iron in the air into spears and sent them flying into the abomination.

"Why not just turn her into muck?" asked Exp 8.

"I can't alter matter of unconsenting living beings. Bob, can you save him?" asked Matteria.

"Already done," said Bob.

Ynottulg's arm collapsed to the ground. Fat gushed out of her wound and crawled toward the team.

Exp 8 jetted up to the demon goddess and sent an orb flying at her face.

Matteria rushed to his lover's side and ripped him out of the mouth's grip.

"I'm bleeding. Am I going to die again?" asked Anthrax in tears.

Matteria solidified the blood. "Nope. You're going to be just fine," he said, cradling his boyfriend.

"Hey guys, I could use a little back up here!" yelled Exp 8 as he strafed in the air to dodge the demon's rapid bites.

Kawai zoomed up to him. "Got it. *Sound Shot.*"

No sound wave was emitted.

"It's like we lost all our artifacts," said Kawai, her shoulders drooping.

"Not all of us! *Hardening Push!*" Nina pressed the ugly thing against the ground with a powerful gravity blast.

Ynottulg's dismembered arm suddenly lunged at the bald man.

"I don't have any artifacts!" yelled D.S., countering the rapid lunges of teeth with his scissors.

"Ego, did you place a tracer on Deerg?" asked Kanasta.

"Affirmative, Boss," said Ego with a salute.

"Good, use long-distance weapons only. Understood?" asked Kanasta.

"Roger," said Tempo, melting the living fat before it could reach him.

"Don't worry guys, I've got this! *INFERNO GAUNTLETS!*" yelled Atatasuki, wearing his flaming oven mitts.

"I leave it in your capable hands," said Riufen, scanning the area for a foe with a sword.

"Don't you even think of getting involved!" yelled Kawai as she distracted the enemy with dynamic flight patterns.

"I may not have any artifacts, but I can still fly!" Opti soared into the air, distracting the big lady further.

Karson switched out his Gatling guns for flamethrowers and torched the living fort's feet. "Nothing is working!"

Devlin pulled his greatest creation out of harm's way. Had he not intervened, his reckless invention would have been bit in half.

"Nice save," said Exp 8 before firing an orb into a lunging mouth.

"We can't lose here. Demonica, isn't there anything you can do?" asked Devlin.

"I can't kill her. It isn't that simple. I'll keep you protected though," said Demonica, slicing a severed gelatinous arm with her sharpened fingernails.

More fat fell to the ground and journeyed toward the team.

"Bullets aren't doing much," said Kaity, pumping the fat full of lead.

"Even its fat is absorbing my flames!" Tempo kicked a blob of fat.

The blob froze in place.

"Hmm, ice seems to work though."

"If we don't wrap this up, we'll be forced back to Absence without a single victory. Move aside everyone, let me deal with her," said Bob.

Exp 8, Kawai, and Opti zoomed behind Bob.

"This had better not be another trick," said Exp 8.

"Oh it is, and a rather simple one at that." Bob zoomed directly below the Sin of Gluttony.

All her mouths lunged at the floating dumpling at once.

Bob phased through them, having the bladed teeth slam into the scorched ground.

The ground beneath the god split in two, followed by cries of misery.

"So the residents are under the molten rock. That means Bob's strategy just killed them," said Exp 8 with eyes of horror.

"She is seriously in danger! Demonica, we have to save her," said Tsul.

"Nothing we can do now but watch and enjoy," said Demonica, biting her lip.

Tsul leaped into action, gripping onto her sister's massive arm with every appendage she had. "Climb up! I won't let you fall!"

"Bit heavy, isn't she?" asked Exp 8, gripping onto the bloated arm and keeping his jets at full throttle.

Ynottulg slipped out of Exp 8's grip. She then skidded down the chasm and into the pool of lava below.

Tsul was almost dragged in but released once the lava set her legs aflame. After the demon goddess spun her tentacles around to put out the flame, she sped up and out of the chasm.

Ynottulg tried to eat the lava but was consumed instead.

"Murderers! You killed her! You all killed her!" yelled Tsul, her whips flailing every which way.

"We didn't kill her. It was her own gluttony that caused her demise. I understand entirely. I promise I won't suffer the same fate," said Atatasuki, lowering his head.

"Another casualty. When the hell will it stop!" yelled Exp 8, slamming his foot down.

"This wasn't supposed to happen! Yvne, kill them!" yelled Tsul in tears.

Yvne landed next to her beautiful sister.

The Sin of Envy was large, green-skinned, and ancient. Two deer-like horns came out from between her long thin strands of silver hair. Wrinkles rode up from the tip of her toes to the top of her forehead. The triple breasted woman's bottom lip quivered. Her tiny pupils had a permanent glimmer of longing and were fixated on Ynottulg.

"What incredible agony. Death...what's it like? I want it. I want to feel it," she said, her curious voice almost like a whisper.

Devlin's fist trembled with rage. "How could someone so pitiful become a god!" he yelled, directing his fist at the privileged wretch.

"Huh? Me?" Yvne pointed at herself.

"Yeah you!" yelled Devlin.

"Are you envious of me? This is the first time anyone's been jealous of my meager accomplishments."

"If you can be a god, then why not me!" yelled Devlin.

"Oh bother, now I feel covetous of your envy," said Yvne, lowering her head.

"She's pathetic," said NoOne.

Yvne spread her wings and landed next to the handsome and charismatic young man. "I heard you were rebels. I wish I could lead a passionate revolution."

"Stop chatting and kill them," said Tsul, chewing on her whip hair.

"Don't you think they should be free!? All these people suffering for crimes they can't even remember?" asked Exp 8.

"Never crossed my mind. If only I could feel that despair again. If only I could go back into that uncertain ascension," said Yvne, staring off into space.

"You know, nothing is more uncertain than a rebellion. Whether we win or lose. Who will die? What happens to us if we win? Where will our revolutionary spirit lead us politically? When, if ever, will our revolt gain public support? How will we create a new society should we succeed? It's all up in the clouds," said Deceivant.

"The clouds...I don't see them. Not here. I wish I could watch them on their journey, just once more," said Yvne, her eyes aching with longing.

"Take out your weapon! Destroy them all!" yelled Tsul.

"We are going after Etah. Once we win, we can take you to Lum to see as many clouds as you want," said Devlin.

"I've thought about being the ruler of Sel, but I've never acted on it. We share the same ambition," said Yvne, beaming at the divine youth.

"That we do," said Devlin.

"Then we're rivals?"

"I guess so," said Devlin with a sly smile.

"An ever-growing conflict of envy, that's what a rivalry is. And now I have it. I feel warm," said Yvne, touching her chest.

Tsul rushed to her airhead sister. "Are you going to fight them or not?"

"Not right now. I want to be alone with this feeling." Yvne walked away, holding her chest.

"Face it sister, the fall of Etah is coming," said Demonica.

"Regna is off fighting Sinner's Fury, but there's still one more sin here. Htols will make all of you into statues," said Tsul.

"You mean she got lost again?" asked Demonica.

"Yes…she got lost," said Tsul, her hand pressed against her forehead.

Htols' grey and meek spider-like body was distorted into the shape of a chair. Her long face drooped, held up by four tiny hands, which were supported by two massive hands. These two hands leaned against her knees. The wretch would collapse if not for having four legs to ground herself.

"What a waste of time," said Htols in a wispy and dreary voice that dragged at each syllable.

"Everyone, stand back. Let me handle her," said Violet.

"You heard her!" hollered Devlin.

Violet approached the lazy wretch.

"So many enemies. Go away," said Htols.

"I know how you can reach your true potential," said Violet.

"Twenty words or less," said Htols.

"Come to Absence and we'll take you to someone who can help you reach a calm state of mind."

Htols made body motions that Violet assumed was a yes.

"This is completely absurd! How flimsy are your loyalties?" asked Tsul.

"Violet, grab her!" yelled Demonica.

The world of Sel dissipated before the Freedom Forcers as they were forcibly brought back to Absence.

# Chapter 68: The First Guardian

The team arrived along with Htols.

"Oh no! They brought in an enemy!" shrieked Eil.

"Why would Sel bother to spy on Absence? You are no threat," said Demonica.

"Ah! Your words pierce me like an arrow! You have a point though. I guess she can stay."

"BoneSaw, turn the timer off. You can put it back on when we next return to Sel," said Kanasta, patting his ally.

Violet walked up to the Second Guardian.

"Don't bother, he can't hear you," said Devlin.

"Yes, but he can sense my spirit." Violet projected her astral self and bowed down. "Oh great and powerful one, can you help us?"

The statue holding the guard suddenly came to life. "The guru is neither great nor powerful. It is simply Void."

"Void, can you enlighten Htols with your unsurpassable neutrality?"

The guard sat down and crossed his legs. "If you stay here, a neutral existence will follow. That is what the guru has conveyed."

"I didn't hear anything," said Devlin.

"Of course not. The great guru lives solely through example. As such Void does not speak. Oh, the guru has re-entered his deep meditation. I'll have to fill in for the time being. Do you have any other questions?" asked the guard, turning once more to face the demon god.

Htols stared blankly.

"Ah, I can hear the song of your soul. It longs to live an existence of inaction. You've come to the right place. It is impossible to accrue karma in Absence and past karmas are naturally shed. This allows each and every resident of Absence to one day reach moksha," said the guard.

Htols' eyes sparkled with intrigue.

Violet took in a deep breath. "Moksha isn't for everyone. It isn't right to force them into enlightenment."

"It's not force; it's more a process of ease. And I agree, moksha should not be the end goal. When reaching moksha the soul is trapped in bliss. It is only by breaking beyond the boundaries of that bliss where one reaches true liberation. Nirvana means extinction. It is a state of infinite power but no will. This is the true goal that we should aspire to," said the guard.

"Enough arguing. Violet communicated with the Second Guardian; doesn't that mean we get a pass?" asked Devlin.

"Yes it does." The guard lifted up Void.

237

Devlin grabbed the now-visible pass. "Good work."

"My pleasure," said Violet with a nod.

"Yes, we make a great team!" exclaimed Ada, grabbing her son's hand.

Devlin pulled away. "Yeah, yeah, whatever. I'm going to go ask the Fourth Guardian for its ticket. The rest of you, stay here."

"And where do you expect to find the guardian?" asked Demonica.

"I can't find it, the guardian must make its presence known to me," said Devlin.

"What do you seek?" asked a deep, guttural voice.

Devlin turned around to face the Fourth Guardian.

The guardian was a seven-foot skull with curved horns. With nostrils above the mouth, the skull looked like that of a dragon. A hooded figure stood atop the massive skull.

"You want my ticket? Why should I assist any of you?" asked the skull.

"We seek to stop the Lord of Hate."

"That does not concern the gods of Absence," said the skull.

"Don't be so sure. Once Etah has taken over Lum, it will only be a matter of time before he comes here with his army," said Devlin.

"Etah has no way of entering Absence without our permission. He is of no threat to us," said the skull.

"So you really did allow him to enter! Why?" asked Devlin, holding in his anger.

"Why we chose what we have chosen is none of your concern," said the skull.

Exp 8 approached from behind. "Let me have a try."

"Go ahead," said Devlin.

"What's your name?"

"I am Loyal," responded the skull.

"I'm Exp 8. We're trying to free the people of Sel from Etah's oppressive reign. There's no harm in helping us."

"My loyalties belong solely to Absence."

"Billions are suffering! They are scared and confused. Why won't you help us stop it?"

"I have no compassion left, only undying loyalty to this realm. You cannot sway me."

"I saw one of the guards in Sel. He was working with Etah. Care to explain?"

"What you claim is not possible."

Bob rose out of the ground.

"Another one?" asked Loyal.

238

"Are you certain Etah has no way to reach here? The angels thought he would be unable to reach Lum, but yet he's found a way again and again. Maybe he doesn't have an Absence god in Sel, but what if there's one in Lum, locked away?" asked Bob with a grin.

"You don't even know how I got here. Seems this place isn't as inaccessible as it claims to be," said Demonica.

The skull breathed flames through its nostrils, searing the ground and revealing a ticket below.

Bob swiped the ticket and handed it to Devlin with a bow.

"Move along," said Loyal.

"I haven't forgotten what you've done. But thanks for the help," said Exp 8.

"Good work," said Devlin.

"You are infinitely welcome," said Demonica, seizing her man in a sudden embrace.

"Hey, you obtained a pass from everyone, good job," said Eil, signaling his guard to give a thumbs-up.

"The second pass we used seemed to last a lot longer than the first one. How long before we're forced back here?" asked Devlin.

"I wasn't quite done. You've gathered a two day pass from each guardian, but…don't you want a week pass?"

"Your two day passes don't even last ten minutes."

"If you want one, then you must fight me."

"Why? For all I know you're lying to us about the weekly passes."

"Because humans need a healthy dose of violence to keep their bloodlust sustained. I don't know; I'm just bored. But I only want to fight one of you at a time, okay?"

"So you were a human. That explains a lot."

"I'll kill him," said Tempo. "I am tired of his nonsense!"

"Without getting paid and without orders from our client?" asked Kanasta, grabbing his hot-headed ally's shoulder.

"Of course not. Hey Exp 8, pay me so I can get us a ticket out of here," said Tempo.

"Sure." Exp 8 handed him eight hundred dollars.

"You stole that from Deerg, didn't you?" asked Deceivant.

"Doesn't matter. Let's get this over with and get out of here," said Exp 8.

"I'll try not to melt the ticket when I kill you," said Tempo, his arm aflame.

The guard took off its black glove. Underneath was a hand constructed of metallic needles. The steel quills spread out, each targeting a different vital spot.

"*TEMPERATURE FALL*." Tempo's body became coated in a cold aura, freezing the spines before they could touch him.

"Is that the best you can do?" asked Tempo, using an ice needle like a toothpick.

The spikes exploded, causing the assassin to lose his balance and fall to the ground.

Tempo kicked off the moment his heel hit the floor. "*FROST BITE*." Ice coated his teeth into blades before plunging into the guard's arm.

"I suppose now would be an apt time to inform you the name of my guard. Its name is Needle. It is a fully obedient and loyal guard who wholeheartedly believes in the system of Absence. It doesn't talk, so please pardon the late introduction!" hollered Eil.

Needle tore the attacker off with a gloved hand. It then took off its cloak, revealing its bullet-shaped body was composed of needles. The guard's vacant eye gleamed like the glint of a weapon.

"Well, well, this should be int—"

Needle's arm shot itself down the resident's throat, filling him with needles. The guard rammed into the mortal who quickly coated his back in ice as a defensive measure.

"Well-played, but once I've melted these—"

The needles inside his stomach exploded.

Tempo's crimson eyes fizzled out. His head drooped. The seasoned assassin fell face-first to the ground.

"Is he dead?" asked Kaity, tugging on Kanasta's arm.

"A split second is all it takes. Everyone, stay vigilant," said Kanasta.

"I'll fight him next," said Nina before kicking the tattered body out of the way.

"Come on, man. Stay with me," said Ego, trying to keep his brother's spasms under control.

"Guard, throw me," commanded Eil.

Needle picked up its master and flung him.

Eil gnawed at the woman's succulent arm, biting through skin and tendons.

"Get off!" Nina ripped him off and tossed him against the floor.

The guard shot out a barrage of needles from his hand.

Nina caught each quill as it zoomed toward her. They exploded in her grip, sending pieces into her enticing hand and curvaceous torso.

"That's the last time you'll touch me." Nina took off her niqab and flung it over the guardian. She tugged on the cloth, bringing the needle guard to the ground. She then pulled the tattered cloak off the guard's face, all the while removing her shirt sensually.

The guard fired an extra large needle at the mortal's chest.

Nina wrapped her shirt around the projectile, spun it around, and released it.

The needle went into Eil's scalp before exploding.

"Congratulations, you win," said Eil unscathed. "Here is your prize." He coughed up yet another ticket.

"I assume you want to fight the Second Guardian now. Well, let me warn you, his guard is ten times more powerful than mine."

Needle lowered its head in shame.


"Let me try to heal him," said Anthrax, crouching down near Tempo.

"Stay with me. You can't go like this. Come on, we've made it through worse," said Ego, shaking his brother's shoulders.

Tempo's body vanished in Ego's arms.

"What just happened?" asked Ego.

"Where did he go?" asked Anthrax, unraveling a large wrap.

"Your buddy is dead. We can't leave corpses lying around in Absence, so we got rid of the body," said Eil.

"Bring him back. He was here a moment ago. Too strong...Tempo's too strong to die like that! Where the hell is he?" asked Ego, gripping onto the skull.

"He's moved to the world beyond the afterlife. I don't know much more than that," said Eil.

"This can't be real. Are we going to die just like last time? How could Tempo have died before me? It doesn't make sense!" yelled Ego, slamming his hand down.

Kanasta picked Ego off his feet. "Even in death he stays concealed. Tempo, you truly are a great assassin. Join me in a silent farewell," he said with a proud smile.

The Viper Squad sent Tempo off with a salute. The rest of the Freedom Forcers soon followed.

Ego broke down in tears.

Kaity approached him from behind and embraced him. "It's okay to cry. He was our big brother," she said with watery eyes.

"No. He'd be disgusted with us if he saw us like this." Ego wiped away the droplets of shame. "We have to move on without him. What kind of assassin gets shaken up over someone's death?" he asked with a strained smile.

"I should feel bad that we lost a teammate, but I feel a lot safer now that he's gone. Still, he saved Atatasuki's life," said Kawai.

"Tempo was beginning to change for the better. I won't forget his sacrifice," said Exp 8, holding his sister close to him.

"I need to make something extremely clear to all of you: Tempo won't be the only casualty we will suffer. If we are going to take down Etah, we all have to be willing to lay down our lives," said Devlin.

"Then you're on your own. I only went after the needle guard because I knew I could take him," said Nina.

"Hey, that reminds me! I have bracelets!" exclaimed Atatasuki.

"Ugh. This is serious. Are you willing to die for our victory?" asked Devlin.

"Not going to happen. I refuse to leave Kawai behind again," said Atatasuki.

"You're being too hasty, Devlin. We should avoid any battles we can. There must be another way to win favor with the guardians of Absence," said Exp 8.

"Hello! Can I have everyone's attention? I have bracelets!" hollered Atatasuki.

"Yes, and we really don't give a damn," said Devlin.

"What about team unity, a promise of victory and a way to meet up if we get separated; does that interest you?" asked Atatasuki.

"Very well, you have the floor," said Devlin, stepping back into the crowd.

"I made allies with some visitors in Lum. One guy in particular is super cool. He said, 'We are all students. We all learn from one another. I only know what I have been taught. Singh, if you treat every being you meet as a teacher, you will be amazed at the lessons you learn.' Badass, right? He's a teacher and a swordsman."

"Sounds like a great man," said Riufen, now fully attentive.

"Who's Singh?" asked Kawai.

"Yeah, he's totally an awesome guy. I don't remember his name, but he gave me these bracelets as a symbol of friendship and as a means to enter his refuge. These bracelets hold important religio-spiritual significance. But don't ask me what that significance is because I have no idea," said Atatasuki.

"They are circlets from the Sikh tradition. They have many symbolic meanings, but most importantly they serve as a reminder. They remind us that God is watching. When we look to our hands and see the circlet, we should contemplate on whether our actions are virtuous or sinful," said Violet.

"A means to re-evaluate our choices, eh? I'm down with that. Hand me one," said Exp 8.

"Not one for jewelry, but I'll make an exception this time," said Nina, already putting one on.

"Whoa, when did you take it?" asked Atatasuki.

"Perhaps you weren't paying attention. Or maybe you forgot," said Nina with a smirk.

"Good work, Failed Experiment. Everyone, let's brainstorm a bit. We'll need a back-up plan in case the angels turn against us," said Devlin, holding out his hand.

"I see no reason why they would. If anything, taking Etah down would end any tension the goddesses have with our presence in Lum," said Violet, placing her new circlet next to her old one.

"I suppose this will be a temporary substitute for our formal contract," said Kanasta, tossing his fellow Viper Squad members the circlets.

"Yay! Look, Sefi-chan, we're matching!" cheered Kaity, pressing their bracelets together.

Ego walked up to Atatasuki. "Hey, can I have two? I…I want to wear an extra one…for Tempo. So I don't forget. Not like I could." He wiped his eyes as they started to tear up.

Kaity grabbed her partner's hand and smiled at him.

"Yeah, of course," said Atatasuki, almost falling over as he rushed to give him the extra bracelet.

"Thanks. You're a cool guy," said Ego with a smile as he slid the bracelet down his arm.

"You seem alright too," said Atatasuki, giving Ego a fist bump.

"Oh yeah, this goes great with my outfit," said Matteria.

"Oh, sorry Bob, I don't think I can put it on you," said Atatasuki.

"Worry not. I'll take your gesture of kindness as a treasure of its own," said Bob with a grin.

Kanasta popped open BoneSaw's top and fitted the bracelet inside.

"I'll take it for now, but if I transform again—I'll try to remember to take it off beforehand," said Anthrax.

"I'm really one of the good guys, aren't I?" asked NoOne, his wrist growing fingers that gripped his heroic circlet.

"Is the one who gave you these treasures the same person who handed that sword down to you?" asked Riufen, cupping his hands together.

"Whoa, you're right, I do have a sword!" exclaimed Atatasuki.

"You should take care of it. That blade is representational of your respect for the one who gave it to you," said Riufen.

"Does that mean I can't fight with it?" asked Atatasuki.

"It means you must fight with it," said Riufen with a nod.

"Awesome! Oh, you want one too?" asked Atatasuki, handing out a bracelet to Demonica.

"Of course. I'm just as much a part of the team as anyone here," said Demonica.

"You've still got some left over. Good. We'll need them when we get some demi-gods on our side," said Devlin.

"Yeah, but I probably shouldn't be the one to keep them," said Atatasuki.

"Agreed," said Kawai.

"Violet, can you keep the remaining seven for me?" asked Atatasuki.

"It would be my honor," said Violet with a smile.

"Hey, Sis, thanks for helping me train," said Exp 8.

"Of course. I can't leave you with any weaknesses! You're already starting to get the hang of it," said Kawai before flooring her beloved's tail to the ground. "But, I've still got you beat," she said with a grin.

"Payment time." Exp 8 embraced his little teacher and pet her.

"Auuh! Amazing!" exclaimed Kawai, hugging back with her stubby arms.

Devlin raised his arm. "We will take down Etah!"

Exp 8 smirked and then shoved his arm in the air. "These bracelets are a reminder of what we stand for! They are proof of us being honorary Freedom Forcers!"

It wasn't long before all the Freedom Forcers raised their symbols of unity up toward the void above Absence.

# Chapter 69: The Second Guardian

"Hey look! Another one!" exclaimed D.S.

The Freedom Forcers turned around to see the second guard.

"I am Occupy and this is Void," said the guard.

"Namaste," said Violet with a bow.

"Namaste," said Occupy in a soothing youthful voice.

"And let me guess, we have to beat you in order to get your ticket, right?" asked Devlin.

"Is that a problem?"

"Why do you guys want to fight anyway, aren't you supposed to practice neutrality?" asked Deceivant.

"There are many reasons. For some, there is excitement to be found in battle. I personally seek to pacify you. Exps are quick to start a fight and hesitant to end one. Such behavior could create problems in Absence. Ah, but there is yet one last reason. As the eyeball said, Etah may be planning on attacking Absence. It would be wise to practice for the coming battle, even if it is highly unlikely that such a battle would occur. Now, who wishes to test their might against my guru?" asked Occupy with a blissful smile.

Anthrax stepped up. "Since it's for a good cause, I'll fight. I'm having difficulty containing myself. Best to get a clear head before we fight Etah."

"Many of you harbor aggression in dire need of an outlet," said Occupy, limbering up his body and focusing his mind with a sun salutation routine.

"Be careful, Thraxy. Are you sure you want to fight him?" asked Matteria.

Anthrax handed Matteria his bracelet. "There is no need to worry. I can't die in my sick form. Everyone stay back. Once my mind is taken over by the virus, I see neither friends nor foes. All I see are bodies in need of improvements.

DISEASE TAKEOVER."

The doctor took out a needle and injected the full vial into his neck. The concentrated disease spread throughout his blood stream. He tore off his clothes as he transformed into his corrosive sick form.

His lean body twisted and expanded as globs of bloated flesh erupted all over the boy's body. The bloated flesh hardened in some areas and burst open in others, oozing pus and blood that drizzled down the wretch's body. Unable to adjust to the developments, Anthrax's mouth tore open and twisted diagonally. Once the new perspective had taken root in his psyche, his large, cataract-laden eye searched for a victim. He raised his motorcycle of a right arm as his fingers locked in a permanent fist.

"You are the embodiment of dukkha, my friend. You must be quite the ascetic to endure such pain on behalf of others. I have much to learn from you," said Occupy, folding his hands before bowing.

Amthraahksh responded with a pained, wet, and guttural battle cry before charging at the guard.

The guard leaped over the plagued ascetic and landed behind him, holding Void out in front of him. "To ensure that there are no escapes, under the seemingly infinite bottom, sides, and sky of Absence there are various transporters. Whatever comes in contact with them will be instantly transmitted to the teleporter on the opposite side. Here, I'll show you." He dropped the weighty guru.

The rounded rock fell, breaking through the floor of Absence.

Amthraahksh turned around and rushed the guard. Suddenly there was a gaping hole in his stomach. He touched his festering insides curiously.

Void rained down again and again, obliterating more of the being's physical body with each trip.

Amthraahksh's legs were destroyed. He collapsed face-first to the ground.

"Shouldn't we do something?" asked Exp 8.

"No, this is his battle. We cannot interfere," said Riufen.

"He knows we're counting on him. He won't let us down," said Matteria.

Occupy put out his hand and grabbed Void as it shot down. "Great guru, you are covered in blood. This will not do. Please, Teacher, let me clean you off." The monk wiped the blood off the rock with gentle swipes of his fingers.

Amthraahksh's fleshy bits molded together into two new legs.

"Still in shape to fight? Most impressive." Occupy tossed Void at a slanted angle into the ground. "Even I don't know where the guru will come from. Isn't the uncertainty exhilarating?"

Amthraahksh stood up as his stomach wound closed.

"I've never witnessed such rapid regeneration. Your power over the mind is phenomenal. This will be a true test of my training."

Amthraahksh shot his arm at the guard who quickly hopped back to avoid it.

"DE-OCCUPY, BODY." Occupy pointed at his attacker over and over.

Amthraahksh's organs vanished one by one. His whole body became limp.

"A yogi must be able to empty the mind of wayward thoughts. My master's guidance has awakened my ability to empty both mental and physical constructs. Can you conquer the power I've uncovered?" asked Occupy as the living plague loomed closer.

Void zoomed by, knocking Amthraahksh's head clear off.

The diseased-ridden freak's neck elongated until it reattached to the head. It then contorted back to its original position.

"So, you still refuse to—"

Void zoomed past Occupy, breaking his neck.

The monk fell to the floor, his eyes peaceful as ever.

"How do we stop this damn thing?" asked Devlin as he jumped around frantically with Kaity in his arms.

"Who cares?" asked Bob as the heavy stone phased through him.

"I'll stop it," said D.S. as he sprawled correction tape over the ground.

Void zoomed right into the mesh of tape, breaking through it with ease.

"He's unstoppable!" yelled D.S., running away with his arms in the air.

Occupy pushed off the ground and grabbed his guru as it skyrocketed toward him.

"I shouldn't have been so careless. It's over. You have won." Occupy fixed his broken neck. "You've earned it." He handed the weekly pass to the young man with golden eyes.


"Pure blind luck! Don't think it will last," said Eil, showing up behind Devlin.

"He's coming this way. How are we going to get Thraxy back to normal?" asked Matteria.

"I'll keep him busy," said Riufen, drawing out his spine.

Amthraahksh leaped over the swordsman. By the time he hit the ground, his body was splitting apart in the middle. His corrosive flesh quickly reconnected as he raised his fist over the frail birdman.

Opti covered his face, bracing for impact. Pesi took over and jumped back. "You moronic, imbecilic, simple-minded buffoon! When someone attacks you, move! We share the same body, and I'll be damned forever in eternal hellfire if I let you ruin it!"

"There's no need to fight him. He can't move from that spot," said NoOne, sitting on the ground.

Amthraahksh's feet were gripped directly by NoOne's shadow.

"It's going to be a bit hard to keep this up. I'm used to having more shadows to work with," said NoOne.

"Everyone, we should stay at a safe distance for now. One of us will have to get injured in the next fight in order to get him to come to his senses," said Devlin.

"Tehtehteh! You'll have a hard time with that. The next Guardian isn't even a tenth as powerful as Void!" exclaimed Eil.

"I could cause some injuries," said Bob, readying a laser.

"Of course Anthrax will come to his senses eventually. Let's stay on target," said Devlin.

"If we continue, we're all going to die miserable deaths. We need to focus our minds," said NoOne.

"He does have a point. Occupy most likely isn't the only guard with mental powers. What do you suggest?" asked Deceivant.

"I suggest we let Violet come up with a solution," said NoOne.

"We could meditate. It wouldn't have to be a complete session. Just long enough to reconnect us with our inner sparks," said Violet.

"Yay! Come on, Pharma! Let's do it! It will be fun!" cheered D.S.

"May I join?" asked Occupy, folding his legs into full lotus.

"It would be our honor," said Violet with a cheerful nod.

"Come on everyone, it's good to clear our thoughts if nothing else," said Exp 8, sitting down next to Opti.

"Not usually one for meditation, but I've got a nice cushion beneath me," said Kawai, plopping down on Exp 8's lap.

"Oh yeah! Let's do this!" cheered Atatasuki.

"I'd rather not waste my time. I'm going to survey the area," said Nina.

"There's nothing to survey. It's best if we all sit down and relax for a while. That means everyone!" hollered Devlin.

The team sat down in a circle.

"Occupy. Would you lead us?" asked Violet.

"It would be an honor."

Occupy lifted his hood. Beneath was a shaved head, a white tilak above a pair of peaceful amber eyes and a placid yet loving smile.

"Join hands with the person next to you, with the receiving palm upright and the giving palm down. Close your eyes. Feel the flow of energy. Will the energy to flow to the person to your right and accept the energy flow from the person to your left. Realize that you are a conduit. Your own energy body interacts and influences the energy bodies of others. Good. Now, center your mind on your goal in this life, whatever it may be. Project your energy toward your goal. In your mind's eye, imagine a growing light in front of you. This light is your inner sun. It illuminates your path. As you focus more energy into the light, it grows larger. Breathe in deeply. Retain your breath. Feel the peace around you, the calming lull of Absence. Release your breath as energy. Now, visualize the ball of energy rising up before bringing it over you. This vital energy enveloping your body is a powerful gravity of bliss. This bliss isn't a euphoric bliss, like what you may have experienced in Lum. It is contentment. You feel at peace. Your goal, which was once the guiding path of your life has now merged with your inner essence, becoming pure energy."

"That's enough," said Devlin. "This meditation is over."

"Where are we?" asked Atatasuki, looking around in a daze.

"You are home," said Occupy with a loving smile.

"Not another word! You're trying to weaken our resolve. That whole meditation was a sham!" yelled Devlin.

"I modified it for this group, but it is still a variation of the standard meditation service I give," said Occupy.

"Hey, Atatasuki, you remember me, right?" asked Kawai.

"Yeah, of course I know you, Sis. But who are they?" asked Atatasuki, pointing at the strangers around him.

"What did you do to him?" asked Kawai.

"Ow! Careful, your tail is crushing mine," said Exp 8.

"The air of Absence. There's something about it. It makes us complacent. It weakens our resolve. That meditation took down our mind's defenses. Occupy was trying to pacify us," said Devlin.

"Ah, see what discoveries you can make with a clear mind?" asked Occupy.

"NoOne's idea wasn't even his, was it? You put it in his head, didn't you?" asked Devlin.

"You are very, very clever. I am impressed," said Occupy.

"You underestimate us. We won't give up so easily," said Devlin.

"Know that all I do, I do on behalf of the residents of Absence. Not for their egos, of course, but for the inner essence imprisoned by their egos. Enduring a suffering existence for infinity is no way to live. Absence is our refuge from life. Once here, there is no need to live again."

"Says you. The idea of a static existence terrifies me. And I refuse to live in solace while others are enslaved. This place is dangerous. If we stay here too long, we will forget what we stand for as Freedom Forcers," said Exp 8.

"We need to find the Third Guardian as soon as possible," said Devlin.

"Hey, Pharma, wake up," said D.S., shaking his pal.

"I'm awake. I suppose I got a bit lost in the moment," said Pharma.

Violet's eyes opened. "I knew you had potential."

"The third one was watching me fight the First Guardian. He should be close by," said Nina.

The Third Guardian appeared directly in front of her, along with its guard.

# Chapter 70: The Third Guardian

"So, you're going to fight me? Very well, but I only fight women," said Plagiarism.

Nina reflexively covered her chest.

Violet approached the reptilian skull, who was seated on the top of a cloaked figure's head. "Then I'll battle you."

"Perorororo, your skin is such a pretty color…like a…oh no. I can't even think of something to compare it to. Have I forgotten all the splendors of nature?" asked Plagiarism.

"Stop being dramatic," said the guard.

"Dramatic! I'm not being dramatic! Plum! Yes, like a plum! That's perfect."

"Plum's aren't light blue. Her skin is more like a blueberry than a plum."

"Yes, yes, pretty like a plum and supple like a plum too. With glistening eyes of gold, like a…hmm, can't think of anything gold other than, well, gold."

"Ugh, I hate this job," said the guard, lowering his head.

"Ah, yes, yes! Golden like a banana in the sunlight. Perororo, I'm quite the wordsmith, aren't I, Crystal?"

"And I hate my name too. What kind of guy is called Crystal? It's pathetic," said the guard in a depressed, rough around the edges tone.

"Please, my allies need to escape this place. Won't you help us?" asked Violet.

"Look at those eyes, that expression…is it longing, devotion, perhaps excitement?" asked Plagiarism, scratching his head with his tongue.

"It's more of a pleading look, if you ask me. Why don't we help her out?" asked Crystal.

"No, no. That won't do at all. I want to see her expressions firsthand. I want those eyes to shiver with tears."

"You mean swell up with tears, right?"

"Is that what they do? Yes, yes! Swell up, big and round…like a bumblebee. Aha, yes! Another thing that is gold. My memories are coming back to me like…well, karma. Make her bleed a bit, would you? I want to hear her sing with pain!"

"Whimper. Nobody sings in pain."

"That's enough out of you. We'll see who's right. I hope I'll be able to taste the shock before it leaves. Let's see how many emotions you can bring out in her. I'll count. Behold mortal, this is my most powerful attack. Guard, attack her!" yelled Plagiarism, smacking the guard with his tongue.

"Ugh, fine." Crystal raised his hands and crystals shot out from his sleeves.

Violet slid out of the way of the assault.

"Keep firing! Her eyes are too placid, calm like a river. I want some ripples!" yelled Plagiarism.

The two mineral streams intersected, fanning out in multiple directions.

One of the serrated crystals pierced into Violet's ankle.

She toppled down.

"No, no! If she runs, then I can't see her face. I completely missed her pained expression! Hurt her again! This time make sure she's facing us!" yelled Plagiarism.

Crystal stopped firing and approached the injured innocent. "There, is that close enough?"

"Yes, yes. But she isn't afraid. Why isn't she bouncing? Make her sweat with terror!" yelled Plagiarism.

"Intimidating a kind-hearted person…it doesn't feel right."

"Are you disobeying me? If you are, I want a look! Defiance is such a splendor to behold!" exclaimed Plagiarism, licking under the guard's hood.

"I apologize. I'll do as you ask." A pearlescent sword came out from the guard's sleeve.

Violet held her cross out in front of her. "God protect me."

"God is indifferent to our suffering. Your faith will fail you," said Crystal before bringing the sword down.

"Suspense!" cheered Plagiarism.

Wires shot out of the ground beneath the devotee, shielding her from the attack.

"Curses! No, no! I missed your expression because of your hood. You must have been quite surprised," said Plagiarism.

"You're rather powerful," said the guard.

"Ever since I came here I've felt a greater bond to my spiritual self." Violet clenched her fist tightly. "God, lay waste to my enemies."

"Ooh, what is that emotion? I can't pinpoint it," said Plagiarism.

Wires shot out from below the guard and wrapped around him. Electricity burst out from the wires as they tightened their grip.

"That won't work on me. Not anymore. **CRYSTAL FIELD**," said the guard.

The crystals in the ground expanded.

Violet leaped back to avoid getting stabbed by the growing minerals.

A barrage of crystals then shot out from the guard's sleeves, aimed at her forehead.

Wires came out from below and swirled around to protect the devotee as she landed.

The mess of wires around the guard slammed him into the ground.

Violet rushed into the guard but was unable to knock him down.

"What's the point of this? Why do you want to escape this place?" asked Crystal, creating thin spears with his free hand.

Violet grabbed one of the spears and tried to wrestle it out of the guard's grip.

"You may have determination, but you can't overpower me." He tore the weapon out from the fighter's grip and slammed his fist into her belly.

Violet dropped to her knees in pain.

"Open mouth, a bit of drool, shrunken pupils. Such a great expression!" cheered Plagiarism.

Crystal pushed off the ground with one spear and lunged the other at the wounded woman below him.

Violet grabbed the spear and then split apart from her astral body. Her astral form held onto the spear, leaving her physical body free to move around.

"Never seen that before," said Crystal.

Violet leaped up to the guard and plunged her scimitar into his throat. The blade cut through the cloak but slid off his fortified neck.

"This is a waste of time. I can't die."

Jagged crystals tore through the front of the guard's cloak and pierced into Violet's chest.

The devotee's astral form tore the spear from the guard's grip and brutally assaulted him with it.

Violet collapsed to the ground, her dress now riddled with holes. There was no blood or wounds to be seen. Her chest had been protected by a row of wires.

The guard was pushed back by the spear assault but quickly countered with his own spear. Plagiarism toppled off his head and fell to the floor.

"No, no. Don't pick me up. I have a splendid view of her succulent legs from here," said the reptilian skull.

The astral Violet kicked off the ground. The spear in its energy-based hand fell to pieces.

"You can't use me against myself." Crystal flung his spear at the beautiful warrior.

Wires burst out from beneath Violet and grabbed the spear.

"Ugh, can you give up already?" asked Crystal.

A fountain of wires erupted from below the guard and swiftly encased him.

Violet reconnected with her astral body and approached the Third Guardian. "Surrender, Plagiarism."

"Perororo. Just because you defeated my guard doesn't mean you can defeat me."

His tongue shot out of his mouth and latched onto the tantalizing woman's cross.

BoneSaw leaped forward and cut Plagiarism's tongue off. It then jumped back and tagged Violet gently with its saw.

"You've done enough. Let BoneSaw take care of the rest," said Kanasta.

"I understand." Violet joined the rest of the group.

"Couldn't you have gotten a bit more beat up? My shadow is having difficulty keeping hold of our sick little doctor," said NoOne.

"My apologies," said Violet with a bow.

"She came out alive. That's what matters," said Devlin.

Violet ran up to her protector and embraced him. She gave him a soft kiss on the cheek.

"Huh?" said Devlin, disoriented.

Violet beamed up at him. "Thank you."

"For what?" asked Devlin, trying to pull her arms off.

"It was your wires that protected me. I love many gods…but you, I love you the most." Violet pulled away with purple flushed cheeks.

"Fathers protect their children. Think nothing of it."

"Foul play! Foul play! Attacking my guard and keeping her safe so I couldn't behold her splendid expressions—you were cheating to protect your soul mate!" exclaimed Plagiarism, his tongue flailing.

Violet buried her face under her hands.

"She isn't my soul mate. I'm already bonded," said Devlin.

"Oh really, then who did you bond with?" asked Plagiarism.

"I…" Devlin glanced at Kaity. "I didn't bond with anyone. But I'm already in love," he said, turning his gaze away from his beloved.

"That's not true! You had a wedding! My boy was a beautiful groom!" cheered Ada.

"I'm not your boy, and I said there wasn't a wedding!" yelled Devlin.

"Hmm, is this what bashful looks like? It's a bit more fiery than I remember. I like it," said Plagiarism.

"Devlin is my god! There's nothing romantic between us," said Violet with a troubled look.

"That's right. And once Etah is defeated, I'll become a real god," said Devlin.

"She's beautiful and in love with you, yet you abstain. Squandering golden opportunities, you're quite the fool," said Plagiarism.

"Violet would you like me to fix your clothes?" asked Sefiwah, holding a needle in her fragile hands.

"That would be wonderful!" exclaimed Violet.

"Oooh, does that mean she is going to be naked? I wonder what color her...oh no, I've forgotten what it's called," said Plagiarism.

"I'll do it. Save us some time," said Demonica.

Violet's clothes were instantly repaired.

"What! That's not fair!" yelled Plagiarism.

"Don't you have a fight to lose?" asked Devlin.

"I have a fight and one that had better not be interrupted by your fatherly affections."

"I'll stay out of it, promise."

"Good. Now let's get this stone rolling!" cheered Plagiarism.


BoneSaw drove up in front of the target.

"A robot? Ugh, why must I fight a robot? No emotion, no feeling, no senses. I'll end this quick. COPY-RIGHT!"

BoneSaw's body reconfigured itself as Plagiarism became coated in metal. Its saws turned into bows with jagged arrows.

Plagiarism turned into an exact replica of BoneSaw. "You are now BowSaw, and I am what you were. You see, my copy-right ability makes me into what you are, or were in this case, and you into something slightly different. You have no idea how to use your new body, so you're at a considerable disadvantage."

"That's the worst BoneSaw impersonation I've ever seen. He never talks," said Kaity.

"What! You dare mock my abilities. I'll show you just how much like that trashcan I am." BoneSaw shot out mini-saws at the sentient mesh of metal.

BowSaw quickly shot off its bows, but the saws cut right through the arrows. It jumped up and fired a volley of metal arrows down, pinning the saws to the floor.

"Not bad for a crude imitation." BoneSaw zoomed up to the rip-off and brought its massive saw down.

BowSaw's sides opened up and fired arrows into the target's front. This caused the saw to slide off the target and slam into the ground.

"Wait, I'm still getting used to the way you operate. I'm accustomed to organics. How do I back up?" BoneSaw pulled the saw out from the ground.

The archer robot connected various bows together and fired a single massive arrow.

The arrow pierced into BoneSaw. It tore through the front and buried itself into the core.

All of BoneSaw's saws became limp before the robot shut down.

BowSaw once more became BoneSaw.

Plagiarism stood where BoneSaw had died, entirely unharmed. "Yes, yes. Good show. You win."

The wires released Plagiarism's guard. Crystal landed on his feet and picked up his boss.

"We won. Hand over the ticket," said Devlin.

"No, no. You cheated the first round. I want another fight and it had better be another female," said Plagiarism.

"You'll just lose again. Your ability is useless," said Devlin.

"Useless? Shape-stealing is fun! How is it useless?"

"You make the original stronger than the copy. That makes it rather challenging to secure a victory in battle," said Deceivant.

"I was a bit disoriented, is all. Won't happen again."

"Excuses. You lost. Now hand it over. Or do you gods not honor your word?" asked Devlin.

"I'll break a promise if it gives me a chance to experience something new. Come on, who wants to fight me next?"

Matteria picked Plagiarism up.

"Ah, it's Ms. Rainbow. You have such dainty fingers," said Plagiarism.

"Would you give us the ticket for a kiss?" asked Matteria.

"If I could nod, you would think I was undergoing a seizure. Peroro. You've got yourself a deal!"

Matteria kissed the lonely creature on both cheek bones. "There you go."

"An angel! Guards, guards, there is an angel in Absence!"

"Aw, you're so flattering," said Matteria as he set the satisfied fan down.

"And you're delectable, or was it adorable? Perhaps both. Yes, yes. Both indeed. Here you are." Plagiarism's regenerated tongue popped out of his mouth, holding the ticket. "Come on, take it."

Matteria bent down and grabbed the ticket with his teeth.

"Such a playful one. Yes, yes," said Plagiarism.

"Well-played. Got us the ticket, all the while trying to bring Anthrax back to his senses by getting him jealous," said Exp 8.

"That's not it. He's a fan of me. I like making my fans happy. It's that simple," said Matteria.

Violet grabbed her living god's hand. "We got another ticket. We'll be out of here in no time."

Devlin slid his hand out from her grip. "I understand you love me, but my heart belongs to the cutest assassin ever. I can't give you what you want. And that goes double for you, Demonica. I am solely devoted to Kaity, understood?" he asked with fierce eyes.

"Are you trying to convince me or yourself?" asked Demonica.

Kaity stomped up to the annoying teenager. "Well, I get you're obsessed with me. But I already have a girlfriend! Like I told you before, I'm not interested," she said, sticking out her tongue.

"Yes. You did say that," said Devlin softly.

"Is he okay?" asked Opti.

"My family is only here because you got us involved. Stay away from me," said Kaity.

"Yeah, I'll uh…give you some space. Let's uh…what are we doing again?" asked Devlin, teetering around in a daze.

"We are getting out of here. We're off to find the next guardian to get his ticket. Stay here too long and we'll forget who we are," said Nina.

"Yeah, you're right. Let's go fight the Fourth Guardian," said Devlin, turning away.

"Not yet. Let's talk," said Sefiwah, grabbing him by his wrist.

"Don't waste your time. He won't give up on me," said Kaity.

Sefiwah patted her girl's head. "It will only take a moment."


Sefiwah led Devlin ten meters away from the group.

"Kaity is right. You'll never convince me to stop loving her. Love doesn't work like that," said Devlin with a quivering smile.

"It's not about that." She placed Devlin's hand on her belly.

"I didn't kill you. You're the one who was being irresponsible. Don't think you can guilt me into following your whims. It was less than a day anyway. All that was lost was potential."

"You didn't fertilize me. As expected, Exps are infertile."

"Maybe you're the one who is barren," said Devlin, pulling his hand away.

"Either way, we had a deal. Kaity said you killed Kanasta. Good work."

"I did it for my own reasons, just like I said I would."

"Does that mean you don't want your reward?" asked Sefiwah, giving the boy's ear an enticing lick.

Devlin shoved the spiteful woman off. "You disgust me."

"Then the deal's off. Such a shame. She has such soft lips," said Sefiwah with a smile.

"You don't get it, do you?"

"I'm not dense. The deal was never on. You thought you were tricking me? I'm an assassin. I could hear the deception in your words."

"Wait, you were playing me?" asked Devlin, grabbing her arm as she turned away.

"I was probing you to find out what kind of person you are. Like you were doing to me."

"Then what you said about Kaity, it wasn't true?"

"Every word was true. I don't lie. The promise I made is still up for grabs too," she said, digging her finger in the boy's chest.

"If Kaity knew the real you…."

"She'd what? Come crawling to you for comfort? I doubt it. Seems more likely she'd go to Kanasta. We both don't want that."

"What do you want?"

"I already have what I want. Just thought I'd make a little suggestion is all. It's like you said: if you wage war against Etah, there will be casualties. Kanasta has to follow your orders. Nobody would blame you if he died fighting. See you later. I'm going to get Kaity frisky and give her a thorough petting." Sefiwah walked back to the team, leaving the boy on his own.

Devlin stomped his foot against the ground in a fit of fury.

# Chapter 71: The Fourth Guardian

After Devlin joined back with the team, the Fourth Guardian appeared about a dozen meters away.

As soon as the Freedom Forcers arrived at the guardian, Atatasuki stepped out of the crowd.

"I'll fight him. Watch my power," said Atatasuki, giving his little sis a thumbs-up.

"Why are you putting yourself in harm's way?" asked Kawai, her tail tightening around Exp 8's.

"I want to impress you. Taking down a dragon is a surefire way to get romantic attention," said Atatasuki, cracking his fingers.

"Ugh, this isn't a game. No. You know what? Go ahead. Die. I don't need you now that my real brother is here." Kawai wrapped her better brother's tail around her body.

"What a fickle creature," said Loyal.

"Don't you dare insult my sister, you fossilized mythical simpleton!" yelled Atatasuki.

"Fossilized…hardly." The skull's flesh came into being layer after layer.

"A dragon! It's a dragon!" cheered D.S.

"I made myself look like a skull so the other guardians wouldn't be offended by my everlasting youth," said the dragon in a wise and thunderous voice.

Smoke erupted from the dragon's nostrils.

The ground shook as the smoke masked the immediate area.

A pearl white dragon with a spiked back and a mace-like tail rose up from the smoke.

"Not bad. Let's see whose fire is stronger," said Atatasuki as his body became super-heated.

"Very well, show me your power," said Loyal, his slit eyes intensifying their gaze.

"*INSTANT BAKE!*" Atatasuki rushed up and punched the dragon's leg, releasing heat through his knuckles upon contact.

Loyal flicked the nuisance aside. "My scales are far too powerful to be penetrated by you."

"My passion knows no limits! *SUPER MEGA…MUFFIN!*" Atatasuki flung a flaming muffin at the mythical reptile.

It crumbled on impact.

Loyal scowled and turned away. "You aren't worth my time. Guard, kill him!"

The guard, standing a couple meters behind Loyal, took off its clear cloak. He was a knight in pearl-white steel armor; the only gaps in the armor were covered by chainmail. The ancient warrior's helmet was shaped like the dragon's head.

The guard shoved his hand in the ground and uncovered a lance. The knight hoisted it up and charged at Atatasuki.

Each jab of the lance was swift and precise. The weapon pulled back the instant after it was thrust forth.

Atatasuki dodged the lance twice and then grabbed it in mid-attack between his searing palms.

The guard thrust with both hands.

Atatasuki slid under the attack and wrapped his feet around the guard's leg. As the knight began to topple to the ground, the living microwave thrust both fists into his opponent's back.

Whilst being propelled into the air, the guard flung his lance into the metal man's palm.

"Why won't it melt!" exclaimed Atatasuki as his pierced hand heated up.

The guard landed into a roll. Once in front of his adversary, he took a bow. "Pardon the late introduction. I am Sir Limit, proud knight of Absence." Though muffled, the heroism in his voice rang through.

"I'm Atatasuki, the one who's going to melt you into oblivion."

"Your pride will not serve you in combat." The guard tore out the lance, spun it around and then shoved it through the metal man's stomach.

Atatasuki's eyes shrank to the size of the lance's tip.

"The fight is over!" yelled Kawai, slamming her tail into the knight's chest.

Limit slid back a bit, guarding with his arms.

Kawai pulled out the lance with her tail and tossed it at her brother's attacker.

Limit grabbed the lance and flung it into the air. "Lord Loyal, let us finish this battle."

Loyal swooped down and consumed the lance and Atatasuki. He landed on the ground and then spit out the lance.

"Give him back!" yelled Kawai, slamming her tail against the dragon's stomach.

"Yeah! Game over! You won! Spit him out!" yelled Exp 8.

Riufen stepped up to the massive winged warrior. "I'll handle this." He tapped Kawai's shoulder and then flung her back to the team.

"Indeed. The battlefield is no place for women and children," said Limit.

"I'll make you spit him out!" yelled Exp 8, powering up an orb.

Riufen gripped Exp 8's arm. "Do you trust me?"

"I do. Get him out there. Please," said Exp 8 before his arm was released.

Riufen walked past the armored warrior and up to the dragon's stomach. "Atatasuki, I had no idea you were so honorable. You fought even though you knew you would die. I have yet to find an opponent who can make that possible for me. But, I will not share this honor now." He turned to the knight, his fingers now gripping the tip of his own spine. "Warrior, draw your blade."

Limit picked up his lance.

"Let us have a fair and honorable fight," said Riufen as he pulled out his spine.

"Is that your weapon? What form of sordid magic are you using?" asked Limit, assuming a defensive stance.

"A warrior and their sword are one. Is this concept foreign to you?"

"You must be from the land of the rising sun."

"Yes, I was created in New Mexico. The sun's rays lay claim to the land."

"What lord do you serve under?"

"I let my honor guide me."

"What about when you were alive? Who was your daimyo? What was the name of your shogun?"

"Devlin was my daimyo and my shogun."

"I see. I too was a renegade knight. I killed my lord to ensure peace for Britain."

"Britain! You heard the man! What an outstanding fellow!" cheered Karson.

"If he killed a British king, then isn't he a traitor to Britain?" asked Pharma.

"Oh shut up! Britain is a land that belongs to no man. He's a true warrior, fighting for a better future for Britain!" cheered Karson.

"A ronin samurai and a renegade knight; this will truly be a battle to remember," said Riufen.

Limit bowed and Riufen bowed back.

Just as the bow finished, the samurai's ribs shot out. Two of them pierced through the chainmail and into the knight's flesh.

Limit tore the samurai's bones out from his chest. "Well played. Let us not dally. I shall fight you without restraints." He removed every piece of armor except his helmet.

"Removing your armor is a bizarre tactic, but thanks to a fellow warrior, it is one I am familiar with," said Riufen, taking a step toward the knight. "𝕽𝖊𝖘𝖙𝖗𝖆𝖎𝖓𝖙 𝕽𝖊𝖒𝖔𝖛𝖆𝖑."

Once dropped, the armor smashed through the floor of Absence, disappearing from view.

The knight vanished from sight.

Riufen's protruding ribs snapped off and fell to the ground.

The samurai spun around to see the knight directly behind him.

"𝕴𝖓𝖍𝖎𝖇𝖎𝖙𝖔𝖗 𝕬𝖉𝖉𝖎𝖙𝖎𝖔𝖓."

Clear weights with chains attached themselves to the samurai.

Riufen's legs shook as he struggled to stand. Once he collapsed to his knees, the lance pierced his chest.

Limit kicked the samurai off the lance and up into Loyal's mouth.

"Knights are the best warriors after all," said Limit, standing proudly.

"Oh yeah, victory for Britain!" cheered Karson.

"Pathetic. I expected better from Riufen," said Bob.

"That knight is incredibly skilled. Bob, I think you should go next. We can't risk any more casualties," said Exp 8, holding his sobbing sister to his chest.

"Sorry, but looks like someone already stepped up to the plate," said Bob.

D.S. approached the knight. His hands were visibly shaking. "You defeated the unstoppable zombie samurai! Gold star! Now it's my turn to play!"

"Sir Limit, allow me to deal with this nuisance." Loyal opened his mouth and a wave of fire consumed his opponent

"Nothing can withstand the might of our loyalty," said Limit.

The smoke cleared and D.S. had kept his ground. His body was partially burnt and he was holding a wire shield. He tossed the shield at the oversized lizard's face.

Loyal jabbed his tail forward, shoving it through the nuisance.

Limit's armor dropped down from above, landing on the dragon's tail.

Loyal let out a pained roar as D.S. slipped off his tail.

After tumbling to the ground and regaining his footing, D.S stood up.

"Eraser Mode!"

His body did not change shape.

"Why aren't my artifacts working?" asked D.S. before he was knocked down by the dragon's tail.

Limit leaped up to his adversary. "𝕴𝖓𝖍𝖎𝖇𝖎𝖙𝖔𝖗 𝕬𝖉𝖉𝖎𝖙𝖎𝖔𝖓!"

D.S. groaned and struggled, but was held firmly in place by clear weights and chains.

"That's three meals today." As soon as Loyal's mouth had stretched to its limit, Riufen jumped out from the dragon's throat.

Loyal's eyes widened, stopping all movement for an instant.

Riufen coughed up his short and long intestines. He wrapped his large intestine around Loyal's mouth to muzzle him. Using his small intestine like a lasso, the stoic samurai yanked Limit's lance out from his grasp.

Before the knight could process the situation, his lance was embedded into Loyal's neck.

"You may have limited my body, but my organs can still move freely. ꞆꞒᒪᒪ ᔑᕼᕑꞇ." Riufen fired out his cells like a microscopic Gatling gun.

"It seems your body can move regardless," said Limit before collapsing to the floor. "What sort of sorcery is this? I don't even have a scratch on me," he said as the samurai approached him.

Riufen swiftly unsheathed his spinal cord. He slowly sliced his own neck until it was detached. He then cut open his stomach and let the stomach acid pour into his mouth. Just as he was about to slam his fist into the warrior's chest, the samurai spit out the acid.

Limit's chain mail did not protect him, the skin on his arms and part of his chest had melted away. He fell to his knees. "I beg of you, don't take off my helmet."

Riufen reattached his head. "I would never de-mask a warrior."

"Hey, what about Atatasuki? Where is he?" asked Kawai, flying up to her powerful ally.

"I never made it to the dragon's stomach. I don't know," said Riufen.

"Loyal, you lost the fight. Spit him out. Atatasuki means a lot to us," said Exp 8, his hands trembling.

"Very well, he's done enough damage anyway." Loyal spit out the nuisance.

"I did it! I broke out!" cheered Atatasuki, his body steaming.

"You almost got eaten, baka," said Kawai, turning away from him.

"I did get eaten, but I'm still alive! Phew, that was a great fight," said Atatasuki, standing up in a bit of a daze.

Exp 8 embraced him tightly. "Good to have you back."

"Hey come on, I'm not going to die so easily," said Atatasuki.

"Kawai's right. You need to be careful," said Exp 8, looking at the acidic damage on his brother's armored legs.

"An intense battle and no casualties. But I'm not quite done yet," said Limit, raising his lance toward the samurai.

D.S. raised his scissors and cut off the knight's head.

Limit's body tumbled to the ground.

After a brief moment, the headless knight stood up and reattached his head. Soon after Loyal handed his partner the lance, the wound in his neck vanished.

D.S. toppled to the ground, holding the massive hole in his chest. "Mommy! Where's my mommy!"

Ada rushed to his side. "I'm right here, baby."

"It hurts, Mommy. Please, make it go away. It really, really hurts," said D.S., clenching her hand.

Ada's head jerked to Deceivant. "Get Anthrax."

"I would but, he's still in his sick form."

"Then get him out of it. Our little boy needs help now!" Ada was in tears.

Deceivant nodded and rushed up to the plagued doctor, who was still being held down by NoOne's shadow. "Hey, Anthrax. D.S., um, my son, he needs your help right now. You're the only one who can save him," he said, staring into the doctor's small eye.

The disease fell off in clumps. The young boy emerged, already in a sprint to the patient. "Don't worry; Dr. Anthrax is on the scene!" He crouched down to the patient's side and got to work on bandaging his stomach wound.

"Tehehugh. You're naked," said D.S.

"Does anyone know where my clothes are?" asked Anthrax.

"They're kind of ripped to shreds," said Matteria.

Demonica snapped her fingers and Anthrax's clothes re-assembled on him.

"Wow! Alright, time to get to work!" cheered Anthrax.

"Yay, I'm going to get a lollipop!" cheered D.S.

"Wait, did you get hurt on purpose to get Anthrax back to normal?" asked Matteria.

"Candy," said D.S., reaching into the doctor's bag.

"Hey, hold still, I'm trying to save you from a mortal wound here," said Anthrax, tearing the wrap with his teeth.

"Where's the candy?" asked D.S., rummaging through the bag.

"Get your hands out! The candy is only after the procedure. Hold still, will you?" asked Anthrax, struggling to push the patient's arm away.

"Heads up," said Matteria.

Anthrax caught the bracelet and put it on. "Thanks. Hope I don't ever have to transform again."


"Here's your pass, Sir Riufen," said Limit with a bow.

Riufen graciously took the ticket and then handed it to Devlin.

Eil appeared directly in front of Devlin. "Tehtehtehteh. Tehtehteh!"

"What is it this time?" asked Devlin, holding his forehead.

# Chapter 72: The Final Guardian

"You think it's over. You think you've won. There is one final guardian you must defeat," said Eil.

"We know," said Devlin.

"Tehteh…what? How can you know?"

"The last guardian appeared a couple times when everyone was fighting. It watched us all very attentively," said Devlin.

"So, where is it hiding now?" asked NoOne.

"Don't know. Come on out. If you want a fight, we'll give you one. But if you give us the ticket, then we'll be on our way," said Exp 8.

The last guardian appeared. It was not a skull at all. This god was an amoeba the size of three Bobs and its guard was shorter than the others.

Kanasta stepped up to the guardian, each step more intense than the one before. He looked up at the guardian. His eyebrows came down.

Exp 8 nudged Kaity. "What's going on with Kanasta?"

"I've seen that look before," said Kaity, her arms instinctively coming to her chest.

"Oh crap, the Boss is pissed," said Ego.

"He's upset? Why?" asked Exp 8.

"Who cares? Hey, would you like to give me a massage?" asked Kawai, stretching out in front of her big brother.

Kanasta's lip quivered. "You remind me of someone."

"Do you know him?" asked Devlin, turning to his crush.

Kaity averted her eyes.

"I've fought his kind before," said Kanasta, keeping his gaze fixed on the amoeba.

"You've fought his—what? He's an amoeba; they're microscopic. How could you—oh no." Deceivant held his forehead.

Violet walked up to her living god. "Did this deity intervene in Kanasta's life?"

"That's not it. I think I figured it out. Two words: gamer grudge," said Devlin.

"Yep. It's a personal vendetta. Boss takes everything seriously," said Ego.

Nina leaped into action. "Enough staring. I'll fight the amoeba. Once I've won, we can go back to Lum and leave this void behind us!"

"Hey Kanasta, I'm right, aren't I? This is about a video game, isn't it?" asked Devlin, his head turning sideways.

"I was so close to a perfect run-through. Every enemy; no lives lost. Took all the right shortcuts. And then…that thing killed me," said Kanasta, his gaze never leaving the target.

"Like I said, a gamer grudge," said Devlin, flashing a smile at Violet.

"I think I understand. I get frustrated sometimes, reading scripture that is. How could Athena be so cruel to Medusa, how could anyone murder Jesus, how come Siva wasn't invited? I think to your brother—"

"He's not my brother," said Devlin, turning his gaze away.

"To Kanasta, the experiences he has in the virtual world…they are real to him. But he must know that you can't punish people in the physical world for actions that took place in mythic time, right?" asked Violet.

"He's looking for an outlet, there's no rational thought behind it," said Devlin.

"I will take care of him, I will." The guard took off its cloak. Beneath was a young human girl, standing on two armadillo-sized tops. Her skirt was shaped like an upside down top and moved in the opposite direction of the tops she was standing on. Two ladles were attached to her earlobes and another top was spinning on her head. "Spinny spin spin," said the guard as she spun in place.

"I didn't expect Absence would have such a cute guard," said Deceivant, wiping his glasses before taking another look.

"She's loopy! I'm waaaay cuter," said Kawai.

"Of course you are. But that in no way undermines her allure," said Deceivant.

"I am Spin the guard of spinning, I am. I guard Separate, God of Division, I guard! *Absence, Spin!*" she exclaimed in a fast paced high pitch voice.

The realm spun around until Kaity among other Freedom Forcers fell down.

"One down, yay!" Spin jumped up with glee.

"Kaity, I will take care of this," said Kanasta.

"Not alone you won't," said Nina.

Spin took off her ladle earrings and set them on the ground.

The earrings gained speed as they closed in.

Nina tossed shurikens at the tops, but they bounced off. She whipped out two machine-guns and opened fire.

"When did you get those?" asked Karson.

"When you weren't looking," said Nina, knocking over the tops.

"*Guns, Spin!*"

The guns revolved rapidly in the seductive warrior's hands.

Nina dropped the weapons and held her hands in pain. "Let's see how your abilities fare against the Gravity Artifact."

Fifteen feet away, Kanasta cracked his neck and took a step closer to his nemesis. "It's just you and me."

Separate divided into two, then four, then eight, until there were sixty-four.

Kanasta took out two decks of cards from his utility belt and rapidly tossed them. Each card hit right on the mark, cutting every amoeba in half.

There were now one-hundred twenty-eight amoebas.

"If you were that easy to kill, I wouldn't detest your existence," said Kanasta, grinding his teeth.

"I'll bring it back together!" yelled Devlin. Wires shot out of his back.

The wires fanned out and hit all the floating amoebas.

" ***CONNECT***." Devlin's wires fused, making one huge amoeba as a result. "It's better to fight just one, isn't that right?" asked Devlin.

"Watch out!" Kanasta leaped into action but not before Separate had covered his little brother.

"Let's see how you handle this." Kanasta took out an ace. He slit his wrist with the card and tossed it aside. In this moment of distraction, he reached into his suitcase. "Seems like the perfect opportunity to try out one of my custom weapons. 𝕽𝕰𝕯 𝕺𝕱 𝕮𝕷𝖀𝕭𝕾 𝕾𝖂𝕺𝕽𝕯"

The sword was black and had a sharp tip in the shape of a club.

Kanasta lashed the blade at Separate. After making contact, the sword got stuck in the amoeba's exterior.

Kanasta pulled the sword out. "I had a perfect Triple S rank, on all the levels before you. Then some giant amoeba kills me and makes me lose all my lives! I tried again and again, but I still died. I wanted nothing more than to kill it, to kill you. I have completed nearly every game I found. And I did beat you, but even then…it was an empty victory. I had already lost so many times that my victory felt like a gluttonous void. I don't care if you're the same amoeba, killing you will finally leave me satisfied," he said, hacking away at the final guardian.

Devlin busted out of the amoeba. "I thought you only killed for pay," he said, creating a shield of wires from his hand.

"I-I do." Kanasta froze up. He dropped the sword and put his arm on his brother's shoulder. "You're right. Thank you. I almost let my old feelings make me do something reprehensible."

Devlin tossed Kanasta's hand off of him. "Don't touch me."

Twenty feet north from where Separate had fallen, Nina was running from the tops. She leaped as they charged, before quickly regaining her footing.

"Damn it, my sexy poses won't do a thing to slow them down. Oh well, only got one option now." Nina did a quick turnaround all the while shielding her face from the leaping ladles. She jumped up, grabbed a kunai in each hand and stabbed them into the guard's throat.

"You can't kill me, you can't." Spin's skin was shredded from within. The moment Nina realized her opponent's body was an assortment of tops was the same moment that her body was bludgeoned from all sides.

"A fake! She was a fake!" yelled Deceivant.

"No surprise," said Kawai.

Nina kicked off, dodging the second round of attacks while posing erotically. "*Softening Pull!* Damn it! *Hardening Push!* What's wrong? It worked fine in Sel. Hmm, I wonder if that meditation session had something to do with it."

The tops picked up speed and rammed into the sides of her feet as the seductive warrior ran.

Bullet fire dispersed the tops and Kaity rushed in.

"I'll take it from here," she said, smiling at her gorgeous ally.

"Thanks! Hey Anthrax, get over here. I'm pretty banged up. Could you heal me? Make sure to put your gloves on first!" hollered Nina, limping up to the young doctor.

The tops spun around the young assassin, waiting for the moment to strike.

"I'm usually the predator; not really used to being the prey," said Kaity, loading a full clip into her pistol.

Separate loomed closer, but the assassin prodigy was more focused on the tops circling a meter away from her.

Just as Separate charged forward, Kaity pumped bullets into the tops. She smacked one aside with her empty gun and then leaped into the amoeba. Her left hand gripped a second sidearm and kept the tops below her at bay. Her right hand reached for Separate's core but was blocked by a viscous sheath. Plasma claws jutted out of her right hand, pierced through the protective layer, and melted the god's core.

The amoeba dissolved.

"We only have to beat the guardian, right?" asked Kaity after she landed.

The tops ended their assault and joined back together.

Separate came back to life and floated above its guard.

"You win, you win," said Spin.

The ticket appeared inside Separate. It fell into Kaity's hand.

"Now we have more than a month out of this place!" exclaimed Devlin.

"That should be more than enough time to end Etah's rein. Let's go to Lum!" exclaimed Exp 8.

"That sounds good," said Nina with a smile.

"I can't bring you there," said Demonica.

"Demonica's the escort to Sel, but there isn't an escort to Lum in this place, is there?" asked Nina, running her fingers through her hair.

"Not that I know of," said Demonica with a shrug.

"She may not know, but the dragon might," said Sefiwah.

"Of course!" Devlin rushed off ahead of the team up to Loyal. "You can get us to Lum, can't you?"

"Not if you were actually banished," said Loyal with a grin.

"We aren't banished?" asked Violet with shimmering eyes.

"Your souls are not bound here, never were," said Loyal.

"I was repelled by the Lum portal when…these two showed up." Devlin pointed to Deceivant and Ada. "If I wasn't truly banished, then explain that."

"Hey come here," said Crystal.

"What is—" Devlin bumped into an invisible wall.

"There's your answer."

"Then I can leave?" asked Devlin.

"That's right," said Crystal.

A white portal appeared in front of him.

"You're the warrior who sent us here," said Riufen.

"I was following orders. And you're lucky I did," said Crystal.

"Thank you for bringing us to Absence to see our son," said Ada, holding her beloved's hand.

"No need to blame or praise me. I'm just doing my job. Not sure why…guess it creates a false sense of purpose for me. Anyway, you guys should get going. This place will sap the resolve out of you," said Crystal.

"Do you think the angels will help us?" asked Exp 8.

"We broke out of Absence, we should at least be able to negotiate," said Devlin.

"It's worth a shot. Freedom Forcers, let's head out!" cheered Exp 8, raising his arm.

The group charged into the portal, escaping the prison of Absence and going headlong into the realm of creation.

# Part 8
# The Goddess Shaped by Misfortune

# Chapter 73: Fate

The Freedom Forcers were dropped upside-down two meters above Lum's grassy landscape. They stood up in a daze.

"What happened here?" asked Sefiwah, her eyes hollow.

"Looks like a turf war," said D.S., making big splashes with his feet.

"Such a waste," said Kanasta.

Ten bodies shaped like humans with torn open stomachs were strewn across the white grass. Their faces were scarred beyond recognition.

"Hmm, looks like something interesting happened while we were gone," said Bob.

"Are they dead?" asked Ada, her hands shielding her eyes.

"I think this one's breathing," said Anthrax, his head to a young girl's chest.

"Then hurry up and heal her!" yelled Deceivant.

"What are the odds of us falling into this mess?" asked Nina, carefully stepping around the blood puddles.

"Forget the girl, we need to get out of here," said Devlin, scanning the bushes for movement.

"My powers still aren't working. Come on, stay with me," said Anthrax, pumping the girl's chest.

"Bob, you can use your spectral hands to get her heart pumping, right?" asked Deceivant.

"Do I look like a doctor to you?" asked Bob.

"I'm begging you," said Deceivant in tears, pressing his head to the blood-soaked grass.

"Oh wow, this is kind of funny. Hmm, make him roll over like a puppy dog," said Demonica.

"I made you Bob, now do it!" yelled Deceivant.

"Calm down, I've been pumping her heart from beneath the ground. She may have some important information to pass down to us," said Bob.

"Like what? We already know it was the angels who did this," said Nina.

"That's impossible," said Violet.

"This is a trap," said Sefiwah.

"Not sure if we were the intended targets, but we've drawn unwanted attention," said Kanasta, pointing past the group at a large redwood tree in the distance.

A group of eleven angels, all clad in armor had them in their sights and were charging toward them.

"But Efil is our friend," said Violet.

"If they want a fight, we'll give them one. Stand ready," said Devlin, positioning himself in front of Kaity.

"They are within range, do I fire?" asked Karson, his twin bazookas ready to unload on the angels.

"Wait, maybe we can scare them off," said Ada.

"Good idea. Once we've killed enough of them, they should disperse," said Bob, focusing energy into his pupil.

"No. We only attack if they attack, understood?" asked Exp 8, trying to make eye contact with his allies while keeping the coming armada of angels in view.

"Wish I could help you all, but I'm forbidden to hurt angels. Unless they strike first, that is," said Demonica with a smile. "I'm going to vanish for the time being." She rushed out of the group and into the forest.

"Um guys, there's more," said D.S., facing the opposite way.

"More what?" Bob spun around. "Ah, so that's what's going on."

A brigade of over fifty warriors, all from Allah's Jannah, were charging down the hill behind them with weapons at the ready.

"Hmm, so which side should we pick?" asked Bob.

"What do you mean?" Exp 8's head jerked around to see the armed humans closing in.

"Forget sides! Let's get out of the way," said Nina before running off.

"Attack the humans," said Devlin.

"What? Why?" asked Anthrax.

"Whether the angels are our allies or enemies, we have nothing to gain by fighting them. Going against their enemies will win us favor with the angels," said Devlin.

"Good point," said Sefiwah.

"Wait, they aren't bad people. We shouldn't hurt them," said Matteria.

"You of all people are questioning me," said Devlin with a sharp look.

"Please be reasonable. The angels don't want the rebels dead. They only want to keep the peace," said Violet.

"At least don't kill any, okay?" asked Matteria, his hands clasped beneath his chin.

"This is survival. Do what's necessary," said Devlin, looking directly at his seasoned samurai.

"No! Plan B. We tackle both groups. We take them down. No casualties," said Exp 8.

"I fail to see the strategy behind this plan. We need to plan ahead or the number of casualties will grow," said Deceivant, cleaning the girl's wounds with his own shirt.

"Strategy? We can prevent these two groups from massacring each other. Deceivant, take Ada and the others who can't fight and follow Nina. Meet up with us once you've found her and when the coast is clear, okay?"

"Now you're making sense." Deceivant signaled Matteria, Anthrax and Ada to follow him. "Kawai, you should come too. This is a dangerous situation," he said, pulling her arm.

"I'm staying with Brother. I can take care of myself," she said, releasing her tail's grip on Exp 8 and raising it above her.

"Keep her safe," said Deceivant with a serious look.

"Absolutely," said Exp 8 with a nod.

Deceivant's group rushed off into the maze of trees with the injured girl in tow.

"Whoever's with me, charge at the angels. We might be able to hold them back long enough for the humans to escape," said Exp 8.

"The worst they can do is banish us. Any place is better than this glorified rehab," said Pharma, pumping himself full of adrenaline.

The leader of the angel squadron, who had a similar aura to Efil, raised its hand. The angels all stopped.

"Don't just stand there! Let's take down those humans!" cheered Devlin, the first to rush off.

"Back him up. Keep casualties to a minimum. Each live one could become a future target. Each dead body is a missed opportunity for payment," said Kanasta before rushing ahead of his brother.

Riufen turned to the team leader. "Apologies, but I am honor bound."

"Only if you choose to be," said Exp 8.

"I am honor bound to stop my ex-daimyo from killing needlessly," said Riufen with a smile.

"That's the spirit," said Exp 8 with a nod.

Riufen nodded and then rushed off to provide support.

Karson looked back at Exp 8's group. "Sorry but war is a bloody affair. We need angelic support if we are to take on Etah." He then charged off into battle against the rebels.

"Are you coming or not?" asked Bob, peering up at the spiritually adept warrior.

"I...don't know what to do," said Violet.

"Too much faith, not enough thought...or are you over thinking things?"

"I'll disarm them, that way they won't be killed. That's it!" Violet rushed off.

"Time for some fun," said Bob, seeping inside the hill.

It wasn't long before the two groups clashed.

"The assassins have returned!" yelled the leader of the rebel battalion.

Arrows carved out of wood and sharpened stone pelted Devlin's group.

BoneSaw rushed ahead, tearing through spears before slicing through flesh and bone.

Devlin parried four spear jabs with wires that burst out from his arm. He gripped one of his attackers by the side and then tore them apart with extra sharp wires.

"Demon!" yelled one of the rebels before stabbing the monster in the back.

Violet tackled the rebel as a stray wire came out from her creator's back.

The wire sliced open her shoulder, but had she not intervened, it would have ended up decapitating the woman.

"Why are you getting in the way?" asked Devlin, turning to his defiant creation as he held back four spears at once.

Kanasta gripped the spears, crushed them, and then knocked down the four rebels with the back of his hand. "Killing them for nothing is despicable." He lifted the future investment up and tossed it aside.

Kaity hopped onto his shoulders and opened fire on the rebels with her sidearm. "A bullet in the knee will keep them down for quite some time," she said, loading the next clip in with her tail.

Karson fired his bazooka a couple meters away from a group of six rebels. "These blokes don't stand a chance. Killing them is completely unnecessary."

The group got back to their feet and scattered, leaving their weapons behind.

"I agree," said Riufen as he diced his attacker's weapons into paper thin shreds.

"Don't let them get away! Round them up!" Devlin's wires grabbed the fleeing humans by their legs and pulled them into the group.

Ego slammed his enlarged fist into the final group that was still fighting and knocked them off their feet.

Meanwhile: Exp 8's group waited for the angels to move.

Four of the angels had already left the group, but the other seven kept their gaze fixed on the group of Exps.

"We can't just stand around! Those angels probably left to hurt my mom!" exclaimed D.S.

"You're right. I'll try to reason with them. Stand ready." Exp 8 broke out of formation and approached the leader of the angel battalion. "We don't want any trouble. Our enemy is Etah, same as you."

"How did you escape banishment?" asked the leader.

"Does it matter? Look, if you call in Efil, I'm sure we can negotiate," said Exp 8.

"And why is that? She's the one who banished you. Or is there something more complicated going on?"

"Why are you fighting those humans? Was it your group that murdered those people?" asked Exp 8, his fist shaking.

"Six angels, their entrails poking out of their bellies, eyes blank, all hoisted up as examples. The time for negotiation is over. Lum sent me to end them all."

"That's horrible. I'm so sorry your friends are gone. But you can't just wipe all the rebels out. It isn't too late to find a peaceful solution," said Exp 8, taking a firm stance.

"Says the one who rallied his people in a pointless battle."

"I…thought I was making the right choice."

"Choice, such a deceptive word."

"I won't let you kill anyone else," said Exp 8, tightening his fingers into a fist.

"Do you think you can stop me? I am Etaf." She pulled off her helmet. "I am the controller of destinies."

Etaf's skin was dark like the night but creamy like sandalwood paste. Black sooty tattoos accentuated her lips. Around her white pupils were twelve black lines, each corresponding to a different hour. A bright white hilt of a sword could be seen just beyond her four clumps of silver hair which were equidistant from one another. She was clad in pearl-white mist armor. The light aura around her was replaced with a thin silver layer of energy.

"What the humans did to your people was horrible," said Exp 8.

"No, it wasn't. It was a reaction to the attack on their leader. They think we sent your assassin friends after their Imam," said Etaf in an inquisitive, detached, and firm voice.

"See? It's all a misunderstanding," said Exp 8.

"I have my orders. The rest of you go on ahead. I will take care of this."

"No! Stay put!" yelled Exp 8.

The angels walked right past him.

"Team, negotiations have failed. Take them down!" hollered Exp 8.

NoOne popped up behind his courageous leader. "No need."

"Huh?"

"Plenty of shadows here. It was easy to get a hold of them. They can't move. The rest of you should go after the angels that are on Nina's trail. Come back here when you've met up with them. Please, don't leave me behind."

"Wouldn't dream of it. Team, let's move out!" hollered Exp 8.

"I don't think so, kuru-guru." Etaf sliced the shadow thread off her with the tip of her sword as she unsheathed it.

"How?" asked NoOne.

The platinum sword radiated with light.

"By carving out a destiny! Behold, the Destiny Sword!"

The blade of the sword was wide near the hilt but thinned out all the way down to its tip. The tip gleamed like a star.

The sword thrust toward Exp 8 but was deflected when Kawai's tail slammed into it.

"I've got her angels pinned. The rest of you attack her!" yelled NoOne.

Etaf slammed the girl's side with the hilt of her sword. Her hand covered the child's face before slamming her to the ground.

Atatasuki jumped on the commander's back and knocked her to the ground.

She rolled back to a standing position with the mechanical man now beneath her feet.

D.S. slammed his scissors into her blade. "Angels are supposed to be nice!" He knocked the weapon out of her hand and held the scissors to her neck.

Etaf called the sword back into her hand.

"What do we do?" asked Opti, looking at his toxic pal.

Pharma exhaled a purple cloud of smoke around Etaf. "We take her on a wild ride. *Breathing Bong.*"

Exp 8 jet-propelled himself into the smoke cloud. He slammed into the commander, grabbed onto her, and lifted her off the ground.

"DESTINY PAUSE. Etaf stabbed her sword into the ground, stopping all momentum instantaneously. She slammed her wrist up into the Exp leader's chin.

Kawai zoomed behind Etaf and smashed her tail into the enemy's head.

Etaf spat and then quickly swiped her blade behind her.

Exp 8 gripped the commander's arm. "Give it up!"

D.S. pulled the sword out from her hand. "Ha! Can't call it back now, can you?" He stuck out his tongue.

"No need," said Etaf.

All at once, wires lifted Exp 8 and his team off the ground.

The team dangled upside-down, except for NoOne who was still keeping the angels from moving.

"That's enough of that," said Devlin, looking up at Exp 8 with a grin.

"Aren't we on the same side?" asked Opti.

"As soon as you raised your hand against Lum, we broke apart." Devlin looked up at the angelic warrior. "You're a goddess, aren't you?"

Etaf's sword broke out of D.S.'s grip and gravitated into her hand.

"I am the Goddess of Fate. And you're merely another one of Etah's pawns," said Etaf.

"Fate? Like the lottery?" asked Kanasta, slightly intrigued.

"Such things are chance, not fate. I bring the near future into the present. I have the ability to pull in or deter the fate of others."

"We rounded them all up, the rebels I mean. You wanted them, right?" asked Devlin.

"You want to strike a deal? Not interested. Once I've dealt with the rebels, I'll decide what to do with you and your allies."

"No strings attached, we only want to help out."

"We both know that isn't true. I only act upon Lum's orders. Tell your ally to release my angels."

Devlin's gaze turned to NoOne.

"Sorry, but I'm working with Exp 8. His heroism is what will triumph against Etah," said NoOne.

"Holy Goddess, we aren't your enemy. Now that Devlin is here with us, we are going to remove Etah from his throne," said Violet.

"Why bother?" asked Etaf.

"I don't understand. I thought all the Lum goddesses would want him out of the picture," said Devlin.

"Etah is a bit too ambitious, but we can handle him. Hmm, looks like my reinforcements have arrived," said Etaf, her gaze shifting upward.

Efil and a group of twenty angelic warriors lined up in a circle around the Freedom Forcers.

"How did they come back if you banished them?" asked Etaf.

"I apologize, but I don't know the answer. I was sent here on Lum's behalf. Our Lord has given us a new mission," said Efil.

"Did Lum speak to you?"

"Lum has tasked me with dealing with the Imam. The purge is off."

"How did you convince the Great Goddess to change her mind?"

"The orders to purge…they weren't from Lum. It was misinformation."

"I doubt the rebels will believe you."

Deceivant's group came out from the foliage and joined up with the other Freedom Forcers.

"Efil! Please, heal this child!" exclaimed Deceivant, holding up the injured girl.

"Wait, that child. She looks familiar. Fatima," said Nina with wide eyes.

"Can you heal her?" asked Deceivant.

"Yes, leave her in my care," said Efil.

"She's a good kid. Don't know how she got caught up in this," said Nina.

"Rest assured. I will save her. But first I must relay a message to Etaf," said Efil.

"I'm listening," said Etaf.

"I alone am to deal with the Imam. Lum's mission for you is to relate to the Exps."

"Relate? I'm supposed to stall them, right?"

"No. Relate to them. She didn't specify how. I must be off," said Efil, signaling her battalion to follow her lead.

"So we're supposed to make friends, right? Want a smoke?" asked Pharma, detaching his cigar thumb.

Etaf sheathed her weapon. "No. Hmm, what should I do?" she asked, looking at the team inquisitively.

"We could share secrets!" cheered Ada.

"Secrets? Yes. I suppose there's no better way to build trust," said Etaf.

"What's your favorite color?" asked Opti.

"Huh?"

"Forget him. Honestly, how is a god supposed to relate to us mortals?" asked Anthrax.

"I wasn't always a god," said Etaf, her eyes flickering.

"Wait, you became a god?" asked Devlin, his eyes alight with intrigue.

"Etaf, were you chosen for your beauty, perhaps your sense of justice? What was it?" asked Matteria.

"So you we're once mortal? Or were you an angel first? How did you become a god?" asked Anthrax.

"If a mortal can become a god, then maybe I can become a hero. It could happen, right?" asked NoOne.

"That's right, buddy," said Opti, patting his shadow pal on the back.

"She's a warrior goddess. No doubt she was a brave soldier in her past life. Her merits in battle led to her divine ascension," said Karson.

"Where to begin?" asked Etaf, gazing inquisitively into the sky.

"Ooh, this story is going to be cool," said D.S., sitting down cross-legged.

"To think I'm getting a chance to hear a tale of apotheosis straight from a goddess!" exclaimed Violet, bouncing up and down.

"Another time perhaps, we have a mission to complete," said Kanasta.

"Yes, we are quite busy indeed. We're on a quest to take down Etah. Something you and your angels should have dealt with long ago," said Bob.

"Shut up! I want to hear it! Etaf, share with us whatever led you to your unique path. Tell us how you gained favor with the gods. I want to know everything!" exclaimed Devlin.

"I told you, my dear, fairy tales only serve to confuse children. Look at him; he's so invested in these fantasies he's practically schizophrenic," said Deceivant with a shrug. "That said, were you a girl in your previous life?"

"Yes," said Etaf.

"Then by all means proceed. It would be best to start off when you were a child. After all it is in those early years of curiosity that we form the skeleton for our moral compass and belief systems. A child's mind is truly a wonder worth exploring," said Deceivant, his golden eyes glimmering.

"So Boss, do we go after the Imam before Efil catches her?" asked Ego.

"Thinking it over, this is a great opportunity to gain Intel," said Kanasta.

"I second that. And it's not like Efil can take on all the rebel forces on her own," said Nina.

"Agreed. Give us the rundown," said Kanasta.

"Tempo used to tell me scary stories when we were little. Those were good times. Everybody's got a story; let's hear it," said Ego with a heartfelt smile, leaning back and stretching his legs.

"Or we could engage in an honorable bout," said Riufen, staring at Etaf's sword.

"So, were you a human in your past life? Or do you just appear this way to seem more relatable to the insurgents?" asked Sefiwah.

Kaity hopped on Sefi-chan's shoulders. "Ooh, this is sounding more and more interesting! Did you fight in a war? Were you chosen or did you just transform into a god?"

"Patience, please," said Etaf with a smile.

"We've got time. It will be nice to sit back and relax," said Exp 8.

"Agreed," said Kawai, sitting in her brother's lap and snuggling him.

"Hey, can I sit with you?" asked Atatasuki.

"Yep, just don't block the view," said Kawai, patting the ground.

"Why not start at the beginning? What was the first moment that shaped you into who you are now?" asked Devlin, lying down.

"Yes. I suppose I should start there. Gather around. You will be witness to my past as I lived it. My inner thoughts shall be made audible." Etaf raised her sword and carved the air into a frame. "This is the story of how a mortal became a god." The goddess' hand emanated light.

The light from her hand filled the frame and created an image.

# Chapter 74: A Mother's Love

There were walls made of wood and a woman in a bed. A boy was crouched down next to the woman. Tears were dripping down his pale cheeks.

Not understanding what was happening, yet still perceptive to the emotions swirling in the room, I began to cry. I whined, wailed, whimpered and sobbed.

I felt as if the sounds I made were only perceivable to me. The woman in bed, my own mother, could not hear me. She could not feel my desire for her warmth. I was trapped and physically incapable of climbing out.

A man came into the room. I reached my hand through the bars of my cage but my presence was unknown to him. The man crouched down next to mother. He pulled out a piece of wood and began shaving it. Once he was done he placed the piece of shaved wood at the center of the room next to the burning wood. He began speaking to someone not present in a low voice.

At one point the boy let go of my mother's hand. He stood up and placed his hand on the man's shoulder. They both fell silent.

I continued to cry the rest of the night. My voice gave out before the sun came around.

That night I learned that the only one I can rely on is myself.

Time went on and after five years another woman came into my life. She was very kind and beautiful, but my brother never spoke a word to her. She taught me how to garden, cook, and embroider. Once I became of age, she decorated my face with sooty tattoos like hers. When I was with her, whether out in the fields or in the cabin, I quickly lost track of time. Before I knew it, two years had passed with us getting closer each day. But the closer I got to her, the more distant my brother became.

One morning I woke up and found her shivering. I fetched my father and tried to get my brother to come along, but to no avail.

An old man came in, along with my father. I had seen him before but only at a ceremony. This was the first time the aged man had come inside our home.

His beard was larger and greyer than father's. The flies buzzing around him and father mingled. Below his thick bushy eyebrows were very small eyes. There was something mystical about those dark brown eyes. They had seen things I doubt I could ever comprehend.

Father grabbed mother's hand and blew air on her to keep her spirit from leaving. "What deed has she done to deserve this? She has always been dutiful and loyal," he said, unaware that his hand was shaking.

"Has she made any enemies? This could very likely be the work of a witch," said the old man, searching through my mother's clothes for intentional cuts.

"A woman so kind cannot be despised. My first wife spoke out of turn, wandered from the cabin, and made enemies. She was an *amiyok-guru*! One time, in a fit of blind rage, she stole the offerings I placed at the altar, making me lose favor with the *kamui*. But this woman is nothing like her; she is calm, as rational as any man, and always courteous. She stays where she should and is always wary of danger," he said, sadness welling up in his eyes.

The old man crouched down to mother and pulled up her eyelids. "A curse has been placed upon her."

"It must have been that boy! He is so arrogant; risking his life and others for nothing other than his own ego! He takes after his mother, that's for sure!" yelled father.

"Brother wouldn't hurt her," I said softly.

"Not intentionally. But his ill will has manifested as a dark spirit and seized her. To think a boy could have the power to bind her spirit. Can this *uoitakushi* be undone?" asked father, sweat building up on his brow.

"I can only do what the chief *kamui* permits." The old man chanted by her bedside and made many *inao* as offerings.

I never once left mother's side for the three days of her illness. Brother never once came to the cabin during this time.

The third night the old man had succeeded in the exorcism. Father, him and I all rattled sticks around the cabin, scaring off the spirit that had possessed her.

My father gave thanks to the fire *kamui* and was in such an ecstatic state he rushed out of the cabin to give praise to every *kamui* he could find.

I confronted the old man as he turned to leave the cabin. "I want to help people. I want to banish evil *kamui*, like you do."

"You want to be a *tusu-guru*?" he asked with a toothy grin.

"Yes. More than anything. Please, teach me all that you know," I said, keeping my voice strong but hushed.

"I cannot teach you," he said, taking another step toward the exit.

"Is it because a woman cannot pray? I've felt the *kamui*'s presence many times. I'm as perceptive as a dog…just not all the time," I said, shuffling my feet.

"Women are fully capable of proper prayer and if you are as perceptive as you say, it is likely you would make a great *tusu-guru*. But teaching such things to a girl or woman is taboo. *Popke no okai un*," he said before walking out.

After approaching him many times a day for a few weeks, he finally spoke to me again.

"Sit down."

I nodded happily and sat down in the grass. "What's my first lesson?"

"I didn't say I would teach you. But I will tell you why I can't teach you. There is a reason that it is *hatto-an* for girls and women to perform rituals."

"And what is the reason?"

"They have no souls and thus their prayers are empty and lifeless," he said, staring into my eyes.

*No souls? What? Every creature, land, air, and sea has a soul. Why wouldn't women?*

"Haha. At least that's what I was told before."

"You, you're not a man?" I asked, my head a bit dizzy.

"Not entirely. As a boy I would dress up in my sister's *amip*. I related to girls more than boys. I prayed every night for the chief *kamui* to correct his one and only mistake: giving me the wrong body. I was such a presumptuous child. I did not understand that there is one supreme, perfect chief of the *kamui*. The *Kotan Kara Kamui* is the only *kamui* that exists outside the universe. He is the maker of all places and worlds. Any faults in the stars or misfortunes are the result of other *kamui* shirking their duties or misinterpreting his orders. I can't say I entirely hated being a boy; it allowed me to perform rituals and become a *tusu-guru*. If they knew I was really a feminine spirit in a masculine body, I likely would be banished. You won't tell anyone, right?" he asked with a wrinkled smile.

"Not a soul," I said, grabbing his hand.

*I can't imagine how strange that must feel. Being born in the wrong body. How can his faith be so strong when his existence is in chaos?*

"Good. Now, the other reason women and girls aren't taught is that, well, they are unable to understand the traditions of the ancients. They lack the mental fortitude and reason to perform proper rituals. Ah, the things men tell themselves," he said, looking up at the clouds.

"So then, you don't believe it?"

"I know it's false. I'm a girl in mind, though not in body. Despite this…malady, I am able to converse with the *kamui*, perform rituals and learn about the secrets of the other worlds. There is one last reason that *matnep* are not allowed to perform rituals or become *tusu-gurus*. Though, the men never speak of it outright."

"What is it?" I asked, scooting up closer.

"Fear. They fear nothing more than a spiteful woman. It is taboo to visit an *ainu moshiri*, but the danger is even greater if the grave belonged to a *matnep*. The idea of witches and the power of a woman's insults are evidence enough of their fear. They know that women are strong, and they want us to think we are *okirasap*. It's more than mere paranoia or a fear that we will make prayers of vengeance. They are scared of our virtuous nature. If a man prays for wine and his wife prays he gets none, who would the *kamui* listen too? Some believe that there was a time when both were allowed to pray, but the wise ancestors decided it was too dangerous. And they made this choice not without reason. Men are afraid that an empowered *matnep* can make them lose favor with the *kamui*. Give women the ability to pray and the whole system changes. And that, my dear, is why I can't teach you," he said with a smile before standing up.

"This is your chance to show them. If I'm a successful *tusu-guru*, you can prove that *matnep* are more than capable of interacting with the *kamui*. The one we pray to, most of all, is the undeniably feminine fire *kamui*—the divine *shongo-kuru-guru*."

"That is correct. After all, it is the *Abe-Kamui* who conjures up the entirety of our *ishu* and judges us accordingly."

"I never knew that. Please, you know so much. This is important. You can uplift all of us out of submission. Please, *ekashi*, I'll do whatever it takes."

He turned his head, only partially facing me. "Things aren't so simple. Customs do not change unless everyone in the village agrees to the change."

"Then we'll show them all. They'll have to admit that girls can become *tusu-gurus*."

"If they found out, I wouldn't be the only one punished. Don't throw away everything you have, my dear. It isn't worth it."

"We'll do it in secret!"

"Nothing is foolproof."

"You must teach me. If my daughter wants to become a *tusu-guru*, then she should be allowed to at least try. I'll take full blame for whatever happens. Even if I am expelled from the tribe, even if they force all the punishments on me, they can't say we aren't capable of interacting with the *kamui*."

*Where did this sudden strength come from?*

"Tomorrow morning, past that hill there is a cave under some vines…don't be late. *Popke no okai un*," he said before walking off.

We would meet in secret during the day, while the other girls took a rest from gardening. Only mother knew where I went. For nearly two years I learned all about medicine, rituals, and *kamui*. I was even given my own staff, topped with fox skulls, which was a special kind of guardian *kamui* called a *shiratki-kamui*. I was taught that the root of an *upcu* plant could cure heavy illness, that crushed dock seeds are for diarrhea, and that a heated nail against the tooth could cure a toothache. I learned there was a willful deity for every phenomenon in nature, each one complete in and of itself. There were male and female *kamuis* of good and evil and of war and peace. Distant beings that overshadow us, the *ehangeko-kamui*, had greater power and sanctity than the *ehange kamui*—the ones who lived with the land alongside us. Not only did my home have its own *kamui* that defended it, our whole village was kept safe by a protector *kamui*. Sure I was told all about *kamui* before, by my mother, but it was only surface knowledge. The stories Teacher told made apparent to me the power and personality of the many *kamuis* around and beyond us. Most of all, I learned that I love medicine, rituals, and all things mystical.

One day, a friend of mine, Hapuru, approached me and begged to come along, if only just once. I led her to the cave, careful not to leave any trace behind. Before the day's lesson began four men rushed into the cave. They seized my teacher and carried him back to the village. I called out to him in tears and raised my staff in retaliation. Teacher told me to lower my staff and was taken away. The next day, after a trial, Teacher was sent away from our village.

    *It was my fault he was banished.*

Time seemed to lose meaning. Dig up soil, sow seeds, eat soup, go to bed, repeat, repeat, repeat. The daily gardening seemed more arduous and my time weaving, though peaceful, lacked any purpose. I would practice in secret what I already knew, but without a teacher I had hit a plateau. Eventually I even stopped honing my skills. After all, what purpose were they if I would never be permitted to use them?

A number of meaningless days later, I found a new passion. One of my mother's friends had fallen ill and mother had volunteered to tend to the baby. Seeing I was sad, she offered to let me hold it.

    *It was light and heavy all at once. It felt warm too.*

    I found such pleasure in holding the *aiai*, though I was still a kid myself. Despite it having no fathom of the world, or perhaps because it did not, the baby exuded profound joy. It was enough to get me out of my slump.

    *I found a new purpose.*

    "How do I make one?" I asked mother while petting the little miracle.

    "You're much too young to be worried about such things, *apohonto*," she said with a smile.

    "Can't be a shaman because I'm a girl and I can't be a mother because I'm a child. What can I do?" I asked, disturbing the baby with my negative energy.

    "You can help me stitch your *akoro yupo*'s *amip*," she said with a peaceful smile.

"If her mother moves on to the next world, can we keep her?" I asked, poking the baby's belly.

"You shouldn't say such things. You'll invite dark spirits in. What we can do is tend to the little one so well that once she recovers, she'll let us watch over him from time to time."

"Then that's what I'll do." I picked up the *aiai* and embraced him. "Hmm. He seems a bit hungry." I lifted up my shirt and held him to my bosom.

"You'll make a wonderful mother," she said, holding up the patched up garment.

*I feel something, but no milk is coming out.*

"Am I doing it wrong?" I asked, switching nipples.

"You're doing fine. It's just that you're too young to make milk. Here, hand him to me," she said, outstretching her arms.

I stood up and carefully placed the baby in her arms. "How long before I can make milk?"

"After you've had a child," she said.

*Of course! Milk is for babies. It only makes sense for it to come after I've had a child.*

"I'm going out," I said.

"Don't wander off too far," she said with a wave.

I left home and rushed to where the boys always gathered. They were on a field, both boys and men, ten on each side. They were playing *karip-pashte*. One side had tossed the vine hoop and one of the more able-bodied boys caught the hoop with a well-timed spear throw. Since he succeeded, he went to the other team. Brother never liked this aspect of the game. He said it reinforces the idea that sides don't matter and could lead to future loyalty issues.

*Time to look for a husband.*

I overheard some of the drunken men talking about making babies with a woman.

*If I want my own little miracle in the future, I should spend my time searching for the perfect husband.*

I waited for the game to end and approached the most handsome boy of the group—the one who switched sides four times before the game's end. "Have your parents picked a wife for you?" I asked, moving my hips side to side in a bewitching way.

"No."

"Perfect." I grabbed his hand and smiled at him.

He pulled his hand away. "But I'm not going to marry an ugly girl like you."

*Ugly.*

He ran off with his friends.

*I'm ugly.*

I rushed back into the cabin, leaving a trail of tears behind.

Brother was in the midst of chanting at the eastern window but stopped once I had entered. "What happened?"

"Am I ugly?" I asked, trying to hold back more tears from coming out.

Brother stood up. "What's his name?"

"I don't know."

"You're too young to be worried about appearances."

"I can't be a *tusu-guru* and I can't have a baby yet. I really want a baby. And I need a boy for that, don't I?"

"You understand so little."

"I understand that I want an *aiai* and I'll do whatever it takes to get one," I said, standing up on my tiptoes.

"You'd die before it even came out. You're too weak to bear a child," he said with a cold gaze.

*Why is he always so cruel to me?*

"I'm stronger than you think!" I yelled.

"Then take me down, right now."

I rushed into him and pushed off the floor with all my strength. I couldn't get him to budge an inch.

*Why am I so weak?*

"I'm the strongest boy my age and you are five years younger than me. If you can't take down a man, there's no way you'll ever have the strength to bear a child. Now get to bed. I have to get up early to go hunting."

He went back to chanting to the fire *kamui.*

I didn't get much sleep that night.


The next two days I spent extra time in the garden, building up strength so I could one day be a mother.

Brother returned early in the morning on the third day.

Men and women gathered around him. In his arms was a fluffy creature, whining in a pained tone.

*It was a bear.*

Brother looked down at me. "You don't need to bear a child to be a mother," he said, handing me the animal.

*It was heavier than a human baby, but it was also cuter.*

"For me?" I asked, looking up at him with bewilderment.

"That's right. I'm entrusting you to look after him. You can name him too, if you'd like."

*Brother smiled at me. Maybe he isn't as mean as I thought.*

The little bear licked my face.

"I'll meet with you back home once I've shared our story," said my brother, turning from me to look at his fellow men.

I nodded and walked back home, making sure the ride was as smooth as possible for my little boy.

Once inside I cooked him up some soup and held up the cup.

The fluffy *aiai* lapped up the soup.

"You haven't eaten in a while, have you?" I asked, rubbing his little belly.

Once he was done with the soup, he began whining again. It all felt so familiar.

*He's crying like I did the night she left. He misses his mother.*

I grabbed him tightly and lowered us both onto my *aputki*. The mat was just barely big enough for the both of us.

"I'll be your mother," I said, kissing him at the center of his forehead.

He continued to whine and pawed at my shirt.

*Of course.*

I lifted my shirt and held him to my bosom.

He suckled for a bit before falling asleep in my arms.

*I know what to call him! Noyuk! A good bear.*


I woke up the next morning with Noyuk licking my face.

I licked him back and giggled.

*How long has it been since I've had a good laugh?*

"You should be more careful, *mataki*. He could bite you. Don't nurse him," said my brother, making a new *inao* with his hunting *chieikip*.

"But he misses his mother," I said.

Brother left the cabin without another word.

"Don't you want breakfast?" hollered mother.

I popped out of bed. "We do," I said, holding up my little boy.

"Here you go. Fresh rice soup for two," she said, setting down the cups.

Noyuk was so excited he knocked over the cup.

*So cute. And he's mine.*

I grabbed hold of him. "Be more careful next time," I said, before releasing him to enjoy his meal.

A year and a half passed by, filled with fun and fulfillment. Noyuk grew from a *peurep* into a *biyap*. But a little extra weight didn't get in our way. We were inseparable.

One day, I was playing with my friends. I had just tagged my *aiai* so it was his turn to chase us.

He leaped at the youngest girl of the group and knocked her down.

She screamed a wretched scream.

The men quickly came and pulled Noyuk off.

Her arm had twisted the wrong way and was now broken.

I rushed to my little one and wrapped my arms around him.

*He really has gotten big.*

The men left me with the bear and went together into the chief's *chisei*. When my brother came back from the hunt, a man whispered in his ear and he went with my *akoro-yupo* inside the chief's home.

I ventured to my friend's *chisei* and apologized to her mother.

"Get out! And keep your monster away from my *apohonto*," she said, holding her daughter's hand as the shaman examined the broken arm.

I left to my *chisei* with Noyuk.

After dinner, we went straight to bed.

When my brother came in he sat down by my bed. "*Chishirikirap*," he said, gently touching my hand.

*Why was he apologizing? That isn't like him at all.*

He then left to his corner and rested.


Mother kept watch over my *aiai* while I went out gardening. When I returned to the cabin during the shift change, he was gone.

Mother looked away, tears welling up in her eyes. "They took Noyuk. I'm so sorry."

I ran out of my home and into a growing crowd of villagers. I pushed through and found my *aiai*. He was trapped in a cage and crying.

*He's alive.*

My hands went between the bars and caressed his head.

"Let him out," I said with a fierce tone.

Brother put his hand on my shoulder and pulled me into an embrace. "*Chishirikirap*."

I socked him in the face. "How could you let this happen?"

"I need you to stay inside the cabin tonight. Please. You owe me at least this much," he said, lifting me off my feet.

"Let me go!" I yelled, slamming my fists against his chest. "I don't owe you anything!"

He kept silent till we were back in the cabin. He tossed me to the ground. "You killed my mother! If you were never born she would be here right now! You're going to stay inside like I said. Understood?"

*I killed her?*

"Understood!" he yelled.

I nodded, tears building up at the edges of my eyes.

He left me sobbing in the cabin.

I walked toward the door.

His malice bit me, causing me to nearly topple over.

*He hates me.*


It wasn't long before I heard cheering and singing.

*I have to save my baby.*

I slammed against the back door but it wouldn't budge.

Mother came up and hugged me. "Stay here tonight, *apohonto*. With me."

"What if that was me out there? What if I was the one in a cage, fearful and lonely?"

Mother was silent.

I put on a cloak and went to the *rorun-puyara*. "I'm going to save him. If the *kamui* curse me for exiting through this window, so be it." I climbed out of the eastern window and landed on my feet.

I ran past drunken men, some I recognized and other's I didn't.

*These patterns. Are they from nearby tribes? Are they planning on sacrificing my aiai for this festival?*

I had never seen the village so crowded. I slipped through the men until I made it to the center of the commotion.

Our shaman was crouched near Noyuk, his hand was on its head. He was asking for forgiveness. Pleading with my baby to not return with a vengeance.

*My little boy looked so scared.*

Two men opened the cage and wrapped a rope around my baby's neck and each foreleg. The other men sat in a circle around the fire.

"Horrible, isn't it? And all to gain favor with the *kamui*," said a voice behind me.

I turned around to see a boy around my age. The white pattern on his cloak revealed him to be from the Isepo tribe.

"Your people do the same?" I asked.

"Depends on what you mean by my people. I walk among them, but I am not one of them. Shamans exist on the fringe of society, not fully in this world or the other. Nice to meet you," he said, scratching his cheek.

"I'm Ebui. I'm a *tusu-guru* too," I said in a hushed voice.

"What?"

"Forget about that. Can you save my baby? Please. I'll do anything."

"I'm still in training. I'm not powerful enough to stop this."

The young people from my tribe and the neighboring tribes all stood up at once. They fired blunt arrows and shouted at my child as he was pulled along by a rope around his neck. Familiar faces all clapped their hands together, intoxicated by the excitement of the ritual.

*Is this a nightmare?*

"Do what you can!" I rushed in and placed my body over my child's back. Blunt arrows continued to fire.

I heard a loud shout.

*Brother.*

He ran up to me and yanked me off. "I told you to stay inside," he said, grabbing my ear.

The boy grabbed a dagger from one of the dunk men and started cutting at the rope. He was soon lifted off his feet.

Two men stood up and grabbed my son's hindquarters and face. A third man went up to my *aiai*. He was holding a piece of wood.

"Stop!" I screamed.

The boy slammed his knee into the teeth of the man holding him. He squeezed out from the man's grip and went back to cutting the rope.

Once it broke, he was pinned down by two men.

"Run!" I yelled to my baby.

Noyuk clawed at the man trying to shove a piece of wood in its mouth.

I slipped out of my brother's grip and pierced a man with his own dagger.

"Ay-oh!" he screamed. The man released my baby's mouth, but two men behind were still strangling my little one with a rope knotted into a noose.

*He's almost free.*

"Get out of here!" I yelled.

The man I hurt raised his hand to strike me, but my *akoro yupo* gripped his wrist. Brother pulled a bow out from his quiver and pierced it through my baby's head.

My little one was dead in an instant.

*This can't be real.*

Brother grabbed me and carried me off.

*My baby is dead. He's dead.*

Through the drunken men and shadowy faces, I was carried back home. Brother set me down on my bed.

My whole body was shaking.

*Noyuk is really gone.*

289

"Get some rest," he said.

"Why does the chief *kamui* hate me?" I asked, tears racing down my cheeks.

*I'm cursed.*

"He doesn't hate anyone. You're being conceited."

"You killed my *aiai*!" I yelled, grabbing whatever I could find and launching it at him.

"And you killed my mother!" he yelled before storming out of the *chisei*.

"Mother! Where are you?" I went to her corner but she wasn't there.

*I'm not leaving. I'll guard this place like a ghost and attack anyone who enters.*

The next three days sapped my essence like a curse. I blocked the doors and threatened to kill anyone who entered. Brother eventually broke through and disarmed me. I cried myself to sleep that night. When mother came back the following morning, I sobbed in her arms. But even her embrace lost its warmth. After all, how long would it be before my curse took her life? On the third day, the oldest woman of the village passed on. Brother forced me into clothes and dragged me along; all the while I spouted all the curses I could think of.

I was supposed to weep with the other girls, but I didn't know the woman who had gone away. The men were solemn too. But who cares? These men and the women too, they were all there when my *aiai* was killed.

*They are all responsible. They all deserve my wrath.*

I mouthed curses to each one but it felt ineffectual. As far as I was concerned, they should all die.

*I should die too.*

I overheard a couple muttering about the resting old woman in their *chisei*. The *paunguru* prohibited them to enter and said that it would be burned down. The couple asked if they could get their belongings out, but the chief outright refused them.

"The ghosts of old women are especially deadly. If you enter that cabin you not only put your life and that of your families at risk, you risk dooming our entire village to her wrath."

*Doom the entire village.*

The couple nodded and left with their neighbors to their home.

"When is it to be burned down?" asked my brother.

"As soon as possible," said the chief.

*I better hurry. An opportunity like this won't come again. None of us deserve to live. We all deserve death.*

# Chapter 75: Taboo

As soon as the funeral service ended, I ran off to find the cabin where the old woman had gone away. Upon arrival, I felt a shift in air pressure. She was here alright, and she was very powerful.

*I need to get her upset, really upset.*

I stomped my way around the cabin and kicked open the front door.

Her presence built up at my feet, but I kept moving.

I grabbed a club from the man's corner and smashed everything I could find.

"That old woman was a total nuisance. Her funeral felt more like a celebration than a ceremony of loss. We all took turns talking about how she made our lives more difficult."

A powerful wind swirled inside, knocking over the *inao* placed by the eastern window.

"They say this place is haunted, but that weak old woman could never have the power to curse someone."

I smelled something…*shupuya.*

*That was fast. Better finish up.*

The front door slammed shut by a powerful gust.

"It sure is windy today," I said before spitting at the holy altar.

*If her wrath isn't sufficient, then enraging the kamui should get the desired result.*

"You feel that heat? That's a fire. They are going to burn this place so you'll have nowhere to go. We don't want you anymore so just leave us alone!"

I turned to the sacred east window. It was now blocked by a tower of flames.

*Okay, back exit.*

I slammed against the back door, but a force greater than my own kept it closed.

*Please let the front be open.*

I rammed my body into the front door. It didn't budge.

*Bad. This is very bad.*

"You may take my life! But what about the others! They all mock you! They all hate you! They are burning down your residence and there is nothing you can do!" I yelled as loud as I could.

*I deserve to die. This is only fair. It's so hot, but I can't stop shivering.*

"Do your worst!"

*Maybe this is for the best. If her hex is insufficient, I'll haunt them all till they die of illness. I'll end the whole village with my motherly wrath.*

"Go ahead and burn me!"

I heard something slam into the door.

The middle portion of the door burst open.

"Get out of here now!" yelled my brother.

"No! I'm going to burn and it's all your fault! This is what you get for killing my baby!"

He squeezed through the broken door, slicing his legs in the process.

"What do you care if I die? I killed your mother, didn't I? You hate me! Well I hate you too!"

*I hate everyone.*

Brother tore off my shirt and tossed it into the flames. He lifted me up and held me to his chest, shielding me from the heat.

He squeezed through the door once more, which now had fire brewing at its bottom.


As soon as we got out, my brother brought me to the shaman's home.

"You are more wounded than she is," said the *tusu-guru*.

"Forget the wounds. My sister was possessed. A *nitnep* took over her," said my brother.

A man rushed into the cabin. "Is she okay?"

Father had returned from his fight with the Horokeu tribe.

"She has been possessed by snakes, father," said my brother.

"The *paunguru* has called for a meeting to discuss her punishment. What did she do?" asked father, examining the wounds on my brother's legs.

"A spirit possessed her to enter another spirit's domain. Foolish sister, you will be made infertile by the ghost's curse," he said, chewing burdock leaves before applying the salve to the burn marks on my arms.

*Even now he mocks me. I hate him.*

"How can I bring a child into a world that raises animals only to kill them? He was my baby!" I yelled, hitting my brother.

Father seized my head and ran his hand down the length of my hair from my crown to my shoulders. "There, there, *apohonto*. You were a splendid mother. I am so very proud of you."

*I never meant to bring him into this. Please let father be safe from my curse.*

"You're praising her after what she's done!" yelled my brother.

"You had her take care of a *hepere*? What were you thinking?" asked father, still stroking me.

"I didn't know she would get so attached. Children tend to play with the cubs and women nurture them, but never has anyone tried to stop the ceremony."

"You killed his mother, brought him to me only to kill him yourself. Why must you torment me? Is it because I killed your mother?" I asked, held down by the shaman.

"The fire *kamui* shirked her duties. It was not your fault she is sleeping," said father in a hushed tone.

The shaman turned to my brother. "Ebui is not possessed. What your sister did, she did of her own accord."

"And so her mother's madness finally shows itself. I will stay with her while she heals. Do your best to mitigate her punishment," said father, looking at my brother while crouching down next to me.

The shaman and my brother left the cabin.

"That boy has caused you great harm, but you must stay *okira*," said father, moving a clump of my hair back.

*Father is always so strong. He has truly lived up to his name.*

"You wouldn't have let them kill my *aiai*, would you?" I asked, starting to tear up.

"Traditions only change by a unanimous vote. I alone can change nothing. I follow the *tuitak*, traditions and customs. I pray daily and with sincerity. When I am called to battle, I fight to protect the village. You cannot change things, *apohonto*. You must simply adjust and move on. If it were up to me, you never would have spent time with that bear cub. To go through such a loss at your age— it isn't right."

"What isn't right is killing someone you know."

"Then killing a stranger is okay?"

"That's not what I meant. Noyuk was my baby. I loved him so much."

"And I'm sure you'll make a wonderful mother."

"I'm done with that. I'm done with love and magic! I'm sick of this village and everyone in it!"

*I should have died in that* chisei, *surrounded by flames.*

"Get some rest, *apohonto*."

"Yeah, I am pretty tired." I closed my eyes and fell asleep.

When I awoke, it was early morning and a shirt was placed on me.

Brother was looming over me. "Get up."

I turned away from him as I slipped into the new shirt.

"What did they decide, Akno?" asked father, holding mother's hand.

Brother gritted his teeth. "Banishment."

*What?*

"Let me talk to the *paunguru*," said father, getting up from the floor.

"I packed your things, *mataki*," said my brother, putting my *korobe* into a single pile.

"Where am I going?" I asked.

"Away from here. And you can't return."

*I've been banished?*

"Calm down. Okira is talking with the chief. I'm sure things will work out. Ebui is only a child," said mother.

"The chief knows she purposefully went into that home. Your little bud tried to curse all of us," said my brother, glaring at mother.

"But how will she survive on her own?" asked mother, her eyes becoming wet.

*I never meant to hurt her.*

"I'll be okay. Teacher taught me what is poisonous and edible. I'll be fine," I said, embracing my mother with all my love.

*I may never hug her again.*

"*Mataki*, it's time." Brother attached all my things to a *tara*, fastened it around my lower back and led me out of the cabin.

Father was shouting at the *paunguru*.

I waved at him.

Father rushed over to me.

No words were exchanged. He embraced me one last time.

Brother and father led me to the edge of the village.

"Stay safe. *Sarampa*," said father, forcing a smile.

"Keep searching for a village that will accept you. Be respectful of your new family. *Sarampa*," said my brother.

I walked past the village borders and entered the forest.

*This wasn't supposed to happen.*

Four days and nights passed without any soup and without the safety of a *chisei*. It rained on the fourth night and the trees provided less shelter than I had hoped. I woke up shivering throughout that night. On the fifth morning, I came across a man, but he had no pattern on his shirt from which to identify his tribe.

*What if he's an enemy?*

"Who's there?" he asked, holding up his bow and arrow.

*If I move, he may shoot on reflex. Don't have many options.*

"I'm just a girl. I'm not armed," I said, coming out of the bushes with my hands raised.

The man lowered his weapon and walked up to me. "You're shivering. Come with me. The *tusu-guru* from my village will heal you," he said, placing his shirt over my shoulders.

"What village are you from?" I asked while following him.

"What about you?"

I stood up proud. "Shitumbe."

"Where you banished as well?"

"What makes you say that?"

"You're either lost or banished. There's no need to be ashamed. I was picked up around here when I was kicked out of my village. I was once a Horokeu."

*He's our enemy.*

I stopped in place. "What did you do?"

"Relax. I'm not going to hurt you. My friend stole some things and got caught. I took the blame for him. He wasn't well liked. The incident would have likely resulted in a severe punishment for him."

"The Horokeu have friends? I thought they were savages, like the *koropok-gurus*."

"Even savages have friends."

"Then you don't eat *ainu*?"

"Is that what your people told you? We may be ruthless in battle, but otherwise we aren't all that *uoaya* from you, *furep*."

"It's Shitumbe," I said, holding my head up high.

"Not anymore. You aren't a fox and I'm no longer a wolf. We're just Ainu," he said with a smile.

*He's wrong. Banished or not, I'm a Shitumbe.*


I followed him all the way to his village and gave him back his shirt once my shivering died down. The village was small, consisting of twenty-two homes, all the same size. As we walked by, I peeked inside, seeing as many as six people per house.

"Do you have a leader?" I asked, covering my red pattern as best I could as their eyes judged me.

"We have a *nupuru-guru* who helped establish this place. His name is Hechaka. And he's aptly named. He cleared the fog away from so many of us." The man who was once a Horokeu opened the door to a *chisei*.

*It's him!*

The one who inspired me, who helped me find my purpose, was seated on a mat in front of me. He was wearing a blend of shamanic garb and women's clothing. He even had a headdress now. The twinkle in his eye meant he recognized me.

My teacher's smile faded as he stood up. "Why were you banished?"

"It's really you." My mind went blank and all of a sudden I was hugging him. He was more than a familiar face; he was my teacher. Once I came to my senses, I immediately broke out of the hug. "My apologies. I meant no disrespect."

*I can't be seen as a child.*

"No need for concern. We do not have the same customs here," said Teacher, showing me the beads in his hair and tapping his now shaved chin. "Lie down. You're still shaking," said Hechaka with a smile.

"Wait. If the customs are different…can you teach me? I want to be a *tusu-guru*! I want to talk with the *kamui*, lose myself in a divination, and help people heal!"

"If you are here, then there is surely a reason behind it. This is the place where those without a destiny can forge a new future. You sent me on this path and now you have come upon the path you brought about. Our destinies are linked, Ebui. I will share with you all I know. Once you get over your sickness, that is," he said, gesturing for me to lie down.


Thirty-two days later, an outsider was brought into our village.

As the shaman's apprentice, it was my duty to assist in tending to the outsiders wounds. Upon entering the cabin, I found a boy. It was the same boy who tried to help me save my baby.

*Did destiny bring him here?*

"Hold onto his hand; we mustn't let his spirit leave. Check his body for wounds," said Hechaka, pulling her hand away from the boy's heated forehead.

I gripped the boy's hand and examined him. I found blood stains on the edges of his shirt but saw no wound on his body.

*Where did the blood come from?*

"Take a look into his eyes. What is your assessment?"

I lifted up his eyelids. They were a nice amber color. "They are heavily dilated. Shall I ask the fire *kamui* to heal him?"

"No. Keep him calm. Make sure his spirit does not leave his body. I will call upon a powerful *kamui* in the meantime."

"I know he has a fever, but do you really think that is necessary?"

"It is."

"Should I bring you some rice wine?"

"A possession cannot be forced. One must make their mind receptive through prayer and contemplation. This is likely your first time witnessing a possession. Worry not; you will be in no danger." Teacher sat down on her knees and faced the eastern window. She chanted beneath her breath.

I took in a deep breath and centered my mind on joy.

"♫ The bunny gets lost in the rain. Lost in the rain.

He is scared, he is hurt, and he is cold.

He was lost in the rain. Lost in the rain.

Spent days searching for his home.

Then one day, when the sun was shining and the rain had cleared,

a fox came by. A fox, oh my.

The fox bared his teeth and the bunny cried. The bunny ran, afraid to die.

But the fox was fast, oh so fast.

He jumped on the bunny. Jumped on the bunny.

He bared his teeth, once again.

Then asked if the bunny would be his friend.

The bunny stood up. Up. Up. Up.

He licked the fox's face with friendly love.

He thought he was lost, but now he was found.

If it rained or snowed. Whether warm or cold.

With a snuggle and love. A kiss and hug.

The fox would always guide him home.

The bunny was lost. Lost in the rain.

But the fox would always guide him home. ♫"

Singing the story my mother used to relax me ended up bringing back an intense longing for home.

*I want to see her...and father too.*

Teacher's eyes slowly opened. Her spine contorted and she leaned over the boy. "Dark spirit. Leave this body." She beat her chest and spoke in monotone. Despite this, there was an otherworldly power to her words.


Teacher came to after the dark spirit had been drawn out of the boy. When I asked her the meaning of her words, which spoke of past, present, and future as if they were happening in the present moment, she could only make vague approximations. The words were not her own after all; she was truly possessed by a *kamui*.

*I'm sure she could teach me much, but I would never be able to conjure up a spirit that was not my own.*

Teacher left to attend to another matter, leaving me alone with the patient.

The boy stirred. He rolled to his side and opened his eyes. He smiled when his eyes met mine. "Have I crossed over?"

"No. You are alive. The men found you in the woods. Your *amip* were drenched. You still have a fever. What happened to you? Why is their blood on your shirt?"

"I don't remember. I don't know how I got here or whose blood that is."

"Well, you should get some rest. We can escort you back home only once you're fully healed," I said, finally letting go of his hand.

"I'm not going back."

"Why not?"

"♫ Because with a snuggle and love. A kiss and a hug. The fox would always guide him home ♫," he said, placing his hand on mine.

*Eyes filled with dreams are truly a beautiful sight.*

I pulled my hand away. I could feel my cheeks getting flushed. "You should rest. I'll watch over you. But don't talk too much. Save your energy. You're still weak. You haven't fully recovered."

He nodded. "Will you hold my hand?"

"Yes...I can do that. It's good to see you again."

"It's the second time I've visited your village now," he said with a weak smile.

"This isn't the Shitumbe village. It's Moyuk, a village of outcasts. After my *aiai* was killed...I...I did something horrible. I was banished, never to return home. But just like the song says, you can find home anywhere. It goes beyond location and transcends tribe."

"I suppose we're both banished, *chiri-po*," he said, lifting up the blood stained section of his shirt.

"Yep. And were both apprentices now, *isepo*," I said, pulling out my special staff topped with a *niwok*.

"This village really is unlike the others. Hey, *chiri-po*, I suppose I never told you my name."

"Yeah, but I did. It's Ebui. Where did you get *chiri-po* from? I'm a proud fox not a little bird."

"You sang to me and you're little, so you're *chiri-po* now."

"And you are?"

"I was named by my father. I was a meek *aiai*, so it's not a very good name."

"How bad can it be?"

He looked away from me. "Eoha. It means to become empty."

"That's a great name!"

"It is?"

"For a shaman becoming empty is a vital skill. And if you're empty, then that means you have plenty of room in your heart," I said with the biggest smile I could muster.

"It's just as my vision said: you will be rescued by a *shiretok* girl," said Eoha, gazing into me.

*Beautiful. Am I really beautiful?*

I looked away and covered my flushed cheeks. "*Haphap.* Now, please, be silent. We can chat once you're feeling better."

"One last thing. Do you have a *chikappo*? The shaman of my village always uses one to drive away illness."

"I don't."

"Well, I see no reason the charm has to be a physical object. Can I have a *chopchose* instead?" he asked, puckering his lips.

*Teasing me even though he's sick. He'll recover in no time.*

"Go to sleep." I leaned over and kissed his forehead.

Eoha smiled at me and closed his eyes.


For four years I stayed at the Moyuk village. Eoha and I trained as apprentices every day. When it came time for possession training, I failed miserably, no matter how hard I tried. Eoha refused to train, if only to not make me feel inferior. Near the end of the third year, I was confident and skilled enough to heal people on my own; we both were. It felt like the curse surrounding me had been lifted. Then one day I received a premonition. It wasn't anything colorful or metaphorical. There wasn't even an image.

It was my teacher's voice. "You've killed me."

That's all it said.

I awoke with cold sweats in my bed.

"Your first vision," said Hechaka, pride beaming from her wrinkled face.

"Yes, I...."

"Congrats!" Eoha picked me up in a heartfelt embrace.

"What was it? No, let me guess. It's about me and about you. *Ainu katu ehange.* The time for me to leave this world is fast approaching," said Teacher in a tone of ease,

"What? No, that's not what it said." I clenched my fists.

"I had the same vision when we first met. I'll admit I was confused at first. I told you our destinies were connected, remember? Ah, this will be a great opportunity for a final lesson." Teacher stared off through the east window.

*Final lesson.*

I felt dizzy.

Three days passed. I avoided Teacher at every turn. I even left the village on the third day but got lost and ended up back where I had started. It was as if all the *kamui* were conspiring against me.

*Could the wrath of that old woman's ghost have been more powerful than I had predicted? Was this my punishment for leaving through the east window? Or was I always a doomed child?*

I sat up on a hill overlooking the village.

*How long before they are all devoured by my curse?*

I gazed up at the stars, searching for answers within their twinkling patterns.

# Chapter 76: Bound by the Cosmos

Complete darkness, then dots of light came into being. The one gazing at them wasn't doing so leisurely. The gaze was intense and fully aware. It noticed patterns in the stars. Each *rikop* shined but the light emitting from them felt ominous.

My gaze shifted back to the earthly plane.

The one who had taught me everything I knew looked up at the starlit sky with a smile.

"How can you smile?" I asked, on the brink of tears.

"Why not?" asked Hechaka, still looking into the night sky.

"You're going to die."

"Yes, and the *Kotan Karo Kamui* has been kind enough to let me know when."

I grabbed onto her hand. "Why can't I save you?"

"You'll make a great *tusu-guru*," she said, placing her hand over mine.

"The stars foretell great misfortune in the coming years. I can't help anyone without you."

"I have never done anything. I am merely a vessel."

"You cured my mother. You've saved so many people. I still have so much to learn. You need to teach me more." Tears were already beginning to well up in my eyes.

"You can't run away from your destiny. It will find you, just as death has found me."

"I...I can't do this," I said, pulling my hand away.

*How can she expect me to kill her?*

"You don't have a choice."

"I refuse to!"

"Look up there. We can't escape what's written. Great calamity is creeping upon us. But remember, after every collapse comes a renewal."

"I can't do the ceremony on my own."

"You have Eoha with you as well and the other shamans."

"No. They are depending on you."

"You're here for a reason. You know this must be done. How you plan to do it...that's up to you."

"Why me? You're *onne*; why not let time take you?"

"*Onne*? By that do you mean valued or aged?"

"I meant aged, but of course I value you. You're my teacher."

"You can't convince me otherwise. It's been decided. Hmm, I wonder how you'll do it."

I put my arms around Hechaka's arm and leaned my head against her. "I can't do it." I hugged her tightly. "I love you. You're my teacher. You're even more than that! You're my grandmother! You can't leave until I'm ready. I'm not ready yet, okay?"

"I have taught you much…but your family is still your blood. You must show your true family *uainu*."

"I can never return to them, so why should I bother feeling anything for them. Even if I went back, the villagers wouldn't allow me in. This is my home, and you are my only family now."

"Stay strong. If you don't decide how you're going to end me…soon enough it will happen and not the way you intended. We don't want that, now do we? The more you postpone destiny, the fewer paths you can take."

"I'm only confident as a mystic because of you. I owe you everything. I can only heal people due to your teachings. You gave my life meaning when it had none. I love you dearly!"

"Ah, that will do," said Hechaka, her voice fading.

The arms became limp around me. Her head fell upon my shoulder.

*I miss her already.*

I stayed in Teacher's limp embrace for a while longer, but eventually I had to stand up. I had to rise to my feet and go back to the village. It was inevitable.


I found my *chisei* in the darkness. Each step I took felt predetermined. I had finally lost my illusion of control. It was as if I had been possessed by a spirit. Each motion was an observation, not an action. I spoke to no one. I had nothing to say anyway. I walked past the sleeping women who shared the cabin with me, careful not to disturb them, and made it to my bed. The night air was cold. I huddled for warmth inside my bear skin blanket. Odd as it may sound, the skin gave me a sense of comfort that no other material could.

*It always made me feel like a little bear cub, cuddling against its mother's warm fur.*

But the warmth didn't last. Soon it made me feel cold, sad, and alone. I put on three blankets, but the chill would not leave.


Morning came as it always does and always will. Now more than ever I realized the futility of my actions.

*I can't stop time. Everyone I know will die, myself included. Such is the fate of mortals.*

My eyes opened on their own and before I knew it, I was back on my feet. I rushed over to teacher's *chisei* for early morning lessons. It was only after I entered that it hit me. I fell to my knees.

*She was gone.*

This must have been how my brother felt. I never knew our blood mother, but he did. He loved her dearly. Even when he smiled at me, his eyes didn't. They always glared. They spoke his thoughts *"You killed her. You took mother away."*

I felt something on my cheek.

*Tears. I was crying.*

I wiped my eyes clean but they kept coming.

"Tears are for those who have yet to accept fate." That was what Teacher would say, and it would always make the flow of sadness stop. But now I realized it was her wrinkled smile that calmed me, not the words themselves.

I was on the ground, sobbing. My hands were clinging onto my sacred staff.

*I don't deserve this.*

If only she knew the truth. I couldn't see spirits. I was never possessed by a *kamui*. The only gift I had was lying. I lied my way into becoming her student. I lied because I thought she could save me, give me power and a purpose that I did not possess. I wanted something to live for. And now I have to keep the lie going until death gives me its mercy.

*No. There is one other option.*

I packed some food and a few of my belongings and, after properly fastening my *tara*, hoisted them up with my head—which was protected by a cotton cloth. I went back to the hill where Hechaka was resting. After digging a hole and placing my teacher inside, I held up my staff.

"Thank you, chief *kamui*, for bringing me and my teacher together."

"So, she's really gone now," said Eoha as he walked up to me.

Together we wrapped Teacher's body in mats and placed the dirt over the mats. We placed *chi-ehoroka-kep*, special *inao* that were shaved from bottom to top and made many prayers for her well being in the next world.

I turned to Eoha after wiping away my tears.

In the four years we had been together, I had seen him transform from a mischievous boy into a wise, but still at times mischievous, young man. His face was still rounded, as was his nose—both which gave him the look of a baby. He had a slender build and lanky arms that could bend in ways I thought weren't possible. His black hair was cut in the shape of a quarter moon, and he tended to it daily for reasons beyond me. Just like my brother, he had yet to grow any hairs on his chin. His clothes were loose and he only carried a single *chitarape*, which was slung around his right arm, filled with potions, leaves, and other remedies. His amber eyes always lit up whenever they met mine, even though he was in many ways superior to me as a shaman. Though I was a year older than him, I felt that he had wisdom far beyond me.

I stood up and looked into his mystical eyes. "I can't stay here. I'm going back home."

Eoha turned to me and gripped my hand. "Stay with me. Please. There are other mystics here. We can continue our training."

"How long before I have a vision leading to your death? I'm done being a shaman. I'm going back to my village. I'll work in the gardens with my mother. You stay here. Become a powerful *tusu-guru* in my stead." I leaned over and kissed his forehead.

"Let me come along. The forest can be deceptive, especially at night."

"Fine, but only as far as the village outskirts. Pack your things and come right back, okay?"

He nodded and rushed off.

I sat by the unmarked grave. "You deserve better than this. You were beloved in our village. I never should have had you train me. It's only led to misfortune. Maybe, they're right. *Matnep* aren't meant to be *tusu-gurus*." I set my staff at her grave and cried.

"I'm ready."

I turned to see Eoha. I got up, grabbed his hand, and headed back to my village.

On our journey we stopped by a lake. After looking up at the cloudy sky—perhaps pondering about the coming weather—Eoha sat down next to me and dropped some berries into my hands.

"This is your chance," he said with a grin.

"For what?" I asked, licking the berry juice off my finger.

"To see what a beautiful Ainu you are, *chiri-po*," he said, gesturing to the lake.

"Oh no. Mother warned me about reflective surfaces. For each second you spend in front of one, months are sapped away from your life."

"Your brother goes fishing, doesn't he? I'm sure he's seen his reflection a number of times. I don't think you need to worry if it's a *heshi*," he said, splashing his feet in the water.

"I suppose you're right."

*I hope I'm not ugly.*

I stepped up to the lake and waited for the *aka* to calm. Ever so gradually my visage formed. I was still a bit shorter than Eoha, which he made apparent by placing his hand on my head. There was a sooty, dark blue tattoo mark around my lips.

I remembered that the skin around my lip was cut off in order to make room to place the blue soot in. It was painful and a bit scary, but the colors matched well with the patterns etched on the backs of my hands. Due to my complaining, mother ended prematurely. This left me with a smaller tattoo, and I actually preferred it this way.

My cheekbones were a bit more elevated than I had thought, and my cheeks had a rosy complexion to them. My blue eyes sparkled despite my fatigue. I suppose the color must have been passed down to me by the one my brother calls mother. The blue beads around my neck complemented my facial features. My long brown *attush*, made from the inner bark of elm trees, was held together with shells. The little fox at the hip was a special design I learned from my mother, and I was never told it was inappropriate at the village of outcasts. Around my wrists were bluish bracelets embroidered by my mother. The only thing out of sorts was my hair, though my headdress was lovingly decorated. My mother usually cut and combed it, so it was too long—now down to my elbows—and it was clumped like a bird's nest. Still, I suppose I was pretty.

"See, what did I tell you?" asked Eoha, handing me a blue shell he found at the bottom of the lake.

"*Haphap*. We should get going," I said, fastening the shell to my dress.

"You are most welcome, *chiri-po*. Onward!" he cheered, rushing off ahead of me.

We arrived by morning and slid past some men who were going out on a hunt.

"Eoha, this is as far as you go. Wait here. They might not accept me. And if they don't, then I want to go back with you."

He suddenly embraced me.

*He felt so warm.*

I kissed his cheek, nodded, and then went back to my village.

Before I made it to my old *chisei*, a hand grabbed my wrist. I was suddenly lifted off the ground and pulled into a hug.

"*Mataki*, you're safe. Father's prayers have been well received."

Brother hated me for killing his mother. He was the one who killed my baby. Despite this, my arms went around his back and returned the affection.

*Just seeing a familiar face after all this time was incredible.*

My brother was now nineteen, a full-fledged man and fully adorned in *tonto* armor. He was strong, squarely built, thick-chested, and taller than any *ainu* I had seen. He had messy long hair and only a few hairs on his rounded chin that stuck up like *inao* at the *rorun-puyara* altar. A bow and arrow, war club, and some offerings were poking out from the pack slung around his shoulders. His eyes sparkled like a *rikop* pattern of good fortune in the night sky.

Once my feet were back on the ground, his eyes lost their shine.

"I'm sad." I buried my face in his chest.

It reeked of fish.

*Dead fish never smelled so good.*

"Sadness does us no good. All my tears could not bring her back. Not even my blood could," he said, pulling me off.

"I want to stay here, with my family," I said, trying to hold back my tears.

"Sister. You must leave. Go back to where you came from."

"No! Hechaka, the one who was banished from our village…all because of me…she's dead now."

"She? Your teacher was a man. All *tusu-gurus* are," said my brother.

"You know nothing! Teacher may have had a man's body, but she had a woman's nurturing spirit."

"I'm sorry for your loss. He…she was a great Ainu," said my brother, putting his hand on my shoulder.

I launched myself into him. "Please, let me come with you. I don't want to go back to that place. Everything there reminds me of Hechaka. It forces me to acknowledge her death. I won't go back."

"You must."

"I refuse!"

"A mere two days after you left, someone in the village became very ill. They moved on that very night," said my brother in a whisper.

"And they think it's my fault!"

"It wasn't long before the plague broke out. We've been fighting it for the past four years. Some have lost husbands, others wives, brothers are without sisters, and sisters without brothers. Whole families have been wiped out. There are only half as many of us as there once were. They think the plague is the tangible wrath of the old woman's ghost. They think it's your fault. If you return, I don't think you'll survive three days."

*Is it my fault? Did I really cause all that pain, all that death? Teacher was right: there is nothing more terrifying than the wrath of a woman.*

"I can't go back there. Please, brother. If you care about me, even a little bit, let me stay," I said, gripping onto his shirt.

"I will talk with the *paunguru*. But it may take time. Go back to your new village. Stay strong, sister. I will find you and bring you back if I can convince the chief."

"Okay. I'll try. Tell father I said hello."

"I will," he said with a smile.

"And give mother a big hug for me," I said with a smile.

"Y-yes. I will tell her you stopped by. Now, hurry, you must leave."

I nodded and turned away from him.

*Why can't I be strong like him?*

Eoha and I went back to the Moyuk village. Upon returning, he told the other shamans the news of our teacher's passing. That night he held me in his arms until I cried myself to sleep. After a few days, I joined him to continue our training under a different teacher. I was easily distracted and refused outright when the vision training began. I never again wanted to see into the future.

*It would only bring misfortune to those around me.*

Around twenty days later, when Eoha and I were staying up late chatting by the hill, we heard something rustling in the bushes.

*Too big to be a raccoon and too small to be a bear.*

It was a man. I raced down the hill and lost my footing. Before Eoha could come to my aid, a familiar rough hand picked me up off the ground.

It belonged to my brother.

"Did they say I can return?" I asked.

"Not exactly," he said, nodding to Eoha to let him know I was in good hands.

"Then what is it?" I asked, pulling at his shirt.

"They sent me here to beg you to return," he said, lowering his head.

"What happened?"

"Our last remaining *tusu-guru*, Eikashu, left this world a few days ago…"

*That's what he gets for leading the ceremony to kill my baby.*

"…as did father."

All the blood in my body froze. The warmth in the world was gone in an instant.

*Father.*

"The shaman was taken from us by the plague, but father…he fought bravely against the Horokeu. But in the end, *an-raige*," said my brother, his bottom lip quivering.

*Father was killed.*

"Who did it? Who took him away from us?"

"There's no way of knowing. But it makes no difference. I swore at his grave that I would kill every last one of them."

My mind shifted back to the Horokeu man who once saved my life, the one who still lived at the Moyuk village. I pictured his face cracked open by my brother's war club. It was refreshing and disturbing all at once.

I put my arm around my brother's.

"Does mother know?"

"Y-yes. I told her. It was the first time I've spoken to Okira's wife in a long time," said my brother, visibly shaken up.

"Did he kill a lot of them? Before...*an-raige*?" I asked, gripping my brother's rough hand.

"Yes. He killed one of their greatest warriors before he succumbed to the *surugu* in their arrows."

"It's *hatto-an* to use poison against another *ainu*, even in warfare."

"The Horokeu have no morals. No doubt the *kamui* they worship are the same dark *kamui* who brought the plague to our village," he said, clenching his free hand into a fist.

"You don't think it's my fault?"

"Please, you're not that powerful and neither was that old woman. This plague is a sign of a shift in power between the *kamui*. The *kunne* is going against the *koshne*, and the dark *kamui* are gaining ground. It's possible that the *nitne kamui* is involved. Of course, I know of no such things, but that is what the *tusu-guru* said when the plague hit him. There will still be those who blame you, but even they know they need you now." He crouched down and wiped a strand of hair away from my face.

*The stars told of great misfortune. Could this plague be the omen they showed us?*

Eoha came up to us and handed me our teacher's staff.

"Was that in your bag?"

"Teacher told me to give it to you once you accepted her passing. I wanted to pass it on earlier, but I was nervous. You're going to be a full-fledged shaman now. Hechaka would be so proud of you," said Eoha, beaming at me.

I took Teacher's staff from his hands. "Has the village been informed of the shaman's passing?" I asked, shifting toward my brother.

"No. The chief has told everyone that the *tusu-guru* is afflicted with *kamui irushka tashum*. The plan is to inform them once you've returned. You will come back, won't you?"

"Yes. I'll get packed up," I said with a strained smile.

"One last thing. There wasn't time to ask before, but why is there no pattern on your clothes?"

"Oh, that's because this village welcomes people from all tribes. We are a village of outcasts. We no longer belong to any tribe. But I still stitched a little fox," I said, showing him the design on my hip.

"You will always be Shitumbe."

"Of course and they don't ask us to denounce our tribe. It's a really peaceful village. We have our own customs and beliefs. In our village it's okay for women to be—"

"Are there any Horokeu there?" asked my brother, his eyes becoming slanted.

"Of course not. We're welcoming but not crazy."

*I hope he believed me.*

"You there, boy. What tribe did you belong to?" asked my brother.

Eoha put two fingers on the top of his head. "Isepo. Well, I was one but now I am a Moyuk."

"Isepo are allies, but what are Moyuk? I've never heard of that tribe."

"We are a tribe of outcasts. We are intelligent and crafty scavengers, just like raccoons."

"I suppose that makes sense. Why were you banished?" asked my brother, stepping up to Eoha.

"Enough! He's my closest friend. I won't let you interrogate him. I'm going back to my *chisei* to pack my things, and then I'll meet with you here."

"Understood. Hey, sister...your old clothes...the ones with the Shitumbe pattern, do you still have them?"

"Yes. I've kept them safe," I said with a little smile.

"Good. Put them on. I'll be waiting right here."

Eoha looked up at me. "Will I see you again?"

"Of course you will! At the next inter-tribal meeting. We'll both lead the ceremony," I said with a grin.

*And we'll rescue the bear cub too.*

"Hey, boy, uh, what's your name?" asked my brother.

"Eoha. And you are?"

"Akno. I'd like to talk to you. You got a moment?"

"Sure."

"Well, go on, *mataki*. We need to head out as soon as we can."

I nodded and headed back to my *chisei*.

After gathering my things, changing into the shirt mother had knit me, and giving a big farewell hug to Eoha, I began my journey back home. Brother and I walked for hours before he finally spoke to me.

"After the plague, like I said, there aren't many of us."

I had almost forgotten.

*Was it really my fault?*

Brother lifted up his bow and aimed it at a bird on a branch. "We can't get enough to eat with only the men doing the hunting. Would you like me to teach you *emoni*?" he asked, releasing the arrow.

The arrow hit the branch and the bird flew away.

"See? Even experts like myself mess up every once in a while. Want to have a go?" he asked, offering me the bow.

*He missed on purpose.*

He probably just wants to embarrass me. No, he's going to make me feel like I'm skilled and then show me just how much better he is.

*I'll just have to prove him wrong.*

"I suppose I could try," I said, grabbing at the bow.

"Uh-uh, not yet. Before every hunt it is important to pray to the fire *kamui*," he said, pulling out a freshly shaved *inao*.

"I'm the *tusu-guru*, so I'll lead, okay?"

"But you don't know what we say," he said, pulling the *inao* out of my reach.

I snatched it and held it between my palms. "Fire *kamui*, divine messenger, I ask that you give us your *inunuke* on the hunt we are about to embark on. May we find plentiful food and return safely." I handed him back the *inao*. "How was that?"

"It's not exact, but you had reverence and that's what counts. So are you ready?"

*Oh yeah, I'm ready.*

I nodded with a big grin.

After handing me the bow and a few arrows, he got behind me and gripped my arms. "That's it, pull back a bit more. Good. Now getting the proper shot is all about concentration and intention. Aim at the center of the tree."

*Concentration and intention—I'm going to do great!*

I focused until the feeling of his hands on my arms left, until the tree itself was gone and all there was before me was that single spot. My fingers let go.

The arrow sped through the air and hit just below the target.

"Yes!" I exclaimed with a hop.

"Heheh! Good show. Still it's harder with a moving target," he said, scanning the trees.

"I bet I could take down a deer," I said, loading up another arrow.

"Not yet you can't. You make too much noise when you walk. A deer wouldn't come within range unless it was deaf."

*I knew it. This is all just to mock me. I'll show him.*

I spotted a squirrel peeking into a hole in the tree.

*Ainu of all tribes behold: the very first girl to be a mystic and the very first shaman who can double as a hunter.*

I released the arrow.

The squirrel fell off the tree. Though I aimed for the head, I only hit its little back. The squirrel was writhing around and crying.

*Crying...just like my little one. My aiai. What have I done?*

"Sister, stay focused." Brother fired an arrow through the squirrel's skull. It stopped moving. "You always want to get a sure kill. Ainu aren't the only ones who have souls, all *chikoikip* do, whether land, air, or sea. We also aren't the only creation that can be vengeful. Not that you should worry about a squirrel, but let's say it's a larger animal, like a b—wolf! Well wolves are difficult, but I've taken down a few. Anyways, you don't want them to see your face. That's also why it's best to blind the creature before the kill. And, if you aren't grossed out by the idea," my brother plucked out the squirrel's right eye and popped it in his mouth, "eat the eyes."

My stomach churned.

"That's disgusting."

"Haha. Yeah, I thought you'd say that. But you know, there was a time, before you and I were even born, that mother was infertile. They found out soon after their marriage. It wasn't long before rumors began that one of them had sinned grievously against the *kamui*. She tried many things, visited many *tusu-gurus*, but still she never got pregnant. One day, after a successful hunt, our father came home and served her the heart of an *at kamui*."

"A *kamui*? How do you eat a *kamui's* heart?" I asked, sticking out my tongue.

"No, *at kamui* means the divine prolific one, it is a type of furry bird. Father served her the bird's heart without her knowledge, and a few months later, she got pregnant with me. If it weren't for that animal giving up its *ishu*, I never would have been born," said my brother softly.

"I don't believe it. I think her desire to have a kid finally broke the curse upon her. That's what happened."

"Well, you definitely got the basics of a bow and arrow. Let's move onto traps," he said, beckoning me closer with an open hand.

"So is that all boys know: how to kill and how to pray?" I asked, sticking out a tongue.

"We're taught how to make bows, arrows, traps, and offerings. We're taught how to hunt, fish and read the weather. We learn names of lakes, hills, mountains, tree *kamui* and some of us are even taught how to make poison. So, we know how to pray, kill, and identify landmarks," he said with a grin.

311

"Well, girls are taught how to cook, make clothes, embroider, make tattoos, garden, cut wood, nurse children, cry at a funeral—which is way more fun than it sounds—and above all we are taught not to disrespect men. So we create art and tools, learn how to properly wail at a funeral, raise children, and make the food. Seems we should be the ones leading the tribe," I said, sticking out my tongue.

*And one day we will.*

"I think the wise should lead, not the ones who work the hardest," said my brother.

"So, were you taught how to make poison?" I asked, squinting at the arrow tips.

"Yes, but that's very advanced and it's dangerous. Let's stick with traps for now, okay?"

I nodded and smiled. "Okay."


On the way back home, my brother taught me how to make *akbe*, a type of spring bow for hunting deer and *akbe-imok*, a spring trap used to catch raccoons, otters, and other small animals.

"Wait, but what if a fox gets caught in it?" I asked.

Brother tossed a rock in the trap. The rock was gripped by the string. "Well then the fox gets hoisted up into the air and we get to eat," he said, flicking the suspended stone.

"But we're Shitumbe!"

"Yes, foxes are our tribal symbol, but they aren't our guardian deity. You've eaten fox before."

"What? I didn't know. I just thought meat was...well, meat," I said, shuffling my feet. "I'm never eating *shumaune* again!"

"Does that mean you don't want any squirrel?" asked my brother, handing me thin slices of flesh.

*That was once part of a living being.*

"Are you kidding? I was the one who shot him. He'll come back and haunt me. Why take the risk? I'm done eating meat. Never, ever, ever again am I going to put something that once had a soul in my mouth."

"Then why did I waste my time teaching you how to hunt?" he asked, air puffing out from his nostrils.

"It's all you know and I...I just wanted to be with you," I said.

*I can't even remember the last time we bonded.*

"What about *chep*? Will you eat *chep*? Do you want to learn how to *emoni*?"

"Fish aren't vegetables. They have a soul too. Last thing I want is them circling around me in my dreams. Let's just head back, okay?"

"Fine. But in case you get lost, I'll show you what plants not to eat," he said, tossing me a mushroom.

"Ooh. Nice find. Did you know if you mix this in with soup it can cure fatigue?"

"Can't say I did. That's good to know."

"Yep, looks like I'll be the one teaching you," I said with a grin.

"I suppose so. Teach me as we move along. We should be able to make it back by nightfall if we pace ourselves."

We arrived at our village the next morning. Everyone was outside of their tents and seated for the early meal. The gatherers had found plentiful amounts of *ratashkep*.

*I'm hungry.*

"First we must tell the *paunguru* you've returned. Come with me. I'm not letting you out of my sight," he said, leading me past the crowd.

We arrived at the chief's *chisei*, which was a bit bigger than the others. In the Moyuk village, all the homes were the same size and rather than one chief and two sub-chiefs, we had three chiefs of equal status and power.

Brother approached the door, cleared his throat and entered.

He sat cross-legged at the hearth near the chief. They rubbed their hands together for a while.

It was the customary greeting for *ainu*. In the village of outcasts, both men and women initiated any conversation by performing the greeting before we entered someone's *chisei*.

The *paunguru* and my brother went back and forth, wishing *inunuke* upon each other, their families, relatives, etc. They ended the ritualistic greeting by stroking their beards, or in my brother's case—the few hairs on his chin, all the while talking about the matter at hand.

It was only after they stopped stroking their chins that I was invited to speak.

*It's been so long. Hope I remember everything.*

I removed my headdress and placed it over my arm. I brushed the front locks of my hair to the side and placed my hand over my mouth.

*Teacher was right. Even with something as simple as a greeting, women are made to know they are inferior.*

After getting an invitation to speak, I cleared my throat and pulled my hand away. "Thank you for allowing me to return."

*I knew not what else to say.*

Brother cleared his throat, wished blessings on the chief, and walked out.

I did the same but had to walk backward out of the cabin. After all, it was taboo for a woman to show her back to a man.

*Wait. This is just another way to keep us women suppressed. These little things are all thin ropes, fastening themselves to our psyche. They keep us bound, just like a scared little bear before it is ridiculed and sacrificed.*

I began to tear up.

Brother grabbed my hand and walked me to our *chisei*. "You must miss mother."

"Oh I can't wait to see her. We have a lot to catch up on. And father too! I missed them both so much!"

Brother shifted his gaze to the ground. "I told you, father is…."

*Dead. That's right, he was killed by the Horokeu. It doesn't seem real.*

"I have to prepare for the funeral. I'll pick you up when it's time. Don't go outside. It isn't safe for you here yet, understood?"

I nodded.

Brother guided me past the chief's *chisei*, which was only a bit larger than the other homes. Before long we arrived.

*Home.*

It looked the same as ever: walls made of reeds fastened together by the inner bark of elm wood, the porch by the west end where I would often gaze at the stars with mother, the south end exit where father would go to get extra fire wood, screens made of reeds, the *rorun-puyara* where my father and brother would sit at daily for prayer, and situated on eight stilts around a small plot of land where mother and I gardened.

*It was nostalgic.*

"I don't ever want to leave again," I said, latching onto his arm.

"You won't have to. The house is under my custody now, and I would never give it up. Welcome home, *mataki*," said my brother, opening our door.

In the center was the *hoka*, currently unlit. This was the vessel where the fire *kamui* gave enough warmth to save mother's life but not enough to save the mother before her.

Mother was seated on an *aputki* in her corner, knitting our pattern into a garment. Her brown eyes met mine and the needle dropped.

It happened so fast. I wasn't sure if her arms coiled around me first or if mine grabbed onto her before them. Either way, she was warm.

*Alive and warm.*

She looked so beautiful. Her forehead and arms were decorated with beautiful patterns—something I wouldn't experience because I would never marry. A beaded necklace, earrings, rings, and bracelets all came together to make her inward beauty project to all who saw her. It took me a moment to realize she was wearing a widow's bonnet, and her head was completely shaved. This was when it really sunk in.

*Father was gone.*

I cried in her arms till my eyes were sore.

She made me up my favorite stew with peas, along with some beans and potatoes. It looked so vital, and it never had dead animals in it anyway. I picked up the cup and sat in mother's lap.

"O, chief *kamui*, our nourisher, I thank thee for this food: bless it to the service of my body," I said before bringing the soup cup to my lips.

*It tastes like home.*

Having finished my soup, I started cleaning my cup with my index finger. Mother suddenly asked me to tell her about my journey.

I set down my cup, grabbed her shoulders, and wept.

I lost track of time telling her all about the Moyuk village, about my teacher, about the apprentice boy, and about all the things I learned. Most of all we talked about father, our fondest memories, his achievements, and how much we will miss him. Soon after the sun went away, my brother came in.

"It's time. We'll need a *tusu-guru* to conduct the service," he said, leaning against the door.

I walked with him into the crowd. Everyone stared at me as I approached. I noticed many of the women had shaved their heads, likely hiding the resulting scars beneath their mourning bonnets. Some of the men had cut their hair short, a few had even torn out not only their hair but most of their beard as a testament to how much the loss of their wives meant to them.

*So much pain and I'm the cause, aren't I?*

Brother grabbed my hand. "Stay strong. They don't know yet but soon they'll be grateful you're here."

*Strong, okira, just like father. I never realized how similar they are. Brother and father have the same fortitude.*

The elder patted the ground next to him.

I sat down next to the *paunguru* of my village.

I looked at his wrinkled face.

*How long before my curse claims his life as well?*

He looked into my eyes and nodded ever so slightly. He raised his hand, immediately calling everyone's attention to him. "Eikashui has moved on." He grabbed my arm and raised it. "Ebuike is our *tusu-guru* now."

*Flower? Well, I suppose I'm no longer a bud anymore.*

I gripped my teacher's staff.

*Banished, trained in a village of outcasts, and journeyed back home. So many things have happened. But here I am now, serving the shaman for my people.*

Silence befell the crowd.

Ainu were taught to respect our elders and the *paunguru* in particular. Still, I doubt even the chief could placate them now.

*They wanted me dead.*

My brother was the first to raise his hand, though out of respect for the chief, not for me. The other's followed, but their gestures were empty.

*Everything feels empty.*

The mystic's funeral was one of the happiest I had been to. As always, the commoners were in the back and there was ample rice wine, which was also known as *tonoto*—the official milk. I didn't mind funerals. It was the day after that would always bother me. Most of the men would reek of *arakke* and go around in a stupor.

I had to hold in my laughter when my brother drank with the other men. As always, he would use a moustache lifter—a long and thin device used to keep the mustache from going in the rice wine—even though he only had a few hairs growing.

Thankfully both my brother and my father always drank in moderation and only did so during a celebration, never out of mourning or for leisure. Father was aware that drinking caused more problems than it solved, and my brother decided to follow father's example. Hopefully, there wouldn't be too much drinking at this ceremony. The man who moved on was already very old. Now that I was going to take up the mantle, our people wouldn't be without their mystic. Still, some glared at me between sips.

"Proceed," said the chief, looking at me.

I stared at him blankly.

*Am I supposed to conduct the ceremony...right now?*

My brother tapped my shoulder. "You'll do fine."

I took a deep breath.

*Okay. It's time. Time to find out what destiny has in store for us.*

I walked to the center of the group and arranged the sticks in the proper order. I had to make sure the central stick was facing east. I created a circle around the pile with the final stick, before tossing it in with the others.

I closed my eyes. I chanted as I knocked the ignition sticks together.

A flame came into being.

*So far, so good.*

With great care I leaned over the batch of sticks and set them aflame.

The heat bit my hand, reminding me that I was only a mediator for its message.

In the sky something whizzed by. It was a broom star and bore special meaning to mystics. War, famine, flood, I knew not what it meant, but I knew that a great calamity was on approach.

*But the misfortune in the stars should already be over. My people suffered a plague. What else could befall us? I felt dizzy.*

I saw my brother looking up at me.

*I have to stay strong.*

I took a deep breath and continued the ritual. I let the fire cook for a bit—placing my awareness on it and further away from the scornful gaze of the people around me.

*I could jump in right now. Sure it would be painful, but it's what they all want. It's probably what's best for the tribe. No. I'm being selfish. Teacher left me with a mission. I have to prove that a woman, or even a girl, can be a proper* tusuguru. *I have to do this right, if only for her.*

The fumes entered my nostrils. I centered my thoughts to shift my awareness.

Fire everywhere. Bodies...so many bodies.

*Is this the future?*

The blood from the bodies crawled toward me.

*This is a nightmare.*

I came to my senses, looking at my brother.

"What did you see?" he asked.

*Strange. His eyes didn't look at me with disdain. They looked at me with worry, maybe even care. My birth killed his mother. Why is he looking at me like this?*

"Sister, you must tell us what you saw."

I now noticed my hands were shaking. No, not only my hands—my whole body was trembling like a raging river.

*I may have been incapable of seeing spirits, but I had a knack for divination. Why did my only talent bring me such misfortune?*

"Tell us exactly what you saw," said the chief, his eyes fixated on me.

"I...there was...a fire. It consumed the cabins. There were many dead."

"How many?" asked my brother.

"I don't know. There were *kaisei* as far as the eye could see. And blood...it was everywhere."

"You trust this child?" asked a voice from the crowd.

My brother turned his head but was unable to locate the voice's point of origination. "Ebuike is not a child. My sister has been through fourteen cycles. If not for Eikashu's passing, she would be searching for a partner for which to wed in two years."

*Why was he defending me?*

"Trust what you want. I am only speaking what I saw," I said with wisdom far beyond my years.

"How soon before the vision becomes the present?" asked the chief.

"I don't…"

*Yes I do.*

"The trees will be taller than the cabins. A few years it seems," I said.

"We must be prepared for anything," said my brother, gripping his spear.

"Do you think it is the Horokeu clan?" asked the elder.

"It must be. Who else would attack our village?" asked my brother.

I tapped my brother's shoulder. "I never said there was an attack."

"You said there was blood. Fire does not make blood, *ainu* do. You are right that it may not be the Horokeu clan. In your vision, do you remember seeing any attackers?"

"No, only bodies. Wait, arrows…yes. There was a bamboo-tipped arrow in the neck of one of the bodies, a few more in the area around it. The Horokeu clan use clubs, spears, and stone-tipped arrows in warfare, like we do. We can't say for certain it was them."

The chief's face became pale. "Are you sure that's what you saw?"

"It happened so fast, but that's what I remember," I said.

"Fast? The fire had gone out before you awoke," said my brother.

"I saw an arrow with a bamboo tip. It seems so familiar," I said.

"Isepo," said the chief. "But they are our allies."

*This is crazy. Why would Eoha's people attack us?*

"We can't be certain of anything. They became our allies out of fear, not kinship. Our ancestors have fought them before," said my brother.

"Careful. We must not incite a battle," said the chief.

"Of course not. I'll take a few men and we'll scope out the area. But we should keep in mind they might not even be preparing to attack yet. It's difficult to place the exact time of the vision. Thank you, *mataki.*"

"For what?" I asked, looking up at him.

"For saving us," he said, his smile genuine and beaming.

*Saving us.*

Brother seized my head and ran his hand down the length of my hair from my crown to my shoulders.

This gesture lit up my spirit. Yet at the same time, it calmed me, reminding me of all the times father used to praise me.

*I wasn't alone. Brother believes in me. He truly does.*

"When are you leaving?" I asked, my hand gripping his arm without me noticing.

"Soon. You should rest. Head back to our *chisei*," he said, pulling away. Before I knew it, he was gone from my sight.

I got up and searched the crowd for my brother.

*He tells me to stay by his side and then he leaves.*

I stepped to the side, covered my mouth, and kept my gaze fixed on the ground, as was customary for women to do when men were crossing.

One of the young men bumped into me.

He pushed me away. "Don't you touch me. Your curse already took my sister away." His gaze pierced past my flesh and wounded my spirit.

"Wait, Hapuru, she is dead?" I asked, a cold chill suddenly coming over me.

*That can't be true. She was always so healthy and happy. Someone like that couldn't be gone.*

"She fell ill the night after you were banished."

"I never meant to hurt her. She was my friend."

*Who else has been taken by my curse?*

"Stay away. All you touch falls to ruin, cursed child," he said as he walked off.

A full-grown man looked at me and spat in my face, one hand raised in a fist, the other holding onto the wrist of his wife. "Murderer. If you take more of my wives from me, I'll kill you myself." He then pulled her along.

*What if the plague really was my fault? She is dead because of me.*

My eyes watered up.

*Where is my brother?*

After navigating through the hateful stares of my people, I found my brother.

"You look shaken up. Were you crying? Was it another vision?" he asked, handing one of the men a freshly sharpened arrow.

"I need to talk to you," I said.

My brother signaled the man to leave us.

I looked up at him and I froze up.

"Well, speak."

"Why are you being like this? You've been acting different ever since you went to fetch me from the village of outcasts. Is it because I'm the only shaman the village has now? Is that why you give me *uainu*?"

Brother looked at me with wet eyes. "I've always respected you."

*Liar!*

"That isn't true. You hated me. You put me outside in the cold mere days after I was born. I heard it from father. You blamed me for mother's death."

*The plague, her death, Teacher, father—did all these horrible things happen because of me?*

"I was so foolish back then. *Mataki*, can you forgive me?"

"Huh? What? What about you? Can you forgive me for mom's death?"

"I can't. But that's due to my own weakness. You inspire me, *mataki*. I can't just accept how powerless we all are. If I did, I wouldn't be able to fight, to kill those who threaten us. You can do what none of us can. You can enter the darkness and bring light to us."

*Was it all in my head? He doesn't hate me? He looks up to me? What's going on?*

"You've saved us all. I can't thank you enough."

As my mind tried to make sense of it all, he drifted further and further away.

*It was my own projection. The look I saw in his eyes was my own guilt, not his hate.*

I nearly fell to the ground.

*He was right. I needed rest.*

"I'll head back home, okay?"

"No. Stay away from our *chisei*. I'm going to go check it out with some of the other men. Is there a safe place you can stay?"

"Well there's the cave where I was taught. But I don't think you have to—"

"It may not be safe there. Do you know a place that nobody else knows about?"

*What was he so worried about?*

"Yes. I do."

"Good. Stay there. You can return in the morning. Understood?"

"Am I in danger?" I asked, grabbing his hand.

"I don't know. It's just a precaution. Stay safe, *mataki*."

*If he believes in me, then I'll trust him too.*

"*Popke no okai un*," I said, with a nod.

"Yes. *Popke no okai un*."

His fingers let go of my hand, and I went into the forest.

Soon enough I found myself deep in the forest in front of a cave.

*This was where Hechaka had always entered to find deeper truths. She warned me of its dangers, but now I am ready to face them.*

I entered the cave and sat on the rocky ground.

A strong scent overcame me. It was noxious, but my nose welcomed it in as a guest.

It wasn't long before I had another vision.

My brother was naked. His face was pale. Blood dripped from his lips. He was shivering. There was a wound in his chest, a deep wound. The weapon was blurred, but the hand holding it was crystal clear—as was the blood on it. I recognized the bracelet on the hand's wrist. It was my own.

# Chapter 77: Eternally Cursed

*How can this be happening? I was going to kill him. Why? Nothing makes sense anymore. Think of what Teacher said, "If I don't understand the vision, it can bring about great misfortune." That's right. She died because I gave her the peace of mind necessary to move on. Things are never as simple as they seem. No force on this planet could make me kill my own brother willingly, especially not now. It's probably more of a nightmare anyway. Then again, my dreams and nightmares have all ended up as realities. Let's say it's true...that I do kill him. Why would that be?"*

"I knew I'd find you here," said a young, happy voice.

I awoke out of my trance and opened my eyes, slowly re-familiarizing myself with my surroundings.

It was Eoha, my fellow shaman in training. I suppose we aren't equals anymore.

*I hope that doesn't change our relationship too much.*

"What are you doing here? Has something happened at your village?"

"I came to see you. Things aren't the same without you there," he said with a warm smile.

I stood up. "You want me to try to convince my *paunguru* to let you in the village. I don't have that kind of power. And right now, tensions are very high, even amongst allies."

*If I tell him more, that will only make things worse.*

"I wouldn't ask you to. What I want is something different, *chiri-po*," he said, gently putting my hand between his.

I looked into his eyes and then turned away.

*He was love-stricken. I mean, he's liked me for a long time. I always found it endearing, but what if it's more than that?*

"Please, hear me out," he said, his eyes beaming at me.

*Did destiny connect him to me? Does he have a role to fulfill for our clan? For what reason have our fates been intertwined?*

"You are my dear friend, but you will never be anything other than that," I said, pulling away from him.

"Life isn't the same without you beside me," he said, taking a step closer.

*I have to stop this now.*

"Okikurumi, the great hero, nearly died from the despair of love. You should learn from his example. You are a powerful shaman. Why can't you just be content with that?"

"Remember that even with the world beneath him and the stars around him, the *chup orosh guru* is lonely. I'd rather die from despair than live with loneliness," he said, putting his arms around me.

"Let go of me!" I yelled, pushing him to the ground.

*I won't let my curse take him away. I won't lose him too!*

Eoha stood up and approached me. "We don't have to have children, but still," he took something out from his pack and placed it around my neck "I want you to marry me."

*He really does think I'm pretty.*

"Wait. I can't."

"Why not?"

*This is only getting worse! What do I do?*

"It isn't common to marry outside your village. I've never heard of an *uiritak* wedding from this village," I said with a shaky voice.

"My father is a Shitumbe and just because it's uncommon doesn't mean it's *hatto-an*. This is the only way I'll be welcomed to stay in your *chisei*. We've lived together for so long. I've wanted to ask for you to marry me for a while now."

*He said it again.*

"I just could never build up the courage to propose. But now I don't have a choice. If marriage is our only means of continuing to share the same home, then I must marry you."

*Why must he be so cute and kind?*

"But what about my parents? I mean, my mother, um, my brother would never approve."

"I spoke with your brother before. He gave more than his *inunuke*. He told me to marry you and keep you happy. He only asked one thing in return," said Eoha with an embarrassed smile.

*Why must destiny be so intrusive in my life?*

"What did he want?"

"Sorry, he asked me not to tell you unless we did marry."

"Well, what about your parents? You would need your parents' approval too."

"It's the children who get the final word. Not even if the parents on both sides will a marriage to be can they force it upon their children."

"Yes, but without their consent we would have to get our own *chisei* and there would be no ceremony."

*Yes. That's it. I'll say whatever it takes. I have to get this idea out of his head before we're both doomed.*

"The ceremony isn't important. What matters is that we're together. Don't you trust me?" His gorgeous amber eyes glistened.

"Of course I do. We switched clothing that one time, remember?"

"Yes. I remember. I suppose considering the dangerous hexes one can place on another through the possession of their *amip*, their truly is no act more trusting. Now that you mention it, it's not uncommon for the betrothed to exchange clothes and live together in their future spouse's *chisei*. I'd like live in your *chisei*," he said, reaching for my hand.

I wanted to pull away, but before I knew it my hand was gripping his. The next moment we were in a warm embrace.

"But I'm cursed. Surely our marriage would only end in disaster," I said, while pressed up against him.

"The necklace I gave you is an *aumshup*. It's the only thing I have to remember my father by. Not only that. It is also a powerful *inao-kike*. It will protect you."

"But who will protect you?"

"I can defend myself. So, will you marry me?"

*All the exits are being closed off. Every route is converging at one point. What can I say to stop this?*

"You're in such a rush. And remember what happened to the impatient Pen'ambe."

"Yes, but he was a fox and I am a rabbit."

*A handsome rabbit.*

"True, but I…well, I'm only fourteen!"

*Yes, of course! I'm too young to marry. Why didn't I think of that earlier?*

"I'm only fifteen," he said with a grin. "But I want something to look forward to when I become a man."

*Two years from now. Is that when it will happen, the prophesized end of my people?*

"I…I…."

"We may be diviners, but it's alright if we make our own future every so often. A promise to marry is like a prophecy in itself. Only a matter of time before it's fulfilled," he said, giving me a kiss on the cheek.

*Hapuru. His kiss was so soft, yet I feel such a strong warmth.*

"I…I'll think it over."

"Thanks, that's all I ask of you," he said with a nod.

*I only hope it isn't too late.*

"May I have some time alone? I just need to calm my thoughts. I've been under so much stress lately," I said, sitting down.

"And I'm here to help you bear it," he said, leaning his head against my shoulder.

*So sweet!*

"Please, Eoha. Just for tonight."

He stood up. "Of course. I'll leave you be, *chiri-po. Popke no okai un.*"

"May you be kept warm too," I said with a smile.

He left the cave with steps of hesitation.

*The annihilation of my people, potential death of my brother, and now marriage—it was all too much to comprehend. What if they were each stepping stones to one another? Which comes first? What do I do?*

I held my teacher's staff to my chest. "Please, give me the strength and the vision to see past all this. How can I save my people?"

I sat in silence and time whisked by.


A hand broke me out of my trance.

"Do you know what's going on?" asked Eoha, pulling me to my feet.

"What do you mean?" I asked, only half aware.

The sun was shining through the vines.

*I was more tired than I had thought.*

"Six men, your brother leading them, they were listening in on a meeting from my old tribe. Next thing I know they take the chief hostage. Please, you have to talk some sense into him. He'll listen to you, right?" asked Eoha.

"He wouldn't do that without a reason. What was said in the meeting?"

"How am I supposed to know? I was lucky I wasn't spotted. Returning from banishment warrants severe punishment," he said, taking a step back.

"What can I do?"

"I need you to ask your brother what happened. If you don't talk to him, things will only get worse. One of my old friends has rounded up a party to save the *paunguru.* Of course they don't want to hurt your brother, but things could escalate."

*He's right. No wait, that's not true. If I'm the one who hurts my brother, then that means as long as I stay away from him, no harm will come to him…at least nothing fatal.*

"Intervening would only make things worse."

"You won't try to reason with him?"

"He knows what he's doing. I have faith in him. But take me to see the rescue group. I'll talk to them."

*I won't just sit here and do nothing.*

"I'm not even supposed to know about them. I can't take you there."

"You will. I know you will," I said, giving him a kiss on the lips.

*Soft and warm.*

"That's the first time you've kissed me there," he said, gently touching his bottom lip.

"Let's get going," I said, flashing him an extra sweet smile.

"Yuh-yeah. It's not too far from here. I'll lead the way," he said, stepping out in front of me.

*I can't live up to his expectations, but that doesn't mean he can't bend to mine a bit. His bond with me can help bring peace to both our tribes.*

Eoha was right; in less time than it took for me to unjumble my thoughts, we had made it to the group. They were each carrying spears and a quiver of arrows…all except for one. He was holding a war club.

*What was a Horokeu warrior doing with the Isepo clan? Did the Isepo get spears from the Horokeu? Nothing makes sense anymore.*

"She means you no harm. She only wants to talk," said Eoha.

I tried to pretend I didn't notice the club. Good thing I was skilled at lying.

"I know my brother well. He will return the chief before the night is up."

"I agree," said the *Horokeu* warrior.

"Good."

"Bring her with us. Now we have bargaining power," he said.

"Hey, wait a minute. You don't have to go that far. I know her brother too. He only attacks when provoked," said Eoha.

"He has our chief hostage. Having a hostage of our own puts us on even ground. The more even we are, the more likely this will not end in bloodshed," said the youngest of the Isepo soldiers.

"And what if he refuses to hand over the *paunguru*? Then what?" asked Eoha.

"We will make him hand over our chief, no matter the cost," said the leader of the specialized squad.

My ankle turned as I made a sprint for safety. Before I knew it, I was on the ground with a spear held to my neck.

*Things are escalating so quickly. No matter what, I mustn't see my brother.*

"Get away from her!" yelled Eoha before he was slugged by the Horokeu warrior. He fell down flat on his back.

"Don't hurt him. I'll cooperate."

*Nobody else will suffer because of me.*

"Bring her along. I still have his trail," said one of the Isepo warriors.

"Run when you get the chance. I will protect you, *chiri-po*." Eoha bit his thumb and made marks under his eyes and cheeks. He took out a special potion from his arm bag and drank it. He rose up slowly, almost like a marionette.

"Eoha, why make this difficult? Do you value this Shitumbe over your old tribe, more than our chief?" asked an Isepo warrior, his spear at the ready.

Eoha's eyes were vacant. He rushed up to the warrior and slashed his face.

*Were his nails always that long and sharp?*

I grabbed the spear in front of me and pushed it away. The warrior slammed his foot on my belly and repositioned the spear. I could feel its tip poke a hole in my skin. I turned my attention back to Eoha. His shirt was partially cut, and there was a trail of blood at his chest.

"Stop!" I yelled.

Eoha's fingernails rode up his attacker's arm, carving it up. He then jabbed his hand into the warrior's neck.

*Did Eoha just kill someone? No, that wasn't him. Unlike me, he had a connection to the kamui. He was channeling a kamui's essence and a strong one at that. This all seemed so surreal.*

The other Isepo warriors made a circle around him. The Horokeu warrior gained ground by a nearby hill. He was aiming his spear.

*Oh no.*

"Wait! I'll come with you, okay? Don't kill him!"

It was too late. The spear had already been thrown.

It stopped as soon as it hit its intended point.

*Simply following its path, like all of us, I suppose. Wait!*

The spear was clenched in Eoha's hand. The feat was even more spectacular considering his head was dangling and thus only able to see the ground.

This display of otherworldly power was enough to scare the others off. They picked me up and ran as fast as they could.

"Eoha is a mystic, right? How can he be so skilled in combat? You knew him, right? Tell me," said one of the warriors, keeping his blade at my throat.

"I've never seen him like that. I heard he could channel *kamui*, but I thought they needed a ritualistic space to operate. I thought he was framed for the murder of Shirara, but what if he really did kill him? We need to keep our distance. Do you think he's still following us?" asked the youngest warrior.

*Murder. That's why he was banished.*

"Doubt it," said one of the warriors before collapsing.

The spear from before had found a new home at the tip of his spine.

*Is this another vision? Am I still in that cave? This can't be real?*

The youngest warrior was already at his ally's side. "Can you hear me?" he asked, his voice barely coming out.

"He's dead. We better move or we'll share his fate," said the eldest warrior.

Five other men met up with the group, all wielding spears.

*More Horokeu?*

"The Isepo's banished prodigy killed one of his own. Be careful when you approach him. We'll meet up with you once their *paunguru* has been recovered," said the Horokeu warrior.

The other's nodded and made their way down the hill.

"Eoha!"

I was shouting, screaming for him. But in the end, what was the point? My love for my dear friend isn't enough to keep him from death. But as long as he channeled a *kamui*, a spirit which has transcended destiny, he should be safe from harm.

By the time I turned my attention to the front, I saw him, my brother, and five other men all holding spears up to the Isepo *paunguru*.

*I heard all about the Isepo chief from Eoha. He was a bit too idealistic, but I never thought he would harm anyone. Yet his own people had sided with the Horokeu to retrieve him.*

The spear fell from my brother's hand once he saw me.

"Tell your men to release the *paunguru*. Now," said the Isepo captain.

My brother's mouth opened, but no words came out.

His fellow warriors turned to him for guidance.

My brother picked up his spear and raised it. "You really have sided with the Horokeu. To think I once called you my brothers," he said, tears finding their way out of his fiery eyes.

"You bring dishonor to all your ancestors by taking our *paunguru*. *Aiona kamui* is watching you, *furep*," said the Isepo captain.

"You worship your chief as if he was the chief *kamui*. Idolatry is against the word of our great ancestor," said my brother.

"Stop! We don't want any more violence. We will trade our chief for your sister. Is that understood?" asked the youngest Isepo warrior.

"A *paunguru* for a *tusu-guru*, that hardly seems fair," said my brother, signaling the others to press their spears closer to the chief.

"We will kill your sister if you don't cooperate!" yelled the Isepo captain.

"A rabbit baring its teeth at a fox. Laughable," said my brother, though I noticed his hands were shaking.

"Cut her," said the leader.

"For every cut you put on her, your chief loses a limb," said my brother, his rage boiling.

"Everyone, calm down!" yelled the youngest warrior. "I just saw my old friend, a dear friend, kill my closest friend. I don't want to see any more death. Please. Let's settle this without bloodshed and go home."

*All I want is to go home with my brother.*

"The Horokeu clan murdered our people. They killed my father! They killed our *tusu-guru*!" yelled my brother.

"And you've killed many of us, Shitumbe," said the Horokeu warrior.

"Brother. You said the shaman moved on due to sickness. Nobody killed him. If anything, I am responsible," I said in a whisper.

"*Surugu.* He was poisoned," he said softly.

"What. You can't know for certain," I said.

"It was at the Isepo clan's bear ceremony. No feuding allowed and they all drink rice wine. A day later, our shaman falls ill and leaves this world that very night. That's too convenient for a coincidence. And our father was poisoned too. Not by drink but by an arrow! I'll kill every Horokeu and all who call them friend!"

*Yet another calamity follows the ceremony.*

"What if you're wrong?" I asked.

"I don't need to prove it. A Horokeu spy told us everything. That is before we cut him open."

"Why would they target him? It makes no sense."

*Please calm down, my brother.*

"The *tusu-guru* is even more important than the *paunguru* in some ways. They heal the sick, mend wounds both physical and spiritual. It is with their power that the *kamui* are channeled and reasoned with. You were their next target. Before I even left with the group, I found two Horokeu warriors outside our *chisei*. With you dead, we would have no shaman to lead our ceremonies," he said, gritting his teeth.

"You know how important she is, both to you and your village. Now let the chief go," said the youngest Isepo warrior.

"Your *paunguru* made secret unions with the enemy, seeking peace with those murders. I took up the spear so that I could usher justice for my people. To allow him to live would be to betray all I believe," he said.

"Would you rather have your sister's death on your conscience? If you need to shed blood, take mine. Let the chief go," said the youngest warrior, breaking down into tears.

"No. Release her now or your *paunguru* loses a limb!" yelled my brother.

"I'll call your bluff. Foxes are tricky creatures, after all. We won't give up our only advantage," said the Isepo warrior leader.

A slice. An arm fell to the ground.

*Did he just...?*

"Chief!"

All the Isepo warriors rushed at my brother.

The spears turned away from the chief and toward the attackers.

Weapons clashing, blood, and muffled screams. It all felt like another vision.

*My brother is safe. If destiny decided I will kill him, then that makes him invincible.*

The Isepo warriors fell. I suppose their emotions left them open to attack.

I felt something cut into my side. It was sharp. It hurt.

An arrow had pierced me. The Shitumbe warriors charged at the Horokeu man who had stabbed me.

*Was I going to die? No. Impossible. My vision said I was alive. It couldn't have been false. It never is!*

The five Shitumbe warriors checked me for wounds.

*Wait...only five? Brother!*

My brother was on the ground, for the first time looking helpless. A spear was in his chest. The wound was deep.

Before I knew it I was at his side, hands gripping the spear.

*Was this the vision? No. He was naked. He is still partially clothed. But here I am, holding the weapon lodged in his chest.*

Brother looked up and smiled at me.

*I knew it. He won't go down from only one spear.*

My brother looked past me and at the men. "Kill him. Kill the Isepo *paunguru*. He couldn't have gone far."

The Shitumbe warriors bowed and then rushed off.

"Let me tend to your wounds," I said.

I lifted up his shirt and placed the salve on his wound. Other than the giant gash, he had no new scars.

"*Mataki*, can you promise me something?" he asked with a smile.

"What?" I asked, carefully cleaning the wound.

"Don't blame yourself. I die a warrior. It isn't your fault. You've saved us. You uncovered the secret alliance," he said, his eyes slowly closing.

"No! You are not dying!" I yelled, griping the spear and slowly pulling it out.

*It was deeper than I thought.*

The spear had pierced through his flesh. It had pierced into his heart.

I grabbed my head. "No. No. No. I shouldn't have come. I shouldn't have," I said, breaking down into tears.

"That's right. You got captured. You need to be more careful. Promise me you'll be more careful," he said, rising up to look me in the eye.

"I'll be more careful. You can't die, right? You have to kill the traitors. You need to usher in justice in this empty world," I said, gripping his hand tightly.

*Please, don't go.*

"You have to convince the *paunguru* for me. I can't rest without knowing that every last treacherous Isepo is dead. Tell him what I told you."

"This is because I had the vision. You went out into harm's way because of me."

"I'm a soldier. It's…*ay-oh*…my *ishu*. It's been a great life. Sister, I'm starting to fade. I don't know if anyone's told you this, but you're very beautiful. When you're focused during a trance, you give off the presence of a benevolent *kamui*. You truly have blossomed, *mataki*."

His hand went limp. His eyes closed. That was his last smile.

*Brother.*

The world no longer felt empty. It was dark. Ominous. It had a *kuroro* of its own. Destiny was conniving and malicious. There was no way to fight it. Worst of all it had chosen me as its target.

I looked up at the night sky.

*The twinkling stars weren't showing their beauty. They weren't even sending a message. They were showing off their power. They were looking down at us mortals and deciding how next to make us suffer.*

# Chapter 78: A Change of Plans

The image faded away. Etaf stared at the Exps, gauging their reaction while remaining stoic herself.

Tears were pouring out of Exp 8's helmet. "You felt so powerless. It's the worst feeling in the world." He approached the victim and embraced her.

"See? Us gods once suffered as mortals," said Etaf.

"It's hard to see your brother die," said Kawai, failing to keep her tears from flowing.

"Hey, Sis. Cheer up. I'm right here," said Atatasuki.

Kawai hugged him tightly and continued to cry.

"Such a wretched existence. Here I thought I was the only one spited by the universe," said NoOne, seeping into his own shadow.

"Don't ever leave me," cried D.S., burying his face in his mom's bosom.

"There, there sweetie. I'm not going anywhere," said Ada, caressing his bald head.

"Things got better after that, right?" asked Opti, his face covered in tears.

"Of course not," said Etaf.

"Then perhaps it's best you stopped there," said Ada, hugging D.S.

"You were such a strong little girl, a loving daughter, a nurturing mother to your little bear and also quite the skeptic," said Deceivant with a benevolent grin.

"She's a survivalist. I can relate," said Nina, posing in front of her allies to get some much needed attention.

"Hey, are there places like that cave here? Those fumes looked incredible," said Pharma.

"Yes, I believe they were sulfur fumes. The clairvoyants in ancient Greece likely used them to attain a shift in consciousness." Violet turned her attention to the cursed goddess. "Your mother was such a beautiful person. She loved you so dearly."

"Yes. She did," said Etaf, factual and cold as ever.

"And your brother had such faith in you," said Kanasta.

"And he died a brave warrior! What an outstanding fellow!" cheered Karson.

BoneSaw nodded.

"Too much faith," said Etaf.

"He was right about you. Here you are now, living as a goddess," said Sefiwah.

"Yeah, you've moved past the loss and became someone he would be proud of," said Ego with tearful eyes.

"Hey, Etaf, so do you know what it is? Soma, I mean? It's spoken of in the Vedas. It's said to be the ultimate drug," said Pharma.

"Not a clue."

"Violet, do you know?" asked Pharma.

"Any liquid taken in a ritual setting can be mind-altering," said Violet with a smile.

"Most likely they were from Psilocybin mushrooms, but it's all conjecture," said Anthrax.

"I suppose it will forever remain a mystery. All of mankind's historical discoveries are meaningless. How could such vital knowledge have been lost? Humans need to get their priorities straight!" yelled Pharma.

"Etaf, I know it can't be easy, but please tell us the rest. How did you become a god?" asked Kaity.

"That is a very good question. You've barely scratched the surface. We were promised a tale of apotheosis," said Devlin.

"Yes, please, tell us more," said Matteria, grabbing Thraxy's hand.

"Can we become gods?" asked Anthrax.

"Perhaps I'll finish it another time," said Etaf.

"Boo! I want to hear the happy ending!" whined D.S.

"Why won't you tell us more?" asked Bob, his eye all watery.

"No bloody way...you're crying," said Karson.

"What!?" snapped Bob. "Absurd!"

"You are," said Riufen, leaning in closer.

"Oh, I am...well, that's different. I suppose something in that story must have hit a nerve. Do continue your tale," said Bob with a bow.

"Yes, you must tell us how you became a goddess," said Violet, her eyes shimmering.

"To surpass such limitations, you must have inherited your brother's fighting spirit," said Riufen.

"Well, you'll have to find out later. I stopped the story for a reason. Lum sent me a message. There's been an unforeseen development," said Etaf, drawing her sword.

Devlin snapped his fingers. "Goddess of Fate, it was you...wasn't it? You're the one who made me lose against Exp 8, right?"

"That was your own insolence. I did not intervene. That said, I will be the one who puts an end to your current existence." Etaf summoned a massive roulette wheel on her arm.

The wheel was around the size of a dart board. It was colored white and was bordered by a golden line. The pointer was as thin as a needle and radiated with an inner light. The wheel had over a hundred different sections that shifted each moment.

"I can also create new tangents of fate, thus altering your destiny."

"Hehehaha! Do you listen to yourself? I've never heard such absurdities in my life," said Deceivant.

"Laugh all you want. This is the manifestation of my soul," said Etaf, holding up the wheel of fate.

"Then what is the sword?" asked Riufen.

"Yet another manifestation. Would you like to challenge it?" asked Etaf, pointing the tip of her blade at him.

"It would be an honor," said Riufen with a bow.

Etaf tossed her sword into the air. Having distracted the team, she flicked the arrow on her shield. "DIVERGENT INTERVENTION!" She held out her arm, pointing at Kaity.

Kanasta rushed at the goddess and lifted her up by her throat. "Whatever you are doing…stop it now."

"It's too late. Once your fate has been spun, it cannot be stopped." Etaf grinned as the pointer came to a halt.

"What does it say?" asked Kaity, her sidearm ready to fire.

"You shall…befriend a white chabe? That can't be right," said Etaf.

"What's a chabe?" asked Kaity.

"I thought all angels spoke in a way that is understood by all beings," said Exp 8.

"Angels do, but gods don't. We are connected to Lum and thus can understand any language, but I'm not using telepathy right now." Etaf turned to Kaity. "Your destiny should come into fruition any moment now."

A white kitty with frazzled fur and a meek body hopped into Kaity's arms.

"So cute. Hmm. I'll call you Napkin," said Kaity, scratching under the kitty's chin.

"Ooh, ooh. I want candy! Spin the wheel! Spin it!" cheered D.S.

"Ugh, simpletons. Forget the wheel. The Destiny Sword shall carve your path to salvation!"

Etaf raised her sword and sliced the air.

Blood gushed out of Riufen's neck before his head fell to the ground.

"What! But she was nowhere near him," said Devlin, firing a wire at the goddess.

"What is distance to destiny? Fate needn't travel anywhere; it need only manifest," she said.

With another slice, Riufen was cut in half.

Bob slammed into the powerful warrior.

She countered with her blade, slicing straight through him.

"Hmm, you missed," said Bob.

A diagonal slash appeared on Opti's chest. He fell to the ground and pulled his legs in. "How did you attack me?" he asked, holding in the pain.

"The Destiny Sword chose you as its target. Within you lie two different souls. Depending on which soul takes center stage—"

Kaity leaped from a crouched position and unloaded a round directly into the target's forehead.

The bullets bounced off the goddess.

Kaity was sent flying by a sudden kick.

"I wasn't done," said Etaf, slicing the air once more.

Opti screamed as both arms were removed.

"We don't stand a chance against her," said Pharma.

"And...boom," said Karson.

Etaf was thrown into the air after stepping on a land mine.

Karson unloaded a full round of bullets at the enemy.

"CONVERGENCE."

The bullets all gravitated toward the Destiny Sword, collecting at the sides of the weapon.

"Take cover!" yelled Karson.

Exp 8 stood between Opti and Etaf, taking the barrage of aura-laden bullets head on. "We don't want to fight you? Why are you trying to kill us? We want to stop Sel from attacking Lum. We have the same agenda!"

"This battle is not yours to stop. The presence of Exps in Sellum only complicates things. And things are already intricate enough." Etaf was about to slash again, but the swordsman countered with his spine.

The spine had been coated in solidified blood, making it extra durable.

Devlin's wires barraged Etaf, leaving her no choice but to parry.

"DESTINY GENESIS."

The sword moved with a will of its own becoming a blur. It blocked every attack, even the added bullet barrage from Kaity.

"If there is a battle, then Lum will fall to Etah. Is that what you want?" asked Exp 8.

"I only want balance. You cannot have life without death. You cannot have light without darkness. And you cannot have Lum without Sel."

"Forget balance. What about justice?" asked Exp 8, powering up an orb.

"Justice is merely a guideline used to keep the oppressed in line. Crime and sin are but deviations to the standards set by the rulers. Criminals are punished for being unable to mold into society. Lum and Sel are the same in this regard.

They both discriminate against those who do not follow prescribed moral actions. Instead of being judged for their unchangeable outsides they are judged for their insides. Corruption is an illusion, don't you see? Neither side is right and neither side is wrong."

"The fight with us for balance," said Devlin.

"The concept of balance has been altered by the rulers and has become a tool for furthering their agendas. Still, only the truth of balance can keep the two sides from destroying one another. ," said Etaf all the while parrying any and all attacks with her levitating blade.

"Are you a Marxist?" asked Violet.

"Far from it. Communism and Marxism are fueled by idealistic notions that underestimate the desires of individuals. Such systems only work when each individual is wholly dependent on the others, such as an ant colony," said Etaf, dodging the incoming orb.

"Finally got you to move." Exp 8 slammed his fist into the Destiny Sword, igniting a power struggle. "None of that matters, right now. Don't you think that Etah should be our priority? He should be Lum's immediate concern."

"He is Lum's concern, not mine. I can't change the outcome, so why bother fighting it?" The Destiny Sword overpowered Exp 8's fist and then sliced through the samurai's armored spine.

"Is there anything that sword cannot cut?" asked Riufen with wide eyes.

"Souls, I presume," said Bob, firing a laser that the warrior goddess quickly deflected.

"DESTINY PAUSE," said Etaf.

All projectiles froze in place.

"Lum's gaze has finally left us. Go on, leave. This distraction won't last," said Etaf, her blade dispersing into energy.

"Huh?" asked D.S.

"Leave this place, the other gods of Lum will not be as understanding."

"Leave and go where?" asked Devlin.

"Back to Absence. You'll need help from the guardians if you hope to challenge Etah's forces," said Etaf before walking off.

A cloaked figure appeared from seemingly nowhere and created an Absence portal.

"I'll go with my group and convince the Absence gods. Devlin, I want you to stay with the others, okay?" asked Exp 8.

"Of course. We'll scope out the area a bit. See what we can find out about the development Efil talked about. We'll find Demonica. When you meet up with us, we'll head to Sel," said Devlin.

"Agreed." Exp 8 clenched his partner's hand.

Karson walked up to Riufen. "Keep an eye on Bob." He rushed to Exp 8's side. "I'll come along with you."

"I will too," said Violet.

"No, stay with Devlin's team. Make sure Opti gets patched up, okay?" asked Exp 8.

"Of course," said Violet.

"Kaity, go with Exp 8. I will keep Sefiwah safe," said Kanasta.

"Roger," said Kaity.

"Alright team, let's go!" cheered Exp 8.

His group rushed into the portal to Absence.


"Back already? Did you forget something? Oh, of course. You miss me, don't you?" asked Eil with a grin.

"What the hell? That's not even funny!" yelled Exp 8.

Kawai approached the annoying skull. "We need your help to fight against Etah. Will you or any of your friends join us?"

"Tehtehteh. You want us to get involved? How foolish," said Eil.

"I would like to, but I don't feel I am quite ready for battle," said Occupy, appearing behind the team.

"You're more than qualified," said Kaity.

"If Absence is in danger, my lance shall defend it. A sword does not attack without command. Going after Etah now would bring unwanted attention to my homeland," said Limit.

"He's got a point! He must protect his homeland! For Britain!" cheered Karson, raising his arm up.

"The moment Etah steps foot into Absence, I will devour him," said Loyal.

"Yes yes yes yes yes! I want out of here. It will be so much fun, fighting angels or demons, whatever. Please, just get me out of here!" yelled Plagiarism.

"I suppose it beats staying here and doing nothing," said Crystal with a shrug.

"Spin! Spin spinny spin spin!" cheered Spin.

"Hold on everyone. If we go out there, then we become mortal. I think once you've thought things through, the thought of thinking of joining this group's thoughtless battle against Etah will be seen as an act of utter foolishness!" yelled Eil.

Occupy bowed to each guardian and then spoke. "Etah cannot travel to Absence unless he breaches the Elysium Asylum. We have an obligation to protect this realm from any threat—potential, ideological or otherwise. If we join the Exps, we are only putting our own lives at risk, not the safety of Absence."

"That speech. It moved me!" exclaimed Plagiarism, flailing his tongue around.

"Such valor," said NoOne.

"If we die, so be it," said Crystal.

"That said, we aren't ready for a battle," said Occupy.

"I am always ready," said Limit, spinning around his lance.

"We all lost our battles. Yes, we were having fun, but the fact remains that we are out of touch with our combative nature," said Occupy.

"Not all of you were messing around, right?" asked Opti.

"Then let us be the fire that ignites your passion!" cheered Atatasuki.

"Yeah, I'll knock you down till your fighting spirit stands up!" cheered Kawai.

"But what's the point if we all die once Etah appears?" asked NoOne.

"Yeah, good point," said Crystal.

"I'd rather die fighting," said Exp 8.

"What better way to die than defending the home front?" asked Limit.

"Spoken like a true warrior!" cheered Karson.

"Alright, everyone. I'm going to assume that we're all going to join their team. If you don't agree, too bad," said Eil.

"The Absence gods have always stood united," said Occupy.

"Fine, we'll all join your team after one final fight. All of you, or at least all who are here at the moment, versus all of us! Rather than playtime, this will be a warm up for the coming battle. We won't hold back; so don't complain if you get killed. Hmm…well I suppose that won't really be a problem, now will it? Anyway, we want the best you've got! Only if we're beaten will we join you," said Eil.

"Let's do this," said Exp 8.

"Count me in!" cheered D.S., raising his scissors.

"The two teammates have been chosen. No one else may enter now."

"But you said ten members, not two," said Exp 8.

"You must have misheard me," said Eil.

"They are already at a numerical disadvantage. All of you, attack us at once. Show us your team unity," said Loyal.

"Hold on a minute. Let's all try not to kill them," said Crystal, eyeing the second guard. "As far as we know, we both want to keep Absence safe."

"I'll pass on this fight. Needle will have to try extra hard on my behalf, tehtehteh," said Eil.

"My guru is beyond such things," said Occupy, setting Void down next to the First Guardian.

"I see no reason for fighting. My skills are well honed," said Limit.

"No! I must fight you! We are both warriors!" cheered Karson.

"Such spirit. Very well, I shan't disappoint you," said Limit, raising his lance.

"Stay close by, Sis. If you need help, I'll intervene, ok," said Exp 8.

"Which one are you going after?" asked Kawai.

"The dragon." Exp 8's jets shot him up into Loyal's chin.

His orb fired off and exploded. In the midst of the explosion, his turrets popped out and opened fire.

Kaity fired at each needle as it shot out while Karson kept Limit at bay with machinegun fire.

D.S. was running from Spin's tops.

NoOne had gripped Separate and Plagiarism by enveloping them with his shadow.

"Thanks. Don't know how long we'll stay here. Gotta make use of our time," said Pharma, heating up a cigarette with his shoulder lighter.

Atatasuki turned toward Pharma. "No way! You're fighting just like the rest of us!"

A barrage of crystals fired at Atatasuki. Kawai zoomed in and knocked each one aside with her tail.

"Thanks, Sis," said Atatasuki.

"Have you found your opponent yet?" asked Kawai, grabbing a particularly large crystal with her tail.

"I'll fight you," said Occupy, appearing in front of the heated metal warrior.

Atatasuki superheated his fist and slammed them into the monk.

After a blurry motion from Occupy, Atatasuki was flat on his back.

"You're fast!" he exclaimed, swiping his tail at the monk.

"Come on. Awaken my fighting spirit!" Occupy lifted his sparring partner up and tossed him into the air.

Loyal spit fire balls at Exp 8 as the little nuisance zoomed around him. "Do you think such a tactic will work against Etah?"

"It worked last time." Exp 8 fired a souped-up orb into Loyal's mouth as the dragon opened for another attack. He then zoomed inside, shooting the orb with his turrets to expand it.

"Well done, Commander!" exclaimed Karson with a salute.

"That's far enough." Limit punched Karson full of holes the moment he was within range.

"Well-played. But I'm not done yet." A cannon came out from the gunman's chest as his feet opened fire at the armored knight.

Atatasuki was being kicked around like a hacky sack, and D.S was still running from the tops.

"I'll be right there as soon as I'm done here!" Kawai got in close to Crystal and was bashing him around with her tail.

"I can't feel that. I don't feel anything anymore," said Crystal, fashioning his arms into mineral blades.

Exp 8 slammed into him from behind.

"Thanks, Brother!" cheered Kawai.

"What about your opponent?" asked Atatasuki as he met the warrior monk's fist barrage with his own.

"Taken care of," said Exp 8, snapping his fingers.

The bloated dragon in the distance burst open. His body parts littered the otherwise spotless ground of Absence.

Karson leaped out of the way of the fellow European's thrust and aimed his cannon. "Got you now. **PARTICLE BEAM**!"

Limit swerved out of the beam's range. The laser then obliterated Separate, who was still pinned by NoOne's shadow.

"You're not the only target here," said Karson, keeping the knight occupied with shotgun fire.

"Aww man. Karson's too busy. Oh! Hey Pharma, help out your uncle!" yelled D.S., blocking Spin's top barrage with his scissors.

"Be right there, unlike that useless gun. *Junkie Jolt*," said Pharma, injecting himself with adrenaline and caffeine.

The drug lord slammed into Occupy, who suddenly appeared in his path. The user was knocked off balance and fell over.

"Sorry, but I have to defend my allies," said Occupy with a slight smile.

Exp 8 fired orbs up to Kawai who knocked them like volleyballs at Crystal.

"Ooh, ooh! We should call this a new attack. Any ideas?" asked Kawai, beaming at her brother.

"ORB..."

"*Volley!*" cheered Kawai, whacking one orb into another to make a bigger orb.

NoOne sent his arm at Plagiarism and sliced the skull in half while still keeping him pinned. "Phew. That was rather tricky."

"If you're free, then go help my little brother!" hollered Kawai, swerving to dodge a mineral storm.

Occupy grabbed Atatasuki and walloped Pharma down to the ground with him. "Awaken me! Fight harder!"

Atatasuki's body heated up and his jets activated. He pummeled the monk with a flurry of kicks before his legs bent back. Bloodied and crushed, he dropped to the ground.

"NoOne, go after Crystal. I'll take down Occupy," said Exp 8, snatching his sister from the air as he zoomed out of the way of a mineral barrage.

Karson fell to the ground, covered in even more holes. "You win. You are a true warrior."

"As are you," said Limit with a swift salute.

"Not good! We lost Karson!" Kaity ran on all fours, gradually closing in on Needle.

"Wait, who am I fighting?" asked Kawai, looking around.

Limit rushed forth at the floating child, his lance gleaming.

"Butter-muffins," said Kawai, clenching her teeth. She swerved out of the way, knocking the lance aside in the process. In that moment she boosted and latched onto his face. "*Energy Drain*"

Seven meters away, the tops sped around D.S.'s scissors, spiraled down them, and then fired off into his chest.

"Sorry. I'm out," said D.S., falling back with a smile.

Spin's tops immediately headed toward the girl with the ballerina slippers.

NoOne and Crystal were rapidly assaulting each other with double-bladed hands. Though, due to their body's composition, neither could harm the other.

"Looks like a stalemate. And so my life hits another wall. Typical," said Crystal.

"If you're going to fight with us, then you must take up a hero's spirit!" cheered the shadow master.

Four arms arose out from the NoOne's shadow. They each morphed into blades and sliced into the ground.

"It's no use. There are no shadows here," said Crystal.

"Yes, this place is rather special," said NoOne.

Occupy blocked each punch the team's leader threw his way. He slid his feet in a rapid motion, avoiding the sudden orb shot and tripping the Exp leader all at once.

Exp 8 grabbed the monk's arm with his tail. "Training really pays off. **LITTLE ORBS OF BIG ORB**!" The large orb fired itself out as ten smaller orbs.

Occupy pulled his arm free and made slight movements to dodge each orb.

By the time Exp 8 hit the ground, he had fused his misfires into a massive orb.

Limit sat down and watched as Kawai fended off Spin's tops. "The resolve they fight with is truly admirable."

"You're a gentleman, right? Help me out!" yelled Kawai before her body suffered another wound from the tops.

"You chose to enter this fight. You are a warrior as of now and my opponent," said Limit.

"NoOne, what about you?" asked Kawai, shielding her face from the deadly ladles.

"Just about done here."

NoOne's shadow came up from beneath the floor of Absence and returned to him.

Crystal fell down a chasm into the nothingness below. "Well played," he said before vanishing completely.

Having dispatched his opponent, NoOne fired shadow balls at the pearl knight as he rushed to Kawai's aid.

"I won't let them down!" Kaity had finally closed in. She leaped up, taking four quills in the chest, and sliced open Needle with her plasma claws.

To her surprise, blood gushed out of the prickly figure's body and splattered her face.

Kaity screamed out as the black blood burned her eyes.

Exp 8's souped-up orb had missed before Occupy's palm slammed into his chest. The Freedom Forcers' founder grabbed onto Occupy's arm with his tail and opened his palm. "Time for a new move. Return to my body. **ORB ORIGIN**!"

All the previously fired orbs now gravitated back to Exp 8's floating wrist ring, slamming into Occupy's back in the process.

Exp 8 jet-boosted to safety as the orbs exploded. He skidded across the ground and stopped in front of his shadow ally. "I need a break. Take it from here, will you?"

"What? You're the hero here! We can't beat them on our own," said NoOne, parrying the knight's lance with one of his own design.

"Surrender begins in the mind," said Limit, rapidly piercing a line up the shadow sorcerer's body.

NoOne's body split in two.

Having blinded her, the needle god gripped Kaity by her calf.

The assassin prodigy reacted on instinct, kicking the guard in the face and slicing open her foot in the process.

She screamed out as the prickly guard's acidic blood ate away at her skin.

"Damn it! You owe me one!" Kawai zoomed through the tops and snatched the wannabe cat-girl off the ground. "Stop writhing so much!"

"Is it just us two now?" asked both halves of NoOne as they continued to attack the knight.

"I'm up," said Exp 8, rising from the ground.

Occupy zoomed by and slammed the leader back to the ground.

"No way. I blew you up!" yelled Exp 8.

"It was a well-timed attack. I should have been more cautious," said Occupy, sending the leader next to his remaining comrades with a sudden kick.

"Damn, he hits hard. How many are left?" asked Exp 8, standing up in a bit of a daze.

"Four!" yelled Kawai, spinning her tail around to deflect Spin's barrage. "I can hardly defend. How am I going to win this?" she asked, flying around to avoid the leaping ladles.

"Nice job taking out Crystal," said Exp 8, waiting for his opponent's next move.

"I didn't. He's on a short trip. He'll be back soon," said NoOne, assaulting the knight with eight shadow limbs.

"You're right," said Exp 8, pointing up at a falling figure. "Time to even the odds!" The Ultimate Exp boosted past Needle's assault and slammed into the guard. He lifted the spiny warrior off the ground and zoomed toward the crystal guard. After firing off the prickly defender with an orb, he sped behind Crystal. The freedom fighter then gravitated Needle into Crystal by pulling in the orb.

"Brother is so incredible!" cheered Kawai, bouncing in place. Her next tail swipe demolished the incoming tops.

"I can be a hero too, damn it!" The shadow master's blades bent upon contact. They curved into the gaps in Limits armor and sliced through the flesh beneath.

Limit fell apart into slabs, his armor unscathed.

"See? Pretty cool, kehkehkeh," said NoOne.

"Brother is counting on me," said Kawai, counterattacking after each successful defense.

"To fell Sir Limit, you are more than mortal," said Occupy, slicing through the shadow blades with one hand.

Exp 8 slammed into the monk and punched him vigorously. "You will go down!" he yelled, firing an orb as each punch connected.

"Such vigor! I think I'm going to burst," said Kawai, her body swaying back and forth. "You're blocking my view!" She slammed her extra hard tail into the tops, smashing them to bits. "Oh wow! The more in love I am, the stronger I get!" she cheered, chasing the fleeing tops.

"Kawai's got it under control. I'll finish off the deadbeat," said NoOne, bringing his two halves back together.

Crystal crashed. He rose up from his invisible crater. "I'm not done yet."

Kawai zoomed up and slammed him to the ground with her rock hard tail. "Don't block my view!"

Exp 8 was knocked off Occupy in an instant. He zoomed right back into another fist barrage.

"Do you, uh, need any help?" asked NoOne, looking at the deranged girl.

"Don't you dare get back up!" yelled Kawai.

"Whatever. I'm sick of this. I'm out," said Crystal, raising his hand in surrender.

Exp 8 was knocked away only to charge right back in ten more times.

"That's it! Keep fighting!" yelled Occupy, landing four hits after receiving one.

"I will! Feel our drive! We will take down Etah!"

"Inspirational!" Occupy's hand burst through his chest. "You've done it! My fighting spirit has been reawakened! Let us bring the battle to Etah!" he exclaimed, raising his new ally with his fist.

"Brother!" Kawai zoomed to her beloved.

"Is he alright?" asked Occupy, setting down the injured warrior.
 "Stay with me." She gripped onto his hand.

"I'll be okay. I just have to rest for a bit," said Exp 8, rubbing her head.

"Do I have to fight you now?" asked NoOne, cringing as the immortal monk took a step toward him.

"No. You've won our allegiance. Heal them up," said Occupy, lifting Crystal back to his feet.

"I can only do so much. These wounds are pretty extensive. They should go to Lum and get healed by the goddesses," said Crystal.

"Then we shall accompany them," said Limit, already fully restored and atop his trusty steed.

"I'll make the portal. But I'm not going back to Lum. We can join them in Sel. Our presence in Lum would only complicate things," said Crystal.

"Good point," said Occupy.

Neutral, the God of Absence, spontaneously generated in front of the Absence gods. "You were fight-ing again? Your low energy tells me your pride has been wound-ed. Were you defeat-ed?"

"Indeed they were. And they made a deal, so they're with us now," said Exp 8.

"Then you all will go into battle, possib-ly never return-ing. Ah, this means actual neutral-ity. Leave now. All the Freedom Forcers are now un-banish-ed to Absence." Neutral turned to face the team, vanishing for an instant from sight. "You all have caus-ed un-necessary occurrences. You are free to leave. You are not free to return."

"Last you'll see of us, promise," said Exp 8.

Crystal created a portal and Occupy and Limit helped the team make it through.

"I'm going with them. We're responsible for the state they are in," said Occupy, bowing to his allies before entering the portal.

The team arrived in a forest clearing.

Occupy closed his eyes. "Your team should be right over that hill." He turned back, looking at the miserable state of the Freedom Forcers. "Stay here. I'll be back as soon as I can with Efil."

"Hey, Brother, stay with me," said Kawai, the blood from her wounds dripping off her face.

Atatasuki's placed his hand on her head. "Don't worry. He's only resting. It will take a lot more than that to take him out."

"What is this stuff?" asked NoOne, yanking at the corrosive black goop on Kaity's face. He pulled his hand away abruptly. "Impossible." His fingers had lost their tips. "How can it harm me?"

"Not sure, but it looks pretty hard core. Let me try." Pharma snorted up the back goop with the bendy straws in his nostrils. "Shit, this is intense!" he yelled, running around in circles.

Kaity writhed around, her screams muffled by the black goop.

"She's going to be okay, right?" asked D.S., the skin from his chest shredded up.

"Hey…things are starting to get blurry," said Karson, riddled with holes and in a puddle of his own oil.

"Nobody is allowed to die…okay?" asked Exp 8, his voice weak and his eyes closed.

"Help has arrived!" exclaimed NoOne as the Goddess of Life landed.

Efil immediately rushed to Kaity's side. She concentrated light energy in her hand and fired it as a concentrated blast. "What happened here? Were you ambushed by demons?"

"You healed me. It doesn't hurt anymore," said Kaity, not a blemish on her face.

Exp 8 raised his head off the ground. "We were fighting the Absence gods. They're pretty tough."

"Where are the rest of you? Were they killed in battle? I haven't been gone long, how could this have happened?" asked Efil, using her life energy to heal the gunman.

"You're a damn good medic," said Karson, stretching out his limbs.

"We did lose someone, but you're not to blame. You were protecting us from Etaf, right? That's why you sent us to Absence back then?" asked Exp 8.

"I am merely an instrument for Lum's will. I followed my orders. We didn't expect you to arrive so soon," said Efil, walking to Exp 8.

"Hey, heal the rest first. I'm their leader, so I should be taken care of last," said Exp 8.

"Wrong. You're the number one priority here," said Kawai.

Efil mended the wound in the leader's chest. The white aura then shot into his scalp, growing back the tendril he had lost. The Goddess of Life then pooled her energy into his stub, reforming his arm.

"Oh, hell yeah! I'm back in action! Hey, Atatasuki is pretty beat up. Can you heal him next?" asked Exp 8, punching the kinks out of his new arm.

"You all plan to fight against Etah, don't you?" asked Efil.

"Yeah, that's right," said Exp 8, patting Kawai's head.

"Lum has ordered the rebels of Allah's Jannah to be killed," said Efil, her eyes quivering.

"Does that mean you were fighting them before coming to help us?" asked Atatasuki.

"No. Etaf and her angels are sufficient for that task. Lum would not ask that of me. She only orders me into battle when truly necessary," said Efil, using an arching beam to heal the remaining Freedom Forcers.

"Wait, but you told Etaf that she tasked you with taking out the Imam," said Exp 8.

"I lied. But I had to. Etaf would have killed all of you and then she would wipe out everyone associated with Allah's Jannah. I couldn't let that happen. It's an unforgivable sin to speak for Lum, but I...I did what I had to," said Efil in tears.

"You did the right thing. I'm sure Lum would be proud of you," said Exp 8.

"You really think so?" asked Efil with shimmering eyes.

"Hey, we should meet up with our allies. Thanks for everything," said Atatasuki with a thumbs-up.

"Of course. But wait. Things have changed. Once the order to kill the rebels came through…well, I don't know how it happened…but the demons attacked. The barrier still stands, but they somehow got through. Etaf is keeping them at bay, as are the other goddesses. Even the Imam's assassination has been postponed. We would like you to help fight the demons here. Etah has made his move. There is no fault in retaliating now. In fact, it would give us a tactical advantage if you would fight as visitors of Lum," said Efil.

"You bought us enough time to create a new option for us. Thanks, Efil. You are a friend to all Exps," said Exp 8, putting his arm around her.

"Does that mean you'll help?" asked Efil with a rosy blush.

"You can tell your fellow goddess that the Exps are fighting to defend Lum, but we can't stay here. If Etah's forces are attacking Lum now, that makes this the opportune time for a direct attack. We're going to find our allies and head straight to Sel. We'll end the battle by taking him down," said Exp 8 with a clenched fist.

"You're an incredible leader. Maybe one day, you'll join us as a god," said Efil with a slight bow.

"Not happening. My duty is to inspire mortals, and I can do so only as long as I am mortal," said Exp 8, signaling his team to get up.

"I shall tell Lum the good news. I wish you the luck of the Goddess," said Efil with a smile.

"Thanks. We'll need it. Team, let's move out!" cheered Exp 8, rushing up the hillside.


Once they reached the top of the hill, they spotted their allies.

They were about a half a mile away and encircled by demons.

Exp 8 boosted ahead, slamming into a particularly prickly demon and shattering its spines.

"How did negotiations go?" asked Devlin, before slicing up six demons with a single wire.

"They were a complete success. And everyone made it out alive," said Exp 8.

"Good work. Well then, no need to stay here. Demonica, bring us to Sel," said Devlin.

"Yes, sir," said Demonica, forming a Sel portal.

The Freedom Forcers rushed in.

"Did you see, Efil?" asked Deceivant.

A blinding light came from above, causing the demons and Demonica to disperse.

Efil landed in front of the inventor. "Are there more who are injured?"

"Forget that. Where's Fatima?" asked Nina.

"She is safe and healthy," said Efil.

"Can you heal Opti?" asked Anthrax.

"No need," said Opti, standing tall and waving.

"Opti, your arms are back! Did my powers return?" asked Anthrax, rolling up his sleeves to look at his hands.

"I healed him. Apparently my connection with the Revive Artifact isn't completely lost," said Sefiwah.

"That's great news! Efil already regenerated my arm, but I'll be sure to keep your healing prowess in mind," said Exp 8.

"I give you all my blessing. May you each return victorious," said Efil with a big smile and a little bow.

"You'll owe us more than a mere blessing. We'll discuss our reward later. You need to go see if there are any other children who were hurt by your fellow angels," said Deceivant.

"You're right!" Efil flew off.

Demonica rose out from a puddle of demon blood. "She's not coming back, right?"

"Not if we hurry. Everyone in!" hollered Exp 8, aiming an orb at the few brave demons who approached.

Once all his allies passed through the portal, Exp 8 entered.

# Part 9
# The Lord of Hate

# Chapter 79: The Forces of Hate

Incredible heat greeted the team. Flames erupted around them as they fell, disoriented onto the scorched earth of Sel.

"If I get fired up, well, it could be fatal in this place. Even staying here too long might kill me," said Atatasuki.

"And without Tempo around, there's no way to cool you down," said Kawai.

"Who's Tempo?" asked Atatasuki.

"Ugh. Forget it," said Kawai.

"Whoa, man. Classic rock is my fave, but heavy metal is rocking too. This place looks like a heavy metal album cover! It's got personality," said Ego, looking far into the distance.

"Stay vigilant. Some of our past targets may be lurking around, seeking vengeance," said Kanasta, scanning the ground for familiar faces.

"Ugh. I can feel their negative energy," said Sefiwah, covering her mouth.

"They were buried under molten rock the last time we came here, but not anymore. This whole world is made of suffering people. This is why we must take down Etah," said Exp 8.

"The hero has returned!" exclaimed a protruding head.

"I have, but keep it under wraps. I don't want Etah knowing I'm here," said Exp 8.

"Mommy, I want to go home. This place is scary," said D.S., tugging her arm.

"Sweetie, I'm sorry but we have to do this. As soon as we're done, we can head back to Lum, okay?" asked Ada.

"Okay," said D.S. with a sullen look.

"Hmm, I'm sensing Etah's soul looming closer. He may be here quicker than expected," said Bob.

"Let him come! We're ready!" cheered Karson.

"I look forward to the coming battle," said Riufen, drawing a second spine from his back.

"I'm not sure how I can help," said Matteria.

"Can we really defeat the God of Hate?" asked NoOne.

"Products of science versus mythical nonsense. I'm sure you'll all do fine," said Deceivant.

"I sure hope so," said Opti, biting his nails.

"We have to win. The people of Lum are counting on us," said Anthrax.

"And so is Efil. She believes in us," said Violet.

"Not to mention you have me. I know all about Etah. And I can tell you, it will be a miracle if you succeed," said Demonica.

The ground quaked. A chasm appeared sixty feet in front of the team. Etah emerged from it, followed by a continuous stream of demons.

"Where are our allies from Absence?" asked Devlin, turning to his co-captain.

"They said they would join us here," said Exp 8, looking around.

"Well, they better hurry up," said Devlin.

"BoneSaw, start up the clock. We're back on the job," said Kanasta.

The Freedom Forcers split into three groups, putting their strongest members in the front lines. Napkin hopped out of Kaity's arms and ran off.

"The cat will be fine. We need to stay focused on the matter at hand," said Kanasta, soothing his apprentice with gentle gestures.

"What are you doing back there? Get up here with us," said Exp 8, beckoning NoOne to the front lines.

Kanasta crouched down to BoneSaw. "If the demons break through, protect my parents. You too, Ego."

The Freedom Forcers all took their battle stance before the demons were within range.

Kaity rushed by Karson. "Thanks!" She rolled into a flat position and centered her sights. She was the first to fire, bursting the heads of twenty demons with a single sniper bullet.

Karson fired rockets into the stampede of demons while Bob cut through entire rows with his lasers.

"I'm sorry, but in order to take down Etah...we'll kill if we must." Exp 8 fired a souped-up orb into the midsection of enemies.

The demons parted around the massive orb, breaking them into two groups.

The Freedom Forcers' front line charged in.

Devlin sped ahead on all fours, slicing through several columns of demons with wires that spun out from his back.

Riufen charged into the area with the most bladed demons and started to cut through their line with his dual-sword style.

With an orb in each hand, Exp 8 pummeled the incoming demons. When a large enough group appeared, he fired off the orbs into the crowd.

NoOne created ten bladed arms and rushed into a nearby hoard of grunts, staying within range of the team's brave leader.

Kanasta charged through a line of demons, braving cuts and bludgeoning.

Unsure of where he was needed most, D.S. made it his duty to finish off the wounded demons.

Demonica elongated her fingernails and tore through the demons, savoring the shock in their eyes as they were cut to pieces.

While staying in place, Bob fired lasers at the demons who weren't taken out by the others in the front line.

Karson provided covering fire, all the while remaining at his station in the middle line.

The ground quaked again. Three more chasms appeared, like gashes in the earth, boxing the Freedom Forcers in.

It wasn't long before hoards of demons charged out of the screaming chasms.

"We were so foolish to come here," said NoOne.

"Damn it! NoOne and I will hold the line here. The rest of you fan out and stop the incoming forces," said Exp 8.

"We can't stay idle! Everyone, grab a gun and open fire!" yelled Nina, taking guns off the living ammo depot's back.

"You could at least ask!" yelled Karson before his head disengaged.

"I don't know what to do with this," said Ada, holding an AK-47 in her arms.

"I can show you," said Ego.

"Wait, hold on a minute. I can't take that. These hands are meant to heal," said Anthrax.

"You're the one who said everyone in Lum is counting on us. Are you going to let your morals get in the way of saving people?" Nina dripped water on her outfit and pushed out her chest.

"No, I…uh…you're right," said Anthrax, cocking the revolver.

A group of demons stopped for a moment and then rushed at Nina with a jolt of vigor.

"Damn it! This isn't effective the way I had hoped it would be," said Nina, splashing water at the demons before kicking them aside.

"Too many are breaking past the front line. We need to split up and defend from all angles," said Kaity, firing Uzis with her feet while unloading sniper rounds into the coming hoards of demons.

"Damn it, even when they're down they keep fighting," said Deceivant, blasting a half torso on the ground with his shotgun.

"So much death," said Violet, tears rushing down her cheeks.

"Yeah, it's like the Baghavad Gita, Ragnarok, or um…the Illiad," said Atatasuki, fighting four demons at once with a sword he just happened to find on his person.

"When you put it that way, it doesn't seem so bad," said Violet with a slight smile.

"You're uh, Violet, right?" asked Atatasuki before slamming his fist into a demon's open mouth.

"Yes, that's right."

"Yeah, yeah, I remember you. Still having trouble remembering some of the others," said Atatasuki, dodging a sickle and grabbing it.

Kawai stayed a few feet above the demons and attacked them with her hardened tail.

Steam poured out from BoneSaw and surrounded a group of approaching demons. The little robot fired mini-saws into the crowd, but even after losing limbs, they persevered onward.

"Umm, guys. I think there are more of them," said Opti, wincing as the revolver in his hand fired off.

An armada of demons came charging down the molten mountainside, releasing a thunderous battle cry.

"How many more must die?" asked Sefiwah, dodging a demon's claw swipe and piercing his throat with her fingers.

"I got a killer hangover. Are there as many of them as it looks?" asked Pharma, poking his rival's shoulder.

"If you've got the energy to talk, then use it to fight!" yelled Karson, mowing down hundreds of demons with dual Gatling guns.

"Fine." Pharma yanked a flamethrower off his rival's back. "Who wants to get cooked?" he asked, shooting a stream of fire into a group of four demons.

Demonica turned her arm into a blood scythe and carved a path to Devlin. "These are all weak demons. Etah's toying with us. They're practically cannon fodder." She slammed her heel on a downed demon.

"And the ones about to join them?" asked Devlin, gesturing to the mountain on his right.

"They're a mixed bunch, but nothing that special," she said.

"We're going to need to put forth even more effort! The reinforcements are here!" yelled Exp 8.

"Understood," said Kawai with a salute, tossing grenades with her tail while gunning down the demons.

The new wave of demons attacked Etah's forces, immediately throwing the army into a state of confusion.

"The hero has returned!" yelled a plump demon with a golden belly.

"What hero?" asked Devlin.

"They're talking about me," said Exp 8.

"A fighting fan club! Brother never ceases to amaze. The tide of battle has turned!" hollered Kawai.

"Wait a minute. I know him," said Exp 8.

"Is he your friend?" asked Kawai, zooming past Karson to get another set of guns.

"Hardly. He calls himself the Führer of Fortune. He's a demon lord who wants to rule Sel by removing Etah from the throne."

"We are here to assist," said the Führer, signaling the demon next to him to wave the flag impaled in its back.

The Baroness of Blades sliced through a line of enemies up to the Hero of Sel.

"What are your orders?" she asked, bent down on her knee.

Exp 8 suddenly embraced her. "Last time I saw you, you were cut in half. I'm glad you survived."

"The Führer patched me up," said the Baroness, showing the solid gold coating that held her body together.

"So you're still allied with that tyrant?" asked Exp 8.

"We are Hero's Militia. Our group was founded by the Führer."

"Wait, so you all renamed your group?"

"Not exactly. We split apart from the Sinner's Fury after your brave battle against Etah."

"Thanks, but I just did what I felt was right. Too bad I lost," said Exp 8, scratching the back of his head.

"There are three demon lords leading the Hero's Militia against the Forces of Hate, but you are our true leader," she said with a bow.

"He's also taken." Kawai opened her mouthpiece, pulled her brother's head in with her tail and kissed his cheek.

"My orders are to fight with the victims in mind. Aim to incapacitate, not kill," said Exp 8.

"I'll relay your orders to the others," said the Baroness before rushing off.

A demon walked up to the hero and stood on the balls of its feet, allowing the hero to use the sound amplifier attached to its shoulder.

"Thanks. Residents of Sel, I accept your title of hero! Etah will fall today! All will be free! But the Hero of Sel cannot win this battle with only his forces! Do whatever you can to stop the Forces of Hate! If you're melted to the ground but you can move your hands, then slow them down as best you can! This battle can only be won by everyone joining together to defeat Etah! If despair fuels him, then we shall fight back with unwavering hope!" exclaimed Exp 8, raising his fist to rally his warriors.

"He's never looked so sexy," said Kawai, squirming in delight.

"To think he rallied an entire army all on his own. He truly is the Ultimate Exp," said Deceivant.

"Again and again he surpasses expectations. Still resolve alone can't carry us to victory," said Devlin.

The ground quaked and split open in three sections, followed by screams of agony.

"Enemy reinforcements, approaching all lines, stay focused everyone!" hollered Exp 8.


The chasm near the first group burst open, causing a quake and nearly caving in the ground. A massive head rose out from the crevice in synch with the symphony of screams. Its arms, nearly the size of oak trees, slammed against the ground.

"Hey, do you know that thing?" asked Exp 8, tripping a demon with his tail before sending it flying with an orb.

"That would be the Daimyo of Death. Don't be frightened though. It's only a title," said Demonica. A thick black aura burst out from her body and came together in her grip. The energy solidified into a black pole. A murky red aura then ran down her hands and into the pole's grip. A crimson jagged blade came out from the tip of the pole, forming it into a scythe. "I'm the real thing."

"Daimyo? Is he Japanese?" asked Riufen, dodging spears thrown his way while he fought one-on-one with the enemy before him.

"Just a name, like I said." Demonica twirled the scythe around, slicing through her kin with an aroused grin.

The Daimyo flung a thick liquid off his arms.

"What is this?" asked NoOne.

"Oil!"

A fireball came from above and ignited the oil.

Kanasta shielded D.S. from the blast.

Standing on the top of the Daimyo's head was the General of Genocide.

"And that would be—"

"No need, Demonica, I know him," said Exp 8 before taking flight.


A demon lord emerged near the back group and was shaped like a ferret. It was fully adorned in spiky armor and an iron helmet. Two thin blades were poised at its side. Atop of his back was a blunderbuss. The furry demon was swiftly surrounded by four-legged demons with saddles and spiked helmets.

"Hmm, first non-human demon I've seen," said Nina.

The ferret demon lord slid under his battalion as they charged the enemy.

"Nina, toss me one a bottle," said Matteria, keeping Anthrax in his sight.

"I don't have many. Don't waste it," she said, throwing it his way.

The ferret climbed up one of his soldier's legs, onto their back and then leaped off, grabbing the bottle with his tail.

"Get down!" Deceivant grabbed his wife and ducked under a blast of screws and nails. "Damn. It's got more range than I expected, are you okay?" he asked, holding his injured shoulder.

"Come on, powers, don't fail me now! LIQUID SPIKE!" exclaimed Matteria, his hands glowing with energy.

The water burst the bottle and jutted out like a sea-urchin.

The demon lord was surprised but not injured. Once it landed, it concealed itself under its forces.

Anthrax fell over after firing his revolver.

The bullet shot into the arm of one of the four-legged soldiers but didn't stop her.

Ada winced each time she fired into the crowd.

"Beheh! Let's see them get through this!" exclaimed Pharma, creating a wall of fire with the flamethrower he swiped from his rival.

The demon lord climbed onto the saddle of one of his soldiers. It leaped off as a shotgun blast came its way and landed on another saddle. "You're rather fast, but not quite quick enough. Greetings, rebels, I am the Captain of Carnage," he said, with a high-pitched and excited tone.

"So polite! I'm Ada! Come on, everyone, we should introduce ourselves."

"I am Etah's personal assassin. If anyone, even a demon lord, becomes a problem, he sends me to end them." The blades at his sides shot out, each one connected to him by a cord.

One of the blades pierced into Nina's leg, the other zoomed right by Matteria and planted itself in the ground.

Nina fired at the armored weasel as he zoomed up to her.

The Captain grabbed a blade hidden beneath him with his tail. He cut into Nina's arm and then ran down her leg, all the while slicing her up. The demon lord dislodged the blade in her leg with his mouth and then scurried across the ground.

"Can you take care of him? We've got more enemies inbound," said Deceivant, firing into an incoming crowd before loading in a fresh round of bullets.

"I can help with that," said Ego, enlarging himself as he rushed into enemy lines.

The demon lord pulled himself toward his blade, all the while dodging the bullets coming his way.

He sliced Matteria as he zoomed by and then fired his other blade at the enemy's foot.

Matteria quickly pulled his foot out of the way.

The demon lord leapt off the ground and reeled in the blade, slicing the enemy in the process.

"Stop hurting my boyfriend!" Anthrax fired three shots. Two missed and the third hit the demon lord's chin.

The Captain pulled himself back toward the blade he had planted as he tried to reorient himself.

"Damn it, they're getting closer," said Nina, using machine-gun fire to disperse the four-legged soldiers.

Fifteen meters ahead, near the middle, a swarm of soldiers in gimp gear rushed out from a hole in the ground, wielding double-ended weapons drenched in fresh blood.

Their leader rolled out of the chasm. Eagles, zebras, cows, pigs, hippos, horses, bears—thirty angels of various species had been melted together to form the gruesome figure. It was a twenty-foot wrecking ball of agony.

"I want to fly," said a head, poking out between three of the screaming angels. A helmet with fox ears covered the burnt face of the demon lord responsible for the abomination.

"I'll keep him busy!" yelled Kaity, rushing ahead.

The wrecking ball demon lord purposefully ran over demons as it chased down the kitty girl.

"Karson, give me more grenades, now!" exclaimed Kawai, sticking her hands in his body.

"Stop that! I'll get them for you, calm down!" he yelled, keeping the incoming demons held back all on his own.

"What are these horrid things?" asked Violet as the gimps approached.

"They are suffering," said Sefiwah with quivering eyes.

The gimp soldiers sliced into their own bodies with the back of their weapons as they thrust the tips at the enemies. With each slash came a muffled scream of pain.

Sefiwah grabbed the blade of a halberd between her hands. She broke it off and ducked under an axe. After leaping, she plunged the sharpened metal into one of their backs. While back-flipping out of the way of a spear, she gripped the blade with her feet and sliced open the gimps back.

Violet's astral hands yanked a double-sided mace out of the gimp's grip. "Should I provide Kaity assistance?" she asked, parrying multiple katana swipes.

"It looks like Kaity can handle it," said Atatasuki, decapitating a gimp after getting his blade stuck in its neck.

BoneSaw sped in the path of the living ball of destruction. It fired saws at a low angle to alter the thing's trajectory.

Kaity shot at the wrecking ball with an Uzi gripped by her tail as she ran circles around it.

"Fly! Fly like a bird in the sky!" The tortured angels who made up the perimeter of the sphere all sprouted wings of light one after the next. The demon lord rose off the ground and into the air.

"Didn't expect that," said Kaity, whipping out the sniper and focusing her sights.

"A beautiful bird! No, an angel! I'm an angel! An angel with wings of light!" cheered the demon lord, in an elated, sing-song voice.

"You're disgusting!" yelled Kawai, sending a grenade flying with her tail. The grenade burst after hitting the ball.

Kaity waited for the smoke to clear and then fired at the demon lord, busting open his head.

The wrecking ball came crashing down and burst open upon impact.


Previously: the front lines were engaged in a battle against two demon lords.

Devlin shot a wire at the Daimyo's eye but it slid off. "Slippery bastard." He turned around to decapitate four demons on approach.

"What the hell are you doing, General? This is our chance to stop Etah! I don't think the Mediator would approve of this!" yelled Exp 8, powering up an orb as he navigated through a storm of fireballs.

"Ha! I don't care what that little cretin wants! This is my chance to show Etah my power! I'd be a fool to miss out!" The General zoomed off the Daimyo, igniting the demon lord's massive bald scalp. "*FURIOUS MORTAR!*" Like a living fireball, he slammed into the hero.

"I'm alive! Not that you were concerned," said NoOne, rising out of his shadow.

"This guy's huge! Like a final boss!" hollered D.S., swinging his scissors at incoming demons as he ran as fast as he could away from the giant's arm.

"I always find that the most rewarding boss is the one that mimics the fighting style of the player. Still, he's more than a mere damage sponge," said Kanasta, leaping over a hand sweep while loading bullets into the giant's knuckles.

"Need any help?" asked Bob, phasing through fireballs that soon slammed into the supposed ultimate Exp.

"No. I got this!" Exp 8 held out his orb, having the General slam into it. With maximum jet propulsion he then zoomed into the ground, ejecting the orb before crashing into a group of demons.

"Where did that coward go!" yelled the General, his flames bursting out and igniting nearby demons.

Demonica rose out of a puddle directly in front of the hot-headed demon lord. "Hi," she said, her scythe nearly touching his neck.

"You joined with the Hero of Sel?" he asked, his pupils shrinking.

"Do you surrender?" she asked with a smile.

The General nodded and then zoomed into the air. Flames came out from his fingertips like bullets and set the Daimyo on fire. "Kill her now!" he yelled, before flying off.

Bob's laser bore through the giant's shoulder.

Devlin's wires gripped the hand. After it was sent up by a powerful punch from Kanasta, the wires slammed the hand into the Daimyo's face.

"Haha! You made him face-palm!" cheered D.S.

Exp 8 flew around, keeping the other hand occupied.

"I've had enough fun." Demonica's fingernails jutted out and pierced into the Daimyo's chest. She took flight and sliced all the way up his face. "The system is stale and outdated. Demon lords will be a thing of the past. Once Devlin takes over, you're all going away." After dousing the flames on his forehead with a blast of blood, she landed. "Bye."

The Death Scythe, fully engorged a murky red aura, tapped against the Daimyo's forehead.

D.S. jumped out of the way as the giant's hand crashed.

The Daimyo collapsed with a quake, his eyes void of vitality.

The ground roared with triumphant cheers.

"Hey Demonica, can you help me out here?" asked Devlin, looking at sheets of seared skin that once belonged to him.

"Yep." She snapped her fingers.

A fresh layer of skin and Devlin's clothes reappeared on his body.

"How do you do that?" he asked with a smile.

"Still a secret." The Death Scythe collapsed into energy and returned into her body.

Previously: the rear forces were locked in battle with the Captain of Carnage.

"Matteria, I just came up with a great idea," said Nina, tossing her empty gun aside. She pulled off her shirt, flung it aside, and exposed her lacy purple bra. "Kill them with my sweat!"

"Well, you've got plenty of it. 𝄞𝄞𝄞𝄞 𝄞𝄞𝄞𝄞," said Matteria, pointing with a smile and a wink.

Sweat droplets shot off the seductive warrior's body like bullets as she transitioned into various erotic poses, which mainly accentuated her bust. The sweat pierced through the four-legged battalion, downing most of them.

"Watch out!" yelled Anthrax.

The Captain was right in front of Matteria. He fired both blades at once.

Matteria shot the blood from his wound at the Captain, but one of the blades still pierced his shoulder.

"Not used to being on the battlefield, but doesn't seem you are either," said the Captain, regaining his footing after being hit by one of the bullets.

The blunderbuss on his back fired a mix of flesh and blood at the matter manipulator.

He leaped up in the midst of the distraction and swiped the blade in his tail at Matteria's neck.

Nina drop-kicked the demon lord and kept him pinned under her foot.

His tail sliced at her leg viciously, but she only pressed down harder.

"Finish him off. Now!" yelled Nina, cringing in pain.

Matteria made the blood slide down his partner's leg and onto the Captain. "SOLIDIFICATION!"

Nina lifted her foot up as the blood froze.

The Captain was frozen solid.

One of the remaining four-legged demons tackled Nina. Another picked up his boss and rushed out of the battlefield.

Nina limped up to Matteria. "Forget about him. More are on their way," she said, tearing off a piece of cloth from the glamour boy and closing her wound.


After being blown up and then sniped, the demon lord crashed down.

The demon lord had fur sewn to his arms, leather grafted to his chest, wool stitched into his back, ivory spikes jutting out from his legs and was wearing a silk cape with the worms still attached. "I am the Viscount of Violence," he said with a grin, standing up with a gaping hole in his head.

"You're just a violent creep who takes from others!" yelled Kawai, smacking one of the demons with her tail.

The Viscount pulled in pieces from the tortured angels and connected them to his body with metallic strings, all the while being pelted by pistol fire.

"Damned for all eternity, that's what they told me. But it was a mistake! I was supposed to go to Lum!" His strings shot out and yanked the sniper out of the cat-girl's grip. "I'm an angel, damn it! One of God's chosen! If I've done something wrong, then tell me what it is!"

The strings sent the bear claws lashing at the girl with the kitty ears.

Kaity dodged three swipes and then sliced through the arm with her own claws.

The Viscount flung body parts with his strings as he slowly approached.

"That's the last one," said Sefiwah, pulling her blade out from the gimp's throat.

The bound soldier, who had his back slit open earlier, suddenly stood up. Light shot out from his back and formed wings.

"It's as I thought," said Sefiwah, wiping away blood off her cheek with a trembling hand.

"They were all once angels. How did they get here?" asked Violet.

"I don't know," said Sefiwah, ducking under the angel as he lunged at her.

Atatasuki lashed his sword at the angel before it burst.

The sudden blast sent him off his feet.

Kawai zoomed up to her brother once he crash-landed. "Are you alright?"

"A little bit dizzy," he said with a smile before closing his eyes.

"Your slaves hurt my brother! This is the last grenade I've got! Die for real this time!" yelled Kawai, sending the explosive flying with her tail.

The Viscount raised his mangled victims up to deflect the explosion and took another step closer to the kitty-girl.

"I'm a fox! Not a human! Foxes should go to heaven! We can't help it if we kill! It's in our blood!" he cheered, gripping the kitty-girl's legs with strings.

"Just go away, creep!" yelled Kawai, rushing in with her tail poised.

The Viscount raised his hand and wrapped Kawai in his strings. "Little girls don't belong here. This is a place for bad men. We should go to Lum together," he said, now pulling the kitten in.

Atatasuki cut the strings with his sword. "Stay away from her, you freak!"

"She's not my target," said the Viscount with a demented grin.

"Kaity!" yelled a voice in desperation.

The young assassin's head jerked.

Sefiwah was being overrun by the gimps; her wounds were growing by the second.

Kaity sliced away the strings and rushed on all fours, not even bothering to defend herself from the searing claws of her attackers.

The gimps had all been piled on top of the pale woman.

Kaity's claws jutted out, slicing the gimps up before they could counterattack. They were all then pulled away by unseen strings.

Sefiwah had been pierced through the chest, a chunk of flesh had been eaten from her face, her eyes were quickly losing luster.

Deceivant fired a shotgun blast at a four-legged demon that was closing in on the young assassin's location.

"I'll get you out of here. Okay?" asked Kaity.

Sefiwah smiled and wiped away a tear from her soul mate's cheek. She took in a pained breath and started shivering.

"No! Stop it! Not again! No!" Kaity shook her lover vigorously.

BoneSaw rushed to the scene and assaulted the demon looming over the assassin prodigy.

"Get away from there!" yelled Deceivant, firing a shotgun blast into a gimp and causing it to explode.

Ten gimps came out from the crowd and charged at the distracted cat-girl.

"Run!" yelled Deceivant, loading up his shotgun.

Kaity gripped her lover's hand. "I'm here. Right here. You can feel me. Stay with me, okay?" she asked, her emerald eyes quivering.

Kanasta pulled his protégé off the ground and rushed out of enemy lines.

"No! No! I can't leave her alone. She needs me! I need her!" screamed Kaity, digging her fingers into Kanasta while trying to escape his grip.

The explosive demons burst once they arrived at the pale woman.

Sefiwah's blood splattered on her lover's tear-ridden face.

Kaity's eyes shrank. She looked out at the field of demons and saw only targets.

Kanasta dodged a sudden swipe from her claws and released her.

Kaity ran to the first target and ripped off its arm. She sliced the body in half as her eyes located her next victim. Rushing headlong into a group of ten demons, she jumped up and sliced off a head with her plasma claws.

Dark energy poured out of the wound and consumed the target. It spread across the ground, forming into a puddle that devoured the surrounding targets.

Kaity rushed on all fours through a line of demons on approach, pushing off the ground with one hand and slashing with the other.

A demon had jabbed its spear-like arm into her side. Kaity turned around and sliced off the attacker's arm. She kept up her killing spree, not even bothering to remove the spear.

A large target puffed up its belly and then released a stream of flame from its mouth.

Kaity used a nearby target as a shield and once within range, pierced her claws through both bodies.

The nimble assassin moved in a flash behind a nearby target.

"You agree, right? I don't deserve this!" yelled the Viscount.

Kaity sliced through the strings and the living armor around the target.

"I'm an angel! I can't die!"

She sliced it, back and forth, over and over, until there was nothing left but a bloody pulp.

Devlin rushed over to confront Kaity.

Kanasta signaled him to stay put and crouched down so his little girl could see him. "It's over. The army has retreated," he said, keeping out of range of her plasma claws.

Kaity blinked, her eyes calmed down a bit. She looked up at all her allies. "We won? Where's Sefiwah?" she asked, drenched in blood.

Ego dropped his head in tears.

Ada opened her mouth to speak but found nothing she could say.

"Sefiwah is no longer with us," said Kanasta.

The images of her lover's half-eaten face must have returned. Kaity clenched her temples and wailed.

"Sadness. We can't have that, now can we?"

The Freedom Forcers turned around. Standing before them was Etah. Behind him were four members of the Sinful Sorority. Over a thousand demons were closing in from the horizon.

"As if all the hatred from my demons wasn't enough of a treat, you've brought so many strong souls to me," said Etah, scanning the Freedom Forcers.

"Shut up. She's suffering," said Devlin.

"We won't back down until you resign your godhood. All forces, keep his army at bay! My team will handle Etah and the Sinful Sorority!" hollered Exp 8.

"You Exps need to know your place. You are artificial creations. The Gods have existed long before your kind. We came into being at the dawn of life. This realm has withstood far worse than your squabble with me," said Etah with a relaxed gaze.

"Yes this is the land of justice, your own twisted justice. Soon I shall reign over it as its king. Then I'll decide what is sin. I'll decide how to punish those who oppress others," said Devlin, coating his arms in wires.

"Such concentrated hate. But it's not enough. I want to see you in your greatest moment of despair."

"Then fight me." Devlin's wires shot out and coiled around Etah's throat.

"Soon, but not yet. All your hatred! I want to see it! I want to live it! **LIVING NIGHTMARE**!"

A giant red vortex came out from Devlin and engulfed the Freedom Forcers. The crimson vortex blotted out their senses.

# Chapter 80: Living Nightmare

Machine-gun fire, bombs, retro chimes. Sounds of all sorts came into being as the world slowly came into focus.

Carpeted floor, light blue walls and a TV the size of a small car emerged from the nothingness.

I was holding a game controller in my hand and staring attentively at the TV.

"Watch out. You'll need to duck this attack," said a voice above me.

I pressed down on the controller and looked up.

My brother was calm and focused no matter the situation. His eyes always seemed to see things that were beyond my sight. His face was firm and his body was large, even for someone twice my age. Brother's arms were wrapped around me and clenching a controller. Even though I was sitting in his lap, I felt like he was beyond my reach.

"Brother! Jump!"

I put my focus back on the game and leaped over the fireball launched by the frog human hybrid on the screen.

*Or did I?*

The tip of my character's foot, I think his name was Daron, hit the edge of the fireball and I died.

The pause screen came up and before I knew it, we were back at the main menu.

"Why did you quit?"

"You died. We cannot get the unlockable unless we win with no deaths. It would have been a waste of time to continue," he said.

"The game cheated me. You saw."

"What I saw was you jumping too early," he said, his eyes still focused on the screen.

"Let's try again."

"There's no point. Back to training," he said, clicking on the dynamic *versus* on the screen.

*I hate playing competitively with him.*

"No. I'm done. I told you I don't like going against you."

"Because you always lose? You should have gotten used to it by now. If you're afraid of losing you'll never win. How do you think I've completed so many games?" asked my brother, gesturing to the shelf in the corner.

It was stacked with retro games at the top and each lower row had games from a newer generation.

"It's not fun. Maybe we can just lie down and relax," I said, leaning back against his chest.

"My time is precious," said my brother, already continuing his file on his portable system.

"I'm going to get something to eat? Are you coming?"

Brother put the portable game away. "Not yet. I'm going to beat that amoeba today. No deaths," he said, his eyes like that of a soldier entering the battlefield.

"Okay, but remember to take a break if you get too frustrated," I said, rising from his lap.

"I've defeated greater foes before. That boss will fall today," said my brother, clenching his fist.

"Do what you want. Do you want anything to drink?"

He shook his head.

Once I turned around I felt his arms around me.

*I'm not a kid anymore. Why does he still hug me?*

"Enjoy your meal," he said with a smile.

"I will."

I left to the kitchen and grabbed a banana.

The doorbell rang.

*Maybe my package arrived! Kitty Cat Invaders! Oh yeah!*

I opened the door.

The guy I'd seen on TV, who always talked about saving our country, was right at the door.

*My father sure is famous.*

"Are your parents home?" he asked.

"Uh, yeah," I said.

The man opened the door himself and walked right in. He went down the hall like he owned the place.

*Something didn't feel right.*

I went to the living room to see my brother fully engrossed.

*Best not to bother him.*

I quickly caught up with the man.

He continued down the hall and to the lab.

*I don't think he's allowed there. I'm not.*

The man opened the door but didn't close it completely.

*How did he open it? I've tried so many times.*

I pressed my body against the wall and sneaked up to the door. I peeked inside.

Mom and father came into focus. They were draped in white lab-coats which swayed along with their movements.

The couple was inside a brightly lit lab room. Sunlight entered the room from the open windows.

There were all manner of devices and materials. I even saw some body parts in the corner of the room.

*This must be where father made Kawai. Now I had to enter.*

I waited for the man to walk up to my parents.

*He was a senator. Can't remember his name though.*

I ran inside and hid under the nearest metal table.

"Is my weapon ready yet?" asked the senator.

"No, not yet," said father, turning away from the senator's gaze.

I watched from under the desk in the corner of the room.

*I knew he was trouble. He didn't even knock. What does this man want?*

The senator approached my father with a clenched fist.

*This looked bad. I need to get Brother. He'll know what to do.*

I crawled out from under the table and silently made my way to the door.

"Hmm, I don't remember seeing this one," said the senator, his eyes catching me as I touched the door.

"Devlin, go to your room. Now," said father, taking a step toward the senator.

The door opened. A person in a black suit was looking down at me, their face concealed by a helmet. Before I knew it, I was in the black-suited man's grip. My feet were suspended in the air.

"Let go!" I yelled, squirming in the man's grip.

"Put him down!" yelled father.

"You promised me a weapon. If it isn't ready, then I'll have to take him as collateral," said the Senator, stepping closer to me.

Mom approached the Senator. "You want an Exp, right? Then I'll come with you."

*What? What's going on?*

"Why isn't my weapon completed yet?"

"We've been working restlessly on Exp 8, but these things take time."

"Your son's an Exp, right?" asked John, his eyes measuring me up.

"Looks like a normal little kid to me," said the black-suit soldier, prying my mouth open.

"I'm not a kid! I'm thirteen!" I bit the man's finger as hard as I could.

"You're going to have to bite harder if you want me to bleed. He doesn't have a lethal bite, and his skin seems natural. He has black hair and his dad's golden eyes. Looks like he's their son, alright. Of course, that could just be a cover up to keep him safe," said the black-suited man.

"Devlin's a human. I gave birth to him. He won't be of any use to you. Please Senator, don't you have children of your own?" asked Mom with a shaky smile.

*I've never seen Mom so worried.*

"What an obvious lie. A thing can't give birth. You can't even get pregnant! I will ask one more time, is your son an Exp? Do not lie to me again!" yelled the Senator, his eyes flaring.

Father approached the Senator. "He is our son and I refuse to let you have him."

"Uhehehahahahahahaa! You refuse me! You fool! You can't refuse me. I am the world government! I could put your wife on a dissecting board and frame you for her murder." The Senator raised his hand.

Black-suited men and women stormed the room and aimed their guns at Deceivant.

"Leave mom alone!" I yelled, thrashing around in the man's grip.

"I'm taking him whether you want me to or not," said the senator.

A metal card zoomed by, cutting the tips off of all their guns.

Brother entered the room. "Put down my little brother now." He whipped out a revolver and aimed it at the man holding me.

Once the soldier dropped me, I hid behind my brother.

*No worries. Brother's here now. Everything will be fine.*

"Hey boss, do I kill the kid?" asked the black-suit commander, his tone so calm it was chilling.

"No. It's time to go. I have an important meeting to attend. I'll be back in a month." John signaled his troops and they all evacuated the building.

"Dad, can I kill that guy?" asked Brother, twirling the gun on his finger.

"Don't even kid about that," said father.

"I know that was stressful, but let's not be negative." Mom put on a big smile and picked me up. "Today Devlin starts his first day of middle school."

I hugged Mom tightly.

*She's safe. We're all safe.*

"I'm still not so sure formal schooling is a good idea," said father.

"Oh he'll be fine. It will be good for him to go out and make some friends," said Mom.

"I don't want to make friends," I said, grabbing Brother's hand.

"These kids will be your age. They won't be like the kids in the neighborhood," said Mom.

"But if I make friends, then I'll have less time to spend with my brother," I said, giving my bro a smile.

"You'll have plenty of time to spend with him once you're home. He can even help you with your homework," said Mom.

Father patted me on the head. "I doubt you'll need any help though. You're a child genius, just like your father."

"What if I don't like the teachers?" I asked, looking up at Mom's pretty white face.

"Oh, I'm sure you'll find at least one you like. Did you already pack your bag?"

"Yeah. Mom, I really don't want to go. After what happened, I want to stay home." I buried my face in her chest.

*The fear and worry seemed to disappear. All I could feel was Mom's warmth.*

"We can't homeschool you forever. Now more than ever, Mommy and Daddy will be very busy. It will be a good experience for you. Now get dressed." Mom set me down.

*She really wants this. Okay, I'll do it for Mom.*

I nodded with a smile and then scurried out of the room. After rushing up the stairs, I entered my room. My burgundy middle school uniform was folded neatly on my bed, right below my poster of planet Earth.

Brother leaned against the doorway as I got dressed. "Anyone gives you any trouble, you tell me."

*No matter what happens, I can always rely on him.*

I slipped into my shirt. "I'll be okay. Mom wouldn't send me to any place that's unsafe." I rushed up to Brother, gave him a hug and then hurried downstairs.

Mom was waiting by the door. "You are so cute in that uniform. Aww, you're growing up so fast," she said with a beaming smile.

"If you make any cute friends, be sure to invite them over," said father in a hushed tone.

"Honey, I think you should stay focused on your work. We can't afford to make John wait again," said Mom with a look of worry.

"A little play between work increases productivity," said father.

"I already had breakfast. Do I head out?" I asked, peeking out the window.

Mom clasped her hands around father's. "Our little Devlin is going to school for the first time."

"Yes, yes. You should get ready too, my dear. You shouldn't be late for work," said father, rubbing her head.

Mom gave father a quick kiss. "I'll get ready." She skipped to her room.

"Why do all the school kids have to dress the same?" I asked.

"That's so you lose your individuality," he said, keeping up his smile.

"Like prison," said Brother, opening the window and looking outside.

"You're too stressed out. It's a harmless dress code used to create school spirit, uniformity and it lets them know who's a student and who isn't," said father.

"It's mainly for security reasons," said Kanasta, running his hand under the kitchen table.

"How dangerous is this school?" I asked.

"It's a regular public school. Your mother thought it would be best for you to be among children of mediocre intellect. If it was up to me, you'd be going to a private school for inventors," said father, trying to hide his disappointment.

"Take my pocket knife in case you get into trouble," said Brother, putting it in the front pocket of my book bag.

*He's always looking out for me.*

"I'll be out as soon as the bell rings," I said, slipping into the bag's straps.

"We'll be parked in the front," said Brother, zipping up my book bag.

"Sweetie, your bus is here!" hollered Mom from her bedroom.

"Bye Brother. Bye Mom! Bye," I said, looking up at father.

*I can't call him father. Not out loud. It doesn't feel right.*

I took a deep breath and then ran to the bus.


I sat down and looked around. I was a bit uneasy, but my heart was also racing due to excitement.

I looked out at the other kids and saw they were also anxious. Most of them were quiet. They seemed nice enough…well most of them did.

A child taller than me and wearing a hoodie was looking at me from the corner of his eye.

I casually moved to the back of the bus, but the staring continued.

*I need to relax. Brother packed my bag, so it should be…aha! There it is!*

I pulled out a portable gaming system and worked on making a new character. I gave him golden eyes like me, but made him strong like my brother. Every so often I would look up to see the same kid, watching. I shifted my focus back to the game.

*Hmmm. Knights are cool, but they can be a bit violent. I'll pick the white mage so I can help people just like Mom!*

The school wasn't far away and the ride was over in fifteen minutes.

I was the first one out of the bus. I rushed to the front of the school and bowed to the principal, standing by the front gates.

"Such nice etiquette. Welcome," said the principal with a smile of ease.

I smiled back.

*What if that kid is still watching me?*

I rushed through the front doors and down the halls. "Thirty-six. Room 36. Ah, there it is." I entered the classroom and sat down. The boy with the hood sat in the back.

*Why did he have to be in the same class?*

The bell rang and the teacher walked in two minutes later. My eyes widened along with my smile.

*It was her! She's really here!*

"Hello class. I'm your home room teacher and I may be your science teacher too."

"Mom!" I jumped out of my seat and hugged her.

"That's Mrs. Kagaku now," she said, her smile extra bright.

Adolescent laughter filled the room.

I looked around in a bit of a daze, found my seat and sat down. I buried my face to hide my embarrassment.

*Why do I feel this way? It's their fault. They're mocking me. Bet they're just jealous because my mom is prettier than their moms.*

"Alright, now let's call roll," said Mom.

At the end of the class, after Mom left, I confronted the hooded kid.

*I wasn't going to let him ruin my whole school year. This had to end, now.*

"Would you please stop staring at me?" I asked.

"Why don't you make me?" asked the tall kid as his eyes flashed.

"Ooooooooooh," said a growing crowd of students.

*What a jerk.*

I turned away.

"That's what I thought," said the kid.

I was quiet for the other periods. I focused my attention on taking notes. I even doodled a bit.

*Each time I drew her, I noticed something new about Kawai. She's so cute!*

When the lunch bell rang, I rushed to get in line.

*Bodies. They were serving dead bodies. I know Mom warned me about this. But experiencing it was different. I could almost feel the pain.*

"Are you aware that she suffered when she died?" I looked up at the cafeteria attendant while pointing at the chicken's severed leg on my metal tray.

"You don't want it, then throw it away," said the attendant with a grimace.

"I'll take it," said the hooded kid, snatching the dismembered body part from my plate.

*I wasn't about to argue with him about the moral implications of eating a fellow living being. It would only fall on deaf ears.*

"Go ahead. Hey can I have something different to drink? I drink soy, almond, rice, and coconut milk. I can't drink this. It was made with cruelty," I said, setting the milk carton down.

"Go to a fountain if you're thirsty," said the attendant.

I broke out of the line and sat down.

"Hey, what's your name?" asked a chipper young boy.

"I'm Devlin. What about you?" I mixed the carrots and mashed potatoes.

*The food looked less vital than what I'm used to eating. It tasted a bit off too. Oh well, at least it was edible.*

"Hey, there's a secret club meeting in room 67 during lunch time. Want to come along?" asked the kid, keeping his voice down.

"What kind of club?"

"You'll know when you get there. It's the first time I've been invited, so even I don't have a clue."

"Can I take my food with me?" I asked, munching on a carrot.

*Kawai is so cute when she eats carrots.*

"Sure."

"Are you coming too?"

"Of course. It's not often a freshmen gets invited to a cool club."

*This is it! This is the opportunity to make new connections. Potential allies for my future endeavors, as father puts it.*

"Hey, uh, do you want to be friends?" I asked.

"Sure." He shook my hand. "Come on, let's go!"

We sped out of the lunch room and entered room 67.

It was guarded by a security guard.

*If he's outside, then I don't need to worry about running into trouble. He was overweight, but I suppose he could pin me down if he needed to.*

As soon as we entered, the security guard outside locked the door and walked away.

*This is bad.*

Standing before me was the hooded kid and three other students.

"Why did he lock the door?" I asked.

The student who escorted me went to the hooded kid. "I brought him here, can I get my phone back now?" he asked with open hands.

The hooded kid smiled and handed him his cell phone.

"Why are we locked in here?" I asked, looking at the window in the back.

371

"I paid off the security guards. I also got a little something special from them." The hooded kid took out a nightstick.

"Hey, you said you wouldn't hurt him," said the escort student.

The hooded kid pushed me to the floor.

In less than a second his knees were on my stomach. He slammed the nightstick down.

*This is really happening.*

I tried to shield my face with my arms.

I looked to my side and saw the fire alarm.

Right above the switch, it said "In case of emergency, push". I did just that and the alarm started blaring.

"You think that's going to save you?" asked the kid before striking my face with the night stick.

*Damn it. Now Kawai won't think I'm cute.*

"Stop hitting him!" yelled my escort.

The hooded kid tossed one of his lackeys the keys. "Get the whiner out of here. I'm taking this outside."

The hooded kid lifted me up and smashed me through the window.

He whispered something to himself as the glass shards pierced my skin.

*I didn't feel much pain. Am I so afraid I can't even process it?*

I fell to the wet grass, pelted by the rain.

The glass had cut deep into the skin below my wrist.

*Wait. I have a weapon. Brother knew I'd need to defend myself.*

I rummaged through the front pocket of my book bag.

"Looking for this?" asked the hooded kid, twirling the knife on his finger.

*I don't understand. I've trained with Brother. I should be able to defend myself, but I'm just so scared.*

"Leave me alone!" I yelled, crawling away in the rain.

"Your little friend, the security guard and me, a total stranger, do you want to know why we all turned against you?"

"Get away from me!" I struggled to get to my feet.

The kid took out a pistol from his jacket pocket. "We all hate you because you aren't one of us! You're not human. You're a freak!"

"My brother is going to kill you!" I yelled before running off.

Three bullets shot into my leg.

*Am I really going to die? Mom is going to be so sad. And Kawai, she'll never know how I truly feel about her.*

"Come on, fight back!" The hooded kid kicked me over and over.

"Help! Help!" I reached out to the cars in the distance.

"No one can hear you! It's raining, moron!" The hooded kid sat on me and pressed the gun to my forehead. "Are you ready to…?"

*My mind when blank.*

A wire was in the hooded kid's throat.

I trembled while following the wire with my eyes. It was in me. The wire came from the wound on my wrist.

The next moment wires burst out from my arm, tearing through his skin.

*This must be a nightmare.*

The wires pierced into the assailant's neck.

The boys head came off his neck and fell on my chest.

Blank eyes. Blood.

*Stop staring at me!*

I knocked the head off my chest.

A car drove by in the rain.

I looked down at the corpse.

"I…I killed someone. He's dead."

*I have to get home! I have to find Brother. He'll protect me.*

I waited for the car to pass and ran across the street. I tripped and fell on the asphalt, scraping my face. I got back to my feet and ran down the sidewalk. I tried to wipe the blood off my uniform, but it smeared across my shirt. I ran down several streets, searching for a familiar name.

*I want to go home.*

I sat down and lowered my head between my knees. I covered the wires with my left hand.

*What am I?*

I looked up to see a police car. Before I could get back on my feet, the policeman confronted me.

"Hey kid, do you need a ride home?"

"Yes! Thank you!" I rose my head up.

The cop whipped out his Taser and shocked me.

The wires from my face wound sliced through the cop's hand.

"Monster!"

The wires shot out from my other arm and sliced the cop's body to pieces.

*No! Not another one! He was scared. He was scared and now he's dead. I'm a murderer.*

I ran and ran. Blood and tears clouded my vision.

Bright lights. A sudden collision.

I tumbled across the asphalt, losing more of my skin.

I landed in front of a dead kitty. Its stomach had been flattened. Blood and guts were seeping out.

*Poor kitty.*

I cradled the cat in my arms. The wires coiled around the cat, bringing it deeper into my embrace. "So, you were hit too. We were both hurt by ignorant humans."

The rainstorm increased in power, creating a pool of water around me.

Bright lights loomed ever closer.

*Stay away.*

Wires burst out from my back, tearing through the car and whoever was inside it. The mangled car slammed into a lamppost.

*After doing it three times it didn't feel so bad. It didn't feel like much of anything. Is this what happens to slaughterhouse workers? Does killing people become just part of a routine?*

I walked to the bushes and set the dead cat down. "They can't hurt you now."

*No. I know better than that. Whatever isn't their species doesn't matter. They think they're the only ones with value. Wait...they. But I'm one of them. I'm a human, aren't I?*

I walked down the sidewalk in a daze, looking for anything even remotely familiar.

After a few minutes, I arrived at Martinak State Park.

*Finally. I'm safe. Brother and I come here all the time. It's close to home. He'll find me here.*

I leaned against the tree and looked out at the dock. Plastic bottles, empty chip bags, and other junk outlined the perimeter of the lake.

*This is how we treat the world. Humans think we're entitled to everything.*

I walked past the playground and onto the nature path.

*This place looks so different at night. It feels cold.*

I jumped at a rustle in the bushes. I left the path and went into the greenery. After finding a place where I would be out of sight, I laid down and closed my eyes.

*The grass is so prickly.*

No. I shouldn't be spoiled. Plenty of animals sleep in the grass. And that's what I am. I'm an animal.

*I'm not a machine.*

That was the first time I didn't spend the night at home. I had to sleep without anyone at my side.

*I was alone.*

# Chapter 81: On the Run

While the moon was still in the sky, a flashlight glared in my face.

*Who is it?*

"Target found," said a dark, gruff voice.

I looked up to see a large man with a thermometer in his mouth and a pistol in his hands.

*Is this real?*

A wire shot out as the pistol fired.

The pistol was knocked out of the man's hand.

A bullet pierced my shoulder.

*Why does everyone want me dead?*

Just as I turned around to flee, a patch of grass rose up in front of me.

A boxy robot emerged with two massive saws poised for the kill.

Three wires came out of my chest but were sliced in two by the saws.

*I must still be dreaming. Brother, please wake me up!*

Something pierced me.

*I never should have left home.*

A spurt of blood came out from a hole in my chest. I rose my arms up as the saws came forward.

The saws cut into the wired tendons of my arms before becoming jammed.

I was suddenly off my feet and soaring through the air. I careened into a tree stump that slammed into my legs. I toppled over the stump and fell to the grass.

The man with the thermometer in his mouth was holding a shotgun. "A kid and a living weapon. Killing you is going to be such a thrill." The man's hand suddenly combusted into flames.

The flames didn't burn him though. It was as if he commanded them.

*Is he a freak, like me?*

When he thrust his burning arm forth, the tree stump was set aflame.

The wires acted on their own, lifting a nearby log and sending it flying at the man.

I heard the man slice through the log as I ran for a new source of cover.

I suddenly realized I was on all fours.

*It felt unfamiliar, but natural.*

I sliced through the park's fence with the wires and rushed through the street. I navigated through the cars while keeping watch.

*My pursuers were nowhere in sight.*

Another bullet pierced my leg.

I lost my footing, tumbled a bit and then continued the sprint, almost getting slammed by a bus in the process.

The bus curved in front of me, blocking my path.

*Gotta keep running.*

I leaped over the bus.

A wondrous sense of weightlessness took over me. My eyes darted down, seeing a police blockade ahead.

Smoke emitted from the bus, coating the entire street.

My eyes shifted focus, almost like a microscope.

The world looked different now. There weren't people or faces, only energy and shapes.

*All the red shapes were closing in on me.*

I was an abomination that the world was trying to get rid of. I was a paradox and their job was to correct me.

*Well I won't go down easy.*

I jumped over a car and onto another one. I sprinted off that car and ran up a building. I had never climbed a building before, but something inside me knew I could do it.

Without looking behind I sensed something following me.

*It was getting closer.*

A metal net descended upon me from above.

A tail shot out from my coccyx and cut the net to pieces.

*What do I really look like?*

I made it to the rooftop and was immediately pelted by machinegun fire.

Four helicopters were positioned around the area.

*Like a video game. This is just a game. And I can beat it! I'm good at games. Not as good as Brother. But I'm still a hardcore gamer!*

Something slammed into me from behind, making me spin in mid-air.

I looked down to see a young man on a motorcycle.

*It's a game. I'm in control. That means there are no consequences to my actions. Just make it out alive. Yeah. Focus on the goal.*

I willed my wires to seize the young man.

*That's right! These wires were me! They listen to me!*

My wires wrapped him around my back, turning him into my meat shield.

The helicopters stopped firing and repositioned themselves as I leaped from rooftop to rooftop.

Four armor-piercing bullets shot through my arms and legs.

The pain was so intense I blacked out for a moment before I tumbled off the building and fell to the ground.

I looked up, a smile spreading across my unfamiliar face in a nearby puddle.

I had made it to my street. Just down the road was home.

*Home.*

An electrical current surged through my body.

The young man rolled off my back and was picked up by…Brother!

My eyes teared up.

*He's here. I'm safe.*

"Boss, you're late," said the young man with a half-hearted smile.

"Tempo, I need you to draw the police's attention," said Brother.

A building in the distance was suddenly consumed in flames.

The helicopters turned around immediately. Only one kept its searchlight fixed on me.

"You found me," I said, my tear ducts overflowing.

"I have," said Brother, pulling me to my feet.

Once I was standing again, he slammed me to the ground, cracking the asphalt with my body.

*Huh?*

"Quite durable indeed. Yes, you'll fetch quite the price," said Brother, slamming his foot down on me over and over.

I screamed out. My wires climbed up Kanasta's legs and flung him into a nearby car.

"It's me, Devlin. I'm your little brother!" I yelled in tears.

Brother climbed out of the imprint on the car. "Yes, you pretended to be a human rather well. In the end though, you can't be controlled. You're dangerous. It's only a matter of time before the government comes back for you. I might as well get some extra cash by selling you myself." He flung a car door in my direction.

*Why does he look like that? His eyes, they don't love me. Why don't they love me?*

The door slammed into my side, sending me tumbling down the asphalt.

*There has to be some explanation for this.*

"What are you doing, Brother?" I asked, struggling back to my feet.

"Apprehending the target," he said, dodging through my unconscious onslaught of wires.

"Stay away from me!"

The imposter coiled some wires around his arm and pulled me in. He slammed me down before unloading a full clip of shotgun bullets into my body.

"The client should arrive shortly."

*His voice was cold, unfamiliar.*

"When Mom and Dad find out about this—"

"They already know. They don't care about you."

*I've had enough of this!*

My wires came together into a fist and knocked him off.

Wires from my torso moved down to my damaged legs and healed them.

I zoomed through the bushes and smashed right through the glass window.

"Mom! Dad! Help me!"

"Get out of here!" yelled father, backed into a corner.

"It's me, your son."

"I thought you would be different, but nothing has changed. You are weak, Devlin, and so am I. You aren't safe here. Get out before I kill you," said father, holding a grenade in his hands.

"Mom! Save me!" I wailed.

"Get out of here! You're not a part of my family! You're a failed creation!" yelled father.

My wires shot out on their own.

Ada rushed into the room.

*Mom! Thank the universe!*

The wires stopped.

"I told you to hide!" yelled father.

"Mommy!" I yelled, rushing toward her.

"Why are you trying to kill your father?" asked Mom in tears.

"Wait, no, that isn't…." I backed away in tears.

"Get out of here!" yelled father.

*No. He's not my father.*

"You were using me all along. You raised me so you could sell me off."

"We are all in danger as long as you are here!" yelled Deceivant, holding Mom close to him.

Mom was crying, unable to look at me.

"I won't let some tool ruin everything I've worked for!" yelled Deceivant.

"I'm not a tool! I'm alive!"

My wires went into a manic frenzy, slicing everything in sight.

Deceivant fell to the ground with Mom and shielded her from the onslaught.

I rushed out the room and into the backyard.

The black-suited men were all waiting, their guns poised.

"Right on time," said the commander.

*They knew. Mom and him both knew.*

The only sounds that existed were guns firing off. For an unperceivable span of time, I was decimated by bullets.

*I suppose that's game over then. Time to wake up?*

A long tube connected to my chest.

Energy left my body, abandoning me just like everything else.

The world went black.

# Chapter 82: Forever an Outcast

Cold air surrounded me. Each breath I made took extra effort to get ample oxygen.

*Do I even need oxygen? What am I?*

My eyes opened.

Steel bars in front, damp floor below and a mildew ceiling above.

My human skin was completely sheared off, leaving me a naked monster.

*I'm not even an animal anymore, am I? Am I a machine?*

I curled up into a ball and closed my eyes.

*Footsteps.*

I peeked between my hands to see a woman. "Mom!" I yelled, grabbing onto the bars.

An electric zap rattled my arms and flung me back against the wall.

"Are you sure it's safe?" asked a male voice from outside the prison cell.

"If he tries anything, we'll just kill him," said the woman.

The tall, short haired woman was not my mom.

Once she opened the door she walked up to me.

"So has the boss decided yet?" she asked, her eyes aware of the slightest movement I made.

"Not yet. Either way it should give us some leverage. Stealing Ada or Kawai would still be preferred," said the young man outside the prison walls.

*They want my mom and Kawai, why?*

"Then I'll hold myself back a bit." The woman set a toolbox down, never looking away from me.

*This woman is dangerous. I have to kill her.*

Thirty wires came out from my body and followed her movements, ready for a counter-attack.

"He doesn't have any artifacts, but he's clearly made for combat," said the woman.

"Maybe Deceivant made him to get rid of us. That would explain why he was so easy to capture. I wouldn't put it past him. He's quite clever," said the man.

The woman stretched her hand out to touch me.

My wires shot out.

She moved her hand out of the way and took a step back.

"The suppressors have worn off a bit, though they've clearly slowed him down."

"What do you want with me?" I asked.

"We only want a few questions answered. That's all," she said with a jaded smile.

All of a sudden her hand slammed into my chest.

I fell to my knees and my wires dropped.

She lifted up my arm and let it fall back down. "He's sedated. Time to get to work," she said, pulling out a wire cutter.

"I can't move." My eyes watered up.

"You can talk and that's all I need." She grabbed my hand and held out my pinky.

*What is she going to do?*

"Leave me alone!"

"Shh. Shh. I didn't ask you a question yet. Only talk when I ask something, okay?" She squeezed the wire cutters around my pinky. "Hmm. They aren't strong enough. Let's see…." She opened her tool box and pulled out plasma wire cutters. She grabbed my hand and sliced off the top of my pinky.

"Let me go," I cried.

"Talk again and you'll lose a whole finger," she said, sliding the cutters up and down my arm.

*She's insane! This woman is insane and I can't even move!*

"Eesh. Okay, it seems like you've got this under control. Give me a call if you need anything. Sis and I are going to shower together," said the man before walking off.

"Yeah, I'll be done in time for lunch," said the woman, looking away for a second.

*This was my chance.*

I concentrated all my energy into a single wire and sent it into the woman's throat.

She snipped the wire, took the tip out from her throat and wiped the blood off. "Hmm. Not sure about a super weapon, but you would make a decent assassin. Maybe it runs in the family," she said with a slight smile.

*There's no way I can beat her. I'm stuck here.*

I looked down and whimpered.

"Alright. First question." She pressed the plasma cutters just hard enough to tear through the protective shell around my fingers.

"Agh! It hurts."

"How many Exps does Deceivant have and what are their names?"

"Kawai. Uhh, umm…Atatasuki. Destructus Supplious. Do I count? Is that what I am?"

"Yes and so is your mommy."

"She is? Is that why I was born as an Exp?"

*Of course. That's what I am. I'm an Exp, like Kawai.*

"No. Exps can't be born, only created. She isn't your mother. You don't have a mother, brother, sister or father. You only have a creator. Is that all of them? Or are there some he keeps secret?" asked the psycho lady.

*She's right about one thing. I have no family.*

"Do I need to repeat myself?" she asked, her smile hiding dark intentions.

"That's all I know. I swear." I wheezed before swallowing.

"Hmm. I believe you. But just in case." She plunged the cutters into my arm and slowly turned them.

"Is there anyone else you might be forgetting?"

"Stop!"

She plunged in deeper. "That's not an answer."

"I don't know anyone else. Stop hurting me."

She pulled the plasma cutters out. "I thought as much. If he did have a secret weapon it's unlikely he'd tell you. He knew it was quite likely we would pick you up."

"Did he sell me to you?"

"That seems to be the case. Maybe he thought he could keep Ada safe by handing you over to us. But he did so in a way that you wouldn't even know. He's a clever man. Now let's move along. How is your creator's progress on Exp 8?"

"I don't know. He spends a lot of time in the basement lab. But he doesn't show me his work. He works with Mom, so they're the only ones who know. Can you let me go now?"

"Ugh, this is going nowhere. This thing knows nothing."

"I'm not a thing. I'm Devlin. See, I have a name. I'm alive, like you. So please don't hurt me anymore."

"Alive, hardly. It's all programming. Look at you. You're only metal and wires. You're a weapon who thinks he's a boy."

"No, I'm alive. I know it."

*What if she's right?*

"Such delusions. I'll ask you more questions later."

"Then can I go home?"

*Anywhere! Anywhere but this room. The air is so thick.*

"Never. And why would you even want to? Your father, mother, brother, they all let you take the fall. It's kind of sad," she said, twirling her tool like a gun in a Western flick.

"Then this is where I'll live for the rest of my life?"

*The thought left a sour taste in my mouth.*

"Can't even cry. Not alive and definitely not human. Still, you can suffer. Let's see some more of that." The crazed woman rubbed her finger's together. Blue energy rose out from her fingertips.

"I'll say whatever you want."

The woman pierced the energy into my chest. She then pulled her hand away, but the energy needles remained.

"My heart. They're scratching against my heart."

"You don't have a heart. You're a soulless machine."

The torturer sliced up and down my legs and my chest. Every so often she would jab the cutters into my chest and twist them. The more I screamed, the more she smiled. She never said a word the entire time. Just as she pulled out a drill the voice of a young woman came from outside.

"Is he here? Can I talk to him?" The hazy figure rushed to the prison bars.

"Don't touch the bars!" yelled the torturer.

The young woman was sent flying back, slamming into the wall.

"Ow! Oww. Am I bleeding? Am I okay?"

The torturer cradled the young woman in her arms. "You're okay. Let's get you to the medical bay. You can talk to him later."

"But he knows so much about Deceivant. I want to talk to him now."

The torturer lifted her up. "Lean on me. After a quick checkup, you can have him for the rest of the day," said the torturer, locking the prison door and walking out of sight.

I closed my eyes, my body was shivering. "I hate you, Deceivant! I hate you! I hate everyone!" My wires thrashed around the prison walls making cuts in the concrete. Beneath the surface of concrete was a thick layer of steel.

*There was no use fighting. I was trapped.*

A guard stood outside the door and watched me with hollow eyes.

"What do you want? Leave me alone!" I yelled.

The large man covered his eyes with his white hair. "I'm here to kill you. Orders from the boss." He grabbed the prison bars. His hands trembled from the shock, but he didn't move an inch. He took one arm off the bars and slammed it into the prison door.

The door smashed into the wall behind Devlin.

"No! No. Stay away." My wires slammed into the man's shoulder.

"Let's see what you can do." He picked me up by my head and walked out of the prison.

*Why is this happening to me?*

I was brought to a spacious room and thrown to the ground. My back slammed against the red concrete below.

"Stand up and fight me."

My body trembled but could not push off the ground.

"I had nearly forgotten we drained you." The man picked me up by my head. He removed each energy needle and then slammed his open palm into my chest.

Energy burst out from the point of impact, filling my whole being.

*This is it. Life or death. I've got to fight to survive! This yearning to live! It proves I'm a living being! It proves it!*

Wires came out from my back and wrapped around the man's arm. They twisted, trying to tear it off.

The man head-butted me and then slammed me to the ground.

My wires lost their grip as he pulled back in pain.

The man stomped his foot on my chest.

My wires all shot out at once and targeted the man's throat. Before they could make contact they were repelled by an unseen force.

"Die! Die! Die!" My wires slashed the man all over.

No wounds appeared. The man put both his fists to my chest.

"**IMPACT RELEASE**."

The world went dark.

# Chapter 83: Artificial Family

I awoke in a place without light. My wires groped around the immediate area. They pushed against the ceiling and opened it.

A full moon was in the starry night sky.

I climbed out of the new prison and fell to the ground.

*What is all this junk?*

I cleaned the grime, food and paper scraps off my body. Apparently I was in a dumpster.

*Trash. Everyone thinks I'm worthless.*

I moved in a daze.

A voice suddenly rang out from seemingly nowhere. It was stiff and cold. It belonged to a man who tried to kill me. "It won't be long before the assassins track you down."

I looked around for the man, even at the top of the building.

"Where are you?" I asked, my wires creeping out my back.

"Not important. The Baltimore-Washington International Airport is nearby. Take Flight 636 to New Mexico. It's at Gate F2."

"Why should I listen to you?" I asked, still looking around.

"I got you out, didn't I? Look, Kanasta has sent his assassins to track you down."

*Brother.*

"The people I work with know you're nearby the airport, but they don't know the flight. You aren't safe anywhere in this country. I have a fellow operative as a pilot for flight 636. Gate F2. It's a normal flight. Make sure you're the only one who get's on it and make sure nobody sees you get on it. They're sending us out to track you down, so I can't stay in contact."

"What's your name? Why are you helping me?"

"Telling you my name would put us both in more danger. I'm helping you because I don't see you as a weapon. You're a child. You may not be an animal, but you're still a little boy. No other reason needed. I won't be able to contact you. Get on that plane by any means necessary. The other operative will fill you in accordingly."

"Hello? Hello? Thank you."

*Just as soon as I had made an ally, that ally abandoned me.*

I peeked out from behind the dumpster.

Sure enough, there was the airport at the end of the winding road.

I waited for the sidewalk to clear and then broke into a four-legged sprint.

Screams from the frightened humans did nothing to deter me. I stayed focused.

Before I could even make it to the entrance door, a group of four guards confronted me.

I knocked the pistols out of their hands as they reached for them, all the while keeping my pace. To bypass the guard at the outside luggage check in, I smashed through the glass window.

Screams and looks of horror pierced me from all sides.

*They were judging me.*

But why should it surprise me. Humans have been known for discrimination, even amongst their own kind.

For the first time I felt good about my inhumanity.

*I'm not like them. I'm something so much more.*

My wire's cleared the way through the crowds, knocking down every worthless judgmental human in my way.

The Thurgood Marshall Tribute Space caught my attention. As I charged past and pushed aside what I once thought were my own people, I saw flashes of his timeline and even a bronze bust of the Civil Rights champion.

*In recognizing the humanity of our fellow beings, we pay ourselves the highest tribute.*

The more I thought about it, the less sense the quote made. It assumed that humanity was something virtuous. Non-humans were plenty virtuous, but they had no humanity. All humans are animals but not all animals are humans, after all.

"Get down!" yelled a guard.

Gunshots soon followed.

My wire's acted on instinct, pulling in a nearby woman and using her to shield my body from the bullets.

*I didn't mean to. No. If it happened, then a part of me thought it. This is survival. I saw an opportunity and I took it. I'm not at fault here.*

I flung the bleeding woman into the wall of guards in front of me.

My eyes caught sight of their guns. The wires obeyed my thoughts, seizing the guns.

Four more guards came out from behind the corner.

My wires shot off the guns, sending bullets into the arms of my attackers. One bullet was misdirected and pierced into the guard's throat.

*Is he going to die? Did I kill him?*

My eyesight became hazy as I skidded to make a sharp turn.

Three bullets shot into my back.

*Who cares if he died? He was an enemy. They all are. Every last human is my enemy.*

My wires became thin. They sliced the guards blocking the security checkpoint into bits.

386

I rammed through them, breaking them to bloody pieces.

*I'm a weapon! A living breathing, killing machine!*

My wires wiped the fleshy chunks off my face.

I vaulted over the security line as I was pelted by bullets.

I caught sight of a passerby. The look in his eyes was that of absolute fear.

*This is how they should see me.*

I was suddenly blockaded by a SWAT team and a pack of twelve police dogs.

My wires sliced through the guns and the humans. They didn't touch the dogs.

*Not human. Alive. Domesticated. Like me.*

My wire's coiled around the dogs' legs and held them in place. Not a single drop of their blood was shed.

*Whatever I think, happens. My wires are me and I am them.*

My body cut across the walls and sliced through any human who dared to get in my path.

A young girl slipped out of her mom's grasp and rushed to the candy store, putting her right in my path.

*Just a child.*

I leaped over her and made my way down the path, all the while pelted by bullets.

*Gate E7, E8. I'll be there soon.*

A SWAT agent popped out from behind the chairs and unloaded a shotgun blast into my back.

My extra appendages spun around, catching all the bullets.

*I'm incredible! I'm invincible!*

I seized the shotgun, tore it from the attacker's hand and then blasted him with it.

*There's nobody strong enough to stop me!*

I arrived at Gate F2.

*F2. 2F. To freedom. Yeah. To freedom.*

I peered at the plane through the glass wall. There was no check-in crew and all the black plastic waiting seats were empty.

My body pried the doors open as I was being shot at from behind.

I rushed down the jetbridge and into the plane.

It was a compact plane with only thirty-six seats. Thankfully the seats were made from vinyl and not cow skin.

"All passengers boarded. Prepare for liftoff," said the pilot over the speakers.

A black-suit soldier approached me from behind.

My body shot out to attack her but stopped.

*No harmful intent.*

She smiled, tossed a smoke bomb into the crowd of SWAT agents and closed the plane doors.

I looked up at her.

*Her heat signature looked familiar. Aha!*

She was the same young woman who was shocked by the prison bars.

"Hey, if you wanted to, you could kill me right now. Is that right?" she asked with shimmering eyes.

The plane started trembling as it gained speed for liftoff.

"Nonstop flight to Alabama Georgia. Fasten your seatbelts, turn off all electronic devices and enjoy the ride," said the pilot over the loudspeaker.

"New Mexico. I was told it was New Mexico. What flight number is this?"

*Another trap! Of course!*

"It's the right flight. We'll be making several stops before we drop you off so nobody can find you. You can relax now. Nobody is going to hurt you," she said with a smile.

The plane lifted off the ground.

"Why is it New Mexico anyway?"

"It's out of the states and therefore out of the boss' immediate surveillance. You won't be one-hundred percent safe, but you'll be much better off. There's a massive facility you can stay at. It's your dad's old lab, but now that he's publicly retired and moved to Maryland, it's abandoned."

"Why are you helping me?"

"You're a sweet little boy. Why wouldn't I help you?" she asked, grabbing my hand.

*Her hands were soft. Wait; stay focused.*

"No. There's another reason. What are you planning?"

"Devlin, there's no need to be confrontational. We're all friends here. I'm actually a super big fan of your father. Can you tell me about him?" she asked, hopping up and down.

"I...don't have a father. He's merely the man who made me. I hate him."

*I hope I never see him again.*

"Oh, okay. I understand. I won't ask you about him. So, uh, can you tell me about yourself? According to this picture my brother sent me, you are quite the cutie pie," she said, waving her phone in my face.

It was a picture of me in my pajamas, the ones with kitty cat faces. I was nestled up against Brother.

*Not Brother, Kanasta.*

"How did you get that?" I asked, plucking the device out of her hands.

*I hardly even use my hands anymore. So much has changed.*

"The boss has had his eye on your family for a long time. To be honest…I've had my eyes on you for a while," she said, holding her cheeks and swaying her hips.

*What?*

"Uh, oh. No. I mean th-thanks but I'm already taken."

"Ohoh, is that so? Who is the lucky girl?"

"I…can't tell you. You'd probably kill her if you found out."

*That's right. I can't trust her. She works for that politician. She's my*

enemy.

"I wouldn't do that. I don't kill people."

"Then what do you do?"

"I, well—it's a very important job. But, uh, I can't tell you. Top secret," she said with a smile.

My appendages coiled around her throat before the suspicion even registered in my conscious mind.

*My subconscious. The wires were my subconscious mind. I didn't kill those people. I can't be judged for my impulses, can I?*

"That hurts. Please stop," she said, her eyes watering up.

"I've figured you out. This is more interrogation. Playing nice to get me to spill my guts—yeah, that's all this is. Well I won't do it. You won't hear another word from me."

Something hit me from behind. Yet again I collapsed.

Surrounded by darkness. I had no dreams, no nightmares. It was pure darkness. But it didn't bother me. It reminded me that I was alone.

*I was okay with being alone now. In fact, I preferred it. Yeah, I'm a killing machine. No friends, no family, I make my own rules and I answer to no one.*

I came to in a queen-sized bed. On top of a pillow next to me was a steel box and a note.

*Where am I now?*

My wires picked up the note, but I couldn't read it.

My eyes adjusted. Heat energy was still visible, but now I could make out words and maybe faces too.

*The thermal vision must have happened because my mind went into combat mode. Now that I'm safe, my vision is normal again. Yeah, that makes sense.*

Disinterested in the letter, I picked it up just so I could read words again.

*After all, reading and building were my two greatest passions. Well that and doting on Kawai. So cute!*

There was no signature and the handwriting style shifted throughout the letter.

"You will find all you need to build yourself a new family in that box and in the lab. Capsules are the clear fist-sized cases which are the heart of Exps. Artifacts are placed inside and will give them special powers. You should have enough for a small army in there. Get to work and enjoy your new life."

Rather than a signature, there was a quote at the bottom by Thurgood Marshall.

"The legal system can force open doors and sometimes even knock down walls but it cannot build bridges. That job belongs to you and me."

*That's right! In the end it's people who make real change, both through technology and the evolution of ethics. After all, Mr. Marshall said to appreciate the differences and discover the similarities.*

*I may not be a human, but I am still the same virtuous person. I'm still disgusted by discrimination and by mankind's treatment of the Earth. If anything, this is an opportunity to look at humans from an outside perspective. Even though my skin and body were different, I am still me. I'm still a freedom fighter and still an inventor.*

Just thinking about building Exps got me excited. I knew it was what they wanted and it was part of some plan to gain new weapons. But I didn't care. If they came here, I would kill them. I'd grow strong enough and I would kill them with my new family.

*Wait, not a family but an army. Yeah, enough for a small army. That's what it said.*

"Oh yes! I'll return home with my army and I'll kill them! Deceivant, my brother, my mom and every human in that city! I'll teach them to fear me as an Exp and as an inventor!"

*Saying it out loud made it sound even more exciting!*

I spun the capsule around in my hands.

I hopped off the bed, all of a sudden staring into a mirror.

I thought I had gotten used to it. Looking like a monster. I thought I liked it. Maybe when I'm killing them it would help. But right now I feel disembodied. I need fake skin.

*I need to be a boy again!*

I rushed down to the lab where there were compartments of different materials. Various textures of synthetic skin were lined up inside one of the drawers. It was below the drawer of fake eyeballs and above the one with little girls' underwear.

*No doubt about it. This was Deceivant's lab. But now it's mine.*

There were blueprints outlining the wall of the lab.

*Ada, D.S., Kawai...*

I felt warm all of a sudden.

*There she was. My future wife. Well not necessarily, but a boy can dream. Either way, I have to save them. They aren't safe with Deceivant. No, no. Not safe at all. But first, I'll need a small army. An army and a family!*

"Yeah, I'll show my so-called family just how replaceable they are! Then I'll break my people out. I'll free them all! We'll kill everyone who sees us as tools. Everyone who dares to say we aren't alive. And after that. Oh, we can accomplish anything! We will be the true stewards of the Earth. With Exps in control, there won't be discrimination. With me in control, all the world's problems will be solved!"

*Being a monster just means I transcend the moral limitations binding mortals. I am willing to do what others won't. I'll make them the monsters and us the people. Then I'll wipe them out like the invasive species they are!*

# Chapter 84: Revenge

The world faded from view. Steam, flames, heat, and Lord Etah arose from the darkness. The nightmare faded and the Freedom Forcers awoke to the realm of Sel.

"So much hate," said Etah, a molten grin spreading from one side of his face to the other.

Devlin was on his knees, his eyes hollowed out.

"Then you felt it. All of you felt it." The God of Hate looked down at his defeated enemies. "Every surge of pain, every tinge of guilt, his overwhelming sadness, his overflowing anger! All of his negative emotions and none of the fleeting moments of joy. This is my power you see. To cripple my enemies with their own hellish memories. I use their hate to destroy them."

Exp 8 struggled to stand. "We're not, destroyed. We can still, hugh, fight."

Opti was on the ground, shaking in misery.

Bob looked around at his allies. "Are you all that hurt by Devlin's sob story? Didn't bother me one bit. Come on people, get over it." He turned to Riufen. "You agree with me, right?"

Tears melted in Riufen's eyes. "Devlin-sama has suffered so much. For no reason…so much suffering."

"Devlin-sama? I thought you were a ronin now," said Bob.

"I will not abandon my creator. I was inspired to act on my own accord and to forge my own destiny. I've made this decision as an individual following his own path, not due to my preprogramming." Riufen walked up to his creator and lowered himself to his knees. "I hereby swear eternal loyalty to you, Devlin-sama. My life is an extension of your will," he said, pressing his face against the ground.

"You haven't changed one bit," said Bob, rolling his pupil.

"No surprise you're still standing," said Etah, glaring at the eyeball.

"You bring up bad memories. You can hardly call that an attack," said Bob.

"Devlin, you understand now, don't you? You are powered by hate. Fueled by vengeance. You came this far not due to some naïve ambition. That was merely a way of rationalizing your rage. You are here, standing before a god because your anger kept you going. You killed your brother and your mother with so much hate! You should be by my side. I can make you a god. At this moment. Right now."

Devlin's fingernails drew blood as they dug into his fists. "I gained power and put my creations, my own children, in jeopardy because I believed in a better world. My hatred for discrimination fuels me, but I don't relish the suffering of others. You enslave others. I fight for their liberation. We are nothing alike."

"Hmmhmmhmmmhuhuh. You have no idea, do you? We share the same blood. And it boils like lava when we're enraged. You've inherited my hatred."

"Shut up. You are not my father. I don't even have a father!"

"Tell him, Deceivant. My words can't bring out the anger in him like yours can," said Etah.

"I'm sorry Devlin. I'm so sorry," said Deceivant, his whole body shaking. Ada was silently crying.

"Don't you see it, Devlin? You and I, we aren't crippled by hatred or pain. It empowers us. You stand before me, stronger than ever. I am not your father, if only I was. Even so, I am Deceivant's father. I'm your grandfather. Divinity is your birthright."

"Why would I believe that nonsense? You've wasted your time. I've come to grips with my past long ago. Your attempts to unhinge me are pathetic," said Devlin, his legs still shaking.

"You are not my father! You're a self-proclaimed god who has mimicked his features!" yelled Deceivant, struggling to stand.

"I've changed, yes, but it's still me."

"Atlas?" asked Kanasta.

"Yes. I was Atlas," said Etah.

"You are him! You sacrificed them. You killed my mother to become a god! What the hell happened to you?" asked Deceivant.

"You're joking. The God of Hate is my grandfather?" asked Devlin.

"Yes, Brother. He is," said Kanasta.

"Don't you dare call me Brother!"

"I finally understand your animosity toward me," said Kanasta.

"Animosity. Strange choice of words. It's more like humanity. I harbor the un-distilled hatred of a human for you. No non-human animal could ever harbor a hate so personal, so transforming."

"You most likely won't believe me. I didn't know my assassins had targeted you," said Kanasta.

"You gave us the mission: capture the Exp. That's thirty grand we never collected. But you didn't tell us the target was your brother. That's hardcore, even for you," said Ego.

"Even your own assassins won't back up your lies," said Devlin with a grin.

"That wasn't me. I would never, could never, harm my little brother." Kanasta's voice cracked and he sobbed.

"Papa wouldn't do that. He loves you...more than anything," cried Kaity.

"He made his choice. They all did," said Devlin.

Etah stepped up to his grandson, shaking the ground with each step. "You've killed them once before. Murder your mother, father, and brother. Then I will turn you into a god of equal power to me."

"I don't need you to tell me to kill them!" yelled Devlin.

His wires shot out at all three, sharpening as they zoomed through the air.

"No!" yelled Kaity, standing firmly in front of her papa.

Exp 8 slammed into the vengeful lunatic. "What the hell are you doing? You already murdered Ada once! Why would you want to repeat your mistake?"

"It wasn't a mistake! They deserve it! All of them!"

"I didn't see a mother who looked the other way as her husband sold out her son. Ada put her faith in Deceivant. He must have told her it was for your sake. Don't think for a second that Ada, the most loving person I know, would ever abandon you. Not to save her life, her husband's life, or any other reason. Ada's not capable of such a choice. I don't know Deceivant's ploy, but Ada is innocent!" yelled Exp 8.

Devlin broke out into tears. "I've wanted to believe that...I truly have."

"No you haven't. You've cocooned yourself in isolation. You painted them all traitors so you could leave them behind. Instead of harboring doubts about their motives, you found it easier to make them enemies."

"You don't know me at all!"

Devlin's wires pummeled his self-righteous creation, reading his every counter attack and finding an opening.

"You ruined my life before you were even created. Everything was always about making Exp 8. I was kidnapped and sold off because Deceivant wanted to keep Exp 8 to himself. That government special ops team rescued me so I could, guess what, make Exp 8. My old crush, Kawai, could only ever love the Ultimate Exp. My own children turned against me because you couldn't just be a good tool and serve your master!"

"Stop hurting him!" Kawai slammed her tail into her creator's back.

It was stopped by a mesh of wires.

"Leave him alone, Devlin! You've got this all wrong!" yelled Deceivant.

"You!" All of Devlin's wires lunged at Deceivant.

Matteria stood in the path.

Devlin's wires parted, went around his beloved son, and plunged into Deceivant's sides.

"Why are we fighting each other!" yelled Anthrax.

"Because Devlin is insane! I told you we couldn't trust him!" yelled Exp 8.

Deceivant took a deep breath, holding in the pain. "I scared you off, made you leave, because I knew they were coming for you. You weren't safe at home…with us. The only way to protect you and Ada was to make sure you wouldn't come back. I didn't know they were outside, waiting for you. As for Ada, I told her this was the only way to keep you safe. She came to see you one last time, despite my instructions," he said in tears.

"Spin whatever story you want now. It won't fool me," said Devlin.

"My, my, this is such an interesting turn of events," said Bob.

Demonica put her hand on Devlin's shoulder. "There's something you should know."

"Demonica. Silence," said Etah.

"The one who sent the assassins after you, the one who attacked you—"

Etah's aura shot out at Demonica but was repelled by her black aura.

"It wasn't Kanasta who attacked you. It was my minion. It was a demon, posing as your brother," said Demonica, unable to look her beloved in the eyes.

"Wh-what?" Devlin's eyes shrank.

"Not another word!" Etah rushed at the treacherous woman and picked her up. The blood clone collapsed in his grip.

The real Demonica popped out from Deceivant's puddle of blood. "The demon who posed as Kanasta set up the whole thing. It was following orders. The boy in the hood who beat you up, the dead cat in the road, the fake Kanasta that ordered the attack and hunted you down—they were all my minion wearing different disguises."

"I can't believe that. Why would you do that to me?"

"We had to break you apart from your family to get you working for us. We used you so you would gather more souls for Sel. Your whole life has been orchestrated from your creation to now," said Demonica, unable to look into Devlin's captivating golden eyes.

Devlin's eyes became hollow.

"Hmmhmmhmmmhuhuh. Now you understand. Demonica never loved you! It was all a ploy. You are merely a pawn who has made some unexpected moves." Etah leaned down to the naïve boy's ear. "You are and always will be my pawn."

Demonica walked to Etah, her head held down.

A massive clear portal appeared and all the Absence gods emerged. They joined up with the Freedom Forcers.

"Hmm, reinforcements. I suppose you're not completely unprepared." Etah turned his attention to Bob and smiled. "There is no need for you to continue this charade."

Bob bowed and moved to Etah's side, waving with a smile at his prior allies.

"No. That's not right. You're my Exp! I made you!" yelled Deceivant.

"He fooled you all from the beginning. He was my ally all along," said Etah with a grin.

Bob shrugged. "It's true. Oh, but it's been a lot of fun."

"Hold on just a damned moment. If Bob is your pawn, then why did he help us get here? Why would he aid us in the fight against you?" asked Deceivant.

"So that all of Sel could bear witness to my triumph. So that the hope the residents harbor can become all-pervasive despair. So that Devlin can take his rightful place as a god of Sel. Hmmhmmhmmmhuhuh. There are so many reasons."

"Bob has always been untrustworthy, but this is…," said Exp 8.

"Not surprised one bloody bit," said Karson.

"Oh stop, you'll make me blush," said Bob, turning away.

"Even with the dishonorable traitor on your side. We will cut you down," said Riufen, his eyes still wet from the tears.

"Karson!" shouted Etah.

"Oh, um, what is it?" asked Karson, arching back.

"It's time to pay up for the infinite lives I gave you."

"Oh, yes of course it is. Sorry everyone. It seems this is where we part ways," said Karson, keeping his eyes to the ground.

"Pathetic. I thought you were a noble warrior," said Pharma.

"I am a soldier. Survival is my immediate priority," said Karson, pushing his chest out.

"Your name is Karson, is that right?" asked Atatasuki.

"Yes, but now is not the time for re-introductions," said Karson.

Atatasuki pointed at the gunman, his hand steaming. "I knew it! I knew you were a spy all along!"

"But I wasn't. It wasn't until—why even bother telling you anything. We are enemies now." Karson walked in front of Bob and aimed his bazooka arms at the Freedom Forcers.

"Absence warriors. This is your only chance to leave. If you attack me, the full power of my armies will be unleashed upon your realm." Etah's eyes shifted to each Absence god.

"This is a losing battle. We will attack when provoked. There is no need for Absence to be caught up in their rebellion," said Limit, creating a clear portal.

"Such wisdom," said Loyal, making a much larger portal before going through.

"We'd just die anyway. Guard, return me to Absence," said Plagiarism.

Crystal tossed Plagiarism into the portal. "I'm staying right here."

"Don't be foolish. There's no need to keep this up. We've held up our end of the bargain. We've brought all the Exps to Etah's welcome mat, all the while pretending we would provide them back up. Tehtehteh. It's time for us to return to Absence and celebrate another battle successfully avoided," said Eil.

"Go ahead. I'm staying," said Crystal.

"You won't hold us all accountable for his actions, right?" asked Eil.

"Most certainly not. He will be destroyed as an example. That is all," said Etah.

"Fair enough. Occupy, are you coming?" asked Eil.

Occupy stepped up to Needle. "Take Master Void with you. I won't abandon them. This is the right path to walk. It's not the middle path. But if I avoided this battle, then I wouldn't be worthy of upholding the values of Absence."

"What a shame. You will be missed. For a time," said Eil.

Needle beckoned Spin and Plagiarism into the portal and then left with Eil and Void.

"Is anyone else going to abandon us? Betray us!" yelled Exp 8.

"Me." D.S. walked to Etah's side. He stopped midway, chuckling. "Fooled ya! I'm done being a bad guy," he said, sticking his tongue out at Etah.

"Shall we proceed?" asked Etah, towering above his allies.


On Etah's side were Demonica, Edirp, Yvne, Deerg, Tsul, Bob, and Karson.

"We still have plenty of allies to take you down," said Exp 8.

The Freedom Forcers' side consisted of Devlin, Exp 8, Ada, Kawai, Atatasuki, NoOne, Nina, Pharma, Kanasta, Kaity, BoneSaw, Ego, Riufen, Matteria, Violet, Anthrax, D.S., Deceivant, Exp 11, Crystal and Occupy.

"You must earn the right to battle me. My minions will take on three of you each in an arena of my choosing."

Atatasuki leaned over to his brother. "We don't have to agree to this, right?"

Exp 8 grabbed his dear brother's shoulders. "Show no fear. We can take him down on his terms. No problem. All of Sel will bear witness to our overwhelming and legitimate victory over Etah!"

The Freedom Forcers raised their arms in the air and cheered.

"Hehheh. You really know how to rally a crowd into a minefield," said Bob.

"Hey, Occupy, Crystal, Napkin. Come here," said Exp 8.

"Napkin, is that his name? He has a powerful soul," said Occupy, holding the kitty.

"Where did you find him?" asked Kaity.

"He came to me soon after we arrived," said Occupy.

"Are you coming or not?" asked Exp 8.

"What, you got some sort of strategy?" asked Crystal.

The leader of the Freedom Forcers wrapped his arms around Crystal, Occupy and he put his hand on Napkin, who was on the monk's shoulder. "Welcome to the team. You three are officially honorary Freedom Forcers. Group hug!"

One by one the Freedom Forcers joined in the embrace.

"Should I attack now? It would be so funny if one of them died," said Bob.

"Patience. They will be crushed in the arenas with all of Sel watching," said Etah, patting his powerful assistant.

"Shall I give them a symbol of our unity?" asked Violet.

"Once the battle is over, sure. For now, let's stay vigilant. Deceivant, take care of Napkin. Ada, you stay behind too," said Exp 8.

"Okay. I understand," said Ada.

"Make him pay," said Deceivant.

"We will," said Exp 8.

"Wait, with them out, there are only…nineteen of us. That isn't divisible by three at all. It's a prime number!" yelled D.S.

"Then it's a good thing Demo isn't here," said Deceivant with a grin.

"Any way you cut it, we never had twenty-four guys on our team. Hey Etah, you suck at math!" hollered D.S.

"I'll take on Demonica. I am going to rip her to shreds!" yelled Devlin, his wires rattling.

"Let me come with you," said Matteria.

"You stay here. You don't have a complete connection to your artifact, and you aren't a warrior. Going in there now is tantamount to suicide," said Devlin, grabbing his creation's hand tightly.

"Okay. I'll stay here, waiting for your return," said Matteria with a teary smile.

"Opti is too shaken up to battle. And it doesn't seem Pesi is coming out. You can count him out as well," said Kanasta, crouched over his broken comrade.

"Then we'll help him get back on his feet," said Matteria, grabbing Ada's hand.

"Good thinking." Exp 8 turned to the skilled doctor. "Go with Devlin. Heal him if he needs it."

"Yeah, good idea," said Anthrax.

Etah created eight separate portals, each leading to a different area of Sel.

"Are we seriously going to go in there?" asked Atatasuki.

"It could be a vicious ambush. Maybe he's right," said Kawai, her tail on end.

"This is the way it's got to be done. Don't worry, I'll personally defend you both," said Exp 8.

Each of Etah's allies stood by a separate portal, waiting for the Freedom Forcers to enter. There was one portal that had nobody next to it.

"Everyone, we are going to make it through this! Keep your wits about you and don't lose hope. We'll meet up once we've beaten them. Then we'll take down Etah together," said Exp 8, raising his fist toward the skies.

Violet took in a deep breath and stepped up to Tsul. "How can you still be on his side after what he's done? Devlin is a kind soul. He never deserved any of that."

"Bad things happen to good people all the time. I fight for the realm of Sel. My loyalty to this place far outweighs any idealistic sense of morality I have toward others. I hope you're ready to die." Tsul cracked her whip and then entered the portal.

"I am," said Violet, standing firm.

"Wait up!" D.S. rushed up to his little sister. "That demon lady is super dangerous and totally nuts. I'll keep you safe." He held his scissors over his shoulder.

"Thank you, brother," said Violet with a smile.

Nina cautiously approached Edirp. "Don't speak. Go in the portal. Let's settle things there."

"I've got your back," said Kaity, releasing her plasma claws.

"Fine with me. You're not worth wasting words on," said Edirp, strutting into the portal.

Kanasta loomed over Deerg. "All of you demons ruined my brother's life. I won't hold back. Your death will pay for itself."

Crystal stood by the assassin's side. "I'll keep her distracted. You go for the kill."

"Sounds like a plan." Kanasta gripped the detestable demon and tossed her into the portal.

Ego rushed up to Yvne. "Now you have something to be envious of," he said, flexing his arms.

"Jealousy is my power," said Yvne before vanishing through the portal.

"If she wasn't here, I wouldn't even bother fighting. But with such a pathetic adversary, how can I lose?" asked NoOne, following Ego into the portal.

Riufen walked up to Bob. "You have dishonored us all with your betrayal. That cannot be forgiven."

Bob gathered energy in his pupil. "Who's asking for forgiveness?"

Occupy put a friendly hand on the swordsman's shoulder. "His spiritual powers are akin to Guru Void's. You need not fight him alone. I will aid you."

"Your assistance may be necessary to defeat him. Even so, let me battle him on my own first. If I fail, then you can intervene," said Riufen.

"Understood," said Occupy.

"Alone, together, either way you'll end up dead," said Bob with a glare as he went through the portal.

Pharma confronted Karson. "I thought you were stronger than this. You are not my rival. You're a pathetic coward."

BoneSaw revved up his saws and zoomed into the portal.

"Say what you will. This will be our final fight," said Karson.

"That it will," said Pharma, entering the portal.

Devlin stepped up to Demonica, digging his heel into the fleshy ground with each step. "You ruined my life!" He grabbed her and plunged with her into the portal.

Anthrax rushed in after them.

Exp 8 looked up at the final portal. "I don't know what's waiting for us at the other side, but I know we can handle it."

"We can do anything as long as we're together," said Kawai, wrapping her tail around his.

"Hey bro, you joining us?" asked Exp 8.

"Yeah. I'm ready," said Atatasuki.

The siblings entered the portal despite not knowing what lurked beyond it.

# Chapter 85: For All to Bear Witness

Violet and D.S. charged out of the portal into a fleshy tunnel.

"It's bouncy," said D.S., getting twice the air time as he hopped off the ground.

"Ah, yes. That feels great." Tsul was biting her lip and her cheeks were flushed.

"It's her. This whole place is her body," said Violet, flicking the wall of the tunnel.

"Ooh, such a clever girl. But no, it isn't. I've just made it so I can feel every sensation in the area," said Tsul, her whips caressing her demon followers.

"That's advanced meditation. You must have worked hard to achieve it," said Violet.

"Indeed. So much humiliation. So much fear. But it all paid off," said Tsul with shaky eyes.

"Yeah! I did it. Three back flips. Wanna see?" asked D.S., landing in front of his sister.

"You three. Take care of them." Tsul whipped the demons, sending them into a frenzy.

The crazed demons rushed right into the protruding scissors.

"These guys are kinda stupid," said D.S., snipping off the legs of another demon.

"What have you done? They are innocents! She is the only one we need to fight," said Violet, dodging the claws of the last demon.

"Don't worry. I'll fix him up." D.S. stapled the legs back onto the demon's torso. "Even without artifacts I can still help people."

"Why are you even fighting for Devlin? Do you love him?" asked Tsul.

"Eww. No. He's my little brother. Weirdo."

"Love is such a simple word. What I feel for Devlin is something spiritual. It's divine. I am his devotee, body, mind, and spirit!" Violet rushed at the goddess before backing off when four more demons came her way.

"I don't see what's so great about Devlin," said Tsul, tickling the fleshy floor with her whips.

"He fights for what he believes in. How can you not admire him?" Violet pulled out a scimitar from her side and turned to her brother. "There's too many. You can hurt them, a little. Nothing too serious, okay," she said, bonking a demon on the head with her sword.

"Got it," said D.S. with a thumbs-up.

"Strange, don't you believe in non-violence and all that preachy nonsense?" asked Tsul, wetting her lips.

401

"As a Jain I abhor violence. But as a Hindu I am aware that violence can be transformative. Just as purity is necessary to the Brahmin, violence is essential to the Kshatriya. Without Kshatriyas ruling and protecting the society, Brahmins would be unable to uphold their vital ritual functions. I will harness my fighting spirit and take you down to defend the society Devlin envisions." Violet pushed out her chest and held up her sword.

"You're completely lost. Don't see why I can't just kill you." Tsul snapped her whip at the devotee, cutting her face.

Violet grabbed the whip before it could rebound.

Tsul smiled and large spikes came out of the whip, piercing through the naïve mortal's hand.

Violet pulled her hand back, causing the goddess to lose her balance and fall toward her. She then plunged her blade into the Asura's chest.

Pink blood spurted out on the scimitar.

Tsul pushed deeper into the blade and bit onto the warrior's arm.

The God of Lust's hair then wrapped around the mortal and ensnared her.

"Let go of her!" D.S. stabbed his scissors into the mean lady's back lots and lots of times.

"*ASTRAL PROJECTION*." Violet's astral self pulled her blade through the goddess' back before slicing off her whip hair.

Violet's body tumbled to the ground, still being constricted by the whips.

"No! No! Not again!" D.S. sliced through the whips as he was being flogged from behind.

Violet's astral self re-entered her body and smiled at her brother.

Two demons yanked away the giant scissors and tossed them to another group of demons.

"Give that back!" yelled D.S., chasing down the thieves.

Violet dragged her fingers down the fleshy ground, making the Asura pause to savor the pleasure. She grabbed her cross from behind her leg as she approached.

The tips of the cross shot out and little knives popped out. The sides of the cross spun around rapidly.

Violet shoved the cross in the goddess' chest. "*ATONEMENT!*"

The spinning cross shot out, taking the rival goddess with it while slicing her insides.

Tsul slammed against the wall, her chest sliced all over.

"I've had enough. You win," said Tsul, snapping her fingers and creating a portal.

"We did it!" D.S. raised his hand.

"Yaay. Good for you," said Tsul, clapping but disinterested.

Violet's astral self came out and gave him a high five.

The two of them entered the portal.

Crystal and Kanasta popped out of the portal and landed on a hilltop of gold.

"Not good. She could be hiding anywhere." Crystal turned to the assassin. "We should stick to…what are you doing?"

Kanasta was washing his body with gold coins and rubbing them all over his face.

"Ugh, of course. Looks like I'm alone in this fight."

The hill suddenly collapsed.

Crystal grabbed his teammate and leaped up.

The rubble of the hill stood up, revealing it to be an armada of demons. Gold was melted into their flesh and gemstones were pierced into their eyes.

Crystal fired six spear-like shards into the crowd. He hopped off the shards all the while pelting the oncoming demons with a continuous stream of mineral flakes. "We have to find her. Oh my…"

The absence god looked up at a tower of jewels. At the peak of the mineral skyscraper was Deerg.

"Kanasta, your brother is counting on us to take her down. If we don't take this seriously, you could die. I'm immortal so, yeah, no problems for me," said Crystal.

Kanasta shook himself to his senses. He looked up at the gemstone tower with an ever-widening smile. "I'm going to climb it." He slammed his elbow into a demon and then tore out its ruby eyeballs with two fingers.

"You're an assassin right. Here." Crystal formed a fist-sized diamond and handed it to the assassin. "I'm paying you to take her down."

Kanasta grabbed the diamond and kissed it. "Job accepted."

Deerg peeked over the edge. "What are you all muttering about? I own every square inch of this arena. You can't stop me! ⟨◇IN ΗΛΙⱯ↑◇ℝΜ."

The loose change from the tower slipped free and rained down.

"Take cover!" Crystal formed a mineral shield and held it above them.

"Good thinking." Kanasta grabbed the edge of the shield and vaulted himself onto the top of it. He kicked off the shield and gripped onto the side of the tower.

"No! No! No! You're supposed to die," said Deerg, stomping her feet while pacing around.

Arms of demons came out from the wall and grabbed onto Kanasta.

"Out of my way." Kanasta flung two demons off him and smashed another into two more that were cropping out. He tore off one of their legs and used it to knock off the demons above him.

"All my possessions! Stop them!" yelled Deerg.

The mountains of gold collapsed into fifty demons each.

"I won't let them get to you!" Crystal's arms sharpened into swords as he rushed into the battalion of golden demons.

"I'll burry you all. ᗪ◊ᘓᘓᗩᖇ ᗩᐯᗩᘓᗩᘓᘓᗴ!" yelled Deerg.

The uncountable amount of dollars that lined the tower all came tumbling down.

Kanasta knocked a demon off his back with a suitcase and then opened it. He filled it to the brim and then jumped off the mountain.

Crystals erupted from the ground as soon as the demons set foot near the tower.

"I've laid them all around the tower. I can back you up now," said Crystal as the demons climbed over the protruding minerals.

Kanasta kicked off the dollars, locating the most dense areas, all the way to the top of the tower. He landed before the golden goddess, covered in cash.

"Welcome to Trickle-down Tower! Oooh, look at all the money! Don't you want it? Don't you need it!" asked Deerg, her tail wagging back and forth.

Kanasta rushed at the fiscal goddess. He was suddenly pulled in and lost his footing.

"I will show you firsthand how greed can consume you in its glory! ᕼᗩᖇᗪ ᗩᔑᔑᗴ† ᗩᖇᗰ◊ᖇ," said Deerg as her skin gradually hardened. An extra layer of silver skin soon covered her whole body.

Kanasta slammed his fists into the shimmering enemy as soon as she was within range, but the attack slid off her sleek body.

Dollars shot out from beneath Kanasta, ensnaring him in a torrent of wealth.

"If you join Etah, he can make you rich beyond compare," said Deerg, riding the dollar storm all the while pelting the mortal with heated coins.

The gold coins seared through his skintight suit and melted his skin.

"I was framed and my brother was tormented by your master!" Kanasta broke free of the cash, quickly stuffing it in his already full suitcase.

"What does that have to do with my offer?" asked Deerg, riding a platform of dollars up to him.

Kanasta smiled. "Besides, your assassination pays for itself." He grabbed onto the wealthy demon and leaped off the platform.

Deerg clawed him as they plummeted. She slammed into the top of the tower headfirst.

Kanasta took out the diamond he received from Crystal and stabbed it into the target's fortified neck until it got stuck.

"Drown in priceless minerals. ⟨ᛂᛗ ᛁᛏᛢᛦᛗ!" A multitude of shining rocks shot out of from Deerg's hand.

Kanasta pushed through the brutal storm and grabbed the target's arm.

The assassin boss knocked her arm up, changing the attack's direction. He then spun her around. "I won't get distracted. This is just another job." The masterful assassin gripped the gemstone with both hands and pierced it deeper into her throat. "I'll keep your head as a luxurious souvenir." Kanasta tore the diamond out.

Red coins shot out of Deerg's open neck wound like a fountain.

Kanasta grabbed her head and spun it.

It spiraled around until it came off, landing right into his hands.

"Hmm, red coins, not rubies. That's a bit disappointing. Still, this should be worth a fortune." Kanasta grabbed the target's head and shoved it in his suitcase.

Crystal climbed to the top of the mountain, his back tinted gold by the heated metal.

Deerg's headless body was motionless on the ground.

"Hey, you did it. Good job." He tossed the assassin boss a crystallized suitcase. "Your payment is inside. Phew. I think I beat them all," said Crystal, looking down at the battlefield.

Kanasta looked at the diamond suitcase and then back at his ally.

His cloak in tatters, it was now clear that Crystal's entire body was composed of minerals. His face was carved into a permanent grimace and he had sockets but no eyes.

"You can regenerate them?" asked Kanasta with wide eyes.

"Yeah, I am a god, after all."

"I want you." Kanasta's eyes shimmered.

"Whoa uh, huh?"

"Come with me to Earth. I'll take good care of you," said Kanasta with a smile.

"One step at a time. Let's take down Etah," said Crystal.

"Yes. Of course." Kanasta looked down to see jagged crystals protruding out all the way down the pillar. "You fought well."

A portal appeared in front of them. "Let's go."

"I will return to this paradise," said Kanasta before entering the portal.

Kaity and Nina leaped out of the portal and landed in a busy city of demons.

Fleshy buildings rose up to the skies just below the perpetual black fog above. Demon gardeners who were sprinkling pain on the ground looked up curiously at the two new arrivals. The head demon broke the gardeners' gaze with a crack of a whip.

"Are they all enemies?" asked Nina, carefully navigating through the crowd.

"Poison," said Kaity, reclining her claws and stopping her partner with her hand.

Right below the sexy survivalist's foot was a puddle of purple corrosive poison.

Nina swerved her head to the side.

Kaity grabbed the dart and examined it. "Fast acting, but not lethal. It's paralysis."

"Of course it is. They don't want me dead. They want me motionless so they can ravage my body. It's probably been years since any of them have seen a woman with all her skin. And even in their previous life, they've never witnessed anything like me. We need to get them to disperse," said Nina, grabbing the arm of a nearby assailant. She floored him to the ground and took off her leggings.

The young assassin's claws jutted out and pierced a demon as he rushed out from the crowd.

"Why are they all targeting you?" asked Kaity, whipping out a pistol.

"Come on. Who would you go after?" asked Nina, triggering her knee-socks to explode as she roundhouse-kicked three approaching demons.

Kaity fired at four demons that burst out from the crowd, their arms drenched in poison. Each bullet landed right between the eyes.

"I've got guns too," said Nina, firing an automatic machinegun in the air.

"I can't believe Karson's an enemy now. I think it was my fault," said Kaity, warding off some demons in close proximity with warning shots.

The crowd dispersed a bit, but certain demons in the distance still watched from the shadows.

"Stay focused," said Nina, watching for any sudden movements.

"Watch out!" Kaity flung herself onto her partner, toppling her to the ground and dodging ten darts that zoomed above them.

Kaity's face was buried in her crush's squishy breasts.

"Convenient landing. I'll let this one slide since you saved me. Do you see them? They're in the flesh towers," said Nina, lying still.

"Yeah there's at least fifteen. Possibly more on the roofs. Wish I held onto that sniper. Oooh, so soft," said Kaity, resting her head on the warm breasts.

"Reach behind my back. There's a little something for you," said Nina.

Kaity put her arms in Nina's shirt and pulled out a retractable sniper rifle.

"Better hurry. They're closing in to check us out. Sexy poses are a bit risky here and they don't have enough range. I'll get rid of the ones in close proximity, you take out the ones in the towers," said Nina, loading a fresh clip into her machinegun.

"Got it." Kaity rolled off of her ally and kept rolling until the dart barrage ended. In the midst of the machine-gun fire she took out the snipers in the three buildings around them. "Fifteen bullet clip. Yes." She zoomed by Nina, grabbing an extra clip from behind her partner's legs.

"I don't see any others," said Nina, scanning the distant crowds for suspicious fingers.

"My heart's racing. This is so exciting. It's like we're on a mission together," said Kaity.

"Hmph. You sure know how to make a date interesting," said Nina, peeking behind an alleyway corner.

"A date! Oh Nina!" The prodigy leaped up to her partner.

Nina jumped into her fan, grabbed her and spun through the air, dodging four rocket blasts. "Damn it, they have guns too! If Pharma hasn't found a way to kill Karson, I will."

Eight bullets shot into the nimble warrior's gorgeous legs all at once.

The seductive survivalist tumbled along the fleshy ground, getting grabbed and grouped by the soon-to-be demons below. "Damn it! Kaity, do you see them?" she asked, limping out of their range of fire.

"Yeah, there's a lot."

Demons crawled out of the windows by the dozen. They climbed down the buildings as snipers pelted the young assassin from behind the crowd on the roof.

"They're using their allies to mask their location. This is not good. Nina, get on my shoulders. We have to get out of here!"

"Grab on to me. If you could get high enough, could you take them out?" asked Nina, patching up her leg wounds by tearing off part of her shirt.

"Yeah, but—."

Nina grabbed her ally's arm. "*Softening Pull.*" She floated off the ground, taking her little fan along for the ride.

"This is incredible! You're incredible!" cheered Kaity. As soon as the snipers were in sight, she took them out.

"I was saving this surprise for when we located Edirp, but I don't see her anywhere," said Nina as she continued her ascent.

Purple directional arrows pierced through the black fog and converged on them.

"Damn her. Purple is my color!" yelled Nina, spraying the arrows with bullets.

Kaity pierced incoming arrows with her plasma claws. "There's something branded on them. 'Insignificant'. 'Ignorant'. 'Short-tempered'. They're all insults."

"Must be her power. Demeaning others to raise her own self-image, how pathetic. Don't let them hit you. We're going into the fog now. It's the only way we'll reach her," said Nina.

"Not a problem. I can hear them coming," said Kaity, slicing three arrows to bits before reloading her rifle.

They ascended higher and higher into the fog until the arrows were coming out directly below them.

"We've made it. Time to go crashing down. *Hardening Push.*" yelled Nina.

They slammed to the ground.

"Do you sense her?" asked Nina, readying her gun.

"I heard her fall."

Kaity's bullet shot into the fog.

"I hit her, but I'm not sure where," said Kaity.

"Hopefully the mouth," said Nina.

The massive pillar began a rapid descent.

Kaity pierced her claws into the ground and held onto the sniper and Nina with her free hand. "Only a point blank shot can hit at this speed," she said, slinging the sniper over her shoulder while grabbing her ally with her legs and scaling the pillar with her plasma claws.

"Damn it, more arrows!" yelled Nina, firing her machinegun above her.

The sniper's tip bumped something in the fog.

Kaity fired the remaining fourteen shots into the target in different areas.

The pillar descended until it reached flat earth.

Edirp's body was ridden with holes and purple blood. Her brain had splattered against the ground.

"Mission accomplished," said Kaity, reloading the sniper.

"You're quite the partner," said Nina, struggling back to her feet.

"We make a great team. Lean on my shoulder."

"Don't have much of a choice, do I?" Nina wrapped her arm over her friend's shoulder and limped toward the portal they came from.

"I'll ask Violet to heal your legs as soon as we get there," said Kaity.

"Do so secretly. Can't let the team see me in such a pitiful state," said Nina.

Kaity nodded and they walked through the portal.

Ego and NoOne arrived on the other side of the portal.

Ego lost his balance and tumbled down a slope before being sent up a ramp.

"The entire place, it's changing." NoOne looked at the football-field-sized rectangular arena.

Bumps and dips flowed out from the end and came rushing down toward the opposite side like waves.

Two demons with sewed on faces of human women, vacant eyes and sharpened bone arms came out from behind the shadow man.

NoOne's shadow shot out as spikes, piercing the demons. He seeped into the ground, becoming synchronized with the waves.

"Whoa man, this is crazy!" cheered Ego, timing his jumps so he could leap over the demons below.

"Where is Yvne? She couldn't have gone far." A demon leaped on NoOne from above before it was sliced in half by his bladed arm. "Do you need any weapons?"

"Nah man. I just got one." Ego landed on a demon and skated it down the slope, directing it to knock aside other demons in its path.

"I can manage them as well." NoOne's shadow gripped the shadows of the demons he had slain. Their corpses rose from the ground and began an assault against a fresh hoard coming down from the hill.

"Dude, I see her!" Ego pointed to the sky.

Yvne floated above, her wings falling apart as her desire to be grounded increased.

"I'll knock her down. You, um, don't get killed," said NoOne, shooting shadow balls from his palms.

Yvne dodged the balls before curiosity got the better of her and she allowed a shadow ball to knock into her wing.

"Perfect lineup," said NoOne.

All the corpses of his victims were positioned with a connection to each of their shadows.

"Come crashing down! *SHADOW ROPE!*" NoOne pulled on the shadow, tugging the pitiful creature to the ground.

Yvne landed at the shadow man's feet, her wounds healing as soon as they yearned for vitality. "You're so great, so powerful. Why can't I be more like you?" she asked, looking up at him solemnly.

NoOne turned around. There was nobody there. "Strange, who was she talking to? No matter." He plunged his bladed arm down the wretch's throat.

Ego slammed into NoOne. "Why are you praising him? I'm the one you should be worshiping!"

"I didn't notice you there," said Yvne, her eyes locked onto the shadow man.

A massive gash tore across Ego's chest.

"No way. She's lying. It's a combat strategy, that's all." Ego willed himself back to his feet.

"Move aside. I will finish this wretch," said NoOne.

"Shut up! This is my battle, man. Keep out of it," said Ego.

"You'll only get yourself killed. As a hero, I must protect you." NoOne's shadow tugged on Ego's, dragging his ally away from the demon god.

"Oh no you don't! You haven't seen anything yet, I'll show you the true size of my ego! *GROWING SELF-RESPECT, SELF*." Ego grew until he was a hundred feet tall.

"You've doomed us," said NoOne.

"Such incredible size!" exclaimed Yvne, wobbling back and forth while gripping her sides. "I don't stand a chance! Unless... *Fan of Envy!*"

The demon goddess' dark green aura erupted out. It collected in her right hand. The aura then materialized as a personal fan.

The fan was as large as an umbrella and was a sickly green color. Sheets of flesh connected to thin metal rods, making up the separate sections. The handle morphed into teeth and dug its fangs into its owners' arm. The fan then coated itself in energy.

Yvne fanned herself with her murky aura.

NoOne slashed at her with his bladed arm, but she blocked each and every strike, continuing to fan herself.

"Look up in awe. I am as great as a skyscraper! I am as powerful as an army!" cheered Ego, flexing his muscles.

"*Winds of Envy!*" Yvne swooshed her fan.

An elephant-sized gust of energy slammed into the massive man's foot and pushed it off the floor.

"Not so fast! I am the king of balance and the emperor of style!" Ego purposefully tumbled backward, falling into a hand stand. He pushed off his hands and kicked furiously at the goddess from above.

"*Tornado of Envy!*" Yvne rapidly spun around, creating a powerful gust of wind.

The gust stopped the mortal's attack and launched him up.

"It's people like you that make me so unbearably jealous. The only way for my self-esteem to return is to knock you down and tear you to shreds!" Yvne grew in size and her fan along with her. Her growth spurt ended when she was one foot shorter than Ego. "Go away!" She spun her fan around before slamming it into the massive man.

Ego was shot into the distance, crashing into a crowd of spectator demons on a mountain.

"Die! Die! Die! Die! *Blades of Envy.*"

The fan sliced the air, turning the wind it created into invisible sickles.

The wind blades sliced the giant man as he made a desperate effort to shield his face.

"I'm not done yet!" Fueled by the hungry audience of demons, Ego pushed off the broken mountain and somersaulted toward the goddess.

"No! You're too cool." Yvne's head dropped.

NoOne dodged her massive tears as they fell.

"Time for a super stylish finisher!" cheered Ego.

The demons in the crowd cheered.

"*GROWING TO THE MAX*!" Ego grew two hundred feet taller.

"No more." Yvne sprouted wings and soared through his rapid kicks, past his flurry of punches and plunged her bladed fan into his neck. "Go away!"

Yvne's fan had been slicing the wind during her ascent.

The air blades sliced Ego all the way up, leaving only his massive head untouched.

"One mistake is all it takes. I'll see you soon, Bro," said Ego with a smile.

The stylish assassin's body fell into thin slices and crashed down on the battleground below. The bracelets made craters once they landed.

"I need your charisma! Your power!" Yvne ravenously devoured the slabs of meat before they could decay.

Ego's face kept its peaceful smile as it was consumed.

NoOne flattened out and escaped the arena.

# Chapter 86: Traitors

Riufen and Occupy were spit out into a forest of thick mist.

"After all those losses you've suffered, somehow you think this time will be any different. Do you honestly believe you could ever beat me?" asked Bob, firing lasers through the mist.

Riufen dodged each laser and rushed toward its origin point, but each time the traitor vanished. "This time your dishonor is intolerable," said the stoic samurai, anger flaring in his eyes.

Riufen's ribcage shot forward into the mist.

The Befriender of Betrayal phased through it and floated toward the inept warrior. "Close, but no."

Bob shifted out of his phase form once the ribcage receded.

Riufen jumped over the traitor and his ribs elongated once more.

The ribs pierced into the eyeball, making white liquid ooze out.

Bob switched back to his phase form and zoomed up to the honor bound imbecile.

Riufen broke off his ribs and caught the traitor inside them.

Bob fired a laser through the ribs. He passed through the simpleton, turned around and then blasted him at point blank range.

The samurai crashed to the misty floor, unable to see his hand in front of his face. He took out his spinal cord and waited.

"Where are you?" asked Occupy, dispelling a cloud of mist with each wave of his hand.

Glowing eyes beamed out from the cloud of fog that encircled the monk.

One of the creatures lunged out of the fog. Its ethereal shark-like teeth bit into its prey's arm.

"I've never seen such a demon before. What a peculiar creature," said Occupy, examining the strange green entity.

Spectral talons popped out before slicing into the prey.

Occupy grabbed the marvel of creation's arm. "It's a soul with preprogrammed responses. Most peculiar indeed."

Three more Jivas emerged from the darkness and bit into the prey's legs.

"No will of their own. Such a wretched existence. What sort of power can extract the will from a soul? Or perhaps they came into being without a will. If so, what purpose do they serve? How does such a being fit into the complex system of Sellum?"

The remaining Jivas opened their mouths.

Occupy's soul particles were pulled out of his body and devoured.

"Aha! There's my answer. You're made to deal with maverick gods. You must be constructs of Sellum itself! You have every right to attack me. I am acting outside my jurisdiction. I won't back down, though. I've chosen this path, and I will see it through to the end." Occupy spun around in place until the Jivas fell off his body.

One of the spectral beings passed through a tree before seeping into the ground.

"Remarkable. I haven't felt the fear of death in so long! This is exhilarating," said Occupy, rushing by and kicking each Jiva in his path.

The creatures ran alongside him on all fours, keeping just enough distance to suck up his soul particles.

"My spirit has been refined by Guru Void's training regimen," said Occupy with a smile.

The Jivas slowly disintegrated, leaving behind a blue orb. The liberated soul then dimmed out and vanished.

"It is my duty as an Absence god to help troubled souls, either by removing their barriers or filling them with bliss. My own particles have freed your souls. I shall help all of you move on," said Occupy, closing his eyes and smiling as his soul was devoured.


Further north, but still in the mist, Riufen waited for his opponent to resurface.

The Atma Blade pierced the samurai from below.

The skilled warrior plunged his spine into the ground, making it shriek with screams of agony.

The treacherous eyeball popped out in his phase form and pulled Riufen into the air with a spectral tentacle. "*Laser Barrage*." He fired six lasers at once, which were all blocked.

The Atma Blade then plunged into Riufen.

The stoic samurai slammed his head forward but it passed right through his foe.

Bob turned around, ensnared the simpleton in spectral tendrils and jabbed his blade into him.

The proud warrior plunged his spinal cord into the traitor's pupil.

"Aah! Aah!" Bob thrashed around in the air.

Riufen ripped his spinal cord out from the pupil and pierced eight more holes into his adversary.

Bob fired lasers blindly, none of which hit their target.

Riufen shot his ribs forward once more, piercing through the traitor. The ribs then spread out, tearing Bob to pieces. "You shall never dishonor this world with your existence ever again."

The Jivas that remained faded out of existence.

"Why did they leave? How can their presence vanish in an instant? I've never witnessed such an entity," said Occupy.

"Over here!" hollered Riufen. "The battle is done."

Occupy zoomed up to the immortal warrior. "Remarkable! Could those entities truly be created by an Exp?"

"Such questions are pointless. The traitor is no more," said Riufen, flinging the fluids off his spine.

"Does that mean he is free from samsara?" asked Occupy, looking at Bob's remains.

Riufen nodded. He turned his head, sheathed his spine and walked toward the portal they came from. "He will never again bring dishonor to Devlin-sama."

Pharma and BoneSaw arrived on scorched ground once they exited the portal.

Karson was standing tall behind a blockade of ten demons with turrets on their backs. "I had the choice of either dying or having infinite lives. It was not a particularly difficult decision."

"We're tools, you and I. Were supposed to be used, enjoyed and then thrown away! You aren't even a gun anymore. You're a coward," said Pharma.

"So you would rather die than be immortal?"

"There is no question about that. My death would prove the potency of drugs. You have to live your life to the fullest. Without the possibility of overdose, drug abuse is just use. Addicts wouldn't be respected for their bravery and neither would soldiers. We'd all be seen as worthless joy junkies."

"I guess we'll never see eye-to-eye. Probably better, honestly," said Karson, revving up his Gatling guns.

"Selling your soul to the Devil is a total cheap shot. You always talk about honor, but now you've abandoned it. What's the point of living, if you aren't yourself anymore?" asked Pharma, walking forward as he was pelted by bullets.

"You've got it all wrong. I'm free from restraints now. I don't need to avoid your weak point. I'm already a lost soul, so there's no point worrying about sinning." Karson's head fired off, heading straight for the drug lord's chest.

Pharma inhaled a full breath of smoke. He then snatched the missile head from the air. "What do you say we finish our tie, once and for all?"

"There was never a tie! You died every time we fought!" Karson's Uzi feet fired rapidly as his head pushed closer to the addict's chest.

Pharma held the head back with one hand and created a smoke screen with his exhale. "That's just it, Karson. Dying isn't losing. If nicotine tar clogged up my lungs so I couldn't breathe, if I got the shakes so bad my capsule popped, or if I accidently injected rat poison into my veins instead of morphine, well then that's a victory for drugs and it's a victory to me." He flung the head into two of the demons, blowing them to bits.

"Sorry soldiers, guess I'm not a very good commander," said Karson, saluting his fallen warriors.

Pharma lit his cigar thumb and then chewed it off. "Overdosing is the only way to leave this miserable world properly. By denying death you've denied both guns and drugs!" He charged toward his fallen rival.

"Cadets, burn him to cinders," said Karson.

The demons activated the flamethrowers on their arms. They then fell back, separated from their feet.

"BoneSaw is here, isn't he? You must have been hiding him under the smoke," said Karson, pelting the ground in search of the little robot.

Pharma plunged a sword into one of the demons, searing a hole through its chest. The flames spewed by the demon crawled up his arms and onto the tip of the blade. "I practiced my swordsman skills in anticipation of our rematch. Nicky and I are one now." The drug lord rushed at the coward and lashed the cigarette sword back and forth.

Karson arm's fell off as he leaped back.

Pharma put Nicky's handle to his lips and puffed smoke in his ex-rival's face.

A cannon came out of Karson's stomach. It fired, launching a cannonball into the doped-up bloke's chest.

Pharma was sent skyrocketing back from the force of the iron ball.

"You weren't even made for combat. Devlin created you so he would have a drinking buddy," said Karson before popping a hole in the loon's head with a shoulder revolver.

"And he made you so he would have a friend. So he wouldn't be alone. He gave you life. I always stood by his side. You betrayed him again and again!"

"I did what anyone would do!" Karson shot his head forward.

Pharma injected himself with an adrenaline needle and was then hit by the explosive head. His tensed up body bolstered him from the blast. Another cannon ball careened into his leg.

"You'll be dead and I'll live on! What meaning is there in living virtuously if it only leads to death?" asked Karson.

Pharma fell to his knees. He lifted himself off the ground with Nicky and broke into a sprint. He tumbled to the ground to dodge an incoming cannonball. "I will show you Nicky's true power!" The drug lord poked holes in his stomach, and alcohol poured out.

His body was set aflame and he tossed Nicky in the air.

Karson's new Gatling-gun arms fired at Pharma, but the drugee just stood smiling as he was torn to shreds.

Karson looked down to see that they were in a large puddle of alcohol.

"Let's end it as a tie," said Pharma with a smile.

Nicky hit the ground and they both exploded.

A few seconds later, BoneSaw popped out, its saw ready. The robot looked around the burnt battlefield. It picked up the two bracelets, left over from the aftermath, before entering the portal.

Exp 8, Kawai and Atatasuki arrived in a forest of spiked trees.

"Ooh, it's kind of romantic," said Kawai, nuzzling up to her beloved brother.

"Stay focused. I don't see the enemy," said Exp 8, watching each step he took.

The branches came off the trees and fell to the ground. They stood up, each one a demon with thick thorns throughout its body.

Exp 8 shot multiple orbs that floated in the air. "Keep moving!" He and his siblings ran through the forest, dodging the demons at each turn.

*Boom!*

Atatasuki pushed his sister out of the way of the blast. He slammed against the ground before standing up. "What were you thinking?!" he yelled, punching his brother in the face.

"How the hell was I supposed to know there was a mine there?" asked Exp 8.

"Your brashness almost got Kawai killed, again!" yelled Atatasuki, lunging at their foolhardy leader.

"Get off my brother!" screamed Kawai as she tugged Atatasuki off.

"I'm your brother too!" he yelled, his head steaming.

"We don't know where their boss is," said Exp 8, firing orbs at the approaching demons.

"And what? You want to take her down!" yelled Atatasuki, kicking Exp 8.

Kawai slammed him down with her tail. "What is going on with you!?"

"Seven Deadly Sisters, right? Each one representing a sin. Of course, wrath is all that remains. Looks like Atatasuki got affected somehow. Kawai, drain his energy. If he overheats, we won't be able to cool him down in this place," said Exp 8.

"You always think you've got it all figured out! Well, I can think too. This time, I'm doing this my way!" yelled Atatasuki, rushing off.

"Not good. They keep coming! And if I move, I could run into another mine. Kawai, I'm trusting you to go after him, okay?" asked Exp 8, using turret-fire to hold back the spiked demons.

"I won't fail you," said Kawai with a salute as she jetted off.

"Just leave me alone! You don't love me!" yelled Atatasuki before his little sister slammed into him.

"I'm trying to save your life, baka!" yelled Kawai, lighting up as she sapped his energy.

"Get off! I don't want your pity!" He ripped Kawai off and threw her aside.

The cutesy prototype screamed as she crashed into a spiked tree. "Moron!" Kawai cringed as she pulled her arm out of the spike. "Fine then! I'll put you into sleep mode myself!" She knocked the demons aside with her tail as she rushed toward her troublesome sibling.

"Just let me die! You hate me, right! Just leave me alone!" yelled Atatasuki.

Kawai slammed her tail into a demon that dropped down to attack Atatasuki. "I don't hate you! But right now, you're really pissing me off!" She spun in place before slamming her tail into him.

Droplets of blood fell from her arm onto the steamy prototype's face.

"Sis…I'm sorry. I hurt you. It's my fault," said Atatasuki, breaking down into tears.

"Get up!" Kawai pulled him back to his feet. She abruptly embraced him. "I have to look after you because you're so incompetent. It's a pain having a brother like you," she said, grinding her teeth.

"Stop. You're burning yourself," said Atatasuki.

"You're my responsibility. And we gotta look out for each other. Just promise to chill a bit, okay?" asked Kawai, pulling away.

Her arms and legs had second degree burns.

"You shouldn't have—"

"Shut it! Maybe all I need is a new look to get Brother's attention," said Kawai, flaunting her burn marks.

Atatasuki burst into passionate tears.

"Let's head back to Brother. Don't get heated up. I can handle these…" Kawai slammed her tail into a demon, knocking him down, "things."

Atatasuki looked at the spikes now piercing her tail. "I understand. I'll stay calm," he said, wiping away his tears.

"Good. Let's get moving. Get on my back. I'll have to carry you."

"Are you sure I'm not too heavy?"

Kawai lifted him up with her tail. "Nope. Not too much of a burden after all," she said with a strained smile. She activated her jets and flew back to her beloved brother.

"You found him!" Exp 8 rushed up to his siblings.

"Wait, don't!"

*Boom!*

Exp 8 was shot into the air as wretched screams erupted from below. He fired out a wall of orbs to shield himself from potential hidden enemies.

"Bad move! ***ANGER EXPLOSION!***"

The orbs exploded, sending their creator skidding across the floor.

A demon jumped on top of the rebel leader, slashing at him furiously with her nails.

Exp 8 kicked her off and got back on his feet.

"What was that? I didn't even see what hit us," said Atatasuki.

"Maybe you should let me handle this. I can fly so I won't be running into mines," said Kawai, setting Atatasuki down.

Exp 8's shoulder turrets fired rapidly at the figure as it shifted through the trees.

The demon jumped out. "My name is Regna. Pleased to kill you."

The last of the Seven Deadly Sisters was slender and had rough red skin with veins visibly pulsating magma inside. Two crimson clear horns protruded from the top of her crown. Her long, messy hair was a mix of red and orange. The demon goddess' eyes pulsed with rage and shifted from a lighter shade of red to a darker one. Clear spikes with flames boiling within covered her segmented body. Her feet had talons instead of toes, and spikes came out from her breasts in place of nipples. When the sin of anger opened her mouth once more, her forehead corrugated and her shark-like teeth quaked with rage.

"Just like I said. Wrath," said Exp 8.

"No. It's Anger! I'm Regna! Aren't you going to introduce yourself!" she yelled, boiling with rage and seething with disdain.

"I have nothing to say to you. I may detest Devlin, but anyone who stands by the side of the one who ruined his life is my enemy. I will assist him in ending Etah's reign and I will take you down if you stand in my path."

"Ugh! Shut up and fight!" yelled Regna, digging her finger into her temple.

"You shut up! He hardly said anything!" yelled Kawai.

"Don't let her fluster you. Her explosions have emotional properties. We need to stay focused. All of us need to make it out alive," said Exp 8.

"She used me to hurt Kawai!" yelled Atatasuki, his fists clenched.

"That's right! I used you! Come on! Rush in and punch me! Release your rage!" she yelled.

"Ignore her," said Kawai.

"Wait, you sent Kawai after me, but you have jets too," said Atatasuki.

"Yeah, well, I uh…I knew she could handle it. I'd probably just make things worse," said Exp 8.

"I'm still waiting for you to tell me your names!" seethed Regna, stabbing her foot into the ground repeatedly and savoring its screams.

"I'm Atatasuki," he said with a wave.

"Stop talking! Fight me!" yelled Regna.

"Why does she have to shout?" asked Atatasuki.

"Your existence enrages me!"

"I'll keep her occupied," said Exp 8.

"*SPONTANEOUS COMBUSTION!*"

The turret shots exploded before they even hit her, blasting Exp 8's shoulder turret open.

Kawai slammed her tail against the attacker, knocking off her arm.

Regna rammed into Atatasuki and then rushed at the leader. "Die already!"

Exp 8 waited for her to get in range and punched her.

The deadly sin bounced off the ground back onto her feet. "You can't spell anger without rage! **SHORT FUSE!**" She ripped off one of her hands and tossed it at the leader.

The nails pierced into his arm and the hand blinked red. The hand then exploded, sending Exp 8 off his feet.

Regna kicked the Freedom Forcers' leader while he flew through the air. Her foot became stuck in his chest. It then exploded, sending him skidding across the ground violently. The Sin of Anger followed him until he finally regained his balance, dodging the small one's tail swipes in the process.

Exp 8 stood up and signaled his teammates to stay put. "While I was skidding across the ground, I was firing my orbs. And you ran right through my path without even noticing them."

Regna looked at herself to see orbs clinging to her body like dew drops.

"*ORB IGNITION.*" Exp 8 flicked an orb. It exploded, triggering all the other orbs to burst along with it.

"So amazing! And you even made a cool name for your special move this time," said Kawai, cuddling her brother's arms.

"Regna, you were blinded by your own pointless anger and fed the flames of your demise," said Exp 8, turning away.

"What demise? I'm very much alive! I'm still kicking and screaming! **ANGER EXFOLIATION**." Regna's red aura erupted out from her palms.

The energy drilled into Exp 8 and Atatasuki.

Kawai swerved out of the way of the third beam and hid behind a spiky tree.

"They're going to tear each other to pieces," said Regna, dispelling her aura.

The crimson energy burst out from Atatasuki and Exp 8, sending them into an instant frenzy.

The cybernetic brothers pummeled each other ruthlessly, too enraged to even acknowledge their own pain.

"Stop! What do want? Whatever it is, I'll do it! Just don't kill them!" yelled Kawai.

"Shut up! I'm trying to watch," said Regna with a twitch.

Atatasuki's slammed his fist into the adversary, sending it sliding back.

Exp 8's working turret popped out and fired at the enemy.

"Stop fighting!" yelled Kawai, rushing in the middle.

The bullets pelted her from the front.

Atatasuki yanked her out of the air, rushed through the bullet-fire and then bludgeoned the larger enemy with her body.

Exp 8's tail gripped the small figure's neck, yanked her out of the enemy's grip and then used her to knock the enemy's arm aside.

"Please stop!" wailed Kawai.

"Ooh! Let me join in!" Regna rushed on all fours into the fight. She sliced Exp 8 and then stole the small one from his grasp. "I'm going to rip you to pieces!" she seethed, digging her nails into Kawai's arms.

Atatasuki grabbed Regna's head, flipped her over and slammed her to the ground.

Exp 8 fired a massive orb and then sent it flying with a punch.

Atatasuki used Regna as a shield and then slid out of the orb's momentum.

Exp 8 zoomed up to him with both fists.

Atatasuki grabbed both fists and assaulted the enemy with his tail.

Exp 8's tail fought back, wrapping around the attacker's tail and crushing it.

"Stop!" wailed Kawai, putting herself in the middle of her brothers.

"*Energy Drain*" With a hand on each of their chests, she sucked up the red energy.

Exp 8 fired orbs at the incoming explosives and embraced Kawai tightly. She squirmed around in his embrace, hissing and clawing him.

Exp 8's tail wrapped around her tail before being smacked down.

"Stay with me. We'll make it through this," he said, keeping her in his grip as he was bludgeoned.

Atatasuki punched one of Regna's projectile explosives. He was knocked off his feet and crashed into a tree.

"You can't dispel the anger! Until the energy is used up, you are its slave!" yelled Regna, tearing off chunks of her own flesh and tossing them at the enemy commander.

Kawai's tail slammed the explosives back into Regna.

Atatasuki kicked off the tree and grabbed the twisted sadist. He pinned her legs and arms. "You made me hurt my sister!" he yelled, slamming his head against hers.

"Calm down! I'm okay now. Any more exertion and you may die," said Kawai.

"Too late!" Regna's whole body blinked. "You're all going down now!"

"Get out of here now!" yelled Atatasuki.

Exp 8 froze up. His eyes went hollow.

Kawai zoomed up and tore her helpless brother free of the demon goddess. Her tail pummeled Regna vigorously. She spun in place three times before upper-cutting the dark goddess.

"Now!" yelled Kawai.

Exp 8 jetted under Regna. One orb after the next was shot into her, sending her higher and higher as he pursued her into the sky.

"Die!" Regna's arms shot out into the leader and burst along with her body.

Kawai caught her big brother with her tail and then fell into Atatasuki's arms. "Are you okay?"

"Been through worse. Hugh. Great teamwork everyone," said Exp 8, back on his feet and patting his sister's head.

"Yeah, we make an incredible team," said Kawai, pulling her siblings into an embrace.

"We're all still standing. We beat a goddess…together," said Exp 8.

Kawai pooled her energy into her big brother. "You'll need to be at maximum power to take down Etah."

"Yeah, give me that energy shot once it's really time to take him down," said Exp 8, patting her head.

"Will do. I've still got plenty more to give," said Kawai with a salute.

"You're badly burnt. Though I suppose that's just a sign of your sisterly love," said Exp 8, his mouthpiece widening as he smiled.

"I'm sorry. Feeling what Devlin went through made me so angry. And to think she would exploit that not once but twice. Regna is truly wicked," said Atatasuki.

"It's not your fault at all. I lost control too," said Exp 8.

"It was hard for all of us, but not everything that happened to Devlin was bad. I was kind of surprised he remembered his crush on me after all he went through. I knew he liked me, but I didn't know he was totally smitten with this kitten, heehee! Devlin is quite the romantic; seems nothing will ever change that. I wonder if he still likes me," said Kawai with a light blush.

"He's not all bad and yeah, he's been through a hell of a lot. Now, we bring the fight to Etah," said Exp 8, walking hand in hand with his siblings into the portal.

Devlin, Anthrax and Demonica entered a barren steamy wasteland.

"Devlin, let me ex—" said Demonica before she was interrupted by a wire through her forehead.

"Don't ever speak to me again," said Devlin softly. He slammed the wire down, and the detestable woman along with it.

Demonica's face was slammed against the floor continuously. She lifted her head, showing that her forehead was bleeding profusely.

"You forgot this," said Devlin, smashing the traitor's neck in with the bracelet she had left behind.

"Don't kill her," said Anthrax with trembling legs.

"Oh I won't." Devlin's wires pierced into Demonica's feet and then drilled up and out of her legs. He turned his head toward his tormentor. "I want you to suffer," he said with a soft but deadly tone.

Demonica's hand reached out for him. "I still lo—"

Multiple wires pierced into Demonica, making holes throughout her face. The wires then receded, brining her to her beloved.

"I can't stomach your existence anymore." Devlin's arms dispersed into hundreds of wires.

The wires tore the treacherous goddess to pieces until all that remained of her was a red puddle of blood.

"Let's go kill Etah."

Devlin's wire dragged Anthrax with him into the portal they came from.

Etah looked into Devlin's eyes upon his arrival. "I can feel your hate! But this isn't over yet! I may yet have one more ally. Pesi, is it true you love suffering?"

"Yes, I will kill every last vile (Switch) strand of evil in the world so bunnies can breed freely and continuously." (Switch) "You incompetent degenerate imbecile, if it's the last thing I do (switch) I shall save the kitties and (switch) crush them all (switch) with my extra warm hugs. (Switch) Enough. Stop twisting my words. I won't join Etah. But I will take his throne." Pesi lunged at the red hot angry war god of flaming rage.

Etah grabbed the winged mortal and flung him aside. "Yvne, finish them off!" bellowed the tyrant god.

"If you try, you'll become envious of all the limbs everyone else has," said Devlin with a dark glare.

"There are...so many enemies. I don't stand a chance," said Yvne with fear in her eyes.

Wires coiled around Yvne's neck and tore off her head. "Your reign is over," said Devlin as the goddess' blood sprayed on the God of Hate.

# Chapter 87: Etah

Etah created a Sel portal and walked through before the wires made contact.

The portal vanished once he entered.

"Fight me!" yelled Devlin, his wires swinging every which way.

"Stop!" yelled Anthrax, shielding himself from the wires.

Devlin's wires seeped back into his skin. "Are you alright?" he asked, crouching down to his son.

"Yeah, I'm okay. Some scratches, that's all. I know it's hard, but you have to calm down. Etah feeds off hatred. If you're going to kill him, you'll need a clear head."

Devlin sat next to his son. "The others haven't arrived yet. What if they're dead?" he asked, his arms trembling.

"They're used to battle. I'm sure most of them will be fine."

"Do you think it will ever end? Do you think our people will ever be free to live without battle?"

"We're organic weapons. If we didn't have a battlefield, we'd be out on the streets fighting for a better future. I think it's good that we fight. Can't say I like fighting, but it keeps the others focused. It keeps them strong."

"How can we ever break free of the destinies preset by our creators? Angels and demons alike want to use us for their own purposes. With Etah dead, will our people finally gain independence?"

"I don't know. I'm just a doctor. We only solve short term problems. We cure people, not eradicate disease. You're the inventor. I'm sure you'll create a path toward a brighter future for us all," said Anthrax with a hopeful smile.

Kaity came out of a portal with Nina leaned against her.

"Kaity, are you injured?" asked Devlin, rushing to her side.

"Not a scratch. They only targeted Nina. Her legs are pretty shot up," said Kaity.

"Lie her down. I'll have her on her feet in no time," said Anthrax, slipping his gloves on.

Kaity set Nina on the ground and the doctor got to work.

"I don't know what the truth is. Demonica's story could have been created to confuse me. Either way, I promise you: I won't kill Kanasta again. I won't hurt you a second time," said Devlin.

"I can't imagine living with vengeance for such a long time. When I thought Ada killed Sefiwah, my mind went blank. I felt I had to kill her just to stay sane. To live all those years with all that anger and all that pain—I don't know how you bared it," said Kaity with a sniffle.

Devlin embraced her. "You truly understand me."

Occupy and Riufen arrived, followed by D.S. and Violet.

"You beat Bob?" asked Deceivant, joining the group along with Ada, Matteria, Napkin and Exp 11.

Riufen nodded.

"We didn't have much trouble with the whip lady," said D.S.

Kanasta and Crystal arrived.

"Papa!" cheered Kaity, leaping into his protective embrace.

"Good to see you too," said Kanasta, hoisting his protégé onto his shoulders.

BoneSaw joined up with the group, searching the area for the primary target.

"He's not here. Save your energy," said Devlin.

NoOne popped out from behind his creator. "Ego is dead. I barely escaped Yvne's wrath myself."

"I didn't have too much trouble with her," said Devlin, tossing her head to his first creation.

The cyber siblings exited from the portal.

"Where's Etah?" asked Exp 8 with an orb ready to fire.

"He fled as soon as he saw me," said Devlin with a shrug.

"Must be waiting for all of us to gather," said Exp 8.

Kanasta lifted BoneSaw off the ground. "Then we're all that remains of the Viper Squad."

"I don't want you to fight Etah," said Kaity, grabbing onto her papa's arm.

"I wasn't there when Devlin needed me most. I was framed, but regardless, I failed my brother. I won't fail him again," said Kanasta.

"Ego's dead? And where's Pharma? Wasn't he with you?" asked Exp 8 to the boxy robot.

BoneSaw shifted his weight left to right.

"He died. We should have a tribute to both him and Ego," said Exp 8.

"There's no time," said Nina, pointing up.

A cube the size of a basketball emerged from the dark sky and floated above the Freedom Forcers.

Etah's visage was projected into the ashy sky. The Deva's molten gaze pierced through the foggy skies and glared down at the Freedom Forcers.

"All shall bear witness to my triumph!" Etah's vocal eruption blotted out the tormented screams throughout the land. Soldiers from the Forces of Hate and the Hero's Militia lowered their weapons and gazed up at the spectacle.

"It's just him in there," said Kaity, peeking through her scope.

"Only one warrior can enter. Once they are dead, another may challenge me. Choose wisely." A Sel portal appeared.

"Great, now we can all charge in at once," said Atatasuki.

"I'll be back as soon as I can with more Absence gods. If you get him out of that arena, we can likely take him down," said Occupy.

Crystal created an Absence portal. "I'll go with you. They already agreed to help. I'll make sure they don't back out again."

The two Absence guards entered the portal before it vanished.

"Should I go first?" asked Exp 8, twirling his wrists.

"We don't know what he's capable of yet. I'll test his strength," said Kanasta, walking toward the portal.

Kaity leaped off his shoulders and into the portal. "Sorry," she said before vanishing.

The assassin prodigy arrived inside the giant cube.

The cube had six sides. The area around Etah's slab of land was a quicksand floor.

The young assassin had to keep consistent movement or else she would be pulled below.

"I didn't expect you to enter first," said Etah.

Kaity ran circles around the God of Hate. "If I kill you now, I won't have to lose Papa," she said, firing her pistol as she ran on all fours.

The bullets burned inside the Deva's fiery aura.

"You can't expect me to be harmed by earthly constructs." The dark god lifted his foot off the ground.

Kaity broke her pattern and rushed at the target. "Of course not! Hope this works! *ETAH, LOVE, GROUND!*"

The God of Hate plummeted face first to the floor. "All of Sel is mine to command! **HATRED EXPULSION!**"

The god's fiery aura poured into the ground. The quicksand in the arena now lifted him up as it consciously dragged the assassin below.

Kaity tore through the muck with her plasma claws, but it did nothing to stop her descent.

A wave collapsed on the girl, burying her beneath it.

"You have a few minutes to decide who will die next," said Etah with a toothy grin.

Devlin's wires slammed against the cube, but were unable to pierce through.

"Don't waste the effort. This arena is made from my own deep-seated hatred of rebels. It can't be accessed without my approval. Look to the skies to see how your beloved is faring," said Etah, pointing up.

The face of Etah faded out into a clear image of Kaity, gasping for air under the quicksand.

Kanasta put his hand on his brother's shoulder. "She's been in worse situations. She'll pull through."

"Love always triumphs over hate, right?" asked D.S.

"Of course it does," said Ada, putting her arm around her little boy.

Kaity pulled herself toward the stagnant sand below the deity. She climbed all the way up to him, bringing the wrath of the pursuing sand upon him. She jumped up and dug her plasma claws into the god's head.

"Clever, but I've had enough of you." Etah grabbed the child's arm and flung her into a portal above.

Kaity zoomed out of the portal, past Devlin's wires and into Kanasta's arms.

"Who wishes to fight the Lord of Hatred next?" The Deva's scorching eyes scanned the Freedom Forcers from the pitch-black skies.

"I'll go," said Atatasuki.

"Don't you dare." Kawai blocked his path with her tail.

"We can't risk losing our leader. You can live without me, but you can't live without him," said Atatasuki, patting her head.

Kawai broke into tears. "I don't want to live without either of you."

She was suddenly pulled from behind.

Kawai looked up to see a cracked molten smile.

"You can wipe your tears away. You'll be dead before either of your siblings. You won't have to suffer their loss," said Etah, bringing her closer to his face.

Kawai squirmed around in his grip. She bit and clawed his arm ferociously.

"Don't you dare!" yelled Exp 8 from below.

"I won't run! I'll take you down!" yelled Kawai, her whole body trembling. She rammed into the deity's stomach with all her strength.

"Is that all?" asked Etah.

Kawai held her extra burnt arm. "Brother, I'm scared," she said with tears in her eyes.

Etah let go of her tail and clenched her neck between two fingers. "I wonder if you can escape before your throat caves in."

Kawai wrapped her arms, legs, and tail around the god's massive hand, cringing as his heated skin pressed against her second degree burns. "*Complete Drain!*" Her entire body lit up as she sapped away his energy.

"Yes, show me that fighting spirit." Etah slammed her against his knee.

"I won't let go!"

The God of Hate pulled back his fist when the nuisance released a laser net that covered his arm. "I could crush you at any moment." He pressed her below the quicksand and released his grip. "I am a god." The Deva tore off the net and put it under the sand. He lifted up the laser net with her now trapped inside.

"I'll allow you to say a quick farewell," said Etah, turning the net to face the Freedom Forcers below.

"Brother, I love you more than anything. I've enjoyed every moment we've shared. Take care of Atatasuki. He'll fall to pieces on his own," said Kawai in tears.

"Etah, take my life instead. I won't struggle, I promise!" yelled Exp 8, about to tear open his chest.

"In due time." Etah smashed Kawai in between his fists. His aura then focused into his hands. When his fists parted, only ashes remained.

"Now to obtain a new…"

Atatasuki was punching Etah as soon as he opened his fist.

Etah stood there, taking the blows head on while smiling.

"I didn't make this portal. How curious," said Etah, looking down at his attacker.

Atatasuki's whole body became super heated and his onslaught grew more and more vicious.

"Yes, that's what I want."

Etah's arm absorbed the living weapon's red hot fury. The hateful god was now pulsating with power.

Etah grabbed the defect's arm and ripped it off. "You run on passion, but your body can't support it. Your design is too weak. I shall make you a proper vessel." He shoved his hand through Atatasuki's chest and pulled out his capsule.

"Avenge our little—" said Atatasuki before his capsule was smashed to bits.

His body lost all energy.

"Now unify with me." Etah summoned up a spiked mace and the tattoo at the center of his chest stopped glowing.

The mace split in two, revealing it had rows of jagged teeth and a central beak. The spherical souls of the prototype Exps were consumed by the beak in a single bite.

428

Atatasuki's body broke down into dust, leaving his bracelet behind as a sole memento.

Etah scattered the remains with a steamy exhale.

Two weapons materialized in Etah's hands: a rusty copper sword with a heated tip and a pink whip with golden razor blades around it.

"Hmm, the Searing Sword and the…Wailing Whip. Who would like to join my collection next?" asked Etah.

Exp 8 rushed to the portal but was held back by wires.

"If you confront him like that, he'll only grow stronger," said Devlin.

"Then let me go. I won't give him any hate…but sadness is okay, right?" asked Violet with watery eyes.

Devlin embraced her. "Don't die."

"You shouldn't worry about that. You gave me life. If I can die in service to you, then I die fulfilled," said Violet, combing her god's hair with her light-blue fingertips.

Devlin clenched her tighter. "Don't die! I forbid it!"

"I will return. Promise." Violet slipped out of his embrace. The reverent devotee bent down and gave her creator's foot a kiss. She rose up and entered the portal.

"You shouldn't keep me waiting," said Etah with a molten grin.

Violet rushed at him.

Etah planted his feet in the ground and held his arms out, waiting for the proper moment to strike.

The devotee's astral self suddenly split from her body. The sentient energy dived under his legs and popped up behind him, grabbing hold of his arms.

Violet then slammed into the Asura king, searing her skin in the process.

Etah tumbled backward into the quicksand.

Violet fired astral bullets at the Deva's hands, keeping him from pulling himself back onto land.

The astral body was pulled back into Violet before being projected once more.

The energy body leaped off the ground, spun in the air and drilled the Asura king under the quicksand.

Violet collapsed to her knees, panting heavily.

Etah's aura-laden fingers bore into the astral being's legs, stopping the momentum. He slammed his head into the entity repeatedly.

The astral body punched him vigorously as it was assaulted.

Etah tore his fingers out of the legs and gripped the hands.

Feeling that her energy was locked in a power-struggle, Violet dove in.

Unable to pull the energy in, she combined with her astral self.

The sudden power combination caught Etah off guard. His hands were pushed to the side.

Violet pulled her legs back and then slammed them into the god.

Etah's fingers lost their grip. He rammed against the bottom of the arena.

His crimson aura gathered at his legs before propelling him up like a rocket. He slammed into Violet before bursting out of the quicksand. By the time they hit the ground, his knees had pinned her arms and his fingers were around her neck. "Time for another soul! **MISERY MACE**!"

The spiked mace appeared in Etah's free hand and plunged into the spiritual warrior.

"What!" Etah thrust the weapon in repeatedly, having it gnaw at the fallen warrior's soul.

"I made a promise to Devlin," said Violet with a bloodied smile.

Energy shot out from her chest like a spike.

The mace reclined in agony and then vanished.

"Such power! Your spirit must always be yearning! Never stop desiring! Never succumb to content!" Etah lifted her by the throat, created a portal and then tossed her in.

Violet fell into a nest of metal, never touching the ground.

"You should rest," said Devlin, his hands gently wiping the blood off her lip as his eyes quaked with rage.

"I only wish I could have been of more use to you," said Violet, placing her hand on her creator's.

"You've done plenty," said Devlin, kissing her forehead.

Anthrax flung his bracelet to Matteria. "If we don't finish this quick, she is going to die." He walked into the portal, already transitioning into his disease form. The monstrosity fired tumors from his arms as soon as he arrived.

The fleshy projectiles melted before they could meld with Etah's skin.

Etah swiped his fists at the abomination, letting his aura make contact, but never his flesh. "Another flawed design. I wonder what sort of weapon you'll make. You have so much untapped potential, incessantly held back by your unconscious desire to spread disease. Only I can free you from this burden." His energy shot out from his arm and bore into the mutated freak.

Amthraahksh lunged forward, his festering chest now pressed to the god's fist.

Etah punched a hole through the wretch's stomach.

Amthraahksh's stomach reassembled with Etah's arm inside. He put his hands on the deity's face. "**Uhrteamait Teasheash Heaksh**!" The abomination roared, channeling all his sickness into the God of Hate.

The sickness pooled into the god's mouth. "I can feel the full wrath of your disease. An entire colony of spores, bacteria and viruses all united to bring me down. Glorious! Let's see if I can stomach their collective hatred!" He gripped the leper's shoulders, allowing the disease to burrow into his pores.

It wasn't long before all the disease entered Etah and his hands were on the shoulders of a young boy.

"How aren't you dying?" asked Anthrax, fear twinkling in his light blue eyes.

"Hmhmhmhmheheheheh. Their aggression sustains me!" Etah, now cloaked in a dark red aura, raised his hand and with one quick move, sliced off the child's head.

Blood shot out from the neck hole like a fountain.

Etah punched Anthrax's chest, bursting the cavity wide open.

The bloody remains seeped into the quicksand.

"Any other immortals want to die?" asked Etah with a smug grin as his mace feasted on the boy's soul.

A white and moldy arrow with a plus-shaped arrowhead appeared in his grasp. "Yes, of course, the Appalling Arrow."

Matteria dropped Anthrax's bracelet and rushed into the portal before anyone could enter.

"Do you have a death wish?" asked Etah, cracking his neck.

"Whatever you did to him…I want it too," said Matteria with a tearful smile.

"Such radiance I sense from you," said Etah, his eyes alight.

"Please, keep our souls close," said Matteria, stepping toward the god.

"Your courage can't be broken, but your soul can be repurposed." Etah stabbed one finger into the Exp's chest and pulled out his capsule.

"I'm sorry Devlin. I…I can't leave him all alone," said Matteria with tearful eyes.

The capsule was smashed between the deity's massive fingers.

Matteria's body became vapor and dispersed in the air. The diva's bracelet fell to the ground.

As soon as his soul appeared it was consumed by the mace.

A rainbow-colored frilly bow with a pink string appeared in the warrior god's hand.

"Hmm, the Bashful Bow, yes."

"Let me go! He'll kill us all!" yelled Exp 8.

"I'm holding myself back too," said Devlin, his wires deeply rooted in the ground.

NoOne looked at the pitiful state of his allies. "We're heroes! This isn't supposed to happen."

"We should give up before we lose anyone else," said Ada, white digits running down her cheeks.

"I understand now. This is my moment." NoOne looked at the bracelet around his wrist. "I'm the only one who can face him." He went into the portal, his goopy body firm and straight.

"This is unexpected," said Etah.

"I know I'm likely to die, but there's still a chance I'll win." The shadow master fired shadow balls at the main villain.

Etah knocked each one right back at his attacker.

"You may have a thick exterior, but your shadow is thinner than paper," said NoOne as he shaped his arm into a blade.

"What does it matter?" asked Etah.

The shadow master chased the shadow around, stabbing at the ground.

Holes appeared in the deity's body were his shadow was wounded. Molten lava poured out of the holes.

"You're dangerous!" Etah gripped the Misery Mace in his hand and plunged it into his opponent.

The mace bit down.

NoOne collapsed into black muck and mixed with the sand.

"The...what is this? I didn't get a weapon!" yelled Etah.

Riufen snatched the bracelet before it was buried within the sand. "I will end you," he said with a steady hand gripping his spine.

"Hmm, no hatred at all. I don't see why I should waste my time fighting you," said Etah.

"If you are truly an honorable warrior, you will fight me without gimmicks," said Riufen, gesturing to the quicksand.

"Very well." Etah's aura shot out and heated the sand until it became glass. "Satisfied?"

Riufen's ribs shot out, splitting his stomach open. They extended further, piercing into the rival warlord.

"Samurai's do not get fearful or angry in battle. We remain stoic as we cut down our enemies." Riufen pulled out his small intestine and lassoed it onto the warlord's neck. He wrapped the intestine around his arm, bringing the warrior closer and thus pushing his ribs in deeper.

"Take out a weapon or I will kill you where you stand," said Riufen.

"But that would be dishonorable. Attacking an unarmed opponent. Hmm, doesn't sound like the way of Bushido to me," said Etah, gripping the ribs and slowly cracking them.

Riufen tossed his spine into the warlord's chest.

"Hypocrite!" yelled Etah, grinding the spine to powder between his hands.

Riufen broke free of his ribs, jumped onto them and rushed at the god.

"Immortal you may be, but I can still grind your bones to dust." Etah grabbed the ribs impaled in his body and crushed them.

Riufen leaped off fragments of shattered ribs toward the warrior deity.

Etah punched the swordsman with both hands. The force was so great, that in an instant, the Exp's chest was reduced to dust.

Etah smashed the samurai's head beneath his foot. "Who is next?"

The bloody pieces reassembled and Riufen was alive, unscathed even.

"That didn't kill you," said Etah with wide eyes.

"Was it supposed to?" asked Riufen with a curious look.

Etah rushed at the samurai with hands ignited by his aura.

Riufen slid out of the way of the warlord's lunge and sliced his side.

"Can such refined skill truly be a product of science?" asked Etah, sharply turning around and firing off his aura.

Riufen strafed to dodge the first blast, jumped out of the way of the second and ducked under the third. Once the barrage was finished, he was directly in front of Etah.

The very tip of the spine was pierced into the Deva's chest.

"Victory is a matter of perseverance," said Riufen, his gaze as still as his blade.

The spine became a blur as it was stabbed into Etah's flesh. It spine melted completely by the fourth jab.

Etah's arm dragged against Riufen's stomach.

The samurai fell back, now split in two halves.

As the dark red aura pooled into the god's open palms, the samurai tore out his own stomach.

"A warrior's entire body is a weapon!" Riufen tossed his stomach just as the warrior god fired.

The energy blast burst on the fleshy projectile.

"I thank you for your sacrifice, my stomach." Riufen fired the bones out of his arms.

The deity's eyes boiled with rage and melted the bones before they could blind him.

The samurai's intestine leapt out from his body and coiled around the god's arm.

"Enough!" Etah slammed his foot down.

His red hot hatred aura erupted from beneath Riufen and obliterated him. Etah pulled the limp intestine off his arm.

Organs grew out from seemingly nowhere around the intestine, followed by muscles and finally skin. The samurai then stood up once more, swiftly unsheathing his blade and entering a fighting stance.

"I killed you twice! Why won't you just die with honor!" yelled Etah.

Riufen's eyes widened. He sheathed his sword and bowed. "I did not mean to dishonor you. You killed me fairly. I concede. This victory is yours." The samurai stood up straight, unsheathed his spine and pointed it at the divine warrior. "But when our paths cross once more, I will emerge the victor." He picked up his bracelets and walked to the portal, ashamed of his self-imposed defeat.

Etah opened his mouth but knew not what to say.

"Good work," said Opti, raising his hand for a high-five.

"Do not show me pity," said Riufen, walking past him.

"Hmm. I wonder if they harbor one or two souls. Opti, come and face hate itself!" yelled Etah, beating his chest.

"Don't. You'll die," said Ada.

"True, without an artifact, I don't stand a chance against him. Even so, I remember my artifact. I remember its power. I hope that power responds to my will," said Opti before entering the portal.

"Bravery or insolence. Hmm, surely the latter," said Etah.

"I only live because of Devlin. I will freely lay down my life for his sake," said Opti.

"Then come at me!" yelled Etah.

Opti's loving eyes filled with un-distilled rage as his other half took over. Pesi flew up to the being of hatred and raised his fist.

Opti opened his fist and handed Etah a flower. "May there be eternal peace."

Etah shoved his hand in the hippie's chest and tore out his capsule. He channeled his hatred into an orb and shoved it inside. He then slammed the capsule back inside its owner's body.

"I will survive!" yelled Opti before he was blown to smithereens.

His smoldering body flew into the portal.

Upon landing, Opti greeted his allies with a blood-soaked smile. "Hey Violet, it's a miracle. My faith protected me," he said weakly.

"Yes it has. Stay strong. I can give you my energy but you need to heal yourself," said Violet, pouring out prana from her palms.

"You've used up enough energy already," said Devlin, gripping his creation's arm.

"I won't watch him die," said Violet, pouring even more energy into her wounded kin.

"Mom. I love you so much!" D.S. embraced Ada with great strength.

"You know I love you," said Ada, kissing his forehead.

D.S. broke the hug and walked to his father. "Dad. I love you," he said, hugging Deceivant.

"We'll make it through this. We have the Ultimate Exp with us," said Deceivant, patting his creation's back.

D.S. hugged his sister as she healed Opti. "You're my best friend and an awesome sister!"

Violet turned to face him with a loving smile. "It's been a blessing to share this life with you."

D.S. let go and stood up proudly.

Ada grabbed his arm.

"Mom. I can do this. I was made to protect you and dad. If I can't beat him, then I'm a loser," said D.S.

"I won't let you," said Ada.

D.S. smiled. He pushed her off him and into his dad's embrace.

"You're all my friends!" he cheered as he rushed into the portal.

"Such camaraderie. The loyalty of a bodyguard joined with the love of a child. What sort of weapon can I carve out from your soul?" asked Etah with a growing smile.

"My scissors are sick of waiting. They want you dead." D.S. Jumped forward and jabbed his scissors through the bad guy's chest.

Etah grabbed D.S.'s arm. He flipped the warrior over his head and into the protruding tips of his own scissors. The god then grabbed the handles of the scissors and opened them, cutting the living weapon in half. "Challenging me was foolish." He dragged the scissors out of his body, which were only partially melted by his molten blood.

D.S.'s upper half was limping on the floor.

"Cut in two by your own scissors. It must be shameful." Etah slammed the scissors down on the upper body.

The half a body rolled over, making the scissors pierce through his back. "Tehehugh! You fell for it."

"Surely you bluff. You're cut in half," said Etah.

The upper-portion flipped up, revealing that the scissors were not only impaled through his back, but also glued to his arms.

"Now, I control the scissors as easily as I control my own arms."

"Why didn't you do that in the first place?" asked Etah.

"It's all a mind game. Take one for the gang. Get you off-guard. You are sooo predictable." D.S. closed his arms over the bad guy's head.

Etah bit onto the two blades. His body then froze.

"Got him. He's all yours," said NoOne, popping out behind the god.

"You were so busy fighting me, you didn't notice my friend. He was setting up a shadow trap and you totally fell for it!" D.S. opened the scissors, slitting the side of the villain's mouth open.

Etah grunted with rage. His gaze heated up, boiling the deceitful boy's skin.

"Get him!" yelled D.S., pulling back.

NoOne's shadow had a string on each finger, holding the god in place. The shadow master grew an extra arm and sharpened it, giving his shadow an extra limb. "For your crimes against the people you reign over, I sentence you to execution! *HERO'S JUDGMENT!*" NoOne readied his shadow blade to decapitate the god's shadow.

A blast of energy came out from Etah's feet, masking his back and blocking access to his shadow.

NoOne pulled back just before the raging villain came rushing through his own barrier of energy.

In the midst of running, Etah gripped the red hot energy barrier and condensed it into a spear. He tossed the spear into the shady coward.

D.S. leaped on Etah's back and desperately stabbed the muscle man's neck with his scissor arms.

NoOne split apart from the portion of his body with the spear and rushed at the god from two angles.

Etah shaped his energy into swords and swiped at the air, having his shadow block the slashes from the living silhouette.

"Why won't you die?" asked D.S., trying to tear open the bad guy's neck.

"I have come too far to fail now!" Etah flung the aura blades into the two halves of the shadow man and fired energy from his palms, triggering them to burst. "You have disgraced me!" Etah reached behind and grabbed onto D.S.'s arms. "Weak!" Etah crushed the joints and pulled the boy off his back. The Deva rammed the two arm-blades into the coward's lower half. "Enjoy a slow death," said the tyrant before he tossed the two halves into the teleporter. Once the boy had been dealt with, his eyes located the other coward. With his heated gaze, he melted the fleeing puddle before it could enter the portal.

Once NoOne's soul popped out, Etah's mace devoured it.

When the ex-gangster landed, he took some glue and rubbed it on his bottom and top half. The two halves stuck together and he stood up in one piece.

"I...I didn't know he could do that," said Etah, shaking his head.

D.S. walked up to the team captain. "I got your brother's bracelet back," he said softly, holding it out.

Exp 8 fastened the bracelet on his left hand. "Looks like it couldn't handle his passion," he said, pressing the heated metal to his forehead.

"NoOne too? I can't take this anymore," said Ada, sobbing in her husband's arms.

"Mother, it's time I go. Etah has been deprived of hatred for the past few battles. Just a bit more and he will fall," said Kanasta.

"No. If my children can risk their lives than so can I." Ada ran into the portal before her husband could stop her.

"This is mockery! I am a warrior. You're the weakest link. You insult all of Sel by challenging me," said Etah, his eyes kindling with rage.

"I am not the weakest; Napkin is, then Deceivant, then me. I'm third," said Ada, shuffling her feet and pushing out her chest.

Etah rushed up to the weakling and shoved his hand through her chest. He kicked her off, holding her capsule in his hand.

Ada was sent flying back into the portal.

"I am tired of wasting time," said Etah as he smashed the capsule to dust.

Ada broke down in her husband's arms.

D.S. looked away.

"I'll kill you!" yelled Deceivant as he ran to the portal.

"You idiot, that's what he wants!" yelled Devlin, his wires zooming toward Deceivant.

Nina kicked the worthless man out of the way. "I am the one who kills him," she said with silent rage. She stepped into the portal. Her eyes went blank and she fell to the floor.

"Strange. This isn't my doing," said Etah, taking a step closer.

Nina stood up. Her eyes were calm and focused.

"I'm really back. I'm finally in control." Nina turned to face the large man. "You're in Devlin's way," she said before unfolding a windmill shuriken and tossing it.

The shuriken zoomed through the god's hands and pierced into his forehead. "You'll need more than that to hurt me," said Etah, walking to the young lady with molten blood dripping down between his eyes.

"Look again," said Nina before jumping through the portal. When she arrived on the other side, her eyes met Devlin's. She then turned her attention back to the arena.

Etah looked up to see explosive tags on each end of the shuriken.

It exploded, sending him skidding back a few feet.

BoneSaw rushed into the portal, flinging six saws at the target.

More explosives activated, pressing the god against the wall.

The saws sliced into his arms.

"You send this puny piece of trash to face me!" Etah kicked himself off the wall despite the continuous blasts knocking him back.

"Kill." BoneSaw layered four saws before sending them at the target's throat.

"Pathetic." Etah knocked the saw aside and snatched the robot from the ground. He ripped the little robot in two.

BoneSaw's two halves pulled back together. It then grinded its saw against the target's chest.

Etah ripped the robot into ten pieces only to have it come back together again. "That's odd."

"I upgraded BoneSaw during my stay in Lum. He won't break so easily," said Kanasta.

Etah tossed the heap of metal into the teleporter. "I'm tired of fighting your lackeys, come and fight me, Hero of Sel."

Kanasta stepped up to the portal. "Brother, allow me to finish this. No payment needed. I feel I owe him for all he's done to you."

The assassin boss' fists clenched till they bled.

A single wire wrapped around Kanasta's hand.

"Stay here. It's my turn to fight him," said Devlin, his fist no longer quaking.

"Hasn't he taken enough from you already!" yelled Kanasta, breaking down into tears.

Devlin walked into the portal and stared into Etah's eyes with cold detachment.

"No! This isn't right. Show me the power of your hate! Consume me in it!" yelled Etah, the muscles in his fingers tightening.

Devlin flipped off Etah.

A wire shot out of his middle finger and connected to the god's chin.

Devlin yanked on the wire and pulled the Deva into the portal.

Etah arrived before all the Freedom Forcers.

The portal vanished.

"Now, the Lord of Hate shall die," said Devlin with a smile.

# Chapter 88: The Hero of Sel

"Ten against one," said Etah, rising from the ground. "No matter. All of Sel will bear witness to my triumph over the hero and his dishonorable rebels."

The sky projected the image of the dark king and the rebels in his path. Standing before the God of Hate were Exp 8, Kaity, Deceivant, Kanasta, BoneSaw, Nina, D.S., Violet, Napkin, Riufen and Devlin. Bleeding profusely on the floor was Exp 11, clearly not up for battle.

"Don't forget Napkin! He's a Freedom Forcer too. There are eleven of us!" cheered Exp 8.

"Make that twelve," said Demonica reappearing from a puddle of blood. "Thanks for the entertainment," she said, blowing the war god a kiss with her sticky fingers.

"You're the one who created that portal," said Etah with wide eyes.

"Devlin, it's true what Etah said. Except for one thing. I do love you. I always have, always will. Before you kill me, let me fight by your side one last time. Please, I know I don't deserve your forgiveness—"

"Shut up. I can't entirely hate you, or even Etah. Without the two of you, I would most likely have never met Kaity. I wouldn't have created any Exps. I would be just another human, passively hoping for a better future. I grew from my isolation, from my hatred. I found out what I was, who I was, and what was worth fighting for." Devlin bowed his head. "For this I thank both of you." He raised his head, his eyes burning with determination. "But only for that, Etah. Now you shall feel the tangible wrath you brought about in my soul."

Twenty wires burst out and shot forth.

The God of Hate grabbed all the wires, stopping them before they could pierce his flesh.

"I am the ruler of this realm! Come, my army! Defend your king!" yelled Etah, his voice reaching his forces.

His demonic army raised their arms and chanted. "Hero! Hero! Hero!" The Hero's Militia saluted and joined the chanting.

"Stay back, fellow freedom fighters! You've fought enough for one day. My forces shall end Etah's reign!" cheered Exp 8, raising his fist.

A group of nearby demons rushed at the injured god.

"I said stay back," said Exp 8, rushing to save them before getting ensnared in Devlin's wires.

"Be more cautious," said Devlin.

"Insolence!" Etah's aura erupted from below and melted away the demons. "Demons are too fickle," he said, brushing off the ash.

"You've lost favor with even your own kind." Devlin raised his hands toward the skies. "Come, my creations. You are all a self-aware portion of my power. You are all a testament to my true strength!"

Nina tossed shurikens lined with explosive tags at the enemy.

The Lord of Hate lifted a chunk off the ground, deflecting the explosive onslaught.

"Stay back, everyone! I'll handle the rest!" Exp 8 jet-boosted around the rock and slammed an orb larger than his fist into the tyrant's back.

Etah's aura pushed away the orb.

"This time I'll make sure to do more than break it!" yelled Exp 8, firing mini-orbs at the Deva's arm.

The orbs were eaten by the fiery aura.

"Your sister wasn't able to give you an energy boost. Face it. Your defeat is imminent." The Deva's aura fired out from his hands.

Exp 8 maneuvered through the shots, all the while expanding the orbs in his grip. He zoomed up to the god, wielding a souped-up orb in each hand.

Etah coated his fists in his red aura before slamming them into the orbs. "You are too weak."

The god's aura slammed Exp 8 into the ground. As he brought his foot down, the hero's tail coiled around his leg.

The leader of the Freedom Forcers used the momentum to move behind the Deva. Energy erupted from his palms into a large orb.

"You've been practicing," said Etah, spinning around and gripping the orb.

"My sister taught me how to fight with my tail." Exp 8 grabbed onto the bracelet on his left hand and fired off the orb. "And my brother is here, fighting alongside me."

Etah's aura ate up the orb.

"Together, as a family, we are taking you down!" He fired orbs and smacked them with his tail into the god, witling away his aura bit by bit.

"You've served your purpose well: accepting your role as hero, splitting the rebel forces, bringing your allies to Sel...all that is left is for you to die!" Etah's aura shot out as a beam.

Exp 8's jets sent him into sudden acceleration. He maneuvered through the sky, dodging the beam. An extra burst of energy sent him behind Etah. The hero charged two orbs to slam into Etah's exposed back.

A burst of energy erupted from the god's back.

The concentrated energy exploded into Exp 8.

The Ultimate Exp was shot back.

"You aren't fast enough! You aren't strong enough!" Etah flung discs of energy at his fabricated hero.

Each time a disc closed in, Exp 8 activated his jets. This allowed him to conserve energy. After forming two massive orbs, he shot one at Etah, the other up into the black skies.

"Not enough!" yelled the god, vertically slicing through the incoming orb. His energy then shot out from his palms and devoured the energy.

Exp 8 used his jets to go up into the foggy skies. "I wasn't just grinding my teeth as you killed my allies! I utilized every second for your demise!"

Exp 8's wrist ring detached from his body and connected to an object beyond the surface of the fog.

"Then come at me, hero!" yelled Etah, planting his feet into the fleshy ground.

An orb the size of Etah's battle arena was pulled out from the fog. "This is the power of our struggle for equality! **FREEDOM'S WILL**."

Both wrist rings connected and Exp 8 sent himself on a crash course toward the God of Hate.

"All the hatred of Sel, I call upon you! **HATRED ABSORBTION**."

The feelings of deep-seated ill-will, held by the not-yet demons of Sel, pooled into the god's body.

Before the orb made contact, Etah's hatred burst out as a furious red aura. The aura battled against the orb's momentum. The sides of it shot out and pierced the orb from multiple angles.

"You can't stop this rebellion! You can't destroy the hope in my soul! I am the Hero of Sel! I will free these living beings from this oppressive system!"

"Hope or despair, let's see which reigns supreme!" Etah slammed his fists together. **HATRED BURST**."

The aura wall shielding Etah's back pulsated with power.

Exp 8's wrist wrings short-circuited. "Not good."

The orb crashed into and enveloped the hero.

Demons and future demons from all around Sel stopped in place, watching the projection from the sky.

**HATRED CONTAINMENT**."

The aura wrapped around the orb and sealed off the explosion from within. It then burned away.

There was not even a shard of metal remaining. In the wrath of the blast, Exp 8 had all but vanished.

"And so the hero falls! Not even a shred of him remains to be enshrined. The rebellion is crushed!" cheered Etah as he got his balance back.

The residents from all regions of Sel were swept in a gravity of despair.

Ferocious surges of hatred poured out from various cracks in the scorched fleshy earth and were then pulled into Etah. "This is it! This is the power I have yearned for!" The god's molten tears burrowed holes in the ground below.

Screams of demons paved a path all the way to Etah.

The Baroness of Blades rushed down and flung throwing knives at the God of Hate.

"He killed the Ultimate Exp," said Deceivant, frozen in fear.

"I suppose that makes you the real Ultimate Exp," said Demonica, massaging Devlin's shoulders.

"Is this really happening?" asked Devlin, his eyes filled with despair.

"Not him too," said Kaity softly.

Napkin ran in the opposite direction before being picked up by the cat-girl.

"He was my friend," cried Opti.

"He was a cool guy," said D.S.

"I will always remember him," said Violet with a shaky smile.

"He was…a great leader, right?" asked Nina, peeking at Devlin.

"Indeed! Exp 8 was a proud warrior and fought bravely in a one-on-one battle to the death. I can only hope to share the same fate," said Riufen.

"Damn it! I made him! All that power! All that potential! Wasted!" yelled Devlin, his finger wires flailing in all directions.

"We should give up before more of us die," said Deceivant, looking up at Kaity with trembling eyes.

"Perhaps he is right," said Kanasta, covering his face.

"We failed!" wailed Opti.

"We can't run away. We have no choice but to fight," said Kaity, holding Napkin to her chest. She walked up to her downed ally and set the kitty in his arms. "Can you hold him?"

"Yeah, but not much else," said Opti, his body still in a state of ruin.

"We owe it to everyone we've lost…to finish this!" exclaimed Kaity, raising her fist in the air.

BoneSaw raised its saws in approval. The remaining Freedom Forcers joined the salute.

The Baroness was rapidly dodging Etah's energy blast, keeping just out of range of his fists. She closed the distance as she dodged a forward jab and dragged a sword up the bottom of the god's arm.

"*IGNITION.*" The Baroness pulled out three swords with her free hand in the blink of an eye, partially shielding her from the sudden burst of energy from

Etah's chest. She leaped up and flung throwing knives at his eyes, but they were melted by his heated gaze.

Before her foot could touch the ground, Etah's aura pressed down on her.

Etah slammed each sword all the way through the demon lord and then lifted her up. "Pathetic." He slammed his head into her, knocking her out. The God of Hate tossed her body aside and then turned his attention over to the Freedom Forcers. "The battle has ended. With your unconditional surrender you will serve under me. Exps shall give Sel an edge in our conquest of Lum."

"We were given a mission. We will complete it." Kanasta rushed at the murderer and slammed both his fists into the target's chest.

Etah took the attack head on, suffering no damage. "You're used to killing mortals. How much longer must you all keep opposing me? How many of your comrades must die before you submit?" He lifted up the assassin boss by his head.

BoneSaw sawed at the target's feet from underground.

The god tossed Kanasta aside. "Another nuisance." Etah's aura dug into the molten earth.

BoneSaw leapt out of the ground as it caved in, his large saw a mere blur.

Etah grabbed the saw as it sliced his hand. Before it came to a complete stop, he tore it off. The Deva shoved the massive saw into the stubborn piece of trash and then tossed it into the sky like a flying disc.

BoneSaw was gone from sight once it reached the black blanket of fog.

Kaity shot sniper bullets into different vital spots on Etah, relentlessly keeping up the pursuit with six extra clips by her side.

The bullets were too swift to be broken down by the fiery aura and pierced into the god's skin.

Etah hardened his body, skidding further back with each bullet.

Violet was already in position behind him. After coating the cross' blades in her own spiritual aura, she stabbed them into the rival god's back.

"*ATONEMENT!*"

The blades bore into his body, and spun around inside.

Etah reached for Violet, extending his range with his hatred aura.

Just as her skin was singed by the heat of his hate, Violet was pulled away by wires.

"Riufen, what are you standing around for? Attack him!" Devlin fired out wires from below, attacking the god from multiple angles at once.

"It is far too dishonorable for me to attack him when the odds are so clearly in our favor. I refuse," said Riufen.

Demonica dive-bombed from above. She flew through the wire assault and shoved her blood-red hand inside the Deva's chest.

Blood spread out and enveloped the Sel god, reaching to his shoulders in mere seconds.

"Your efforts are all wasted." Etah punched the traitor.

The Goddess of Death spontaneously exploded into blood.

"I wonder which weapon I should use," said Etah to himself, inquisitively looking at the puddle of blood collecting nearby. "Yes, that should be more than sufficient. **AGONY AXE**!"

The axe-shaped tattoo on his chest lost its glow as the weapon materialized. It was a meaty axe with bone spurs jutting out from its grip and with a blade made from sharpened bones. The axe was clenched in Etah's powerful grip.

Demonica reassembled as the puddle of blood took her form. She shot out her fingers, hitting the deity directly, but only barely piercing his body.

Etah smiled and pushed the fingers in deeper, getting closer and closer to the traitor.

Devlin fired wires at the murderer's back and tugged with all his might.

Etah swiped his axe at the traitor, before being pulled back.

The tip of the weapon sliced Demonica's cheek.

"You missed!" hollered Devlin.

Demonica collapsed. She writhed around the scorched fleshy ground, screaming in agony.

The Deva was lifted off the ground toward Devlin.

Kanasta leaped up with his successor's feet pressed against his palms.

Kaity leaped off, rising above the target. She, snapped in her clip, aimed her sniper at the chest and fired rapidly.

The bullets sent the god crashing to the ground, right into a net of explosive tags.

"Surrender already!" yelled Etah, brushing the tags off his legs.

Nina tossed one shuriken at the net and triggered the explosion.

Etah's body, covered in ash was sent flying limply into the air.

" **WIRE SNAKE**!"

Devlin's wires burst out from below. They coiled around each other, creating a single reinforced wire the size of a tree trunk. The wire dodged Etah's desperate axe swipe and then slammed down on him from above. The cords pressed him against the floor before dispersing into thousands of wires, slicing up his whole body.

"My rage consumes all! **HATRED BURST**!" Etah's aura erupted out from his chest and melted the wires.

"Finally, he's open." Kanasta picked up the god by his bald scalp and pummeled him with rockets at point blank range.

Shards of shrapnel stabbed into the assassin boss' body, but he showed no signs of stopping the assault.

Demonica was still writhing on the floor.

Devlin's wires lifted her from the ground and into his embrace. "Calm down. You're not hurt. There's nothing to worry about."

Demonica's rampant flailing calmed until she was back in control. She embraced Devlin with tears welling up in her eyes.

"Kanasta, finish it," said Devlin.

The assassin boss tossed the Deva two feet forward.

As soon as Etah hit the ground he was enveloped in an impenetrable wall.

The Death Die surrounded him before cloaking itself.

"Etah will eternally be imprisoned. Victory belongs to me," said Devlin.

"Hatred cannot be contained!"

The Death Die exploded, its sides shot out, slicing Violet's arm open.

The devotee fell to her knees, her tendons and muscles unable to be mended by her Reiki.


The God of Hate stood tall before the Freedom Forcers. Every wound he suffered was filled in by his aura. In his hand was a chain and attached to its end was the Misery Mace.

"Leave him to me, everyone! I will finish this," said Devlin, stripping out of his clothes.

"What is he doing?" asked Nina with wide-eyes.

"There won't be any more sacrifices. Get as far away as you can! If it's just me and him, then I won't need to hold back."

Demonica flew to safety.

"Keep my family safe," said Devlin, smiling at his loyal creation.

Nina bowed, hoisted Devlin's father over her shoulders, and evacuated the battlefield.


Etah lunged the chain forward and the mace followed.

Devlin shot twenty wires into Etah's forehead. When he endeavored to reel in the murderer, he was pulled instead. "Fine with me." He smacked the Deva's face with his tail, causing the chain to reverberate violently. The vengeful inventor's whole body quaked after he was struck with the mace. He was sent flying back and slid across the ground, tearing the remaining patches of skin off his arms.

Etah flicked his wrist and the Misery Mace shot forward.

Violet stepped up to intervene, but wires burst out from below and ensnared her legs.

"Let's see if you can handle all the hate you've given me," said Devlin as wires shot out of his whole body, ripping his fleshy disguise to shreds.

The wires stopped the mace seconds before it made contact.

Devlin coated his fists in rotating wires and punched the mace, sending it back.

Since his wires had attached to the mace, Devlin was pulled along with them.

The God of Hate grabbed the mace from the air and slammed it down on his defiant grandson.

Devlin smashed against the floor. A geyser erupted from below, melting most of the wires that made up his stomach.

Devlin's arm and leg wires coiled around the tyrant's legs.

"Why are you not miserable?" asked Etah.

"I carry my misery with me at all times." Devlin took a step toward Etah. "No weapon can create more misery than what you've already forced upon me!"

Devlin's hand shot out wires, sending the mace straight up.

Etah lost his balance as the chain slipped out of his hand.

Devlin propelled himself into the air by pressing his back wires against the ground. His tail shot through the tyrant's chest. It stabbed his exposed capsule mercilessly, trying to pierce through the hatred aura.

Wires from the inventor's back pressed off the ground and lifted them up thirty feet.

Etah's slammed his aura-laden fist into his challenger as Devlin created multiple wire shields to defend from the assault.

All the wires receded into Devlin. A single cord came out from his chest and attached to the god's chest. "I'm a living weapon! A killing machine!" Blades jutted out from his hands, feet, and mouth.

Using the single wire as leverage, Devlin spun around the God of Hate, eviscerating him with his claws before they melted away.

Etah tore out the cord only to have Devlin's fangs plunge into his hand. He opened his fist, dislocating the boy's jaw. He then fired a heated blast inside the warrior's mouth.

Smoke came out from Devlin's mouth and his eyes lost their luster.

Once Etah landed, wires burst out from the ground, connecting to his arms and legs. The wires withdrew, stretching the god's limbs.

Etah growled in pain as the flesh of his arm was ripped open.

Devlin landed on all fours and leaped off the ground. A fresh set of talons dug into the body while his arms sliced the head.

Etah gripped his attacker's torso with one hand and cooked his insides. "Your fallen allies are mine to command!" The warrior god summoned the Wailing Whip in his mouth and jabbed it into Devlin.

Both of their bodies shook violently as they tried to endure.

Etah broke free of the wires. He was lifted off the floor by a black puddle below. "Yes! Sel, grant me the power to destroy this rebellion!"

The puddle pooled into his feet.

"This world has chosen me as its king! The realm itself has accepted me as a worthy tyrant!" Darkness oozed from the god's muscles. His arms and legs were soon shrouded in a thick black fog. A dark aura enveloped the rest of his body.

Devlin ripped the whip out of his body and fell to his knees, shivering. "Kawai is not yours to command."

"Her soul has been refined into my weapon! I can do with her as I please!"

The pink whip with gold blades sprang out from the darkness and flogged the Exp.

Devlin's wires knocked the whip aside each time. His body shivered as it rose off the ground.

The dark energy pouring out of Etah ate at Devlin's hands and feet once the pool reached him.

"You were foolish to challenge me!"

The ground beneath Devlin collapsed. He fell into a chasm.

Devlin rushed up the walls of the chasm as the black energy ate away at him.

Once he reached the surface he lunged at the god and pierced his tail into his throat.

Four wires connected to the ground and began to pull Etah down.

"Utter foolishness." The deity's log of an arm slammed into his grandson.

The dark energy pooled off his arm and burrowed into Devlin, eating away at him like acid.

Devlin's tail sliced open Etah's throat but red energy swiftly filled in the wound. He was pressed against the collapsing ground, fully immersed in the black aura.

Violet rushed in and stabbed her sword into the Asura king's chest.

"Farewell. **HATRED ERUPTION**!" Etah's aura focused in his palm and erupted out, completely consuming Devlin and making a hole that bore through the residents all the way to the ocean of lava below.

Violet tore out the blade and jabbed it into the enemy warrior's neck vigorously. She then leaped out of the way of a monstrous punch.

"We will finish this another time." The wounded deity turned around to see Occupy, Crystal, and Limit.

"OCCUPY, BODY, BOMBS."

Etah's muscles stiffened as his insides exploded. Despite the internal barrage, he created a portal and limped toward it.

"Complete Limit."

Clear weights with chains fastened themselves onto Etah's physical and energy body.

Etah's mobility stopped. Even the Deva's fiery aura ceased to move.

"CRYSTAL CRUCIFIXION."

Mineral spikes jutted out from the ground, piercing through the warrior god's foot and into his hands.

Occupy helped Devlin back to his feet. "You must be the one to finish him."

"I destroyed you!" yelled Etah, rising despite the clear chains holding him down.

"This…is the product of all the hatred you have given me." Devlin stumbled up to the wounded god and overlapped his wires continuously into a ball. "WIRE GRENADE." He shoved the mesh of wires in Etah's mouth and kicked the Deva's jaw up, shattering his teeth in the process.

Wires connected to Etah's head and shoulders and lifted him off the ground. The grenade exploded, causing wires to shoot from all sides of the warrior Deva's body. The wires branched out and into the ground, holding the divinity's mangled body like a grotesque totem for all to see.

The fall of the tyrant was seen all across Sel by demons gazing up at a hopeful future.

Devlin fell to the ground, spent from the battle.

"Revenge…at last! I did it. I defeated a god," said Devlin after his head hit the floor.

Dark energy pooled out from the ashy floor and enveloped him.

The great burden of consciousness was lifted from Devlin. After the long battle, he finally rested.

Despite being raised to be Etah's pawn, Devlin carved his own path and transformed into the Hero of Sel.

# Sneak Peek of Book 3, *Sellum*: **Resurrection of the Exps**

Devlin awoke, surrounded entirely by darkness. Spurts of flame sporadically erupted out in the distance, but never enough for him to get a clear image of where he was.

The young inventor cringed in pain and writhed around as the darkness around him filled his insides.

A pitch black cloud, somehow darker than the rest of the area, steadily approached.

An ominous low voice came out from the cloud. "You have proven yourself most worthy."

Darkness hardened around Devlin's body, enveloping him in a heavy material.

The energy climbed up his neck and covered his head. It solidified into a black helmet with a row of sharpened teeth. The helmet covered everything but Devlin's golden eyes.

"Looks like I finally got your attention," said Devlin, his voice deepened by the helmet.

"Don't be so modest. By dethroning the God of Hate, your grandfather, you have earned the right to become a god! You've surpassed my expectations."

A bright red light gleamed inside the black cloud.

"Then you're the one who did it. You gave the orders. You ruined my life," said Devlin, his eyes like a blade.

"Etah's soul yearned for power. That made it easy to manipulate him. But, you were quite the tricky one. The only way to make you follow my wishes was if you believed them to be your own. By isolating you from your family and identity, I bent your beliefs. Ever so slowly, you became my pawn."

"You planned for me to kill Etah?" asked Devlin.

"Etah was certainly useful. But his soul could never be bent to my will. If he gained too much power, he would surely seek to destroy me. This made him a liability. Now that he has been beaten, he will never again be hailed as a ruler. You've created the perfect opportunity for me to reclaim my kingdom."

"Etah was just another stepping stone for my godhood. I took him out for my own reasons," said Devlin.

"Ah, yes and that is the beauty of it. I control both sides of the chess board. I put my pawns in the proper spaces. From there they willingly follow my wishes. I needn't even speak. I simply watch as my pawns fight one another. No matter what side wins, I benefit. Each death brings me more power."

The darkness took form around Devlin's body, enveloping him in sleek black armor. The black plates moved around his body like corrosive sludge. The armor parted in the back as Devlin's tail came out. The dark energy then blanketed the tail and solidified.

"You must be pretty confident to tell me all this! News flash: I used you to become a god."

"Pretentious as ever, I see."

"I've gotten what I needed from you. I'll be back to end you once I've mastered my powers," he said, pooling his dark energy into a portal.

"You belong with me. You've always been a child of darkness. I merely set you on a path that would cultivate the darkness within you."

"That's a load of human shit! The darkness in me came from my separation from my family! It was a lie you forced on me!" yelled Devlin.

"Yes, it's all coming along splendidly. There is no longer a need for subtle manipulation. I have power over your soul. You are mine to control. From now on, you will address me as Lord Sel."

Devlin's eyes lost their fire. They were blank, like that of a corpse.

"Understood, Lord Sel."

# Book 3, *Sellum*: **Resurrection of the Exps**

The Freedom Forcers meet up with Devlin, only to find out he has allied with Sel—the true ruler of the Realm of Destruction. They head to the Elysium Asylum in a desperate attempt to gain new allies. Sel too has his eye on the prison, and his forces have been sent there on a mission that could shift the tides of the coming war in his favor. Even with reinforcements, can the Freedom Forcers save Sellum from destruction incarnate?

Find out Fall 2017.

# About the Author

Alexander McCarty is an animal born on Earth who actively seeks freedom for his fellow animals. At age five, once he realized the chickens he loved and the chickens he was eating were one in the same, he became vegetarian along with his nine-year-old brother. In middle-school he decided to make use of his free time by writing a book. At the age of twenty-one he met vegan activist Gary Yourofsky and vowed to live vegan alongside his brother. They have since dedicated their lives to animal liberation through educational activism. Alexander recently graduated with a bachelor's degree in Religious Studies, and holds certificates in Jainism, Asiatic Studies, and Spirituality. He is now a full-time writer and the president of Sphere of Compassion Inc, which he runs alongside his brother. The SOC company's purpose is to spread innovative media and promote a vegan worldview. When Alexander isn't writing, he is watching anime, reading, or playing videogames. He listens to any and all comments, suggestions, reflections and criticism.

Please contact me with a link to where you placed a review for any of my books and I will answer any single question as one of my characters for **FREE**. If you do a review (and point out where) in addition to submitting fan art, I will write a **FREE** 2–4 page story (with my characters) in a scenario of your choosing. =(:3)* Bloggers who wish to review my book may request "Review Copies" of *Exp 8: Rebellion of the Exps* at the links below.

authoralexandermccarty@gmail.com
alexanderjmccarty@facebook.com

# Paradise on Earth Can Become a Reality

The Golden Rule: "do unto others what you would have them do unto you" is seen as the core of moral action. Is there any reason this rule should not apply to our treatment of our fellow animals who have hearts, nervous systems, and brains functioning just like our own? All species want to live and be free; who are we to intrude upon that freedom? Thankfully, there is much wisdom in scripture and no religion mandates animal product usage. The Abrahamic traditions speak of Eden: a paradise where humans and every other animal species live in peace, eating fruits and not each other. Hinduism talks of reincarnation and how when we eat meat we may be eating a beloved family member from another life. Jainism is centered on non-violence (ahimsa) and non-stealing (asteya); it therefore ideologically condemns both eating meat (violence) and using animal products (stealing). In the end, we don't need to be a part of any religion or philosophy to realize that deeming someone expendable or less valuable, based on the species they were born as, is unfair, cruel, and immoral. The idea that one group is more important than another is discrimination. Discrimination is the primary root of violence. We are taught to discriminate against others, both knowingly and unknowingly. Thankfully, what has been learned can be unlearned by living our ethics.

Living a vegan life is the moral way to treat our fellow animals with the respect they deserve. We need to take responsibility and stand against the exploitation and enslavement of our fellow living beings by transitioning to a VEGAN lifestyle. We can all make a difference in the lives of those who are enslaved and executed for not being born human. Every time we make a purchase, we are casting a vote which either supports or opposes exploitation and violence. If we follow our ethics by living vegan, we can end systemic slavery worldwide!

Below are links where we can get informed and get involved:
http://www.adaptt.org/
www.serv-online.org
http://www.abolitionistapproach.com
veganeducationgroup.com